ANATHEM

wm

WILLIAM MORROW

An Imprint of HarperCollins*Publishers*

ANATHEM

neal stephenson

ANATHEM. Copyright © 2008 by Neal Stephenson. All rights reserved. Printed in the United States of America. No part of this book may be used or reproduced in any manner whatsoever without written permission except in the case of brief quotations embodied in critical articles and reviews. For information address HarperCollins Publishers, 10 East 53rd Street, New York, NY 10022.

HarperCollins books may be purchased for educational, business, or sales promotional use. For information please write: Special Markets Department, HarperCollins Publishers, 10 East 53rd Street, New York, NY 10022.

FIRST EDITION

Book design by Shubhani Sarkar

Library of Congress Cataloging-in-Publication Data
Stephenson, Neal.
    Anathem / Neal Stephenson. —1st ed.
        p. cm.
    ISBN 978-0-06-147409-5
    1. Life on other planets—Fiction. 2. Disasters—Fiction.
    3. Monasteries—Fiction. 4. Philosophy—Fiction.
    5. Mathematics—Fiction. I. Title.
    PS3569.T3868A53 2008
    813' .54—dc22

                                                    2008013175

08 09 10 11 12 WBC/RRD 10 9 8 7 6 5 4 3 2 1

OOOOOOOOOOOOOOOOOOOOOOOOOOOOOOOOOOOOOOOOOOOO TO MY PARENTS

Anathem: (1) In Proto-Orth, a poetic or musical invocation of Our Mother Hylaea, which since the time of Adrakhones has been the climax of the daily liturgy (hence the Fluccish word *Anthem* meaning a song of great emotional resonance, esp. one that inspires listeners to sing along). *Note:* this sense is archaic, and used only in a ritual context where it is unlikely to be confused with the much more commonly used sense 2. (2) In New Orth, an aut by which an incorrigible fraa or suur is ejected from the math and his or her work sequestered (hence the Fluccish word *Anathema* meaning intolerable statements or ideas). See **Throwback.**

—THE DICTIONARY, *4th edition, A.R. 3000*

CONTENTS

NOTE TO THE READER

IF YOU ARE ACCUSTOMED to reading works of speculative fiction and enjoy puzzling things out on your own, skip this Note. Otherwise, know that the scene in which this book is set is not Earth, but a planet called Arbre that is similar to Earth in many ways.

Pronunciation hints: Arbre is pronounced like "Arb" with a little something on the end. Consult a French person for advice. In a pinch, "Arb" will do. Two dots above a vowel are a dieresis, meaning that the vowel in question gets a syllable all its own. So, for example, *Deät* is pronounced "day ott" rather than "deet."

Arbran measurement units have been translated into ones used on Earth. This story takes place almost four thousand years after the people of Arbre settled on their common system of units, which now seem ancient and time-worn to them. Accordingly, old Earth units (feet, miles, etc.) are used here instead of the newer ones from the metric system.

Where the Orth-speaking culture of this book has developed vocabulary based on the ancient precedents of Arbre, I have coined words based on the old languages of Earth. *Anathem* is the first and most conspicuous example. It is a play on the words *anthem* and *anathema,* which derive from Latin and Greek words. Orth, the classical language of Arbre, has a completely different vocabulary, and so the words for *anthem, anathema,* and *anathem* are altogether different, and yet linked by a similar pattern of associations. Rather than use the Orth word, which would be devoid of meaning and connotations to Earth readers, I have tried to devise an Earth word that serves as its rough equivalent while preserving some flavor of the Orth term. The same thing, *mutatis mutandis,* has been done in many other places in the book.

Names of some Arbran plant and animal species have been translated into rough Earth equivalents. So these characters may speak of carrots, potatoes, dogs, cats, etc. This doesn't mean that Arbre has exactly the same species. Naturally, Arbre has its own plants and animals. The names of those species' rough Earth equivalents have been swapped in here to obviate digressions in which, e.g., the phenotype of the Arbre-equivalent-of-a-carrot must be explained in detail.

A very sparse chronology of Arbre's history follows. None of this will make very much sense until one has read some pages into the book, but after that it may be useful for reference.

- 3400 TO - 3300:	Approximate era of Cnoüs and his daughters Deät and Hylaea.
- 2850:	Temple of Orithena founded by Adrakhones, the father of geometry.
- 2700:	Diax drives out the Enthusiasts, founds theorics on axiomatic principles and gives it its name.
- 2621:	Orithena destroyed by volcanic eruption. Beginning of Peregrin period. Many surviving theors gravitate toward city-state of Ethras.
- 2600 TO - 2300:	Golden Age of Ethras.
- 2396:	Execution of Thelenes
- 2415 TO - 2335:	Life span of Protas
- 2272:	Ethras forcibly absorbed into Bazian Empire
- 2204:	Foundation of the Ark of Baz
- 2037:	Ark of Baz becomes state religion of the Empire
- 1800:	Bazian Empire reaches its peak
- 1500S:	Various military setbacks lead to dramatic

shrinkage of the Bazian Empire. Theors retreat from public life. Saunt Cartas writes *Sæculum* **thereby inaugurating the Old Mathic Age.**

- 1472: Fall of Baz, burning of its Library. Surviving literate people flock to Bazian monasteries or Cartasian maths.

- 1150: Rise of the Mystagogues

- 600: The Rebirth. Purging of the Mystagogues, Opening of the Books.

- 500: Dispersal of the mathic system, Age of Exploration, discovery of laws of dynamics, creation of modern applied theorics. Beginning of the Praxic Age.

- 74: The First Harbinger

- 52: The Second Harbinger

- 43: Proc founds The Circle

- 38: Proc's work repudiated by Halikaarn

- 12: The Third Harbinger

- 5: The Terrible Events

0: The Reconstitution. The First Convox. Foundation of the new mathic system. Promulgation of the Book of Discipline and the first edition of the Dictionary.

+ 121: Avout of the Concent of Saunt Muncoster split into two groups, the Syntactics and the Semantics, founding the Procian and Halikaarnian Orders respectively. Thereafter, orders proliferate.

+ 190 TO + 210: Avout of Saunt Baritoe make advances in manipulation of nucleosynthesis using syntactic techniques. Creation of New Matter.

+ 211 TO + 213: The First Sack

+ 214: Post-Sack Convox abolishes most forms of New Matter. Promulgation of the Revised Book of Discipline. Faanian order splits away from Procian. Evenedrician order splits away from Halikaarnian.

+ 297:	Saunt Edhar establishes his own order out of the Evenedricians.
+ 300:	At the Centennial Apert, it is found that several Centenarian maths have gone off the rails ("gone Hundred") since 200.
+ 308:	Saunt Edhar founds the Concent of the same name.
+ 320 TO + 360:	Advances in praxis of genetic sequences made at various concents, frequently arising from collaboration between Faanians and Halikaarnians.
+ 360 TO + 366:	Second Sack.
+ 367:	Post-Sack Convox. Manipulation of genetic sequences abolished. Sharper lines drawn between syntactic and semantic orders. Faanians disbanded. New Revised Book of Discipline promulgated. Syntactic devices removed from the mathic world. The Ita are created; many ex-Faanians join them. The Inquisition is created as a means of enforcing the new rules. Wardens Regulant installed in all concents; modern system of hierarchs instituted in the form that will endure for at least the next three millennia.
+ 1000:	First Millennial Convox
+ 1107 TO + 1115:	Detection of a dangerous asteroid (the "Big Nugget") prompts the Sæcular Power to summon an extraordinary Convox.
+ 2000:	Second Millennial Convox
+ 2700:	Growing rivalry between Procian and Halikaarnian Orders gives rise to Sæcular legends of the Rhetors and the Incanters.
+ 2780:	During a Decennial Apert, the Sæcular Power becomes aware of extraordinary kinds of praxis being developed by Rhetors and Incanters.
+ 2787 TO + 2856:	Third Sack depopulates all concents except for the Three Inviolates.
+ 2857:	Post-Sack Convox reorganizes the concents.

Dowments outlawed. Various measures taken to reduce perceived luxury of mathic life. Number of Orders reduced. Remaining Orders redistributed to bring about greater "balance" between Procian and Halikaarnian tendencies. Promulgation of the Second New Revised Book of Discipline.

+ 3000:   Third Millennial Convox

+ 3689:   Our story opens.

Part 1

PROVENER

Extramuros: (1) In Old Orth, literally "outside the walls." Often used in reference to the walled city-states of that age. (2) In Middle Orth, the non-mathic world; the turbulent and violent state of affairs that prevailed after the Fall of Baz. (3) In Praxic Orth, geographical regions or social classes not yet enlightened by the resurgent wisdom of the mathic world. (4) In New Orth, similar to sense 2 above, but often used to denote those settlements immediately surrounding the walls of a math, implying comparative prosperity, stability, etc.

—THE DICTIONARY, *4th edition, A.R. 3000*

o your neighbors burn one another alive?" was how Fraa Orolo began his conversation with Artisan Flec.

Embarrassment befell me. Embarrassment is something I can feel in my flesh, like a handful of sun-warmed mud clapped on my head.

"Do your shamans walk around on stilts?" Fraa Orolo asked, reading from a leaf that, judging by its brownness, was at least five centuries old. Then he looked up and added helpfully, "You might call them pastors or witch doctors."

The embarrassment had turned runny. It was horrifying my scalp along a spreading frontier.

"When a child gets sick, do you pray? Sacrifice to a painted stick? Or blame it on an old lady?"

Now it was sheeting warm down my face, clogging my ears and sanding my eyes. I could barely hear Fraa Orolo's questions: "Do you fancy you will see your dead dogs and cats in some sort of after-life?"

Orolo had asked me along to serve as amanuensis. It was an impressive word, so I'd said yes.

He had heard that an artisan from extramuros had been al-lowed into the New Library to fix a rotted rafter that we could not reach with our ladders; it had only just been noticed, and we didn't have time to erect proper scaffolding before Apert. Orolo meant to interview that artisan, and he wanted me to write down what hap-pened.

Through drizzly eyes, I looked at the leaf in front of me. It was as blank as my brain. I was failing.

But it was more important to take notes of what the artisan said. So far, nothing. When the interview had begun, he had been dragging an insufficiently sharp thing over a flat rock. Now he was just staring at Orolo.

"Has anyone you know ever been ritually mutilated because they were seen reading a book?"

Artisan Flec closed his mouth for the first time in quite a while. I could tell that the next time he opened it, he'd have something to say. I scratched at the edge of the leaf just to prove that my quill had not dried up. Fraa Orolo had gone quiet, and was looking at the artisan as if he were a new-found nebula in the eyepiece of a telescope.

Artisan Flec asked, "Why don't you just speel in?"

"Speel in," Fraa Orolo repeated to me, a few times, as I was writing it down.

I spoke in bursts because I was trying to write and talk at the same time: "When I came—that is, before I was Collected—we—I mean, they—had a thing called a speely . . . We didn't say 'speel in'—we said 'cruise the speely.'" Out of consideration for the artisan, I chose to speak in Fluccish, and so this staggering drunk of a sentence only sounded half as bad as if I'd said it in Orth. "It was a sort of—"

"Moving picture," Orolo guessed. He looked to the artisan, and switched to Fluccish. "We have guessed that 'to speel in' means to partake of some moving picture praxis—what you would call technology—that prevails out there."

"Moving picture, that's a funny way to say it," said the artisan. He stared out a window, as if it were a speely showing a historical documentary. He quivered with a silent laugh.

"It is Praxic Orth and so it sounds quaint to your ears," Fraa Orolo admitted.

"Why don't you just call it by its real name?"

"Speeling in?"

"Yeah."

"Because when Fraa Erasmas, here, came into the math ten years ago, it was called 'cruising the speely' and when I came in almost thirty years ago we called it 'Farspark.' The avout who live on the other side of yonder wall, who celebrate Apert only once every hundred years, would know it by some other name. I would not be able to talk to them."

Artisan Flec had not taken in a word after Farspark. "Farspark is completely different!" he said. "You can't watch Farspark content on a speely, you have to up-convert it and re-parse the format. . . ."

Fraa Orolo was as bored by that as the artisan was by talk of the Hundreders, and so conversation thudded to a stop long enough for me to scratch it down. My embarrassment had gone away without my noticing it, as with hiccups. Artisan Flec, believing that the conversation was finally over, turned to look at the scaffolding that his men had erected beneath the bad rafter.

"To answer your question," Fraa Orolo began.

"What question?"

"The one you posed just a minute ago—if I want to know what things are like extramuros, why don't I just speel in?"

"Oh," said the artisan, a little confounded by the length of Fra Orolo's attention span. *I suffer from attention surplus disorder,* Fraa Orolo liked to say, as if it were funny.

"First of all," Fraa Orolo said, "we don't have a speely-device."

"Speely-device?"

Waving his hand as if this would dispel clouds of linguistic confusion, Orolo said, "Whatever artifact you use to speel in."

"If you have an old Farspark resonator, I could bring you a down-converter that's been sitting in my junk pile—"

"We don't have a Farspark resonator either," said Fraa Orolo.

"Why don't you just buy one?"

This gave Orolo pause. I could sense a new set of embarrassing questions stacking up in his mind: "*do you believe that we have money? That the reason we are protected by the Sæcular Power is because we are sitting on a treasure hoard? That our Millenarians know how to convert base metals to gold?*" But Fraa Orolo mastered the urge. "Living as we do under the Cartasian Discipline, our only media are chalk, ink, and stone," he said. "But there is another reason too."

"Yeah, what is it?" demanded Artisan Flec, very provoked by Fraa Orolo's freakish habit of announcing what he was about to say instead of just coming out and saying it.

"It's hard to explain, but, for me, just aiming a speely input device, or a Farspark chambre, or whatever you call it . . ."

"A speelycaptor."

". . . at something doesn't collect what is meaningful to me. I need someone to gather it in with all their senses, mix it round in their head, and make it over into words."

"Words," the artisan echoed, and then aimed sharp looks all round the library. "Tomorrow, Quin's coming instead of me," he announced, then added, a little bit defensively, "I have to counter-strafe the new clanex recompensators—the fan-out tree's starting to look a bit clumpy, if you ask me."

"I have no idea what that means," Orolo marveled.

"Never mind. You ask him all your questions. He's got the gift of gab." And for the third time in as many minutes, the artisan looked at the screen of his jeejah. We'd insisted he shut down all of its communications functions, but it still served as a pocket-watch. He didn't seem to realize that in plain sight out the window was a clock five hundred feet high.

I put a full stop at the end of the sentence and aimed my face at a bookshelf, because I was afraid that I might look amused. There was something in the way he'd said *Quin's coming instead of me* that made it seem he'd just decided it on the spot. Fraa Orolo had probably caught it too. If I made the mistake of looking at him, I would laugh, and he wouldn't.

The clock began chiming Provener. "That's me," I said. Then I added, for the benefit of the artisan: "Apologies, I must go wind the clock."

"I was wondering—" he said. He reached into his toolbox and took out a poly bag, blew off sawdust, undid its seal (which was of a type I had never seen before), and withdrew a silver tube the size of his finger. Then he looked at Fraa Orolo hopefully.

"I don't know what that is and I don't understand what you want," said Fraa Orolo.

"A speelycaptor!"

"Ah. You have heard about Provener, and as long as you are here, you'd like to view it and make a moving picture?"

The artisan nodded.

"That will be acceptable, provided you stand where you are told. Don't turn it on!" Fraa Orolo raised his hands, and got ready to avert his gaze. "The Warden Regulant will hear of it—she'll make me do penance! I'll send you to the Ita. They'll show you where to go."

And more in this vein, for the Discipline was made up of many rules, and we had already made a muddle of them, in Artisan Flec's mind, by allowing him to venture into the Decenarian math.

○○

Cloister: (1) In Old Orth, any closed, locked-up space (Thelenes was confined in one prior to his execution, but, confusingly to younger fids, it did not then have the mathic connotations of senses 2, etc., below). (2) In Early Middle Orth, the math as a whole. (3) In Late Middle Orth, a garden or court surrounded by buildings, thought of as the heart or center of the math. (4) In New Orth, any quiet, contemplative space insulated from distractions and disturbances.

—THE DICTIONARY, *4th edition, A.R. 3000*

I'd been using my sphere as a stool. I traced counterclockwise circles on it with my fingertips and it shrank until I could palm it. My bolt had shifted while I'd been sitting. I pulled it up and yanked the pleats straight as I careered around tables, chairs, globes, and slow-moving fraas. I passed under a stone arch into the Scriptorium. The place smelled richly of ink. Maybe it was because an ancient fraa and his two fids were copying out books there. But I wondered how long it would take to stop smelling that way if no one ever used it at all; a lot of ink had been spent there, and the wet smell of it must be deep into everything.

At the other end, a smaller doorway led to the Old Library, which was one of the original buildings that stood right on the Cloister. Its stone floor, 2300 years older than that of the New Library, was so smooth under the soles of my feet that I could scarcely feel it.

I could have found my way with my eyes closed by letting my feet read the memory worn into it by those gone before.

The Cloister was a roofed gallery around the perimeter of a rectangular garden. On the inner side, nothing separated it from the weather except the row of columns that held up its roof. On the outer side it was bounded by a wall, openings in which gave way to buildings such as the Old Library, the Refectory, and various chalk halls.

Every object I passed—the carven bookcase-ends, the stones locked together to make the floor, the frames of the windows, the forged hinges of the doors and the hand-made nails that fastened them to the wood, the capitals of the columns that surrounded the Cloister, the paths and beds of the garden itself—every one had been made in a particular form by a clever person a long time ago. Some of them, such as the doors of the Old Library, had consumed the whole life-times of those who had wrought them. Others looked as though they'd been tossed off in an idle afternoon, but with such upsight that they had been cherished for hundreds or thousands of years. Some were founded on pure simple geometry. Others reveled in complication and it was a sort of riddle whether there was any rule governing their forms. Still others were depictions of actual people who had lived and thought interesting things at one time or another—or, barring that, of general types: the Deolater, the Physiologer, the Burger and the Sline. If someone had asked, I might have been able to explain a quarter of them. One day I'd be able to explain them all.

Sunlight crashed into the Cloister garden, where grass and gravel paths were interwoven among stands of herbs, shrubs, and the occasional tree. I reached back over my shoulder, caught the selvage end of my bolt, and drew it up over my head. I tugged down on the half of the bolt that hung below my chord, so that its fraying edge swept the ground and covered my feet. I thrust my hands together in the folds at my waist, just above the chord, and stepped out onto the grass. This was pale green and prickly, as the weather had been hot. As I came out into the open, I looked to the south dial of the clock. Ten minutes to go.

"Fraa Lio," I said, "I do not think that slashberry is among the

One Hundred and Sixty-four." Meaning the list of plants that were allowed to be cultivated under the Second New Revised Book of Discipline.

Lio was stockier than I. When younger he had been chubby, but now he was just solid. On a patch of disturbed earth in the shade of an apple tree, he was squatting, hypnotized by the dirt. He had wrapped the selvage end of his bolt around his waist and between his thighs in the basic modesty knot. The remainder he had rolled up into a tight cylinder which he had tied at each end with his chord and then slung diagonally on his back, like a bedroll. He had invented this wrap. No one else had followed his lead. I had to admit that it looked comfortable, if stupid, on a warm day. His bottom was ten inches off the ground: he had made his sphere about the size of his head, and was balancing on it.

"Fraa Lio!" I said again. But Lio had a funny mind that sometimes did not respond to words. A slashberry cane arched across my path. I found a few thornless inches, closed my hand around it, jerked it up by its roots, and swung it round until the tiny flowers at its tip grazed Fraa Lio's stubbly scalp. "Thistlehead!" I said, at the same moment.

Lio tumbled backward as if I'd smacked him with a quarterstaff. His feet flew up and spun back to find purchase on the roots of the apple tree. He stood, knees bent, chin tucked, spine straight, pieces of dirt trickling down from his sweaty back. His sphere rolled away and lodged in a pile of uprooted weeds.

"Did you hear me?"

"Slashberry is not one of the Hundred and Sixty-four, true. But neither is it one of the Eleven. So it's not like I have to burn it on sight and put it down in the Chronicle. It can wait."

"Wait for what? What are you doing?"

He pointed at the dirt.

I stooped and looked. Many would not have taken such a risk. Hooded, I could not see Fraa Lio in my peripheral vision. It was believed you should always keep Lio in the corner of your eye because you never knew when he might commence wrestling. I had endured more than my share of headlocks, chokeholds, takedowns, and pins at Lio's hands, as well as large abrasions from brushes with his scalp. But I knew that he would not attack me now because I was showing respect for something that he thought was fascinating.

Lio and I had been Collected ten years ago, at the age of eight, as part of a crop of boys and girls numbering thirty-two. For our first couple of years we had watched a team of four bigger fraas wind the clock each day. A team of eight suurs rang the bells. Later he and I had been chosen, along with two other relatively large boys, to form the next clock-winding team. Likewise, eight girls had been chosen from our crop to learn the art of ringing the bells, which required less strength but was more arduous in some ways, because some of the changes went on for hours and required unbroken concentration. For more than seven years now, my team had wound the clock each day, except when Fraa Lio forgot, and three of us had to do it. He'd forgotten two weeks ago, and Suur Trestanas, the Warden Regulant, had sentenced him to do penance, in the form of weeding the herb beds during the hottest time of the year.

Eight minutes to go. But nagging Lio about the time wouldn't get me anywhere; I had to go through, and out the other side of, whatever it was that he wanted to talk about.

"Ants," I said. Then, knowing Lio, I corrected myself: "Ant vlor?"

I could hear him smiling. "Two colors of ants, Fraa Raz. They're having a war. I regret to say I caused it." He nudged a pile of uprooted slashberry canes.

"Would you call it a war, or just mad scrambling around?"

"That's what I was trying to figure out," he said. "In a war, you have strategy and tactics. Like flanking. Can ants flank?"

I barely knew what that meant: attacking from the side. Lio worried such terms loose from old books of vlor—Vale-lore—as if pulling dragon's teeth from a fossil jaw.

"I suppose ants can flank," I said, though I sensed that it was a trick question and that Lio was flanking me with words at this very moment. "Why not?"

"By accident, of course they can! You look down on it from above and say, 'Oh, that looked like flanking.' But if there's no commander to see the field and direct their movements, can they really perform coordinated maneuvers?"

"That's a little like Saunt Taunga's Question," I pointed out ("Can a sufficiently large field of cellular automata think?").

"Well, can they?"

"I've seen ants work together to carry off part of my lunch, so I know they can coordinate their actions."

"But if I'm one of a hundred ants all pushing on the same raisin, I can feel the raisin moving, can't I—so the raisin itself is a way that they communicate with one another. But, if I'm a lone ant on a battlefield—"

"Thistlehead, it's Provener."

"Okay," he said, and turned his back on me and started walking. It was this penchant for dropping conversations in the middle, among other odd traits, that had earned him a reputation as being less than intact. He'd forgotten his sphere again. I picked it up and threw it at him. It bounced off the back of his head and flew straight up in the air; he held out a hand, barely looking, and caught it on the drop. I edged around the battlefield, not wanting to get combatants, living or dead, on my feet, then hustled after him.

Lio reached the corner of the Cloister well ahead of me and ducked in front of a mass of slow-moving suurs in a way that was quite rude and yet so silly that the suurs all had a chuckle and thought no more of it. Then they clogged the archway, trapping me behind them. I had alerted Fraa Lio so he wouldn't be late; now I was going to arrive last and be frowned at.

Aut: (1) In Proto- and Old Orth, an act; an action deliberately taken by some entity, usually an individual. (2) In Middle and later Orth, a formal rite, usually conducted by an assembly of avout, by which the math or concent as a whole carries out some collective act, typically solemnized by

singing of chants, performance of coded gestures, or other
ritual behavior.

—THE DICTIONARY, 4th edition, A.R. 3000

In a sense the clock was the entire Mynster, and its basement. When
most people spoke of "the clock," though, they meant its four dials,
which were mounted high on the walls of the Præsidium—the
Mynster's central tower. The dials had been crafted in different
ages, and each showed the time in a different way. But all four were
connected to the same internal works. Each proclaimed the time;
the day of the week; the month; the phase of the moon; the year;
and (for those who knew how to read them) a lot of other cosmographical arcana.

The Præsidium stood on four pillars and for most of its height
was square in cross-section. Not far above the dials, however, the
corners of the square floor-plan were cleaved off, making it into an
octagon, and not far above that, the octagon became a sixteen-sided
polygon, and above that it became round. The roof of the Præsidium was a disk, or rather a lens, as it bulged up slightly in the middle
to shed rainwater. It supported the megaliths, domes, penthouses,
and turrets of the starhenge, which drove, and was driven by, the
same clock-works that ran the dials.

Below each dial was a belfry, screened behind tracery. Below
the belfries, the tower flung out plunging arcs of stone called buttresses to steady itself. Those found footing amid the topmost spires
of four outlying towers, shorter and squatter than the Præsidium,
but built to the same general plan. The towers were webbed to one
another by systems of arches and spans of tracery that swallowed
the lower half of the Præsidium and formed the broad plan of the
Mynster.

The Mynster had a ceiling of stone, steeply vaulted. Above the
vaults, a flat roof had been framed. Built upon that roof was the ae-
rie of the Warden Fendant. Its inner court, squared around the Præsidium, was roofed and walled and diced up into store-rooms and
headquarters, but its periphery was an open walkway on which the
Fendant's sentinels could pace a full circuit of the Mynster in a few

minutes' time, seeing to the horizon in all directions (except where blocked by a buttress, pier, spire, or pinnacle). This ledge was supported by dozens of close-spaced braces that curved up and out from the walls below. The end of each brace served as a perch for a gargoyle keeping eternal vigil. Half of them (the Fendant gargoyles) gazed outward, the other half (the Regulant gargoyles) bent their scaly necks and aimed their pointy ears and slitted eyes into the concent spread below. Tucked between the braces, and shaded below the sentinels' walkway, were the squat Mathic arches of the Warden Regulant's windows. Few places in the concent could not be spied on from at least one of these—and, of course, we knew them all by heart.

○○

Saunt: (1) In New Orth, a term of veneration applied to great thinkers, almost always posthumously. *Note:* this word was accepted only in the Millennial Orth Convox of A.R. 3000. Prior to then it was considered a misspelling of **Savant**. In stone, where only upper-case letters are used, this is rendered SAVANT (or ST. if the stonecarver is running out of space). During the decline of standards in the decades that followed the Third Sack, a confusion between the letters *U* and *V* grew commonplace (the "lazy stone-carver problem"), and many began to mistake the word for SAUANT. This soon degenerated to *saunt* (now accepted) and even *sant* (still deprecated). In written form, *St.* may be used as an abbreviation for any of these. Within some traditional orders it is still pronounced "Savant" and obviously the same is probably true among Millenarians.

—THE DICTIONARY, *4th edition, A.R. 3000*

The Mynster erupted from the planed-off stump of what had once been the end of a mountain range. The crag of the Millenarian math loomed above it on the east. The other maths and compounds were spread below it on the south and west. The one where I lived with the other Tenners was a quarter of a mile away. A roofed gallery, consisting of seven staircases strung together by landings, connected our math to a stone patio spread before the portal that we used to get into the Mynster. This was the route being taken by most of my fellow Tenners.

Rather than wait for that clot of old suurs to clear the bottleneck, though, I doubled back into the Chapterhouse, which was really just a wide spot in the gallery that surrounded the Cloister. This had a back exit that got me into a covered alley between chalk halls and workshops. Its walls were lined with niches where we stuffed work in progress. Ends and corners of half-written manuscripts projected, slowly yellowing and curling, making the passage seem even narrower than it was.

Jogging to its end and ducking through a keyhole arch, I came out into a meadow that spread below the elevated plinth on which the Mynster was built, and that served as a buffer separating us from the math of the Centenarians. A stone wall sixteen feet high sliced it in half. The Hundreders used their side for raising livestock.

When I had been Collected, we had used our side as a haymow. A few years ago, in late summer, Fraa Lio and Fraa Jesry had been sent out with hoes to walk it looking for plants of the Eleven. And indeed they had happened upon a patch of something that looked like blithe. So they had chopped it out, piled it in the middle of the meadow, and set fire to it.

By day's end, the entire meadow on our side of the wall had become an expanse of smoking carbonized stubble, and noises coming over the top of the wall suggested that sparks had blown onto the Hundreders' side. On our side, along the border between the meadow and the tangles where we grew most of our food, the fraas and suurs had formed a battle line that ran all the way down to the river. We passed full buckets up the line and empty ones down it and threw the water onto those tangles that seemed most likely to burst into flames. If you've ever seen a well-tended tangle in the late summer, you'll know why; the amount of biomass is huge, and by that time of the year it's dry enough to burn.

At the inquisition, the deputy Warden Regulant who had been on duty at the time had testified that the initial fire had produced so much smoke that he'd been unable to get a clear picture of what Lio and Jesry had done. So the whole thing had been Chronicled as an accident, and the boys had got off with penance. But I know, because Jesry told me later, that when the fire in the blithe had first spread to the surrounding grass, Lio, instead of stamping it out, had proposed that they fight fire with fire, and control it using fire vlor. Their attempt to set counterfires had only made matters worse. Jesry had dragged Lio to safety as he was attempting to set a counter-counterfire to contain a system of counterfires that was supposed to be containing the original fire but that had gotten out of hand. Having his hands full with Lio, he'd had to abandon his sphere, which to this day was stiff in one place and could never quite become transparent. Anyway, the fire had provided an excuse for us finally to do something we'd been talking about forever, namely to plant it in clover and other flowering plants, and keep bees. When there was an economy extramuros, we could sell the honey to burgers in the market stall before the Day Gate, and use the money to buy things that were difficult to make inside the concent. When conditions outside were post-apocalyptic, we could eat it.

As I jogged toward the Mynster, the stone wall was to my right. The tangles—now just as full and ripe as they'd been before the fire—were mostly behind me and to my left. In front of me and somewhat uphill were the Seven Stairs, crowded with avout. Compared to the other fraas all swathed in their bolts, half-naked Lio, moving twice as fast, was like an ant of the wrong color.

The chancel, the heart of the Mynster, had an octagonal floor-plan (as theors were more apt to put it, it had the symmetry group of the eighth roots of unity). Its eight walls were dense traceries, some of stone, others of carved wood. We called them screens, a word confusing to extramuros people for whom a screen was something on which you'd watch a speely or play a game. For us, a screen was a wall with lots of holes in it, a barrier through which you could see, hear, and smell.

Four great naves were flung out, north-east-south-west, from the base of the Mynster. If you have ever attended a wedding or a funeral in one of the Deolaters' arks, a nave would remind you of the big part where the guests sit, stand, kneel, flog themselves, roll on the floor, or whatever it is that they do. The chancel, then, would correspond to the place where the priest stands at the altar. When you see the Mynster from a distance, it's the four naves that make it so broad at its base.

Guests from extramuros, like Artisan Flec, were allowed to come in the Day Gate and view auts from the north nave when they were not especially contagious and, by and large, behaving themselves. This had been more or less the case for the last century and a half. If you visited our concent by coming in through the Day Gate, you'd be channeled into the portal in the north façade and walk up the center aisle of the north nave toward the screen at the end. You might be forgiven for thinking that the whole Mynster consisted of only that nave, and the octagonal space on the other side of the screen. But someone in the east, west, or south nave would make the same mistake. The screens were made dark on the nave side and light on the chancel side, so that it was easy to see into the chancel but impossible to see beyond it, creating the illusion that each nave stood alone, and owned the chancel.

The east nave was empty and little used. We'd ask the older fraas and suurs why; they'd give a wave of the hand and "explain" that it was the Mynster's formal entrance. If so, it was so formal that no one knew what to do with it. At one time a pipe-organ had stood there, but this had been ripped out in the Second Sack, and later improvements of the Discipline had banned all other musical instruments. When my crop had been younger, Orolo had strung us along for several years telling us that there was talk of making it a sanctuary for ten-thousand-year fraas if the Concent of Saunt Edhar ever got round to building a math for such. "A proposal was submitted to the Millenarians 689 years ago," he'd say, "and their response is expected in another 311."

The south nave was reserved for the Centenarians, who could reach it by strolling across their half of the meadow. It was much too big for them. We Tenners, who had to cram ourselves into a much smaller space just next to it, had been annoyed by this fact for more than three thousand years.

The west nave had the best stained-glass windows and the finest stone-carving because it was used by the Unarians, who were by far the best-endowed of all the maths. But there were easily enough of them to fill the place up and so we didn't resent their having so much space.

There remained four screen-walls of the chancel—northeast, southeast, southwest, and northwest—that were the same size and shape as the four that lay in the cardinal directions but that were not connected to proper naves. On the dark sides of these screens lay the four corners of the Mynster, cluttered by structural works that were inconvenient for humans but necessary for the whole thing to remain standing. Our corner, on the southwest, was by far the most crowded of these, since there were about three hundred Tenners. Our space had therefore been expanded by a couple of side-towers that bulged out from the walls of the Mynster and accounted for its obvious asymmetry in that corner.

The northwest corner connected to the Primate's compound, and was used only by him, his guests, the wardens, and other hierarchs, so there was no crowding there. The southeast corner was for the Thousanders; it connected directly to their fantastical hand-carved stone staircase, which zoomed, veered and rambled down the face of their crag.

The northeastern corner, directly across from us, was reserved for the Ita. Their portal communicated directly with their covered slum, which filled the area between that side of the Mynster and the natural stone cliff that, in that zone, formed the concent's outer wall. A tunnel supposedly gave them access to the subterranean workings of the clock, which it was their duty to tend. But this, like most of our information concerning the Ita, was little better than folklore.

So there were eight ways into the Mynster if one only counted the formal portals. But Mathic architecture was nothing if not complicated and so there were also any number of smaller doors, rarely used and barely known about, except by inquisitive fids.

I shuffled through the clover as quickly as I could without stepping on any bees. Even so I made better time than those on the Seven Stairs, and soon reached the Meadow door, which was set into a masonry arch that had been grafted onto the native rock. A flight of stone steps took me up to the level of the Mynster's main floor. I dodged through a series of odd, mean little store-rooms where vestments and ceremonial objects were kept when out of season. Then I came out into that architectural hodgepodge in the southwest corner that we Tenners used in place of a nave. Incoming fraas and suurs obstructed me. But there were lanes of open space wherever the view was obstructed by a pillar. Planted in one of those lanes, right up against the base of a pillar, was our wardrobe. Most of its contents had been dumped out onto the floor. Fraa Jesry and Fraa Arsibalt were standing nearby, already swathed in scarlet and looking irritated. Fraa Lio was swimming through silk trying to find his favorite robe. I dropped to one knee and found something in my size among the ones he had discarded. I threw it on, tied it, and made sure it wouldn't get in the way of my feet, then fell in behind Jesry and Arsibalt. A moment later Lio came up and stood too close behind me. We came out from the shadow of that pillar and threaded our way through the crowd toward the screen, following Jesry, who wasn't afraid to use his elbows. But it wasn't that crowded. Only about half of the Tenners had shown up today; the rest were busy getting ready for Apert. Our fraas and suurs were seated before the southwest screen in tiered rows. Those in the front sat on the floor. The next row sat on their spheres, head-sized. Those behind them had made their spheres larger. In the back row, the spheres were taller than those who sat on them, stretched out like huge filmy balloons, and the only thing that kept them from rolling about and spilling people onto the stone was that they were all packed in together between the walls, like eggs in a box.

Grandfraa Mentaxenes pulled open the little door that penetrated our screen. He was very old, and we were pretty sure that doing this every day was the only thing that kept him alive. Each of us stepped into a tray of powdered rosin so that his feet could better grip the floor.

Then we filed out and, like grains of sugar dropped in a mug of tea, dissolved in a vast space. Something about the way the chancel was built made it seem a cistern storing all of the light that had ever fallen upon the concent.

Looking up from a standpoint just inside the screen, one saw the vaulted Mynster ceiling almost two hundred feet above, illuminated by light pouring in through stained-glass windows in the clerestory all around. So much light, shining down onto the bright inner surfaces of the eight screens, rendered them all opaque and made it seem as though the four of us had the whole Mynster to ourselves. The Thousanders who had clambered down their walled and covered stair to attend Provener were now seeing us through their screen, but they could not see Artisan Flec, with his yellow T-shirt and his speelycaptor, in the north nave. Likewise Flec could not see them. But both could view the aut of Provener, which would take place entirely within the chancel, and which would be indistinguishable from the same rite performed one, two, or three thousand years ago.

The Præsidium was supported by four fluted legs of stone that rammed down through the middle of the chancel and, I imagined, through the underlying vault where the Ita looked after the movements of their bits. Moving inward we passed by one of those pillars. These were not round in cross-section but stretched out diagonally, almost as if they were fins on an old-fashioned rocketship, though not nearly as slender as that implies. We thus came into the central well of the Mynster. Looking up from here, we could see twice as far up, all the way to the top of the Præsidium where the starhenge was. We took up our positions, marked by rosin-stained dimples.

A door opened in the Primate's screen, and out came a man in robes more complicated than ours, and purple to indicate he was a hierarch. Apparently the Primate was busy today—also probably getting ready for Apert—and so he had sent one of his aides in his place. Other hierarchs filed out behind. Fraa Delrakhones, the Warden Fendant, sat in his chair to the left of the Primate's, and Suur Trestanas, the Warden Regulant, sat to the right.

Fifteen green-robed fraas and suurs—three each of soprano, alto, tenor, baritone, and bass—trooped out from behind the screen of the Unarians. It was their turn to lead the singing and chanting, which probably meant we were in for a weak performance, even though they'd had almost a year to learn it.

The hierarch spoke the opening words of the aut and then threw the lever that engaged the Provener movement.

As the clock would tell you, if you knew how to read it, we were still in Ordinal time for another two days. That is, there was no particular festival or holiday going on, and so the liturgy did not follow any special theme. Instead it defaulted to a slow, spotty recapitulation of our history, reminding us how we'd come to know all that we knew. During the first half of the year we would cover all that had gone before the Reconstitution. From there we would work our way forward. Today's liturgy was something to do with developments in finite group theorics that had taken place about thirteen hundred years ago and that had caused their originator, Saunt Bly, to be Thrown Back by his Warden Regulant and to live out the remainder of his days on top of a butte surrounded by slines who worshipped him as a god. He even inspired them to stop consuming blithe, whereupon they became surly, killed him, and ate his liver out of a misconception that this was where he did his thinking. If you live in a concent, consult the Chronicles for more concerning Saunt Bly. If you don't, know that we have so many stories in this vein that one can attend Provener every day for one's whole life and never hear one repeated.

The four pillars of the Præsidium I have mentioned. Right in the middle, on the central axis of the whole Mynster, hung a chain with a weight at its end. It reached so high in the column of space above us that its upper reaches dissolved into dust and dimness.

The weight was a blob of grey metal shot through with voids, as if it had been half eaten by worms: a nickel-iron meteorite four billion years old, made of the same stuff as the heart of Arbre. During the almost twenty-four hours since the last celebration of Provener, it had descended most of the way to the floor; we could almost reach up and touch it. It descended steadily most of the time, as it was responsible for driving the clock. At sunrise and sunset though, when it had to supply the power for opening and closing the Day Gate, it dropped rapidly enough to make casual spectators scurry out of its way.

There were four other weights on four other, independently moving chains. They were less conspicuous because they did not hang down in the middle, and they didn't move much. They rode on metal rails fixed to the four Præsidium pillars. Each of these had a regular geometric shape: a cube, an octahedron, a dodecahedron, and an icosahedron, all wrought from black volcanic stone quarried from the Cliffs of Ecba and dragged on sledge trains over the North Pole. Each rose a little bit every time the clock was wound. The cube descended once a year to open the Year Gate and the octahedron every ten years to open the Decade Gate, so both of these were now quite close to the tops of their respective tracks. The dodecahedron and the icosahedron did the same for the century and millenium gates respectively. The former was about nine-tenths of the way to the top, the latter about seven-tenths. So just from looking, you could guess it was about 3689.

Much higher in the Præsidium, in the upper reaches of the chronochasm—the vast airy space behind the dials, where all of the clock-work came together—was a hermetically sealed stone chamber that contained a sixth weight: a sphere of grey metal that rode up and down on a jack screw. This kept the clock ticking while we were winding it. Other than that, it would only move if the meteorite was on the floor—that is, if we failed to celebrate the daily aut of Provener. When this happened, the clock would disengage most of its machinery to conserve energy and would go into hibernation, driven by the slow descent of the sphere, until such time as it was wound again. This had only ever occurred during the three Sacks and on a few other occasions when everyone in the concent had been so sick that they'd not been able to wind the clock. No one knew how long the clock could run in that mode, but it was thought to be on the order of a hundred years. We knew it had continued to run all through the time following the Third Sack when the Thousanders had holed up on their crag and the rest of the concent had been uninhabited for seven decades.

All of the chains ran up into the chronochasm where they hung from sprockets that turned on shafts, connected by gear-trains and escapements that it was the Ita's business to clean and inspect. The main drive chain—the one that ran up the middle, and supported the meteorite—was connected to a long system of gear-trains and linkages that was artfully concealed in the pillars of the Præsidium as it made its way down into the vaulted cellar below our feet. The only part of this visible to non-Ita was a squat hub that rose up out of the center of the chancel floor, looking like a round altar. Four horizontal poles projected like spokes from this hub at about the height of a person's shoulder. Each pole was about eight feet long. At the proper moment in the service, Jesry, Arsibalt, Lio, and I each went to the end of a pole and put his hands on it. At a certain beat in the Anathem, each of us threw himself behind his pole, like a sailor trying to weigh anchor by turning a capstan. But nothing moved except for my right foot, which broke loose from the floor and skidded back for a few inches before finding purchase. Our combined strength could not over-come the static friction of all the bearings and gears between us and the sprocket hundreds of feet above from which the chain and the weight depended. Once it became unstuck we would be strong enough to keep it going, but getting it unstuck required a mighty thrust (supposing we wanted to use brute force) or, if we chose to be clever, a tiny shake: a subtle vibration. Different praxics might solve this problem in different ways. At Saunt Edhar, we did it with our voices.

Back in very ancient times, when the marble columns of the Halls of Orithena still rose from the black rock of Ecba, all the world's theors would gather beneath the great dome just before noon. Their leader (at first, Adrakhones himself; later, Diax or one of his other fids) would stand on the analemma, waiting for the shaft of light from the oculus to pass over him at midday: a climax celebrated by the singing of the Anathem to our mother Hylaea who had brought us the light of her father Cnoüs. The aut had fallen into disuse when Orithena had been destroyed and the surviving theors had em-barked on the Peregrination. But much later, when the theors retreated to the maths, Saunt Cartas drew on it to anchor the liturgy that was then practiced all through the Old Mathic Age. Again it fell into disuse during the Dispersal to the New Periklynes and the Praxic Age that followed, but then, after the Terrible Events and the Reconstitution, it was revived again, in a new form, centered on the winding of a clock.

The Hylaean Anathem now existed in thousands of different versions, since every composer among the avout was likely to take at least one crack at it during his or her lifetime. All versions used the same words and structure, but they were as various as clouds. The most ancient were monophonic, meaning each voice sang the same note. The one used at Saunt Edhar was polyphonic: different voices singing different melodies that were woven together in a harmonious fashion. Those One-offs in their green robes sang only some of the parts. The rest of the voices came out through the screens. Traditionally the Thousanders sang the deepest notes. Rumor had it they'd developed special techniques to loosen their vocal chords, and I believed it, since no one in our math could sing tones as deep as the ones that rumbled out from their nave.

The Anathem started simple, then got almost too complicated for the ear to follow. When we'd had an organ, it had required four organists, each using both hands and both feet. In the ancient aut, this part of the Anathem represented the Kaos of non-systematic thought that had preceded Cnoüs. The composer had realized it almost too well, since during this part of the music the ear could scarcely make sense of all the different voices. But then, sort of as when you are looking at some geometric shape that looks like a tangle having no order at all, and you rotate it just a tiny bit, and suddenly all its planes and vertices come into alignment and you see what it is, all of those voices fell in together over the course of a few measures and collapsed into one pure tone that resonated in the light-well of our clock and made everything vibrate in sympathy with it. Whether by a lucky accident, or by a feat of the praxics, the vibration was just enough to break the seal of static friction on the winding-shaft. Lio, Arsibalt, Jesry and I, even though we knew it was coming, practically fell forward as the hub went into motion.

Moments later, after the backlash in the gear train had been taken up, the meteorite above our heads began to creep upwards. And we knew that twenty beats later we could expect to feel the day's accumulation of dust and bat droppings raining down on our heads from hundreds of feet above.

In the ancient liturgy, this moment had represented the Light dawning in the mind of Cnoüs. The singing now split apart into two competing strains, one representing Deät and the other Hylaea, the two daughters of Cnoüs. Trudging counterclockwise around the shaft, we worked up to a steady pace that fell into synchrony with the rhythm of the Anathem. The meteorite began to rise at about two inches every second, and would continue to do so until it reached its upper stop, which would take about twenty minutes. At the same time, the four sprocket-wheels from which the four other chains were suspended were also turning, though much more slowly. The cube would rise by about a foot during this aut. The octahedron would rise by about an inch, and so on. And up above the ceiling, the sphere was slowly descending to keep the clock going during the time it took us to wind it.

I should stipulate that it does not really take so much energy to run a clock—even a huge one—for twenty-four hours! Almost all of the energy that we were putting into the system went to run the add-ons, like bells, gates, the Great Orrery just inside the Day Gate, various lesser orreries, and the polar axes of the telescopes on the starhenge.

None of this was in the front of my mind while I was pushing my pole around and around the hub. True, I did look at these things afresh during the first few minutes, simply because I knew that Artisan Flec was watching, and I was trying to imagine how I might explain these things to him, supposing he asked. But by the time we had found our rhythm, and my heart had begun to thump along at a steady pace, and the sweat had begun to drip from my nose, I had forgotten about Artisan Flec. The chanting of the One-offs was better than I'd expected—not so bad as to call attention to itself. For a minute or two I thought about the story of Saunt Bly. After that, I thought mostly of myself and my situation in the world. I know that this was selfish of me, and not what I should have been doing during the aut. But unbidden and unwanted thoughts are the hardest to expel from one's mind. You might find it in poor taste that I tell you of what I was thinking. You might find it unnecessarily personal, perhaps even immoral—a bad example for other fids who might one day find this account sticking out of a niche. But it is part of this story.

As I wound the clock on that day I was wondering what it would be like to climb up to the Warden Fendant's ledge and jump off.

If you find such a thing impossible to comprehend, you probably are not avout. The food that you eat is grown from crops whose genes partake of the Allswell sequence, or even stronger stuff. Melancholy thoughts may never come into your mind at all. When they do, you have the power to dismiss them. I did not have that power, and was becoming weary of keeping company with those thoughts. One way to silence them forever would have been to walk out of the Decenarian Gate in a week's time, go to live with my birth family (supposing they would have me back), and eat what they ate. Another would have involved climbing the stair that spiraled up our corner of the Mynster.

○○○

Mystagogue: (1) In Early Middle Orth, a theorician specializing in unsolved problems, esp. one who introduced fids to the study of same. (2) In Late Middle Orth, a member of a suvin that dominated the maths from the middle of the Negative Twelfth Century until the Rebirth, which held that no further theoric problems could be solved; discouraged theoric research; locked libraries; and made a fetish of mysteries and conundrums. (3) In Praxic and later Orth, a pejorative term for any person who is thought to resemble those of sense 2.

—THE DICTIONARY, *4th edition, A.R. 3000*

"Are people starving to death? Or are they sick because they are too fat?"

Artisan Quin scratched his beard and thought about that one. "You're talking of slines, I assume?"

Fraa Orolo shrugged.

Quin thought that was funny. Unlike Artisan Flec, he was not afraid to laugh out loud. "Sort of both at the same time," he finally admitted.

"Very good," said Fraa Orolo, in a *now we're getting somewhere* tone, and glanced at me to make sure I was getting it down.

After the Flec interview, I had had words with Fraa Orolo. "Pa, what are you doing with that five-hundred-year-old questionnaire? It's crazy."

"It is an eight-hundred-year-old copy of an eleven-hundred-year-old questionnaire," he had corrected me.

"It would be one thing if you were a Hundreder. But how could things have changed that much in only ten years?"

Fraa Orolo had told me that since the Reconstitution there had been forty-eight instances in which radical change had occurred in a decade, and that two of these had culminated in Sacks—so perhaps the sudden ones were the most important. And yet ten years was a long enough span of time that people who lived extramuros, immersed in day-to-day goings-on, might be oblivious to change. So a Tenner reading an eleven-hundred-year-old questionnaire to an artisan could perform a service to the society extramuros (assuming anyone out there was paying attention). Which might help to explain why we were not only tolerated but protected (except when we weren't) by the Sæcular Power. "The man who looks at a mole on his brow every day when he shaves may not see that it is changing; the physician who sees it once a year may easily recognize it as cancer."

"Beautiful," I'd said. "But you've never cared about the Sæcular Power before, so what's your *real* reason?"

He had pretended to be bewildered by the question. But, seeing I wasn't going to back off, he had shrugged and said "Just a routine check for CDS."

"CDS?"

"Causal Domain Shear."

This had as much as proved that Orolo was only having me on. But sometimes he had a point when he was doing that.

Correction: he *always* had a point. *Sometimes* I was able to see it. So I had rested my face on my hands and muttered, "Okay. Open the floodgates."

"Well. A causal domain is just a collection of things linked by mutual cause-and-effect relationships."

"But isn't *everything in the universe* so linked?"

"Depends on how their light cones are arranged. We can't affect things in our past. Some things are too far away to affect us in any way that matters."

"But still, you can't really draw hard and fast boundaries between causal domains."

"In general, no. But you are much more strongly webbed together with *me* by cause and effect than you are with an alien in a faraway galaxy. So, depending on what level of approximation you're willing to put up with, you could say that you and I belong together in one causal domain, and the alien belongs in another."

"Okay," I had said, "what level of approximation *are* you willing to put up with, Pa Orolo?"

"Well, the whole point of living in a cloistered math is to reduce our causal linkages with the extramuros world to the minimum, isn't it?"

"Socially, yes. Culturally, yes. Ecologically, even. But we use the same atmosphere, we hear their mobes driving by—on a pure theoric level, there is no causal separation at all!"

He hadn't seemed to have heard me. "If there were another universe, altogether separate from ours—no causal linkages whatsoever between Universes A and B—would time flow at the same rate between them?"

"It's a meaningless question," I'd said, after having thought about it for a moment.

"That's funny, it seemed meaningful to me," he'd retorted, a little cross.

"Well, it depends on how you measure time."

He'd waited.

"It depends on what time *is*!" I'd said. I had spent a few minutes going up various avenues of explanation, only to find each of them a dead end.

"Well," I'd said finally, "I guess I have to invoke the Steelyard. In the absence of a good argument to the contrary, I have to choose the simplest answer. And the simplest answer is that time runs independently in Universe A and Universe B."

"Because they are separate causal domains."

"Yes."

Orolo said, "What if these two universes—each as big and as old and as complicated as ours—were entirely separate, except for a single photon that managed to travel somehow between them. Would that be enough to wrench A's time and B's time into perfect lockstep for all eternity?"

I had sighed, as I always did when one of Orolo's traps closed over me.

"Or," he'd said, "is it possible to have a little bit of time slippage—shear—between causal domains that are connected only loosely?"

"So—back to your interview with Artisan Flec—you want me to believe that you were just checking to see whether a thousand years might have gone by on the other side of that wall while only *ten* have gone by on *this* side!?"

"I saw no harm in making inquiries," he'd said. Then he'd gotten a look as if something else were on the tip of his tongue. Something mischievous. I had headed him off before he could say it:

"Oh. Is this anything to do with your crazy stories about the wandering ten-thousand-year math?"

When we'd been new fids, Orolo had once claimed that he had found an instance in the Chronicles where a gate somewhere had ground open and some avout had walked out of it claiming to be Ten-thousanders celebrating Apert. Which was ridiculous because avout in their current form had only existed for (at that time) 3682 years. So we'd reckoned that the whole purpose of the story had been to see if we had been paying any attention whatsoever to our history lessons. But perhaps the story had been meant to convey a deeper point.

"You can get a lot done in ten millennia if you put your mind to it," Orolo had said. "What if you found a way to sever all causal links to the world extramuros?"

"That is utterly ridiculous. You are giving Incanter-like powers to these people."

"But if one could do it, then one's math would become a separate universe and its time would no longer be synchronized with the rest of the world's. Causal Domain Shear would become possible—"

"Nice thought experiment," I'd said. "Point taken. Thank you for the calca. But please tell me you don't *really* expect to see evidence of CDS when the gates open!"

"It is what you don't expect," he'd said, "that most needs looking for."

"Do you have, in your wigwams or tents or skyscrapers or wherever you live—"

"Trailers without wheels mostly," said Artisan Quin.

"Very well. In those, is it common to have things that can think, but that are not human?"

"We did for a while, but they all stopped working and we threw them away."

"Can you read? And by that I don't just mean interpreting Logotype . . ."

"No one uses that any more," said Quin. "You're talking about the symbols on your underwear that tell you not to use bleach. That sort of thing."

"We don't have underwear, or bleach—just the bolt, the chord, and the sphere," said Fraa Orolo, patting the length of cloth thrown over his head, the rope knotted around his waist, and the sphere under his bottom. This was a weak joke at our expense to set Quin at ease.

Quin stood up and tossed his long body in a way that made his jacket fly off. He was not a thick-built man but he had muscles from working. He whirled the jacket round to his front and used his thumbs to thrust out a sheaf of tags sewn into the back of the collar. I could see the logo of a company, which I recognized from ten years ago, though they had made it simpler. Below it was a grid of tiny pictures that moved. "Kinagrams. They obsoleted Logotype."

I felt old: a new feeling for me.

Orolo had been curious until he'd seen the Kinagrams; now he looked disappointed. "Oh," he said, in a mild and polite tone of voice, "you are talking bulshytt."

I got embarrassed. Quin was amazed. Then his face turned red. It looked as if he were talking himself into being angry.

"Fraa Orolo didn't say what you think!" I told Quin, and tried to punctuate it with a chuckle, which came out as a gasp. "It is an ancient Orth word."

"It sounded a lot like—"

"I know! But Fraa Orolo has forgotten all about the word *you* are thinking of. It's not what he meant."

"What did he mean, then?"

Fraa Orolo was fascinated that Quin and I were talking about him as if he weren't there.

"He means that there's no real distinction between Kinagrams and Logotype."

"But there *is*," Quin said, "they are incompatible." His face wasn't red any more; he drew breath and thought about it for a minute. Finally he shrugged. "But I see what you mean. We could have gone on using Logotype."

"Why do you suppose it became obsolete, then?" asked Orolo.

"So that the people who brought us Kinagrams could gain market share."

Orolo frowned and considered this phrase. "That sounds like bulshytt too."

"So that they could make money."

"Very well. And how did those people achieve that goal?"

"By making it harder and harder to use Logotype and easier and easier to use Kinagrams."

"How annoying. Why did the people not rise up in rebellion?"

"Over time we were led to believe that Kinagrams really were better. So, I guess you're right. It really is bul—" But he stopped in mid-word.

"You can say it. It's not a bad word."

"Well, I won't say it, because it feels wrong to say it here, in this place."

"As you wish, Artisan Quin."

"Where were we?" Quin asked, then answered his own question: "You were asking me if I could read, not these, but the frozen letters used to write Orth." He nodded at my leaf, which was growing dark with just that sort of script.

"Yes."

"I could if I had to, because my parents made me learn. But I don't, because I never have to," said Quin. "My son, now, he's a different story."

"His father made him learn?" Fraa Orolo put in.

Quin smiled. "Yes."

"He reads books?"

"All the time."

"His age?" Obviously this was not on the questionnaire.

"Eleven. And he hasn't been burned at the stake yet." Quin said that in a very serious way. I wondered if Fraa Orolo understood that Quin was making a joke—taking a dig at him. Orolo made no sign.

"You have criminals?"

"Of course." But the mere fact that Quin responded in this way caused Orolo to jump to a new leaf of the questionnaire.

"How do you know?"

"What?!"

"You say *of course* there are criminals, but if you look at a particular person, how do you know whether or not he is a criminal? Are criminals branded? Tattooed? Locked up? Who decides who is and isn't a criminal? Does a woman with shaved eyebrows say 'you are a criminal' and ring a silver bell? Or is it rather a man in a wig who strikes a block of wood with a hammer? Do you thrust the accused through a doughnut-shaped magnet? Or use a forked stick that twitches when it is brought near evil? Does an Emperor hand down the decision from his throne written in vermilion ink and sealed with black wax, or is it rather that the accused must walk barefoot across a griddle? Perhaps there is ubiquitous moving picture praxis—what you'd call speelycaptors—that know all, but their secrets may only be unlocked by a court of eunuchs each of whom has memorized part of a long number. Or perhaps a mob shows up and throws rocks at the suspect until he's dead."

"I can't take you seriously," Quin said. "You've only been in the concent, what, thirty years?"

Fraa Orolo sighed and looked at me. "Twenty-nine years, eleven months, three weeks, six days."

"And it's plain to see you are boning up for Apert—but you can't really think that things have changed so much!"

Another look in my direction. "Artisan Quin," said Fraa Orolo, after a pause to make his words hit harder, "this is anno three thousand, six hundred, and eighty-nine of the Reconstitution."

"That's what my calendar says too," Quin affirmed.

"3690 is tomorrow. Not only the Unarian math, but we Decenarians as well, will celebrate Apert. According to the ancient rules, our gates will open. For ten days, we shall be free to go out, and visitors such as you shall be welcome to come in. Now, ten *years* hence, the Centenarian Gate will open for the first, and probably the last, time in my life."

"When it closes, which side of that gate will you be on?" Quin asked.

I got embarrassed again, because I'd never dare ask such a question. But I was secretly delighted that Quin had asked it for me.

"If I am found worthy, I should very much like to be on the inside of it," said Fraa Orolo, and then glanced at me with an amused look, as if he'd guessed my thoughts. "The point is that in nine or so years, I can expect to be summoned to the upper labyrinth, which separates my math from that of the Centenarians. There I shall find my way to a grate in a dark room, and on the other side of that grate shall be one of those Hundreders (unless they have all died, vanished, or turned into something else) who shall ask me questions that shall seem just as queer to me as mine do to you. For they must make preparations for their Apert just as we do for ours. In their books they have records of every judicial practice that they, and others in other concents, have heard of in the last thirty-seven-hundred-odd years. The list that I rattled off to you, a minute ago, is but a single paragraph from a book as thick as my arm. So even if you find it to be a ridiculous exercise, I should be most grateful if you'd simply describe to me how you choose your criminals."

"Will my answer be entered in that book?"

"If it is a new answer, yes."

"Well, we still have Magistrate Doctors who roam about at the new moon in sealed purple boxes . . ."

"Yes, those I remember."

"But they weren't coming round as often as we needed them—the Powers That Be weren't doing a good job of protecting them and some got rolled down hills. Then the Powers That Be put up more speelycaptors."

Fraa Orolo jumped to a new leaf. "Who has access to those?"

"We don't know."

Orolo began moving to yet another new leaf. But before he found it, Quin continued: "But if someone commits a bad enough crime, the Powers That Be clamp a thing on their spine that makes them sort of crippled, for a while. Later it falls off and then they are normal again."

"Does it hurt?"

"No."

A new page. "When you see someone wearing one of those devices, can you tell what crime they committed?"

"Yes, it says right on it, in Kinagrams."

"Theft, assault, extortion?"

"Sure."

"Sedition?"

Quin waited a long time before saying, "I've never seen that."

"Heresy?"

"That would probably be handled by the Warden of Heaven."

Fraa Orolo threw his hands up so high that his bolt fell away from his head and even bared one of his armpits. Then he brought them down again, the better to clamp them over his face. It was a sarcastic gesture that he liked to make in a chalk hall when a fid was being impossibly block-headed. Quin clearly took its meaning, and became embarrassed. He shifted back in his chair and pointed his chin at the ceiling, then lowered it again and looked at the window he was supposed to be mending. But there was something in Fraa Orolo's huge gesture that was funny, and gave Quin the feeling that it was okay.

"All right," Quin finally said, "I never thought of it like this, but now that you mention it, we have *three* systems . . ."

"The chaps in the purple boxes, the spine clamps, and this new thing that neither I nor Fraa Erasmas has ever heard of called the Warden of Heaven," said Fraa Orolo, and began pushing through many leaves of his questionnaire—digging deep.

Something had occurred to Artisan Quin. "I never mentioned them because I thought you'd know all about them!"

"Because," Fraa Orolo said, finding the page he'd been looking for, and scanning it, "they claimed that they came from the concent . . . bringing the enlightenment of the mathic world to a worthy few."

"Yeah. Didn't they?"

"No. They didn't." Seeing just how taken aback Quin was, Orolo continued: "This sort of thing happens every few hundred years. Some charlatan will appear and make a claim on Sæcular Power based on an association with the mathic world—which happens to be fraudulent."

I knew the answer to the following question before I blurted it out: "Does Artisan Flec—is he a follower, a disciple, of the Warden of Heaven?"

Quin and Orolo both looked at me, agog for different reasons. "Yes," Quin said. "He listens to their casts while he works."

"That's why he made a speely of Provener," I said. "Because this Warden of Heaven claims to be part of us. If there's anything mysterious or . . . well, magnificent about this place, why, that just makes the Warden of Heaven seem that much bigger and more powerful. And to the extent that Artisan Flec is a disciple of the Warden of Heaven, he feels some of that belongs to him."

Orolo said nothing, which made me embarrassed at the time. When I thought about it later, though, I understood that he didn't need to say anything because what I'd said was obviously true.

Quin was looking a little confused. "Flec didn't make a speely."

"I beg your pardon?" I said.

Fraa Orolo was still distracted, thinking about the Warden of Heaven.

"They wouldn't allow it. His speelycaptor was too good," Quin explained.

Being old and wise, Fraa Orolo went rigid, pursed his lips, and looked uneasy. Being neither, I said: "What on earth does that mean?"

Fraa Orolo's hand came down on my wrist and prevented me from writing any more. And I suspect that his other hand wanted to clamp down on Quin's mouth. Quin went on, "The Eagle-Rez, the SteadiHand, the DynaZoom—put those all together, and it could have seen straight across into the other parts of your Mynster, even through the screens. Or at least that's what he was told by the—"

"Artisan Quin!" Fraa Orolo trumpeted, loud enough to draw looks from everyone else in the library. Then he made his voice quite low: "I am afraid you are about to tell us something that your friend Flec learned from talking to the Ita. And I must remind you that such a thing is not allowed under our Discipline."

"Sorry," Quin said. "It's confusing."

"I know it is."

"All right. Forget about the speelycaptor. I'm sorry. Where were we?"

"We were talking about the Warden of Heaven," Fraa Orolo said, relaxing a little, and finally letting go my wrist. "And as far as I'm concerned, the only thing we need to establish is whether he is a Throwback-turned-Mystagogue, or a Bottle Shaker, as the former can be quite dangerous."

Kefedokhles: (1) A fid from the Halls of Orithena who survived the eruption of Ecba to become one of the Forty

Lesser Peregrins. In his old age, he appears to have turned up on the Periklyne, though some scholars believe that this must have been a son or namesake of the Orithenan. He appears as a minor character in several of the great dialogs, most notably *Uraloabus,* where his timely and long-winded interruption enables Thelenes—who has been thrown back on his heels by the heavy sarcasm of his adversary—to recover his equilibrium, change the subject, and embark upon the systematic annihilation of Sphenic thought that accounts for the last third of the dialog and culminates in the title character's public suicide. From the Peregrin phase of Kefedokhles's career, three dialogs survive, and from his years on the Periklyne, eight. Though talented, he gives the impression of being insufferably smug and pedantic, whence sense 2. (2) An insufferably smug or pedantic interlocutor.

—THE DICTIONARY, *4th edition, A.R. 3000*

"I can puzzle out 'Throwback-turned-Mystagogue,'" I told Fraa Orolo later. I was chopping carrots in the Refectory kitchen, and he was eating them. "And I can even guess why they are dangerous: because they're angry, they want to come back to the place that Anathematized them, and even the score."

"Yes, and that's why Quin and I spent the whole afternoon with the Warden Fendant."

"But what's a Bottle Shaker?"

"Imagine a witch doctor in a society that doesn't know how to make glass. A bottle washes up on the shore. It has amazing properties. He puts it on a stick and waves it around and convinces his fellows that he has got some of those amazing properties himself."

"So Bottle Shakers aren't dangerous?"

"No. Too easily impressed."

"What of the slines who ate Saunt Bly's liver? Apparently they weren't so impressed."

To hide a smile, Fraa Orolo pretended to inspect a potato. "The point is well taken, but remember that Saunt Bly was living alone on a butte. The very fact of his having been Thrown Back separated him from the artifacts and auts that are most impressive to Bottle Shaker–producing societies."

"So what did you and the Warden Fendant decide?"

Fraa Orolo glanced around in a way that made it obvious I should have been more discreet.

"Expect more precautions at Apert."

I lowered my voice. "So, the Sæcular Power will send . . . I don't know . . . ?"

"Robots with stun guns? Echelons of horse archers? Cylinders of sleeping gas?"

"I guess so."

"That depends on to what extent the Warden of Heaven has become the same as the Panjandrums," Fraa Orolo said. He liked to call the Sæcular Power the Panjandrums. "And that is very difficult for us to make out. Obviously, I can't make heads or tails of it. It is just the kind of thing for which the office of Warden Fendant was created, and I'm certain that Fraa Delrakhones is working the problem as we speak."

"Could it lead to . . . you know . . ."

"A Sack? Local or general? I certainly don't think that this is going to culminate in Number Four. Fraa Delrakhones would have heard rumblings from other Wardens Fendant. Even a local sack is most improbable. I wouldn't be surprised to see a bit of roughhousing on Tenth Night; but that's why we prepare for Apert by moving all of the stuff we really care about to the labyrinths."

"You said to Quin that radical changes extramuros had twice culminated in Sacks," I reminded him.

Fraa Orolo let a moment go by and said, "Yes?" Then, before I could go on, he put on the merry-fraa face that he used when he was trying to humor a chalk hall full of bored fids. "You're not actually worrying about Number Four, are you?"

I murdered a carrot and said Diax's Rake three times under my breath.

"Three Sacks-General in 3700 years is not bad," he pointed out. "The statistics for the Sæcular world are far more alarming."

"I was worrying about it *a little bit*," I said. "But that is not what I was going to ask before you went Kefedokhles on me."

Orolo said nothing, perhaps because I was gripping a large knife. I was tired and testy. Earlier, I had punched in my sphere to make it a bushel basket and ventured into the tangles nearest the Cloister, only to find they'd already been stripped of produce. To find all the stuff we needed to make the stew, I'd had to cross the river and ransack some of the tangles between it and the wall.

I snatched a hard-earned carrot and aimed it at the sky. "You have only taught me of the stars," I said. "History I have learned from others—mostly from Fraa Corlandin."

"He probably told you that the Sacks were our fault," said Orolo—using *our*, I noted, in a very elastic way, to mean every avout all the way back to Ma Cartas.

Sometimes, when I was chatting with Thistlehead, he would reach out and give me a little push on the collarbone, and just like that I'd be flailing my arms, aware that one more push would topple me. It was Lio's charming way of letting me know that he had noticed I was standing in the wrong way, according to his books of Vale-lore. I thought it nonsense. But my body always seemed to agree with Fraa Lio, because it would over-react. Once, in trying to recover my balance, I had pulled a muscle deep in my back that had hurt for three weeks.

Fraa Orolo's last sentence touched my mind in a similar way. And in a similar way, I over-reacted. My face flushed and my heart beat faster. It was just like the moment in a dialog when Thelenes has tricked his interlocutor into saying something stupid and is about to begin slicing him up like a carrot on a plank.

"Each Sack *was* followed by a reform, was it not?" I said.

"Let us Rake your sentence, and say that each Sack led to changes in the maths that are still observed to this day."

That Fraa Orolo was now talking in this style confirmed that we were in dialog. The other fraas stopped peeling potatoes and chopping herbs, and gathered around to watch me get planed.

"All right, call them whatever you wish," I said, and then snorted, because I knew I had left myself open; this was the equivalent of me falling on my arse after one little nudge from Fraa Lio. I should never have brought up Kefedokhles. I was going to pay for that.

I couldn't stop myself from shooting a glance out the window. The kitchen faced south into an herb garden that filled most of the space between it and the closest of the tangles—the ones cultivated by the very oldest fraas and suurs, so that they wouldn't have to walk very far to get their chores done. The roof on that side had a deep overhanging eave to prevent sun from shining in and making the kitchen even hotter than it already was. Suur Tulia and Suur Ala were sitting together in the shade of that eave, directly beneath the window, cutting up tires to make sandals. I didn't want Tulia to hear me get planed because I had a crush on her, and I didn't want Ala to hear it because she would enjoy it so much. Fortunately, they were explaining something to each other as usual, and had no idea what was happening in here.

"Call them whatever you wish? What a curious thing to say, Fid Erasmas," Orolo said. "Let me see . . . may I call them carrots or floor-tiles?" Titters flew out from all around, like sparrows flushed from a belfry.

"No, Pa Orolo, it would not make sense to say that each Sack was followed by a carrot."

"Why not, Fid Erasmas?"

"Because the word *carrot* has a meaning different from *reform* or *change in the maths.*"

"So because words have this remarkable property of possessing specific meanings, we must take care to use the correct ones? Is that a just statement of what you have said, or am I in error?"

"It is correct, Pa Orolo."

"Perhaps some of the others, who have learned so much from the New Circle and the Reformed Old Faanians, have noted some error in this, and would like to correct us." And, with the placid eye of a viper tasting the air, Fraa Orolo looked about at the half-dozen fids who had encircled us.

No one moved.

"Very well, no one here wishes to support the novel hypothesis of Saunt Proc. We may continue under the assumption that words mean things. What is the difference between saying that the Sacks were followed by reforms, and saying that they were followed by changes in the maths?"

"I suppose it has to do with the connotations of the word *reform*," I said. For I had given up and was willing to let myself be planed, not because I liked it but because it was so unusual for Fraa Orolo to expose his views about anything other than stars and planets.

"Ah, perhaps you could elaborate on that, for I am not gifted with your faculty for words, Fid Erasmas, and would be chagrined if I failed to follow your argument."

"Very well, Pa Orolo. To say that there were *changes* seems like a more Diaxan phrasing—raked clean of subjective emotional judgments—whereas, when we say *reforms*, it gives the feeling that something was wrong with how the maths were run before, and that—"

"We *deserved* to be sacked? The Panjandrums *needed* to come in and mend us?"

"When you put it that way, Pa Orolo, and in that tone of voice, you seem to suggest that the changes that were made, need not have been—that they were forced on us wrongly by the Sæcular Power." I stumbled over a few words, because I was excited. I had glimpsed a way to corner Orolo. For those reforms—those changes—were as fundamental to the maths as going to Provener every day, and he could hardly take a stand against them.

But Fraa Orolo only shook his head sadly, as if he could scarcely believe what thin gruel was being spooned out to us in the chalk halls. "You need to review the *Sæculum* of Saunt Cartas."

Avout who spent a lot of time peering through telescopes were known for taking an eccentric approach to the study of history, and so I did not laugh at this. A few of the others exchanged smirks.

"Pa Orolo, I read it last year."

"What you read was probably selections from a translation into Middle Orth. Many of those translations were influenced by a sort of ur-Procian mentality that took hold during the Old Mathic Age, not long before the rise of the Mystagogues. You giggle, but it is obvious once you begin to notice it. Certain bits of it they translate poorly, because they are skittish about what it means; then, when they get around to choosing selections, they leave those bits out because they're ashamed of them. Instead you should go to the effort of reading Cartas in the original. It is not as difficult to follow Old Orth as some would have you believe."

"And when I do this, what shall I learn?"

"That in the very founding document of the mathic world, Saunt Cartas herself emphasizes that it is not an accommodation to the Sæculum but a kind of opposition to it. A counterbalance."

"The Concent-as-fortress mentality?" suggested one of the listeners—trying to bait Orolo.

"That is not a designation I love," said Orolo, "but if I hold forth on that, the stew will never get made, and we'll soon have two hundred and ninety-five hungry avout calling for our heads. Suffice it to say, Fid Erasmas, that Saunt Cartas would never have accepted the notion that the Sæcular Power can or should 'reform' the maths. But she would have admitted that it does have the power to wreak changes on us."

○○

Proc: A late Praxic Age metatheorician who is assumed to have been liquidated in the Terrible Events. During the brief window of stability between the Second and Third Harbingers, Proc was the leading figure in a like-minded group called the Circle, which claimed that symbols have no meaning at all, and that all discourse that pretends to mean anything is nothing more than a game played with syntax, or the rules for putting symbols together. Following the Reconstitution, he was made patron Saunt of the Syntactic Faculty of the Concent of Saunt Muncoster. As such, he is viewed as the progenitor of all orders that trace their descent to that Faculty, as opposed to those originating from the Semantic Faculty, whose patron was Saunt Halikaarn.

—THE DICTIONARY, *4th edition, A.R. 3000*

"I understand that some planning took place in the kitchen?"

"Believe me, it was not one for ink or even chalk."

Fraa Corlandin, the FAE—First Among Equals—of the Order of the New Circle, had sat down across the table from me.

For the first nine and three-quarters years of my time at the Concent, he had ignored me, except in chalk hall where he was obliged to pay attention; lately he was acting as if we were friends. This was to be expected. With luck, thirty or forty new avout would be joining us at Apert. Even though they were not here yet, they seemed to surround us like ghosts, which made me seem older by contrast.

Not long after, if things went according to the usual pattern, the bells would signal the aut of Eliger, and all the Tenners would come together to watch me take a vow that would bind me to one order or another.

Eleven of my crop had been Collected—brought straight into the math from extramuros. The other twenty-one had joined the Unarian math first and spent at least a year under their Discipline before graduating to the Tenners; they tended to be a little bit older than us Collects. All Collection, and most graduation, happened during Apert. Though if a One-off showed exceptional promise, he or she could graduate early by passing through the labyrinth that connected the Unarian to the Decenarian math. But this had only happened three times while I'd been here. The full wiring diagram of how avout came here from extramuros and from small feeder maths in the region, and how they moved from one math to another, was complicated, and not really worth explaining. The upshot was that in order to maintain our nominal strength of three hundred, we Tenners would need to take in about forty new people at Apert. Some—we couldn't know how many—would be graduating from the Unarian math. The balance would be made up by Collection, and by trolling through hospitals and shelters for abandoned newborns.

Once that was all done, I'd be facing a choice. Fraa Corlandin was sounding me out, perhaps even recruiting me, for the New Circle.

I had always been seen as a fid of Orolo and a few other Edharians who assisted him in his theorics. They spent whole days together in tiny chalk halls, and when they came out, I would go in and see their handwriting all tangled together on the slates—snarled skeins of equations and diagrams of which I understood perhaps one symbol in twenty. At this very moment, I was supposed to be working on a problem that Orolo had set for me: a photomnemonic tablet bearing an image of Saunt Tancred's Nebula, from which I was supposed to answer certain questions about the formation of heavy nuclei in the cores of stars. Definitely not a New Circle kind of exercise. So why would the New Circle take it into their heads, now, that I might choose them at Eliger?

"Orolo is an impressive theorician," Fraa Corlandin said. "I regret that I haven't been suvined by him more."

The flaw in this was obvious: odds were that Corlandin was going to spend sixty or seventy more years in the same math with Orolo. If he really meant what he said, why didn't he simply pick up his stew-bowl and walk across the Refectory to Orolo's table?

Fortunately my mouth was full of bread, and so I did not subject Fraa Corlandin to a withering blast of Thelenean analysis. Chewing my food gave me time to realize that he was just speaking polite nothings. Edharians never talked this way. Spending all my time around Edharians, I'd forgotten how to do it.

I tried to unlimber those parts of my mind that were used for polite conversation: probably a good thing to do anyway, on Apert eve. "I'm sure you could arrange to be suvined by Orolo, if you sat down near him and said something wrong."

Fraa Corlandin chuckled at my joke. "I'm afraid I don't know enough about the stars even to say something wrong."

"Well, today for once he said something that wasn't about stars."

"That's what I heard. Who could have guessed that our cosmographer was an enthusiast for dead languages?"

This entire sentence went by me—a little like when you are eating a slice of canned fruit and suddenly it slides down your throat before you've had a chance to chew it. Having finally got the hang of polite chitchat, I returned the favor of chuckling at his remark. But before I could really think about what he was saying, I noticed Lio and Jesry carrying their bowls to the kitchen. Two other fids stood, as though caught up in their wake, and followed them.

Following their glances, I noticed Grandsuur Tamura standing by the exit with her arms folded.

She reacted as if I had hit her with a spitball from across a crowded chalk hall, swiveling her head to strafe me with her eyes. I still had no idea what was going on, but I excused myself from Fraa Corlandin and carried my bowl into the kitchen. Seven of the other fids were there, hurriedly cleaning their bowls, but none of them knew any more than I did.

○○○○○○○○○○○○○○○○○○○○○○○○○○○○○○○○○○○○○○○

Incanter: A legendary figure, associated in the Sæcular mind with the mathic world, said to be able to alter physical reality by the incantation of certain coded words or phrases. The idea is traceable to work conducted in the mathic world prior to the Third Sack. It was wildly inflated in popular culture, where fictionalized Incanters (supposedly linked to Halikaarnian traditions) dueled their mortal foes, the Rhetors (supposedly linked to Procians), in more or less spectacular style. An influential suvin among historical scholars holds that the inability of many Sæculars to distinguish between such entertainments and reality was largely responsible for the Third Sack.

—THE DICTIONARY, *4th edition, A.R. 3000*

A few minutes later, all thirty-two fids and Grandsuur Tamura were together in Saunt Grod's chalk hall, which was normally considered to hold eighteen. "Shall we move over to Saunt Venster where there's more room?" suggested Suur Ala. She was the self-appointed boss of the bell-ringing team—and of everyone else in range of her searchlight eyes. Behind Ala's back, people liked to say that, of all the current crop of fids, she was the most likely to end up being Warden Regulant.

Grandsuur Tamura pretended not to hear. She had lived here

seventy-five years and well knew the sizes of the available halls. She must have chosen this one for a reason—probably, I realized, because no one could hide ignorance, or boredom, when we were packed in so tightly. There wasn't room to make our spheres into stools, and so we kept them pilled up and tucked inside our bolts.

I noticed that some of the suurs were standing even closer together than was strictly necessary, and sniffling into one another's shoulders. One of them was Tulia, whom I liked quite a bit. I was eighteen. Tulia was a bit younger. Lately I had dreamed of having a liaison with her once she had come of age. In general I looked at her more often than was strictly necessary. Sometimes she looked back. But when I tried to meet her eye now, she pointedly looked away, and fixed her red and swollen eyes on the big stained-glass window above the slate. Since (a) it was dark outside and (b) the window depicted Saunt Grod and his research assistants being beaten with rubber hoses in the dungeons of some Praxic Age spy bureau and (c) Tulia had already spent something like a quarter of her life in this room, I reckoned that inspecting the window wasn't really the point.

Dense though I am, I finally put it together that this was the last time that our crop of thirty-two fids would be gathered together, as such, in our lives. The girls with their preternatural ability for noticing such things were responding, the boys with our equally uncanny obtuseness were only affected inasmuch as the girls we fancied were crying.

Grandsuur Tamura was not doing this to be sentimental, though. "Our topic is the Iconographies and their origins," she announced. "If I am satisfied that you know enough and that you understand the importance of what you know, then you shall be free to roam about extramuros during the ten days of Apert. Otherwise, you shall remain in the Cloister for your own safety. Fid Erasmas, what are the Iconographies and why do we concern ourselves with them?"

Why had Grandsuur Tamura directed the first question at me? Probably because I'd been transcribing those interviews with Fraa Orolo, and had an advantage over the others. I decided to frame my answer accordingly. "Well, the extras—"

"The Sæculars," Tamura corrected me.

"The Sæculars know that we exist. They don't know quite what to make of us. The truth is too complicated for them to keep in their heads. Instead of the truth, they have simplified representations—caricatures—of us. Those come and go, and have done since the days of Thelenes. But if you stand back and look at them, you see certain patterns that recur again and again, like, like—attractors in a chaotic system."

"Spare me the poetry," said Grandsuur Tamura with a roll of the eyes. There was a lot of tittering, and I had to force myself not to glance in Tulia's direction.

I went on, "Well, long ago those patterns were identified and written down in a systematic way by avout who make a study of extramuros. They are called Iconographies. They are important because if we know which iconography a given extra—pardon me, a given Sæcular—is carrying around in his head, we'll have a good idea what they think of us and how they might react to us."

Grandsuur Tamura gave no sign of whether she liked my answer or not. But she turned her eyes away from me, which was the most I could hope for. "Fid Ostabon," she said, staring now at a twenty-one-year-old fraa with a ragged beard. "What is the Temnestrian Iconography?"

"It is the oldest," he began.

"I didn't ask how old it was."

"It's from an ancient comedy," he tried.

"I didn't ask where it was from."

"The Temnestrian Iconography . . ." he rebegan.

"I know what it's called. *What is it?*"

"It depicts us as clowns," Fraa Ostabon said, a little brusquely. "But . . . clowns with a sinister aspect. It is a two-phase iconography: at the beginning, we are shown, say, prancing around with butterfly nets or looking at shapes in the clouds . . ."

"Talking to spiders," someone put in. Then, when no reprimand came from Grandsuur Tamura, someone else said: "Reading books upside-down." Another: "Putting our urine up in test tubes."

"So at first it seems only comical," said Fraa Ostabon, regaining the floor. "But then in the second phase, a dark side is shown—an impressionable youngster is seduced, a responsible mother lured into insanity, a political leader led into decisions that are pure folly."

"It's a way of blaming the degeneracy of society on us—making us the original degenerates," said Grandsuur Tamura. "Its origins? Fid Dulien?"

"*The Cloud-weaver,* a satirical play by the Ethran playwright Temnestra that mocks Thelenes by name and that was used as evidence in his trial."

"How to know if someone you meet is a subscriber to this iconography? Fid Olph?"

"Probably they will be civil as long as the conversation is limited to what they understand, but they'll become strangely hostile if we begin speaking of abstractions . . . ?"

"Abstractions?"

"Well . . . let's say anything that comes to us from our mother Hylaea."

"Level of dangerousness, on a scale of 1 to 10?"

"Given what happened to Thelenes, I'd say 10."

Grandsuur Tamura didn't favor the answer. "I can't be too hard on you for *over*-estimating the risk, but—"

"Thelenes was executed in an orderly judicial proceeding by the Sæcular Power—not a mob action," volunteered Lio, "and mob actions are less predictable, thus, more difficult to defend against."

"Very good," said Grandsuur Tamura, obviously surprised to hear such a cogent answer coming from Lio. "So let us rate its level of danger as 8. Fid Halak, what is the origin of the Doxan Iconography?"

"A Praxic Age moving picture serial. An adventure drama about a military spaceship sent to a remote part of the galaxy to prevent hostile aliens from establishing hegemony, and marooned when their hyperdrive is damaged in an ambush. The captain of the ship was passionate, a hothead. His second-in-command was Dox, a theorician, brilliant, but unemotional and cold."

"Fid Jesry, what does the Doxan Iconography say of us?"

"That we are useful to the Sæcular Power. Our gifts are to be celebrated. But we are blinded, or crippled—take your pick—by, er . . ."

"By the very same qualities that make us useful," said Fid Tulia. Which was why I couldn't get her out of my mind: in a heartbeat, she could go from blubbering to being the cleverest person in the room.

"How to identify one who is under the influence of the Doxan Iconography? Fid Tulia, again?"

"They'll be curious about our knowledge, impressed by us, but patronizing—certain that we must be subordinated to intuitive, common-sense leaders."

"Danger level? Fid Branch?"

"I would put it very low. It is basically the situation we are living in anyway."

This got a laugh, which Grandsuur Tamura didn't like very much. "Fid Ala. What does the Yorran Iconography have in common with the Doxan?"

Suur Ala had to think for a minute before trying: "Also from a Praxic Age entertainment serial? But it was an illustrated book, wasn't it?"

"Later they made moving pictures of it," put in Fraa Lio.

Someone muttered a hint into Ala's ear, and then she remembered everything. "Yes. Yorr is identified as a theorician, but if you see how he actually spends his time, he's really more of a praxic. He has turned green from working with chemicals, and he has a tentacle sprouting from the back of his skull. Always wears a white laboratory smock. Criminally insane. Always has a scheme to take over the world."

"Fraa Arsibalt, what iconography surrounds the Rhetors?"

He was *so* ready. "Fiendishly gifted at twisting words and confusing Sæculars—or, what is worse, influencing them in ways so subtle they don't even know it's happening. They use Unarian maths to recruit and groom minions, whom they send out into the Sæcular world to get influential positions as Burgers—but in truth they are all puppets of a Rhetor conspiracy."

"Well, *that* one makes sense, anyway!" said Fid Olph.

Everyone looked at him to make out whether he was joking. He looked taken aback.

"Guess we know which order *you'll* be signing up for!" said one irritated suur, who everyone knew was headed for the New Circle.

"Because he's a Procian-hater? Or just because he's socially inept?" said one of her companions in a low voice that was, however, clearly audible.

"That's enough!" said Grandsuur Tamura. "The Sæculars don't know about the differences between our Orders and so all of us—not just the Procians—are equally vulnerable to the iconography that Fraa Arsibalt has just explained. Let's move on."

And so it went. The Muncostran Iconography: eccentric, lovable, disheveled theorician, absent-minded, means well. The Pendarthan: fraas as high-strung, nervous, meddling know-it-alls who simply don't understand the realities; lacking physical courage, they always lose out to more masculine Sæculars. The Klevan Iconography: theor as an awesomely wise elder statesman who can solve all the problems of the Sæcular world. The Baudan Iconography: we are grossly cynical frauds living in luxury at the expense of the common man. The Penthabrian: we are guardians of ancient mystical secrets of the universe handed down to us by Cnoüs himself, and all of our talk about theorics is just a smoke-screen to hide our true power from the unwashed multitude.

In all, there were a round dozen iconographies that Grandsuur Tamura wanted to talk about. I'd heard of all of them, but I hadn't realized that there were so many until she made us sort through them one by one. Particularly interesting was the rating of their relative dangers. After much back-and-forth we concluded that the most dangerous of the lot was not the Yorran, as one might have expected, but rather the Moshianic, which was a hybrid of the Klevan and the Penthabrian: it held that we were going to emerge from the gates and bring enlightenment to the world and usher in a new age. It tended to peak every hundred or thousand years, as people got ready for the Centenarian or Millenarian gates to open. It was dangerous because it raised people's expectations to the point of delirium, and drew many pilgrims and much attention.

Because of my work with Fraa Orolo, I knew that the Moshianic Iconography was ascendant, in the guise of the so-called Warden of Heaven. Our hierarchs had become aware of this, and the Warden Fendant had asked Grandsuur Tamura to lead us in this discussion.

In the end, she gave the whole crop permission to go extramuros during Apert, which surprised no one: the threat of locking us up had only been to make us pay heed.

The discussion had actually become quite interesting, and the only thing that ended it was the ringing of the curfew bell. It was part of our Discipline never to sleep two nights in a row in the same cell. Assignments were posted each evening on a slate in the refectory. We had to go back there to find out where we'd be sleeping and whom we'd be chumming with. So the entire group made its way out of the chalk hall and around the Cloister, chattering and laughing about Dox and Yorr and the other funny characters that the extras had dreamed up in an effort to make sense of us. Older fraas and suurs sat on the benches that faced into the Cloister, assembling sandals—normally our sort of job—and giving us dirty looks.

It was important that I not let any one of the sandal-makers catch my eye, so I looked elsewhere. I noticed Fraa Orolo emerging from one of the other chalk halls with a sheaf of leaves, cluttered with calculations, tucked under his arm. He started one way, then, seeing our crowd, turned into the garden instead, and headed off in the direction of the Mynster. This gave me a little twinge, for a certain tablet of Saunt Tancred's Nebula was gathering dust on a table in a workroom up in the starhenge, holding down a couple of leaves stained with inconclusive notes and scratch-outs in my handwriting. Orolo would notice, and know I hadn't worked on it in days.

A few minutes later I was in the cell that I was to share that night with two other fraas, wrapping myself up in my bolt and making my sphere a pillow. You might expect that, as I lay there trying to get to sleep, I'd be thinking about Apert or about the iconographies. But spying Fraa Orolo in the Cloister had put me in mind of the slippery sentence that Fraa Corlandin had spoken at dinner, and that I'd swallowed without tasting. Now it had become one of those unwelcome thoughts I didn't know how to get rid of.

That's what I heard, Fraa Corlandin had said. But my dialog with Orolo had taken place only an hour before dinner. Who among the spectators had run off to spread the story in the New Circle chapter-house? Why did anyone care?

Until last year, Corlandin had been in a liaison with Suur Tresta-nas, also of the New Circle. Then one day the bells had rung to sig-nal the aut of Regred, meaning that someone had made the decision to go into retirement. We had convened in the Mynster and the Pri-mate had called out a name: that of our Warden Regulant. Despite all of the penance that this man had meted out to us over the years, we all felt sorrow as we sang the chants of the aut, for he'd been reasonable and wise.

Statho—the Primate—had then named Suur Trestanas the new Warden Regulant. It was a little bit of a surprise because she was young, but not controversial since everyone knew she was bright. She'd moved to the Primate's Compound where she now had a cell to herself, and took her meals with the other hierarchs. But rumor had it that her liaison with Fraa Corlandin continued. Some avout, of a suspicious mindset, believed that the hierarchs had devices salted around the concent that enabled them to know what we were say-ing. Believing so was a fad that came and went depending on what people thought of the hierarchs at a given time. It had been on the rise since Suur Trestanas had been appointed Warden Regulant. It was impossible for me not to think of it now. Perhaps she had lis-tened to my dialog with Orolo and then passed it on to Corlandin.

On the other hand (said the part of my mind that pleaded with such thoughts to go away), I had to admit that I myself had thought it strange that Orolo would suddenly take an interest in Old Orth translation errors.

Who could have guessed that our cosmographer was an enthusiast for dead languages? Well, *enthusiast* was one of those unkillable words that had passed almost unchanged from Proto-Orth all the way up into Fluccish. In Fluccish—which was how I assumed, at first, Cor-landin had used it—it simply meant one who liked something. The

Proto-Orth meaning, however, was not a very complimentary one to hang on a fraa, especially a theorician like Orolo. And *dead languages* too was an interesting choice of words. Was it really dead if Orolo was reading it? And if Orolo was right about the translations, then by calling the original "dead," wasn't Corlandin sort of making a point—and doing it in a sneaky way, without going to the effort of proving it?

After what seemed like hours of lying awake and worrying about this, I had the upsight that the things Fraa Orolo said—even when they caused me embarrassment or outright pain—never made me wrestle with my bolt in the night-time in the way that these words from Fraa Corlandin had. This made me think I'd rather join the Edharians.

If, that is, the Edharians would have me. I was not so confident that they would. I'd never been as quick to grasp pure theorics as some of the other fids. This must have been noticed. I wondered: why had Grandsuur Tamura asked me the first, and easiest, question? Was it because she didn't think I could handle anything more difficult? Why did Orolo have me working as an amanuensis instead of doing theorics? Why was Corlandin now trying to recruit me? Putting it all together, I came to the conclusion that everyone knew I just wasn't fit to join the Edharian order, and some were trying to prepare a soft landing for me.

Part 2

APERT

Ita: (1) In late Praxic Orth, an acronym (therefore, in ancient texts sometimes written ITA) whose precise etymology is a casualty of the loss of shoddily preserved information that will forever enshroud the time of the Harbingers and the Terrible Events. Almost all scholars agree that the first two letters come from the words *Information Technology,* which is late Praxic Age commercial bulshytt for syntactic devices. The third letter is disputed; hypotheses include Authority, Associate, Arm, Archive, Aggregator, Amalgamated, Analyst, Agency, and Assistant. Each of these, of course, suggests a different picture of what role the Ita might have performed in the years before the Reconstitution, and so each tends to be advocated by a different suvin. (2) In early New Orth (up to the Second Sack), a faculty of a concent devoted to the praxis of syntactic devices. (3) In later New Orth, a proscribed artisanal caste tolerated in the thirty-seven concents that were built around the Great Clocks, all of which are in technical violation of the Second Sack reforms in that their clocks were built with subsystems that employ syntactic devices; the task of the Ita is to operate and maintain those subsystems while observing strict segregation from the avout.

—THE DICTIONARY, *4th edition, A.R. 3000*

○○○

T
he last night of 3689 I dreamed that something was troubling Fraa Orolo, and that everyone had noticed, but on no account would he or anyone else speak of it openly. So it was a mystery. And yet everyone knew what it was: the planets were deviating from their courses, and the clock was wrong. For part of the clock was an orrery: a mechanical model of the solar system that displayed the current positions of the planets and many of their moons. It was in the narthex or lobby between the Day Gate and the north nave. It had been exactly correct for thirty-four centuries, but now it had gone out of whack. The marble, crystal, steel, and lapis spheres that represented the planets had moved to positions that were at odds with what Fraa Orolo could plainly see even in the smallest of telescopes. Never mentioned in the dream, but understood by me, was that the problem must have something to do with the Ita, because the orrery was one of the systems driven by the devices that they tended in the vaulted cavern beneath the floor of the Mynster.

The same system, it was rumored, effected subtle corrections to the rate of the main clock. If the error down in the cellar were not fixed, it would lead to greater errors that would be obvious to all, such as the bells chiming midday when the sun was not at its zenith, or the Day Gate opening before or after sunrise.

In a universe governed by the usual logic, those errors would have cropped up later than the tiny discrepancies between the orrery and the planets. But in dream-logic, it all happened at the same time, so that I was wondering what was troubling Fraa Orolo even as I saw the orrery show the phase of the moon wrong, which happened at the same time as burgers were wandering in through the Day Gate at midnight. But for some reason, none of those errors troubled me as much as the sounds emanating from the belfry: the bells ringing the wrong changes. . . .

I opened my eyes to hear Apert ringing. Or so the other fraas in my cell speculated. There was no way of telling unless you listened carefully for a few minutes. The belfry movement could play fixed tunes, for example to chime the hours. But to announce auts and other events, our team of ringers would disengage that mechanism and ring changes, or permutations of tones. There was a pattern or code in them that we were taught to understand. This was supposedly so that messages could be cast to a sprawling concent without the people extramuros knowing what was being said.

Not that there was anything secret about Apert. This was the first day of 3690; therefore, not only the Day Gate but the Unarian and Decenarian Gates would open at sunrise. Any extra who glanced at a calendar knew this perfectly well, and so did we. But for some reason none of us would get out of bed and act upon it until we heard the right sequence of tones ring out from the belfry: a melody reversed, flipped upside-down, and turned back on itself in a particular way.

We sat up, three naked fraas in a cold cell with our bolts and chords and spheres all disheveled on the pallets. Such a day called for a formal wrap, which was difficult to manage alone. Fraa Holbane's feet had touched the floor first, so I leaned over and rummaged through his warm, stirred-up bolt until my fingers felt the fraying end, which I drew toward me. Fraa Arsibalt, the third one in the cell, was the last to wake up; after some strong language from me and Holbane, he finally took up the selvage end. We went out into the corridor and stretched it between us. Fraa Holbane had made it short, thick, and fuzzy for warmth.

Arsibalt and I pleated Holbane's bolt and then backed away from each other as Holbane made it three times as long and much thinner. Chord wadded in his hand, he crawled under it and then stood so that it was tented over his left shoulder. Then all he had to do was swivel this way and that, and raise and lower his arms at the right times, while Arsibalt and I moved about him, like planets in an orrery, winding the bolt, spreading or bunching pleats as necessary. The finished wrap was notoriously unstable, so we held it in place for a minute while Holbane passed his chord over it in several places and tied a few important knots. Then he was free to partner with Arsibalt in getting my bolt around me. Finally, Holbane and I did it for Arsibalt. Arsibalt always liked to go last, so that he would get the best results. Not that he was vain. On the contrary, of all of our crop, he seemed best suited to live in a math. He was big and portly, and kept trying to grow a beard so that he could look more like the old fraa that he was destined to be. But unlike, say, Fraa Lio, who invented new wraps all the time, Arsibalt insisted on having it done right.

When we were all clothed, we spent a few more minutes making extra passes with our chords and shaping the pleats that hooded our heads: just about the only part of this wrap where it was possible to show any individual style.

Completed sandals were heaped on the ground next to the exit of the cell-house. I kicked through them looking for a pair big enough for my feet. The Discipline had been created by people who lived in warm places. It allowed each of the avout to own a bolt, a chord, and a sphere, but it said nothing about footwear. That didn't trouble us much during the summer. But the weather was getting ready to turn cold. And during Apert we might go extramuros and walk on city streets with broken glass and other hazards. We stretched the Discipline a little bit, wearing tire sandals during Apert and soft-soled mukluks during the winter months. The avout of Saunt Edhar had been doing this for a long time now and the Inquisition hadn't come down on us yet, so it seemed that we were safe. I made a pair of sandals mine, and tied them onto my feet.

Finally, each of us took his sphere and made it fist-sized. As we strolled in the direction of the Mynster, we passed the knotted ends of our chords around these, weaving simple nets to entrap them, then made the spheres inhale and swell to draw the chords taut. Each of us then made his sphere glow with a soft scarlet light. The light was so that we could see where we were going and the color was to mark ourselves as Tenners, which was necessary since before long we'd be mixed up with One-offs.

When all of these preparations were finished, the sphere dangled from the right hip and swung against the thigh, which looked fascinating when a couple of hundred of us were converging on the Mynster in the dark. If you wanted to look like a real Saunt in a statue, you could cup the glowing sphere in one hand and stroke it with the other while staring off into the distance as though mesmerized by the Light of Cnoüs.

Forty avout had risen earlier and gathered in the chancel. They were singing the processional of Decennial Apert as we came in. Woven into this chant was a melody I had not heard in ten years, or since I had stood inside the Decade Gate at sunrise and watched its stone-and-steel doors grind shut on everything I had ever known. To hear that melody now penetrated so deep into my brain that it literally threw me off balance, and I leaned into another fraa: Lio, who for once did not use it as an excuse to flip me over his hipbone and slam me to the ground, but rather pushed me back up straight, as if I were a crooked ikon, and turned his attention back to the aut.

All of the music was synchronized to the clock, which served as metronome and conductor. It went on for another quarter of an hour: no reading, no homily, just music.

The sky was clear, and so at the moment of sunrise, light washed down the well from the quartz prism at the top of the starhenge. The music stopped. We extinguished our spheres. I had an impression that the light from above was emerald-colored at first, or perhaps that was a trick of my eyes; by the time I'd blinked once, it had gone the color of the back of your hand when you shine a light through it in a dark cell. There was an unbearable moment of stillness when we all feared that (as in my dream) the clock was wrong and nothing would happen.

Then the central weight began to drop. This happened every day at sunrise to open the Day Gate. But today it was the signal for everyone to crane their necks and look up to where the Præsidium's pillars pierced the Mynster's vault. We heard, then saw movement. It was happening! Two of the weights were descending, riding down their rails to open the Year Gate and the Decade Gate.

We all gasped and exclaimed and cheered and many of us had

to wipe our eyes. I could even hear the Thousanders reacting to it behind their screen. The cube and the octahedron descended into plain view and everyone roared. We applauded them as if they were celebrities at an awards ceremony. As they neared the chancel floor we hushed, as if fearing that they might smash into the ground. But as they got closer they slowed, and finally crept to a halt only a hand's-breadth above the floor. Then we all laughed.

In some ways this was ridiculous. The clock was but a mechanism. It had no choice at this moment but to let those weights drop. Yet to see it happen created a feeling that can't be conveyed to one who was not there. The choir were supposed to break into polyphonic singing now, and they almost couldn't. But the raggedness of their voices was a music of its own.

Outside, beneath the singing, I could hear the sound of running waters.

○○○○○○○○○○○○○○○○○○○○○○○○○○○○○○○○○○○○

Avout: (1) A person who has sworn a vow to submit himself or herself to the Cartasian Discipline for one or more years; a fraa or suur. (2) A plurality of such persons. (3) A formally constituted community of such persons, e.g., a chapter or a math.

—THE DICTIONARY, *4th edition, A.R. 3000*

"There's no right way to build a clock," Fraa Corlandin used to say when he was teaching us modern (post-Reconstitution) history. This was his euphemistic way of saying that Saunt Edhar's praxics had been a little bit crazy.

Our concent was nestled in the crook of a river where it dodged around one end of a range of rocky bluffs—the terminus of a mountain range that stretched for hundreds of miles to the northeast and whose glaciers and snowpacks formed the river's headwaters. Just upstream was a series of cataracts. We could hear them at night if the slines weren't making too much noise. Below them, the river, as though resting from all of the excitement, ran still and gentle for some distance, curving across a well-drained prairie. Part of that prairie, and a mile and a half of the river, were encompassed by our walls.

Up at the cataract, the river was easily bridged, and so a settlement tended to be there. During some eras it would grow and engulf our walls, and office workers in skyscrapers would gaze down on the tops of our bastions. At other times it would ebb and recede to a tiny fueling-station or gun emplacement at the river crossing. Our stretch of the river was hazardous with rust-eaten girders and lumps of moss-covered synthetic stone, the remains of bridges that had been raised at that crossing and, in later ages, collapsed and washed downstream.

Most of our land and almost all of our buildings were on the inside of the riverbend, but we had claimed a strip on the far bank and built our fortifications there: walls parallel to the river where it ran straight, bastions where it bent. Three of those bastions housed gates, one each for the Unarian, Decenarian, and Centenarian maths (the Millenarian Gate was up on the mountain and worked differently). Each gate was a pair of doors, supposed to swing open and closed at certain times. This had posed a problem for the praxics, in that the gates were situated far away, and on the opposite side of a river, from the clock that was supposed to command the opening.

The praxics had done it with water power. Far outside of our walls, upstream of the cataract—therefore, at an altitude well above our heads—they had carved a pool, like an open cistern, out of the river's stony course, and made it feed an aqueduct that cut due south toward the Mynster, bypassing the cataract, the bridge, and the bend. After rushing through a short tunnel and loping on stone stilts across half a mile of broken terrain, this dove into the ground and became a buried pipe that passed beneath what was now a settled neighborhood of burgers. The water in that pipe, pressurized by gravity, erupted in a pair of fountains from the pond that lay just outside of the Day Gate. A causeway ran across the middle of that pond, connecting the central square of the burgers' town, at its northern end, to our Day Gate at its southern, and passing right between those two fountains.

The elevation of the pond was still above that of the river and plain. Drains were plumbed into its bottom and throttled by monumental ball-valves of polished granite. One of them fed a series of ponds, canals, and fountains that beautified the Primate's compound and, farther downstream, formed part of the barrier between the Unarian and the Decenarian maths. Three other drains were connected to systems of pipes, siphons, and aqueducts that ran out toward the Year, Decade, and Century Gates. Those systems were dry except at Apert. Now the clock's descending weights had opened two valves and allowed water to rush from the pond to flood the Year and Decade systems.

In some ways maybe this *was* a crazy and ramshackle way to do it, but there was one advantage that wasn't obvious to me until that day. The waterworks had been designed to fill up slowly. So after the rite concluded, we were able to spill out of the Mynster and follow the water at a brisk walking pace as it charged an aqueduct that ran along beside the Seven Stairs, skirted the Cloister, and reached across the Back toward the river.

A stone bridge crossed the river there, anchored on the near bank by a round tower and on the far by a bastion in the concent's outer wall. Within the round tower was a cistern, now being filled by water from the aqueduct, with a pitcher-lip poised above the petals of a water-wheel. Most of us reached it in time to see the cistern overflow and the wheel begin to turn, accepting energy from the water before exhausting it into the river. By stainless steel gears the wheel rotated a shaft, as thick as my thigh, that ran across the bridge (you might mistake it for a very stout railing if you didn't know what it was for). Across the river, inside of the bastion, the shaft drove another set of gears that was connected directly to the hinge-pins around which the gates swung.

Hearing them move, we ran toward them, but slowed as we got closer, not knowing what was about to happen.

Well . . . actually, we had a pretty good idea. But I was still young enough that I could let myself forget about Diax's Rake when I was in love with some idea. Orolo's yarn about a math that floated freely in time, surfing on crosscurrents of Causal Domain Shear, had really stirred my emotions, and so for a few moments I let my imagination run away, and pretended that I lived in such a math and that I really had no idea what might be found outside its gates when they opened: Mobs of jumped-up slines rushing in with pitchforks or molotovs. Starving ones crawling in to worry potatoes out of the ground. Moshianic pilgrims expecting to see the face of some god or other. Corpses strewn to the horizon. Virgin wilderness. The most interesting moment was when the gap between the gates grew just wide enough to admit a single person. Who would it be? Male or female, old or young, carrying an assault rifle, a baby, a chest of gold, or a backpack bomb?

As the doors continued to open, we were able to make out perhaps thirty Sæculars who had gathered to watch. Several were planted facing the gate, all sharing the same awkward stance; after a while I figured out that these were aiming speelycaptors at us, or holding up jeejahs to send feeds to people far away. A small child sat on her father's shoulders, eating something; she was already bored, and wriggling to be let down; he bent and twisted at the hips and in-sisted through clenched teeth that she watch, just for another min-ute. Eight children in identical clothes stood in a row, watched over by a lady. These must have come from one of the Burgers' suvins. A desolate woman, looking as though she'd survived a natural disas-ter that hadn't touched anyone else, walked slowly toward the gate carrying a bundle that I suspected was a newborn infant. Half a dozen men and women were gathered around something that smoked. This artifact was surrounded by a loose revetment of large brightly colored boxes, on which some of them sat, the better to eat their enormous drooling sandwiches. Half-forgotten Fluccish words came to me: *barbecue, cooler, cheesburg.*

One man had planted himself in a disk of open space—or per-haps the others were just avoiding him—and was waving a banner on the end of a pole: the flag of the Sæcular Power. His posture was defiant, triumphant. Another man shouted into a device that made his voice louder: some sort of a Deolater, I guessed, who wanted us to join his ark.

The first to enter were a man and woman dressed in the kinds of clothes that people wore extramuros to attend a wedding or make an important commercial transaction, and three children in miniature renditions of those clothes. The man was towing behind him a red wagon carrying a pot with a sapling growing out of it. Each of the children had a hand on the rim of the pot so that it wouldn't topple as the wagon's wheels felt their way over the cobbles. The woman, unencumbered, moved faster, but in a gait that looked all wrong until I recollected that women extramuros wore shoes that made them walk so. She was smiling but also wiping tears from her eyes. She headed straight for Grandsuur Ylma, whom she seemed to recognize, and began explaining that her father, who had died three years ago, had been a great supporter of the concent and liked to go in the Day Gate to attend lectures and read books. When he had died, his grandchildren had planted this tree, and now they hoped to see it transplanted to a suitable location on our grounds. Grandsuur Ylma said that that would be fine provided it was of the One Hundred Sixty-four. The Burger lady assured Ylma that, knowing our rules, they had gone to all sorts of trouble to make sure that this was so. Meanwhile, her husband was prowling around taking pictures of this conversation with a jeejah.

Seeing that we had not massacred the Burger family or inserted probes into their orifices, a young assistant to the man with the sound amplification device came in and began to approach us one by one, handing us leaves with writing on them. Unfortunately they were in Kinagrams and so we could not read them. We had been warned that it was best to accept such things politely and claim we would read them later—not engage such persons in Thelenean dialog.

This man noticed the desolate woman. Guessing that she meant to leave her baby with us, he began trying to talk her out of it in slangy Fluccish. She recoiled; then, understanding that she was probably safe, began cursing at him. Half a dozen suurs moved forward to surround her. The Deolater became furious and looked as if he might strike someone. I noticed Fraa Delrakhones for the first time, watching this fellow closely and making eye contact with several burly fraas who were moving closer to him. But then the man with the sound device chirped out a word that must have been the younger fellow's name. Having got his attention, he looked up at the sky for a moment ("The Powers that Be are watching, idiot!") then glared at him ("Simmer down and keep handing out the all-important literature!").

A tall man was walking toward me: Artisan Quin. Next to him was a shorter copy of Quin, without the beard. "Bon Apert, Fraa Erasmas," Quin said.

"Bon Apert, Artisan Quin," I returned, and then looked at his son. His son was looking at my left foot. His gaze traveled quickly up to the top of my hood but did not catch or linger on my face, as if this were of no more note than a wrinkle in my bolt. "Bon—" I began, but he interrupted: "That bridge is built on the arch principle."

"Barb, the fraa is wishing you Bon Apert," said Quin, and held out his hand in my direction. But Barb actually reached out and pulled his father's arm down—it was blocking his view of the bridge.

"The bridge has a catenary curve because of the vectors," Barb went on.

"Catenary. That's from the Orth word for—" I began.

"It's from the Orth word for chain," Barb announced. "It is the same curve that a hanging chain makes, flipped upside-down. But the driveshaft that opens the gates has to be straight. Unless it was made with newmatter." His eyes found my sphere and studied it for a few moments. "But that can't be, because the Concent of Saunt Edhar was built after the First Sack. So it must have been made with old matter." His eyes went back to the driveshaft, which seemed to follow the arch of the bridge, passing through blocks of carved stone at regular intervals. "Those stone things must contain universal joints," he concluded.

"That is correct," I said. "The shaft—"

"The shaft is put together from eight straight pieces connected by universal joints hidden inside the bases of those statues. The base of a statue is called a plinth." And Barb began to walk very fast; he was the first extra to cross over the bridge into our math. Quin gave me a look that was difficult to interpret, and hustled after him.

An altercation had flared up between the desolate woman and the suurs. Apparently, this woman had been told by some ignorant person that we'd give her money for the baby. The suurs had set her straight as gently as they knew how.

Several more extras had come in. A group of half a dozen, mostly men, all wearing clothes that were respectful, but not expensive. They had engaged a small group of mostly older avout. The foremost of the visitors was draped in a thick, gaudy-colored rope with a globe at the end. I reckoned he was the priest of some newfangled counter-Bazian ark. He was talking to Fraa Haligastreme: big, bald, burly, and bearded, looking as if he'd just stepped off the Periklyne after a brisk discussion of ontology with Thelenes. He was a theorical geologist, and the FAE of the Edharian chapter. He was listening politely, but kept throwing significant glances at a pair of purple-bolted hierarchs standing off to the side: Delrakhones, the Warden Fendant, and Statho, the Primate.

Circumventing this group, I passed in earshot of a side conversation. One of the women visitors had engaged Fraa Jesry. I put her age at about thirty, though the way that extramuros women did their hair and faces made it difficult to guess such things; on second thought, she was a dressed-up twenty-five. She was paying close attention to Jesry, asking him questions about life in the math.

After what seemed like a long time, I got Jesry's attention. He politely told the woman that he had made arrangements to go extramuros with me. She looked at me, which I enjoyed. Then her jeejah spat out a burst of notes and she excused herself to take a call.

⭘⭘⭘⭘⭘⭘⭘⭘⭘⭘⭘⭘⭘⭘⭘⭘⭘⭘⭘⭘⭘⭘⭘⭘⭘⭘⭘⭘⭘⭘⭘⭘⭘⭘⭘⭘⭘

Sline: (1) In Fluccish of the late Praxic Age and early Reconstitution, a slang word formed by truncation of **baseline,** which is a Praxic commercial bulshytt term. It appears to be a noun that turned into an adjective meaning "common" or "widely shared." (2) A noun denoting an extramuros person with no special education, skills, aspirations, or hope of acquiring same. (3) Derogatory term for a stupid or uncouth person, esp. one who takes pride in those very qualities. Note: this sense is deprecated because it implies that a sline is a sline because of inherent personal shortcomings or perverse choices; sense (2) is preferred because it does not convey any such implication.

—THE DICTIONARY, 4th edition, A.R. 3000

Jesry and I walked out for the first time in ten years.

The first thing I noticed was that people had leaned a lot of junk against the outside of our walls. Apparently some of it had even been leaned against the gates, but someone had cleared it off to the sides in preparation for Apert.

During this era, the neighborhood outside the Decade Gate was where artisans kept their shops, and so the stuff leaned against the walls tended to be lumber, pipes, reels of cable or tubing, and long-handled tools. We walked silently for a while, just looking. But sooner than you might think, we got used to it and forgot we were fraas.

"Do you think that woman wanted to have a liaison with you?" I asked.

"A—what do you call it—"

"An Atlanian Liaison." Named after a Decenarian fraa of the Seventeenth Century A.R. who saw his true love for ten days every ten years and spent the rest of the time writing poems to her and sneaking them out of the math. They were really fine poems, carved in stone some places.

"Why do you think a woman would want that?" he wondered.

"Well, no risk of getting pregnant, when your partner is a fraa," I pointed out.

"That might be important sometimes, but I think it's easy for them to obtain contraception in this epoch."

"I was kind of joking."

"Oh. Sorry. Well . . . maybe she wants me for my mind."

"Or your spiritual qualities."

"Huh? You think she's some kind of Deolater?"

"Didn't you see who she was with?"

"Some sort of—who knows—a *contingent,* I think is what they call that."

"Those were Warden of Heaven people, I'll bet. Their leader was got up in a kind of imitation of a chord."

We had gone far enough that the Decade Gate was lost to view around a curve. I glanced up at the Præsidium. The megaliths rising up from the perimeter of the starhenge served as compass points to help me establish my bearings. We had come to a larger road now, running roughly parallel to the river. If we crossed it and kept going, we'd climb into a neighborhood of big houses where burgers lived. If we followed it to the right, it would take us to the commerce district and we could eventually loop back in through the Day Gate. To the left, it ran out into the fauxburbs where I had spent my first eight years.

"Let's get this over with," I said, and turned left.

After we had gone a few paces, Jesry said "Again?" which was his annoying way of requesting clarification. "The Warden of Heaven?"

"Moshianics," I said, and then spent a while telling him about Fraa Orolo's interviews with Flec and Quin.

As we went along, the nature of the place changed: fewer workshops, more warehouses. Barges could navigate this stretch of the river and so it was where people tended to store things. We saw more vehicles now: a lot of drummons, which had up to a dozen wheels and were used for carrying large, heavy objects around districts like this. These looked the same as I remembered. A few fetches scurried around with smaller loads secured to their backs. These were more colorful. The men who owned them tended to be artisans, and it was clear that they spent a lot of time altering the vehicles' shape and color, apparently for no reason other than to amuse themselves. Or maybe it was a kind of competition, like plumage on birds. Anyway, the styles had changed quite a bit, and so Jesry and I would stop talking and stare whenever a particularly strange or gaudy fetch went by. Their drivers stared right back at us.

"Well, I was oblivious to all that Warden of Heaven stuff," Jesry concluded. "I've been very busy computing for Orolo's group."

"Why did you think Tamura was drilling us last night?" I asked.

"I *didn't* think about it," Jesry said. "All I can say is, it's good you are around to be aware of all this. Have you considered—"

"Joining the New Circle? Angling to become a hierarch?"

"Yeah."

"No. I don't have to, because everyone else seems to be considering it for me."

"Sorry, Raz!" he said, not really sounding sorry—more miffed that I had become miffed. He was hard to talk to, and sometimes I'd go months avoiding him. But slowly I'd learned it could be worth the aggravation.

"Forget it," I said. "What have Orolo's group been up to?"

"I've no idea, I just do the calculations. Orbital mechanics."

"Theorical or—"

"Totally praxic."

"You think they have found a planet around another star?"

"How could that be? For that, they have to collate information from other telescopes. And we haven't gotten anything in ten years, obviously."

"So it's something nearer," I said, "something that can be picked out with our telescopes."

"It's an asteroid," Jesry said, fed up with my slow progress on the riddle.

"Is it the Big Nugget?"

"Orolo would be a lot more excited in that case."

This was a very old joke. The Panjandrums had almost no use for us, but one of the few things that might change that would be the discovery of a large asteroid that was about to hit Arbre. In 1107 it had almost happened. Thousands of avout had been brought together in a convox that had built a spaceship to go nudge it out of the way. But by the time the ship had been launched in 1115, the cosmographers had calculated that the rock would just miss us, and so it had turned into a study mission. The lab where they'd built the ship was now the concent of Saunt Rab, after the cosmographer who had discovered the rock.

To our right, the hill where the burgers lived had petered out. A tributary of the river cut across our path from that direction. The road crossed it on an ancient steel bridge, built, rusted, decayed, condemned, and pasted back together with newmatter. A dotted line, worn away to near invisibility, hinted to motorists that they might consider showing a little civility to pedestrians between the right-most lane and the railing. It was a bit late for us to double back now, and we could see another pedestrian pushing a cart, piled high with polybags, so we hustled over as quickly as we could manage, trusting the drummons, fetches, and mobes not to strike us dead. To our left we could see the tributary winding through its floodplain toward the join with the main river a mile away. When I'd been younger, the angle between the two watercourses had been mostly trees and marsh, but it looked as though they had put up a levee to fend off high water and then shingled it with buildings: most obviously, a large roofless arena with thousands of empty seats.

"Shall we go watch a game?" Fraa Jesry asked. I couldn't tell whether he was serious. Of all of us, he looked the most like an athlete. He didn't play sports often, but when he did, he was determined and angry, and tended to do well even though he had few skills.

"I think you need money to get in."

"Maybe we could sell some honey."

"We don't have any of that either. Maybe later in the week."

Jesry did not seem very satisfied with my answer.

"It's too early in the morning for them to be having a game," I added.

A minute later he had a new proposal: "Let's pick a fight with some slines."

We were almost to the end of the bridge. We had just scurried out of the path of a fetch operated by a man about our age who drove it as if he had been chewing jumpweed, with one hand on the controls and the other pressing a jeejah to the side of his face. So we were physically excited, breathing rapidly, and the idea of getting into a fight seemed a tiny bit less stupid than it would have otherwise. I smiled, and considered it. Jesry and I were strong from winding the clock, and many of the extras were in terrible condition—I understood now what Quin had meant when he'd said that they were starving to death and dying from being too fat at the same time.

When I looked back at Jesry he scowled and turned his face away. He didn't really want to get into a fight with slines.

We had entered into the fauxburb where I had come from. A whole block had been claimed by a building that looked like a megastore but was apparently some new counter-Bazian ark. In the lawn before it was a white statue, fifty feet high, of some bearded prophet holding up a lantern and a shovel.

The roadside ditches were full of jumpweed and slashberry poking up through sediments of discarded packaging. Beneath a grey film of congealed exhaust, faded Kinagrams fidgeted like maggots trapped in a garbage bag. The Kinagrams, the logos, the names of the snacks were new to me, but in essence it was all the same.

I knew now why Jesry was being such a jerk. "It's disappointing," I said.

"Yeah," Jesry said.

"All these years reading the Chronicles and hearing strange tales told every day at Provener . . . I guess it sort of . . ."

"Raised our expectations," he said.

"Yeah." Something occurred to me: "Did Orolo ever talk to you about the Ten-thousanders?"

"Causal Domain Shear and all that?" Jesry looked at me funny, surprised that Orolo had confided in me.

I nodded.

"That is a classic example of the crap they feed us to make it seem more exciting than it really is." But I sensed Jesry had only just decided this; if Orolo was talking to *all* the fids about it, how special could it be?

"They're not feeding us crap, Jesry. It's just that we live in boring times."

He tried a new tack: "It's a recruiting strategy. Or, to be precise, a retention strategy."

"What does that mean?"

"Our only entertainment is waiting for the next Apert—to see what's out there when the gates open. When the answer turns out to be the same crap except dirtier and uglier, what can we do besides sign up for another ten years and see if it's any different next time?"

"Or go in deeper."

"Become a Hundreder? Haven't you realized that's worthless for us?"

"Because their next Apert is *our* next Apert," I said.

"And then we die before the next one after that."

"It's not that rare to live to 130," I demurred. Which only proved that I had done the same calculation in my head and come to the same conclusion as Jesry. He snorted.

"You and I were born too early to be Hundreders and too late to be Thousanders. A couple of years earlier and we might have been foundlings and gone straight to the crag."

"In which case we'd both die before seeing an Apert," I said. "Besides, *I* might have been a foundling, but from what you've said of your birth family, I don't think *you'd* have."

"We'll see soon enough," he said.

We covered a mile in silence. Even though we didn't say anything, we were in dialog: a peregrin dialog, meaning two equals wandering around trying to work something out, as opposed to a suvinian dialog where a fid is being taught by a mentor, or a Periklynian dialog, which is combat. The road dovetailed into a larger one lined with the mass-produced businesses where slines obtained food and stuff, enlivened by casinos: windowless industrial cubes wrapped in colored light. Back in some day when there had been more vehicles, the full width of the right-of-way had been claimed by striped lanes. Now there were a lot of pedestrians and people getting around on scooters and wheeled planks and pedal-powered contraptions. But instead of going in straight lines they, and we, had to stitch together routes joining the pavement slabs that surrounded the businesses as the sea surrounds a chain of islands. The slabs were riven with meandering cracks marked by knife-thin hedges of jumpweed that had been straining dirt and wrappers out of the wind for a long time. The sun had gone behind clouds shortly after dawn but now it came out again. We ducked into the shade of a business that sold tires of different colors to young men who wanted to prettify their fetches and their souped-up mobes, and spent a minute rearranging our bolts to protect our heads.

"You want something," I said. "You're grumpy you don't have it yet. I don't think that what you want is stuff, because you've paid no attention at all to any of this." I jerked my head at a display of iridescent newmatter tires. Moving pictures of naked women with distended breasts came and went on the sides of the wheels.

Jesry watched one of the moving pictures for a while, then shrugged. "I suppose I could leave, and learn to like such things. Frankly it seems pretty stupid. Maybe it helps if you eat what they eat."

We moved on across the pavement-slab. "Look," I said, "it's been understood at least since the Praxic Age that if you have enough allswell floating around in your bloodstream, your brain will tell you in a hundred different ways that everything is all right—"

"And if you don't, you end up like you and me," he said.

I tried to become angry, then surrendered with a laugh. "All right," I said, "let's go with that. A minute ago, we passed a stand of blithe in the median strip—"

"I saw it too, and the one by the pre-owned-pornography store."

"That one looked fresher. We could go pick it and eat it, and eventually the level of allswell in our blood would go up and we could live out here, or *anywhere*, and feel happy. Or we could go back to the concent and try to come by our happiness honestly."

"You are so gullible," he said.

"*You're* supposed to be the Edharians' golden boy," I said, "*you're* supposed to be the one who swallows this stuff without question. I'm surprised, frankly."

"And what are you now, Raz? The cynical Procian?"

"So people seem to think."

"Look," Jesry said, "I see the older avout working hard. Those who have upsight—who are illuminated by the light of Cnoüs"—he said this in a mocking tone; he was so frustrated that he veered and lunged in random ways as he moved from one thought to the next—"they do theorics. Those who aren't so gifted fall back, and cut stone or keep bees. The really miserable ones leave, or throw themselves off the Mynster. Those who remain seem happy, whatever that means."

"Certainly happier than the people out here."

"I disagree," Jesry said. "These people are as happy as, say, Fraa Orolo. They get what they want: naked ladies on their wheels. He gets what he wants: upsight to the mysteries of the universe."

"Let's get down to it then: what do you want?"

"*Something to happen,*" he said, "I almost don't care what."

"If you made a great advance in theorics, would that count?"

"Sure, but what are the odds I'll do that?"

"It depends on the givens coming in from the observatories."

"Right. So it's out of my control. What do I do in the meantime?"

"Study theorics, which you're so good at. Drink beer. Have Tivian liaisons with as many suurs as you can talk into it. Why is that so bad?"

He was devoting way too much attention to kicking a stone ahead of him, watching it bound across the pavement. "I keep looking at the shrimpy guys in the stained-glass windows," he said.

"Huh?"

"You know. In the windows depicting the Saunts. The Saunts themselves, they're always shown big. They fill most of the window. But if you look close, you can see tiny little figures in bolts and chords—"

"Huddled around their knees," I said.

"Yeah. Looking up at the Saunt adoringly. The helpers. The fids. The second-raters who proved a lemma or read a draft somewhere along the way. No one knows their names, except maybe the cranky old fraa who takes care of that one window."

"You don't want to end up as a knee-hugger," I said.

"That is correct. How does that work? Why some, but not others?"

"So, you want a window all to yourself?"

"It'd mean that something interesting happened to me," he said, "something more interesting than this."

"And if it came to a choice between that, and having enough allswell in your blood?"

He thought about that as we waited for a huge, articulated drummon to back out of our way.

"Finally you ask an interesting question," he said.

And after that, he was quite a pleasant companion.

Half an hour later I pronounced us lost. Jesry accepted it with pleasure, as if this were more satisfactory than being found.

A boxy vehicle rolled past. "That is the third coach full of children that has gone by us recently," Jesry pointed out. "Did you have a suvin in your neighborhood?"

"Places like this don't have suvins," I reminded him. "They have stabils."

"Oh yes. That comes from—it's an old Fluccish word—uh, cultural . . ."

"Stabilization Centers. But don't say that because no one has called them that in something like three thousand years."

"Right. Stabils it is."

We turned where the coaches turned. For the next minute or so, things were fragile between us. Inside the math, it didn't matter that he had come from burgers and I had come from slines. But as soon as we had stepped out of the Decade Gate, this fact had been released, like a bubble of swamp gas deep in dark water. Invisibly it had been rising and expanding ever since, and had just now erupted in a great, flaming, stinking belch.

My old stabil looked, in my eyes, like a half-scale reproduction of itself thrown together by a sloppy modelmaker. Some of the rooms had been boarded up. In my day they'd been crowded. So that confirmed that the population was declining. Perhaps by the time I was a grandfraa there would be a young forest here.

An empty coach pulled out of the drive. Before the next drew up to take its place, I glimpsed a crowd of youngsters staggering under huge backpacks into a canyon of raucously colored light: a breezeway lined with machines dispensing snacks, drinks, and attention-getting noises. From there they would carry their breakfasts into rooms, which Jesry and I could see through windows: in some, the children all watched the same program on a single large screen, in others each had his or her own panel. To one end, the blank wall of the gymnasium was booming with low-frequency rhythms of a sports program. I recognized the beat. It was the same one they had used when I was there.

Jesry and I had not seen moving pictures in ten years and so we stood there for a few minutes, hypnotized. But I had got my bearings now, and once I had nudged Jesry back into motion, I was able to lead us down the streets I had wandered as a boy. People here were as keen to modify their houses as their vehicles, and so when I did recognize a dwelling, it would have a new, freestanding roof lofted above the old one, or new modules plugged and pasted onto the ones I saw when I dreamed about the place. But I was helped by the fact that the neighborhood was half the size of what I remembered.

We found where I'd lived before I was Collected: two shelter modules joined into an L, another L of wire mesh completing a weedy cloister that housed one dead mobe and two dead fetches, the oldest of which I had personally helped set up on blocks. The gate was decorated with four different signs of varying ages promising to kill anyone who entered, which, to me, seemed much less intimidating than a single sign would've. A baby tree, about as long as my forearm, had sprouted from a clogged raingutter. Its seed must have been carried there by wind or a bird. I wondered how long it would take to grow to a size where it would tear the gutter clean off. Inside, a loud moving picture was showing on a speely, so we had to do a lot of hallooing and gate-rattling before someone emerged: a woman of about twenty. She'd have been a Big Girl to me when I'd been eight. I tried to remember the Big Girl's names.

"Leeya?"

"She moved away when *those* guys left," the woman explained, as if hooded men came to her door every day incanting the names of long-lost relations. She glanced back over her shoulder to watch a fiery explosion on the speely. As the sound of the explosion died away we could hear a man's voice demanding something. She explained to him what she was doing. He didn't quite follow her explanation, so she repeated the same words more loudly.

"I infer that some kind of factional schism has taken place within your family while you were gone," Jesry said. I wanted to slug him. But when I looked at his face I saw he wasn't trying to be clever.

The woman turned to look at us again. I was peering at her through an aperture between two signs that were threatening to kill me, and I wasn't certain that she could see my face.

"I used to be named Vit," I said.

"The boy who went to the clock. I remember you. How's it going?"

"Fine. How are you?"

"Keeping it casual. Your mama isn't here. She moved."

"Far away?"

She rolled her eyes, vexed that I had leaned on her to make such a judgment. "Farther than you can probably walk." The man inside yelled again. She was obliged to turn her back on us again and summarize her activities.

"Apparently she does not subscribe to the Dravicular Iconography," Jesry said.

"How do you figure?"

"She said you went to the clock. Voluntarily. Not that you were taken by or abducted by the avout."

The woman turned to face us again.

"I had an older sib named Cord," I said. I nodded at the oldest of the broken fetches. "Former owner of that. I helped put it there."

The woman had complex opinions of Cord, which she let us know by causing several emotions to ripple across her face. She ended by exhaling sharply, dropping her shoulders, setting her chin, and putting on a smile that I guessed was meant to be obviously fake. "Cord works all the time on stuff."

"What kind of stuff?"

This question was even more exasperating to her than my earlier "Far away?" She looked pointedly at the moving picture.

"Where should I look?" I tried.

She shrugged. "You passed it on the way probably." And she mentioned a place that we had in fact passed, shortly after leaving the Decade Gate. Then she took a step back inside, because the man in there was demanding an account of her recent doings. "Keep it casual," she said, and waved, and disappeared from our view.

"Now I really want to meet Cord," Jesry said.

"Me too. Let's get out of here," I said, and turned my back on the place—probably for the last time, as I didn't imagine I'd come back at next Apert. Perhaps when I was seventy-eight years old. Reforestation was a surprisingly quick process.

"What's a sib? Why do you use that word?"

"In some families, it's not entirely clear how people are related."

We walked faster and talked less, and got back across the bridge in very little time. Since the place where Cord worked was so close to the concent, we first went up into the burger neighborhood and found Jesry's house.

When we'd gone out the Decade Gate, Jesry had been quiet and distracted for a few minutes before he had gone on his rant. Now I had an upsight, which was that he'd been expecting his family to be standing in front of the gate to meet him. So as we approached his old house I actually felt more anxious than I had when approaching mine. A porter let us in at the front gate and we kicked off our sandals so that the damp grass would clean and soothe our blasted feet. As we passed into the deep shade of the forested belt around the main residence, we threw back our hoods and slowed to enjoy the cool air.

No one was home except for a female servant whose Fluccish was difficult for us to make out. She seemed to expect us; she handed us a leaf, not from a leaf-tree such as we grew in the concent, but made by a machine. It seemed like an official document that had been stamped out on a press or generated by a syntactic device. At its head was yesterday's date. But it was actually a personal note written to Jesry by his mother, using a machine to generate the neat rows of letters. She had written it in Orth with only a few errors (she didn't understand how to use the subjunctive). It used terms with which we were not familiar, but the gist seemed to be that Jesry's father had been doing a lot of work, far away, for some entity that was difficult to explain. But from the part of the world it was in, we knew it had to be some organ of the Sæcular Power. Yesterday, she had with great reluctance and some tears gone to join him, because his career depended on her attending some kind of social event that was also difficult to explain. They had every intention of making it back for the banquet on Tenth Night, and they were bending every effort to round up Jesry's three older brothers and two older sisters as well. In the meantime, she had baked him some cookies (which we already knew since the female servant had brought them out to us).

Jesry showed me around the house, which felt like a math, but with fewer people. There was even a fancy clock, which we spent a lot of time examining. We pulled down books from the shelves and got somewhat involved in them. Then the bells began to ring in the Bazian cathedral across the street, followed by the chimes in the fancy clock, and we realized that we could read books any day and sheepishly re-shelved them. After a while we ended up on the veranda eating the rest of the cookies. We looked at the cathedral. Bazian architecture was a cousin to Mathic, broad and rounded where ours was narrow and pointy. But this town was not nearly as important to the Sæcular world as the Concent of Saunt Edhar was to the mathic world, so the cathedral looked puny compared to the Mynster.

"Do you feel happy yet?" Jesry joked, looking at the cookies.

"It takes two weeks," I said, "that's why Apert is only ten days long."

We wandered out onto the lawn. Then we marched back out and headed down the hill.

Cord worked in a compound where everything was made of metal, which marked it as an ancient place—not quite as ancient as a place made of stone, but probably dating back to the middle of the Praxic Age when steel had become cheap and heat engines had begun to move about on rails. It was situated a quarter of a mile from the Century Gate on the end of a slip that had been dug from the river so that barges could penetrate into this neighborhood and connect to roads and rails. The property was a mess, but it drew a kind of majesty just from being huge and silent. It had been outlined by a fence twice my height made from sheets of corrugated steel anchored in earth or concrete, welded together, and braced against wind by old worn-out railroad rails, which seemed like overkill for a wind brace. In fact it was such conspicuous overkill that Jesry and I interrupted each other trying to be the first to point it out, and got into an argument about what it meant. Other parts of the perimeter were made of the steel boxes used later in the Praxic Age to enclose goods on ships and trains. Some of these were filled with dirt, others stuffed with scraps of metal so tangled and irregular that they looked organic. Some *were* organic because they had been colonized by slashberry. There was a lot of green and growing matter around the edges of the compound, but the center was a corral of pounded earth.

The main building was little more than a roof on stilts straddling the last two hundred feet of the canal. Its trusses were oversized to support a traveling crane with a great hook dangling from a rusty chain, each of whose links was as big as my head. We had seen this structure from the Mynster but never given much thought to it. Teed into its side was a high-roofed hall enclosed by proper walls of brick (below) and corrugated steel (above). Grafted to the side of that, down low, was a shelter module with all sorts of homey touches, such as a fake wood door and a farm-style weathervane, that looked crazy here. We knocked, waited, then pushed our way in. We made lots of noise, just in case this was another one of those places where visitors were put to death. But no one was there.

The module had been designed to serve as a home, but everything in it had been bent to serve the purposes of an office. So for example the shower stall was occupied by a tall cabinet where records were filed. A hole had been sawed into a wall so that little pipes could be routed to a hot-beverage machine. A freestanding urinal had been planted in the bedroom. The only decoration, other than those crazy-looking rustic touches that had shipped with the module, was oddly shaped pieces of metal—parts from machines, I reckoned—some of which had been bent or snapped in traumatic events we could only imagine.

A trail of oily bootprints led us to the back door. This opened straight into the cavernous hall. Both of us hunched our shoulders as we stepped over the threshold. We hesitated just inside. The place was too big to illuminate, so most of the light was natural, shining through translucent panels high up in the walls, each surrounded by a hazy nimbus. The walls and floors were dark with age, congealed smoke, and oil. More hooks and chains dangled from overhead beams. The light washing round these gave them a spindly, eroded look. The floor sprawled away into haze and shadow. Widely spaced around it were crouching masses, some no bigger than a man, others the size of a library. Each was built around a hill of metal: from a distance, smooth and rounded, from up close, rough, which led me to guess that these had been made in the ancient process of excavating molds from sand and pouring in a lake of molten iron. Where it mattered, the rough iron had been cut away to leave planes, holes, and right angles of bare grey metal: stubby feet by which the castings were bolted to the floor, or long V-shaped ways on which other castings could slide, driven by great screws. Huddled beside these things or crouching under them were architectures of wound copper wire, rife with symmetries, and, when they moved, brilliant with azure-tinged lightning. Tendrils of wire and of artfully bent tubing had grown over these machines like ivy exploring a boulder, and my eye followed them to concentrations where I was sometimes surprised to see a human being in a dark coverall. Sometimes these humans were doing something identifiable as work, but more often they were just thinking. The machines emitted noise from time to time, but for the most part it was quiet, pervaded by a low hum that came from warm resonating boxes strewn all round and fed by, or feeding, cables as thick as my ankle.

There were perhaps half a dozen humans in the entire place, but something in their posture made us not dare approach them.

One came our way pushing a rusty cart exploding with wild helices of shaved metal.

"Excuse me," I said, "is Cord here?"

The man turned and extended his hand toward something big and complicated that stood in the middle of the hall. Above it, the rational adrakhonic geometry of the roof-trusses and the infinitely more complex manifolds of swirling mist were magnified and made more than real by the sputtering blue light of electrical fire. If I saw a star of that color through a telescope, I would know it as a blue dwarf and I could guess its temperature: far hotter than our sun, hot enough that much of its energy was radiated as ultraviolet light and X-rays. But, paradoxically, the house-sized complex that was the source of the energy looked orange-red, with only a fringe of the killing radiance leaking out round edges or bouncing from slick places on the floor. As Jesry and I drew closer, we perceived it as a giant cube of red amber with two black forms trapped in it: not insects but humans. The humans shifted position from time to time, their silhouettes rippling and twisting.

We saw that this machine had been robed in a curtain of some red jelly-like matter suspended from an overhead track. The blue light could blast straight up and kill germs in the rafters but it could not range across the floor and blind people. Obviously to me and Jesry, the curtain was red because it had been formulated to let only low-energy light—which our eyes saw as red—pass through it. To high-energy light—which we saw as blue, if we could see it at all—it was as opaque as a steel plate.

We walked around the perimeter, which was about the size of two small shelter modules parked side by side. Through the red jelly-wall it was difficult to resolve fine details of the machine, but it seemed to have a slab-like table, big enough to sleep ten, that eased to and fro like a block of ice on a griddle. Planted in its center was a smaller, circular table that made quick but measured spins and tilts. Suspended above all of this, from a cast-iron bridge, was a mighty construct that moved up and down, and that carried the spark-gap where the light was born.

An arm of tubular steel was thrust forth from the apex of the bridge toward a platform where the two humans stood. Pendant from its end was a box folded together from sheet metal, which looked out of place; it was of a different order of things from the sand-cast iron. Glowing numbers were all over it. It must be full of syntactic processors that measured what the machine was doing, or controlled it. Or both; for a true syntactic processor would have the power to make decisions based on measurements. Of course my thought was to turn away and get out of the room. But Jesry was rapt. "It's okay, it's Apert!" he said, and grabbed my arm to turn me back around.

One of the two humans inside said something about the x-axis. Jesry and I looked at each other in astonishment, just to be sure we'd actually heard such a thing. It was like hearing a fry cook speak Middle Orth.

Other fragments came through above the sputtering of the machine: "Cubic spline." "Evolute." "Pylanic interpolation."

We could not keep our eyes off the banks of red numbers on the front of the syntactic processor. They were always changing. One was a clock counting down in hundredths of a second. Others—as we gradually perceived—reflected the position of the table. They were literal transcriptions of the great table's x and y position, the angles of rotation and tilt of the smaller table in the middle, and the altitude of the sizzling blaster. Sometimes all would freeze except for one—this signaled a simple linear move. Other times they would all change at once, realizing a system of parametric equations.

Jesry and I watched it for half an hour without speaking another word. Mostly I was trying to make sense of how the numbers changed. But also I was thinking of how this place was similar in many respects to the Mynster with its sacred clock in the center, in its well of light.

Then the clock struck, as it were. The countdown stopped at zero and the light went out.

Cord reached up and threw back the curtain. She peeled off a pair of black goggles, and raised one arm to wipe her brow on her sleeve.

The man standing next to her—who I gathered was the

customer—was dressed in loose black trousers and a black long-sleeved pullover, with a black skullcap on his head. Jesry and I realized at the same moment what he was. We were dumbstruck.

Likewise, the Ita saw what we were, and took half a step back. His long black beard avalanched down his chest as his mouth fell open. But then he did something remarkable, which was that he mastered the reflex to cringe and scuttle away from us, which had been drilled into him since birth. He thought better of that half-step back. He resumed his former stance, and—hard to believe, but Jesry and I agreed on this later—*glared* at us.

Not knowing how to handle this, Jesry and I backed away and stood out of earshot while Cord did one small quick necessary chore after another, celebrating some aut of shutting down the machine and making it ready for re-use.

The Ita peeled off his skullcap—which was how they covered their heads when they were among their own kind—and drew it out into the slightly mushroomed stovepipe that they wore when they were out and about so that we could identify them from a distance. He then set this back on his head while sending another defiant look our way.

Just as we would never let the Ita come into the chancel, he saw it as sacrilege that *we* would come *here*. As if we were guilty of a profanation.

Perhaps obeying a similar impulse, Jesry and I hooded ourselves.

It was almost as if, far from chafing under the stereotype of the sneaky, scheming, villainous Ita, this one was embracing it—taking pride in it, and pushing it as far as he could without actually talking to us.

As we waited for Cord and the Ita to conclude their business, I kept thinking of all the ways that this place was similar to the Mynster: for example, how I had been taken aback when I'd stepped into the hall, so dark and so light at the same time. A voice in my head—the voice of a Procian pedant—admonished me that this was a Halikaarnian way of thinking. For in truth I was looking at a collection of ancient machines that had no meaning: all syntax, no semantics. I was claiming I saw a meaning in it. But this meaning had no reality, outside of my mind. I had brought it into the hall with me, carrying it in my head, and now I was playing games with semantics by pasting it onto these iron monuments.

But the longer I thought about it, the more certain I became that I was having a legitimate upsight.

Protas, the greatest fid of Thelenes, had climbed to the top of a mountain near Ethras and looked down upon the plain that nourished the city-state and observed the shadows of the clouds, and compared their shapes. He had had his famous upsight that while the shapes of the shadows undeniably answered to those of the clouds, the latter were infinitely more complex and more perfectly realized than the former, which were distorted not only by the loss of a spatial dimension but also by being projected onto terrain that was of irregular shape. Hiking back down, he had extended that upsight by noting that the mountain seemed to have a different shape every time he turned round to look back at it, even though he knew it had but one absolute form and that these seeming changes were mere figments of his shifting point of view. From there he had moved on to his greatest upsight of all, which was that these two observations—the one concerning the clouds, the other concerning the mountain—were themselves both shadows cast into his mind by the same greater, unifying idea. Returning to the Periklyne he had proclaimed his doctrine that all the things we thought we knew were shadows of more perfect things in a higher world. This had become the essential doctrine of Protism. If Protas could be respected for saying so, then what was wrong with me thinking that our Mynster, and this machine hall, were both shadows of some higher thing that existed elsewhere—a sacred place of which they were both shadows, and that cast other shadows in such places as Bazian arks and groves of ancient trees?

Jesry meanwhile had been staring at Cord's machine. Cord had manipulated some controls that had caused the lightning-head to retract as far up as it would go and the table to thrust itself forward. She vaulted up onto that steel slab. In small premeditated steps she came to the part of it that tilted and rotated (which, by itself, was a machine of impressive size). Before resting her weight on a foot she would wiggle it to and fro, scattering shards and twists of silver metal to either side. They made glinting music as they found their way to the floor, and some left corkscrews of fine smoke along their paths. A helper approached with an empty cart, a broom, and a shovel, and began pushing the scraps into a pile.

"It carves the metal from a block," Jesry said. "Not with a blade but with an electrical discharge that melts the stuff away—"

"More than melts. Remember the color of the light?" I said. "It turns the metal to—"

"Plasma," we said in unison, and Jesry went on: "It just carves off all the bits that aren't wanted."

This raised the question of what *was* wanted? The answer was clamped to the top of the rotating table: a sculpture of silver metal, flowing and curved like an antler, swelling in places to knobs pierced by perfect cylindrical holes. Cord drew a wrench from the thing she was wearing, which seemed more harness than garment, as its chief purpose was to secure tools to her body. She released three vises, put the wrench back in its ordained pocket, threw back her shoulders, bent her knees, made her spine long, raised her hands, and clasped them around two prongs of this thing she had made. It came up off the table. She carried it down off the machine as if it were a cat rescued from a tree and set it upon a steel cart that looked older than a mountain. The Ita ran his hands over it. His tall hat turned this way and that as he bent to inspect certain details. Then he nodded and exchanged a few words with Cord and pushed the cart off into smoke and quiet.

"It's a part for the clock!" Jesry said. "Something must have broken or worn out down in the cellar!"

I agreed that the style of the thing reminded me of some parts of the clock, but I shushed him because I was more interested in Cord just now. She was walking toward us, almost but not quite stepping on strewn shards of metal, wiping her hands on a rag. Her hair was cut short. I thought at first that she was tall, perhaps because that was how I remembered her. In truth she was no taller than I. She seemed stocky with all that hardware strapped to her, but her neck and forearms were firm. She drew to within a couple of paces and clanked to a stop and planted herself. She had a quite solid and deliberate manner of standing. She seemed as though she could sleep standing up, like a horse.

"I guess I know who you are," she said to me, "but what is your name?"

"Erasmas, now."

"Is that the name of an old Saunt?"

"That's right."

"I never did get that old fetch to run."

"I know. I just saw it."

"Took part of it here, to be machined, and never left." She gazed at the palm of her right hand, then looked up at me. I understood this to mean "my hand is dirty but I will shake it if you please."

I extended my hand and clasped hers.

The sound of bells drifted in.

"Thank you for letting us see your machine," I said. "Would you care to see ours? That's Provener. Jesry and I have to go wind the clock."

"I went to Provener one time."

"Today, you can see it from where we see it. Bon Apert."

"Bon Apert," she returned. "Okay, what the heck, I'll come see it."

We had to run across the meadow. Cord had left her big tool-harness behind at the machine hall, only to reveal a smaller, vestlike one that I guessed held the stuff she'd not be without under any circumstances. When we broke into a run, she clanked and jounced for a few paces until she cinched down some straps, and then she was able to keep pace with us as we rushed through the clover. Our meadow had been colonized by Sæculars who were having midday picnics. Some were even grilling meat. They watched us run by as if our being late were a performance for their amusement. Children were chivvied forward for a better view. Adults trained speelycaptors on us and laughed out loud to see us caring so much.

We came in the meadow door, ran up stairs into a wardroom where stacks of dusty pews and altars were shoved against the walls, and nearly tripped over Lio and Arsibalt. Lio was sitting on the floor with his legs doubled under him. Arsibalt sat on a short bench, knees far apart, leaning forward so that the blood streaming from his nostrils would puddle neatly on the floor.

Lio's lip was puffy and bleeding. The flesh around his left eye was ochre, suggesting it would be black tomorrow. He was staring into a dim corner of the room. Arsibalt let out a shuddering moan, as if he'd been sobbing, and was just now managing it.

"Fight?" I asked.

Lio nodded.

"Between the two of you or—"

Lio shook his head.

"We were *set upon!*" Arsibalt proclaimed, shouting at his blood-puddle.

"Intra or extra?" Jesry demanded.

"*Extra*muros. We were en route to my pater's basilica. I wished only to learn whether he would speak to me. A vehicle drove by once, twice, thrice. It circled us like a lowering raptor. Four men emerged. One had his arm in a sling; he looked on and cheered the other three."

Jesry and I both looked at Lio, who took our meaning immediately.

"Useless. Useless," he said.

"What was useless?" Cord asked. The sound of her voice caused Arsibalt to look up.

Lio was not the sort to care that we had a visitor—but he did answer her question. "My vlor. All of the Vale-lore I have ever studied."

"It can't have been that bad!" Jesry exclaimed. Which was funny since, over the years, no one had been more persistent than Jesry in telling Lio how useless his vlor was.

By way of an answer Lio rolled to his feet, glided over, grasped the edge of Jesry's hood, and yanked it down over his face. Not only was Jesry now blind, but because of how the bolt was wound around his body, it interfered with his arms and made it surprisingly difficult for him to expose his face again. Lio gave him the tiniest of nudges and he lost his balance so badly that I had to hug him and force him upright.

"That's what they did to you?" I asked. Lio nodded.

"Tilt your head *back,* not forward," Cord was saying to Arsibalt. "There's a vein up here." She pointed to the bridge of her nose. "Pinch it. That's right. My name is Cord, I am a sib of . . . Erasmas."

"Enchanted," Arsibalt said, muffled by his hand, as he had taken Cord's advice. "I am Arsibalt, bastard of the local Bazian arch-prelate, if you can believe such a thing."

"The bleeding is slowing down, I think," Cord said. From one of her pockets she had drawn out a pair of purple wads which unfolded to gloves of some stretchy membranous stuff. She wiggled her hands into them. I was baffled for a few moments, then realized that this was a precaution against infection: something I never would have thought of.

"Fortunately, my blood supply is simply enormous, because of my size," Arsibalt pointed out, "otherwise, I fear I should exsanguinate."

Some of Cord's pockets were narrow and tall and ranked in neat rows. From two of these she drew out blunt plugs of white fibrous stuff, about the size of her little finger, with strings trailing from them. "What on earth are those?" Arsibalt wanted to know.

"Blood soaker-uppers," Cord said, "one for each nostril, if you would like." She gave them over into Arsibalt's gory hands, and watched, a little bit nervous and a little bit fascinated, as Arsibalt gingerly put them in. Lio, Jesry, and I looked on speechless.

Suur Ala came in with an armload of rags, most of which she threw on the floor to cover the blood-puddle. She and Cord used the rest to wipe the blood off Arsibalt's lips and chins. The whole time, they were appraising each other, as if in a competition to see which was the scientist and which was the specimen. By the time I got my wits about me to make introductions, they knew so much about each other that names hardly mattered.

From yet another pocket Cord produced a complex metal thing all folded in on itself. She evoluted it into a miniature scissors, which she used to snip off the strings dangling from Arsibalt's nostrils.

So bossy, so stern a person was Suur Ala that, until this moment, I had feared that she and Cord were going to fall upon each other like two cats in a pillowcase. But when she drew focus on those blood soaker-uppers, she gave Cord a happy look which Cord returned.

We frog-marched Arsibalt out of there, hid his carnage under a huge scarlet robe, and came out for Provener only a few minutes late. We were greeted by titters from some who assumed we'd been extramuros getting drunk. Most of these wags were Apert visitors, but I heard amusement even from the Thousanders. I was expecting that Jesry and I would have to do most of the work, but, on the contrary, Lio and Arsibalt pushed with far more than their usual strength.

After Provener, the Warden Fendant crossed the chancel and came through our screen to interview Lio and Arsibalt. Jesry and I stood off to one side. Cord stood close and listened. This influenced Lio to use a lot of Fluccish, to the annoyance of Fraa Delrakhones. Arsibalt, on the other hand, kept using words like *rapscallions*.

From his description of the vehicle the thugs had driven and the clothes they had worn, Cord knew them. "They are a local—" she said, and stopped.

"Gang?" Delrakhones offered.

She shrugged. "A gang that keeps pictures of fictional gangs from old speelys on their walls."

"How fascinating!" Arsibalt proclaimed, while Fraa Delrakhones was absorbing this detail. "It is, then, a sort of meta-gang. . . ."

"But they still do gangy stuff for real," Cord said, "as I don't have to tell you."

It became clear from the nature of the questions Delrakhones asked that he was trying to work out which iconography the gang subscribed to. He did not seem to grasp something that was clear enough to me and Cord: namely, that there were extras who would beat up avout simply because it was more entertaining than *not* beating them up—not because they subscribed to some ridiculous theory of what we were. He was assuming that rapscallions bothered to have theories.

Cord and I therefore became frustrated, then bored (and as Orolo liked to say, boredom is a mask that frustration wears). I caught her eye. We drifted to one side. When no one objected, we fled.

As mentioned, we Tenners had a bundle of turrets instead of a proper nave. The skinniest turret was a spiral stair that led up to the triforium, which was a sort of raised gallery that ran all the way around the inside of the chancel above the screens and below the soaring clerestory windows. At one end of our triforium was another little stair that led up to the bell-ringers' place. Cord was interested in that. I watched her gaze traveling up the bell-ropes to where they vanished into the heights of the Præsidium. I could tell she wouldn't rest until she had seen what was at the other ends of those ropes. So we went to the other end of the triforium and began to climb another stair. This one zigzagged up the tower that anchored the southwestern corner of the Mynster.

Mathic architects were helpless when it came to walls. Pillars they could do. Arches they were fine with. Vaults, which were just three-dimensional arches, they knew everything about. But ask them to construct a simple wall and they would go to pieces. Where anyone else in the world would construct a wall, they'd fill in the space with a system of arches and tracery. When people complained about wind, vermin, and other things that would be kept out of a normal building by walls, they might be troubled to fill up a vacancy with a stained-glass window. But we hadn't got round to putting all of those in yet. On a windy and rainy day it made buildings like this hellish. But on a day like this one it was fine because you could always see. As we scaled the flights of the southwestern tower we had views down into the Mynster, and out over the concent.

The upper reaches of this tower—the place where it devolved into piers and pinnacles, the highest part, in other words, that you could get to without ladders and mountaineering equipment—was at about the same altitude as the Warden Regulant's headquarters. It sported one of the most elaborate works of stone-carving in the whole concent, a sort of cupola/tower/walk-through statue depicting planets and moons and some of the early cosmographers who had studied them. Built into the middle of this was a portcullis: a grid of bars that could be cranked up and down. At the moment, it had been drawn up out of the way, giving us the freedom to attack yet another stair. This one was cut right into the top of a flying buttress. It would take us up and inwards to the Præsidium. If the portcullis had been closed, we'd have had nowhere else to go, unless we wanted to cross over a sort of bridge into the Warden Regulant's quarters.

Cord and I passed through the cupola, moving slowly so that she could take in the carvings and the mechanism. Then we were on our way up. I let her go ahead of me so that she could get an unobstructed view, and so that I could steady her if she got dizzy. For we were high above the ground here, climbing over the curve of a stone buttress that seemed about as thick as a bird's bone when you looked at it from the ground. She gripped the iron banisters with both hands and took it slowly and seemed to enjoy it. Then we passed through an embrasure (sort of a deep complicated Mathic archway), built into the corner of the Praesidium at about the level of the belfries.

From here there was only one way up: a series of stairs that spiraled up the inside of the Præsidium just within its tracery walls. Few tourists were game for that much climbing, and many of the avout were extramuros, so we had the whole Præsidium to ourselves. I let her enjoy the view down to the chancel floor. The courts of the Wardens, immediately below us, were cloister-shaped, which is to say that each had a big square hole in the middle where the Præsidium shot through it, lined with a walkway with sight-lines down to the chancel and up to the starhenge.

Cord traced the bell-ropes up from the balcony and satisfied herself that they were in fact connected to a carillon. But from here it was obvious that other things too were connected to the bells: shafts and chains leading down from the chronochasm, where automatic mechanisms chimed the hours. It was inevitable that she'd want to see this. Up we went, trudging around like a couple of ants spiraling up a well shaft, pausing now and then to catch our breaths and to give Cord leisure to inspect the clock-work, and to figure out how the stones had been fitted together. This part of the building was much simpler because there was no need to contend with vaults and buttresses, so the architects had really gotten out of hand with the tracery. The walls were a fractal foam of hand-carved, interlocking stone. She was fascinated. I couldn't stand to look at it. The amount of time I had spent, as a fid, cleaning bird droppings off this stone, and the clock-works inside . . .

"So, you can't come up here except during Apert," she asserted at one point.

"What makes you think that?"

"Well, you're not allowed to have contact with people outside your math, right? But if you and the One-offs and the Hundreders and Thousanders could all use this stairway any time you wanted, you'd be bumping into each other."

"Look at how the stairway is designed," I said. "There's almost no part of it that we can't see. So, we just keep our distance from each other."

"What if it's dark? Or what if you go to the top and bump into someone at the starhenge?"

"Remember that portcullis we went through?"

"On top of the tower?"

"Yeah. Well, remember there's three more towers. Each one has a similar portcullis."

"One for each of the maths?"

"Exactly. During the hours of darkness, all but one of them is closed by the Master of the Keys. That's a hierarch—a deputy of the Warden Regulant. So on one night, the Tenners might have sole access to the stair and the starhenge. Next night it might be the Hundreders. And so on."

When we reached the altitude where the Century weight was poised on its rail, we paused for a minute so that Cord could look at it. We also looked out through the tracery of the south wall to the machine hall where she worked. I retraced my morning's walk, and picked out the house of Jesry's family on the hill.

Cord was still looking for flaws in our Discipline. "These wardens and so on—"

"Hierarchs," I said.

"They communicate with all of the maths, I guess?"

"And also with the Ita, and the Sæcular world, and other concents."

"So, when you talk to one of them—"

"Well, look," I said, "one of the misconceptions people have is that the maths are supposed to be hermetically sealed. But that was never the idea. The kinds of cases you are asking about are handled by disciplined conduct. We keep our distance from those not of our math. We are silent and hooded when necessary to avoid leakage of information. If we absolutely must communicate with someone in another math, we do it through the hierarchs. And they have all sorts of special training so that they can talk to, say, a Thousander in a way that won't allow any Sæcular information to pass into his mind. That's why hierarchs have those outfits, those hairstyles—those literally have not changed in 3700 years. They speak only in a very conservative ancient version of Orth. And we also have ways to communicate without speech. So, for example, if Fraa Orolo wishes to observe a particular star five nights in a row, he'll explain his plan to the Primate, and if it seems reasonable, the Primate will direct the Master of the Keys to keep our portcullis open those nights but leave all the others closed. All of them are visible from the maths, so the Millenarian cosmographers can look down and see how it is and know that they won't be using the starhenge tonight. And we can also use the labyrinths between the maths for certain kinds of communication, such as passing objects or people back and forth. But there's nothing we can do to prevent aerocraft from flying over, or loud music from being heard over the walls. In an earlier age, skyscrapers looked down on us for two centuries!"

That last detail was of interest to Cord. "Did you see those old I-beams stacked in the machine hall?"

"Ah—were those the frames of the skyscrapers?"

"It's hard to imagine what else they'd be. We have a box of old phototypes showing those things being dragged to our place by teams of slaves."

"Do the phototypes have date prints?"

"Yeah. They're from about seven hundred years ago."

"What does the landscape in the background look like? A ruined city, or—"

She shook her head. "Forest with big trees. In some of those pictures they are rolling the beams over logs."

"Well, there was a collapse of civilization right around 2800, so it all fits together," I said.

The chronochasm was laced through with shafts and chains that in some places converged to clock-movements. The chains that led up from the weights terminated up here in clusters of bearings and gears.

Cord had been growingly exasperated by something, and now, finally, she let it out: "This just isn't the way to do it!"

"Do what?"

"Build a clock that's supposed to keep going for thousands of years!"

"Why not?"

"Well, just look at all those chains, for one thing! All the pins, the bearing surfaces, the linkages—each one a place where something can break, wear out, get dirty, corrode . . . what were the designers thinking, anyway?"

"They were thinking that plenty of avout would always be here to maintain it," I answered. "But I take your point. Some of the other Millennium Clocks are more like what you have in mind: designed so that they can run for millennia with no maintenance at all. It just depends on what sort of statement the designer wanted to make."

That gave her much food for thought, so we climbed in silence for a while. I took the lead, since, above a certain point, there was no direct route. We had to dodge and wind among diverse catwalks and stairs, each of which had been put there to provide access to a movement. Which was fine with Cord. In fact she spent so much time working out how the clock functioned that I became restless, and thought about the meal being served at this moment in our re-fectory. Then I recollected that it was Apert and I could go extra-muros if I wanted, and beg for a cheeseburg. Cord, accustomed to being able to eat whenever she pleased, wasn't concerned about this at all.

She watched a complex of bone-like levers wrestling with one another. "Those remind me of the part I made for Sammann this morning."

I held up my hands. "Don't tell me his name—or *anything*," I pleaded.

"Why can't you talk to the Ita?" she asked, suddenly irritated. "It's stupid. Some of them are very intelligent."

Yesterday I would have laughed at any artisan who was so pre-sumptuous as to pass judgment on the intelligence of anyone who lived in a concent—even an Ita—but Cord was my sib. She shared a lot of my sequences and had as much intrinsic intelligence as I. Fraas were kept sterile by substances in our food so that we could not impregnate suurs and breed a species of more intelligent hu-mans inside the concents. Genetically, we were all cut from the same cloth.

"It's kind of like hygiene," I said.

"You think the Ita are dirty?"

"Hygiene isn't really about dirt. It's about germs. It's to prevent the spread of sequences that are dangerous if they are allowed to propagate. We don't think the Ita are dirty in the sense of not wash-ing. But their whole purpose is to work with information that spreads in a promiscuous way."

"Why—what is the point? Who came up with all these stupid rules? What were they afraid of?"

She was quite loud. I'd have cringed if she'd talked this way in the Refectory. But I was happy to hear her out alone in this chasm of patient, deaf machines. As we resumed our ascent, I searched for some explanation to which her mind might be open. We had passed above most of the complicated stuff now—the machines that moved the clock's dials. All that remained were half a dozen vertical shafts that ran up through holes in the roof to connect with things on the starhenge: polar drives for the telescopes, and the zenith synchronizer that adjusted the clock's time every day at noon—every clear day, anyway. Our final approach to the starhenge was a spiral stair that coiled around the largest of those shafts: the one that rotated the great Telescope of Saunts Mithra and Mylax.

"That big machine you use to cut the metal—"

"It's called a five-axis electrical discharge mill."

"I noticed it had cranks, made for human hands. After the job was finished, you turned them to move the table this way and that. And I'll bet you could also use those cranks to cut a shape, couldn't you?"

She shrugged. "Sure, a very simple shape."

"But when you take your hands off the cranks and turn control over to the syntactic device, it becomes a much more capable tool, doesn't it?"

"Infinitely more. There's almost no shape you couldn't make with a syndev-controlled machine." She slid her hand down to her hip and drew out a pocket-watch, and let it dangle at the end of a silver chain made of fluid, seamless links. "This chain is my journeyman piece. I cut it from a solid bar of titanium."

I took a moment to feel the chain. It was like a trickle of ice water over my fingers.

"Well, syndevs can have the same amplifying effect on other kinds of tools. Tools for reading and writing genetic sequences, for example. For adjusting proteins. For programmatic nucleosynthesis."

"I don't know what those are."

"Because no one does them any more."

"Then how do *you* know about them?"

"We study them—in the abstract—when we are learning about the First and Second Sacks."

"Well, I don't know what those are either, so I wish you would just get to the point."

We'd been standing at the top of the stair that led up to the starhenge. I pushed the door open and we walked outside, squinting in the light. Cord had gotten a little testy. From watching Orolo talk to artisans like Flec and Quin, I knew how impatient they could be with what they saw as our winding and indirect way of talking. So I shut up for a minute, and let her look around.

We were on the roof of the Præsidium, which was a great disk of stone reinforced by vault-work. It was nearly flat, but bulged up slightly in the middle to shed rainwater. Its stones were graven and inlaid with curves and symbols of cosmography. Around its perimeter, megaliths stood to mark where certain cosmic bodies rose and set at different times of the year. Inside of that ring, several free-standing structures had been erected. The tallest of these, right in the center, was the Pinnacle, wrapped in a double helix of external stairs. Its top was the highest part of the Mynster.

The most voluminous structures up here were the twin domes of the big telescope. Dotted around from place to place were a few much smaller telescope-domes, a windowless laboratory where we worked with the photomnemonic tablets, and a heated chapel where Orolo liked to work and to lecture his fids. I led Cord in that direction. We passed through two consecutive doors of massive iron-bound hardwood (the weather could get rough up here) and came into a small quiet room that, with its arches and its stained-glass rosettes, looked like something out of the Old Mathic Age. Resting on a table, just where I'd left it, was the photomnemonic tablet that Orolo had given me. It was a disk, about the size of my two hands held side by side, and three fingers thick, made of dark glassy stuff. Buried in it was the image of Saunt Tancred's Nebula, dull and hard to make out until I slid it away from the pool of sunlight coming in the window.

"That's about the bulkiest phototype I've ever seen," Cord said. "Is that like some ancient technology?"

"It's more than that. A phototype captures one moment—it doesn't have a time dimension. You see how the image seems close to the upper surface?"

"Yeah."

I put a fingertip to the side of the tablet and slid it downwards. The image receded into the glass, following my finger. As it did, the nebula changed, contracting into itself. The fixed stars around it did not change their positions. When my fingertip reached the bottom of the tablet, the nebula had focused itself into a single star of extraordinary brilliance. "At the bottom layer of the tablet, we're looking at Tancred's Star, on the very night it exploded, in 490. Practically at the same moment that its light penetrated our atmosphere, Saunt Tancred looked up and noticed it. He ran and put a photomnemonic tablet, just like this one, into the great telescope of his concent, and aimed it at that supernova. The tablet remained lodged there, taking pictures of the explosion every single clear night, until 2999, when finally they took it out and made a number of copies for distribution to the Thousanders."

"I see things like this all the time in the background of spec-fiction speelys," Cord said, "but I didn't realize that they were explosions." She traced her finger up the side of the tablet a few times, running it forward thousands of years in a second. "But it couldn't be more obvious."

"The tablet has all kinds of other functions," I said, and showed her how to zoom in on one part of the image, up to its resolution limit.

That's when Cord saw the point I was making. "This," she said, pointing at the tablet, "this has got to have some kind of syndev built into it."

"Yes. Which makes it much more powerful than a phototype—just as your five-axis mill is much more powerful because of its brain."

"But isn't that a violation of your Discipline?"

"Certain praxes were grandfathered in. Like the newmatter in our spheres and our bolts, and like these tablets."

"They were grandfathered in—when? When were all of these decisions made?"

"At the Convoxes following the First and Second Sacks," I said. "You see, even after the end of the Praxic Age, the concents obtained a huge amount of power by coupling processors that had been invented by their syntactic faculties to other kinds of tools—in one case, for making newmatter, and in the other, for manipulating sequences. This reminded people of the Terrible Events and led to the First and Second Sacks. Our rules concerning the Ita, and which praxes we can and can't use, date from those times."

This was still too abstract for Cord's taste, but suddenly she got an idea, and her eyes sprang open. "Are you talking about the Incanters?"

Out of some stupid, involuntary reflex, I turned my head to look out the window in the direction of the Millenarian math, a fortress on a crag, on a level with the top of this tower, but shielded from view by its walls. Cord took this in. Worse, she seemed to have expected it.

"The myth of the Incanters originated in the days leading up to the *Third* Sack," I said.

"And their enemies—the what-do-you-call-'em . . ."

"Rhetors."

"Yeah. What's the difference exactly?" She was giving me the most innocent, expectant look, twirling her watch chain around her finger. I couldn't bear to level with her—to let her know what stupid questions she was asking. "Uh, if you've been watching those kinds of speelies, you know more about it than I do," I said. "One sort of glib explanation I heard once was that Rhetors could change the past, and were glad to do it, but Incanters could change the future—and were reluctant."

She nodded as if this weren't a load of rubbish. "Forced to by what the Rhetors had done."

I shrugged. "Again: it all depends on what work of fiction you happen to be enjoying—"

"But *those* guys would be Incanters," she said, nodding at the crag.

I was getting a little restless, so I led her back out onto the open roof, where she immediately turned her gaze back to the Thousanders' math. I finally worked it out that she was merely trying to reassure herself that the strange people living up there on the crag that loomed over her town were not dangerous. And I was happy to help her, especially if she might go out and spread the good news to others. That sort of fence-mending was the whole purpose of Apert.

But I didn't want to lie to her either. "Our Thousanders are a little different," I said. "Down in the other maths, like the one where I live, different orders are mixed together. But up on the crag, they all belong to one order: the Edharians. Who trace their lineage back to Halikaarn. And to the extent there is any truth whatsoever in the folk tales you're talking about, that would put them on the Incanter side of things."

That seemed to satisfy her where Rhetor/Incanter wars were concerned. We continued wandering around the starhenge, though I had to give wide berth to an Ita who emerged from a utility shack with a coil of red cable slung over his shoulder. Cord noticed this. "What's the point of having the Ita around if you have to go to all of this trouble to avoid them? Wouldn't it be simpler to send them packing?"

"They keep certain parts of the clock running . . ."

"I could do that. It's not that hard."

"Well . . . to tell you the truth, we ask ourselves the same question."

"And being who you are, you must have twelve different answers."

"There is a sort of traditional belief that they spy on us for the Sæcular Power."

"Ah. Which is why you despise them."

"Yeah."

"What makes you think they're spying on you?"

"Voco. An aut where a fraa or suur is called out from the math—Evoked—and goes to do something praxic for the Panjandrums. We never see them again."

"They just vanish?"

"We sing a certain anathem—a song of mourning and farewell—as we watch them walk out of the Mynster and get on a horse or climb into a helicopter or something, and, yes, 'vanish' is fair."

"What do the Ita have to do with that?"

"Well, let's say that the Sæcular Power needs a disease cured. How can they possibly know which fraa or suur, out of all the concents, happens to be an expert in that disease?"

She thought about this as we clambered up the spiral stair that wrapped up and around the Pinnacle. Each tread was a slab of rock cantilevered straight out from the side of the building: a daring design, and one that required some daring from anyone who would climb it, since there was no railing.

"This all sounds pretty convenient for the Powers That Be," Cord commented. "Has it ever occurred to you that all this fear about the Terrible Events and the Incanters is just a stick they keep handy to smack you with to make you do what they want?"

"That is Saunt Patagar's Assertion and it dates from the Twenty-ninth Century," I told her.

She snorted. "I'll bite. What happened to Saunt Patagar?"

"Actually, she flourished for a while, and founded her own Order. There might still be chapters of it somewhere."

"It's frustrating, talking to you. Every idea my little mind can come up with has already been come up with by some Saunt two thousand years ago, and talked to death."

"I really don't mean to be a smarty pants," I said, "but that is Saunt Lora's Proposition and it dates to the Sixteenth Century."

She laughed. "Really!"

"Really."

"Literally two thousand years ago, a Saunt put forth the idea that—"

"That every idea the human mind could come up with, had already been come up with by that time. It is a very influential idea . . ."

"But wait a minute, wasn't Saunt Lora's idea a new idea?"

"According to orthodox paleo-Lorites, it was the Last Idea."

"Ah. Well, then, I have to ask—"

"What have we all been doing in here for the 2100 years since the Last Idea was come up with?"

"Yeah. To be blunt about it."

"Not everyone agrees with this proposition. Everyone loves to hate the Lorites. Some call her a warmed-over Mystagogue, and worse. But Lorites are good to have around."

"How do you figure?"

"Whenever anyone comes up with an idea that they think is new, the Lorites converge on it like jackals and try to prove that it's actually 5000 years old or something. And more often than not, they're right. It's annoying and humiliating but at least it prevents people from wasting time rehashing old stuff. And the Lorites have to be excellent scholars in order to do what they do."

"So I take it you're not a Lorite."

"No. If you like irony, you might enjoy knowing that, after Lora's death, her own fid determined that her ideas had all been anticipated by a Peregrin philosopher 4000 years earlier."

"That's funny—but doesn't it prove Lora's point? I'm trying to figure out what's in it for you. Why do you stay?"

"Ideas are good things to have even if they are old. Even to understand the most advanced theorics requires a lifetime of study. To keep the existing stock of ideas alive requires . . . all of this." And I waved my arm around at the concent spread out below us.

"So you're like, I don't know, a gardener. Tending a bunch of rare flowers. This is like your greenhouse. You have to keep the greenhouse up and running forever or the flowers will go extinct . . . but you never . . ."

"We *rarely* come up with new flowers," I admitted. "But sometimes one will get hit with a cosmic ray. Which brings me to the subject of this stuff you see up here."

"Yeah. What is it? I've been looking at this poky thing my whole life and thinking it had a telescope on top, with a crinkly old fraa peering through it."

We'd reached the top of the "poky thing"—the Pinnacle. Its roof was a slab of stone about twice as wide as I was tall. There were a couple of odd-looking devices up here, but no telescopes.

"The telescopes are down in those domes," I said, "but you might not even recognize them as such." I got ready to explain how the newmatter mirrors worked, using guidestar lasers to probe the atmosphere for density fluctuations, then changing their shape to cancel out the resulting distortions, gathering the light and bouncing it into a photomnemnonic tablet. But she was more interested in deciphering what was right in front of her. One was a quartz prism, bigger than my head, held in the grip of a muscular Saunt carved out of marble, and pointed south. Without any explanation from me, Cord saw how sunlight entering into one face of the prism was bounced downwards through a hole in the roof to shine on some metallic construct within. "This I've heard of," she said, "it synchronizes the clock every day at noon, right?"

"Unless it's cloudy," I said. "But even during a nuclear winter, when it can be cloudy for a hundred years, the clock doesn't get too far out of whack."

"What's this thing?" she asked, pointing to a dome of glass about the size of my fist, aimed straight up. It was mounted at the top of a pedestal of carven stone that rose to about the same height as the prism-holding statue. "It's got to be some kind of a telescope, because I see the slot where you put in the photomnemonic tablet," she said, and poked at an opening in the pedestal, just beneath the lens. "But this thing doesn't look like it can move. How do you aim it?"

"It can't move, and we don't have to aim it, because it's a fisheye lens. It can see the entire sky. We call it Clesthyra's Eye."

"Clesthyra—that's the monster from ancient mythology that could look in all directions at once."

"Exactly."

"What's the use of it? I thought the point of a telescope was to focus in on one thing. Not to look at everything."

"These things were installed in starhenges all over the world around the time of the Big Nugget, when people were very interested in asteroids. You're right that they're useless if you want to focus in on something. But they're great for recording the track of a fast-moving object across the sky. Like the long streak of light that a meteorite draws. By recording all of those and measuring them, we can draw conclusions about what kinds of rocks are falling out of the sky—where they come from, what they're made of, how big they are."

But as Clesthyra's Eye lacked moving parts, it didn't hold Cord's attention. We'd gone as high as we could go, and reached the limit of her cosmographical curiosity. She drew out her pocket-watch on its rippling chain and checked the time, which I pointed out was funny because she was standing on top of a clock. She didn't see the humor. I offered to show her how to read the time by checking the sun's position with respect to the megaliths, but she said maybe some other time.

We descended. She was feeling late, worrying about jobs to do and errands to run—the kinds of things that people extramuros spent their whole lives fretting about. It wasn't until we reached the meadow, and the Decade Gate came in view, that she relaxed a little, and began reviewing in her mind all that we'd discussed.

"So—what do you think of Saunt What's-her-name's Assertion?"

"Patagar? That the legend of the Incanters is trumped up so that the Panjandrums can control us?"

"Yeah. Patagar."

"Well, the problem with it is that the Sæcular Power changes from age to age."

"Lately from year to year," she said, but I couldn't tell whether she was being serious.

"So it's awfully hard to see how they could maintain a consistent strategy over four millenia," I pointed out. "From our point of view, it changes so often we don't even bother keeping track, except around Apert. You could think of this place as a zoo for people who just got sick of paying attention to it."

I guess I sounded a little proud. A little defensive. I said goodbye to her on the threshold of the Decade Gate. We had agreed to meet again later in the week.

As I walked back over the bridge, I thought that of all the people I'd talked to today, I was probably the least content in my situation. And yet when I heard the system being questioned by Jesry and by Cord, I lost no time defending it and explaining why it was a good thing. This seemed crazy on the face of it.

Newmatter: A solid, liquid, or gas having physical properties not found in naturally occurring elements or their compounds. These properties are traceable to the atomic nuclei. The process by which nuclei are assembled from smaller particles is called nucleosynthesis, and generally takes place inside of old stars. It is subject to physical laws that, in a manner of speaking, congealed into their current forms shortly after the inception of the cosmos. In the two centuries following the Reconstitution, these laws became sufficiently understood that it became possible for certain of the avout to carry out nucleosynthesis in their laboratories, and to do it according to sets of physical laws that differed slightly from those that are natural in this cosmos. Most newmatter proved to be of little practical value, but some variants were discovered and laboriously improved to produce substances that were unusually strong or supple or whose properties could be modulated under syntactical control. As part of the First Sack reforms, the avout were forbidden to carry out any further work on newmatter. Within the mathic world, it is still produced in small quantities to make bolts, chords, and spheres. Extramuros, it is used in a number of products.

—THE DICTIONARY, *4th edition, A.R. 3000*

Fraa Lio perfected a new wrap that made him look like a parcel that had fallen from a mail train, but that could not under any circumstances be pulled over the face by a foe. We proved as much by trying to do it for a quarter of an hour, Lio getting more and more pleased with himself until Jesry ruined the mood by asking whether it could stop bullets.

Cord came back, accompanied by one Rosk, a young man with whom she was having some sort of liaison. They had supper with us in the Refectory. She wore fewer wrenches and more jewelry, all of which she had made herself out of titanium.

Arsibalt managed to walk to the basilica unmolested, but his father refused to talk to him, unless his purpose in coming was to repent and be consecrated into the orthodox Bazian faith.

Lio roamed the fauxburbs in the hopes that he would be set

upon by a gang of thugs, but instead people kept offering him rides and buying him drinks.

Jesry's family filtered back into town, and he went to visit them from time to time. I accompanied him once and was struck by their intelligence, their polish, and (as usual) how much stuff they owned. But there was nothing underneath. They knew many things but had no idea why. And strangely this made them more, rather than less, certain that they were right.

Stung by Jesry's earlier remarks, Lio persuaded some of his new friends to take him out to an abandoned quarry in the foothills where people amused themselves by discharging projectile weapons at things that didn't move. His bolt and sphere became targets. Lio took up arms against two of his three possessions, assaulting them with bullets and broad-headed arrows. Bullets apparently passed through the weave of the bolt—the newmatter fibers stretched to let them go through, leaving gaps that could later be massaged away. But the razor-sharp arrows cut some of the fibers and left irreparable holes in the garment. The sphere, however, distorted and stretched without limit, like a sheet of caramel if you try to shove your finger through it. The bullets poked it nearly inside-out and knocked it back like a batted balloon. Lio's verdict was that the sphere could be used as a defense against gunfire: the bullet would still penetrate your body, but it would pull a long stretchy finger of sphere-stuff behind it, which would prevent fragmentation or tumbling, and which could be used to pull the bullet out of the wound. We were all much comforted by this.

Cord came back for yet another visit, this time without Rosk. We had a nice stroll around the math and even went into the upper labyrinth for a look round. The conversation was first about where various members of our family had ended up, and later about where she hoped she'd be at the next Apert.

Eight days into Apert, I was sick of it, and thoroughly mixed up. I had a crush on my sib. This might mean all kinds of bad things about me. As I thought about it more, though, I saw it was not the kind of crush where I wanted to have a liaison with her.

I would think about her all day, care too much what she thought of me, and wish she would come around more often and pay attention to me. Then I'd remember that in a few days the gate would close and I wouldn't have any contact with her for ten years. She seemed never to have lost sight of this, and had kept a certain distance. Anyway, I reckoned, the parts of the concent that were most interesting to her were those that concerned the Ita, and, in a sense, she had access to that all the time because she made stuff for them.

On any given day of Apert I could have written an entire book about what I was thinking and feeling, and it would have been completely different from the previous day's book. But by the end of the eighth day, the thing had been settled in such a way that I can sum it up much more briefly.

○○

Liaison: (1) In Old and later Orth, an intimate (typically sexual) relationship among some number of fraas and suurs. The number is almost always two. The most common arrangement is for one of these to be a fraa and the other a suur of approximately the same age. Liaisons are of several types. Four types were mentioned by Ma Cartas in the Discipline. She forbade all of them. Later in the Old Mathic Age, a liaison between Saunt Per and Saunt Elith became famous when their hoards of love-letters were unearthed following their deaths. Shortly before the Rebirth, several maths took the unusual step of altering the Discipline to sanction the Perelithian liaison, meaning a permanent liaison between one fraa and one suur. The Revised Book of Discipline, adopted at the time of the Reconstitution, described eight types and sanctioned two. The Second New Revised Book of Discipline describes seventeen, sanctions four, and winks at two others. Each of the sanctioned liaisons is subject to certain rules, and is solemnized by an aut in which the participants agree, in the presence of at least three witnesses, to abide by those rules. Orders or concents that deviate from the Discipline by sanctioning other types of liaisons are subject to disciplinary action by the Inquisition. It is permissible, however, for an order or concent to sanction fewer types; those that sanction zero types are, of course, nominally celibate. (2) A Late Praxic Age bulshytt term, as such, impossible to define clearly, but apparently having something to do with contacts or relations between entities.

—THE DICTIONARY, *4th edition, A.R. 3000*

Fraa Orolo had noticed how distracted I was and summoned me to the starhenge shortly before sunset. He'd reserved the Telescope of Saunts Mithra & Mylax for the night. The weather was cloudy, but in the hope that it would clear up, he had gone there late in the afternoon to aim the telescope and blank a photomnemonic tablet. I found him at the controls of the M & M just as he was finishing these preparations. We went out and strolled around the ring of megaliths. My tongue was a long time in loosening, but after a while I told Orolo of what I'd been feeling and thinking about Cord. He asked all sorts of questions I'd never have thought of, and listened carefully to my answers, all of which seemed to confirm in his mind that I wasn't feeling anything about her that was inappropriate for a sib.

Orolo reminded me that Cord was all the biological family I had left, not to mention the only person I really knew from extramuros, and assured me that it was normal and healthy for me to think about her a lot.

I told him about the conversations I'd been having lately that called into question all kinds of things about the Discipline and the Reconstitution. He assured me that this was an unwritten tradition of Apert. This was a time for the avout to get all of that out of their systems so that they did not have to spend the next ten years worrying about it.

He slowed and stopped as we rounded the northeastern limb. "Did you know that we live in a beautiful place?" he asked.

"How could I not know it?" I demanded. "Every day, I go into the Mynster, I see the chancel, we sing the Anathem—"

"Your words say yes, your defensive tone says something else,"

Orolo said. "You haven't even seen this." And he gestured to the northeast.

The range of mountains leading off in that direction was obscured during winter by clouds and during summer by haze and dust. But we were between summer and winter now. The previous week had been hot, but temperatures had fallen suddenly on the second day of Apert, and we had plumped our bolts up to winter thickness. When I had entered the Præsidium a couple of hours earlier, it had been storming, but as I'd ascended the stair, the roar of the rain and the hail had gradually diminished. By the time I'd found Orolo up top, nothing remained of the storm except for a few wild drops hurtling around on the wind like rocks in space, and a foam of tiny hailstones on the walkway. We were almost in the clouds. The sky had hurled itself against the mountains like a sea attacking a stony headland, and spent its cold energy in half an hour. The clouds were dissolving, yet the sky did not get any brighter, because the sun was going down. But Orolo with his cosmographer's eye had noted on the flank of a mountain a stretched patch that was brighter than the rest. When I first saw what he was pointing at, I guessed that hail had silvered the boughs of trees in some high vale. But as we watched, the color of it warmed. It broadened, brightened, and crept up the mountainside, setting fire to individual trees that had changed color early. It was a ray coming through a gap in the weather far to the west, levering up as the sun sank.

"That is the kind of beauty I was trying to get you to see," Orolo told me. "Nothing is more important than that you see and love the beauty that is right in front of you, or else you will have no defense against the ugliness that will hem you in and come at you in so many ways."

From Fraa Orolo, of all people, this was an astonishingly poetic and sentimental remark. I was so startled that it didn't occur to me to wonder what Orolo was referring to when he spoke of the ugliness.

At least my eyes were open, though, to what he wanted me to see. The light on the mountain became rich in hues of crimson, gold, peach, and salmon. Over the course of a few seconds it washed the walls and towers of the Millenarian math with a glow that if I were a Deolater I'd have called holy and pointed to as proof that there must be a god.

"Beauty pierces through like that ray through the clouds," Orolo continued. "Your eye is drawn to where it touches something that is capable of reflecting it. But your mind knows that the light does not originate from the mountains and the towers. Your mind knows that something is shining in from another world. Don't listen to those who say it's in the eye of the beholder." By this Orolo meant the Fraas of the New Circle and the Old Reformed Faanites, but he could just as well have been Thelenes warning a fid not to be seduced by Sphenic demagogues.

The light lingered on the highest parapet for a minute, then faded. Suddenly all before us was deep greens, blues, and purples. "It'll be good seeing tonight," Orolo predicted.

"Will you stay?"

"No. We must go down. We're already in trouble with the Master of the Keys. I must go fetch some notes." Orolo hustled away and left me alone for a minute. I was surprised by a little sunrise above the mountains: the ray, sweeping invisibly up through empty sky, had found a couple of small wispy clouds and set them alight, like balls of wool flung into a fire. I looked down into the dark concent and felt no desire to jump. Seeing beauty was going to keep me alive. I thought of Cord and the beauty that she had, in the things she made, the way she carried herself, the emotions that played on her face while she was thinking. In the concent, beauty more often lay in some theoric proof—a kind of beauty that was actively sought and developed. In our buildings and music, beauty was always present even if I didn't notice. Orolo was on to something; when I saw any of those kinds of beauty I knew I was alive, and not just in the sense that when I hit my thumb with a hammer I knew I was alive, but rather in the sense that I was partaking of something—something was passing through me that it was in my nature to be a part of. This was both a good reason not to die and a hint that death might not be everything. I knew I was perilously close to Deolater territory now. But because people could be so beautiful it was hard not to think that there was something of people that came from the other world that Cnoüs had seen through the clouds.

Orolo met me at the top of the stairs, notes under his arm. Before we began our descent, he took one last look at the stars and planets beginning to come out, like a butler counting the spoons. We went down in silence, lighting our way with our spheres.

Fraa Gredick, the Master of the Keys, was waiting by the portcullis just as Fraa Orolo had predicted. Another, slighter person stood next to him. As we came down the buttress, we saw that it was Gredick's superior: Suur Trestanas. "Ugh, looks like we're going to get penance," I muttered. "This just demonstrates your point."

"Which point do you mean?"

"The ugliness coming in from all directions."

"I don't think this is that," Fraa Orolo said. "This is something exceptional."

We stepped down into the stone cupola and crossed the threshold. Gredick slammed the grid down behind us with too much force. I looked at his face, thinking he was angry we'd made him wait. But that wasn't it. He was unsettled. He only wanted to get out of there. We all watched him fumble with his key ring. As he was locking the portcullis down, I looked north to the Unarians' cupola and then east to the Centenarians'. Both of their gridirons were also closed. The whole thing seemed to have been shut down. Perhaps a security precaution for Apert?

I expected Gredick to leave so that Suur Trestanas could give me and Orolo a scolding. But Gredick looked me in the eye and said, "Come with me, Fid Erasmas."

"Where to?" I asked. It was unusual for the Master of the Keys to make such a request; it wasn't his job.

"Anywhere," he said, and then nodded toward the head of the stairs that would lead us down.

I looked at Orolo, who shrugged and made the same nod. Then I looked at Suur Trestanas, who only stared back at me, putting on a show of patience. She was early in her fourth decade of life, and not unattractive. She was brisk and organized and confident—the kind of woman who in the Sæcular world might have gone into commerce, and scampered up the hierarchy of a firm. During her first months as Warden Regulant, she had handed out a lot of penance for small infractions that her predecessor would have ignored. Older avout had assured me that this was typical behavior for a new Warden Regulant. I was so certain that she was going to give me and Orolo penance for being late that I hesitated to leave before she had done so. But it was clear that she had come here for another purpose. So I took my leave of Trestanas and Orolo, and began descending the stairs, followed by Fraa Gredick.

When Trestanas judged that Gredick and I were far enough away, she began telling Orolo something in a low voice. She talked for a minute or so, as if delivering a little speech that she had prepared.

When Orolo answered—which he did only after a long pause—it was in a voice that was wound up tight. He was making some kind of argument. And it was not the cool voice that he used when he was in dialog. Something had upset him. From this I knew that Suur Trestanas had not given him penance, because that was something one had to accept meekly, lest it be doubled and doubled again. They were talking about something more important than that. And Suur Trestanas had obviously told Gredick to get me out of that place so that she and Orolo could have privacy.

This was not a very satisfying end to the conversation that Orolo and I had shared on the starhenge! But it was further proof of the point he had made, and a challenge for me to put the idea into practice.

You must have this and hold to it or you'll die. By the time I awoke the next morning I could not recall whether this was something Orolo had said in so many words, or a resolution that had formed in my own mind. Anyway I woke up exhilarated and determined.

In the Refectory I saw Fraa Orolo, sitting alone, several tables away. He gave me a tight smile and looked away in the next instant. He did not wish to fill me in on his argument with Suur Trestanas. He ate quickly, then got up and headed in the direction of the Decade Gate for another day on the town.

More important than the argument with Trestanas was my conversation with Orolo just before. I knew I could not talk about this in the Refectory. It would not survive Diax's Rake; it would not be considered sound by the avout. Those of a more Procian bent would say I'd become a kind of Deolater. I'd be unable to defend myself without invoking all kinds of ideas that would sound ridiculously fuzzy-minded to them. At the same time, though, I knew that this was how the Saunts had done it. They judged theorical proofs not logically but aesthetically.

I wasn't the only one with a lot on his mind. Arsibalt sat alone, ate practically nothing, and then skulked out. Later Tulia picked up her bowl and came over and sat by me, which made me happy until I understood that she only wanted to talk about him. Arsibalt had been doing a lot of brooding, and he had been doing it in conspicuous places, as much as demanding that we ask him what was wrong. I'd refused to do so because I found it such an annoying tactic. But Suur Tulia had been checking on him from time to time. She let me know I ought to go and see him. I did so only because the request had come from her.

After the Reconstitution, the first fraas and suurs of the Order of Saunt Edhar had come to this place where the river scoured around a ramp of stone and attacked it with explosives and water-jet cutters, cleaning away the scree and rotten rock—which they moved to the perimeter and piled up to fashion the concent's walls—until they hit the sound stone at the heart of the mountain. This they cleaved off in slabs and prisms that tumbled to the valley floor, sometimes rolling almost to the walls before they came to rest. The ramp became a knob, the knob was sharpened to a crag. The first Thousanders whittled a narrow meandering stair up its face and went up there one day and never came back again, but pitched a camp on its top and set to work building their own walls and towers. The valley below remained a rubble-field for centuries. The avout swarmed over the strewn stones wherever they had come to rest and carved out of them the pieces of the Mynster. Almost all of them were now gone, and the land was flat, fertile, and stoneless. But a few of the great boulders were still dotted around the meadow, partly for decoration and partly as raw materials for our stonecutters, who were still fiddling with the Mynster's gargoyles, finials, and such.

I found Arsibalt perched on the top of a boulder, surrounded by empty beverage containers that had been strewn around the place by slines. All around him, visitors were sleeping it off in the tall grass. Across the meadow, Lio was cavorting around a statue of Saunt Froga, flinging the end of his bolt out and letting it waft over the statue's head, then snapping it back like a whip. I wouldn't have looked twice if this hadn't been Apert. But there were visitors on the meadow, watching, pointing, laughing, and speelycaptoring. Another useful function of Apert: to be reminded of how weird we were, and how fortunate to live in a place where we could get away with it.

Exhibit A: Fraa Arsibalt. Speaking whole paragraphs, complete with topic sentences, in perfect Middle Orth, with footnotes in Old and Proto-Orth, he explained that he felt aggrieved by his father's refusal to talk to him, because he was not so much abjuring his father's faith as trying to build a bridge between it and the mathic world.

This struck me as an ambitious project for a nineteen-year-old to undertake, seven thousand years after the two daughters of Cnoüs had stopped speaking to each other. Still, I heard him out. Partly so that I could later impress Tulia with what a good guy I was. Partly because I didn't want to be a Lorite. But also partly because what Arsibalt was saying was nearly as crazy as my discussion with Orolo the evening before. And so perhaps, after I had heard Arsibalt out, he would let me confide some of my thoughts. But as the conversation (if listening to Arsibalt talk could be called that) went on, this hope curdled. It had not crossed his mind that I too might have some things I wanted to discuss—perhaps not as clever or as momentous as what was on his mind, but important to me. I bided my time. And just when I saw an opening, he changed the subject altogether and ambushed me with a rhapsody about "the exquisite Cord." And so instead of talking about what I wanted to talk about, I was forced to come to grips with the idea of Cord as being exquisite. He wondered whether she might be open to an Atlanian liaison. I thought not, but who was I to judge? And a boyfriend who was (a) sterile and (b) only allowed out once every ten years seemed like a safe boyfriend to have, so I shrugged and allowed that anything was possible.

Then, back to Suur Tulia to file a report.

Seventeen years ago, Tulia had been found at the Day Gate, wrapped in newspapers and nestled in a beer cooler with the lid ripped off. The stump of her umbilical cord had already fallen off, which meant that she was too old and too touched by the Sæcular world to be accepted by the Thousanders. Anyway she had been sickly at first and so she had been kept in the Unarian math, which was more convenient to Physicians' Commons. There she had been raised (as I pictured it) by the doting burgers' wives and daughters who populated that math until she'd graduated through the labyrinth at the age of six. She had emerged, all alone, from our side of the maze and gravely introduced herself to the first suur she saw. Anyway, she had no family on the outside. Watching the rest of us cope with our families during Apert had led her to understand how very fortunate she might be. She was too deft to say anything, but it was clear she'd spent the whole time being bemused at the rest of us. She had seen me strolling around chatting with my sib and concluded that everything was fine and simple for me. I sensed it would boot me nothing to try to explain to her what I had discussed with Orolo.

So, instead, I talked to groups of total strangers from extramuros who showed up to take tours of the Unarian math.

My math was small, simple, and quiet. The Unarian math, by contrast, had been built to overawe people who came in from outside: ten days out of each year, groups of extramuros tourists, and the rest of the time, those who'd made a vow to spend at least one year in it. Few of these graduated to the Decenarian math. "Burgers' wives trying to feel something," was an especially cruel description I had once heard from an old fraa. As often, they were younger, unmarried, and looking for the final coat of polish and prestige needed to go out into adult society and seek a mate. Some studied under Halikaarnians and became praxics or artisans. Others studied under Procians; these tended to go into law, communications, or politics. Jesry's mother had done two years here just after she'd turned twenty. Not long after coming out, she'd married Jesry's father, a somewhat older man who had put in three years and used what he'd learned to start a career doing whatever it was he did.

Plane: (1) In Diaxan theorics, a two-dimensional manifold in three-dimensional space, having a flat metric. (2) An analogous manifold in higher-dimensional space. (3) A flat expanse of open ground in the Periklyne of ancient Ethras, originally used by theoricians as a convenient place to scratch proofs in the dirt, later as a place to conduct dialogs of all types. (4) Used as a verb, utterly to destroy an opponent's position in the course of a dialog.

—THE DICTIONARY, *4th edition, A.R. 3000*

Around dawn of the tenth day of Apert, Suur Randa, who was one of the beekeepers, discovered that during the night some ruffians had found their way into the apiary shed, smashed some crockery, and made off with a couple of cases of mead. Nothing so exciting had happened in eons. When I came into the Refectory to break my fast, everyone was talking about it. They were still talking about it when I left, which was at about seven. I was due at the Year Gate at nine. The easy way to get there would have been to go extramuros through the Decade Gate, walk north through the burgers' town, and approach it from the outside. But thinking about Tulia yesterday had given me the idea of getting there through our lower labyrinth—retracing the steps she'd taken at the age of six. Supposedly she had made it through in about half a day. I hoped that at my age I could get through it in an hour, but I allowed two hours just to be on the safe side. It ended up taking me an hour and a half.

As the clock struck nine, I stood, formally wrapped and hooded, at the foot of the bridge that led to the Year Gate, which rose up before me in its crenellated bastion. Bridge and gate were of similar design to those in the Decenarian math, but twice as big and much more richly decorated. On the first day of Apert, four hundred had thronged the plaza that I could now see through the Year Gate, and cheered as their friends and family had poured out at sunrise to end their year of seclusion.

This morning's tour group numbered about two dozen. A third of them were uniformed ten-year-olds from a Bazian Orthodox suvin, or so I guessed from the fact that their teacher was in a nun's habit. The others seemed a typical mix of burgers, artisans, and slines. The latter were recognizable from a distance. They were huge. Some artisans and burgers were huge too, but they wore clothes intended to hide it. The current sline fashion was to wear a garment evolved from an athletic jersey (bright, with numerals on the back) but oversized, so that shoulder seams hung around the elbows, and extremely long—descending all the way to the knee. The trousers were too long to be shorts and too short to be pants—they hung a hand's-breadth below the jersey but still exposed a few inches of chunky calf, plunging into enormous, thickly padded shoes. Headgear was a burnoose blazoned with beverage logos whose loose ends trailed down the back, and dark goggles strapped over that and never removed, even indoors.

But it was not only clothing that set the slines apart. They had also adopted fashions in how they walked (a rolling, sauntering gait) and how they stood (a pose of exaggerated cool that somehow looked hostile to me). So I could see even from a distance that I had four slines in my tour group this morning. This troubled me not at all, because during the previous nine days there had been no serious trouble on the tours. Fraa Delrakhones had concluded that the slines of this era subscribed to a harmless iconography. They were not half as menacing as their postures.

I backed up onto the crest of the bridge to get a little altitude. Once the group had formed up below me I greeted them and introduced myself. The suvin kids stood in a neat row in the front. The slines stood together in the back, maintaining some distance to emphasize their exceptional cool, and thumbed their jeejahs or suckled from bucket-sized containers of sugar water. Two latecomers were hustling across the plaza and so I went a little slowly at first so as not to strand them.

I had learned not to expect much in the way of attention span and so after pointing out the orchard of page trees and the tangles on this side of the river, I led them over the bridge into the heart of the Unarian math. We skirted a wedge-shaped slab of red stone, carved all over with the names of the fraas and suurs whose remains lay underneath it. It was our policy not to talk about this unless someone asked. Today, no one did, and so a lot of awkwardness was avoided.

The Third Sack had opened with a week-long siege of the concent. The walls were far too long to be defended by so few, and so on the third day the Tenners and Hundreders had broken the Discipline and withdrawn to the Unarian math, which was somewhat easier to defend because it had a smaller perimeter that included some water barriers. The Thousanders of course were safe up on their crag.

By the time the siege was two weeks old, it had become obvious that the Sæcular Power had no intention of coming to their aid. Before dawn one day, most of the avout gathered behind the Year Gate, threw it open, and stormed out across the plaza in a flying wedge, driving through the surprised besiegers and into the town. For one hour they sacked the town and the besiegers' supply dumps, gathering medicines, vitamins, ammunition, and all that they could find of certain chemicals and minerals that could not be obtained within the concent. Then they did something even more astonishing to the attackers, which was that instead of running away they formed up into another wedge—much smaller, by this point—and fought their way back across the plaza and went back in the gate. They didn't stop until they'd crossed the bridge, which was immediately dropped by explosives. There they threw down the stuff they had scavenged and collapsed. Five hundred had stormed out. Three hundred had come back. Of those, two hundred died on the spot from wounds suffered during the operation. This wedge of granite was their tumulus. The stuff that they had gathered was sent up to the Thousanders. The rest of the concent fell the next day. The Thousanders lived alone and untouched on their crag for the next seventy years. Besides ours, only two other Millenarian maths in the world had made it through the Third Sack unviolated and unsacked. Though in many cases there had been enough warning that avout had been able to run away, carrying what they could in the way of books, and live in remote places for the next decades.

The wedge monument was aimed, not out toward the city, but in toward the clock. This was to emphasize that those buried under it had returned.

Fifty paces from its vertex lay the entrance of the Hylaean Way. After the Mynster, this was the dominant architectural feature of the concent. The style of these buildings was more Bazian than Mathic—less vertical, more horizontal, reminding people of arks, which traditionally spread wide to welcome all comers.

I held the door open long enough for the two latecomers to scurry inside, then closed it, content—maybe even smug—in the knowledge that Barb was not with us. During the first two days of Apert, the son of Quin had attended almost every one of these tours. After memorizing every word that the guides said, he had begun to ask crippling numbers of questions. From there he'd moved on to correcting the fraas and suurs whenever they'd said something wrong, and amplifying their remarks when they were insufficiently long-winded. A couple of wily suurs had found other ways to keep him busy, but it was difficult to keep him focused for long and so he would still make occasional strafing runs. Quin and his ex-wife seemed content to give Barb the run of the concent at all hours, which was as good as telling us that they wanted him Collected.

The architects of the Hylaean Way had played a little trick by making its grand-looking entrance lead to a space that was unexpectedly dark and close—suggestive of a labyrinth, but not nearly that complicated. The walls and floors were made from slabs of greenish-brown shale quarried from a deposit that fascinated naturalists because of the profusion of early life-forms fossilized in it. I explained as much to the group as we all waited for our eyes to adjust to the dimness, then invited them to spend a few minutes looking at the fossils. Those who'd had the foresight to bring a source of light, such as the suvin kids and some of the retired burgers, dispersed into the corners of the chamber. The nun had brought a map so that she knew just where to look for the really weird fossils. I circulated among the others with a basket of hand-lights. Some accepted them. Some waved me off. Probably these were counter-Bazian fundamentalists who believed that Arbre had been created all at once in its present form shortly before the time of Cnoüs. They ignored this phase of the tour as a silent protest. A few more wore earbuds and listened to recorded tours on jeejahs. The slines only stared at me and made no response. I noticed that one of them had his arm in a sling. It took me a few moments to place this memory. Then I drew the obvious conclusion that this was the very group that had attacked Lio and Arsibalt. I felt helpless in my formal wrap—the one that could easily be pulled down over the face—and wished I'd paid more attention to how Lio had been wearing his bolt lately.

Backing away from them, I announced: "This chamber is two things at once. On the one hand, it's an exhibit of ancient fossils—mostly weird and funny-looking ones that did not evolve into any creatures known to us today. Evolutionary dead ends. At the same time, this place is a symbol for the world of thought as it existed before Cnoüs. In that age there was a zoo of different thought-ways, most of which would seem crazy to us now. These too were evolutionary dead ends. They are extinct except among primitive tribes in remote places." As I was saying this I was leading them around a couple of turns toward a much bigger and brighter space. "They are extinct," I continued, "because of what happened to this man as he was walking along a riverbank seven thousand years ago." And I stepped forth into the Rotunda, quickening my pace to draw the group along in my wake.

A long pause now, so as not to ruin the moment. The central sculpture was more than six thousand years old; it had been a world-famous masterpiece for almost that long. How it had found its way to this continent and this rotunda was a long and lively story in itself. It was of white marble, double life size, though it seemed even bigger because it was up on a huge stone pedestal. It was Cnoüs, aged but muscular, with long wavy beard and hair, sprawled back against the gnarled roots of a tree, staring up in awe and astonishment. As if to shield himself from the vision, he had raised a hand, but could not resist the temptation to peek over it. Gripped in his other hand was a stylus. Tumbled at his feet were a ruler, a compass, and a tablet graven with precisely constructed circles and polygons.

Barb hadn't looked at the ceiling when he'd come in here for the first time. This was because Barb's brain was so organized that he was blind to facial expressions. Everyone else—even I, who'd seen it many times—looked up to see what was having such an effect on poor old Cnoüs. The answer (at least, ever since the statue had been installed here) was an oculus, or a hole at the apex of the Rotunda dome, shaped like an isosceles triangle, and letting in a beam of sunlight.

"Cnoüs was a master stonemason," I began. "On one ancient tablet, which was made before he had his vision, he is described by an adjective that literally means one who is elevated. This might mean either that he was especially good at being a stonemason or that he was some kind of holy man in the religion of his place and time. At the command of his king, he was building a temple to a god. The stone was quarried from a place a couple of miles upriver and floated down to the building site on rafts."

Here one of the slines broke in with a question, and I had to stop and explain that all of this had happened far away, and that I was not speaking of our river or our quarries. A jeejah began to crow a ridiculous tune; I waited for its owner to stifle it before I continued.

"Cnoüs would draw up measurements on a wax tablet and then walk up to the quarry to give instructions to the stonecutters. One day he was trying to work out a particularly difficult problem in the geometry of the piece he needed to have cut. Under the shade of a tree that grew on the riverbank, he sat down to work on this problem, and there he had a vision that changed his mind and his life.

"Everyone agrees on that much. But his description of that vision comes to us indirectly, through these women." I extended my arm toward a pair of slightly smaller sculptures, which (inevitably) formed an isosceles triangle with that of Cnoüs. "His daughters Hylaea and Deät, thought to be fraternal twins."

The counter-Bazians were way ahead of me. They had already moved to the foot of Deät and knelt down to pray. Some were rummaging in their bags for candles. Others, peering into their jee-jahs as they snapped phototypes, stumbled and collided. Deät was a cloaked figure sunk to her knees, facing toward Cnoüs, her garment shielding her face from the light of the oculus.

Our Mother Hylaea, by contrast, stood erect, pulling her cloak back to bare her head, the better to gaze straight up into the light. With her other hand she was pointing at it, and her lips were parted as if she were just beginning to offer up some observation.

I recited a legend concerning these two statues. They had been commissioned in -2270 by Tantus, the Bazian Emperor, specifically as companion-pieces to the older one of Cnoüs, which he had just acquired by sacking what was left of Ethras. He had also acquired the quarry whence the marble for the original statue had come, and so he had caused two more great blocks to be extracted from it and shipped to Baz in specially made barges. The finest sculptor of the age had spent five years carving these.

At the formal unveiling, Tantus had been so taken by the look on Hylaea's face that he had ordered the sculptor to be brought before him and had asked him what it was that Hylaea was about to say. The sculptor had declined to answer the question. Tantus had insisted. The sculptor had pointed out that all of the art, and all of the virtue, in this statue lay in that very ambiguity. Tantus, fascinated, had asked him a number of questions on that theme, then drew the Imperial sword and plunged it into the sculptor's heart so that he would never be able to undermine his own work of art by answering the question. Later scholarship had cast doubt on this story, as it did on all good stories, but to tell it at this point in the tour was obligatory, and the slines got a kick out of it.

In my opinion, these two sculptures were such bald pro-Hylaea, anti-Deät propaganda that I was almost embarrassed by them. The Deolaters, however, seemed to take precisely the opposite view. Over the course of Apert, Deät's pedestal had become bedizened with so many candles and charms, flowers, stuffed animals, fetishes, phototypes of dead people, and slips of paper that the One-offs would be cleaning it up for weeks after the gates closed.

"Deät and Hylaea went out searching for their father and found him lost in contemplation under the tree. Both saw the tablet on which he had recorded his impressions, and both listened to his account. Not long after, Cnoüs said something so offensive to the king that he was sent into exile, where he soon died. His daughters began telling people different stories. Deät said that Cnoüs had looked up into the sky and seen the clouds part to give him a vision of a pyramid of light, normally concealed from human eyes. He was seeing into another world: a kingdom of heaven where all was bright and perfect. According to her, Cnoüs drew the conclusion that it was a mistake to worship physical idols such as the one he had been building, for those were only crude effigies of actual gods that lived in another realm, and we ought to worship those gods themselves, not artifacts we made with our own hands.

"Hylaea said that Cnoüs had actually been having an upsight about geometry. What her sister Deät had misinterpreted as a pyramid in heaven was actually a glimpse of an isosceles triangle: not a crude and inaccurate representation of one, such as Cnoüs drew on his tablet with ruler and compass, but a pure theorical object of which one could make absolute statements. The triangles that we drew and measured here in the physical world were all merely more or less faithful *representations* of perfect triangles that existed in this higher world. We must stop confusing one with the other, and lend our minds to the study of pure geometrical objects.

"You'll notice that there are two exits from this room," I pointed out, "one on the left near the statue of Deät, the other on the right near Hylaea. This symbolizes the great forking that now took place between the followers of Deät, whom we call Deolaters, and of Hylaea, who in the early centuries were called Physiologers. If you pass through Deät's door you'll soon find yourself outside where you can easily find your way back to the Unarian Gate. A lot of our visitors do that because they don't think that anything beyond this point is relevant to them. But if you follow me through the other door, it means you are continuing on the Hylaean Way." And after giving them a few minutes to roam around and take pictures, I went out, leading all but the Deät-pilgrims into a gallery lined with pictures and artifacts of the centuries following the death of Cnoüs.

This in turn gave on to the Diorama Chamber, which was rectangular, with a vaulted ceiling, and clerestory windows letting in plenty of light to illuminate the frescoes. The centerpiece was a scale model of the Temple of Orithena. As I explained, this had been founded by Adrakhones, the discoverer of the Adrakhonic Theorem, which stated that the square of a right triangle's hypotenuse was equal to the sum of the squares of the other two sides. To honor this, the floor of the chamber was adorned with numerous visual proofs of the said theorem, any of which you could puzzle out if you stood and stared at it for long enough.

"We're now in the period from about 2900 years before the Reconstitution to about negative 2600," I said. "Adrakhones turned Orithena into a temple devoted to exploration of the HTW, or the Hylaean Theoric World—the plane of existence that had been glimpsed by Cnoüs. People came from all over. You'll notice that this chamber has a second entrance, leading in from the out of doors. This commemorates the fact that many who had taken the other fork and sojourned among the Deolaters came in from the cold, as it were, trying to reconcile their ideas with those of the Orithenans. Some were more successful than others."

I looked over at the slines. Back in the rotunda, they had spent some time speculating as to the size of certain parts of the anatomy of Cnoüs (which were hidden under a fold of his garment) and then gotten into a debate as to which they fancied more: Deät, who was conveniently kneeling, or Hylaea, who was beginning to take her clothes off. In this chamber, they had gathered beneath the most prominent fresco, which depicted a furious dark-bearded man charging down the steps of the temple swinging a rake, striking terror in a group of deranged, eye-rolling dice-players. It was clear that the slines loved this picture. So far, they'd seemed docile enough. So I drew closer to them and explained it. "That's Diax. He was famous for his disciplined thought. He became more and more distressed by the way Orithena was being infiltrated by Enthusiasts. Those were people who misunderstood how the Orithenans used numbers. They dreamed up all kinds of crazy number-worshipping stuff. One day Diax was coming out of the temple after the singing of the Anathem when he saw these guys casting fortunes using dice. He was so furious that he grabbed a rake from a gardener and used it to drive the Enthusiasts out of the temple. After that, he ran the place. He coined the term *theorics,* and his followers called themselves 'theors' to distinguish themselves from the Enthusiasts. Diax said something that is still very important to us, which is that you should not believe a thing only because you like to believe it. We call that 'Diax's Rake' and sometimes we repeat it to ourselves as a reminder not to let subjective emotions cloud our judgment."

This explanation was too long for the four slines, who turned their backs to me as soon as I got past the rake fight. I noticed that one of them—the one with his arm in a sling—had a curious, bony ridge running up his spine and protruding a few inches above the collar of his jersey. Normally this was concealed by his trailing burnoose, but when he turned away from me I saw it clearly. It was like a second, exoskeletal spine attached to the natural one. At its top was a rectangular tab, smaller than the palm of my hand, bearing a Kinagram in which a large stick figure struck a smaller one with his fist. It was one of the spine clamps Quin had described to me and Orolo. I guessed it had disabled the man's right arm.

A fresco on the ceiling at the far end showed the eruption of Ecba and the destruction of the temple. The following series of galleries contained pictures and artifacts from the ensuing Peregrin period, with separate alcoves dedicated to the Forty Lesser and the Seven Great Peregrins.

From there we came out into the great elliptical chamber with its statues and frescoes of the theoric golden age centered on the city-state of Ethras. Protas, gazing up at the clouds painted on the ceiling, anchored one end. His teacher Thelenes commanded the other, striding across the Plane with his interlocutors—variously awed, charmed, chastened, or indignant. The two bringing up the rear had their heads together, conspiring—a foreshadowing of Thelenes's trial and ritual execution. A large painting of the city made it easy for me to point out the Deolaters' temples atop its highest hill, where Thelenes had been put to death; its market, the Periklyne, wrapped around the hill's base; a flat open area in the center of the

Periklyne, called 'the Plane,' where geometers would draw figures in the dust or engage in public debate; and the vine-covered bowers around the edges, in whose shade some theors would teach their fids, from which we got the word *suvin,* meaning "under the vines." As far as the nun was concerned, that one moment made the whole trip worth the trouble.

As we worked our way to the farther end, we began seeing theors standing at the right hands of generals and emperors, which led naturally enough to the last of the great chambers in the Hylaean Way, which was all about the glory that was Baz, its temples, its capitol, its walls, roads, and armies, its library, and (increasingly, as we approached the end) its Ark. After a certain point it was priests and prelates of the Ark of Baz, instead of theors, advising those generals and emperors. Theors had to be sought out as small figures in the deep background, reclining on the steps of the Library or going into the Capitol to spill wise counsel into the dead ears of the high and mighty.

Frescoes depicting the Sack of Baz and the burning of the library flanked the exit: an incongruously narrow, austere archway that you might miss if it weren't for the statue of Saunt Cartas cradling a few singed and tattered books in one arm, looking back over her shoulder to beckon us toward the exit. This led to a high stone-walled chamber, devoid of decoration and containing nothing except air. It symbolized the retreat to the maths and the dawn of the Old Mathic Age, generally pegged at Negative 1512.

From there the Hylaean Way took a lap around the Unarian Cloister and petered out. There was room on the other side where exhibits might one day be added about the rise of the Mystagogues, the Rebirth, the Praxic Age, and possibly even the Harbingers and the Terrible Events. But we had seen all the good stuff, and this was customarily the end of the tour.

I thanked them all for coming, invited them to backtrack if they wanted to spend more time with any of what they'd seen, reminded them that all were welcome at the Tenth Night supper, and told them I'd be happy to answer questions.

The slines seemed happy for now to savor the pictures of Imperial Bazian galley combat and library-burning. A retired burger stepped up to thank me for my time. The suvin kids asked me what sorts of things I had been studying lately. The two visitors who had rushed in at the last minute bided their time as I tried to explain to the kids certain theorical topics that they'd never heard of. After a minute the nun took pity on me (or possibly on the kids) and hustled them away.

The latecomers were a man and a woman, both probably in their fifth decades of life. I did not get the sense that they were having a liaison. Both were attired for commerce, so perhaps they were colleagues in a business. Around each one's neck was a lanyard leading to a flasher of the type used extramuros to demonstrate one's identity and control access to places. Since such things weren't needed here, both of them had tucked their flashers into their breast pockets. They had been appreciative tourists, trailing the group, cocking their heads toward each other to discuss fine details that one or the other had noticed.

"I was intrigued by your remarks about the daughters of Cnoüs," the man announced. His accent marked him as coming from a part of this continent where cities were bigger and closer together than around here, and where a concent might house a dozen or more chapters in contrast to our three.

He went on, "It's just that normally I would expect an avout to emphasize what made them different. But I almost got the idea you were hinting at a—" And here he stopped, as though groping for a word that was not in the Fluccish lexicon.

"Common ground?" suggested the woman. "A parallel between them?" Her accent—as well as the bone structure of her face and the hue of her skin—marked her as coming from the continent that, in this age, was the seat of the Sæcular Power. And so by this point I had made up a reasonable story in my head about these two: they lived in big cities far away, they worked for the same employer, a business of global scope, they were visiting its local office for some purpose, they'd heard it was the last day of Apert and had decided to spend a couple of hours taking in the sights. Both, I guessed, had spent at least a few years in a Unarian math when younger. Perhaps the man's Orth had grown some rust and he was more comfortable confining the discussion to Fluccish.

"Well, I think many scholars would agree that Deät and Hylaea both say that one should not confuse the symbol with the thing symbolized," I said.

He looked as if I'd poked him in the eye. "What kind of way to begin a sentence is that? 'I think many scholars would agree . . .' Why don't you just say what you mean?"

"All right. Deät and Hylaea both say that one should not confuse the symbol with the thing symbolized."

"That's better."

"For Deät the symbol is an idol. For Hylaea it's a triangular shape on a tablet. For Deät, the thing symbolized is an actual god in heaven. For Hylaea, it's a pure theorical triangle in the HTW. So, do you agree that I can speak about that commonality in itself?"

"Yes," the man said, reluctantly, "but an avout rarely takes an argument that far only to drop it. I keep waiting for you to base some further argument on it, the way they do in the dialogs."

"I take your point clearly," I said. "But I was not in dialog at the time."

"But you are now!"

I took this as a joke and chuckled in a way I hoped would seem polite. His face showed a trace of dry amusement but on the whole he looked serious. The woman seemed a bit uneasy.

"But I wasn't *then*," I said, "and *then* I had a story to tell, and it had to make sense. It makes sense if Deät and Hylaea took the same idea and mapped it onto different domains. But if I'd described them as saying totally contradictory things about their father's vision, it wouldn't have made sense."

"It would have made perfect sense if you had made Deät out to be a lunatic," he demurred.

"Well, that's true. Maybe because there were so many Deolaters in the group I avoided being so blunt."

"So you said something you don't actually believe, just to be polite?"

"It's more a matter of emphasis. I *do* believe what I said before about the commonality—and so do you, because you agreed with me to that point."

"How widespread do you suppose that mentality is within this concent?"

Hearing this, the woman looked as if she had got a whiff of something foul. She turned sideways to me and spoke in a subdued voice to the man. "Mentality is a pejorative term, isn't it?"

"All right," the man said, never taking his eyes off me. "How many here see it your way?"

"It's a typical Procian versus Halikaarnian dispute," I said. "Avout who follow in the way of Halikaarn, Evenedric, and Edhar seek truth in pure theorics. On the Procian/Faanian side, there is a suspicion of the whole idea of absolute truth and more of a tendency to classify the story of Cnoüs as a fairy tale. They pay lip service to Hylaea just because of what she symbolizes and because she wasn't as bad as her sister. But I don't think that they believe that the HTW is real any more than they believe that there is a Heaven."

"Whereas Edharians do believe in it?"

The woman shot him a look, and he made the following adjustment: "I specify Edharians only because this is the Concent of Saunt Edhar, after all."

If this man had been one of my fraas I might have spoken more freely now. But he was a Sæcular, strangely well-informed, and he behaved as though he were important. Even so, I might have blurted something out if this had been the first day of Apert. But our gates had been open for ten days: long enough for me to grow some crude political reflexes. So I answered not for myself but for my concent. More specifically for the Edharian order; for all of the Edharian chapters in other concents around the world looked to us as their mother, and had pictures of our Mynster up in their chapterhouses.

"If you ask an Edharian flat out, he'll be reluctant to admit to it," I began.

"Why? Again, this *is* the Concent of Saunt Edhar."

"It was broken up," I told him. "After the Third Sack, two-thirds of the Edharians were relocated to other concents, to make room for a New Circle and a Reformed Old Faanite chapter."

"Ah, the Powers That Be put a bunch of Procians in here to keep an eye on you, did they?" This actually caused the woman to reach out and put her hand on his forearm.

"You seem to be assuming I'm an Edharian myself," I said, "but I have not yet made Eliger. I don't even know if the Order of Saunt Edhar would accept me."

"I hope so for your sake," he said.

The conversation had become steadily odder from its very beginning and had reached a point where it was difficult for me to see a way forward. Fortunately the woman got us out of the jam: "It's just that with all that's been going on with the Warden of Heaven, we were speculating, as we were on our way here, whether the avout were feeling any pressure to change their views. And we wondered if your take on Deät and Hylaea might have reflected some Sæcular influence."

"Ah. That's an interesting point," I said. "As it happens, I'd never heard of the Warden of Heaven until a few days ago. So if my take on Deät and Hylaea reflects anything at all, it's what I've been thinking about lately for my own reasons."

"Very well," the man said, and turned away. The woman mouthed a "thank you" at me over her shoulder and together they strolled off into the Cloister.

Not long after, the bells began to chime Provener. I walked across the Unarian campus, which had been turned inside-out. Many avout, as well as some extramuros contract labor, were cleaning the dormitories to make them ready for the crop that would be starting their year tomorrow.

For once, I reached the Mynster with plenty of time to spare. I sought out Arsibalt and warned him to be on the lookout for those four slines. Lio overheard the end of that conversation and so I had to repeat it as we were getting our robes on. Jesry showed up last, and drunk. His family had thrown a reception for him at their house.

When the Primate entered the chancel, just before the beginning of the service, he had two purple-robed visitors in tow. It was not unusual for hierarchs from other concents to show up in this way, so I didn't think twice about it. The shape of their hats was a little unusual. Arsibalt was the first to recognize them. "It appears that we have two honored guests from the Inquisition," he said.

I looked across the chancel and recognized the faces of the man and woman I'd been talking to earlier.

I spent the afternoon striping the meadow with rows of tables. Fortunately, Arsibalt was my partner. He might be a little high-strung in some ways, but beneath the fat he had the frame of an ox from winding the clock.

For three thousand years it had been the concent's policy to accept any and all folding chairs and collapsible tables made available to it, and never throw one away. On one and only one occasion, this had turned out to be a wise policy: the millennial Apert of 3000, when 27,500 pilgrims had swarmed in through the gates to enjoy a square meal and see the End of the World. We had folding chairs made of bamboo, machined aluminum, aerospace composites, injection-molded poly, salvaged rebar, hand-carved wood, bent twigs, advanced newmatter, tree stumps, lashed sticks, brazed scrap metal, and plaited grass. Tabletops could be made of old-growth lumber, particle board, extruded titanium, recycled paper, plate glass, rattan, or substances on whose true nature I did not wish to speculate. Their lengths ranged from two to twenty-four feet and their weights from that of a dried flower to that of a buffalo.

"You'd think that after all this time someone might have invented . . . oh, say . . . *the wheel*," Arsibalt mentioned at one point, as we were wrestling with a twelve-foot-long monster that looked like it might have stopped spears during the Old Mathic Age.

Dragging these artifacts up from the cellars and down from the rafters was an almost perfectly stupid task. It was not much more difficult to get Arsibalt talking about Inquisitors and the Inquisition.

The gist of it was that the arrival of two Inquisitors wasn't a big deal at all, unless it was a big deal, in which case it was a really big deal. The Inquisition long ago had become a "relatively non-psychotic, even bureaucratized, process." This was evidenced by the fact that we saw the Warden Regulant and her officers all the time even when we *weren't* in trouble. Though they reported to the Primate, they were technically a branch of the Inquisition. They even had the power to depose a Primate in certain circumstances (Arsibalt, warming to the task, here threw in some precedents of yore involving insane or criminal Primates). Consistent standards had to be maintained across all the world's concents, or else the Reconstitution would be null and void. And how could that be achieved unless there existed this elite class of hierarchs—typically, Wardens Regulant who had doled out so much penance to their long-suffering fraas and suurs that they'd been noticed, and promoted—who traveled from concent to concent to poke around and keep an eye on things? It happened all the time. I just hadn't noticed it until now.

"I'm a little rattled by something that happened just before Provener," I told him.

We were out in the meadow, working on our second acre of tables. Suurs and younger fraas were scurrying around in our wake, lining the tables with chairs, covering them with paper. Older and wiser fraas were hauling on lines, causing a framework of almost weightless struts to rise up above our heads; later these would support a canopy. In an open-air kitchen in the center of the meadow, older suurs were trying to kill us with the fragrance of dishes that were many hours away from being served. Arsibalt and I had been trying for ten minutes to defeat the latching mechanism on the legs of an especially over-designed table: military surplus from a Fifth Century world war. Certain levers and buttons had to be depressed in the right sequence or the legs would not deploy. A dark brown leaf, folded many times, had been wedged into the undercarriage: helpful instructions written in the year 940 by one Fraa Bolo, who had succeeded in getting the table open and wanted to brag about it to generations of unborn avout. But he used incredibly recondite terminology to denote the different parts of the table, and the leaf had been attacked by mice. At a moment when we were about to lose our tempers, throw the table off the Præsidium, consign Fraa Bolo's useless instructions to the fires of Hell, and run out the Decade Gate in search of strong drink, Fraa Arsibalt and I agreed to sit down for a moment and take a break. That was when I told Arsibalt about my conversation with Varax and Onali—as the male and female Inquisitors were called, according to the grapevine.

"Inquisitors in disguise, hmm, I don't think I've heard of that," Arsibalt said. Gazing worriedly at the look on my face, he added: "Which means nothing. It is selection bias: Inquisitors who can't be distinguished from the general populace would of course go unnoticed and unremarked on."

Somehow I didn't find that very comforting.

"They have to move about *somehow*," Arsibalt insisted. "It never occurred to me to wonder how exactly. They can't very well have their own special aerocraft and trains, can they? Much more sensible for them to put on normal clothing and buy a ticket just like anyone else. I would guess that they happened to come in from the aerodrome just as your tour was beginning, and decided on the spur of the moment to tag along so that they could view the statues in the Rotunda, which anyone would want to see."

"Your words make sense but I still feel . . . burned."

"Burned?"

"Yeah. That Varax tricked me into saying things I'd never have said to an Inquisitor."

"Then why on earth did you say them to a total stranger?"

This wasn't helpful. I threw him a look.

"What did you say that was so bad?" he tried.

"Nothing," I concluded, after I'd thought about it for a while. "I mean, I probably sounded very HTW, very Edharian. If Varax is a Procian, he hates me now."

"But that is still within normal limits. There are whole orders that have prospered for thousands of years, saying much more ridiculous things, without running afoul of the Inquisition."

"I know that," I said. Looking across the meadow I happened to see Corlandin and several others of the New Circle getting in position to rehearse a carol that they would sing tonight. From a hundred feet away I could see them grinning and exchanging handshakes. I could smell their confidence as if I were a dog. I wanted to be like that. Not like the crusty Edharian theoricians carrying on bitter debates about the vector sums on the vertices of the canopy struts.

"When I say burned, maybe what I'm getting at is that I burned my bridge. What I said to Varax is going to get repeated to Suur Trestanas and then filter down to the rest of her lot."

"You're afraid the New Circle won't want you for Eliger?"

"That is correct."

"You can avoid the stink then. Better for you."

"What stink, Arsibalt?"

"The stink that's going to permeate this place when most of our crop join the Edharians. The New Circle and the Reformed Old Faanians are going to be left with floor-sweepings."

Trying to seem casual, I looked around to be sure that we were not in earshot of any of the fids Arsibalt considered to be floor-sweepings. But the only person nearby was the primeval Grandfraa Mentaxenes, shuffling around waiting for a purpose, but too proud to ask for one. I approached him with the gnawed table-opening codex of Fraa Bolo and asked him to translate it. He couldn't have been more ready. Arsibalt and I left him to it, and trudged back toward the Mynster for the next table.

"What makes you think that's going to happen?" I said.

"Orolo has been talking to many of us—not just you," Arsibalt said.

"Recruiting us?"

"Corlandin recruits—which is why we don't trust him. Orolo simply talks, and lets us draw our own conclusions."

Bulshytt: (1) In Fluccish of the late Praxic Age and early Reconstitution, a derogatory term for false speech in general, esp. knowing and deliberate falsehood or obfuscation. (2) In Orth, a more technical and clinical term denoting speech (typically but not necessarily commercial or political) that employs euphemism, convenient vagueness, numbing repetition, and other such rhetorical subterfuges to create the impression that something has been said. (3) According to the Knights of Saunt Halikaarn, a radical order of the 2nd Millennium A.R., all speech and writings of the ancient Sphenics; the Mystagogues of the Old Mathic Age; Praxic Age commercial and political institutions; and, since the Reconstitution, anyone they deemed to have been infected by Procian thinking. Their frequent and loud use of this word to interrupt lectures, dialogs, private conversations, etc., exacerbated the divide between Procian and Halikaarnian orders that characterized the mathic world in the years leading up to the Third Sack. Shortly before the Third Sack, all of the Knights of Saunt Halikaarn were Thrown Back, so little more is known about them (their frequent appearance in Sæcular entertainments results from confusion between them and the Incanters).

Usage note: In the mathic world, if the word is suddenly shouted out in a chalk hall or refectory it brings to mind the events associated with sense (3) and is therefore to be avoided. Spoken in a moderate tone of voice, it takes on sense (2), which long ago lost any vulgar connotations it may once have had. In the Sæculum it is easily confused with sense (1) and deemed a vulgarity or even an obscenity. It is inherent in the mentality of extramuros bulshytt-talkers that they are more prone than anyone else to taking offense (or pretending to) when their bulshytt is pointed out to them. This places the mathic observer in a nearly impossible position. One is forced either to use this "offensive" word and be deemed a disagreeable person and as such excluded from polite discourse, or to say the same thing in a different way, which means becoming a purveyor of bulshytt oneself and thereby lending strength to what one is trying to attack. The latter quality probably explains the uncanny stability and resiliency of bulshytt. Resolving this dilemma is beyond the scope of this Dictionary and is probably best left to hierarchs who make it their business to interact with the Sæculum.

—THE DICTIONARY, *4th edition, A.R. 3000*

Somehow that canopy got raised. The struts were newmatter dating back to the founding of the Concent; as dusk fell, they began to emit a soft light that came from all directions and made even Fraa Mentaxenes look healthy. Beneath it, twelve hundred visitors, three hundred Decenarians, and five hundred Unarians celebrated Tenth Night.

This had originated as a harvest festival, coinciding with the end of the calendar year. Thanks to some adroit sequence-writing that had been done before the Second Sack, we had a few crops that could grow almost year-round. In our greenhouses we could cultivate less hardy plants in midwinter. But that stuff wasn't glorious in the way that tangle food was at this time of the year.

The tangle had been invented way back before Cnoüs, by people who lived on the opposite side of the world from Ethras and Baz. Cob grew straight up out of the ground to the height of a man's head and bore rich heads of particolored kernels late in the summer. In the meantime, it served as a trellis for climbing vines of podbeans that gave us protein while fixing nitrogen in the soil to nourish the cob. In the web that the podbean vines spun among the cob stalks, three other kinds of vegetables grew: highest from the ground, where bugs couldn't get to them, red, yellow, and orange tommets to give us vitamins and flavor our salads, stews, and sauces. Snaking along the ground, gourds of many varieties. In the middle, hollow pepperpods. Tubers of two kinds grew beneath the ground, and leaf vegetables gathered whatever light remained. The original, ancient tangle had comprised eight plants, and the people who cultivated them had over thousands of years bred them to be as efficient as they could be without actually reaching in and tinkering with their sequences. Ours were more efficient yet, and we had added four more types of plants, two of which had no purpose other than to replenish the soil. At this time of year, the tangles we'd been cultivating since thaw were in their glory and sported a variety of color and flavor that couldn't be had extramuros. That's why Apert took place now. It was a way for those inside the math to share their good fortune with their neighbors extramuros, as well as to relieve them of any babies not likely to survive the winter.

I saved seats for Cord and her boyfriend Rosk. Cord also brought with her a cousin of ours: Dath, a boy of fifteen. I remembered him vaguely. He'd been the kind of youngster who was always being rushed to Physicians' Commons for repair of astonishing traumas. Somehow he'd survived and even put on passable clothing for the event. His dents and scars were hidden beneath a mess of curly brown hair.

Arsibalt made sure he was seated across from "the exquisite" Cord; he didn't appear to understand the significance of Rosk. Jesry caused his entire family to sit at the next table, which placed him back to back with me. Then Jesry flagged down Orolo and persuaded him to sit in our cluster. Orolo attracted Lio and several other lonely wanderers, who proceeded to fill out our table.

Dath was the kind of sweet untroubled soul who could ask very basic questions with no trace of embarrassment. I tried to answer them in the same spirit.

"You know I'm a sline, cousin," I said. "So the difference between slines and us is not that we're smarter. That is demonstrably not the case."

This topic had come up after people had been eating, drinking, talking, and singing old carols just long enough to make it obvious that there really were no differences. Dath, who had come through his early mishaps with his good sense intact, had been looking about and taking note of this—I could read it on his face. And so he had raised the question of why bother to put up walls—to have an extramuros and an intramuros?

Orolo had caught wind of this and turned around to get a look at Dath. "It would be easier for you to understand if you could see one of the pinprick maths," he said.

"Pinprick maths?"

"Some are no more than a one-room apartment with an electrical clock hanging on the wall and a well-stocked bookcase. One avout lives there alone, with no speely, no jeejah. Perhaps every few years an Inquisitor comes round and pokes his head in the door, just to see that all is well."

"What's the point of that?" Dath asked.

"That is precisely the question I am asking you to think about," Orolo said, and turned back round to resume a conversation with Jesry's father.

Dath threw up his hands. Arsibalt and I laughed, but not at his expense. "That's how Pa Orolo does his dirty work," I told him.

"Tonight, instead of sleeping, you'll lie awake wondering what he meant," Arsibalt said.

"Well, aren't you guys going to help me? I'm not a fraa!" Dath pleaded.

"What would motivate someone to sit alone in a one-room apartment reading and thinking?" Arsibalt asked. "What would have to be true of a person for them to consider that a life well spent?"

"I don't know. Maybe they're really shy? Scared of open spaces?"

"Agoraphobia is not the correct answer," Arsibalt said, a little huffy.

"What if the places you went and the things you encountered in your work were more interesting than what was available in the physical world around you?" I tried.

"Okayyy . . ."

"You might say that the difference between us and you is that we have been infected by a vision of . . . another world." I'd been about to say "a greater" or "a higher" but settled for "another."

"I don't like the infection metaphor," Arsibalt started to say in Orth. I kneed him under the table.

"You mean like a different planet?" Dath asked.

"That's an interesting way of looking at it," I said. "Most of us don't think it's another planet in the sense of a speculative fiction speely. Maybe it's the future of *this* world. Maybe it's an alternate universe we can't get to. Maybe it's nothing but a fantasy. But at any rate it lives in our souls and we can't help striving toward it."

"What's that world like?" Dath asked.

Behind me, a jingle began to play from someone's jeejah. It wasn't that loud, but something about it made my brain lock up. "For one thing, it doesn't have any of *those*," I told Dath.

After the jeejah had been singing for a little while, I turned around. Everyone in a twenty-foot radius was staring at Jesry's older brother, who was slapping himself all over trying to determine which of the pockets in his suit contained the jeejah. Finally he extracted it and silenced it. He stood up, as if he had not drawn enough attention to himself, and bellowed his own name. "Yes, Doctor Grane," he went on, staring into the distance like a holy man. "I see. I see. Can they infest humans as well? *Really!?* I was only joking. Well, how would we be able to tell if that had happened?"

People turned back to their meals, but conversations were slow to restart, because of sporadic incursions from Jesry's brother.

Arsibalt cleared his throat as only Arsibalt could; it sounded like the end of the world. "The Primate's about to speak."

I turned around and looked at Jesry, who had realized the same thing and was waving his arms at his brother, who stared right through him. He was negotiating a bulk rate on biopsies. He was a *very* tough negotiator. Women in the party—sisters and sisters-in-law of Jesry—had begun to feel ashamed and to tug at the man's elbows. He spun around and stalked away from us: "Excuse me, Doctor, I didn't catch that last part? Something about the larvae?" But in his defense, as I looked around I could see that he was only one of many who were using jeejahs for one purpose or another.

Statho had already addressed us twice. The first time had been ostensibly to greet everyone but really to nag us into taking our seats. The second time had been to intone the Invocation, which had been written by Diax himself while the rake blisters were still fresh on his hands. If you could understand Proto-Orth and if you happened to be a mushy-headed, number-worshipping Enthusiast, the Invocation would make you feel distinctly unwelcome. Everyone else just thought it added a touch of class to the proceedings.

Now he told us we were going to be entertained by a contingent of Edharians. Statho's grasp of Fluccish was weak; the way he phrased it, he was *commanding* us to be entertained. This made laughter run through the crowd, which left him nonplussed and asking the Inquisitors (who were flanking him at the high table) for explanations.

Three fraas and two suurs sang a five-part motet while twelve others milled around in front of them. Actually they weren't milling; it just looked that way from where we sat. Each one of them represented an upper or lower index in a theorical equation involving certain tensors and a metric. As they moved to and fro, crossing over one another's paths and exchanging places while traversing in front of the high table, they were acting out a calculation on the curvature of a four-dimensional manifold, involving various steps of symmetrization, antisymmetrization, and raising and lowering of indices. Seen from above by someone who didn't know any theorics, it would have looked like a country dance. The music was lovely even if it was interrupted every few seconds by the warbling of jeejahs.

Then we ate and drank more. Then the New Circle fraas sang their piece, which was much better received than the tensor dance. Then we ate and drank more. Statho made it all tick along, like Cord running her five-axis mill. We weren't used to seeing him do a lot of work, but he was earning his beer this evening. To the visitors, this was just a free feed with weird entertainment, but in truth it was a ritual as old and as important as Provener and so there were certain boxes that had to be checked if we were to get out of it without drawing a rebuke from the Inquisition. And Statho was the kind who would have done it the right way even if Varax and Onali hadn't been sitting there asking him to pass the salt.

Fraa Haligastreme was introduced to say a few words on behalf of the Edharian chapter. He tried to talk about what I had mentioned to Dath earlier, and bungled it even worse. He was the funniest man in the world if you just walked up to him and asked him a question, but he was helpless when given the opportunity to prepare, and the sporadic alarums of the jeejahs shattered his concentration and reduced his talk to a heap of shards. The only shard that lodged in my memory was his concluding line: "If this all seems ambiguous, that's because it is; and if that troubles you, you'd hate it here; but if it gives you a feeling of relief, then you are in the right place and might consider staying."

Next up was Corlandin for the New Circle chapter.

"I've been with my family the last ten days," he announced, and smiled over at a table of Burgers who smiled back at him. "They were kind enough to organize a family reunion during Apert. All of them have busy lives out there, just as I do in here, but for these days we suspended our routines, our careers, and our other commitments so that we could be together."

"Myself, I've been out watching speelys," Orolo remarked. Only about five of us could hear him. "Ones with plenty of explosions. Some are quite enjoyable."

Corlandin continued, "Making dinner—normally a routine chore we perform to avoid starvation—became something altogether different. The pattern of cuts my Aunt Prin made in the top crust of a pie was not just a system of vents to relieve internal pressure, but a sort of ritual going back who knows how many generations—an invocation, if you will, of her ancestors who did it the same way. The conversations we had about, say, when Grandpa Myrt fell off his porch roof while cleaning the gutters, were not just debriefings about the hazards of home renovation but celebrations— full of laughter, tears, and sometimes laughter and tears at the same time—of how much we loved each other. So you could say that nothing was about what it superficially *seemed* to be about. Which in another context might make it sound all just a bit sinister. But obviously it was nothing of the kind. We all got it. You'd have gotten it too. And that's a lot like what we fraas and suurs do in this concent all the time. Thank you." And Corlandin sat down.

Slightly indignant murmuring from avout—not at all certain that they agreed with him—was drowned out by applause from the majority of visitors. Poor Suur Frandling had to get up next and say a few words for the Reformed Old Faanians, but she could have been reading from an economic database for all anyone cared. Most of the avout were peeved by Corlandin's eloquence—or glibness—and

Orolo was among them. But to his credit he pointed out that Corlandin had smoothed over an awkward moment and probably won us some sympathy extramuros.

"How do you know when someone is *really* glib?" Jesry muttered to me.

"I'll bite. How?"

"It doesn't cross your mind that he's glib until someone older and wiser points it out. And then, your face turns hot with shame."

More music then, as most of us avout got up to clear plates and fetch dessert. The entertainment, which earlier had been so intimidating, had become a little easier to enjoy. Many of the carols traditionally played over loudspeakers in stores and elevators at this time of year were derived from liturgical music that had originated in the maths and filtered out at Apert, and so many of the visitors were pleasantly surprised to hear familiar melodies spilling from the lips of these bolt-wrapped weirdos.

Dessert was sheet cakes baked and served in broad trays. One of them ended up in front of Arsibalt—not a coincidence. He picked up the spatula that had arrived with it: a flat metal blade about the size of the palm of a child's hand. Just before he plunged it into the cake, I had an idea, and stopped him. "Let's have Dath do it," I said.

"As hosts, it is our duty to serve," Arsibalt demurred.

"Then you can serve, but I want Dath to do the cutting," I insisted. I wrenched the spatula from Arsibalt's grip and handed it across to Dath, who took it a little uncertainly.

I then talked him through cutting the cake; but I had him go about it in a very specific way, working through the steps of an old geometry proof* that Orolo had taught me when I had been a brand-new fid, up all night crying because I missed my old life. This took a little while, but when all was said and done, it was clear from the look on Dath's face that he understood it, and I was able to tell him: "Congratulations. You have just worked out a geometric proof that is thousands of years old."

---

* See Calca 1.

"They had sheet cakes back then?"

"No, but they had land and other things they needed to measure, and the same trick works for those things too."

"Uh huh," Dath said, gobbling a vertex from his serving.

"You say uh huh like it is not a big deal, but it is a big deal to us," I said. "Why should a proof that works for sheet cake work as well for a plot of land? Cake and land are different things."

We had gone a little over the head of Dath, who just wanted to eat his cake, but Cord saw it. "I guess I have an unfair advantage here since I spend so much time thinking about geometry in my work. But the answer is that geometry is . . . well . . . geometry. It's pure. It doesn't matter what you're applying it to."

"And it turns out that the same is true for other kinds of theorics besides geometry," I said. "You can prove something. Later the same thing might be proved in a totally different way; but you always end up with the same answer. No matter who is discussing these proofs, in what age, whether they are speaking of sheet cake or pasture-land, they always arrive at the same answer. These truths seem to come out of another world or plane of existence. It's hard not to believe that this other world really exists in some sense—not just in our imaginations! And we would like to go there."

"Preferably without having to die first," Arsibalt put in.

"When I'm cutting a part, sometimes I get obsessed with it," Cord said. "I lie awake in my bed thinking about its shape. Is that—perhaps—related to how you all feel about what you study?"

"Why not? You're carrying this geometry around in your head that fascinates you. Some would say it's only a pattern of neurons firing in your brain. But it has an independent reality. And for you, thinking about that reality is an interesting and rewarding way to spend your life."

Rosk was a manual therapist—he put his hands on people to fix them. "I've been working on someone who has a pinched nerve because he has lousy posture," he said. "I was discussing it with my teacher, over the jeejah—no pictures, just our voices. We had this long talk about this nerve and the muscles and ligaments around it and how I should manipulate them to help alleviate the problem, and suddenly I just flashed on how weird the whole thing was—two of us both relating to this image—this model—of another person's body that was in *his* mind and in *my* mind, but—"

"Also seemingly in a third place," I suggested, "a shared place."

"That's what it felt like. It freaked me out for a little while, but then I put it out of my mind because I thought I was just being weird."

"Well, it's been freaking people out since Cnoüs and this is like an asylum for people who can't stop thinking about it," I said. "It's not for everyone, but it's harmless."

"Since the Third Sack anyway," Rosk said.

That he said it so innocently made it ten times as rude as it was to begin with. I saw Cord's face flush, and guessed she'd probably have words with him after dinner. It was anyone's guess whether he'd ever really understand why it was such an abhorrent thing to say.

People were shushing us because we had reached that part of the aut where the newcomers were presented at the high table.

Eight foundlings had been Collected. One was sickly and would stay in the Unarian math where it would be easier for the physicians to keep an eye on her. Two of them still had the stumps of their umbilical cords attached, which meant that they were destined for the Millenarian math, by way of a brief sojourn among the Hundreders. We would pass them along via our upper labyrinth. The remaining five were a little bit older, and so would be passed to the Hundreders.

Thirty-six youngsters were to be Collected. Seventeen of these, including Barb, would come directly to our math. The others would stay with the One-offs, at least at first. With any luck, some of them might graduate to our math later.

Twelve of the One-offs had decided to graduate to our math. Nine more had arrived from another, smaller concent in the mountains that acted as a feeder to ours.

All of these were brought up before the high table, welcomed, and applauded. Tomorrow, after the gate closed, we would celebrate their arrival in a much more tedious ceremony. Tonight was the time for the extramuros authorities to supply their own special brand of tedium. By ancient tradition, the highest-ranking Panjandrum present at this dinner was supposed to stand up and formally hand the newcomers over to us. At that moment, they passed out of Sæcular, and into mathic jurisdiction. We became responsible for housing them and feeding them, caring for them when they ailed, burying them when they died, and punishing them when they misbehaved. It was as if they ceased in this moment to be citizens of one country and became citizens of another. It was, in other words, a big deal from a legal standpoint, and it had to be solemnized by the speaking of certain oaths and the ringing of a bell. And there was an almost as ancient tradition that the official in question would use it as an excuse to "deliver some remarks."

This turned out to be the rope-draped oddity who had appeared at the Decade Gate with his contingent on the first morning of Apert. He was, as it turned out, the mayor.

After thanking everyone from God on down and then back up to God again, and then, as a precaution, tacking on a blanket thank-you for any persons or supernatural beings he had left out, he began: "Even those of you who live at Saunt Edhar must be aware by now that the extraordinary re-configuration of prefectural boundaries mandated by the Eleventh Circle of Arch-Magistrates has literally transformed the political landscape. The Plenary Council of the Recovered Satrapies has passed through a tipping point of no return, placing five of the eight Tetrarchies within the grasp of a new generation of leaders who I can promise you will be far more sensitive than their predecessors to the values and priorities of New Counterbazian constituencies and our many friends who may belong to other Arks, or even to no Ark at all, but who share our concerns . . ."

"If there are eight of them, why are they called Tetrarchs?" Orolo demanded, drawing an exasperated look from Jesry's father, who had been listening intently—he was *taking notes.*

"There were four of them originally and the name stuck," Arsibalt said.

Jesry's father seemed to relax a bit, thinking that the interruption was over. But we were just beginning.

"What's a New Counterbazian?" Lio wanted to know. Jesry's brother shushed him. To my surprise Jesry rose to Lio's defense. "We didn't tell you to shut up when you were bellowing about your infestation."

"Yes you did."

"I'll bet it's a euphemism for one of those Warden of Heaven nut jobs," I said to Lio. This brought a cataract of shushing down on me. Jesry's father sighed as if he could thereby rise above all of this, and cupped a hand to his ear, but it was too late; we'd planted a branching tree of arguments and recriminations. The mayor was going on and on about the beauty of our clock, the majesty of our Mynster, and the magnificent singing of the fraas and suurs. At no point did he say anything that was not as sugary as words could be, and yet the feeling I got was one of foreboding, as if he were urging all of his constituents to mass before our gates with bottles of gasoline. The argument between Jesry and his brother decayed into sporadic sniper fire across the table, suppressed by glares and arm-squeezings from exasperated females who had wordlessly squared up into a peacekeeping force. Jesry's brother had decided that with our hair-splitting debates about how many Tetrarchs there were, we'd shown ourselves to be a lot of insignificant pedants. Jesry informed him that this was an iconography that dated back to before the founding of the city-state of Ethras.

In some eerily quiet way that he must have learned from a book of Vale-lore, Lio had vanished. Strangely for one who studied fighting so much, he hated conflict.

I waited until the bell had rung to induct the newcomers, then excused myself and walked out during the standing ovation. I felt like getting some fresh air. By tradition, the revelry would wind down and the cleanup gather momentum until the gates closed at dawn, so it was unlikely I'd miss much.

The meadow was lit partly by the harvest moon and partly by light diffusing through the skirts of the great canopy, which, when I turned around to look back on it, looked like an enormous straw-colored moon half sunk into a dark sea. Lio was silhouetted against it. He was moving in an odd, dance-like fashion, which for him was hardly unusual. One end of his bolt was modesty-wrapped, but the other was all over the place—flinging out like a bucket of suds, then wafting down for a few moments only to be snapped back and regathered: the same thing he'd been practicing on the statue of Saunt Froga. It was strangely fascinating to watch. I was not his only spectator: a few visitors had gathered around him. Bulky men. Four of them. All wearing the same color. Numbers on their backs.

Lio's bolt slapped down on top of Number 86 and draped him, making him look like a ghost. The lower part was all in a thrash as he flailed his arms to throw it off. His head was a stationary knob at the top—hence a fine target for the ball of Lio's foot, which was delivered in a perfectly executed flying kick.

I started running toward them.

86 went down backwards. Lio's momentum carried him to the same place. He used 86's torso to cushion his landing, and rolled off smartly, staying low like a spider and snapping his bolt free. 79 was coming in high. Lio spun clear of the line of attack and in so doing got his bolt around 79's knees. Then he stood up, bringing 79's knees with him; 79's face dove at the ground and he didn't get his arms up—excuse me, *down*—fast enough to avoid getting a mouthful of turf. For just a moment after Lio spiraled his bolt loose, 79 remained poised upside-down with his legs splayed. Lio absent-mindedly rammed his elbow down into the vee as he turned to see who was next.

Answer: Number 23, running right at him. Lio turned and ran away. But not very fast. 23 gained on him. It was his fate to step on Lio's bolt, which was dragging behind Lio on the grass. This demolished his gait, which had been clumsy to begin with. Lio sensed it—as how could he not, since the other end of that bolt was lashed around his crotch. He whirled and yanked. 23 somehow remained on his feet, but the price he paid for doing so was that he ended up staggering, bent forward at the waist, leading with his head. Lio planted a foot in his path, got a hand on the back of 23's head, and used the other's momentum to flip him over his knee. 23 didn't know how to fall. He came down hard on his shoulder and pivoted around that to a hard landing on his back. I knew what was coming next: Lio would follow with a "death blow" to the exposed throat. And that is just what he did; but he pulled it, as he always had with me, and refrained from staving in the man's windpipe.

One remained. And I do mean one, for he had a large numeral 1 on his back. This was the man with his arm in a sling. With his good arm, he had been been rummaging through the pockets of the fallen 86. He found what he had been looking for and stood up, holding something that I was pretty sure was a gun.

His spine-clamp exploded in light, flashing alternately red and blue. He uttered a common profanity. He dropped the gun and collapsed. Every muscle in his body had lost tone in the same instant, jammed by signals from the clamp. All four of the attackers were down now, and the meadow was quiet except for the plaintive warbling of their jeejahs.

A solitary person, somewhere nearby, began clapping. I assumed it was a sline who'd had too much to drink. But looking toward the sound, I was surprised to see a hooded figure in a bolt. He kept shouting an ancient Orth word that meant "hail, huzzah, well done."

Stalking toward this fraa, I shouted, "I hope you're stinking drunk, because if not, you're an idiot. He could have gotten killed. And even if you really are that big of a jerk—don't you know there's a couple of Inquisitors skulking around?"

"It's okay, one of them skulked out to get away from that idiotic speech," the fraa said.

He pulled back his hood to reveal that he was Varax of the Inquisition.

I can't guess what my face looked like, but I can tell you that the sight of it was the most entertaining thing Varax had seen in a long time. He tried not to show it too much. "It never ceases to amaze me, what people think of us and why we're here," he said. "Will you please forget about this. It is nothing." He looked up at the top of the Præsidium. "Larger matters are at stake than whether a young fraa at the remote hermitage of Saunt Edhar practices his vlor on some local runagates. For God's sake," he continued (which sounded funny to me since few of us believed in God, and he didn't seem like one of them; but maybe it was just an oath used by cosmopolitan people in the sorts of places where our concent was thought of as a "remote hermitage"). "For God's sake, raise your sights. Think bigger—the way you were doing this morning. The way your friend, there, does when he decides to tackle four larger men." And with that Varax drew his hood back over his head and walked back toward the canopy.

He passed the Warden Fendant and the Warden Regulant hurrying the other way. The two of them parted and stood aside to let him pass. Each nodded and uttered some term of respect that no one had ever bothered to teach me.

Both of the Wardens were looking rather tightly wound. In ordinal time, the boundary between their jurisdictions was clear: it was the top of the wall. During Apert, things became complicated as the wall ceased to exist for ten days.

Suur Trestanas was for throwing the Book at Lio. Fraa Delrakhones was satisfied with how things had come out, with a few quibbles: when Lio had noticed the four slines sneaking out the back, he ought to have alerted someone instead of going out to confront them himself.

"Well, is that an offense or isn't it?" demanded Suur Trestanas.

"It is an overlookable offense, as far as I am concerned," said Delrakhones, "but I'm not the Warden Regulant."

"Well, I am," said Suur Trestanas unnecessarily, "and for one of our fraas to be brawling, during Apert, when he's supposed to be welcoming newcomers and busing tables, strikes me as something that could even lead to being Thrown Back."

This was such an outrageous thing to say that I spoke immediately—as if Lio's impulsiveness had jumped like a spark into my head. "If I were you, I'd run that by Inquisitor Varax before taking it any further," I said.

Trestanas turned and looked at me, head to toe, as if she'd never seen me before. And perhaps she hadn't. "The amount of private time you are spending with our honored guests is remarkable. Extraordinary."

"And accidental, I promise you." But Suur Trestanas was—I realized too late—*jealous* of me for this. Almost as if she pined to be in a liaison with Varax and Onali, but they had a crush on me. And she'd never believe that my encounters with them had been mere accidents. You didn't get to be Warden Regulant by believing such things.

"It is obvious that you have no conception of the power that the Inquisition may wield over us."

"Uh, not true. They may put the concent on probation for up to one hundred years, during which time our diet will be restricted to the basics—nutritional but not so interesting. If we haven't mended our ways after a century they can come in and clean the place out top to bottom. And they have the power to fire any hierarch and replace him or . . . her . . . with . . . a new one of their choosing . . ." I was faltering because my brain—too late—was working through the implications. I had only been spewing back what Arsibalt had told me earlier in the day. But to Trestanas it would, of course, sound like a taunt.

"Maybe you think that Saunt Edhar's current hierarchs are not handling their responsibilities well," Suur Trestanas proposed, too calmly. "Perhaps Delrakhones—or Statho—or I—ought to be replaced?"

"I have never thought anything of the sort!" I said, and bit my tongue before I could add *until now*.

"Then why all of these secret assignations with the Inquisitors? You are the *only* non-hierarch who has spoken to them *at all*—and now you have done so *twice*, both times under circumstances that were extraordinarily *private*."

"This is crazy," I said, "this is crazy."

"More is at stake than a boy of your age can comprehend. Your naïvete—combined with your refusal to admit just how naïve you are—imposes risks on us all. I am throwing the Book at you."

"No!" I couldn't believe it.

"Chapters One through . . . er . . . oh . . . *Five*."

"You have got to be kidding!"

"I believe you know what to do," she said, and looked across the meadow to the Mynster.

"Fine. Fine. Chapters One through Five," I repeated, and turned toward the canopy.

"Halt," Suur Trestanas said.

I halted.

"The Mynster is *that* way," she said, sounding amused. "You seem to be going the wrong direction."

"My sib and my cousin are in there. I just need to go and explain to them that I have to leave."

"The Mynster," she repeated, "is in that direction."

"I can't do five chapters before sunrise," I pointed out. "The gates are going to be closed when I come out of that cell. I have to say goodbye to my family."

"*Have* to? Curious choice of words. Let me bring you up to date on semantics, since you who worship at Hylaea's feet are so keen on such things. You *have to* go to the Mynster. You *want to* say goodbye to your family. The whole point of being a fraa is to be free of those *wants* that enslave people who live extramuros. I am doing you the favor of forcing you to make a choice *now,* in this instant. If you *want to* see your family so badly, go see them—and keep on walking, right out the gate, and don't ever come back. If you will remain here, you *have to* walk straight to the Mynster *now.*"

I looked for Lio, hoping he might convey a message to Cord and Dath, but he was some distance away now, recounting the fight to Delrakhones, and anyway I didn't want to give Suur Trestanas the additional pleasure of telling me I couldn't.

So I turned my back on what remained of my family and started walking toward the Mynster.

Part 3

ELIGER

*B*oredom is a mask that frustration wears. What better place to savor the truth of Fraa Orolo's saying than a penance cell of the Warden Regulant? Some cunning architect had designed these things to be to frustration what a lens was to light. My cell did not have a door. All that stood between me and freedom was a narrow arch, shaped in the pointed ogive of the Old Mathic Age, framed in massive stones all scratched with graffiti by prisoners of yore. I was forbidden to stray through it or to receive visitors until the penance was complete. The arch opened onto the inner walkway that made the circuit of the Warden Regulant's court. It was trafficked at all hours by lesser hierarchs wandering by on one errand or another. I could look straight out across that walkway into the vault-work of the upper chancel, but because of its parapet I could not see down to the floor two hundred feet below where Provener was celebrated. I could hear the music. I could gaze straight out and see the chain moving when my team wound the clock and the bell-ropes dancing when Tulia's team rang changes. But I could not see the people.

On the opposite side of the cell, my view was better. Framed in another Mathic arch was a window affording a fine view of the meadow. This was just another device to magnify frustration and hence boredom, since, if I wanted, I could spend all day looking down on my brothers and sisters strolling at liberty around the concent and (I supposed) discussing all sorts of interesting things, or at least telling funny stories. Above, the Warden Fendant's overhanging ledge blocked most of the sky, but I could see to about twenty degrees above the horizon. My window faced roughly toward the Century Gate, with the Decade Gate visible off to the right if I put my face close to the glass. So when the sun rose the morning after Tenth Night, I was able to hear the close-of-Apert service. Looking out my cell's doorway, I could see the chains move as the water-valves were actuated. Then by stepping across the cell and looking out my window I was able to see a silver thread of water negotiate the aqueduct to the Decade Gate, and to watch the gate grind closed. Only a few spectators were strewn about extramuros. For a little while I tortured myself with the idea that Cord was standing there forlornly expecting me to run out at the last moment and give her a goodbye hug. But such ideas faded quickly once the gates closed. I watched the avout take down the canopy and fold up the tables. I ate the piece of bread and drank the bowl of milk left at my door by one of Suur Trestanas's minions.

Then I turned my attention to the Book.

Since the sole purpose of the Book was to punish its readers, the less said of it the better. To study it, to copy it out, and to memorize it was an extraordinary form of penance.

The concent, like any other human settlement, abounded in nasty or tedious chores such as weeding gardens, maintaining sewers, peeling potatoes, and slaughtering animals. In a perfect society we'd have taken turns. As it was, there were rules and codes of conduct that people broke from time to time, and the Warden Regulant saw to it that those people performed the most disagreeable jobs. It was not a bad system. When you were fixing a clogged latrine because you'd had too much to drink in the Refectory, you might not have such an enjoyable day, but the fact of the matter was that latrines were necessary; sometimes they clogged up; and some fraa or suur had to clean them out, as we couldn't very well call in an outside plumber. So there was at least some satisfaction in doing such penance, because there was a point in the work.

There was no point at all to the Book, which is what made it an especially dreaded form of penance. It contained twelve chapters. Like the scale used to measure earthquakes, these got exponentially worse as they went on, so Chapter Six was ten times as bad as Chapter Five, and so on. Chapter One was just a taste, meted out to delinquent children, and usually completed in an hour or two. Two meant at least one overnight stay, though any self-respecting trou-blemaker could bang it out in a day. Five typically meant a stay of several weeks. Any sentence of Chapter Six or higher could be ap-pealed to the Primate and then to the Inquisition. Chapter Twelve amounted to a sentence of life at hard labor in solitary confinement; only three avout had finished it in 3690 years, and all of them were profoundly insane.

Beyond about Six, the punishment could span years. Many chose to leave the concent rather than endure it. Those who stuck it out were changed when they emerged: subdued, and notably di-minished. Which might sound crazy, because there was nothing to it other than copying out the required chapters, memorizing them, and then answering questions about them before a panel of hier-archs. But the contents of the Book had been crafted and refined over many centuries to be nonsensical, maddening, and pointless: flagrantly at first, more subtly as the chapters progressed. It was a maze without an exit, an equation that after weeks of toil reduced to $2 = 3$. Chapter One was a page of nursery-rhymes salted with nonsense-words that almost rhymed—but not quite. Chapter Four was five pages of the digits of pi. Beyond that, however, there was no further randomness in the Book, since it was easy to memorize truly random things once you taught yourself a few tricks—and everyone who'd made it through Chapter Four knew the tricks. Much harder to memorize and to answer questions about were writings that almost but did not quite make sense; that had internal logic, but only to a point. Such things cropped up naturally in the mathic world from time to time—after all, not everyone had what it took to be a Saunt. After their authors had been humiliated and Thrown Back, these writings would be gone over by the Inquisi-tion, and, if they were found to be the right kind of awful, made even more so, and folded into later and more wicked editions of the Book. To complete your sentence and be granted permission to walk out of your cell, you had to master them just as thoroughly as, say, a student of quantum mechanics must know group theory. The punishment lay in knowing that you were putting all of that effort into letting a kind of intellectual poison infiltrate your brain to its very roots. It was more humiliating than you might imagine, and after I'd been toiling on Chapter Five for a couple of weeks I had no difficulty in seeing how one who completed a sentence of, say, Chapter Nine would emerge permanently damaged.

Enough of the Book. A more interesting question: why was I here? It seemed that Suur Trestanas wanted me removed from the community for as long as the Inquisitors were among us. Chapter Three wouldn't have taken me long enough. Four might have done it, but she'd given me Five just in case I happened to be one of those persons who was good at memorizing numbers.

The dawn aut—which was attended only by a smattering of avout who were especially fond of ceremonies—woke me every morning. I snapped my bolt off the wooden pallet that was the cell's only furniture and wrapped it around myself. I pissed down a hole in the floor and washed in a stone basin of cold water, ate my bread and drank my milk, set the empty dishes by the door, sat on the floor, and arranged the Book, a pen, a bottle of ink, and some leaves on the surface of the pallet. My sphere served as a rest for my right elbow. I worked for three hours, then did something else, just to clear my head, until Provener. Then, during the whole time that Lio and Jesry and Arsibalt were winding the clock, I was doing pushups, squats, and lunges. My team were working harder and getting stronger because of my absence, and I didn't want to be weak when I emerged.

My teammates must have somehow figured out which cell I was in, for after Provener they'd have a picnic lunch in the meadow right beneath my window. They didn't dare look up or wave to me—Trestanas must be glaring down at them, just waiting for such a mistake—but they'd begin each lunch by hoisting tankards of beer in someone's honor and quaffing deeply. I got the message.

Plenty of ink and leaves were available, so I began to write down the account you have been reading. As I did so, I became haunted by the idea that there was some pattern woven through the last few weeks' events that I had failed to notice. I put this down to the altered state of mind that comes over a solitary prisoner with nothing to keep him company save the Book.

One day about two weeks into my penance, my morning work-shift was interrupted by strange bells. Through my door I could see a stretch of the bell-ropes that ran from the ringers' balcony up toward the carillon. I moved round to the other side of the pallet, turning my back to the window, so that I could observe the jerking and recoiling of those ropes. All avout were supposed to be able to decode the changes. I had never been especially good at it. The tones melted together in my ears and I could not shape them into patterns. But watching the movements of the ropes somehow made it easier; for such work my eyes were better suited than my ears. I could see the way in which a given rope's movement was conditioned by what its neighbors had done on the previous beats. In a minute or two, without having to ask anyone's help, I was able to recognize this as the call to Eliger. One of my crop was about to join an order.

After the changes were rung, half an hour passed before the aut began, and it was another half an hour of singing and chanting before I heard Statho intone the name of Jesry. This was followed by the singing of the Canticle of Inbrase. The singing was vigorous but rough around the edges—so I knew it was the Edharians who were inducting him. During all of that time, it was difficult for me to concentrate on the Book, and afterwards I could get very little done until after Provener.

The next day those changes rang again. Two more joined the Edharians and one—Ala—joined the New Circle. No surprise there. We'd always expected her to end up as a hierarch. For some reason, though, this one kept me awake late into the night. It was as if Ala had flown off to some other concent where I'd never see her again, never get into another argument with her, never compete with her to see who could solve a theorics problem first. Which was absurd, since she was staying right here at Edhar and I'd be dining with her in the Refectory every day. But some part of my brain insisted on seeing Ala's decision as a personal loss for me, and punished me by keeping me awake.

There was a little lesson hidden in the way I had deciphered the Eliger changes by seeing them. For as I continued to write out my account of the preceding weeks—all the while nagged by the sense that I was missing something—I eventually came to the part where I set down my conversation with Fraa Orolo on the starhenge, and his muffled argument with Trestanas immediately afterwards, down by the portcullis. As I wrote this, I looked out my window to the place where it had happened, and noted that the portcullis was closed—even though it was daytime. I also had a view of the Centenarians' portcullis. It too was closed. Both of them had been closed the whole time I'd been here. With each day that went by I became more and more certain that the starhenge had been altogether sealed off, and had been from the very moment that the Master of the Keys had slammed the grate down behind me and Orolo on the eighth day of Apert. This closure of the starhenge—which I was pretty sure was unprecedented in the entire history of the Concent of Saunt Edhar—must have been the topic of the angry conversation between Orolo and Trestanas.

Was it too much of a stretch to think that the arrival of the Inquisitors, a couple of days later, had been no coincidence? Ours looked at the same sky as every other starhenge in the world. If ours had been closed—if there was something out there we weren't supposed to see—the others must have been closed too. The order must have gone out over the Reticulum on the eighth day of Apert and been conveyed by the Ita, to Suur Trestanas; at the same moment, I reckoned, Varax and Onali had begun their journey to the "remote hermitage" of Saunt Edhar.

All of which made a kind of sense but did nothing at all to help me with the most perplexing and important question: why would they want to close the starhenge? It was the *last* part of the concent one would ever expect the hierarchs to concern themselves with. Their duty was to preserve the Discipline by preventing the flow of Sæcular information to the minds of the avout. The information that came in through the starhenge was by nature timeless. Much of it was billions of years old. What passed for current events might be a dust storm on a rocky planet or a vortex fluctuation on a gas giant. What could possibly be seen from the starhenge that would be considered as Sæcular?

Like a fraa who wakes in his cell in the hours before dawn smelling smoke, and who knows from this that a slow fire must have been smoldering and gathering heat for many hours while he slumbered in oblivion, I felt not only alarm but also shame at my own slowness.

It didn't help that Eliger was being celebrated almost every day now. For the last year or so, I'd sensed myself falling slowly behind some of the others in theorics and cosmography. At times I'd resigned myself to joining a non-Edharian order and becoming a hierarch. Then, immediately before Trestanas had thrown the Book at me, I'd made up my mind to angle for a place among the Edharians and devote myself to exploring the Hylaean Theoric World. Instead of which, I was stuck in this room reading nonsense while the others raced even further ahead of me—and filled up the available spaces in the Edharian chapter. Technically there was no limit—no quota. But if the Edharians got more than ten or a dozen new avout at the expense of the others, there'd be trouble. Thirty years ago, when Orolo had come in, they'd recruited fourteen, and people were still talking about it.

One afternoon, just after Provener, the bell team began to ring changes. I assumed at first that it was Eliger again. For by that time, five had joined the Edharians, three the New Circle, and one the Reformed Old Faanians. But some deep part of my brain nagged me with the sense that these were changes I had not heard before.

Once more I set down my pen—wishing I'd been given this penance in less interesting times—and sat where I could watch the ropes. Within a few minutes I knew for certain that this was not Eliger. My chest clenched up for a few moments as I worried that it was Anathem. It was over, though, before I could make sense of it. So I sat motionless for half an hour listening to the naves fill up. It was a big crowd—all of the avout in all of the maths had stopped whatever they'd been doing and come here. They were all talking. They sounded excited. I couldn't make out a word. But I sensed from their tone that something momentous was about to happen. In spite of my fears, I slowly convinced myself it could not be Anathem.

People would not be talking so much if they had gathered to watch one of their number be Thrown Back.

The service began. There was no music. I could make out the Primate speaking familiar phrases in Old Orth: a formal summoning of the concent. Then he switched to New Orth, and read out some formula that by its nature had to have been written around the time of the Reconstitution. At the end of it he called out distinctly: "Voco Fraa Paphlagon of the Centenarian Chapter of the Order of Saunt Edhar."

So this was the aut of Voco. It was only the third one I'd ever heard. The first two had occurred when I'd been about ten years old.

As I absorbed that, a gasp and then a deep moan welled up from the floor of the chancel: the gasp, I reckoned, from most of the avout, and the moan from the Hundreders who were losing their brother forever.

And now I did something crazy, but I knew I could get away with it: I stepped over the threshold of my cell. I crossed the walkway, and looked over the railing.

Only three people were in the chancel: Statho in his purple robes and Varax and Onali, identifiable by their hats. The rest of the place, hidden behind the screens, was in an uproar that had stopped the aut.

I'd only meant to peek over the rail for an instant so that I could see what was going on. But I had not been struck by lightning. No alarm had sounded. *No one was up here.* They couldn't possibly be here, I realized, because Voco had rung, and everyone had to gather in the Mynster for that—*had to* because there was no way of knowing in advance whose name would be called.

Come to think of it, *I* was probably supposed to be down there! Voco must be one of the few exceptions to the rule that someone like me must remain in his cell.

Then why hadn't the Warden Regulant's staff come and rousted me? It had probably been an oversight, I reckoned. They didn't have procedures for this. If they were like me, they hadn't even recognized the changes. They hadn't realized it was Voco until it had started—and then it had been too late for them to come up and fetch me. They were stuck down there until it was over.

They were stuck down there until it was over.

I was free to move about, at least for a little while, as long as I was back in my cell when the Warden Regulant and her staff trudged back up here. Whereupon I'd be in trouble anyway for having ignored Voco! So why not get in trouble for something that people would be talking about in the Refectory fifty years from now?

All of those exercises I'd been doing were going to pay off. I tore around the walkway, took the stairs up through the Fendant court three at a time, and so came into the lower reaches of the chronochasm. Here I had to move with greater care so as not to clatter and bang on the metal stairs. But by the same token I had a clear view down, so I could keep track of what was going on. Nothing had changed that I could see, but a new sound was rising up the well: the hymn of mourning and farewell, addressed by the Hundreders to their departing brother. This had taken a little while to get underway. No one had it memorized. They'd had to rummage for rarely-used hymnals and page through them looking for the right bit. Then it took them a minute to get the hang of it, for this was a five-part harmony. By the time the hymn really fell together and began to work, I was halfway to the starhenge—clambering up behind the dials of the clock, trying to stay collected, trying to move as Lio would, and not let the end of my bolt get caught between gears. The song of mourning and farewell was really hair-raising— even more emotional, somehow, than what we sang at funerals. Of course I had not the faintest idea who Fraa Paphlagon was, what he was like, or what he studied. But those who were singing did, and part of the power of this music was that it made me feel what they felt.

And—given that Fraa Paphlagon and I were both striking out alone for unknown territory—perhaps I felt a little of what *he* felt.

The main floor of the starhenge was just above my head now—I'd come up against the inward curve of the vault that spanned the top of the Præsidium and supported all that rested on its top. A few shafts penetrated the stonework, delivering power to the polar drives. A stair spiraled around the largest of these. I ran to the top of it and rested my hand on a door latch. Before passing through, I looked down to check the progress of the aut. The door through the Centenarians' screen had been opened. Fraa Paphlagon stepped out into the middle and stood there alone. The door closed behind him.

At the same moment I opened the door to the starhenge. Daylight flooded through. I cringed. How could this possibly go unnoticed?

Calm down, I told myself, only four people are in the well where they can see this. And all eyes are on Fraa Paphlagon.

Looking down one more time, I discovered a flaw in that logic. All eyes were on Fraa Paphlagon—*except for Fraa Paphlagon's!* He had chosen this moment to tilt his head back and gaze straight up. And why not? It was the last time he would ever look on this place. If I'd been in his situation, I'd have done the same.

I could not read his facial expression at this distance. But he must have seen the light flooding through the open door.

He stood frozen for a moment, thinking, then slowly lowered his gaze to face Statho. "I, Fraa Paphlagon, answer your call," he said—the first line in a litany that would go on for another minute or two.

I passed onto the starhenge and closed the door softly behind me.

I had been expecting that everything would be filmed with dust and speckled with bird droppings—Orolo's fids spent an inordinate amount of time up here keeping things clean. But it wasn't too bad. Someone must have been coming up here to look after it.

I came to the windowless blockhouse that served as laboratory, passed through its light-blocking triple doors, and fetched a photomnemonic tablet, blanked and wrapped in a dust jacket.

What image should I record on it? I had no clue what it was that the hierarchs didn't want us to see, so I had no way of knowing where I should aim a telescope.

Actually, I had a pretty good idea what it must be: a large asteroid headed in our direction. That was the only thing I could imagine that would account for the closure of the starhenge. But this didn't help me. I couldn't take a picture of such a rock unless I aimed Mithra and Mylax directly at it, which was impossible unless I knew its orbital elements to a high degree of precision. To say nothing of the fact that aiming the big telescope in these circumstances would draw everyone's attention.

But there was another instrument that didn't need to be aimed, because it couldn't move: Clesthyra's Eye. I started jogging toward the Pinnacle as soon as this idea entered my head.

As I climbed the spiral stair, I had plenty of time to review all of the reasons that this was unlikely to work. Clesthyra's Eye could see half of the universe, from horizon to horizon, it was true. The fixed stars showed up as circular streaks, owing to the rotation of Arbre on its axis. Fast-moving objects showed up as straight paths of light. But the track made by even a large asteroid would be vanishingly faint, and not very long.

By the time I'd reached the top of the Pinnacle, I'd put these quibbles out of my mind. This was the only tool I had. I had to give it a try. Later I'd sort through the results and see what I could see.

Beneath the fisheye lens was a slot carved to the exact dimensions of the tablet in my hand. I broke the seal on the dust jacket, reached in, and got my palm under the opaque base of the tablet. I drew off the dust jacket. The wind tore it out of my grip and slapped it against the wall, just out of reach. The tablet was a featureless disk, like the blank used for grinding a telescope mirror, but darker—as if cast in obsidian. When I activated its remembrance function, its bottom-most layer turned the same color as the sun, for that was the origin of all the light now striking the tablet's surface. Because the tablet was out in the open with no lenses or mirrors to organize the light coming into it, it could not form an image of anything it saw—not of the bleak winter sun lobbing across the southern sky, not of the icy clouds high in the north, and not of my face.

But that was about to change, and so before doing anything else I drew my bolt over my head and shaped it into a long dark tunnel. If this precaution actually turned out to be *necessary*—that is, if this tablet ever found its way to the Warden Regulant—I'd probably be found out anyway. But as long as I was up to something sneaky, I felt an obligation to do a proper job of it.

I introduced the tablet into the slot below the Eye and slid it home, then closed the dust cover behind it. It would now record everything the Eye saw—beginning with a distorted image of my bolt-covered backside scurrying out of view—until it filled up, which at its current settings would take a couple of months.

Then I'd have to come back up here and retrieve it—a small problem I had not even begun to think about.

As I was descending the Pinnacle, thinking about this, something big and loud and fast clattered across the empty space between me and the Millenarians' crag. It scared the life out of me. It was a thousand feet away, but it felt as immediate as a slap in the face. In tracking its progress, I sacrificed my balance and had to collapse my legs to avoid toppling from the rail-less stair. It was a type of aerocraft that could rotate its stubby wings and turn into a two-bladed helicopter. It made a slicing downward arc, as if using the Mynster as a pylon, and settled into a steep glide path aimed at the plaza before the Day Gate. My view of this was blocked from here, so I rose carefully to my feet, ran down to the base of the Pinnacle, then sprinted across the lid of the starhenge. Realizing that I was about to hurl myself from the Præsidium—something I no longer cared to do—I aimed myself at one of the megaliths, put on the brakes, and stopped myself by slamming into it with my hands. Then I peered around its corner just in time to see the aerocraft—rotors now pointed up—settling in for a landing on the plaza. The rotor wash made visible patterns in the surface of the pond and splayed the twin fountains.

A few moments later, two purple-robed figures came into view, having just emerged from the Day Gate. Varax and Onali stripped off their hats so that the wind from the rotors wouldn't do it for them. Two paces behind was Fraa Paphlagon, leaning forward into the hurricane and hugging himself, clawing up handfuls of wayward bolt so that he wouldn't be stripped nude. Varax and Onali paused flanking the aerocraft's door and turned back to look at him.

Each extended an arm and they helped Paphlagon clamber inside. Then they piled in behind him. Some automatic mechanism pulled the hatch closed even as the rotors were spinning up and the aerocraft beginning to lose its grip on the plaza. Then the pilot rammed the throttles home and the thing jumped fifty feet into the air in a few heartbeats. The wings tilted. It took on some forward velocity and accelerated up and away over the pond and the burgers' town, then banked away to the west.

It was just about the coolest thing I'd ever seen and I couldn't wait to talk about it in the Refectory with my friends.

Then I remembered that I was an escaped prisoner.

By the time I got into the chronochasm, Voco was long since over. The sound of voices still crowded the well, but it was dwindling rapidly as the naves emptied. Most were leaving the Mynster but some would ascend the stairs in the corner towers to resume their work in the Wardens' courts. I banged and clanged in my haste. As I got lower, though, I had to be more judicious in my movements in spite of the fear that the quickest of the climbers would get there before I could.

The first ones up were two young hierarchs on the Warden Fendant's staff who were climbing as fast as they could in the hope that they could get to their balcony and catch a glimpse of the aerocraft before it flew out of sight. I reached the Fendant court from above just before they reached it from below. Caught on the walkway, I looked for a place to hide. This level of the Mynster was cluttered with things that only a Warden Fendant could think of as ornaments: mostly, busts and statues of dead heroes. The most awful of these was a life-sized bronze of Amnectrus, who had been the Warden Fendant at the moment of the Third Sack. He was depicted in the pose where he'd spent the last twenty hours of his life, kneeling behind a parapet peering through the optics of a rifle that was as long as he was tall. Amnectrus was cast in bronze but the rifle and the lake of spent shell-casings in which he was immersed were actual relics. The pedestal was his sarcophagus. I dove behind it. The two fleet-footed ones sprinted down the walkway, headed for the west side of the balcony. They passed right by me. I got up, took the long way round to avoid any more such, and plunged down the steps to the Regulant court. I dove to the floor behind the half-wall that ran around the walkway, then levered myself up to hands and knees. In that attitude I scurried round until I found my cell. I'd never thought I'd be happy to see the place.

Now there was only the small problem that I was streaming with sweat, my chest was heaving, my heart was throbbing like the rotors of that aerocraft, I had abrasions on my knees and palms, and was trembling with exhaustion and nervousness. There was only so much I could do. I used some blank leaves to wipe sweat from my face, drew my bolt around me to cover as much as I could, and arranged myself on my sphere before my window, back to the doorway, as if I'd been gazing out at the scene below. Then it was just a matter of trying to control my breathing as I waited for the moment when someone from the Warden Regulant's staff came to look in on me.

"Fraa Erasmas?"

I turned around. It was Suur Trestanas—looking a bit flushed herself from the climb.

She stepped into the cell. I had not spoken to her since Tenth Night. She seemed oddly normal and human now—as if we were just two cordial acquaintances having a chat.

"Mm-hmm?" I said, afraid to say more in case my voice would sound funny.

"Do you have any idea what just happened?"

"It's difficult to make out from here. It sounded almost like Voco."

"It *was* Voco," she said, "and you should have been there."

I attempted to look aghast. Maybe this was easy given the state I was in. Or maybe she wanted me to be aghast so badly that she was easily fooled. Anyway, she let a few moments go by so that I could twist in the wind. Then she said: "I'm not going to throw the Book at you, not this time, even though it is technically a serious offense."

Besides which, I thought, *you'd have to give me Chapter Six—which I could appeal—and you don't want to have to defend that.*

"Thank you, Suur Trestanas," I said. "In the unlikely event that we have another Voco while I'm here, should I go down for it?"

"That is correct," she said, "and view it from behind the Primate's screen. Return here immediately afterward."

"Unless it's I whose name gets called," I said.

She wasn't looking for humor in this situation and so this only flustered her. Then she was annoyed at having become flustered. "How are you progressing on Chapter Five?" she asked.

"I hope I'll be ready for examination in one or two weeks," I said.

Then I wondered how I was going to retrieve that tablet from Clesthyra's Eye and sneak it out of here in that amount of time.

Suur Trestanas actually showed me the beginnings of a smile before she took her leave. Maybe it had something to do with the fact that the two Inquisitors had just left, and whatever strange motivation lay behind her throwing the Book at me had departed along with them. Anyway, I got the idea that for all intents and purposes my punishment was finished now, and the rest was just a formality. This made me most impatient to get on with it. During the rest of the day I made more progress on Chapter Five than I had in the previous week.

The next day Eliger rang again. Two more joined the Edharians, two the New Circle, and again the Reformed Old Faanians came up with nothing.

One of the names called out for the New Circle was Lio. I was astonished by this, and wondered for a time if I'd heard it right. It's difficult to say why, because it made perfect sense. Lio was an obvious candidate for Warden Fendant. His fight with the slines on Tenth Night must have impressed Fraa Delrakhones to no end. Working for the Warden Fendant meant being a hierarch, and for some reason that was associated with being in the New Circle. So why did it surprise me? Because (as I figured out, lying awake on my pallet that night) Lio and I had been on the same Provener team for so long that I'd grown used to his being there, and had assumed that he and I and Jesry and Arsibalt would always be together in the same group. And I had believed that they shared these feelings and assumptions. But feelings can change, and I was beginning to see that they had been changing rapidly while I'd been up in this cell.

Two days later, Arsibalt joined the Reformed Old Faanians. It was just dumb luck that no one down below heard me yelling, *"What!?"* I could lie awake all night long if I pleased and no upsight would be forthcoming to explain this. The Reformed Old Faanians had been a dying order for almost as long as they'd been in existence.

The only thing for it was to get out of this cell. I gave up on daily exercise and stopped writing the journal and did nothing but study Chapter Five after that. By the time I gave word that I was ready to be examined, eleven had joined the Edharians, nine the New Circle, and six the Reformed Old Faanians. My options, assuming I still had any, were narrowing by the hour. In my gloomier moments I wondered if throwing the Book at me had been a sort of recruiting tactic on the part of Suur Trestanas—a way of forcing me to join some non-Edharian order and thereby pushing me down the path that would lead to my toiling in the Primate's compound as a lesser hierarch, always under someone's thumb. Ordinary fraas and suurs answered to no one except the Discipline. But hierarchs were in a chain of command: it was the price they paid for the powers they wielded.

My examination took place the next day, following an Eliger in which one more went to the New Circle and three to the Reformed Old Faanians. Of those, two were what Arsibalt had had in mind when he had spoken of floor-sweepings. One was unusually bright. Of my crop, only I and one other now remained. Since I hadn't been writing names down, I probably would have lost track, by this point, of who the other one was—if not for the fact that it was Tulia.

The examiners numbered three. Suur Trestanas was not among them. At first I was relieved by this, then irritated. I had just sacrificed a month of my life doing this penance, and thrown away any chance I'd ever had of getting into the Order of Saunt Edhar. The least she could have done was show up.

They began by asking me some trick questions about Chapter Two in the hopes that I'd have rushed through it on the first day and then forgotten it. But I had anticipated this, and had spent a couple of hours reviewing the first three chapters the day before.

When I recited the 127th through 283rd digits of pi, the fight went out of them. We only spent two hours on Chapter Five. This was exceptionally lenient. But Eliger had pushed everything back to late in the day. We were nearing the solstice, so it got dark early, which made it seem even later. I could actually hear the examiners' stomachs growling. The head of the panel was Fraa Spelikon, a hierarch in his seventh decade who'd been passed over for Warden Regulant in favor of Suur Trestanas. At the last minute he seemed to decide I hadn't been grilled hard enough, and began putting up a fight. But I snapped out an answer to his first question, and the other two examiners said with their postures and their tones of voice that it was over. Spelikon snatched up his spectacles, held them in front of his face, and read something from an old leaf that said my penance was over and I was free to go.

Though it felt later, a whole hour remained before dinner. I asked if I could go back to my cell to collect some notes I had left there. Spelikon wrote out a pass giving me permission to remain in the Regulant court until the dinner hour.

I thanked them, took my leave, and walked around to my cell, waving my pass at any hierarchs who crossed my path. By the time I had reached my cell and pulled my journal out from beneath my pallet, an idea—which had not even existed thirty seconds earlier as I had bid goodbye to the examiners—had flourished inside my head and taken control of my brain. Why not sneak up to the starhenge right now and collect that tablet?

Of course my better sense prevailed. I wrapped my journal up in the free end of my bolt and walked out of that cell—forever, I hoped. Fifty paces down the walkway took me to the southwest corner, the head of the Tenners' stair. A few fraas and suurs were passing up and down, getting ready for a change of guard at the Fendant court. I stood aside to make way for one who was on his way up. He was hooded, and not looking where he was going. Then my feet came into his view. He pulled his hood back to reveal a freshly shaved head. It was Lio.

There was so much to say that neither of us knew where to begin, so we just stared at each other and made incoherent sounds for a few moments. Which was probably just as well since I didn't want to say *anything* in the Regulant court. "I'll walk with you," I said, and turned to fall in step alongside him.

"You have to talk to Tulia," he muttered, as we were ascending to the Fendant court. "You have to talk to Orolo. You have to talk to *everyone.*"

"Going to your new job?"

"Delrakhones has me doing an internship. Hey, Raz, where the heck are you going?"

"The starhenge."

"But that's—" He grabbed my arm. "Hey, idiot, you could be Thrown Back!"

"It's more important that I do this than that I not be Thrown Back," I said. Which was pretty stupid, but I was feeling rebellious and not thinking very hard. "I'll explain it to you later."

I had led Lio off the inner walkway, which was too crowded for comfort, and out toward the periphery of the Fendant court as if we were going to stand on the ledge. Along the way we had to pass through a narrow arch. He made an after-you gesture. I stepped into the arch—and realized at the same instant that I'd just turned my back on him. By the time that had penetrated my brain, he had my arm wrapped up the wrong way. I had a choice: move, and spend the next two months with my arm in a sling, or not move. I chose not to move.

My tongue still worked. "Good to see you again, Thistlehead. First you get me in trouble—now this."

"You got your own self in trouble. Now I'm going to make sure you don't do it again."

"Is this how they do things in the New Circle?"

"You shouldn't even try to speak of how Eliger came out until you know what's going on."

"Well, if you'll let go of me so I can get up to the starhenge, my next step will be the Refectory where I'll get all the latest."

"*Look,*" he said, and levered me around so that I could see back the way we had come. A hush had fallen over the stairs. I was half afraid we'd been seen. But then I saw a procession of black-clad figures in tall hats on their way up. They passed into the chasm above and began to clang on the ironwork.

"Huh," I said, "no wonder it's so clean up there."

"*You've been up there!?*" Lio was so startled that he tightened his grip on me in a way that hurt.

"Let go! I promise I won't go any farther up," I said.

Lio released my arm. I slowly and judiciously got it arranged in a more human position before standing up to face him.

"What did you see?" Lio wanted to know.

"Nothing yet, but there's a tablet up there I have to retrieve that might—*might*—give us a hint."

He considered it. "That will be a challenging operation."

"Is that a promise, Lio?"

"Just an observation."

"Do those Ita go up there on some kind of a predictable schedule?"

Lio parted his lips to answer, then got a shrewd look on his face and said, "I'm not going to tell you that." Then something occurred to him. "Look, I'm late."

"Since when do you care about *that*?"

"A lot has changed. I have to go. *Now*. Talk to you later, okay?"

"Lio!"

He turned to look back at me. "*What!?*"

"Who was Fraa Paphlagon?"

"He taught Fraa Orolo half of what he knew."

"Who taught him the other half?" I asked, but Lio was already gone. For a minute I stood there listening to the upward progress of the Ita, wondering whether they checked the equipment for tablets. Wondering where I could get myself an Ita disguise.

Then my stomach growled. As if it were wired directly to my feet, I headed for the Refectory.

It had been ten years and a couple of months since I had watched a moving picture, but I could still remember a kind of scene where a spaceman walks into a starport bar, or a steppe rider into a dusty saloon, and all goes silent for a few moments. That was how it was when I entered the Refectory.

I had arrived early—a mistake, since it gave me no way of controlling who I would sit with. A few of the Edharians had come early and staked out tables, but they glanced away from me when I tried to catch their eye. I got in the queue behind a couple of Edharian cosmographers, but they turned their backs on me and put on a show of discussing, with great intensity, some new proof that they had found in the ten years' worth of books and journals that had been dumped on the threshold of the library at Apert.

It was the Reformed Old Faanians' night to serve dinner. Arsibalt gave me an extra dollop of stew and shook my hand—the first warm greeting I had received. We agreed to talk later. He seemed happy.

I decided to sit down at an empty table and see what happened. Within a few minutes, fraas and suurs of the New Circle began to cluster around me, and each had some jovial remark to throw my way about my time in the cell.

After a quarter of an hour, Fraa Corlandin showed up cradling something old, dark, and crusty, like a mummified infant. He set it down on the table and peeled off some wrappings. It was an ancient firkin of wine. "From our chapterhouse to you, Fraa Erasmas," he announced, in lieu of a greeting. "One who has endured extraordinary penance deserves an extraordinary libation. This won't give you those weeks back. But it will help you forget everything about the Book!"

Corlandin was being a little bit clever. I was glad of it. Given his liaison with Suur Trestanas—which I assumed was still going on—this moment was bound to be awkward. The wine was both a kind gesture and a way of sliding past that awkwardness. Though as he fussed with the stopper I felt a little uneasy. Was this also meant to be a celebration of my joining their order?

Fraa Corlandin seemed to be reading my mind. "This is strictly to celebrate your freedom—not to encroach on it!" he said.

Someone else had fetched a wooden case and opened it to reveal a matched set of silver thimbles, each engraved with the crest of the New Circle. A fraa and a suur plucked these one by one from their velvet-lined niches and polished them with their bolts. Corlandin busied himself with the stopper, a brittle contraption of clay and beeswax, difficult to remove without shattering it and contaminating the wine. Just to watch Fraa Corlandin was to feel a link to a time when concents had been richer, classier, more well-endowed, and—though this made no sense at all—somehow *older* than they were now.

The cask was obviously made of Vrone oak, which meant that the wine inside of it had been made, in some other concent, from the juice of the library grape, and sent here to age.

The library grape had been sequenced by the avout of the Concent of the Lower Vrone in the days before the Second Sack. Every cell carried in its nucleus the genetic sequences, not just of a single species, but of every naturally occurring species of grape that the Vrone avout had ever heard of—and if those people hadn't heard of a grape, it wasn't worth knowing about. In addition, it carried excerpts from the genetic sequences of thousands of different berries, fruits, flowers, and herbs: just those snatches of data that, when invoked by the biochemical messaging system of the host cell, produced flavorful molecules. Each nucleus was an archive, vaster than the Great Library of Baz, storing codes for shaping almost every molecule nature had ever produced that left an impression on the human olfactory system.

A given vine could not express all of those genes at once—it could not be a hundred different species of grape at the same time—so it "decided" which of those genes to express—what grape to be, and what flavors to borrow—based on some impossibly murky and ambiguous data-gathering and decision-making process that the Vrone avout had hand-coded into its proteins. No nuance of sun, soil, weather, or wind was too subtle for the library grape to take into account. Nothing that the cultivator did, or failed to do, went undetected or failed to have its consequences in the flavor of the juice. The library grape was legendary for its skill in penetrating the subterfuges of winemakers who were so arrogant as to believe they could trick it into being the same grape two seasons in a row.

The only people who had ever really understood it had been lined up against a wall and shot during the Second Sack. Many modern winemakers chose to play it safe and use old-fashioned grapes. Developing a fruitful relationship with the library grape was left to fanatics like Fraa Orolo, who had made it his avocation. Of course, library grapes hated the conditions at Saunt Edhar, and were still reacting to an incident fifty years ago when Orolo's predecessor had pruned the vines incorrectly, poisoning the soil with bad memories encoded in pheromones. The grapes chose to grow up small, pale, and bitter. The resulting wine was an acquired taste, and we didn't even try to sell it.

We had better luck with trees and casks. For while the Vrone avout had been busy creating the library grape, their fraas and suurs a few miles up the valley at the rustic math of Upper Vrone Forest had been at similar pains with the trees that were traditionally fashioned into casks. The cells of the Vrone oak's heartwood—still half alive, even after the tree had been chopped down, sliced into staves, and bound into a cask—sampled the molecules drifting around in the wine, releasing some, making others percolate outward until they precipitated on the outside of the cask as fragrant sheens, rinds, and encrustations. This wood was as choosy about the conditions under which it was stored as the library grape was about weather and soil, so a winemaker who treated the casks poorly, and didn't provide them with the stimulation they liked, would be punished by finding them crusted and oozing with all the most desirable resins, sugars, and tannins, with nothing left on the inside of the cask but cleaning solvent. The wood liked the same range of temperature and humidity as humans, and its cellular structure was responsive to vibrations. The casks, like musical instruments, resonated in sympathy with the human voice, and so wine that had been stored in a vault used for choir rehearsals would taste different from that stashed along the walls of a dining room. The climate at Saunt Edhar's was well suited to growing Vrone oaks. Better yet, we were somewhat renowned for our prowess with aging. Casks felt comfortable in our Refectory and our Mynster, and responded warmly to all the talking and singing. Less fortunate concents shipped their casks here to age. We ended up with some pretty good stuff. We weren't really supposed to drink it, but every so often we would cheat a little.

Corlandin got the stopper out without incident and decanted the wine into a blown-quartz laboratory flask, and from there served it out into the thimbles. The first of these was passed to me, but I knew better than to drink from it right away. Everyone at the table had to get one—last of all Fraa Corlandin, who raised his, looked me in the eye, and said, "To Fraa Erasmas, on the occasion of his freedom—long may it last, richly may he enjoy it, wisely may he use it."

Then clinking all around. I was uneasy about the "wisely may he use it" part, but I drank anyway.

The stuff was tremendous, like drinking your favorite book. The others had all stood for the toast. Now they sat down, allowing me to see the rest of the Refectory. Some tables were watching the toast and hoisting tankards of whatever they were drinking. Others were involved in their own conversations. Standing around the edges of the place, mostly alone, were the ones I most wanted to talk to: Orolo, Jesry, Tulia, and Haligastreme.

Dinner became quite long, and not very ascetic. They kept refilling my glass. I felt very well taken care of.

"Someone get him to his pallet," I heard a fraa saying, "he's finished."

Hands were under my arms, helping me to my feet. I let them escort me as far as the Cloister before I shook them off.

My time in the Mynster had made me well aware of which parts of the concent could not be seen from the Warden Regulant's windows. I made several orbits around the Cloister, just to clear my head, and then went into the garden and sat down on a bench that was shielded from view.

"Are you even a sentient being at this point or should I wait until the morning?" a voice asked. I looked over to discover that Tulia had joined me. I was pretty sure she had woken me up.

"Please," I said, and patted the bench next to me. Tulia sat down but kept her distance, the better to get a thigh up on the bench and turn sideways to face me.

"I'm glad you're out," she said, "a lot has been going on."

"So I gathered," I said. "Is there any way to sum it up quickly?"

"Something's . . . funny with Orolo. No one knows what."

"Come on! The starhenge has been locked! What else is there to know?"

"That's obvious," she said, a little bit annoyed at my tone, "but no one knows why. We think Orolo knows, but he's not telling."

"Okay. Sorry."

"It has been shaping Eliger. Some fids who were expected to join the Edharians have gone to other orders."

"I noticed that. Why? What's the logic?"

"I'm not so sure it *is* logical. Until Apert, all the fids knew exactly what they wanted to do. Then so many things happened at once: the Inquisitors. Your penance. The closure of the starhenge. Fraa Paphlagon's Evocation. It shook people up—made them rethink it."

"Rethink it how?"

"It got everyone thinking politically. They made decisions they might not have done otherwise. For one thing, it cast doubt on the wisdom of joining the Edharians."

"You mean because they are on the outs politically?"

"They're *always* on the outs politically. But seeing what happened to you, people got to thinking that it was unwise to turn one's back on that side of the concent."

"I'm starting to get it," I said. "So a guy like Arsibalt, by going to the Reformed Old Faanians, who want him desperately—"

"Can become *important* in the Reformed Old Faanians, *right away.*"

"I noticed he was serving the main course at supper." That was an honor normally reserved for senior fraas.

"He could become the FAE. Or a hierarch. Maybe even Primate. And he could fight some of the idiotic things that have been going on lately."

"So the ones who *have* been going to the Edharians—"

"Are the best of the best."

"Like Jesry."

"Exactly."

"We're going to screen you Edharians, protect you on the political front, so that you can be free to do what you do best," I said.

"Uh, that's the gist of it—but who's this 'you' and 'we' you're talking about?"

"Clearly where this is going is that tomorrow you join the Edharians and I join the New Circle."

"That's what everyone *expects*. It's not what is going to *happen*, Raz."

"You've been—*holding a space for me* in the Edharians?"

"That's an awfully blunt way of putting it."

"I can't believe the Edharians want me that badly."

"They don't."

"*What!?*"

"If they held a secret ballot, well, it's not clear that they would vote for you over me. I'm sorry, Raz, but I have to be honest. A lot of the suurs in particular want me to join them."

"Why don't we *both* join them?"

"It is considered impossible. I don't know the particulars—but some sort of deal has been made between Corlandin and Haligastreme. It's decided."

"If the Edharians don't want me, why are we even discussing this?" I asked. "Did you see that keg the New Circle tapped for me? They want me bad. So why don't I join them and you go to the loving embrace of the suurs of the Edharian chapter?"

"Because it's not what Orolo wants. He says he needs you as part of his team."

That affected me so much that between it and the wine I almost cried. I sat quietly for a while.

"Well," I said, "Orolo doesn't know everything about what is going on."

"What are you talking about?"

I looked around. The Cloister was too small and quiet for my taste. "Let's go for a walk," I said.

I said no more until we were on the other side of the river, strolling in the moon-shadow of the wall, and then I told her about what I had done during Voco.

"Well!" she said, after a long silence. "That settles that, anyway."

"What settles what?"

"You have to go to the Edharians."

"Tulia, first of all, no one knows besides you and Lio. Second, I'll probably never come up with a way to retrieve the tablet. Third, it's probably not going to contain any useful information!"

"Details," she scoffed. "You're missing my whole point. What you did shows that Orolo is correct. You do belong on his team."

"What about you? Where do you belong, Tulia?"

She wasn't comfortable with that. I had to ask her again.

"What happened, on Tenth Night, happened. All of us made decisions. Maybe later we'll think better of them."

"And to what extent is this seen as my fault?"

"Who cares?"

"*I* care. I wish I could have come down out of that cell to talk people out of it."

"I don't like the way you are thinking about this at all," she said. "It's like the rest of us became adults while you were up there—and you didn't."

That one made me stop in my tracks and blow air for a while. Tulia kept going for a couple of paces, then rounded on me. "To what extent is this seen as my fault?" she said, mimicking me. "Who cares? It's done. It's over."

"I care because it has a big effect on how I am seen by the rest of the Edharians—"

"*Stop caring,*" she said, "or at least stop talking about it."

"Okay," I said, "sorry, but I've always thought of you as a person others could talk to about those kinds of feelings—"

"You think I want to spend the rest of my life being that person? For everyone in the concent?"

"Apparently you don't."

"All right. We're done. You go find Haligastreme. I'll find Cor-

NEAL STEPHENSON

[180]

landin. We'll tell them that we are joining their respective orders tomorrow."

"Okay," I said with a fake-nonchalant shrug, and turned around to walk back toward the bridge. Tulia caught up with me and fell in step alongside. I was silent for a while—a little bit distracted by the prospect of joining a chapter that didn't want me, many of whose members might blame me for taking Tulia's place.

Some part of me wanted to hate Tulia for being so hard on me. But by the time we had crossed over the bridge, that voice, I'm happy to say, had been silenced. I was to hear it again from time to time in the future, but I would do my best to ignore it. I was scared to death to be joining the Edharians under these circumstances. But to forge ahead and just do it without leaning on Tulia's, or anyone else's, shoulder felt better—felt right. As when you just know you're on the right track with a theorical proof, and all the rest is details. A splinter of the beauty Orolo had spoken of was reaching out toward me through the dark, and I would follow it like a road.

"Do you want to talk to Orolo?" was Fraa Haligastreme's question, after I broke the news to him. He wasn't surprised. He wasn't overjoyed. He wasn't anything except tired. Just looking at his face in the candlelight of the Old Chapterhouse told me how exhausting the last few weeks had been for him.

I considered it. Talking to Orolo seemed like such an obvious thing to do, and yet I'd made no move to do it. Considering how the conversation had gone with Tulia, I was no longer inclined to stay up half the night telling people about my feelings.

"Where is he?"

"I believe he is in the meadow with Jesry conducting naked-eye observations."

"Then I don't think I'll disturb them," I said.

Haligastreme seemed to draw energy from my words. *The fid is beginning to act his age.* "Tulia seems to think that he wants me . . . here," I said, and looked around the Old Chapterhouse: just a wide spot in the Cloister gallery, rarely used except for ceremonial purposes—but still the heart of the worldwide Order, where Saunt Edhar himself had once paced to and fro developing his theorics.

"Tulia is correct," Haligastreme said.

"Then here is where I want to be, even if the welcome is luke-warm."

"If it seems that way to you, it's largely out of concern for your own well-being," he said.

"I'm not sure I believe that."

"All right," he said, a bit irritated, "maybe some don't want you for other reasons. You used the word *lukewarm,* not *chilly* or *hostile.* I refer now only to those who are lukewarm."

"Are you one of those?"

"Yes. We, the lukewarm, are only concerned—"

"That I won't be able to keep up."

"Exactly."

"Well, even if that's how it works out, you can always come to me if you need to know some digits of pi."

Haligastreme did me the courtesy of chuckling.

"Look," I said, "I know you're worried about this. I'll make it work. I owe that much to Arsibalt and Lio and Tulia."

"How so?"

"They've sacrificed something to make the concent work better in the future. Maybe with the result that the next generation of hi-erarchs will be better than what we have now—and will leave the Edharians to work in peace."

"Unless," said Fraa Haligastreme, "being hierarchs changes them."

Part 4

ANATHEM

S ix weeks after I joined the Edharian order, I became hopelessly stuck on a problem that one of Orolo's knee-huggers had set for me as a way of letting me know that I didn't really understand what it meant for two hypersurfaces to be tangent. I went out for a stroll. Without really thinking about it I crossed the frozen river and wandered into the stand of page trees that grew on the rise between the Decade Gate and the Century Gate.

Despite the best efforts of the sequencers who had brought these trees into being, only one leaf in ten was high-grade page material, suitable for a typical quarto-sized book. The most common flaw was smallness or irregularity, such that when placed in the cutting-frame, it would not make a rectangle. That was the case for about four out of ten leaves—more during cold or dry years, fewer if the growing season had been favorable. Holes gnawed by insects, or thick veins that made it difficult to write on the underside, might render a leaf unusable save as compost. These flaws were especially common in leaves that grew near the ground. The best yield was to be found in the middle branches, not too far out from the trunk. The arbortects had given them stout boughs in the midsection, easy for young ones to clamber on. Every autumn when I'd been a fid, I'd spent a week up on those branches, picking the best leaves and skimming them down to older avout who stacked them in baskets. Later in the day we'd tie them by their stems to lines stretched from tree to tree, and let them dry as the weather turned colder. After the first killing frost we would bring them indoors, stack them, and pile on tons of flat rocks. It took about a century for them to age properly. So once we'd gotten the current year's crop under stone we'd go back and find similar piles that had been made about a hundred years earlier, and, if they seemed ready, take the rocks off and peel the leaves apart. The good ones we stacked in the cutting-frames and made into blank pages for distribution to the concent or for binding into books.

I'd rarely gone into the coppice after harvest time. To walk through it in this season was to be reminded that we only collected a small fraction of its leaves. The rest curled up and fell off. All those blank pages made an uproar as I sloshed through them, searching for one especially grand tree I'd always loved to climb. My memory played me false and I wandered lost for a few minutes. When I finally found it, I couldn't resist climbing up to its lower boughs. When I'd done this as a boy I'd imagined myself deep in the middle of a vast forest, which was much more romantic than being walled up in a math surrounded by casinos and tire stores. But now, with the branches bare, it was plain that I was close to the eastern limit of the coppice. The ivy-snarled ruin of Shuf's Dowment was in plain sight. I felt foolish, thinking Arsibalt must have seen me from a window, so I let myself to the ground and began walking that way. Arsibalt now spent most of his days there. He had been pestering me to come out and visit him, and I'd been making excuses. I couldn't slink away now.

I had to get over a low hedge that bounded the coppice. Shoving the snarled foliage out of my way I felt cold stone against my hand, pain an instant later. This was actually a stone wall that had become a trellis for whatever would grow on it. I vaulted over it and spent some time yanking my bolt and chord free from hedge-plants. I was standing on someone's tangle, brown and shriveled now. The black earth was gouged where people had been digging up the last potatoes of the season. Going over the wall made me feel as though I were trespassing. To elicit such feelings was probably why Shuf's Lineage had put it there in the first place. And that explained why those who'd found themselves on the wrong side of that wall had eventually become fed up with it and broken the lineage. Tearing the wall down was too much trouble and so that work had been left to ants and ivy. The Reformed Old Faanians had more recently got in the habit of using this place as a retreat, and when no one had objected, they'd slowly begun to make themselves more comfortable there.

Gardan's Steelyard: A rule of thumb attributed to Fraa Gardan (-1110 to -1063), stating that, when one is comparing two hypotheses, they should be placed on the arms of a metaphorical steelyard (a kind of primitive scale, consisting of an arm free to pivot around a central fulcrum) and preference given to the one that "rises higher," presumably because it weighs less; the upshot being that simpler, more "light-weight" hypotheses are preferable to those that are "heavier," i.e., more complex. Also referred to as Saunt Gardan's Steelyard or simply the Steelyard.

—THE DICTIONARY, *4th edition, A.R. 3000*

Very comfortable, as I saw when I came up the steps and pushed the door open (again fighting the sense that I was a trespasser). ROF carpenters had been at work furnishing the stone shell with wooden floors and paneled walls. Actually "cabinet-makers" was a fairer description than "carpenters" for avout who chose woodworking as their avocation, and so the place was all fitted and joined to tolerances that Cord might have envied. It was mostly one great cubical room, ten paces square, and lined with books. To my right a fire burned on a hearth, to my left, clear northern sky-light rushed in through a bay window so large that it formed a sort of alcove, as broad, round, and comfortable as Arsibalt, who sat in the middle of it reading a book so ancient he had to handle the pages with tongs. So he had not seen me tree-climbing after all. I could have slunk away. But now I was glad I hadn't. It was good to see him here.

"You could be Shuf himself," I said.

"Ssh," he commanded, and looked about the place. "People will be cross if you talk that way. Oh, all the orders have their special hideaways. Islands of luxury that must make Saunt Cartas roll over in her chalcedony sarcophagus."

"Pretty luxurious, that, come to think of it—"

"Come off it, it's cold as hell in the winter."

"Hence the expression 'cold as Cartas's—'"

"Ssh," he said again.

"You know, Arsibalt, if the Edharian chapter has a luxurious hideaway, they've yet to show it to me."

"They are the odd ones out," he said, rolling his eyes. He looked me up and down. "Perhaps when you have attained more seniority—"

"Well, what are *you,* at the age of nineteen? The FAE of the Reformed Old Faanians?"

"The chapter and I have become most comfortable with each other in, yes, a short time. They support my project."

"What—reconciling us with the Deolaters?"

"Some of the Reformed Old Faanians even believe in God."

"Do you, Arsibalt? All right, all right," I added, for he was getting ready to shush me for a third time. He finally began to move. He took me on a little tour, showing me some of the artifacts of the Dowment's halcyon days: gold drinking-cups and jeweled book-covers now preserved under glass. I accused his order of having more of the same hidden away somewhere for drinking out of, and he blushed.

Then, as all this discussion of utensils had put him in mind of food, he shelved his book. We left Shuf's Dowment behind us and began walking back for the midday meal. We had both skipped Provener, a luxury that was possible only because some younger fraas had begun to spell us winding the clock a few days a week.

When we gave up altogether on clock-winding, which would happen in two or three years, each of us would have enough free time to settle on an avocation—something practical that one could do to help improve life at the concent. Between now and then, we had the luxury of trying different things just to see how we liked them.

Fraa Orolo, for example, and his ongoing conversation with the library grape. We were too far north. The grapes were not happy. But we did have a south-facing slope, between the page trees and the outer wall of the concent, where they deigned to grow.

"Beekeeping," Arsibalt said when I asked him what he was interested in.

I laughed at the image of Arsibalt enveloped in a cloud of bees. "I always thought you'd end up doing indoor work," I said, "on dead things. I thought you'd be a bookbinder."

"At this time of year, beekeeping *is* indoor work on dead things," he pointed out. "Perhaps when the bees come out of hibernation I won't favor it so much. How about you, Fraa Erasmas?"

Though Arsibalt didn't know it, this was a sensitive subject. There was another reason you needed an avocation: so that if you turned out to be incapable of doing anything else, you could give up on books and chalk halls and dialog and work as a sort of laborer for the rest of your life. It was called "falling back." There were plenty of avout like that, making food, brewing beer, and carving stone, and it was no secret who they were.

"You can pick some funny thing like beekeeping," I pointed out, "and it'll never be anything more than an eccentric hobby—because you'll never need to fall back. Not unless the ROF suddenly re-cruits a whole lot of geniuses. For me the odds of falling back are a little greater and I need to pick something I could actually do for eighty years without going crazy."

Arsibalt now blew an opportunity to assure me that I was really smart and that this would never happen. I didn't mind. After my rough conversation with Tulia six weeks ago I was spending less time agonizing and more time trying to get things accomplished. "There are some opportunities," I told him, "making the instru-ments on the starhenge work the way they're supposed to."

"Those opportunities would be much brighter if you in fact had access to the starhenge," he pointed out. It was safe for him to talk this way since we were sloshing through leaves and no one was near us, unless Suur Trestanas was hiding in a leaf pile with a hand cupped to her ear.

I stopped and raised my chin.

"Are you expecting an Inquisitor to fall out of a tree?" Arsibalt asked me.

"No, just looking at it," I said, referring to the starhenge. From here, on this little rise, we had a good view of it. But nestled as we were in the coppice, we'd be difficult to make out from the Mynster and so I felt comfortable taking a long look. The twin telescopes of Saunts Mithra and Mylax were in the same position where they had rested during the three months or so we'd been locked out: slewed around to aim at the northern sky.

"I was thinking that if Orolo was using the M & M to look at something they didn't want him to see, then we might get some clues from where he pointed it the last day he had access to it. Maybe he even took some pictures that night, yet to be seen."

"Can you draw any conclusions from where the M & M is pointed now?" Arsibalt asked.

"Only that Orolo wanted to look at something above the pole."

"And what is above the pole? Other than the pole star?"

"That's just it," I said. "Nothing."

"What do you mean? There must be something."

"But it messes up my hypothesis."

"What, pray tell, is that? And can you explain it as we walk toward a place that is warm and has food?"

I started moving my feet again, and talked to the back of Arsibalt's head as I let him break trail through the leaves. "I had been guessing it was a rock."

"Meaning an asteroid," he said.

"Yeah. But rocks don't come over the pole."

"How can you say such a thing? Don't they come from all directions?"

"Yeah, but they mostly have low inclinations—they are in the same plane as the planets. So you'd look near the ecliptic, which is what we call that plane."

"But that is a statistical argument," he pointed out. "It could simply be an unusual rock."

"It fails the Steelyard."

"Saunt Gardan's Steelyard is a useful guideline. All sorts of real things fail it," Arsibalt pointed out, "including you and me."

Orolo sat with us. It was the first time I'd talked to him in ages. He sat where he could gaze out a window at the mountains, in much the same mood as I'd been looking at the starhenge a few minutes earlier. It was a clear day, and the peaks were all standing out, seeming as if they were close enough to throw stones at. "I wonder what the seeing will be like tonight on top of Bly's Butte," he sighed. "Better than here, anyway!"

"Is that the one where the slines ate Saunt Bly's liver?" I asked.

"The same."

"Is that around here? I thought it was on another continent or something."

"Oh no. Bly was a Saunt Edhar man! You can look it up in the Chronicle—we have all of his relics salted away somewhere."

"Do you really mean to suggest that there's an observatory there? Or are you just pulling my leg?"

Orolo shrugged. "I've no idea. Estemard built a telescope there, after he renounced his vow and stormed out the Day Gate."

"And Estemard is—"

"One of my two teachers."

"Paphlagon being the other?"

"Yes. They both got fed up with this place at about the same time. Estemard left, Paphlagon went into the upper labyrinth one night after supper and then I didn't see him for a quarter of a century, until—well—you know." A thought occurred to him. "What were *you* doing during Paphlagon's Evocation? At the time, you were still a guest of Autipete."

Autipete was a figure of ancient mythology who had crept up on her father as he lay sleeping and put out his eyes. I had never heard Suur Trestanas referred to this way. I bit my lip and shook my head in dismay as Arsibalt blew soup out his nostrils. "That is not fair," I said, "she's only following orders."

Orolo squared off to plane me. "You know, during the Third Harbinger it was quite common for those who had committed terrible crimes to say—"

"That they were just following orders, we all know that."

"Fraa Erasmas is suffering from Saunt Alvar's Syndrome," Arsibalt said.

"Those people during the Third Harbinger were shoving children into furnaces with bulldozers," I said. "And as far as Saunt Alvar goes—well, he was the sole survivor of his concent in the Third Sack and was held captive for three decades. Locking the door to the telescopes for a few weeks doesn't really measure up, does it?"

Orolo conceded the point with a wink. "My question stands. What did you do during Voco?"

Of course I'd have loved to tell him. So I did—but I made it into a joke. "While no one was looking, I ran up to the starhenge to make observations. Unfortunately, the sun was out."

"That damned luminous orb!" Orolo spat. Then something crossed his mind. "But you know that our equipment can see some things during the daytime, if they are very bright."

Since Orolo had decided to play along with my joke, it would not have been sporting for me to drop it at this point. "Unfortunately the M & M was pointed in the wrong direction," I said. "I didn't have time to slew it around."

"The wrong direction for *what*?" Orolo asked.

"For looking at anything bright—such as a planet or . . ." I faltered.

Jesry sat down at an empty table nearby, facing me and Orolo, and remained still, ignoring his food. If he'd been a wolf his ears would have been erect and swiveled toward us.

Orolo said, "Would it be too much trouble for you to bring your sentence to a decent conclusion?"

Arsibalt looked as rattled as I felt. This had started as a joke. Now, Fraa Orolo was trying to get at something serious—but we couldn't make out what.

"Aside from supernovae, very bright objects tend to be nearby—within the solar system—and things in the solar system are, by and large, confined to the plane of the ecliptic. So, Fraa Orolo, in this absurd fantasy of me running to the starhenge to look at the sky in broad daylight, I'd have to slew the M & M from its current polar orientation to the plane of the ecliptic in order to have a chance of actually seeing anything."

"I just want your absurd fantasy to be internally consistent," Fraa Orolo explained.

"Well, are you happy with it now?"

He shrugged. "Your point is well reasoned. But don't be too dismissive of the poles. Many things converge there."

"Like what? Lines of longitude?" I scoffed.

Arsibalt, in similar spirit: "Migratory birds?"

Jesry: "Compass needles?"

Then a higher-pitched voice broke in. "Polar orbits."

We turned and saw Barb coming toward us with a tray of food. He must have been listening with one ear as he stood in line. Now he was giving the answer to the riddle in a pre-adolescent voice that could have been heard from Bly's Butte. It was such an odd thing to say that it had turned heads all over the Refectory. "By definition," he continued, in the singsong voice he used when he was rattling off something he had memorized from a book, "a satellite in a polar orbit must cross over each of the poles during each revolution around Arbre."

Orolo stuffed a piece of gravy-sopped bread into his mouth to hide his amusement. Barb was now standing right next to me with his tray a few inches from my ear, but he made no move to sit down.

I had the feeling I was being watched. I looked over at Fraa Corlandin a few tables distant, just in the act of glancing away. But he could still hear Barb: "A telescope aimed north would have a high probability of detecting—"

I yanked down on a loose fold of his bolt. One arm dropped. All the food slid to that end of his tray and threw it out of balance. He lost control and it all avalanched to the floor.

All heads turned our way. Barb stood amazed. "My arm was acted on by a force of unknown origin!" he stated.

"Terribly sorry, it was my fault," I said. Barb was fascinated by the mess on the floor. Knowing by now how his mind worked, I rose, squared off in front of him, and put my hands on his shoulders. "Barb, look at me," I said.

He looked at me.

"This was my fault. I got tangled up with your bolt."

"You should clean it up, if it was your fault," he said matter-of-factly.

"I agree and that is what I shall do now," I said. I went off to fetch a bucket. Behind me I could hear Jesry asking Barb a question about conic sections.

○○

Calca: (1) In Proto- and Old Orth, chalk or any other such substance used to make marks on hard surfaces. (2) In Middle and later Orth, a calculation, esp. one that consumes a large amount of chalk because of its tedious and detailed nature. (3) In Praxic and later Orth, an explanation, definition, or lesson that is instrumental in developing some larger theme, but that, because of its overly technical, long-winded, or recondite nature, has been moved aside from the main body of the dialog and encapsulated in a footnote or appendix so as not to divert attention from the main line of the argument.

— THE DICTIONARY, *4th edition, A.R. 3000*

One form of drudgery led straight into another as Suur Ala helpfully reminded me that it was my day to clean up the kitchen following the midday meal. I hadn't been at it for long before I noticed that Barb was in there with me, just following me around, making no move to help. Which irked me at first: yet another case of his almost perfect social cluelessness. But once I got over that, I decided it was better that way. Some things were easier to do alone. Communicating and coordinating with others was often more trouble than it was worth. Many tried to help anyway because they thought it was the polite thing to do, or because it was an avenue for social bonding. Barb's thinking wasn't muddled by any such considerations. Instead, he talked to me, which in my view was preferable to being "helped."

"Orbits are about as much fun as what you are doing," he observed gravely, watching me get down on my knees and reach elbow-deep into a grease-choked drain.

"I gather that Grandsuur Ylma has been teaching you about

such things," I grunted. Drain-cleaning made it easy to hide my chagrin. I hadn't learned about orbits until my second year. This was Barb's second *month*.

"A lot of xs and ys and zs!" he exclaimed, which forced a laugh out of me.

"Yes," I said, "quite a few."

"You want to know what's stupid?"

"Sure, Barb. Lay it on me," I said, hauling a fistful of vegetable trimmings up out of the drain against the back-pressure of twenty gallons of dammed-up dishwater. The drain gargled and began to empty.

"Any sline could stand out on the meadow at night and see *some* satellites in polar orbits, and *other* satellites in orbits around the equator, and know that those were two different kinds of orbits!" he exclaimed. "But if you work out the xs and ys and zs of it, guess what?"

"What?"

"They just look like a lot of xs and ys and zs, and it is not as obvious that some are polar and some are equatorial as it would be to any old dumb sline looking up into the sky!"

"Worse than that," I pointed out, "staring at the xs and ys and zs doesn't even tell you that they *are orbits*."

"What do you mean?"

"An orbit is a stationary, stable thing," I said. "The satellite's moving all the time, of course, but always in the same way. But that kind of stability is in no way shown by the xs and ys and zs."

"Yeah! It's like knowing all of the theorics only makes us stupider!" he laughed excitedly, and cast a theatrical glance over his shoulder, as if we were up to something incredibly mischievous.

"Ylma is having you work it out in the most gruesome way possible," I said, "using Saunt Lesper's Coordinates, so that when she teaches you how it's *really* done, it'll seem that much easier."

Barb was dumbfounded. I went on, "Like hitting yourself in the head with a hammer—it feels so good when you stop." This was the oldest joke in the world, but Barb hadn't heard it before, and he became so amused that he got physically excited and had to run back and forth across the kitchen several times to flame off energy. A few weeks ago I would have been alarmed by this and would have tried to calm him down, but now I was used to it, and knew that if I approached him physically things would get much worse.

"What's the right way to do it?"

"Orbital elements," I said. "Six numbers that tell you everything that can be known about how a satellite is moving."

"But I already have those six numbers."

"What are they?" I asked, testing him.

"The satellite's position on Saunt Lesper's x, y, and z axes. That's three numbers. And its velocity along each one of those axes. That's three more. Six numbers."

"But as you pointed out you can look at those six numbers and still not be able to visualize the orbit, or even know that it *is* an orbit. What I am telling you is that with some more theorics you can turn them into a different list of six numbers, the orbital elements, that are infinitely easier to work with, in that you can glance at them and know right away whether the orbit goes over the poles or around the equator."

"Why didn't Grandsuur Ylma tell me that to begin with?"

I couldn't tell him, *because you learn too damned fast.* But if I tried to be overly diplomatic, Barb would see through it and plane me.

Then I had an upsight: it was *my* responsibility, just as much as it was Ylma's, to teach fids the right stuff at the right time.

"You are now ready to stop working in Saunt Lesper's Coordinates," I announced, "and begin working in other kinds of spaces, the way real, grown-up theors do."

"Is this like parallel dimensions?" said Barb, who apparently had been watching the same kinds of speelies as I had before coming here.

"No. These spaces I'm talking about aren't like physical spaces that you can measure with a ruler and move around in. They are abstract theorical spaces that follow different rules, called action principles. The space that cosmographers like to use has six dimensions: one for each of the orbital elements. But that's a special-purpose tool, only used in that discipline. A more general one was developed early in the Praxic Age by Saunt Hemn . . ." And I went on to give Barb a calca* about Hemn spaces, or configuration spaces, which Hemn had invented when he, like Barb, had become sick of xs and ys and zs.

to go Hundred: (Derogatory slang) To lose one's mind, to become mentally unsound, to stray irredeemably from the path of theorics. The expression can be traced to the Third Centennial Apert, when the gates of several Hundreder maths opened to reveal startling outcomes, e.g.: at Saunt Rambalf's, a mass suicide that had taken place only moments earlier. At Saunt Terramore's, nothing at all—not even human remains. At Saunt Byadin's, a previously unheard-of religious sect calling themselves the Matarrhites (still in existence). At Saunt Lesper's, no humans, but a previously undiscovered species of tree-dwelling higher primates. At Saunt Phendra's, a crude nuclear reactor in a system of subterranean catacombs. These and other mishaps prompted the creation of the Inquisition and the institution of hierarchs in their modern forms, including Wardens Regulant with power to inspect and impose discipline in all maths.

—THE DICTIONARY, *4th edition, A.R. 3000*

I caught up with Fraa Orolo late in the afternoon as he was coming out of a chalk hall, and we stood among page-stuffed pigeonholes and chatted. I knew better than to ask him what he had been getting at earlier with his weird discussion of daytime cosmography. Once he had made up his mind to teach us in that mode, there was no way to get him to say the answer straight out. Anyway, I was more worried about the things he had been referring to earlier. "Listen, you're not thinking of leaving, are you?"

---

* See Calca 2.

He got a slightly amused look but said nothing.

"I always worried you were going to go into the labyrinth and become a Hundreder. That would be bad enough. But the way you were talking I got the idea you were going to go become a Feral like Estemard."

This was Orolo's idea of an answer: "What does it mean that you worry so much?"

I sighed.

"Describe worrying," he went on.

"*What!?*"

"Pretend I'm someone who has never worried. I'm mystified. I don't get it. Tell me how to worry."

"Well . . . I guess the first step is to envision a sequence of events as they might play out in the future."

"But I do that all the time. And yet I don't worry."

"It is a sequence of events with a bad end."

"So, you're worried that a pink dragon will fly over the concent and fart nerve gas on us?"

"No," I said with a nervous chuckle.

"I don't get it," Orolo claimed, deadpan. "That is a sequence of events with a bad end."

"But it's nonsensical. There are no nerve-gas-farting pink dragons."

"Fine," he said, "a blue one, then."

Jesry had wandered by and noticed that Orolo and I were in dialog, so he approached, but not too close, and took up a spectator's position: hands folded in his bolt, chin down, not making eye contact.

"It has nothing to do with the dragon's color," I protested. "Nerve-gas-farting dragons don't exist."

"How do you know?"

"One has never been seen."

"But I have never been seen to leave the concent—yet you worry about that."

"All right. Correction: the whole idea of such a dragon is incoherent. There are no evolutionary precedents. Probably no metabolic pathways anywhere in nature that could generate nerve gas. Animals that large can't fly because of basic scaling laws. And so on."

"Hmm, all sorts of reasons from biology, chemistry, theorics . . . I suppose then that the slines, who know nothing of such matters, must worry about pink nerve-gas-farting dragons all the time?"

"You could probably talk them into worrying about it. But no, there's a . . . there's some kind of filter that kicks in . . ." I pondered it for a moment, and shot a glance at Jesry, inviting him to join us. After a few moments he took his hands out of his cloak and stepped forward. "If you worried about pink ones," he pointed out, "you'd have to worry about blue, green, black, spotted, and striped ones. And not just nerve-gas farters but bomb droppers and fire belchers."

"Not just dragons but worms, giant turtles, lizards . . ." I added.

"And not just physical entities but gods, spirits, and so on," Jesry said. "As soon as you open the door wide enough to admit pink nerve-gas-farting dragons, you have let in all of those other possibilities as well."

"Why not worry about all of them, then?" asked Fraa Orolo.

"I *do!*" claimed Arsibalt, who had seen us talking, and come over to find out what was going on.

"Fraa Erasmas," said Orolo, "you said a minute ago that it would be possible to talk slines into worrying about a pink nerve-gas-farting dragon. How would you go about it?"

"Well, I'm not a Procian. But if I were, I suppose I'd tell the slines some sort of convincing story that explained where the dragons had come from. And at the end of it, they'd be plenty worried. But if Jesry burst in warning them about a striped, fire-belching turtle, why, they'd cart him off to the loony bin!"

Everyone laughed—even Jesry, who as a rule didn't like jokes made at his expense.

"What would make your story convincing?" Orolo asked.

"Well, it'd have to be internally consistent. And it would also have to be consistent with what every sline already knew of the real world."

"How so?"

Lio and Tulia were on their way to the Refectory kitchen, where it was their turn to prepare dinner. Lio, having heard the last few lines, chimed in: "You could claim that shooting stars were dragon farts that had been lit on fire!"

"Very good," said Orolo. "Then, whenever a sline looked up and saw a shooting star, he'd think it was corroboration for the pink dragon myth."

"And he could refute Jesry," Lio said, "by saying 'you idiot, what do striped fire-belching turtles have to do with shooting stars?'" Everyone laughed again.

"This is straight from the later writings of Saunt Evenedric," Arsibalt said.

Everyone got quiet. We'd thought we were just being playful, until now. "Fraa Arsibalt is jumping ahead," Orolo said, in a tone of mild protest.

"Evenedric was a theor," Jesry pointed out. "This isn't the kind of stuff he would have written about."

"On the contrary," Arsibalt said, squaring off, "later in his life, after the Reconstitution, he—"

"If you don't mind," Orolo said.

"Of course not," said Arsibalt.

"Restricting ourselves to nerve-gas-farting dragons, how many colors do you think we could distinguish?"

Opinions varied between eight and a hundred. Tulia thought she could distinguish more, Lio fewer.

"Say ten," Orolo said. "Now, let us allow for striped dragons with alternating colors."

"Then there would be a hundred combinations," I said.

"Ninety," Jesry corrected me. "You can't count red/red and so on."

"Allowing for different stripe widths, could we get it up to a thousand distinguishable combinations?" Orolo asked. There was general agreement that we could. "Now move on to spots. Plaids. Combinations of spots, plaids, and stripes."

"Hundreds of thousands! Millions!" different people were guessing.

"And we are only considering nerve-gas-farting dragons, so far!" Orolo reminded us. "What of lizards, turtles, gods—"

"Hey!" Jesry exclaimed, and shot a glance at Arsibalt. "This *is* becoming the kind of argument that a theor would make."

"How so, Fraa Jesry? Where is the theorical content?"

"In the numbers," Jesry said, "in the profusion of different scenarios."

"Please explain."

"Once you have opened the door to these hypotheticals that don't have to make internal sense, you quickly find yourself looking at a range of possibilities that might as well be infinitely numerous," Jesry said. "So the mind rejects them as being equally invalid, and doesn't worry about them."

"And this is true of slines as well as of Saunt Evenedric?" Arsibalt asked.

"It has to be," Jesry said.

"So it is an intrinsic feature of human consciousness—this filtering ability."

As Arsibalt grew more confident, Jesry—sensing he was being drawn into a trap—became more cautious. "Filtering ability?" he asked.

"Don't play stupid, Jesry!" called Suur Ala, who was also reporting for kitchen duty. "You just said yourself that the mind rejects and doesn't worry about the overwhelming majority of hypothetical scenarios. If that's not a 'filtering ability' I don't know what is!"

"*Sorry!*" Jesry snapped back, and looked around at me, Lio, and Arsibalt, as if he'd just been mugged, and needed witnesses.

"What then is the criterion that the mind uses to select an infinitesimal minority of possible outcomes to worry about?" Orolo asked.

"Plausibility." "Possibility," people were murmuring, but no one seemed to feel confident enough to stake a claim.

"Earlier, Fraa Erasmas mentioned that it had something to do with being able to tell a coherent story."

"It is a Hemn space—a configuration space—argument," I

blurted, before I'd even thought about it. "That's the connection to Evenedric the theor."

"Can you please explain?" Orolo requested.

I wouldn't have been able to if not for the fact that I'd just been talking to Barb about it. "There's no way to get from the point in Hemn space where we are now, to one that includes pink nerve-gas-farting dragons, following any plausible action principle. Which is really just a technical term for there being a coherent story joining one moment to the next. If you simply throw action principles out the window, you're granting the world the freedom to wander any-where in Hemn space, to any outcome, without constraint. It be-comes pretty meaningless. The mind—even the sline mind—knows that there *is* an action principle that governs how the world evolves from one moment to the next—that restricts our world's path to points that tell an internally consistent story. So it focuses its worry-ing on outcomes that are more plausible, such as you leaving."

"You're leaving!?" Tulia exclaimed, utterly horrified. Others who'd joined the dialog late reacted similarly. Orolo laughed and I explained how the dialog had gotten started—and I did it hastily, before anyone could run off and start rumors.

"I don't think you're wrong, Fraa Erasmas," said Jesry, when everyone had settled down, "but I think you have a Steelyard prob-lem. Bringing in Hemn space and action principles seems like an unnecessarily heavyweight way of explaining the fact that the mind has an instinctive nose for which outcomes are plausible enough to worry about."

"The point is conceded," I said.

But Arsibalt was crestfallen—disappointed in me for having backed down without a fight. "Remember that this came up in con-nection with Saunt Evenedric," Arsibalt said, "a theor who spent the first half of his life working rigorous calculations having to do with principles of action in various kinds of configuration spaces. I don't think he was merely speaking poetically when he suggested that human consciousness is capable of—"

"Don't go Hundred on us now!" Jesry snorted.

Arsibalt froze, mouth open, face turning red.

"It is sufficient for now to have broached this topic," Orolo decreed. "We'll not settle it here—not on empty stomachs, anyway!" Taking the hint, Lio, Tulia, and Ala took their leave, headed for the kitchen. Ala shot a frosty look over her shoulder at Jesry, then leaned in close to Tulia to make some remark. I knew exactly what she was complaining about: Jesry had been the one who had brought up the profusion-of-outcomes argument in the first place—but when Arsibalt had tried to develop it, he had gotten cold feet and backed out—even mocked Arsibalt. I tried to throw Ala a grin, but she didn't notice. There was too much else going on. I ended up standing there grinning into empty space, like an idiot.

Arsibalt began to pursue Jesry across the cloister, disputing the point.

"Back to where we were," Orolo continued. "Why do you worry so much, Erasmas? Are you doing nothing more productive than imagining pink nerve-gas-farting dragons? Or do you have a particular gift for tracing possible futures through Hemn space—tracing them, it seems, to disturbing conclusions?"

"You could help me answer that question," I pointed out, "by telling me whether you are thinking of leaving."

"I spent almost all of Apert extramuros," Orolo said with a sigh, as if he had finally been run to ground. "I was expecting that it would be a wasteland. A cultural and intellectual charnel house. But that's not exactly what I found. I went to speelys. I enjoyed them! I went to bars and got into some reasonably interesting conversations with people. Slines. I liked them. Some were quite interesting. And I don't mean that in a bug-under-a-microscope way. They have stuck in my mind—characters I'll always remember. For a while I was quite seduced by it. Then one evening I had an especially lively discussion with a sline who was as bright as anyone within this concent. And somehow, toward the end, it came out that he believed that the sun revolved around Arbre. I was flabbergasted, you know. I tried to disabuse him of this. He scoffed at my arguments. It made me remember just how much careful observation and theorical work is necessary to prove something as basic as that Arbre goes around the sun. How indebted we are to those who went before us. And this got me to thinking that I'd been living on the right side of the gate after all."

He paused for a moment, squinting off toward the mountains, as if judging whether he should go on to tell me the next part. Finally he caught me giving him an expectant look, and made a little gesture of surrender. "When I got back, I found a packet of old letters from Estemard," he said.

"Really!"

"He'd been posting them from Bly's Butte once every year or so. Of course he knew that they'd be impounded until the next Apert. He told me of some observations he'd made, using a telescope he'd built up there, grinding the mirror by hand and so forth. Good ideas. Interesting reading. Certainly not the quality of work he'd produced here, though."

"But *he* was allowed to go up *there*," I said, gesturing toward the starhenge.

Orolo thought that was funny. "Of course. And I trust that we shall be re-admitted to it one day before too long."

"Why? How? What basis do you have for that?" I had to ask, though I knew he wouldn't answer.

"Let us say I too am gifted with the faculty that you have, for envisioning how things might play out."

"Thanks a lot!"

"Oh, and I can also put that faculty to work imagining what it would be like to be a Feral," he said. "Estemard's letters make it plain that this is a hard way to live."

"Do you think he made the right choice?"

"I don't know," Orolo said without hesitation. "These are big questions. What does the human organism seek? Beyond food, water, shelter, and reproduction, I mean."

"Happiness, I guess."

"Which is something you can get, in a shallow way, simply by eating the food that they eat out there," Orolo pointed out. "And yet still the people extramuros yearn for things. They join different kinds of arks all the time. What's the point in that?"

I thought about Jesry's family and mine. "I guess people like to think that they are not only living but propagating their way of life."

"That's right. People have a need to feel that they are part of some sustainable project. Something that will go on without them. It creates a feeling of stability. I believe that the need for that kind of stability is as basic and as desperate as some of the other, more obvious needs. But there's more than one way to get it. We may not think much of the sline subculture, but you have to admit it's stable! Then the burgers have a completely different kind of stability."

"As do we."

"As do we. And yet it didn't work for Estemard. Perhaps he felt that living by himself on a butte would fill that need better."

"Or maybe he just didn't need it as much as some of us," I suggested.

The clock chimed the hour. "You're going to miss a fascinating talk by Suur Fretta," Orolo said.

"That sounded kind of like changing the subject," I pointed out.

Orolo shrugged. *Subjects change. You'd best adapt.*

"Well," I said, "all right. I'll go to her talk. But if you're going to leave, don't just walk out of this place without letting me know, please?"

"I promise to give you as much advance knowledge as I can if such a thing is going to happen," he said, in an indulgent tone, as if talking to a mentally unhinged person.

"Thank you," I said.

Then I went to Saunt Grod's chalk hall and took a seat in the large empty space that, as usual, surrounded Barb.

Technically, we were supposed to call him Fraa Tavener now, for that was the name he had adopted when he had taken his vow. But some people took longer than others to grow into their avout names. Arsibalt had been Arsibalt from day one; no one even remembered his extramuros name any more. But people were going to be addressing Barb as Barb for a long time.

Whatever his name, that boy was going to save me. There was a lot he didn't know, but nothing he was afraid to ask about, and ask about, and ask about, until he understood it perfectly. I decided to make him my fid. People would think I was doing it to be charitable. Maybe some would even think I was getting ready to fall back, and was making the care of Barb my avocation. Let them think so! In truth it was mostly self-interest. I had learned more theorics in six weeks, simply by being willing to sit next to Barb, than I had in six months before Apert. I saw now that in my desire to know theorics I had taken shortcuts that, just like shortcuts on a map, turned out to be longcuts. Whenever I'd seen Jesry get it quicker than me, I had misread equations in a way that had seemed easier at the time but made things harder—no, impossible—later. Barb didn't have that fear that others were getting it faster; because of how his brain was set up, he couldn't read that in their faces. And he did not have the same desire to reach a distant goal. He was altogether self-centered and short-sighted. He wanted only to understand this one problem or equation chalked on the slate before him *now, today,* whether or not it was convenient for the others around him. And he was willing to stand there asking questions about it through supper and past curfew.

Come to think of it, Ala and Tulia had come up with a similar way of learning a long time ago. *The creature with two backs* was a term Jesry had coined for those two girls when they stood together outside of a chalk hall discussing—endlessly—what they had just heard. It wasn't enough for one of them to understand something. Nor for both of them to understand it in different ways. They both had to understand it in the same way. The sound of them furiously explaining things to each other gave the rest of us headaches. Especially when we'd been younger, we'd always clap our hands over our ears and run away when we spotted the creature with two backs. But it worked for them.

Barb's willingness to do things the hard way in the near term was making his advancement toward the long goal—even though he didn't *have* one—swifter and surer than mine had ever been. And now I was advancing in step with him.

As a possible avocation, I had been teaching the new crop how to sing. Extramuros, everyone *heard* music but only a few actually knew how to *make* it. These new fids had to be taught everything. It was excruciating. I already knew this wasn't going to be my avocation. We met three afternoons a week in an alcove in what passed for our nave.

One day as I was leaving one of these practices I happened to run into Fraa Lio, who was coming in to do whatever he did at the Warden Fendant's court. "Come up with me," he offered, "I want to show you something."

"A new nerve pinch?"

"No, nothing like that."

"You know I'm not supposed to look out from the high levels."

"Well, I haven't gone through hierarch training—yet—so neither am I," he said. "That's not what I want to show you."

So I began to follow him up the stair. As we climbed, I became nervous that he was going to carry out a plot to raid the starhenge. Then I recalled what Orolo had said the other day about worrying too much, and tried to put this out of my mind.

"You're not supposed to look out beyond the walls," he reminded me, as we were getting closer to the top of the southwest tower, "but you are allowed to remember what you saw there during Apert, right?"

"I suppose so."

"Well, did you notice anything?"

"Say again?"

"Extramuros, did you notice anything?"

"What kind of a question is that? I noticed a ton of stuff," I sputtered. Lio turned around and gave me a brilliant smile, letting me know this was just his goofy sense of humor at work. Humor vlor.

"All right," I said, "what was I supposed to notice?"

"Do you think the city's getting bigger or smaller?"

"Smaller. No question about it."

"Why are you so sure? Did you look up the census data?" Another smile.

"Of course not. I don't know. Just a feeling. Something about how the place looked."

"How did it look?"

"Sort of . . . weedy. Overgrown."

He turned around and held up his index finger like a statue of Thelenes declaiming on the Periklyne. "Hold that idea," he said, "while we pass through enemy territory."

We looked at the closed and locked portcullis, but didn't say anything. We crossed the bridge into the Regulant court and followed its inner walkway round to the stair that led up. When we had reached safe ground above—the statue of Amnectrus—he said, "I was thinking of making gardening my avocation."

"Well, considering all of the weeds you've pulled over the years doing penance for beating me up, you are well qualified," I said. "But why on earth would you want to?"

"Let me show you what has been going on in the meadow," he said, and led me out to the Fendant's ledge. A couple of sentinels were making the rounds, swathed in bulky winter-bolts, their feet swallowed up in furry mukluks. Lio and I were hot from climbing the stairs and so the cold didn't bother us much. We took a moment to hood ourselves. This was a way of showing respect for the Discipline. Our bolts, drawn far out in front of our faces, gave us tunnel vision. When we walked to the parapet and leaned forward, we could see down into the concent but not up and out to the world beyond.

Lio pointed down at the back fringe of the meadow. Shuf's Dowment rose up just on the other side of the river. With the exception of a few evergreen shrubs, everything down there was dead and brown. It was easy to see that, near the riverbank, the clover that carpeted most of the meadow became thin and patchy, and blotched with darker, coarser stuff: colonies of weeds that favored the sandy soil near the bank. Nearer the river I could see a distinct front where the clover gave way altogether to a snarl of woody trash: slashberry and the like. Behind that front I could see splats and rambling trails of green; some of the stuff back there was so tough that not even hard frost could kill it.

"I guess your theme today is weeds. But I don't see where you're going with it," I said.

"Down there, come spring, I am going to stage a re-enactment of the Battle of Trantae," he announced.

"Negative 1472," I answered in a robotic voice, that being one of the dates drilled into the head of every fid. "And I suppose you want me to play the role of a hoplite who gets a Sarthian arrow in the ear? No, thanks!"

He shook his head patiently. "Not with people," he said, "with plants."

"Say again?"

"I got the idea during Apert from seeing how weeds and even trees are invading the town. Taking it back from humans so slowly that the humans don't notice. The meadow is going to represent the fertile Plains of Thrania, the breadbasket of the Bazian Empire," Lio said. "The river represents the river Chontus separating it from the northern provinces. By Negative 1474 those have long since been lost to the Horse Archers. Only a few fortified outposts hold out against the barbarian tide."

"Can we imagine that Shuf's Dowment is one of those?"

"If you like. It doesn't matter. Anyway, during the cold winter of Negative 1473, the steppe hordes, led by the Sarthian clan, cross the frozen river and establish bridgeheads on the Thranian bank. By the time the campaigning season has opened, they've got three whole armies ready to break out. General Oxas deposes the Bazian Imperator in a military coup and marches forth promising to drive the Sarthians into the river and drown them like rats. After weeks of maneuver, the legions of Oxas finally meet the Sarthians in the flat countryside near Trantae. The Sarthians stage a false retreat. Oxas falls for it like a total dumbass and charges into a pincer. He's surrounded—"

"And three months later Baz is on fire. But how are you going to do all of that with weeds?"

"We'll allow the invasive species from the riverbank to make inroads into the clover. The starblossom vines run along the ground like light cavalry—it's incredible how fast they advance. The slashberry is slower, but better at holding ground—like infantry. Finally the trees come along and make it permanent. With a little weeding and pruning, we can make it all work out just like Trantae, except it'll take six months or so to play out."

"That is the craziest idea I have ever heard," I said. "You are some kind of a nut."

"Would you rather help me, or go on trying to teach those brats down there how to carry a tune?"

"Is this a trick to get me to pull weeds?"

"No. We're going to let the weeds *grow*—remember?"

"What's going to happen after the weeds win? We can't set fire to the Cloister. Maybe we could sack the apiary and drink all the mead?"

"Someone already did that, during Apert," he reminded me gravely. "No, we'll probably have to clean it all up. Though if people like it we could let nature take its course and let a grove of trees grow on the conquered territory."

"One of the things I like about this is that, come summer, it will put me in a good position to watch Arsibalt being chased around by angry swarms of bees," I said.

Lio laughed. I thought to myself that his plan had another advantage as well: it was flagrantly silly. Until now, I had been dabbling in avocations, such as looking after Barb and teaching fids how to sing, that were sensible and virtuous. Typical behavior for someone who was getting ready to fall back. To spend the summer doing something absolutely ridiculous would flaunt the fact that I had no such intentions. Those members of the Edharian chapter who hadn't wanted me would be furious.

"I'll do it," I said. "But I guess we have to wait a few more weeks before anything starts to grow."

"You're pretty good at drawing, aren't you?" Lio asked.

"Better than you—but that's not saying much. I can make technical illustrations. Barb is freakishly good at it. Why?"

"I was thinking we should make a record of it. Draw pictures of how it looks as the battle goes on. This would be an excellent vantage point."

"Should I ask Barb if he's interested?"

Lio looked a little uneasy at that. Maybe because Barb could be so obnoxious; probably because Barb was a new fid and shouldn't have an avocation yet. "Never mind, I'll do it myself," I said.

"Great," Lio said, "when can you start?"

Lio and I read some histories of the Battle of Trantae during the next week, and pounded stakes into the ground to mark important sites, such as where General Oxas, pierced by eight arrows, had fallen on his sword. I constructed a rectangular frame, about the size of a dinner tray, with a grid of strings stretched across it. The idea was that I'd set this up on the parapet and look through it like a windowframe as I sketched; if I continued to use it in the same way throughout the summer, then each illustration would tally with the next. One day we'd be able to line them up in a row and then people would walk down the line and see the weed-war unfold like a speely.

Lio spent a lot of time thrashing around in the brush along the riverbank looking for particularly aggressive specimens of various kinds of weeds. Yellow starblossom was going to represent the Sarthian cavalry, red and white their allies.

We were both waiting for the moment when we would get in trouble.

Sure enough, a couple of weeks into the project, I looked up during supper to see Fraa Spelikon come into the Refectory, accompanied by a younger hierarch of the Regulant staff. Conversation dimmed for a moment—sort of like when the power threatens to go out and the room becomes brown. Spelikon looked around the Refectory until he found my face. Then, satisfied, he snatched up a tray and demanded some food. Hierarchs were allowed to dine with us, but they rarely did. They had to concentrate pretty fiercely not to let Sæcular information slip out and so this was no way to have a relaxing meal.

Everyone had noticed the way Spelikon had looked at me and so, following the brownout, there was a brief jovial uproar at my expense. For once in my life I wasn't worried. What could they accuse me of? Conspiring to let weeds grow? Probably they had misinterpreted what

Lio and I were up to. The only hard part was going to be explaining it to a man like Spelikon.

The younger hierarch—Rotha was her name—ate quickly, then rose and walked out of the Refectory hugging a fat wallet of papers that swiveled as her hips moved. Spelikon ate more heartily but refused offers of beer and wine. After a few minutes he pushed back, wiped his lips, stood up, and came over to me. "I wonder if I might have a word with you in Saunt Zenla's," he said.

"Certainly," I said, then glanced across the room at Lio, who was dining at another table. "Would you like Fraa Lio to join us or—"

"That will not be necessary," Spelikon said. Which struck me as odd, and left me with physical symptoms of anxiety—pounding heart, moist palms—as I followed Spelikon around the Cloister to Saunt Zenla's.

This was one of the smallest and oldest chalk halls, traditionally used by the most senior Edharian theoricians to collaborate or to teach their senior students. I'd only been in the room a couple of times my whole life, and would never have dared to barge in there and claim it like this. It had one small table, large enough for at most four people to sit around it on their spheres. Rotha had already covered the table with stuff: a constellation of glow-buds whose pools of soft light merged to illuminate a stack of blank leaves and a few manuscripts, or excerpts of them. Several pens lay in a neat row next to an uncapped ink-bottle.

"Interview with Fraa Erasmas of the Edharian chapter of the Decenarian math of the Concent of Saunt Edhar," Spelikon said. Rotha scribbled out a row of marks on a blank leaf—not the customary Bazian characters, but a kind of shorthand that hierarchs were trained to use when taking down transcripts. Spelikon went on to tell the date and the time. I was mesmerized by Rotha's skill with the pen—her hand swept across the whole width of the leaf in as little time as it took to draw breath, leaving in its wake a row of simple one-stroke glyphs that, it seemed to me, couldn't possibly convey as much meaning as the words we were speaking.

My eyes wandered to the other manuscripts that Rotha had set out on the table. Most of them were also written in that same short-hand. But at least one was in traditional script. *My* script. Bending closer, I was able to make out several words. I recognized it as the journal I had started keeping when I'd been in the penance cell in the Mynster. I saw the names Flec and Quin, and Orolo.

My movements had gone all jerky. Some primitive threat-response mechanism had taken over. "Hey, that's mine!"

Spelikon saw to it that this was written down. "The subject admits that Document Eleven is his."

"Where did you get that?" I demanded, now sounding no older than Barb. Rotha's hand flitted across the leaf and immortalized it.

"From where it *was*," Spelikon answered, amused. "You do know the whereabouts of your own journal, don't you?"

"I *thought* I did." One of the niches outside of Saunt Grod's chalk hall, up high where only a few people could reach it. But to take someone else's leaves out of a niche was just about the rudest thing an avout could do. It was only acceptable when someone had died or been Thrown Back. "But," I went on, "but you're not supposed to—"

"Why don't you let me be the judge of what we are and are not supposed to do," Spelikon said. As he spoke these words he made a gesture with his hand that stilled Rotha's hand, so none of it was written down. Then he made a different gesture that undid the spell, and she began to write again. "This inquiry does not concern you directly and, in fact, need not take up very much of your time. You have already supplied most of what we wish to know in the leaves of your journal. Clarification and confirmation are all that we require. On the day before Apert, did you serve as amanuensis during an interview conducted in the New Library between Fraa Orolo and an artisan from extramuros named Quin?"

"Yes."

"Document Three, please," Spelikon said. Rotha drew out another manuscript, also written in my hand: my transcript of Orolo's interview with Quin. I didn't bother asking where they'd gotten it. Obviously they'd been rooting around in Fraa Orolo's niches too. Outrageous! But for all that, I was beginning to relax. There was nothing wrong with the conversations Orolo had had with those artisans. Even if the Warden Regulant wouldn't take my word for it, well, others had been in the library the whole time and could vouch that it had all been harmless. This must be some petty and misguided harassment of Fraa Orolo that would come to nothing, and—I hoped—make Fraa Spelikon look like an idiot.

Spelikon had me confirm that Document Three was mine before going on: "There are discrepancies between the account of the Orolo-Quin conversation as you transcribed it at the time, and the version you later set down in your journal."

"Yes," I said. "I'm not like her." I nodded at Rotha. "I can't take shorthand. I only wrote down what was germane to the research that Orolo was doing."

"Which research do you mean?" Spelikon asked.

I'd thought that was obvious, but I explained, "His study of the political climate extramuros—part of normal preparations for Apert."

"Thank you. There are several such discrepancies, but I'd like to draw your attention to one, late in the Quin interview, concerning the technical capabilities of speelycaptors."

This was so unexpected it blanked my mind. "Uh, I vaguely remember that topic coming up."

"Your memory was not vague at all when you wrote this," he said, and reached down over Rotha's shoulder and picked up the journal. "According to this, Artisan Quin said, at one point, and I quote, 'Flec didn't make a speely.' Does that make your memory any less vague?"

"Yes. The day before, at Provener, we had sent Artisan Flec to see the Ita so that they could show him to the north nave. Flec wanted to make a speely. But later Quin told us that it hadn't gone as planned. The Ita didn't allow Flec to operate his speelycaptor in the Mynster."

"Why not?"

"The image quality was too good."

"Too good in what way?" Spelikon asked.

"Quin rattled off some commercial bulshytt that I tried to capture in the journal," I said.

"When you say you tried to capture it, are you saying that what you wrote in the journal is only a guess at what it said? Here it reads—quoting again—'the Eagle-Rez, the SteadiHand, the DynaZoom—put those all together, and it could have seen straight across into the other parts of your Mynster, even through the screens.' Did Quin actually use those words?"

"I don't know. It's partly my recollection and partly an educated guess."

"Explain what you mean by an educated guess in this case."

"Well, the point of the story—the basic technical reason that the Ita wouldn't allow Flec to use the speelycaptor—was that from where he was going to be sitting, behind the north screen, he would have been able to take pictures of the Thousanders and Hundreders by pointing his speelycaptor across the chancel. With our naked eyes, we can't see through the screens into the other naves because of the contrast between the screen, which is light-colored—cosmographers would say it has high albedo—and the dark space beyond. Also because of distance and other factors. The gist of it was that the Ita had looked up the specifications on Flec's speelycaptor and figured out that it had some combination of features that would make it possible to see things that the naked eye couldn't. Now, it's a fool's game trying to make sense of the commercial bulshytt that the makers of speelycaptors use to describe those features. But from my experience with cosmography, I have a pretty good idea what it would entail: some kind of zoom or magnification feature, a way of detecting faint images against a noisy background, and image stabilization, to correct for shaking of the hands."

"And that is what you mean by an educated guess," Spelikon said. "Educated, in the sense that anyone with a knowledge of cosmographical instruments would be able to infer what you inferred about the capabilities of Flec's speelycaptor."

"Yes."

"It says in your journal," Spelikon continued, "that Fraa Orolo's hand came down on your wrist just after that, and stopped you from writing. Why?"

"Being older and wiser," I said, "Orolo saw where the conversation was headed. Quin was about to go off chattering about Sæcular stuff, and about what had happened between Flec and the Ita, which obviously is not the kind of information we ought to be exposed to."

"But if your ears were going to be exposed to it *anyway*, why did Orolo stop your *hand*? Why did he not plug your ears?"

"I don't know. Maybe it wasn't the most logical thing for him to do. People don't always think clearly at such moments."

"Except when they *do*," Spelikon said. "Well, at any rate, that is all I have for you concerning the Orolo-Quin interview. There is only one other question."

"Yes?"

"Where were you on the ninth night of Apert?"

I thought for a minute, and frowned. "That's one of those simple-sounding questions that is hard for a normal person to answer."

Spelikon was almost too quick to agree with me. "If by 'normal person' you mean 'non-hierarch,' then let me assure you I have no specific memories of what *I* did that evening."

"Well, I was scheduled to give a tour the next morning, so I didn't stay up late. I had supper. Then I'm pretty sure I went to bed. I was doing a lot of thinking."

"Really?" Spelikon asked. "About what?"

I must have gotten a very strange look on my face. He chuckled and said, "I'm just curious. I don't think it matters." He drew up another leaf. "According to the Chronicle, on that night you were assigned to share a cell with Fraa Branch and Fraa Ostabon. If I were to ask them, they'd both say you were in the cell with them that night?"

"I can't imagine why they'd say anything else."

"Very well," Spelikon said, "that will be all. Thank you for your time, Fraa Erasmas."

Spelikon opened the door for me. I stepped through it to discover Fraa Branch and Fraa Ostabon waiting in the gallery.

My talent for envisioning things, and spinning yarns in my head, failed me that evening, as if it had gone on vacation. I could make no sense of my interview with Spelikon. I put it down as further evidence that Suur Trestanas was cracking, and would soon be sent to Physicians' Commons to get better—hopefully very slowly.

The next day I was up early to help serve breakfast. I spent the morning in a chalk hall with Barb, working on some fundamentals of exterior calculus that I should have understood years earlier but was only now getting a real grip on. As I was reaching the point where my brain couldn't take any more, and noticed myself making dumb mistakes, Provener rang.

This was one of the days that my old team was supposed to wind the clock, so I went to the Mynster. It was sparsely attended, with few hierarchs in evidence. I didn't see Fraa Orolo or any of his senior students, and Jesry didn't show up, so Lio and Arsibalt and I had to do it without his help.

Between that and the long morning in the chalk hall, I was famished, and ate like a dog in the Refectory. When I was almost finished, Orolo came in, fetched himself a light lunch, and sat down alone in what had become his favorite spot: the table from which he could look out the window and down the mountains when the weather was clear. Today, it wasn't; but it felt as though the clouds might later be rinsed away by a cold clear river of wind. When I had finished eating, I went over and sat with him. I guessed that Spelikon must have been pestering him with questions too. But I didn't want to bring it up. He must be sick of it.

He gave me a little smile. "Thanks to the hierarchs," he said, "I shall soon be making observations again."

"They're going to open the starhenge? That's great news!" I exclaimed. Orolo smiled again. Things were beginning to make sense. Something had spooked the hierarchs. They had misinterpreted Orolo's pre-Apert activities in a way I still didn't understand. Now finally they were coming to see that they'd been mistaken, and things were about to go back to normal.

"I must admit, I have a tablet up in the M & M that I've been dying to get my hands on," he said.

"When are they going to open it?"

"I don't know," Orolo said.

"What are you going to look at first?"

"Oh, I'd rather not say just now. Nothing that requires the power of the M & M. A smaller telescope would suffice, or even a commercial speelycaptor."

"Spelikon was asking me all kinds of questions about those—"

He put his finger to his lips. "I know," he said, "and it is good that you answered his questions as you did."

I was distracted for a few moments, working through the implications. The news was good. But when people began going up to the starhenge again, they might find the tablet I'd left in Clesthyra's Eye, which could get me in a lot of trouble. I felt stupid now for having put it there. How was I going to fetch it back?

Orolo looked out a different window, reading the time from the clock. "I saw Tulia a few minutes ago. She and Ala were rounding up the team. She asked me to give you a message."

"Yes?"

"She won't be turning up for this meal. She'll see you at supper."

"That's the message?"

"Yes. The team have got some unusual changes to ring—it's going to require their full attention. They'll be starting in half an hour or so. She seemed to think that you of all people would find this especially important. I've no idea why."

Voco.

It had to be another Voco. So I was going to get my chance to sneak up to the starhenge again—*that* was the real message that Tulia was trying to send me.

Did Orolo understand all of this? Did he know what was going on?

But once the changes began to ring, I couldn't very well go charging up the Mynster stairs against the traffic of Regulant and Fendant staff coming down to attend the aut. This was only going to work if I ascended first, *before* the bells sounded, and hid myself up there.

And I had a perfect excuse for doing so, thanks to Lio.

I stood up. "See you in the Mynster," I said to Orolo.

"Yes," he said, and then winked. "Or perhaps not."

I was frozen for a moment, again wondering how much he knew. This made him smile broadly. "All I meant," Orolo said, "was that one never knows who will remain in the Mynster after one of these auts, and who will depart."

"You think you might be called up at Voco?"

"It is most unlikely!" Orolo said. "But just in case *you* are called—"

I snorted. Now he was just having fun with me.

"Just in case *you* are called," he said, "know that I have seen the progress you have been making in recent months. I am proud of you. Proud, but not *surprised*. Do keep at it."

"All right," I said. "I'll keep at it. In fact, I have some questions for you later. But I have to run."

"Run then," he said. "Mind your step on those stairs."

I turned around and forced myself to saunter, not sprint, out of the Refectory. I fetched my drawing-frame and sketches from the niche where I'd been stashing them, and walked as quickly as I could, without looking like I was in a hurry, to the Mynster. When I had ascended to the triforium, I looked over to the bell-ringers' balcony and saw Ala and Tulia and their team there, going through the motions of the changes they were about to ring without actually pulling on the ropes. Tulia saw me. I looked away, not wanting to be obvious, then went the other way and climbed the southwest tower stairs as briskly as I could.

The Regulant court was as crowded as I had ever seen it, but quiet, as everyone seemed intent on something. Which made sense, just before a Voco. I actually saw Suur Trestanas for a moment as she was passing from one office to another. She looked a little surprised, but then her gaze dropped to take in my drawing equipment, and she saw me attacking the next flight of stairs. Something clicked into place in her mind and she forgot about it.

Lio was waiting for me by the statue of Amnectrus, looking a little flushed himself from climbing the stairs. He fell in step beside me. "Don't go to the ledge," he said, "too conspicuous. Come with me."

I hooded myself as I followed him around the inner walkway. Neither of us spoke, as we always seemed to be in earshot of someone. Finally he dodged into a chamber that was lined with heavy wooden doors all around—a muster room, they called it, where a squad might gather to brief and equip before a mission.

"You planned this whole thing, didn't you?" I whispered.

"I created opportunities, in case we might need them." Lio slid one of the doors open to reveal a storage chamber lined with metal boxes, neatly stacked. Then he grabbed my bolt in front of my chest, yanked me forward, and shoved me into the locker. By the time I'd got my balance back, he'd slid the door shut behind me. It was dark. I was hidden.

No more than a minute later, the bells began to ring strange changes.

My eyes had adjusted to the darkness. I took the minor risk of making my sphere give off a faint glow. The boxes stacked around me were stenciled with incomprehensible words and numbers, but I was growing certain that they contained ammunition. I had heard stories. The lifetime of this stuff was a few decades. Then it had to be flung off the Mynster and shoveled into wagons to be carted off for disposal. The whole concent would then queue up on the stairs and convey the fresh ammunition up to this level by passing the boxes from hand to hand. This hadn't been done in a while, but some of the older avout remembered it clearly.

Anyway it gave me something to think of while I waited through the ringing of the changes and the half-hour of assembly time that followed. No one up here needed half an hour. They could go on about their business for fifteen or twenty minutes and then hustle down at the last minute. So it took a while for the place to empty out. At some point Fraa Delrakhones himself made a sweep, commanding *everyone* to leave *now*. He wanted to be the last one down, and he didn't want to have to run.

After that, I felt it was safe to go out into the muster room. I cracked the door of the locker and paused to let my eyes adjust, then crept out and squatted behind the exit door for a minute, just listening. But there was nothing to hear—not even from the Chancel and the naves, which sounded as if they had been abandoned.

I was afraid that Delrakhones might still be hunting for stragglers, and there was no particular reason to hurry, so I waited until the voice of Statho resonated up the well, intoning the Convocation. Then I bolted from cover, charged around to the stairs, and raced into the space above. Statho went on at some length, pausing from time to time as though sifting through hastily assembled notes, or gathering strength.

I was about halfway to the starhenge, high up behind the face of the clock, when I first heard the word *Anathem*.

My knees collapsed, like those of a beast when something unexpectedly touches its back. I lost my stride and had to stop myself and crouch down lest I bang into something.

It couldn't be real. The aut of Anathem had not been celebrated in this place for two hundred years.

And yet I had to admit that the changes Tulia had rung had sounded new to my ears—different from Voco. The crowd in the Mynster had been dead quiet before the aut. Now they were muttering, producing a gravelly sound the likes of which I'd never heard.

Everything that had happened since Apert now made sense in a new way, as if a pile of shattered fragments had been thrown up in the air and reassembled itself into a mirror.

Some part of me said that I must keep moving. That this was my only chance to fetch that tablet. Not that the images stored on it mattered any more. But Orolo had gone out of his way to tell me, a few minutes ago, that he wanted the tablet from the M & M. I had to get both of them. If I blew it, I'd get in huge trouble—perhaps be Thrown Back. Worse, I'd fail Orolo.

How long had I been crouched on this catwalk not moving? Wasted time! Wasted time! I made myself move.

Whose name would they call? Perhaps mine? What would happen then if I failed to step out? There was some dark humor in that. It got darker as I imagined one way to answer the call: by jumping down the center of the well. With luck I'd land on Suur Trestanas. Now *that* would be a story that would live on forever in the lore of Saunt Edhar and the mathic world beyond. Perhaps it would even make the local newspapers.

But it would not get that tablet from Clesthyra's Eye, nor the one that Orolo wanted from the M & M. That was a prize worth taking risks for.

I climbed as Statho read some ancient prattle about the Discipline and how it must be enforced. Maybe I didn't climb as quickly as I might have, for I could tell he was leading up to the moment when he would call out the name of the one who was to be Thrown Back, and I wanted to hear it. I reached the top, and put my hand on the door that led to the starhenge, and actually killed time for a minute.

Finally he said "Orolo." Not "Fraa Orolo," for in that instant he had ceased to be a fraa.

How could I be surprised? From the moment I had heard "Anathem" I had known that it would be Orolo. Still I said "No!" out loud. No one heard me, because everyone else was saying it in the same moment; it came up the well like the beat of a drum. As it died away, a very weird sound replaced it, something I'd never heard the likes of before: people were *screaming* down there.

Why did I cry out "No!" when I'd known it all along? Not out of disbelief. It was an objection. A refusal. A declaration of war.

Orolo was ready. He emerged through the door in our screen immediately, and closed it firmly behind him before his former brothers and sisters could begin to say goodbye, for that would have taken a year. Better to just be gone, like one who is killed by a falling tree. He walked out into the chancel and tossed his sphere to the floor, then began to untie his chord. This dropped around his ankles. He stepped out of it and then reached down, grabbed the lower fringes of his bolt, and shrugged it off over his shoulders. For a moment, then, he was standing there naked, holding a wad of bolt in his arms, and gazing straight up the well, just as Fraa Paphlagon had done at Voco.

I opened the door to the starhenge and let the light flood in. Orolo saw it and bowed his head like a Deolater praying to his god. Then I passed through and closed the door behind me. The entire, terrible scene in the Mynster was eclipsed, and replaced by the lonely vista of the starhenge.

In the same moment I began sobbing out loud. My face drew back from my skull as if I were vomiting and tears ran from my eyes like blood from gashes. I was sad—rather than surprised—because I had known that this was coming from the moment Fraa Spelikon had begun asking about speelycaptors. I hadn't foreseen it only because it was too dreadful to think about until I could not escape it any more—until it had happened. Until now. So I didn't have to waste any time being astonished, like those fraas and suurs down below me; I went straight to the most intense and saturating grief I had ever known.

I found my way to the Pinnacle more by groping than by sight, as I could perceive little more than light and dark. By the time I'd reached the top, I'd moved on to hysterical blubbering, but I wiped my face a couple of times with my bolt, took some deep breaths, and settled myself long enough to get the dust cover open and withdraw the tablet from Clesthyra's Eye. This I wrapped in my bolt, which called to mind the memory of Orolo stripping his off.

He would stand there naked while the avout sang a wrathful song to Anathematize him. They were probably singing it now. You were supposed to sing it like you meant it. Maybe that would be easy for the Thousanders and the Hundreders who had never known him. But I suspected that little coherent sound was coming from behind the Tenners' screen.

I went into the control chamber of the M & M and looked for the tablet that Orolo had placed in its objective when he and I had been here just before the whole place had been locked down. But it was empty. Someone had been here before me and confiscated it. Just as they would now go through the niches that he had used and take all of his writings.

Then I did something that might have been foolish, but that was necessary: I went to the same place where I'd watched Fraa Paphlagon and the Inquisitors take off in their aerocraft. I crouched at the base of the same megalith, and waited until Orolo walked out of the Day Gate. Once he had passed out of the chancel, and out of sight of the avout, they had given him a sort of gunny sack to cover his body, and an emergency blanket made of crinkly orange foil, which he pulled around his shoulders as he got out into the plaza and the wind hit him. His skinny white ankles were lost in a pair of old black work boots and he had to shuffle lest they fall off. He moved away from the concent without once gazing back over his shoulder. After a few moments he disappeared behind the spray of one of the fountains. I chose that time to turn my back on him and head back down.

As I passed back into the chronochasm and heard the aut of Anathem concluding, I thought it was a small mercy for me that I'd had this last sight of Orolo extramuros. Those in the Mynster merely saw him be swallowed by the unknowable beyond, which was (and was meant to be) terrifying. But I had at least seen him making his way out there. Which didn't make things any less horrible and sad. But to glimpse him still alive and moving under his own power in the Sæculum was to have hope that someone would help him out there—that maybe, before dark, he'd be sitting in hand-me-down clothes in one of those bars he had frequented during Apert, having a beer and looking for a job.

The remainder of the service was a reaffirmation of vows and a rededication to the Discipline. I was happy to miss it. I wrapped up the tablet in a leaf of drawing paper and stashed it behind a can of ammunition; Lio could always retrieve it later.

The one question was: would my absence have been marked by any of the Tenners? But in a group of three hundred, it was easy for such a thing to go unnoticed.

In case anyone asked, I concocted a story that Orolo had dropped a hint of what was going to happen (which—come to think of it—he had, though I'd been too dense to get it) and that I had skipped the aut because I was afraid I couldn't bear it. This would still get me in trouble. I didn't much care. Let them Throw me Back; I'd figure out where Orolo had gone—probably to Bly's Butte—and join him there.

But as it came out, I never had to tell anyone that lie. No one had noticed I was missing; or if they had, they didn't care.

The story of how Orolo had come to be Thrown Back had to be reconstructed over the next few weeks, like a skull in an archaeological dig being fitted together one shard at a time. We would get lost for days as rumor or convincingly wrong data sent us up some promising path that only later proved a logical cul-de-sac. It didn't help that all of us had suffered the psychic equivalent of third-degree burns.

He had somehow known, days before Apert, that there would be trouble related to the starhenge. He'd put Jesry to work doing some computations. He had not allowed Jesry to see the photomnemonic tablets from which the givens had been extracted; indeed, he'd gone to a lot of effort to obscure the nature of the work from Jesry and his other students, perhaps to shield them from any consequences.

When Artisan Quin had spoken of the technical capabilities of Flec's speelycaptor, the idea had come into Orolo's head that he might use such a device to make cosmographical observations. On the ninth night of Apert, after the starhenge had been locked, Orolo had gone to the apiary and stolen several crates of mead. He put on clothes that made him look like a visitor from extramuros and went out the Decade Gate with a large wheeled beer cooler in which he hid the loot. He made a rendezvous with a shady character of some description whom he had presumably met while hanging around in bars extramuros. Indeed, his entire motive for having frequented such places during Apert might have been to recruit such a person. In exchange for the mead, Orolo had taken delivery of a speelycaptor.

The little vineyard where Orolo pursued his avocation was difficult to see from the Mynster. During the winter, he sometimes went there to mend trellises and prune vines. In the weeks following Apert he devised a rudimentary observatory there, consisting of a vertical pole somewhat taller than a man, free to rotate, with a crosspiece lashed athwart it at eye level that could be swiveled up and down. Into this crosspiece he'd whittled a niche to fit the speelycaptor. The pole and crosspiece enabled him to hold the speelycaptor steady for long periods as he tracked his target across the sky. The device's image-stabilization, zoom, and low-light enhancement features enabled him to get a decent look at whatever he was so curious about.

The idea of Orolo stealing from the concent, conspiring with a criminal during Apert, and making forbidden observations in the vineyard was shocking to everyone, but the story did make sense, and it was just the kind of logical plan that Orolo would have come up with. Sooner or later we all came to terms with it.

My role in the story led some Edharians to view me as a traitor—as the guy who had sold Orolo out to the Warden Regulant. This was the kind of thing that, before Anathem, would have kept me up all night, every night, feeling bad. On even-numbered nights I'd have felt guilty about what I had divulged to Spelikon and on odd-numbered nights I'd have seethed with impotent rage at those in my chapter who so misunderstood me. But against the backdrop of all that had been going on, being worried about these things was a little bit like attempting to see distant stars against the daytime sky. Even though Orolo was not my father, and even though he was still alive, I felt about Fraa Spelikon as I would have about a man who had murdered my father before my eyes. And my feelings toward Suur Trestanas were even darker since I suspected that, in some sneaky way, she was behind it.

What had Orolo seen? We might have been able to get some clues from the computations Jesry had been doing before Apert. But the Warden Regulant had confiscated these from their niche and so all we had to go on were Jesry's recollections. He was fairly certain that Orolo had been trying to calculate the orbital parameters of an object or objects in the solar system. Normally this would imply an asteroid moving in a heliocentric (sun-centered) orbit that happened to be similar to the orbit of Arbre. A Big Nugget type of scenario, in other words. But Jesry had a hunch, based on certain of the numbers he remembered seeing, that the object in question was orbiting, not the sun, but Arbre. This was extremely unusual. In all the millenia that humans had been observing the heavens, only one permanent moon of Arbre had been found. It was possible for an asteroid in a sun-centered orbit to pass near a libration point and be captured into an Arbre-centered orbit, but all such orbits were unstable, and ended with the rock striking Arbre or the moon, or being ejected from the Arbre-moon system.

It might have been that Orolo was looking at the triangular libration points of the Arbre-moon system, which harbored concentrations of rocks and dust that were visible as faint clouds chasing or being chased by the moon in its orbit about Arbre. But it was not clear why such a project would create so much hostility in the Warden Regulant. And as Barb had pointed out, the orientation of the M & M suggested that Orolo had been using it to take pictures of an object in a *polar* orbit, which was unlikely in a natural object.

Of our group, it was Jesry who first had the courage to give voice to what was implied by all of this: "It is not a natural object. It was made and put there by humans."

It was not exactly spring. Winter was over, but frost still threatened; bulbs were thrusting green spears up through crystalline mud-ice. Several of us had spent the afternoon chopping down the dead stalks and vines of our tangles. We left these up through most of the winter to prevent soil erosion and provide a habitat for small animals, but the time of year had come when we had to take it all down and burn it so that the ashes could fertilize the soil. Now, following supper, we had gone out into the dark and set fire to the slash we'd heaped up during the day, creating a huge gaseous fire that would not last for very long. Jesry had found a bottle of the peculiar wine that Orolo used to make and we were passing it around.

"It could also have been made by some other praxic civilization," said Barb. Technically, of course, he was right. Socially, he was annoying us. By putting forth his suggestion, Jesry had stuck his neck out—had exposed himself to the risk of ridicule. By agreeing with him, silently or not, we were accepting the same risk. The last thing we needed was Barb speculating about bug-eyed space monsters.

Another thing about Barb: he was the son of Quin, who in a sense had instigated all of this by making indiscreet remarks about the excellence of modern speelycaptors. This was hardly Barb's fault but it did create a negative association in one's mind that bobbed to the surface at awkward moments—and Barb was a copious source of awkward moments.

"That would explain the closure of the starhenge," Arsibalt said. "Let us suppose, for the sake of argument, that the Sæcular Power has divided into two or more factions—perhaps arming for war. One may have launched a reconnaissance satellite into a polar orbit."

"Or several of them," Jesry said, "since I got the impression I was making calculations for more than just one object."

"Could it have been one object that changed its orbit from time to time?" Tulia asked.

"Unlikely. It takes a lot of energy to change an orbit from one plane to another—almost as much energy as launching the satellite in the first place," Lio said.

Everyone looked at him.

"Spy satellite vlor," he said sheepishly, "from a Praxic Age book on space warfare. Plane change maneuvers are expensive!"

"A satellite in a polar orbit doesn't need to change its plane!" Barb snorted. "It can see all parts of Arbre by waiting long enough."

"There's one big reason why I like Jesry's hypothesis," I said. Everyone turned and looked at me. I hadn't been talking much. But in the weeks since Anathem, I had come to be seen as an authority on all things Orolo. "Orolo's behavior in the days just before Apert suggests that he knew there was going to be trouble. Whatever it was that he had seen, he knew that it was a Sæcular event and that the hierarchs would make him stop looking at it as soon as they found out. That wouldn't have been true if it was just a rock."

I was only agreeing with the consensus. Most of the others nodded. But Arsibalt of all people seemed to take what I'd said as a challenge. He cleared his throat and came back at me as if we were in dialog. "Fraa Erasmas, what you have said makes sense as far as it goes. But it doesn't go very far. Since Anathem was rung down on Orolo, it's easy for us to fall in the habit of thinking of him as a malcontent. But would you have identified him as such before Apert?"

"Your point is well taken, Fraa Arsibalt. Let's not waste time taking a poll of everyone standing around this fire. Orolo was as happy to abide under the Discipline as any avout who ever lived."

"But the launching of a new reconaissance satellite is clearly a Sæcular event, is it not?"

"Yes."

"And, moreover, since that kind of praxis has been around for millenia—long enough that Fraa Lio here can read of it in ancient books—there is nothing new that Orolo could have learned by making observations of such a satellite, is there?"

"Presumably not—unless it embodied some newly developed praxis."

"But such a new praxis would also be a Sæcular event, would it not?" Tulia put in.

"Yes, Suur Tulia. And therefore no concern of the avout."

"So," said Arsibalt, "if we accept the premise that Fraa Orolo was a true avout who respected the Discipline, we cannot at the same time believe that the thing he saw in the sky was a satellite recently launched from the surface of Arbre."

"Because," said Lio, completing the thought, "he'd have identified any such thing as being of no interest to us."

All of which made sense; but it left us with nowhere to go. Or at least, nowhere we were *willing* to go.

Except for Barb. "Therefore it must be an alien ship."

Jesry inhaled deeply and let out a big sigh. "Fraa Tavener," he said, using Barb's avout name, "remind me to show you some research, back in the Library, showing just how unlikely that is."

"Unlikely but not impossible?" Fraa Tavener shot back. Jesry sighed again.

"Fraa Jesry," I said, and managed to catch his eye and throw him a wry look—exactly the kind of signal to which Barb was oblivious. "Fraa Tavener seems very keen on the topic. The fire's dying fast. We only have a few more minutes here. Why don't you go on ahead of us and show him that research. We'll put out the fire and tidy up."

Everyone was quiet for a while, because every one of us—including I—was startled by what had just happened: I had bossed Jesry around. Unprecedented! But I didn't care. I was too busy caring about other things.

"Right," Jesry said, and stomped off into the dark with Barb in tow. The rest of us stood there silently until the sound of Barb's questions had been drowned out by the seething of the fire and the burble of the river over ice-shoals.

"You want to talk about the tablet," Lio predicted.

"It's time to bring that thing down and look at it," I said.

"I'm surprised you haven't been in more of a hurry," Tulia said. "I've been dying to see that thing."

"Remember what happened to Orolo," I said. "He was incautious. Or maybe he just didn't care whether he got caught."

"Do *you* care?" Tulia asked. It was a blunt question that made the others uneasy. But no one edged away. They all looked at me, keen to hear my answer. The grief that had hit me at the moment Statho had called Orolo's name was still with me all the time, but I had learned that it could transform in a flash to anger. Not jumping-up-and-down anger but cold implacable fury that settled in my viscera and made me think some most unpleasant thoughts. It was distorting my face; I knew this because younger fids who had used to give me a pleasant greeting when I encountered them in a gallery or on the meadow now averted their eyes.

"Frankly no," I said. This was a lie, but it felt good. "I don't care whether I get Thrown Back. But you guys are all involved in it too, and so I'm going to be careful for your sakes. Remember, this tablet might have no useful information whatsoever. Even if it does, we might have to stare into the thing for months or even years before we see anything. So we are talking about a lengthy and secret campaign."

"Well, it seems to me that we owe it to Orolo to try," Tulia said.

"I can bring it down whenever you like," Lio said.

"I know of a dark room beneath Shuf's Dowment where we could view it," Arsibalt said.

"Very well," I said. "I only need a little bit of help from you guys. I'll do the rest myself. If I get caught, I'll say you knew nothing and I'll take responsibility for whatever happens. They'll give me Chapter Six, or worse. And then I'll walk out of here and try to find Orolo."

These words made Tulia and Lio quite emotional in different ways. She looked ready to weep and he looked ready to fight. But Arsibalt was merely impatient with me for being so slow. "There is a larger matter at stake than getting in trouble," he said. "You are avout, Fraa Erasmas. You swore a vow to keep the Discipline. It's the most solemn and important thing in your life. *That* is what you are putting into play. Whether or not you get caught and punished is a detail."

Arsibalt's words had a strong effect on me because they were true. I had an answer ready-made, but it wasn't one that I could speak aloud: I no longer respected that oath. Or at least, I no longer trusted those who were charged with enforcing the Discipline to which I had sworn. But I couldn't very well say as much to these friends of mine who *did* still respect it. My mind worked for a while, looking for a way to answer Arsibalt's challenge, and the others were content to stand there and poke at the dying fire and wait for me to speak.

"I trust Orolo," I finally said. "I trust that, in his mind, he was in no way violating the Discipline. That he was punished by lesser minds who don't understand what is really going on. I think he is—that he will be—a—"

"Say it!" Tulia snapped.

"Saunt," I said. "I will do this for Saunt Orolo."

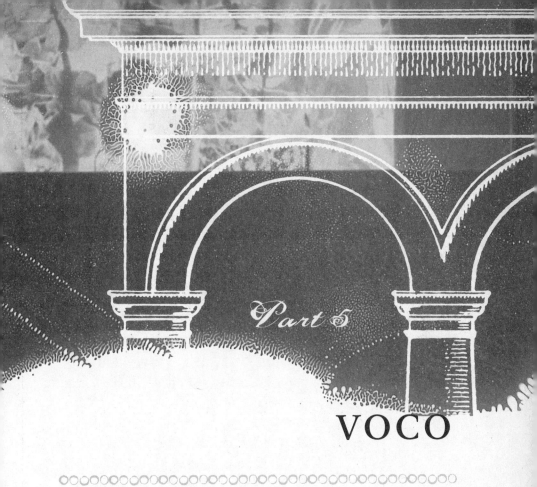

Part 5

VOCO

Lineage: (1) *(Extramuros)* A line of hereditary descent. (2) *(Intramuros)* A chronological sequence of avout who acquired and held property exceeding the bolt, chord, and sphere, each conferring the property upon a chosen heir at the moment of death. The wealth (see **Dowment**) accumulated by some Lineages (or at least, rumors of it) fostered the Baud Iconography. Lineages were eliminated as part of the Third Sack reforms.

—THE DICTIONARY, *4th edition, A.R. 3000*

Whatever you might say of his rich descendants, Fraa Shuf had had little wealth and no plan. That became obvious as soon as you descended the flagstone stairs into the cellar of the place that he had started and his heirs had finished. I write *cellar*, but it is more true to say that there was some number of cellars—I never made an exact count—cemented to one another in some graph that no one fully understood. It was a real accomplishment, in a way, to have left such a mess under a building so small. Arsibalt, of course, had an explanation: Shuf's avocation was stone-mason. He had begun the project, circa 1200, as a sort of eccentric pastime. He'd meant only to build a narrow tower with a room at the top where one avout could sit and meditate. That done, he'd passed it on to a fid who had noticed the tower beginning to lean, and had spent much of his life replacing the foundation—a tetchy sort of undertaking that involved digging out cavities beneath what was already there and socking huge stone blocks into the holes. He'd ended up with more foundation than was really needed, and passed it on to another mason who had done more digging, more foundation work, and more wall-building. And so it had gone for some generations until the Lineage had begun to gather wealth beyond the building itself and had needed a place to store it. The old foundation-work had then been rediscovered, re-excavated, walled, floored, vaulted, and extended. For one of the toxic things about Lineages was that rich avout could get not-so-rich ones to do things for them in exchange for better food, better drink, and better lodging.

Anyway, by the time that the Reformed Old Faanians had begun sneaking back to the ruin of Shuf's Dowment, hundreds of years after the Third Sack, the earth had reclaimed much of the cellars. I wasn't sure how the dirt got into those places and covered the floor so deep. Some process humans couldn't fathom because it went on so gradually. The ROF, who had been so diligent about fixing up the above-ground part, had almost completely ignored the cellars. To your right as you reached the bottom of the stairs there was one chamber where they stored wine and some silver table-service that was hauled out for special occasions. Beyond that, the cellars were a wilderness.

Arsibalt, contrary to his reputation, had become its intrepid explorer. His maps were ancient floor-plans that he found in the Library and his tools were a pickaxe and a shovel. The mystical object of his quest was a vaulted sub-basement that according to legend was where Shuf's Lineage had stored its gold. If any such place had ever existed, it had been found and cleaned out during the Third Sack. But to rediscover it would be interesting. It would also be a boon for the ROF since, in recent years, avout of other orders had entertained themselves by circulating rumors to the effect that the ROF had found or were accumulating treasure down there. Arsibalt could put such rumors to rest by finding the sub-basement and then inviting people to go and see it for themselves.

But there was no hurry—there never was, with him—and no one was expecting results before Arsibalt's hair had turned white. From time to time he would come tromping back over the bridge covered with dirt and fill our bath with silt, and we would know he had gone on another expedition.

So I was surprised when he took me down those stairs, turned left instead of right, led me through a few twists and turns that looked too narrow for him, and showed me a rusty plate in the floor of a dirty, wet-smelling room. He hauled it up to expose a cavity below, and an aluminum step-ladder that he had pilfered from somewhere else in the concent. "I was obliged to saw the legs off—a little," he confessed, "as the ceiling is quite low. After you."

The legendary treasure-vault turned out to be approximately one arm-span wide and high. The floor was dirt. Arsibalt had spread

out a poly tarp so that perishable things—"such as your bony arse, Raz"—could exist here without continually drawing up moisture from the earth. Oh, and there wasn't any treasure. Just a lot of graffiti carved into the walls by disappointed slines.

It was just about the nastiest place imaginable to work. But we had almost no choices. It wasn't as if I could sit up on my pallet at night and throw my bolt over my head like a tent and stare at the forbidden tablet.

We employed the oldest trick in the book—literally. In the Old Library, Tulia found a great big fat book that no one had pulled down from the shelf in eleven hundred years: a compendium of papers about a kind of elementary particle theorics that had been all the rage from 2300 to 2600, when Saunt Fenabrast had proved it was wrong. We cut a circle from each page until we had formed a cavity in the heart of this tome that was large enough to swallow the photomnemonic tablet. Lio carried it up to the Fendant court in a stack of other books and brought it back down at suppertime, much heavier, and handed it over to me. The next day I gave it to Arsibalt at breakfast. When I saw him at supper he told me that the tablet was now in place. "I looked at it, a little," he said.

"What did you learn?" I asked him.

"That the Ita have been diligent about keeping Clesthyra's Eye spotless," he said. "One of them comes every day to dust it. Sometimes he eats his lunch up there."

"Nice place for it," I said. "But I was thinking of night-time observations."

"I'll leave those to you, Fraa Erasmas."

Now I only wanted an excuse to go to Shuf's Dowment a lot. Here at last politics worked in my favor. Those who looked askance at the ROF's fixing up the Dowment did so because it seemed like a sneaky way of getting something for nothing. If asked, the ROF would always insist that anyone was welcome to go there and work. But New Circles and especially Edharians rarely did so. Partly this was the usual inter-Order rivalry. Partly it was current events.

"How have your brothers and sisters been treating you lately?" Tulia asked me one day as we were walking back from Provener. The shape of her voice was not warm-fuzzy. More curious-analytical. I turned around to walk backwards in front of her so that I could look at her face. She got annoyed and raised her eyebrows. She was coming of age in a month. After that, she could take part in liaisons without violating the Discipline. Things between us had become awkward.

"Why do you ask? Just curious," I said.

"Stop making a spectacle of yourself and I'll tell you."

I hadn't realized I was making a spectacle of myself but I turned back around and fell in step beside her.

"There is a new strain of thought," Tulia said, "that Orolo was actually Thrown Back as retribution for the politicking that took place during the Eliger season."

"Whew!" was the most eloquent thing I could say about that. I walked on in silence for a while. It was the most ridiculous thing I'd ever heard. If you couldn't be Thrown Back for stealing mead and selling it on the black market to buy forbidden consumer goods, then what *wouldn't* bring down the Anathema? And yet—

"Ideas like that are evil," I said, "because some creepy-crawly part of your brain wants to believe in them even while your logical mind is blasting them to pieces."

"Well, some among the Edharians have been letting their creepy-crawly brains get the better of them," Tulia said. "They don't want to believe in the mead and the speelycaptor. Apparently, Orolo brokered a three-way deal that sent Arsibalt to the ROF in exchange for—"

"Stop," I said, "I don't want to hear it."

"You know what Orolo did and so it's easier for you to accept," she said. "Others are having trouble with it—they want to make it into a political conspiracy and say that the thing with the mead never happened."

"Not even I am that cynical about Suur Trestanas," I said. In the corner of my eye I saw Tulia turn her head to look at me.

"Okay," I admitted, "Let me put it differently. I don't think she's a conspiracist. I think she's just plain evil."

That seemed to satisfy Tulia.

"Look," I said, "Fraa Orolo used to say that the concent was just like the outside world, except with fewer shiny objects. I had no idea what he was getting at. Now that he's gone, I see it. Our knowledge doesn't make us better or wiser. We can be just as nasty as those slines that beat up Lio and Arsibalt for the fun of it."

"Did Orolo have an answer?"

"I think he did," I said, "he was trying to explain it to me during Apert. Look for things that have beauty—it tells you that a ray is shining in from—well—"

"A true place? The Hylaean Theoric World?" Again her face was hard to read. She wanted to know whether I believed in all that stuff. And I wanted to know if *she* did. I reckoned the stakes were higher for her. As an Edharian, I could get away with it. "Yeah," I said. "I don't know if he would have called it by that name. But it's what he was driving at."

"Well," she said, after giving it a few moments' thought, "it's better than spending your life swapping conspiracy theories."

That's not saying much, I thought. But I didn't say it out loud. The decision Tulia had made to join the New Circle was a real decision with real consequences. One of which was that she must be guarded when talking about ideas like the HTW that they considered to be superstitions. She could believe in that stuff if she wanted; but she had to keep it to herself, and it was bad form for me to try to pry it out of her.

Anyway I now had an excuse to hang around at Shuf's Dowment: I was trying to act as a peacemaker among the orders by accepting the ROF's standing invitation.

After breakfast each morning I would attend a lecture, typically with Barb, and work with him on proofs and problems until Provener and the midday meal. After that I would go out to the back part of the meadow where Lio and I were getting ready for the weed war, and work, or pretend to, for a while. I kept an eye on the bay window of Shuf's Dowment, up on the hill on the other side of the river. Arsibalt kept a stack of books on the windowsill next to his big chair. If someone else was there, he would turn these so that their spines were toward the window. I could see their dark brown bindings from the meadow. But if he found himself alone, he would turn them so that their white page-edges were visible. When I noticed this I would stop work, go to a niche-gallery, fetch my theorics notes, and carry them over the bridge and through the page-tree-coppice to Shuf's Dowment, as if I were going there to study. A few minutes later I'd be down in the sub-cellar, sitting crosslegged on that tarp and working with the tablet. When I was finished I would come back up through the cellars. Before ascending the flagstone steps I would look for another signal: if someone else was in the building, Arsibalt would close the door at the top of the stairs, but if he were alone, he'd leave it ajar.

One of the many advantages that photomnemonic tablets held over ordinary phototypes was that they made their own light, so you could work with them in the dark. This tablet began and ended with daylight. If I ran it back to the very beginning, it became a featureless pool of white light with a faint bluish tinge: the unfocused light of sun and sky that had washed over the tablet after I had activated it on top of the Pinnacle during Fraa Paphlagon's Voco. If I put the tablet into play mode I could then watch a brief funny-looking transition as it had been slid into Clesthyra's Eye, and then, suddenly, an image, perfectly crisp and clear but geometrically distorted.

Most of the disk was a picture of the sky. The sun was a neat white circle, off-center. Around the tablet's rim was a dark, uneven fringe, like a moldy rind on a wheel of cheese: the horizon, all of it, in every direction. In this fisheye geometry, "down" for us humans—i.e., toward the ground—was always outward toward the rim of the tablet. Up was always inward toward the center. If several people had stood in a circle around Clesthyra's eye, their waists would have appeared around the circumference of the image and their heads would have projected inward like spokes of a wheel.

So much information was crammed into the tablet's outer fringe that I had to use its pan and zoom functions to make sense of it. The bright sky-disk seemed to have a deep dark notch cut into it at one place. On closer examination, this was the pedestal of the zenith mirror, which stood right next to Clesthyra's Eye. Like the north arrow on a map, this gave me a reference point that I could use to get my bearings and find other things. About halfway around the rim from it was a wider, shallower notch in the sky-disk, difficult to make sense of. But if I turned it about the right way and gave my eye a moment to get used to the distortion, I could understand it as a human figure, wrapped in a bolt that covered everything except one hand and forearm. These were reaching radially outward (which meant down) and became grotesquely oversized before being cropped by the edge of the tablet. This monstrosity was me reaching toward the base of the Eye, having just inserted the tablet and secured the dust cover. The first time I saw this I laughed out loud because it made my elbow look as big as the moon, and by zooming in on it I could see a mole and count the hairs and freckles. My attempt to hide my identity by hooding myself had been a joke! If Suur Trestanas had found this tablet she could have found the culprit by going around and examining everyone's right elbow.

When I let the tablet play forward, I could see the notch-that-was-me melt into the dark horizon-rim as I departed. A few moments later, a dark mote streaked around the tablet in a long arc, close to the rim: the aerocraft that had taken Fraa Paphlagon away to the Panjandrums. By freezing this and zooming in I could see the aerocraft clearly, not quite so badly distorted because it was farther away: the rotors and the streams of exhaust from its engines frozen, the pilot's face, mostly covered by a dark visor, caught in sunlight shining through the windscreen, his lips parted as if he were speaking into the microphone that curved alongside his cheek. When I ran the time point forward a few minutes I was able to see the aerocraft flying back in the other direction, this time with the face of Fraa Paphlagon framed in a side-window, gazing back at the concent as if he'd never seen it before.

Then, by sliding my finger up along the side of the tablet for a short distance, I was able to make the sun commit its arc across the sky-disk and sink into the horizon. The tablet went dark. Stars must be recorded on it, but my eyes couldn't see them very well because they hadn't adjusted to the dark yet. A few red comets flashed across it—the lights of aerocraft. Then the disk brightened again and the sun exploded from the edge and launched itself across the sky the next morning.

If I ran my finger all the way up the side of the tablet in one continuous motion, it flashed like a strobe light: seventy-eight flashes in all, one for each day that the tablet had lodged in Clesthyra's Eye. Coming to the last few seconds and slowing down the playback, I was able to watch myself emerging from the top of the stairs and approaching the Eye to remove the tablet during Fraa Orolo's Anathem. But I hated to see this part of it because of the way my face looked. I only checked it once, just to be sure that the tablet had continued recording all the way until the moment I'd retrieved it.

I erased the first and last few seconds of the recording, so that if the tablet were confiscated it would not contain any images of me. Then I began reviewing it in greater detail. Arsibalt had mentioned seeing the Ita in this thing. Sure enough, on the second day, a little after noon, a dark bulge reached in from the rim and blotted out most of the sky for a minute. I ran it back and played it at normal speed. It was one of the Ita. He approached from the top of the stairs carrying a squirt-bottle and a rag. He spent a minute cleaning the zenith mirror, then approached Clesthyra's Eye—which was when his image really became huge—and sprayed cleaning fluid on it. I flinched as if the stuff were being sprayed into my face. He gave it a good polish. I could see all the way up into his nostrils and count the hairs; I could see the tiny veins in his eyeballs and the striations in his iris. So there was no doubt that this was Sammann, the Ita whom Jesry and I had stumbled upon in Cord's machine-hall. In a moment he became much smaller as he backed away from the Eye. But he did not depart from the top of the Pinnacle immediately. He stood there for several moments, bobbed out of view, re-appeared, approached and loomed in Clesthyra's Eye for a little bit, then finally went away.

I zoomed in and watched that last bit again. After he polished the lens, he looked down, as if he had dropped something. He stooped over, which made all but his backside disappear beyond the rim of the tablet. When he stood up, bulging back into the picture again, he had something new in his hand: a rectangular object about the size of a book. I didn't have to zoom in on this to know what it was: the dust jacket that, a day previously, I had torn off this very tablet.

The wind had snatched it from my hand, and in my haste to leave, I had, like an idiot, left it lying where it had fallen.

Sammann examined it for a minute, turning it this way and that. After a while he seemed to get an idea of what it was. His head snapped around to look at me—at Clesthyra's Eye, rather. He approached and peered into the lens, then cocked his head, reached down, and (I guessed, though I couldn't see) prodded the little door that covered the tablet-slot. His face registered something. If I'd wanted, I could have zoomed in on his eyeballs and seen what was reflected in them. But I didn't need to because the look on his face told all.

Less than twenty-four hours after I had slipped that tablet into Clesthyra's Eye, someone else in this concent had known about it.

Sammann stood there for another minute, pondering. Then he folded up the dust jacket, inserted it into a breast-pocket of his cloak, turned his back on me, and walked away.

I moved the tablet forward to a cloudy night, thereby plunging myself into almost total blackness, and I sat there in that hole in the ground and tried to get over this.

I was remembering the other evening, standing around the campfire, when I had criticized Orolo for being incautious, and told my friends that I'd be much more careful. What an idiot I was!

Watching Sammann pick up that dust jacket and put two and two together, my face had flushed and my heart had thumped as if I were actually there on top of the Pinnacle with him. But this was just a recording of something that had happened months ago. And nothing had come of it. Granted, Sammann could spill the beans any time he chose.

That was unnerving. But I could do nothing about it. Feeling embarrassed by a mistake I'd made months ago was a waste of time. Better to think about what I was going to do now. Sit here in the dark worrying? Or keep investigating the contents of this tablet? Put that way, it wasn't a very difficult question. The fury that had taken up residence in my gut was a kind of anger that had to be acted upon. The action didn't need to be sudden or dramatic. If I'd joined one of the other orders, I might have made acting upon it into a sort of career. Using it as fuel, I could have spent the next ten or twenty years working my way up the hierarch ranks, looking for ways to make life nasty for those who had wronged Orolo. But the fact of the matter was that I'd joined the Edharians and thereby made myself powerless as far as the internal politics of the concent were concerned. So I tended to think in terms of murdering Fraa Spelikon. Such was my anger that for a little while this actually made sense, and from time to time I'd find myself musing about how to carry it off. There were a lot of big knives in the kitchen.

So how fortunate it was that I had this tablet, and a place in which to view it. It gave me something to act on—something, that is, besides Fraa Spelikon's throat. If I worked on it hard enough and were lucky, perhaps I could come up with some result that I could announce one evening in the Refectory to the humiliation of Spelikon, Trestanas, and Statho. Then I could storm out of the concent in disgust before they had time to Throw me Back.

And in the meantime, studying this thing answered that need in my gut to take some kind of action in response to what had been inflicted on Orolo. And I'd found that taking such action was the only way to transmute my anger back into grief. And when I was grieving—instead of angry—young fids no longer shied away from me, and my mind was no longer filled with images of blood pumping from Fraa Spelikon's severed arteries.

So I had no choice but to put Sammann and the dust cover out of my mind, and concentrate instead on what Clesthyra's Eye had seen during the night-time. I had kept track of the weather those seventy-seven nights. More than half had been cloudy. There had only been seventeen nights of really clear seeing.

Once I allowed my eyes to adjust to the darkness, it was easy to find north on this thing, because it was the pole around which all the stars revolved. If the image was frozen, or playing back at something like normal speed, the stars appeared as stationary points of light. But if I sped up the playback, each star, with the exception of the pole star, traced an arc centered on the pole as Arbre rotated beneath it. Our fancier telescopes had polar axis systems, driven by the clock, that eliminated this problem. These telescopes rotated "backwards" at the same speed as Arbre rotated "forwards" so that the stars remained stationary above them. Clesthyra's Eye was not so equipped.

The tablet could be commanded to tell what it had seen in several different ways. To this point I'd been using it like a speelycaptor with its play, pause, and fast-forward buttons. But it could do things that speelycaptors couldn't, such as integrate an image over a span of time. This was an echo of the Praxic Age when, instead of tablets like this one, cosmographers had used plates coated with chemicals sensitive to light. Because many of the things they looked at were so faint, they had often needed to expose those plates for hours at a time. A photomnemonic tablet worked both ways. If you were to "play back" such a record in speelycaptor mode, you might see nothing more than a few stars and a bit of haze, but if you configured the tablet to show the still image integrated over time, a spiral galaxy or nebula might pop out.

So my first experiment was to select a night that had been clear, and configure the tablet to integrate all the light that Clesthyra's Eye had taken in that night into a single still image. The first results weren't very good because I set the start time too early and the stop time too late, so everything was washed out by the brightness in the sky after dusk and before dawn. But after making some adjustments I was able to get the image I wanted.

It was a black disk etched with thousands of fine concentric arcs, each of which was the track made by a particular star or planet as Arbre spun beneath it. This image was crisscrossed by several red dotted lines and brilliant white streaks: the traces made by the lights of aerocraft passing across our sky. The ones in the center, made by high-flying craft, ran nearly straight. Over toward one edge the star-field was all but obliterated by a sheaf of fat white curves: craft coming in to land at the local aerodrome, all following more or less the same glide path.

Only one thing in this whole firmament did not move: the pole star. If our hypothesis was correct as to what Fraa Orolo had been looking for—namely, something in a polar orbit—then, assuming it was bright enough to be seen on this thing, it ought to register as a streak passing near the pole star. It would be straight or nearly so, and oriented at right angles to the myriad arcs made by the stars—it would move north-south as they moved east-west.

Not only that, but such a satellite should make more than one such streak on a given night. Jesry and I had worked it out. A satellite in a low orbit should make a complete pass around Arbre in about an hour and a half. If it made a streak on the tablet as it passed over the pole at, say, midnight, then at about one-thirty it should make another streak, and another at three, and another at four-thirty. It should always stay in the same plane with respect to the fixed stars. But during each of those ninety-minute intervals Arbre would rotate through twenty-two and a half degrees of longitude. And so the successive streaks that a given satellite made should not be drawn on top of each other. Instead they should be separated by angles of about twenty-two and a half degrees (or pi/8 as theoricians measured angles). They should look like cuts on a pie.

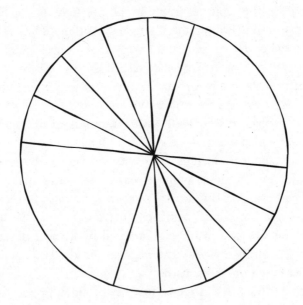

My work on that first day in the sub-cellar consisted of making the tablet produce a time exposure for the first clear night, then zooming in on the vicinity of the pole star and looking for something that resembled a pie-cutting diagram. I succeeded in this so easily that I was almost disappointed. Because there was more than one such satellite, what it looked like was more complex:

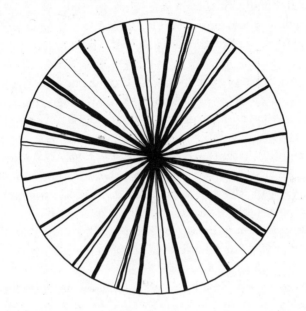

But if I looked at it long enough I could see it as several different pie-cut diagrams piled on top of each other.

"It's an anticlimax," I told Jesry at supper. We had somehow managed to avoid Barb and sit together in a corner of the Refectory.

"Again?"

"I'd sort of thought that if I could see anything at all in a polar orbit, that'd be the end of it. Mystery solved, case closed. But it is not so. There are several satellites in polar orbits. Probably have been ever since the Praxic Age. Old ones wear out and fall down. The Panjandrums launch new ones."

"That is not a new result," he pointed out. "If you go out at night and stand facing north and wait long enough, you can see those things hurtling over the pole with the naked eye."

I chewed a bit of food as I struggled to master the urge to punch him in the nose. But this was how things were done in theorics. It wasn't only the Lorites who said *that is not a new result*. People re-invented the wheel all the time. There was nothing shameful in it. If the rest of us oohed and aahed and said, "Gosh, a wheel, no one's ever thought of that before," just to make that person feel good, nothing would ever get done. But still it stung to risk so much and do so much work to get a result, only to be told it was nothing new.

"I don't claim it is a new result," I told him, with elaborate patience. "I'm only letting you know what happened the first time I was able to spend a couple of hours with the tablet. And I guess I am posing a question."

"All right. What is the question?"

"Fraa Orolo must have known that there were several satellites in polar orbits and that this wasn't a big deal. To a cosmographer, it's no more remarkable than aerocraft flying overhead."

"An annoyance. A distraction," Jesry said, nodding.

"So what was it that he risked Anathem to see?"

"He didn't just *risk* Anathem. He—"

I waved him off. "You know what I mean. This is no time to go Kefedokhles."

Jesry gazed into space above my left shoulder. Most others would have been embarrassed or irritated by my remark. Not him! He couldn't care less. How I envied him! "We know that he needed a speelycaptor to see it," Jesry said. "The naked eye wasn't good enough."

"He had to see all of this in a different way. He couldn't make time exposures on a tablet," I put in.

"The best he could do, once the starhenge had been locked, was to stand out in that vineyard, freezing his arse off, looking at the pole star through the speelycaptor. Waiting for something to streak across."

"When it showed up, it would zoom across the viewfinder in a few moments," I said. We were completing each other's sentences now. "But then what? What would he have learned?"

"The time," Jesry said. "He would know what time it was." He shifted his gaze to the tabletop, as if it were a speely of Orolo. "He makes a note of it. Ninety minutes later he looks again. He sees the same bird making its next pass over the pole." Lio referred to satellites as birds—this was military slang he'd picked up from books—and the rest of us had adopted the term.

"That sounds about as interesting as watching the hour hand on a clock," I said.

"Well, but remember, there's more than one of these birds," he said.

"I don't *have* to remember it—I spent the whole afternoon looking at them!" I reminded him.

But Jesry was on the trail of an idea and had no time for me and my petty annoyance. "They can't all be orbiting at the same altitude," he said. "Some must be higher than others—those would have longer periods. Instead of ninety minutes they might take ninety-one or a hundred three minutes to go around. By timing their orbits, Fraa Orolo could, by making enough observations, compile sort of—"

"A census," I said. "A list of all the birds that were up there."

"Once he had that in hand, if there was any change—any anomaly—he'd be able to detect it. But until such time as he had completed that census, as you call it—"

"He'd be working in the dark, in more ways than one, wouldn't he?" I said. "He'd see a bird pass over the pole but he wouldn't know which bird it was, or if there was anything unusual about it."

"So if that's true we have to follow in his footsteps," Jesry said. "Your first objective should be to compile such a census."

"That is much easier for me than it was for Orolo," I said. "Just looking at the tracks on the tablet you can see that some are more widely spread—bigger slices of the pie—than others. Those must be the high flyers."

"Once you get used to looking at these images, you might be able to notice anomalies just by their general appearance," Jesry speculated.

Which was easy for him to say, since he wasn't the one doing it!

For the last little while he had seemed restless and bored. Now he broke eye contact, gazed around the Refectory as if seeking someone more interesting—but then turned his attention back to me. "New topic," he announced.

"Affirmative. State name of topic," I answered, but if he knew I was making fun of him, he didn't show it.

"Fraa Paphlagon."

"The Hundreder who was Evoked."

"Yes."

"Orolo's mentor."

"Yes. The Steelyard says that his Evocation, and the trouble Orolo got into, must be connected."

"Seems reasonable," I said. "I guess I've sort of been assuming that."

"Normally we'd have no way of knowing what a Hundreder was working on—not until the next Centennial Apert, anyway. But before Paphlagon went into the Upper Labyrinth, twenty-two years ago, he wrote some treatises that got sent out into the world at the Decennial Apert of 3670. Ten years later, and again just a few months ago, our Library got its usual Decennial deliveries. So, I've been going through all that stuff looking for anything that references Paphlagon's work."

"Seems really indirect," I pointed out. "We've got all of Paphlagon's work right here, don't we?"

"Yeah. But that's not what I'm looking for," Jesry said. "I'm more interested in knowing who, out there, was paying attention to Paphlagon. Who read his works of 3670, and thought he had an interesting mind? Because—"

"Because *someone*," I said, getting it, "someone out there in the Sæcular world must have said 'Paphlagon's our man—yank him, and bring him to us!'"

"Exactly."

"So what have you found?"

"Well, that's the thing," Jesry said. "Turns out Paphlagon had two careers, in a way."

"What do you mean—like an avocation?"

"You could say his avocation was philosophy. Metatheorics. Procians might even call it a sort of religion. On the one hand, he's a proper cosmographer, doing the same sort of stuff as Orolo. But in his spare time he's thinking big ideas, and writing it down—and people on the outside noticed."

"What kind of ideas?"

"I don't want to go there now," Jesry said.

"Well, damn it—"

He held up a hand to settle me. "Read it yourself! That's not what I'm about. I'm about trying to reckon who picked him and why. There's lots of cosmographers, right?"

"Sure."

"So if he was Evoked to answer cosmography questions, you have to ask—"

"Why him in particular?"

"Yeah. But it's rare to work on the metatheorical stuff he was interested in."

"I see where you're going," I said. "The Steelyard tells us he must have been Evoked for *that*—not the cosmography."

"Yeah," Jesry said. "Anyway, not that many people paid attention to Paphlagon's metatheorics, at least, judging from the stuff we got in the deliveries of 3680 and 3690. But there's one suur at Baritoe, name of Aculoä, who really seems to admire him. Has written two books about Paphlagon's work."

"Tenner or—"

"No, that's just it. She's a Unarian. Thirty-four years straight."

So she was a teacher. There was no other reason to spend more than a few years in a Unarian math.

"Latter Evenedrician," Jesry said, answering my next question before I'd asked it.

"I don't know much about that order."

"Well, remember when Orolo told us that Saunt Evenedric worked on different stuff during the second half of his career?"

"Actually, I think Arsibalt's the one who told us that, but—"

Jesry shrugged off my correction. "The Latter Evenedricians are interested in exactly that stuff."

"All right," I said, "so you reckon Suur Aculoä fingered Paphlagon?"

"No way. She's a philosophy teacher, a One-off . . ."

"Yeah, but at one of the Big Three!"

"That's my point," Jesry said, a little testy, "a lot of important Sæculars did a few years at Big Three maths when they were younger—before they went out and started their careers."

"You think this suur had a fid, ten or fifteen years ago maybe, who's gone on to become a Panjandrum. Aculoä taught the fid all about how great and wise Fraa Paphlagon was. And now, something's happened—"

"Something," Jesry said, nodding confidently, "that made that ex-fid say, 'that tears it, we need Paphlagon here yesterday!'"

"But what could that something be?"

Jesry shrugged. "That's the whole question, isn't it?"

"Maybe we could get a clue by investigating Paphlagon's writings."

"That is obvious," Jesry said. "But it's rather difficult when Arsibalt's using them as a semaphore."

It took me a moment to make sense of this. "That stack of books in the window—"

Jesry nodded. "Arsibalt took everything Paphlagon ever wrote to Shuf's Dowment."

I laughed. "Well then, what about Suur Aculoä?"

"Tulia's going through her works now," Jesry said, "trying to figure out if she had any fids who amounted to anything."

○○○

Ringing Vale: (1) A mountain valley renowned for the many small streams that spill down its rocky walls from glaciers poised above, producing a musical sound likened to the ringing of chimes. Also known as the Rill Vale, or (poetically) Vale of a Thousand Rills. (2) A math founded there in A.R.17, specializing in study and developments of martial arts and related topics (see Vale-lore).

Vale-lore: In New Orth, an omnibus term covering armed and unarmed martial arts, military history, strategy, and tactics, all of which are strongly associated, in the Mathic world, with the avout of the Ringing Vale, who have made such topics their specialty since a math was founded there in A.R.17. Note: in informal speech and in Fluccish, the word is sometimes contracted to *vlor*. However, note that this variant emphasizes the martial-arts side of Vale-lore at the expense of its more academic and bureaucratic aspects. Extramuros, *Vlor* is an entertainment genre, and (for those Sæculars who can be moved to stand up and practice such things, as opposed to merely watching them) a type of academy.

—THE DICTIONARY, *4th edition, A.R. 3000*

Working in a hole in the ground had made me ignorant of all these goings-on. But now that Jesry had let me know that my fraas and suurs were working so hard, I redoubled my efforts with the tablet. Stored on that thing I had all of seventeen clear nights. Once I got the knack, it took me about half an hour's work to configure the tablet to give me the time exposure for a given night. Then, using a protractor, I would spend another half hour or so measuring the angles between streaks. As Jesry had predicted, some birds made slightly larger angles than others, reflecting their longer periods, but the angle for a given bird was always the same, every orbit, every night. So in a sense it only took a single night's observations to make a rough draft of the census. But I went ahead and did it for all seventeen of the clear nights anyway, just to be thorough, and because frankly I had no idea what to do next. I could polish off one, sometimes two nights' observations every time I got a chance to go down into that sub-cellar, but I didn't get that chance every day.

By the time I finished, I had been at it for about three weeks. Buds were out on the page trees. Birds were flying north. Fraas and suurs were poking around in their tangles, arguing about whether it was time to plant. The barbarian weed-horde was marshaling on the riverbank and getting ready to invade the fertile Plains of Thrania. Arsibalt was two-thirds of the way through his pile of Paphlagon.

The vernal equinox was only a few days away. Apert had begun on the morning of the autumnal equinox—half a year ago! I could not understand where the time had gone.

It had gone the same place as all the thousands of years before it. I had spent it working. It didn't matter that my work was secret, illicit, and could have got me Thrown Back. The concent didn't care about that. Certain persons would have cared a lot. But this was a place for the avout to spend their lives working on such projects. And now that I *had* a project, I was a part of that concent in a way I'd never been before, and the place was the right place for me.

Since Arsibalt, Jesry, and Tulia had their minds on other projects, I didn't tell them about Sammann. That was a topic reserved for Lio when we were out in the meadow coaxing the starblossom to grow in the right direction. Or, since it was Lio, doing whatever else had most recently jumped into his mind.

We had reacted in different ways to the loss of Orolo. In my case, it was bloody revenge fantasies that I kept to myself. Lio, on the other hand, had become entranced by ever weirder varieties of vlor. Two weeks ago, he had tried to get me interested in rake vlor, which I guessed was inspired by the story of Diax casting out the Enthusiasts. I had declined on grounds of not wanting to get a blood infection—a weaponized rake could give you mass-produced puncture wounds. Last week he had developed a keen interest in shovel vlor, and we had spent a lot of time squatting on the riverbank sharpening spades with rocks.

When he led me down to the river again one day, I assumed it was for more of the same. But he kept looking back over his shoulder and leading me in deeper. I'd been on enough furtive expeditions as a fid to know that he was checking the sight-lines to the Warden Regulant's windows. Old habits kicked in; I became silent, and moved from one shady place to another until we had reached a place where the bending river had cut away the bank to form an overhang, sheltered from view. Fortunately no one was there having a liaison just now. It would have been a bad place for it anyway: mucky ground, lots of bugs, high probability of being interrupted by avout messing around on the river in boats.

Lio turned to face me. I was almost worried that he was going to make a pass at me.

But no. This was Lio we were talking about.

"I'd like you to punch me in the face," he said. As if he were asking me to scratch his back.

"Not that I haven't always dreamed of it," I said, "but why would *you* want it?"

"Hand-to-hand combat has been a common element of military training down through the ages," he proclaimed, as if I were a fid. "Long ago it was learned that recruits—no matter how much training they had received—tended to forget everything they knew the first time they got punched in the face."

"The first time *in their lives,* you mean?"

"Yeah. In peaceful, affluent societies where brawling is frowned on, this is a common problem."

"Not being punched in the face a lot is a *problem?*"

"It is," Lio said, "if you join the military and find yourself in hand-to-hand combat with someone who is actually trying to kill you."

"But Lio," I said, "you *have* been punched in the face. It happened at Apert. Remember?"

"Yes," he said, "and I have been trying to learn from that experience."

"So why do you want me to punch you in the face *again?*"

"As a way to find out whether I *have learned.*"

"Why me? Why not Jesry? He seems more the type."

"That is the problem."

"I see your point. Why not Arsibalt, then?"

"He wouldn't do it for real—and then he'd complain that he'd hurt his hand."

"What are you going to tell people if you show up for dinner with a busted face?"

"That I was battling evildoers."

"Try again."

"That I was practicing falls, and landed wrong."

"What if I don't want to mess up my hand?"

He smiled and produced a pair of heavy leather work gloves. "Stuff some rags under the knuckles," he suggested, as I was pulling them on, "if you're that worried about it."

Grandsuurs Tamura and Ylma drifted by on a punt. We pretended to pull weeds until they were out of sight.

"Okay," Lio said, "my objective is to perform a simple takedown on you—"

"Oh, *now* you tell me!"

"Nothing we haven't done a hundred times," he said, as if I would find this reassuring. "That's why we came here." He stomped the damp sand of the riverbank. "Soft ground."

"Why—?"

"If I put up my hands to defend my face, I won't be able to complete my objective."

"I get it."

Suddenly he came at me and took me down. "You lose," he proclaimed, getting up.

"Okay." I sighed, and clambered to my feet. Immediately he wheeled around and took me down again. I threw a playful blow at his head, way too late. This time he took me down a lot harder. Every one of the small muscles in my head felt as if it had been strained. He planted a dirty hand on top of my face and shoved off while getting back to his feet. The message was clear.

The next time I tried for real, but I didn't have my feet planted and wasn't able to hit very hard. And he was coming in too low.

The time after that, I got my center of gravity low, planted my feet in the mud, made a bone connection from hip to fist, and drilled him right on the cheekbone. "Good!" he moaned, as he was climbing off me. "See if you can actually slow me down though—that's the whole point, remember?"

I think we did it about ten more times. Since I was suffering a lot more abuse than he was, I sort of lost track. On my best go, I was able to throw him off stride for a moment—but he still took me down.

"How much longer are we going to do this?" I asked, lying in the mud, in the bottom of an Erasmas-shaped crater. If I refused to get up, he couldn't take me down.

He scooped up a double handful of river water and splashed it on his face, rinsing away blood from nostrils and eyebrows. "That should do," he said. "I've learned what I wanted."

"Which is?" I asked, daring to sit up.

"That I've adjusted, since what happened at Apert."

"We did all that to obtain a *negative result*?" I exclaimed, getting to my knees.

"If you want to think of it that way," he said, and scooped up more water.

I'd never get such a fine opportunity again, so I rolled up, put a foot in his backside, and sent him headlong into the river.

Later, as Lio was engrossed in the comparatively normal and sane activity of shovel-sharpening, I got us back on the topic of what I'd been seeing in the tablet: specifically, Sammann's behavior during his noon visits.

Once I'd gotten over that sick feeling of having been found out, I'd begun to brood over some other questions. Was it merely a coincidence that the Ita who had discovered the dust jacket was the same one who had visited Cord in the machine hall? I reckoned that either it *was* a simple coincidence, or else that this Sammann was some kind of high-ranking Ita who was responsible for important tasks having to do with the starhenge. In any case, it booted me nothing to speculate about it.

"Has dis Ita tried to cobbudicade wid you?" Lio asked through puffy lips.

"You mean, like, sneaking into the math at night to slip me notes?"

Lio was baffled by my answer. He showed this in his usual way: by correcting his posture. The scrape of the rock on the shovel paused for a moment. Then he got it. "No, I don't mean *in real time*," he said. "I mean, *on the tablet* does he—you know."

"No, Thistlehead, I have to confess I haven't the faintest idea—"

"If anyone understands surveillance, it's those guys," Lio pointed out.

"If you buy into Saunt Patagar's Assertion, sure."

Lio seemed disappointed that I was so naïve as not to believe this. He went back to work on that rock. The scraping really set my teeth on edge but I reckoned it must be putting the hurt on any spies who might be eavesdropping.

Apparently my new role at the Concent of Saunt Edhar was to be the sheltered innocent. I said, "Well, answer me this. If they have us under total surveillance, they must know everything about me and the tablet, right?"

"Well, yeah, you'd think so."

"So why hasn't anything happened?" I asked him. "It's not like Spelikon and Trestanas have soft spots for me."

"That doesn't surprise me," he insisted. "I don't think there's anything strange about that."

"How do you figure?"

He paused long enough to give me the idea he was making up an answer on the spot. He dipped his sharpening-rock into the river. "The Ita can't be telling the Warden Regulant everything they know. Trestanas would have to spend every minute of every day with them, to take in so much intelligence. The Ita must make decisions as to what they will pass on and what they will withhold."

What Lio was saying opened up all sorts of interesting scenarios that would take me some time to sort out. I didn't want to stand there with my mouth hanging open any longer than I already had, so I bent down and grabbed the handle of the shovel. It wasn't going to get any sharper. I looked around for a stand of slashberry that needed to be massacred. It didn't take long to find one. I made for it and Lio followed me.

"That's giving the Ita a lot of responsibility," I said, raising the shovel, then driving it down and forward into the roots of the slashberry canes. Several of them toppled. Most satisfying.

"Assume that they are as intelligent as we are," Lio said. "Come on! They operate complicated syntactic devices for a living. They created the Reticulum. No one knows better than they do that knowledge is power. By employing strategy and tactics in what they say and what they don't, they must be able to get things they want."

I took down a square yard of slashberry while thinking about what he said.

"You're saying there's a whole world of Ita/hierarch politics going on over there that we know nothing about."

"Has to be. Or else they wouldn't be human," Lio said.

Then he used Hypotrochian Transquaestiation on me: he changed the subject in such a way as to imply that the question had just been settled—that he had won the point and I had lost. "So, back to my question: does Sammann do anything else on the tablet that sends you a message—or at least indicates he knows that his image is being recorded?" He chucked his sharpening-rock into the river.

The correct response to Hypotrochian Transquaestiation was *Hey, not so fast!* but Lio's question was so interesting that I didn't make a fuss. "I don't know," I had to admit, after I'd spent an enjoyable minute or so taking down more slashberry. "But I'm getting bored measuring pie-slices. And I honestly don't know what else to look at next. So I'll have a look."

After that I couldn't get into the cellar for almost a week. The concent was getting ready for some equinox celebrations and so I had chant rehearsals. The weed war was entering a stage that demanded I draw at least one sketch of it. I had to get my tangle planted. When I was free, there always seemed to be other people at Shuf's Dowment. The place was becoming hip!

"Be careful what you wish for," Arsibalt moaned to me, one afternoon. I was helping him carry a stack of beehive frames into a wood shop. "I invited one and all to use the Dowment—now they are doing so—and I can't work there!"

"Nor I," I pointed out.

"And now this!" He picked up a putty knife, which I was pretty sure was the wrong tool for the job, and began to pick absent-mindedly at a patch of rotten wood on the corner of a frame. "Disaster!"

"Do you know anything about woodworking?" I asked.

"No," he admitted.

"How about the metatheorical works of Fraa Paphlagon?"

"That I know a few things about," he said. "And what is more, I think Orolo wanted us to learn about them."

"How so?"

"Remember our last dialog with him?"

"Pink nerve-gas-farting dragons. Of course."

"We must come up with a more dignified name for it before we commit it to ink," Arsibalt said with a grimace. "Anyway, I believe that Orolo was pushing us to think about some of the ideas that were—*are*—important to his mentor."

"Funny he didn't mention Paphlagon, in that case," I pointed out. "I remember talking about the later works of Saunt Evenedric, but—"

"One leads to the other. We would have found our way to Paphlagon in due course."

"You would've, maybe," I said. "What's it all about?" This seemed a reasonable question. But Arsibalt flinched.

"The sort of stuff Procians hate us for."

"Like, the Hylaean Theoric World?" I asked.

"That's what they would call it, as a backhanded way of suggesting we are naïve. But, starting at least as early as Protas, the idea of the HTW was developed into a more sophisticated metatheorics. So you could say that Paphlagon's work is to classical Protan thought what modern group theory is to counting on one's fingers."

"But still related to it?"

"Certainly."

"I'm just thinking back to my conversation with that Inquisitor."

"Varax?"

"Yeah. I'm wondering whether his interest in the topic—"

"Correction: he was interested in *whether we were interested in it*," Arsibalt pointed out.

"Yeah, exactly—whether that might be further evidence for the existence of the Hypothetical Important Fid of Suur Aculoä."

"I think we should be careful speculating about the HIFOSA until Suur Tulia has actually found evidence of his or her existence,"

Arsibalt said. "Otherwise we'll be coming up with all manner of speculations that would never make it past the Rake."

"Well, without telling me everything you know about it," I said, "can you give me a clue as to why anyone in the Sæcular world would think Paphlagon's work might be of practical importance?"

"Yes," he said, "if you fix this beehive for me."

"You know about atom smashers? Particle accelerators?"

"Sure," I said. "Praxic Age installations. Huge and expensive. Used to test theories about elementary particles and forces."

"Yes," Arsibalt said. "If you can't test it, it's not theorics—it's metatheorics. A branch of philosophy. So, if you want to think of it this way, our test equipment is what defines the boundary separating theorics from philosophy."

"Wow," I said, "I'll bet a philosopher would really jump down your throat for talking that way. It's like saying that philosophy is nothing more than bad theorics."

"There are some theors who would say so," Arsibalt admitted. "But those people aren't really talking about philosophy *as philosophers would define it*. Rather, they are talking about something that theors begin to do when they get right up to the edge of what they can prove using the equipment they've got. They drive philosophers crazy by calling it philosophy or metatheorics."

"What kind of stuff are you talking about?"

"Well, they speculate as to what the next theory might look like. They develop the theory and try to use it to make predictions that might be testable. In the late Praxic Age, that usually meant constructing an even bigger and more expensive particle accelerator."

"And then came the Terrible Events," I said.

"Yes, no more expensive toys for theors after that," Arsibalt said. "But it's not clear that it actually made that much of a difference. The biggest machines, in those days, were already pushing the limits of what could be constructed on Arbre with reasonable amounts of money."

"I hadn't known that," I said. "I always tend to assume there's an infinite amount of money out there."

"There might as well be," Arsibalt said, "but most of it gets spent on pornography, sugar water, and bombs. There is only so much that can be scraped together for particle accelerators."

"So the Turn to Cosmography might have happened even without the Reconstitution."

"It was already happening," Arsibalt said, "as the theors of the very late Praxic Age were coming to terms with the fact that no machine would be constructed during their lifetimes that would be capable of testing the theorics to which they were devoting their careers."

"So those theors had no alternative but to look to the cosmos for givens."

"Yes," Arsibalt said. "And in the meantime we have people like Fraa Paphlagon."

"Meaning what? Both theors and philosophers?"

He thought about it. "I'm trying to respect your earlier request that I not simply bury you in Paphlagon," he explained, when he caught me looking, "but this forces me to work harder."

"Fair is fair," I pointed out, brandishing a crosscut saw that I had been putting to use.

"You could think of Paphlagon—and presumably Orolo—as *descendants* of people like Evenedric."

"Theors," I said, "who turned to philosophy when theorics stopped."

"Slowed down," Arsibalt corrected me, "waiting for results from places like Saunt Bunjo's."

Bunjo was a Millenarian math built around an empty salt mine two miles underground. Its fraas and suurs worked in shifts, sitting in total darkness waiting to see flashes of light from a vast array of crystalline particle detectors. Every thousand years they published their results. During the First Millennium they were pretty sure they had seen flashes on three separate occasions, but since then they had come up empty.

"So, in the meantime, they've been fooling around with ideas that people like Evenedric came up with when they reached the edge of theorics?"

"Yes," Arsibalt said. "There was a profusion of them, right around the time of the Reconstitution, all variations on the theme of the polycosm."

"The idea that our cosmos is not the only one."

"Yes. And that's what Paphlagon writes about when he isn't studying *this* cosmos."

"Now I'm a little confused," I said, "because I thought you told me just a minute ago that he was working on the HTW."

"Well, but you could think of Protism—the belief that there is another realm of existence populated by pure theorical forms—as the earliest and simplest polycosmic theory," he pointed out.

"Because it posits two cosmi," I said, trying to keep up, "one for us, and one for isosceles triangles."

"Yes."

"But the polycosmic theories I've heard about—the circa-Reconstitution ones—are a whole different kettle of fish. In those theories, there are multiple cosmi separate from our own—but similar. Full of matter and energy and fields. Always changing. Not eternal triangles."

"Not always as similar as you think," Arsibalt said. "Paphlagon is part of a tradition that believed that classical Protism was just another polycosmic theory."

"How could you possibly—"

"I can't tell you without telling you everything," Arsibalt said, holding up his fleshy hands. "The point I'm getting at is that he believes in some form of the Hylaean Theoric World. *And* that there are other cosmi. Those are the topics Suur Aculoä is interested in."

"So if the HIFOSA really exists—" I said.

"He or she summoned Paphlagon because the polycosm somehow became a hot topic."

"And we are guessing that whatever made it hot, also triggered the closure of the starhenge."

Arsibalt shrugged.

"Well, what could that possibly be?"

He shrugged again. "That's one for you and Jesry. But don't forget that the Panjandrums might simply be confused."

Finally one day I made it down into the sub-cellar of Shuf's Dowment and spent three hours watching Sammann eat lunches. He made the trip almost every day, but not always at the same time. If the weather was fine and the time of day was right, he would sit on the parapet, spread out some food on a little cloth, and enjoy the view while he ate. Sometimes he read a book. I couldn't identify all of his little morsels and delicacies, but they looked better than what we had for lunch. Sometimes, if the wind blew out of the northeast, we could smell the Ita cooking. It always seemed as if they were taunting us.

"Results!" I proclaimed to Lio the next time I was alone with him in the meadow. "Sort of."

"Yeah?"

"You were right, I think."

"Right about what?" For so much time had passed that he had forgotten our earlier talk about Sammann. I had to remind him. Then, he was taken aback. "Wow," he said, "this is big."

"Could be. I still don't know what to make of it," I said.

"What does he do? Hold up a sign in front of the Eye? Use sign language?"

"Sammann's too clever for that," I said.

"What? It sounds like you're speaking of an old friend."

"I almost feel that way about him by this point. He and I have had a lot of lunches together."

"So, how does he—*did* he—talk to you?"

"For the first sixty-eight days, he's a real bore," I said. "Then on Day Sixty-nine, something happens."

"Day Sixty-nine? What does that mean to the rest of us?"

"Well, it's about two weeks after the solstice and nine days before Orolo got Thrown Back."

"Okay. So what does Sammann do on Day Sixty-nine?"

"Well, normally, when he gets to the top of the stair, he unslings a bag from his shoulder and hangs it around a stone knob that sticks up from the parapet there. He cleans the optics. Then he goes over and sits on the parapet—it has a flat top about a foot wide—and takes his lunch out of that bag and spreads it out there and eats it."

"Okay. What happens on Day Sixty-nine?"

"In addition to the shoulder bag, he is carrying something cradled in one arm like a book. The first thing he does is set this down on the parapet. Then he goes about his usual routine."

"So it's sitting there in plain view of the Eye."

"Exactly."

"Can you zoom in on it?"

"Of course."

"Can you read its title?"

"Turns out it's not a book at all, Lio. It is another dust jacket—just like the one Sammann found up there the first day. Except this one is big and heavy because it contains—"

"Another tablet!" Lio exclaimed, then paused to consider it. "I wonder what that means."

"Well, we have to assume he had just picked it up elsewhere in the starhenge."

"He doesn't leave it there, I assume."

"No, when he's finished eating he takes it with him."

"I wonder why he'd choose that day of all days to snatch a tablet."

"Well, I'm thinking it must have been around Day Sixty-nine that Fraa Spelikon's investigation of Orolo really began to pick up steam. Now, you might remember that when I sneaked up there during the Anathem, on Day Seventy-eight, I checked the M & M—"

"And found it empty," Lio said with a nod. "So. On Day Sixty-nine, Spelikon probably ordered Sammann to fetch the tablet that Orolo had left in the M & M. Which Sammann did. But Spelikon didn't know about the one you'd put in Clesthyra's Eye, so he didn't ask for it."

"But *Sammann* knew," I reminded him. "He had noticed it on Day Two."

"And had made up his mind not to tell Spelikon. But on Day Sixty-nine he didn't try to hide the fact that he'd just grabbed Orolo's tablet." Lio shook his head. "I don't get it. Why would he risk letting you know that?"

I threw up my hands. "Maybe it's not such a risk for him. He's already Ita. What can they do to him?"

"Good point. They can't be nearly as afraid of the Warden Regulant as we are."

I was a little bit irritated to be reminded that we were afraid, but, considering all of the skulking around I'd been doing lately, I couldn't argue.

I'd been getting better, I realized. Recovering from the loss of Fraa Orolo. Forgetting how sad and angry I was. And when Lio mentioned the Warden Regulant, it reminded me.

Anyway, there was a long silence now as Lio assimilated all of this. We actually got some work done. On the weeds I mean.

"Well," he finally said, "what happens after that?"

"Day Seventy, cloudy. Day Seventy-one, snowing. Day Seventy-two, snowing. Can't see anything because the lens is covered. Day Seventy-three, it's brilliant weather. Most of the snow has melted off by the time Sammann gets there. He cleans the place up and has lunch. He's wearing goggles."

"Like sunglasses?"

"Bigger and thicker."

"Like what mountain climbers wear?"

"That's what I thought at first," I said. "Actually, I had to watch Day Seventy-three several times before I got it."

"Got what?" Lio asked. "It was bright, there was snow, he wore dark goggles."

"*Really* dark," I said. "I don't think that these were ordinary goggles like an outdoorsman would wear. I've *seen* these goggles before, Lio. When I saw Cord and Sammann in the machine hall, during Apert, they were wearing these things to shield their eyes from the arc. An arc that's as bright as the sun."

"But why would Sammann suddenly start wearing such a getup to clean the lenses?"

"He doesn't actually have them on while he's cleaning. They're dangling around his neck on a strap," I said. "Then he puts them on and eats his lunch as usual. But the entire time that he's eating, he's staring directly into the sun. *Sammann is watching the sun.*"

"And he never did this before Day Sixty-nine?"

"Nope. Never."

"So do you think that he learned something—?"

"Something from Fraa Orolo's tablet, maybe?" I said. "Or something Spelikon told him? Or perhaps scuttlebutt from other Ita in other concents, talking, or whatever they do, over the Reticulum?"

"Why watch the sun? That is completely off the track of what you have been doing, isn't it?"

"*Completely.* But it's *something.* It is a big fat hint. A gift from Sammann."

"So, have you started looking at the sun too?"

"I don't have goggles," I reminded him, "but I do have twenty-odd clear sunny days recorded on that tablet. So starting tomorrow I can at least look at what the sun was doing three and four months ago."

Big Three: The Concents of Saunt Muncoster, Saunt Tredegarh, and Saunt Baritoe, which are geographically close to one another and which have numerous characteristics in common, e.g., founded in 0 A.R., relatively populous, richly endowed, and enjoying high status for past achievements.

—THE DICTIONARY, *4th edition, A.R. 3000*

The next morning, after a theorics lecture, Jesry and Tulia and I went talking in the meadow. It was the first really fine spring day and everyone was out walking around, so it felt as though we could do this without being conspicuous.

"I think I found the IFOSA," Tulia announced.

"You mean the HIFOSA," Jesry corrected her.

"No," I said, "if Tulia has found such a person, it is no longer Hypothetical."

"I stand corrected," Jesry said. "Who is the Important Fid?"

"Ignetha Foral," Tulia said.

"The surname sounds vaguely familiar," Jesry said.

"The family has been wealthy for a few hundred years, which makes them old and well-established by Sæcular standards. They have a lot of ties to the mathic world—especially Baritoe."

Saunt Baritoe was adjacent to landforms that made a huge and excellent harbor when the sea level was behaving itself, when it wasn't buried in pack ice, and when the river that emptied into it had not dried up or been diverted. For about a third of the time since the Reconstitution, a large city had existed around Baritoe's walls—not always the same city, of course—and so it had the reputation of being urban and worldly, with many ties to families such as, apparently, the Forals. The Procians were powerful there, and in their Unarian math they trained many young Sæculars who later went into law, politics, and commerce.

"What are we allowed to know of her?" Jesry asked.

The question was aptly phrased. Once a year, at Annual Apert, our Unarians reviewed summaries of the Sæcular news of the year just ended. Then, once every ten years, just before Decennial Apert, they reviewed the previous ten annual summaries and compiled a decennial summary, which became part of our library delivery. The only criterion for a news item to make it into a summary was that it still had to seem interesting. This filtered out essentially all of the news that made up the Sæcular world's daily papers and casts. Jesry was asking Tulia what Ignetha Foral had done that was interesting enough to have made it into the most recent Decennial summary.

"She had an important post in the government—she was one of the dozen or so highest-ranking people—and she took a stand against the Warden of Heaven, and he got rid of her."

"Killed her?"

"No."

"Threw her into a dungeon?"

"No, just fired her. I speculate that she has some other job now where she still has enough pull to Evoke someone like Paphlagon."

"So, she was a fid of Suur Aculoä?"

"Ignetha Foral spent six years in the Unarian math at Baritoe and wrote a treatise comparing Paphlagon's work to that of some other, er . . ."

"People like Paphlagon," Jesry said impatiently.

"Yeah, of previous centuries."

"Did you read it?"

"We didn't get a copy. Maybe in another ten years. I already went into the Lower Labyrinth and shoved a request through the grille."

Someone at Baritoe—presumably a Unarian fid—would have to copy Foral's treatise by hand and send it to us. If a book were very popular, fids would do this without being asked, and copies would circulate to other maths.

"You'd think a rich family would have had copies machine-printed," Jesry said.

"Too vulgar," Tulia said. "But I know the title: *Plurality of Worlds: a Comparative Study of Polycosmic Ideation among the Halikaarnians.*"

"Hmm. Makes me feel like a bug under the Procians' magnifying glass," I said.

"Baritoe *is* Procian-dominated," Tulia reminded me. "She wasn't going to get anywhere calling it *Why the Halikaarnians Are So Much Smarter than Us.*" Too late I remembered that Tulia belonged to a Procian order now.

"So, she was interested in the polycosm," Jesry said before this could flourish into a spat. "What could have happened that would be observable from the starhenge and that would make the polycosm relevant?" It was the sort of question Jesry would never ask unless he already knew the answer, which he now supplied: "Something's gone wrong with the sun, I'll bet."

I was poised to scoff, but held back, reflecting that Sammann had, after all, been looking at the sun. "Something visible with the naked eye?"

"Sunspots. Solar flares. These can affect our weather and so on.

And ever since the Praxic Age, the atmosphere doesn't protect us from certain things."

"Well, if that's where the action is, why was Orolo looking at the North Pole?"

"The aurora," Jesry said, as if he actually knew what he was talking about. "It responds to solar flares."

"But we haven't had a single decent aurora this whole time," Tulia pointed out, with a catlike look of satisfaction on her face.

"That we could see with the naked eye," Jesry returned. "This tablet of ours could be the perfect instrument for observing not only auroras but the disk of the sun itself."

"I notice it's 'our' tablet now that it's got something good on it," I pointed out.

"If Suur Trestanas finds it, it'll go back to being 'your' tablet," Tulia said. She and I laughed but Jesry was determined not to be amused.

"Seriously," Tulia continued, "that hypothesis doesn't explain why they Evoked Paphlagon. Any cosmographer can look at solar flares."

"What's the connection to the polycosm, you're asking?" Jesry said.

"Exactly."

"Maybe there *is* none," I speculated, "maybe Ignetha Foral just wanted a cosmographer, and happened to remember Paphlagon's name."

"Maybe she's being persecuted as a heretic, and they yanked Paphlagon so that they could burn him too," Jesry suggested. And we chatted about such ideas for a few minutes before discarding all of them in favor of the proposition that Paphlagon must have been chosen for some good reason.

"Well," Jesry said, "the way that the theors of old found themselves talking about the polycosm in the first place was by thinking about stars: how they formed, and what went on inside them."

"Formation of nuclei and so on," Tulia said.

"And not only that but, when the stars die, how do those nuclei get blown out into space so that they can form planets and—"

"And us," I said.

"Yeah," Jesry said. "It leads to the question, why are all of those processes so fine-tuned to produce life? A sticky question. Deolaters would say, 'Ah, see, God made the cosmos just for us.' But the polycosmic answer is, 'No, there must be lots of cosmi, some good for life, most not—we only see one cosmos in which we are capable of existing.' And *that* is where all of this philosophical stuff originated that Suur Aculoä likes to study."

"I think I see where you're going now when you guess something's gone wrong with the sun," I said. "Maybe there are some new solar observations that contradict what we thought we knew about the theorics of what goes on in the cores of stars. And maybe this has ramifications that extend all the way to those polycosmic theories that Paphlagon's interested in."

"Or—more likely—Ignetha Foral mistakenly *thinks* so, so she's yanked Paphlagon, and is now sending him on a wild goose chase," Jesry said.

"I think she's pretty smart," Tulia demurred, but Jesry didn't hear her because a resolution was forming in his head. He turned toward me. "I want to go down there and view this with you," he said. "Or without you, if you are busy."

For about twelve different reasons I hated this idea, but I couldn't say so without making it look like I was trying to be a pig and monopolize the tablet. "Fine," I said.

"Are you sure that's a good idea?" Tulia said—sounding as if she were pretty sure it wasn't. But before this could develop into a proper fight, we all took notice of the approach of Suur Ala, who was heading straight for us across the meadow. "Uh-oh," Jesry said.

Suur Ala was unusual-looking in a way I'd never been able to pin down; sometimes I found myself staring at her during lectures or at Provener trying to make sense of her face. She had a round head on a slender neck, lately accentuated by a short haircut she had gotten during Apert; since then, one of the other suurs had been maintaining this for her. She had huge eyes, a delicate sharp nose, and a wide mouth. She was small and bony where Tulia was generous. Anyway there was something about her physical form that matched her soul.

She didn't waste time greeting us. "For the eight-hundredth time in the last three months, Fraa Erasmas is at the center of a heated conversation. Carefully out of earshot of others. Complete with significant glances at the sky and at Shuf's Dowment," she began. "Don't bother trying to explain it away, I know you guys are up to something. Have been for weeks and weeks."

We all stood there for a long moment. My heart was pounding. Ala was squared off against the three of us, scanning our faces with those searchlight eyes.

"All right," Jesry said, "we won't bother." But that was all he said. There followed another long silence. I was expecting a look of fury to come over Ala's face. For her to make a threat to bring down the Inquisition on us. Instead of which her face slowly collapsed. For a moment I thought she might show some other emotion—I couldn't guess what. But she passed from there to a blank resolute look, turned her back on us, and began walking away. After she'd gone a few paces, Tulia went after her, leaving Jesry and me alone. "That was weird," he observed.

I could hardly respond. The miserable feeling that had kept me awake in my cell on the night that Ala had joined the New Circle had come over me again.

"You think she'll rat us out?" I asked him.

I tried to put it in an incredulous tone of voice, as in *are you really stupid enough to think she'd rat us out?* but Jesry took it at face value. "It would be a great way to score points with the Warden Regulant."

"But she was careful to approach us when no one else was around," I pointed out.

"Maybe in hopes of negotiating some kind of deal with us?"

"What do we have to offer in the way of a deal!?" I snorted.

Jesry thought about it and shrugged. "Our bodies?"

"Now you're just being obnoxious. Why don't you say 'our affections' if you're going to make such jokes."

"Because I don't think I have any affection for Ala," Jesry said, "and I don't think she has any for me."

"Come on, she's not that bad."

"How can you say that after the little performance she just put on?"

"Maybe she was trying to warn us that we're being too obvious."

"Well, she might have a point there," Jesry admitted. "We should stop talking out in the open where the whole math can observe us."

"You have a better idea?"

"Yeah. The sub-cellar of Shuf's Dowment, next time Arsibalt sends us the signal."

As it turned out, this was only about four hours later. It all worked fine—superficially. Arsibalt sent the signal. Jesry and I noticed it from different places and converged on Shuf's Dowment. No one was there except for Arsibalt. Jesry and I went below and got to work.

But in every other way it was wrong from the start. Whenever I went to Shuf's Dowment, I took a circuitous route through the back of the page-tree-coppice. I never went the same way twice. Jesry, on the other hand, just crossed the bridge and made a beeline for it. But I couldn't say his way was any worse than mine, because that day I encountered no fewer than four different people, or groups of people, out strolling around to enjoy the weather. Within a stone's throw of the Dowment I almost tripped over Suur Tary and Fraa Branch who were enjoying a private moment together, all wrapped up in each other's bolts.

When I finally reached the building, it was with the intent of calling the thing off. But Jesry wasn't about to walk away. He talked me into going down there as Arsibalt looked on, growingly horrified, eyes jumping from door to window to door. So down we went, and crammed ourselves into that tiny place where I had spent so many hours by myself. But it wasn't the same with him there. I'd grown used to the geometric distortion wreaked by the lens; he hadn't, and spent a lot of time zooming in on different things just to see what they looked like. It was no different from what I had done on my first few sessions with it, but it made me want to scream. He didn't seem to understand that we did not have time for this. When he got really interested in something, he would talk much too loudly. Both of us had to go out and urinate; I had to teach him about the "all clear" signal involving the door.

It seemed like two or three hours went by before we actually got around to observing the sun. The tablet worked as well for this as it did for looking at distant stars. It could only generate so much light, and so the sun appeared, not as a blinding thermonuclear fireball, but as a crisp-edged disk—the brightest thing on the tablet, certainly, but not so bright you couldn't look at it. If you zoomed in on it and turned down the brightness, you could observe sunspots. I couldn't really say whether there was an exceptional number of these. Neither could Jesry. By blacking out the sun's disk and observing the space around it, we could look for solar flares, but there was nothing unusual going on that we could see. Not that either of us was an expert on such things. We'd never paid much attention to the sun before, considering it an obnoxious, wayward star that interfered with our observations of all the other stars.

After we became discouraged, and convinced ourselves that the hypothesis about Sammann and the goggles was wrong, and that we'd wasted the whole afternoon, we attempted to leave, and found the door at the top of the stairs closed. Someone else was in the building; it wasn't safe to go out.

We waited for half an hour. Maybe Arsibalt had closed the door in error. I crept up and put my ear to it. He was carrying on a conversation with someone there, and the longer I listened to their muffled voices the more certain I became that the other person was Suur Ala. She had tracked us here!

Jesry had uncomplimentary things to say about her when I came back down to report this news. Half an hour later she was still there. Both of us were starving. Arsibalt must be in a state of animalistic terror.

Clearly our secret was out, or soon to be out, to at least one person. Squatting there in the darkness, trapped like rats, we had more than enough time to think through the implications. To go on as if this had not happened would be senseless. So, having nothing else to do, we pulled the poly tarp up off the floor and wrapped the tablet in it. Then we maneuvered and squirmed into the remotest place we could find—the utmost frontier of Arsibalt's explorations—and used his shovel to bury the tablet four feet deep. When we were finished with that project, and nicely covered with dirt, I went up and put my ear to the door again. This time I heard no conversation. But the door was still closed.

"I think Arsibalt has abandoned us in favor of supper," I told Jesry. "But I'll bet she's still up there."

"It's not in her character to leave at this point," Jesry said.

"Say, that's the nicest thing you've ever said about her."

"What do you think we should do, Raz?"

It was strange to hear Jesry asking for my views on any topic. I savored this novel experience for a few moments before saying, "If she intends to rat us out, I'm dead no matter what. But you have a chance. So, let's go out together. You hood yourself and go straight out the back door and make yourself scarce. I'll approach Ala and talk to her—she'll be distracted long enough for you to melt into the darkness."

"It's a deal," Jesry said. "Thanks, Raz. And remember: if it's your body that she wants—"

"Shut up."

"Okay, let's do it," Jesry said, pulling his bolt over his head. But I could see him shaking his head at the same time. "Can you believe this is what passes for excitement around this place?"

"Maybe someday your wish will be granted and something will happen in the world."

"I thought this might be it," he said, nodding toward the sub-cellar. "But, so far, there's nothing but sunspots."

The door opened and a light shone on us.

"Hello, boys," said Suur Ala, "lose your way?"

Jesry was hooded; she couldn't see his face. He bounded up the stairs, pushed his way past Ala, and headed for the back door. I was right behind him. I came face to face with Suur Ala just in time to hear a terrible thud from down the hall. Jesry was sprawled over the threshold, covered by a mess of bolt—from the waist up.

"No point hiding, Jesry. I'd know your smile anywhere," Ala called.

Jesry got his legs under him, let his bolt drop back down over his arse, and ran off. Now that my eyes had adjusted to the light I could see that Ala had stretched her chord across the doorway at ankle level and tied it off between a couple of chairs flanking the exit. Lacking any other way to keep her bolt on, she had thrown it over herself loosely and was holding it up with one arm. She turned her back on me and shuffled over to retrieve the chord.

"Arsibalt left an hour ago," she said. "I think he lost half his weight in perspiration."

I couldn't muster a lot of amusement, since I knew she was in a position to say equally funny things about me or Jesry if she wanted.

"Cat got your tongue?" she asked, after a good long while.

"How many other people know?"

"You mean, how many have I told? Or how many have figured it out on their own?"

"I guess . . . both."

"I've told no one. As to the other question, I guess the answer would be, anyone who pays as much attention to you as I do, which probably means . . . no one."

"Why would you pay attention to me?"

She rolled her eyes. "Good question!"

"Look, what do you want, Ala? What are you after?"

"It's part of the rules of the game that I mustn't tell you."

"If this is about you trying to be some sort of junior Warden Regulant—her little protégée—then get it over with! Go and tell her. I'll march out of the Day Gate at sunrise and go find Orolo."

She was winding her chord about herself as I said this. Suddenly the bolt seemed to grow twice as large as all of the breath went out of her. Her chest collapsed and her head drooped. The big eyes closed for a few moments. Here was where any other girl would have gone to pieces.

It is hard to say just how monstrous I felt. I leaned back against the wall and let my head thud back as if attempting to escape from my own, hideously guilty skin. But there was no way out of it.

She had opened her eyes. They were gleaming, but they saw everything. *Anyone who pays as much attention to you as I do, which means no one.*

In a voice almost too quiet to hear, she said, "You need to take a bath."

For once in my life I actually managed to see the double meaning. But Ala was already gone.

○○○

Eleven: The list of plants forbidden intramuros, typically because of their undesirable pharmacological properties. The Discipline states that any specimen noticed growing in a math is to be uprooted and burned without delay, and that the event is to be noted in the Chronicle. The list originally drawn up by Saunt Cartas included only three, but their number was increased over the centuries as Arbre was explored and new species were discovered.

—THE DICTIONARY, *4th edition, A.R. 3000*

I'd have become a Deolater and gone on a pilgrimage of any length to find a magic bath that would wash away the mess I'd just made. The hardships of the journey would have been pleasant compared to my next week or so in the math. Not that Ala told anyone. She was too proud for that. But all the other suurs, beginning with Tulia, could tell she was suffering. And by breakfast the next morning, everyone had decided it must be my fault. I wondered how this worked. My first hypothesis was wrong on the face of it: that Ala had run home and narrated the story to a chalk hall full of appalled suurs. My second hypothesis was that she had been seen coming home miserable after having missed supper; I had been seen skulking home a little while later; ergo, I had done a bad thing to her. It wasn't until later that I understood the much simpler truth: others had noticed that Ala had her eye on me, and so if Ala were miserable, it could only be because I had done something—it didn't matter what—bad.

In a stroke I had been Thrown Back by every young female in the math. All the girls seemed to be aghast, all the time, because that was the look that would come over every girl's face when she saw me.

The thing grew over time. If Ala had simply written up an account of what I'd done and stapled it to my chest, it wouldn't have been so bad; but because the amount of information about what I had done was exactly zero, people's imaginations went crazy. Young suurs cringed away from me. Older ones glared at me through supper. It doesn't matter what you did, young man . . . we know you did *something*.

I did not see Ala again for four days, which was statistically improbable. It suggested that other suurs were acting as lookouts, tracking my movements so that they could tell Ala where not to be.

Arsibalt was so rattled that he could hardly speak until three days later, when he came to supper all dirty, and told me in a whisper that he had dug up the tablet from where Jesry and I had buried it ("ridiculously easy to find") and hid it in a much better place ("safe and sound").

Jesry and I knew better than to try to find any object that Arsibalt considered to be safe and sound. All we could do was wait for him to calm down.

I figured out why I never saw Ala: she and Tulia were spending an inordinate amount of time at the Mynster, doing some maintenance on the bells, practicing weird changes, and passing their knowledge down to the younger girls who would eventually replace them.

Sunny days came more frequently. I could look up to the top of the spire sometimes and see Sammann eating his lunch and staring fixedly into the sun through his goggles. Jesry and I discussed smoking a pane of glass and using it to do likewise, but we knew that if we did it wrong we'd go blind. I even contemplated going over the wall, running off to the machine hall, and borrowing a welding mask from Cord. But all of these were really nothing more than distractions to get my mind off the Ala problem. Early on, I had thought of this as a matter of salvaging my reputation. But as time went by, and I thought about it harder, the real nature of the thing became clear: I had made a mess inside of someone else's soul at a moment when that soul had been open to me. Now it was closed. I was the only one who could clean up the mess; but in order to do this I first had to get in there. And I had no idea how, especially in the case of someone as fierce as Ala.

But it occurred to me, one day, as I was pursuing the weed project, that unilateral disarmament might work with someone like her. The work Lio and I had been doing along the riverbank was bringing me into contact with many spring wildflowers. The girls were up in the Mynster doing maintenance on the belfry. Suddenly it all seemed obvious. I put the plan into motion before I'd really thought it through. Ten minutes later I was sleep-walking up the Mynster stairs with a bunch of flowers on my arm, covered under a fold of my bolt because one of them was of the Eleven and I was about to carry it straight through the Warden Regulant's court.

The portcullis was still locked down, the stair up the buttress inaccessible, the upper Præsidium off limits. Our carillon was in the lower reaches of the chronochasm, reachable by a ladder that ran up from the Fendant court. This route dead-ended in a sort of maintenance shack just below the carillon; you couldn't go any higher up the Præsidium that way, so I could go there without arousing any concern that I might be attempting to look at the forbidden sky.

The bells themselves were open to the weather. Below them was this shack that sheltered some of the machinery that made the bells ring. I could hear Ala and Tulia up there talking. The ladder led up to a trapdoor in its floor. My heart was bonging like a bell as I climbed; I gripped the rungs hard so I wouldn't fall off. I'd stuffed the flowers into my bolt to leave both hands free, and now I was sweating all over the blossoms. Disgusting. Ala laughed at some witty remark of Tulia's. I was happy to hear that she was capable of laughter, then chagrined, in a weird way, that she'd already gotten over me.

There was no way to make a smooth entrance. I shoved the trapdoor up and out of my way. The girls became silent. I heaved the bouquet through the aperture and dumped it on the floor to one side, thinking that this would make a more favorable first impression than my face, which of late had practically made young females run screaming. But this was only delaying the inevitable. My face was attached to the rest of me. It and I would have to arrive together. I poked the sorry thing up through the door and looked around, but couldn't see a thing; the shack had windows, but they'd been covered. The girls, however, recognized me with their dark-adjusted eyes, and became even more silent, if such a thing is possible. I hauled the rest of me up through the door.

Tulia made her sphere emit light. She and Ala were sitting side by side on the floor, leaning back against the wall. I wondered why. But I was leery of opening my mouth for any purpose other than the one at hand. So I knelt to one side of the trapdoor and regathered the bouquet. This gave me a few moments to realize I had no plan and nothing to say. But having grown up with Suur Ala and knowing how she reacted to things, I reckoned I couldn't go wrong asking permission. "Ala, I would like to give you these, if it wouldn't kill you."

At least one of them inhaled. Neither raised an objection. The place was larger than I imagined, but so cluttered with beams and shafts I wasn't certain I could stand up, so I knee-walked over to where they were sitting. Something brushed past me—a bat? But the next time I took a count of persons in the room—which was much later—there were only two of us. So it must have been Tulia teleporting herself out of the place like a space captain in a speely.

"Thank you," Ala said—guardedly. "Did you carry these things up through the Regulant court? I guess you must have."

"I did," I said. "Why?" Though I already knew why.

"This one here is Saunt Chandera's Bane, isn't it?"

"Saunt Chandera's Bane makes a weird-looking blossom around this time of year, which I have decided is beautiful." I was getting ready to make an analogy to Ala's appearance but faltered, wondering how to phrase the part about her being kind of weird-looking.

"But it's one of the Eleven!"

"I'm aware of it," I said, getting a little tense, as she had broken into my analogy only to start a dispute. "Look, I put it there because it's forbidden. And this thing between you and me—this mess that I made—is all about something else that's forbidden."

"I can't believe you carried this right up the stairs under the nose of the Inquisition."

"Okay. Now that you mention it, it was pretty stupid."

"That wasn't the word I was going to use," she said. "Thanks for bringing these."

"You're welcome."

"If you sit next to me I'll show you something I'll bet you never expected," she said. And here I was pretty sure there *wasn't* a double meaning. By the time I'd gotten myself seated in Tulia's former spot, Ala had already climbed to her feet—*she* could stand up in here, at least—and padded over to the trapdoor, which Tulia had left open. Ala closed it. She sat next to me and extinguished her light. It was totally dark in here now. Totally dark, that is, except for a single splotch of white light, about the size of the palm of Ala's hand, that seemed to hover in space just in front of us. I didn't imagine that this was a coincidence; the girls had been sitting here *because* of the splotch of light. I reached out and explored it with my right hand (the left, curiously, was beyond use, as it had somehow ended up around Ala's shoulders). There was a plank leaning against the wall, with a blank leaf pinned to it, and the light-splotch was being projected against that leaf. Now that my eyes had adjusted, I could see that the splotch was round. Perfectly circular, in fact.

"Do you remember the total eclipse of 3680 when we made a camera obscura so we could see it without burning our eyes?"

"A box," I recalled, "with a pinhole at one end and a sheet of white paper at the other."

"Tulia and I have been spring cleaning up here," she said. "We noticed these patches of sunlight moving around on the floor and the walls. They were shining through from an old opening up high in the wall, over thataway." She squirmed as she pointed invisibly in the dark, and somehow ended up closer to me. "We think it was put there to ventilate the place, then boarded up because bats were getting in. The light was leaking in through chinks between the boards. We fixed it—almost."

"That 'almost' being a nice neat little pinhole?"

"Exactly, and we set up the screen down here. We have to move it, obviously, as the sun moves across the sky."

Ala could insert the word *obviously* into an otherwise polite sentence like nobody's business. I'd spent more than half of my life being sporadically annoyed by it. Here, finally, I let it go. I was too busy admiring the cleverness of Tulia and Ala. I wished I'd thought of this. You didn't need a lens or a mirror of ground and polished glass to see things far away. A simple pinhole could serve as well. The image that it cast was faint, though, and so you had to view it in a dark room—a camera obscura.

Apparently Tulia had told Ala everything about the tablet, about Sammann, and about my observations. But it seemed like years since I had cared about that stuff as much as I cared about fixing my mess. In fact, as we sat there in the dark together I was finding it difficult to muster even the least bit of interest in the sun. It was shining. Photosynthesis was safe. There were no major flares, and only a few spots. Who cared?

It was even harder to care a few minutes later. Kissing was not a subject taught in chalk halls. We had to learn by trial and error. Even the errors were not too bad.

"A spark," Ala said—muffled somewhat—a while later.

"I'll say!"

"No, I thought I saw a spark."

"I'm told it's normal to see stars at times like this—"

"Don't flatter yourself!" she said, and heaved me aside. "I just saw another one."

"Where?"

"On the screen."

Somewhat bleary-eyed, I turned my attention to it. Nothing was on that page except the same pale-white disk.

And . . .

a spark. A pinprick of light, brighter than the sun, gone before I could be certain it was there.

"I think—"

"There it is again!" she exclaimed. "It moved a little though."

We watched a few more. She was right. All of the sparks were below and to the right of the sun's disk. But each one was slightly higher and farther to the left. If you plotted them on the page, they'd form a line aimed right at the sun.

What would Orolo do? "We need a pen," I said.

"Don't have one," she said. "They're coming about once a second. Maybe faster."

"Is there anything sharp?"

"The pins!" Ala and Tulia had used four stick-pins to fix the page to the plank. I worried one loose and let it tumble into her warm little hand.

"I'm going to hold the plank still. You poke a hole in the page wherever you see a spark," I said.

We missed a few more while we were getting ourselves arranged. I knelt to one side, bracing the plank against the wall with my hand, holding its base steady with my knee. She threw herself down on her belly and propped herself up on her elbows, her face so close to the page that I could see her eyes and the curve of her cheek in the faint illumination scattering from the page. She was the most beautiful girl in the concent.

I saw the next spark reflected in her eye. Up came her hand as she poked it on the page.

"It would be really good if we knew the exact time," I said.

Poke. "In a few minutes this is," poke, "going to migrate off the page, obviously." Poke. "Then we can run out and look at," poke, "the clock." Poke.

"Notice anything funny about these sparks?" Poke.

"They're not instant on-off." Poke. "They flare up quickly," poke, "but fade slowly." Poke.

"I was referring to the color." Poke.

"Kind of blue-y?" Poke.

A sudden grinding noise nearly gave me a heart attack. It was the belfry's automatic mechanism going into action. The clock was striking two. At this time it would have been traditional to plug one's ears. I didn't dare; Ala would have assailed me with that jabbing pin. Poke . . . poke . . . poke . . .

"So much for knowing the time," I said, when I thought she might be able to hear again.

"I made a triple hole on the spark that came closest to the stroke of two," she said.

"Perfect."

"I think it's been curving," she said.

"Curving?"

"Like—whatever makes these sparks isn't moving in a straight line. It is changing its course," she said. "It's obviously flying between us and the sun—it's passing right across the sun's disk, at the moment. But the line of pinholes doesn't look straight to me."

"Well, assuming it's in orbit, that's really weird," I said. "It ought to go straight."

"Unless it's in the act of changing its course," she insisted. "Maybe these sparks are something to do with its propulsion system."

"I remember now where I've seen that shade of blue before," I said.

"Where?"

"Cord's shop. They have a machine that uses plasma to cut metal. The light that comes from it is that shade of blue. The same as a hot star."

"It's passing off the edge of the sun's disk," she said. Then: "Hey!"

"Hey what?"

"It stopped."

"No more sparks?"

"No more sparks. I'm sure of it."

"Well, before I move this thing, make some pinpricks around the edge of the disk of the sun, so we know where it stood in relation to all this. Between that and the time—we can find this thing!"

"Find it how?"

"We can work out where in the sky the sun stood at two P.M. on this day of the year. That is, which of the so-called fixed stars it's passing in front of. This plasma-spark thing that we were tracking—it was in the same place. That means that unless it changes its orbit again, it will pass over the same fixed stars on each orbit. We can find it in the sky."

"But it seems to have no difficulty changing its orbit," said Ala, meticulously outlining the sun's disk with a series of closely spaced pinpricks.

"But part of the puzzle we've failed to understand until now—maybe—is that it only does so when it's passing near the sun. So as long as we have this camera obscura, we can be on the look-out for that."

"Why should the sun's position make any difference?"

"I think it's hiding," I said. "If it did what it just did in the night sky, anyone could see it with the naked eye."

"But we were able to detect it with a pinhole and a sheet of paper!" Ala pointed out. "So it's a pretty ineffective way to hide."

"And Sammann can apparently see it with welding goggles," I said. "But the difference is that people like you and me and Sammann are . . ."

"Are what?" she said. "Knowledgeable?"

"Yeah. And whoever, or whatever this thing is, it doesn't or they don't care if knowledgeable people know they are up there. They are letting their existence be known *to us*—"

"Which the Sæcular Power doesn't like—"

"Which is why Orolo got Thrown Back for looking at it."

It took us a while to get out of there. Too much was going on. I rolled up the page and stuck it inside my bolt. Ala picked up the bunch of flowers. This reminded me of why I'd come up here in the first place and of what we'd been doing before Ala had noticed the sparks. I felt like a jerk for letting this slip my mind. By that time, though, Ala had remembered about the Saunt Chandera's Bane and was wondering what to do with it. So we traded; I gave her the chart and she gave me the flowers so that I could accept the risk of sneaking them back down.

"What should we do next?" I wondered out loud.

"About . . . ?"

We had opened the trapdoor. There was plenty of light. I was about to blurt "what we just saw" when I noticed a look on her face—steeling herself to get hurt again. I think I stopped myself just in time.

"Do you want to—should we—" I began, then closed my eyes and just said it. "I think we should be honest about this in front of everyone."

"I'm fine with that," she said.

"I'll set it up for tomorrow, I guess. After Provener."

"I'll tell Tulia," she said, and something about the way she pronounced that name informed me that she knew everything; she knew I'd once had a crush on her best friend. "Who do you want as your witness?"

I had been about to say Lio, but Jesry had been such a jerk about this that I decided he had to be the one. "And our free witness can just be Haligastreme or whoever is handy," I said.

"What kind of liaison are we to publish?" she asked.

This was not a difficult question. Liaisons were supposed to be announced when they were formed and when they were dissolved. It was a way to curtail gossip and intrigue, which could so easily run rampant in a math. The Concent of Saunt Edhar recognized several types. The least serious was Tivian. The most serious— Perelithian—was equivalent to marriage. That was out of the question for two kids of our age who'd hated each other's guts until forty-five minutes ago. If I said *Tivian*, Ala would throw me out the trapdoor to my death, and I'd spend the last four seconds of my life wishing I'd said *Etrevanean*.

"Could you stand having people know that you were in an Etrevanean liaison with that big jerk Fraa Erasmas?"

She smiled. "Yes."

"Okay." Then awkwardness. It seemed appropriate to kiss her one more time. This went over well.

"Now, are we going to talk about the fact that we have just discovered an alien spacecraft hiding in orbit around Arbre?" she asked in a tiny, coy voice—most unlike her. But she wasn't as used to being in big trouble as I was and so I think she felt as though, on such questions, she had to defer to a hardened criminal.

"To a few people. I'm pretty sure Lio's down in the Fendant court. I'll stop there and tell him—"

"That works. We should go about separately, anyway, until our liaison is published."

Her agility in jumping between the love topic and the alien spacecraft was making me dizzy. Or perhaps giddy. "So I'll meet you below later. We'll spread the news to the others as we have opportunity."

"Bye," she said. "Don't forget your forbidden flower."

"I won't," I said.

Just like that she was gone down the ladder.

I followed a minute later and found Lio in the reading room in the Fendant court. He was studying a book about a Praxic Age battle that had been conducted in the abandoned subway tunnels of a great city by two armies that had run out of ammunition and so had to fight with sharpened shovels. He looked at me blankly for a while. I must have looked even blanker. Then I realized that the recent events weren't written on my face. I would actually have to communicate.

"Incredible things have happened in the last hour," I announced.

"Such as?"

I didn't know what to say first but concluded that alien spaceships were a better topic for the Warden Fendant's reading room. So I gave him a full account of that. He looked a little deranged until I got to the point about how the spark track curved, and mentioned plasma. Then his face snapped like a shutter. "I know what it is," he said.

He was so certain that doubting him never crossed my mind. Instead, I just wondered how he knew. "How can you—"

"I know what it is."

"Okay. What is it?"

For the first time he took his eyes off mine, and let his gaze wander around the reading room. "It might be here . . . or it might be in the Old Library. I'll find it. I'll show it to you later."

"Why don't you simply tell me?"

"Because you won't believe me until I show it to you in a book that was written by someone else. That's how weird it is."

"Okay," I said. Then I added, "Congratulations!" since that seemed like the right thing to say.

Lio slammed his book shut, stood up, turned his back on me, and headed for the stacks.

Back at the Cloister I came to understand that things were going to move much more slowly than I wanted them to. I was on supper duty, so I spent the remainder of the afternoon in the kitchen. Ala and Tulia didn't have to cook, but they did have to serve. While dumping a hot potato into my bowl Ala gave me a look that moved me in a way I won't describe here. While burying it with stew Tulia gave me a look that proved Ala had told her everything. "The pinhole: nice!" I told her. Fraa Mentaxenes, who'd been nudging me in the kidney with his bowl, trying to get me to move faster, had no idea what I meant and only became more irritated.

Lio didn't show up for supper. Jesry was there, but I couldn't talk to him because we were at a crowded table with Barb and several others. Arsibalt sat as far from us as he could, as had been his habit of late. After supper he was on cleanup duty. Jesry went off to a chalk hall to work with some of the other Edharians on a proof. Those guys might work until dawn. But I couldn't have talked to him anyway because I had to corner Fraa Haligastreme and set up the little aut tomorrow where Ala and I would declare our liaison before witnesses and have it entered in the Chronicle.

I did have time to work out where in the sky the sun had stood at two in the afternoon. After curfew, when the fids had gone to bed, I went out into the meadow alone, sat on a bench, and stared at that place in the sky for an hour, hoping I might get lucky and see a satellite pass through. Which was irrational, because if this spaceship could be seen with the naked eye, none of this intrigue would have been necessary. It was some combination of too small, too dark, and/or too high to bounce back enough light for our eyes to see it. But I needed to sit there alone for a while and stare into the black just to settle my thoughts. My brain zinged back and forth between the Two Topics for an hour. When I was totally exhausted I got up and crawled into a vacant cell where I slept soundly.

Lio was in the Refectory at breakfast. When I caught his eye, he glanced significantly at a big old book he'd dug up: *Praxic Age Exoatmospheric Weapons Systems.*

Cheerful.

Jesry skipped breakfast. Afterward, Ala and I squandered most of the morning getting things ready for this afternoon. You could announce a Tivian liaison at the drop of a hat but for the Etrevanean each participant was supposed to discuss it first with an older fraa or suur. I was finishing that up when Provener rang. This was one of those increasingly rare days when my old team was supposed to wind the clock. I found the cell where Jesry was still asleep, yanked him off his pallet, and got him moving. We ended up sprinting to the Mynster, late as usual. But it felt good to have the team back together, after all that had been happening lately, and I enjoyed the simple physical work of winding the clock more than I'd used to.

After, the four of us went to the Refectory to take the midday meal. But there was no question of talking about the spaceship there. Instead it was all about the aut that Ala and I were to celebrate later. Of all the team, I was the first to go so far as to join in such a liaison and so this was sort of like a rehearsal for a bachelor party. We became so loud and so funny (at least, we believed we were funny) that we were asked on two separate occasions to tone it down, and threatened with severe penance—which only made us louder and funnier.

At some point during all of this I mentally stepped back from it all and took a moment to enjoy the looks on my friends' faces and to reflect on everything that had been going on lately. And as part of that, I recollected that Orolo had been Thrown Back and that he was out there, somewhere, extramuros, trying to find his way. Which made me sad, and even brought back a spark of the old anger. But none of it stopped me from being happy with my friends. Part of this was the sheer thrill of what had happened with Ala. But part of it too was the growing certainty that Ala and Tulia and I had scored a victory over those like Spelikon and Trestanas who had locked us out of the starhenge and tried to control what we knew and what we thought about. We just needed to find a way to announce it that wouldn't lead to my getting Thrown Back. I didn't want to leave the concent any more. Not as long as Ala lived here.

She and Tulia were nowhere to be seen, and before long we found out why: they had duties in the Mynster. Bells began to ring not long after we had finished eating. We sat and listened for a couple of minutes, trying to decipher the changes. But Barb had been memorizing these things and figured it out first. "Voco," he announced, "the Sæcular Power will Evoke one of us."

"Apparently Fraa Paphlagon couldn't get the job done," Jesry cracked, as we were draining our beers.

"Or he's calling for reinforcements," Lio suggested.

"Or he had a heart attack," said Arsibalt. Lately he had been full of gloomy ideas like this, and so the rest of us gave him dirty looks until he held up his hands in submission.

We sauntered across the meadow to the Mynster. Even so, we got there in plenty of time, and ended up in the front row, closest to the screen. Voco continued ringing for some minutes after we arrived. Then the eight ringers filed down from their balcony and found places farther back. A choir of Hundreders came out into the chancel and began a monophonic chant. I thought of going back to be near Ala but it was part of the Discipline that you didn't engage in any of that clingy couple-like behavior before your liaison was published, so it would have to wait for a few more hours.

This time Statho didn't have any Inquisitors with him, as he'd had during Fraa Paphlagon's Voco. He went through the opening rounds of the rite as before, and for the first time since the bells had begun to ring, it sank in that this was for real. I wondered which avout we would say goodbye to—whether it would be one of us Tenners this time, or someone like Fraa Paphlagon whom we'd never met because they were of a different math.

By the time Statho reached the place in the aut where he was to call out the name of the Evoked, I had become quite anxious. The Mynster was as silent as that sub-basement beneath Shuf's Dowment. So I almost wanted to scream when he chose that moment to pause and fumble around in his vestment. He took out a page that had been folded in on itself and sealed shut with a dollop of beeswax. It took him forever to pick the thing open. He unfolded it, held it up in front of his face, and looked astonished.

It was such an awkward moment that even he felt the need to explain. He announced, "There are six names!"

Pandemonium was the wrong word to describe a few hundred avout standing still and muttering to each other, but it conveys the right feeling. A single Voco was rare enough. Six at a stroke had never happened—or had it? I looked at Arsibalt. He read my mind. "No," he whispered, "not even for the Big Nugget."

I looked at Jesry. "This is it!" he told me. Meaning the something different he'd been waiting for.

Statho cleared his throat and waited for the murmuring to subside.

"Six names," he went on. The Mynster now became silent again, except for the faint wail of police sirens outside the Day Gate, and the rumble of engines. "One of them is no longer among us."

"Orolo," I said. About a hundred others said it at the same time. Statho's face reddened. "Voco," he called, but his voice choked up and he had to swallow before trying it again. "Voco Fraa Jesry of the Edharian chapter of the Decenarian math."

Jesry turned and socked me on the shoulder, hard enough to leave a charley horse that would still ache three days later. Something to remember him by. Then he turned his back on us and walked out of our lives.

"Suur Bethula of the Edharian chapter of the Centenarian math . . . Fraa Athaphrax of the same . . . Fraa Goradon of the Edharian chapter of the Decenarian math . . . and Suur Ala of the New Circle, Decenarians."

By the time I had regained consciousness she was already on the threshold of the door through the screen. She was as shocked as

I was. Tears began to run out of her eyes as she hesitated, there, and looked my way.

When I'd watched Fraa Paphlagon step out, all those months ago, I'd understood clearly that no one in this place would ever see him again. The same thing was now happening to Ala. But it didn't sink in. The only thing that got through to me was the look on her face.

They told me later I knocked two people down as I made my way over to her.

She hooked an elbow over my neck and kissed me on the lips, then pressed her wet cheek against mine for an instant.

When Fraa Mentaxenes closed the door between us, I looked down to discover a rolled-up page stuck in my bolt. It was perforated with tiny holes. By the time I'd finished taking that in, and stepped forward to put my face to the screen, Jesry, Bethula, Athaphrax, Goradon, and Ala had already walked out the same way that Paphlagon and Orolo had gone before. Everyone was singing except for me.

Terrible Events: A worldwide catastrophe, poorly documented, but generally assumed to have been the fault of humans, that terminated the Praxic Age and led immediately to the Reconstitution.

— THE DICTIONARY, *4th edition, A.R. 3000*

"You see what I mean," Lio said, "that it's so crazy, you wouldn't have believed me unless I showed it to you in a book."

He and I, Arsibalt, Tulia, and Barb were all sitting around the big table at Shuf's Dowment. *Praxic Age Exoatmospheric Weapons Systems* was sprawled out like an autopsy. We were looking at a double-ended foldout. It had taken us a quarter of an hour just to get the thing unfurled without tearing the ancient leaves: real paper made in a factory. We were looking at a huge, exquisitely detailed diagram of a spaceship. At one end, it sported a proper nose cone, as a rocket should. Everything else about it looked weird. It did not have engines per se. At the aft end, where the nozzle bells of a proper rocket ought to be, there was instead a broad flat disk, looking like a pedestal on which the vessel might be stood upright. Forward of that were several stout columns that ran up to what I assumed was the spaceship proper: the family of rounded pressure vessels sheltered beneath that nose cone.

"Shock absorbers," Lio said, pointing to the columns, "except bigger." He drew our attention to a tiny hole in the center of the big disk astern. "This is where it would spit out the atomic bombs, one after another."

"That's the part I still can't get my mind to accept."

"Have you ever heard of those Deolaters who walk barefoot over hot coals to show that they have supernatural powers?" He looked over toward the hearth. We'd lit a fire there. Not that we needed one. We had a couple of windows cracked open to admit a fresh green-scented breeze that was blowing in over the young clover in the meadow. Sad songs were carried on that air. Most of the avout were so shocked by the six-fold Voco that to make music about it was all that they could do. Those of us in this room had another way to come to terms with our loss, but only because we knew things that the others didn't. We'd lit the fire as soon as we'd arrived, not to keep warm but as a primitive way to get some comfort. It was what humans had done, long before Cnoüs, long before even language, to claim a bit of space in a dark universe that they did not understand and that was wont to claim their family and friends suddenly and forever. Lio went over to that fire and assaulted a glowing log with a poker until he had knocked off several lumps of glowing charcoal. He raked one of these out onto the stones. It was about the size of a nut, and red hot.

I was already getting nervous.

"Raz," he said, "would you put this in your pocket and carry it around?"

"I don't have pockets," I joked.

No one laughed.

"Sorry," I said. "No, if I had a pocket I would not put that into it."

Lio spat into the palm of his left hand, then put the fingertips of his right into the pool of saliva. He then used them to pick up that coal. There were sizzling noises. We cringed. He calmly tossed the coal back into the fire, then slapped his hot fingertips against his thigh a few times. "Slight discomfort. No damage," he announced. "The noise was spit being vaporized by the heat of the coal. Now imagine that the plate on the back of that ship was coated with something that served the same purpose."

"The same purpose as spit?" Barb asked.

"Yes. It was vaporized by the plasma from the atomic bombs, and as it expanded into space, it would spank that plate. The shock absorbers would even out the impact and turn it into steady thrust so that the people up at the forward end would feel nice smooth acceleration."

"It's just hard to imagine being that close to an atomic bomb going off," Tulia said. "And not just one, but a whole series of them."

Her voice sounded pretty raw. All of ours did, except for Barb's. He'd been perusing the book earlier. "They were special bombs. Really tiny," he said, making a circle of his arms to show their size. "Designed not to blow out in all directions but to spew a lot of plasma in one direction—toward that ship."

"I too find it unfathomable," Arsibalt volunteered, "but I vote we suspend our disbelief and move forward. The evidence is before us, in this"—he gestured toward the book—"and this." He rested his hand on the sheet that Ala had pinpricked the day before. Then he looked stricken. I think he had seen something on my face, or Tulia's, or both. For us, this leaf was now like one of the mementoes of bygone Saunts that the avout cherished in reliquaries.

"Perhaps," Arsibalt said, "it is too early for us to have this discussion. Perhaps—"

"Perhaps it's too late!" I said. Which earned me a grateful look from Tulia, and seemed to settle it for everyone.

"I'm surprised—pleasantly—you're here at all, Arsibalt," I said.

"You are referring to my, ah, apparent skittishness of recent weeks."

"Your words, not mine," I said, working to keep a straight face.

He raised his eyebrows. "I do not recall—do you?—any *diktat* from the hierarchs to the effect that we must not make tiny holes in pieces of foil and allow the light of the sun to fall on paper. Our position is unassailable."

"I hadn't thought of it that way," I said. "I almost feel a little let down that we are no longer breaking any rules."

"I know it must be an odd sensation for you, Fraa Erasmas, but you may get used to it after a while."

Barb didn't get the joke. We had to explain it. He still didn't get it.

"So I wonder if—perhaps—one of these ships went missing," Tulia said.

"Went missing?" Lio repeated.

"Like—its crew mutinied and they headed out for parts unknown. Now, thousands of years later, their descendants have returned."

"It might not even be their descendants," Arsibalt pointed out.

"Because of Relativity!" Barb exclaimed.

"That's right," I said. "Come to think of it, if the ship could travel at relativistic velocity, they might have gone on a round-trip journey that lasted a few decades to them—but thousands of years to us."

Everyone loved this hypothesis. We had already made up our minds it must be true. There was only one problem. "None of these ships was ever built," Lio said.

"*What!?*"

He looked as if we were about to blame him for it. "It was just a proposal. These are nothing more than conceptual drawings from very late in the Praxic Age."

"Just before the Terrible Events!" Barb footnoted.

We were all silent for a while. It takes time and effort to tear down and stow away an idea you were that excited about.

"Besides," Lio went on, "this ship was only for military operations inside the solar system. They had ideas for ones that could go to relativistic velocity, but they would have been much bigger and they'd have looked different."

"You wouldn't need a nose cone!" said Barb—which was *his* idea of hilarious.

"So if we buy the idea that what Ala and I saw—the blue sparker—was a ship in orbit that was using this kind of propulsion system—" I began, nodding at the diagram.

"—Then it must have come from an alien civilization," Arsibalt said.

"Fraa Jesry believes that advanced life forms must be extremely rare in the universe," Barb told us.

"He followed the Conjecture of Saunt Mandarast," Arsibalt said, nodding agreement. "Billions of planets infested with unicellular glop. Almost none with multicellular organisms—to say nothing of civilizations."

"Let's speak of him in the present tense—it's not as though he's dead!" Tulia pointed out.

"I stand corrected," said Arsibalt, none too wholeheartedly.

"Barb, when you were talking to Jesry of this, did he have some alternate theory?" Tulia asked.

"Yes—an alternate theory about an alternate universe!" Barb cracked. Tulia mussed his hair and gave him a shove, which was a mistake because then he wanted to get rambunctious. We had to threaten him with Anathem and make him go outside and run five laps around Shuf's Dowment before he would settle down.

"Talking about where this thing might have come from is a side track to the main discussion," Lio pointed out.

"Agreed," said Arsibalt, so authoritatively that we *did* agree.

"It came from somewhere. Who cares. It settled into a polar orbit around Arbre and stayed there for a while—doing what?" I said.

"Reconaissance," said Lio. "That's what polar orbits are for."

"So they were learning about us. Mapping Arbre. Eavesdropping on our communications."

"Learning our language," Tulia said.

I went on, "Somehow Orolo became aware of it. Maybe he happened to see the deceleration burn that took it into polar orbit.

Perhaps others did too. The Panjandrums knew. They sent word to the hierarchs: 'we are putting you on notice that we deem this to be a Sæcular matter, it is none of your business, so butt out.' And the hierarchs dutifully sent out the order to close every star-henge."

"Inquisitors were sent to make sure it was done," Lio said.

"Fraa Paphlagon was Evoked to go somewhere and study this thing," Tulia said.

"He," said Arsibalt, "and perhaps others like him from other concents."

"The ship stayed in orbit. Maybe sometimes it would adjust its trajectory by firing those engines. But it would only do so when it was passing between Arbre and the sun—to hide its traces."

"Like a fugitive who walks in a river not to leave footprints," Barb put in.

"But yesterday something changed. Something big must have happened."

"Gardan's Steelyard says that the course change you and Ala witnessed, and the unprecedented six-fold Voco less than a day later, must be connected," Arsibalt said.

I had been avoiding the sacred relic. That had to end. Ala had given it to me for a reason. We unrolled it on the table and weighed its corners down with books.

"We can't figure out what it did unless we know the darn geometry!" Barb complained.

"You mean, of the pinhole, and where the screen was situated up in the Præsidium. Which way was up. Which way was north," I said. "I agree that we have to take all of those measurements."

Barb started backing toward the exit—ready to take those measurements *at once.*

But I held back. I wanted to do those things as badly as he did. But here was where Orolo would have proposed something brilliantly simple. Something that would have made me feel like an idiot for having made it too complicated. I could think of nothing like that.

"Why don't we at least measure the angle," I said. "It comes in from one direction. That's its initial orbit. By firing those bombs, it curves until it is going a different direction. That's its final orbit. We could at least measure that angle."

So we did. The answer was something like a quarter of pi—forty-five degrees.

"So if we assume it started out in a polar orbit, then by the time this maneuver was finished, it was in a new orbit, roughly halfway between polar and equatorial," Lio said.

"And what do you suppose would be the point of that?" I asked, since Lio knew so much more of exoatmospheric weapons systems than anyone else in the room.

"If you plot its ground track on a globe or a map of the world, well, it's never going to ascend higher than forty-five degrees of latitude, in such an orbit. It'll sine-wave back and forth between forty-five degrees north and forty-five south."

"Which is where ninety-nine percent of the people live," Tulia pointed out.

"Which they would know by now, since they have had time to compile maps of every square inch of Arbre," Arsibalt reminded us.

"They have finished Phase One: reconaissance," Lio concluded, "and yesterday began Phase Two: which is—who knows?"

"Actually doing something," Barb said.

"And the Panjandrums know it," I said. "Have been worrying about it. They've had a contingency plan ready for months—we know this because Orolo's name was on that list! So it must have been written out and sealed before his Anathem."

"I'll bet Varax and Onali handed it to Statho during Apert," Tulia said. "Statho's been carrying it around ever since, awaiting the signal to break the seal and read out those names." She got a distracted look on her face. "It bothers me that they chose Ala."

"I never fully understood until last week how close the two of you were," I said.

But Tulia wanted none of it. "It's not just that," she said. "I mean, it *is*. I love her. I can't stand that she's gone. But why her? Paphlagon—Orolo—Jesry—fine. I get it. But why would *you* choose Ala? What would you want someone like her for?"

"To organize a lot of other people," Arsibalt said without hesitation.

"That," said Tulia, "is what troubles me."

For God's sake, raise your sights.

Mention of the Inquisitors had put me in mind of the conversation I'd had with Varax on Tenth Night. This had slipped my mind because of what had happened a few moments afterward. But I could remember him gazing up at the starhenge—or perhaps he'd been raising his sights a little higher, looking off into space. Come to think of it, he'd been facing north at the time. *Larger matters are at stake than whether a young fraa at the remote hermitage of Saunt Edhar practices his vlor on some local runagates . . . think bigger . . . the way your friend does when he decides to tackle four larger men.*

What on earth did *that* mean? That the alien ship was a threat? That we would soon have to tackle it against long odds? Or was I reading too much into it? And why, during my earlier conversation with Varax, had he grilled me concerning my opinions on the Hylaean Theoric World? It was an odd time for someone like him to be so concerned with metatheorics.

Or maybe I was reading way too much into these conversations. Maybe Varax was just one of those guys who thought out loud.

The "raise your sights" part of it seemed pretty clear.

I didn't need a lot of encouragement to get to work. After Orolo's Anathem, the only thing that had kept me from going crazy had been working on the photomnemonic tablet. Ala's loss wasn't quite as dreadful—at least she hadn't been Thrown Back—but unlike Orolo's it had been entirely surprising to me. I was still feeling bad that I'd just stood there like a stunned animal while she'd walked out of my life. To have lost her, just after we'd begun something— well, suffice it to say that I really needed a project to work on.

Our group invaded the shack above the belfry with every measuring device we could scare up. Arsibalt found some architectural drawings of the Mynster dating back to the Fourth Century. We calculated the geometry of the camera obscura in three different ways, and compared the results until we got them all to agree. We were able to refine the rough measurement we had made at Shuf's Dowment: the ship's new orbit was inclined at about fifty-one degrees to the equator, which meant that it passed over essentially all populated areas. When the weather had become hot and dry in the centuries after the Terrible Events, people had tended to move poleward. More recently, reductions in the amount of carbon dioxide in the atmosphere had begun to gentle the climate, and people had migrated back towards the equator to get away from the solar radiation near the poles. As a matter of fact, fifty-one degrees was a higher orbit than the ship really needed, if all it wanted was to keep an eye on most of the world's population.

We thought this mysterious until Arsibalt pointed out that if you looked at all the world's major concents—meaning ones that had Millennium Clocks and that housed hundreds or thousands of avout—the one that was farthest from the equator was at 51.3 degrees north latitude.

That one happened to be the "remote hermitage" of Saunt Edhar.

Word got around. Within a month of the big Voco, everyone in the Decenarian math knew most of what we knew about the ship. The hierarchs could do nothing to suppress it. But still they didn't open the starhenge. I found myself getting invited to a lot more late-night chalk hall sessions. We studied the diagram Lio had found in that book and worked out the theorics of how such a ship would function, and how much bigger it would have to be to journey between stars. Some of it was simple praxic calculations about the shock absorbers. Some—such as predicting what the plasma would do when it hit the plate—was extraordinarily challenging work. The theorics was too advanced for me. It felt like we were proving the Lorites wrong, because some of the other avout, just a little older than I, were coming up with proofs that we were pretty sure had never been thought of by anyone before—anyone on Arbre, that is.

"It makes you wonder about the Hylaean Theoric World," Arsibalt volunteered, one summer evening, about eight weeks after the big Voco. He had been pretending to look after his bees and I had been pretending to tend the weeds. By that time, the Sarthian cavalry had penetrated deep into the Plains of Thrania and driven a wedge between the Fourth and the Thirty-third Legions of General Oxas. So it wasn't surprising that Arsibalt and I bumped into each other. At our latitude, days were very long at this time of year, and we still had some light remaining even though supper had ended hours ago.

"What's on your mind?" I asked him.

"You are toiling in chalk halls with the other Edharians, trying to work out the theorics of this alien ship," he said, "theorics that the aliens must have mastered long ago, to build such a thing and drive it among stars. My question is: are they the same theorics?"

"You mean, ours and the aliens'?"

"Yes. I see the chalk-dust on your bolt, Fraa Erasmas, from equations you were drawing after supper. Did some two-headed, eight-limbed alien draw the same equations on the equivalent of a slate on another planet a thousand years ago?"

"I'm pretty sure the aliens use different notation," I began.

"Obviously!" he barked.

"You sound like Ala."

"Maybe they use a little square to represent multiplication and a circle for division, or something," he went on, rolling his eyes in annoyance, then whirling his hand to indicate he wanted the conversation to go faster.

"Or maybe they don't write out equations at all," I said. "Maybe they prove things with music, or something." Which wasn't far-fetched at all, since we did something like that in our chants, and there had been whole orders of avout who had done all of their theorics that way.

"Now we're getting somewhere!" He was so thrilled by this idea that I regretted having mentioned it. "Suppose they have a system of doing theorics that uses music, as you said. And perhaps if it leads to a harmonious chord, or a pleasing tune, it means that they have proved that something is true."

"You really are going off the deep end now, Arsibalt."

"Tolerate your friend and fraa. Do you think it's the case that, for every proof you and the other Edharians work out on a slate, the aliens have a proof in their own system that corresponds to it? That says the same thing—expresses the same truth?"

"We couldn't do theorics at all if we didn't think that was the case. But Arsibalt, this is old stuff we're talking about. Cnoüs saw it. Hylaea understood it. Protas formalized it. Paphlagon thought about it—which is why he got Evoked. What's the point of going over it now? I'm tired. As soon as it gets a little darker, I'm going to bed."

"How are we to communicate with the aliens?"

"I don't know. It's been speculated that they have been learning our language," I reminded him.

"What if they can't talk?"

"A minute ago you had them singing!"

"Don't be tedious, Fraa Erasmas. You know what I'm getting at."

"Maybe I do. But it's late. I was up until three talking about plasma. Hey, I think it *is* dark enough for me to go to bed now."

"Hear me out. I'm saying that it is through the Protan forms—the theoric truths—in the Hylaean Theoric World that we might end up communicating with them."

"It sounds like you're just itching for an excuse to barricade yourself in Shuf's Dowment behind a stack of old books and work on this. Are you asking me for—permission? Approval?"

He shrugged. "You are the resident expert on the alien ship."

"Okay. Fine. Knock yourself out. I'll back you up. I'll tell everyone you're not crazy—"

"Capital!"

"—if you help me with one thing that really has me scratching my head right now."

"And what would that be, Fraa Erasmas?"

"Why does the Millenarian math appear to be glowing?"

"What?"

"Look at it," I said.

He turned around and raised his chin to gaze up at the crag.

It was glowing ruby red. This was not a normal thing for it to be doing.

Of course, we saw soft lights up there all the time. And if the weather was right, the walls would sometimes catch the light of the setting sun, as when Orolo and I had looked on it during Apert. For the last few minutes, as the twilight had been deepening, I'd noticed a red glow about the place, and reckoned it must be that again. But the sun was absolutely down now. And this light was a shade of red that was most un-sun-like. It had a grainy, sparkly quality.

And it was coming from the wrong direction. Sunlight would have lit up the west-facing surfaces of the math and the crag. But this weird red light was striking the roofs, parapets, and tower-tops. Everything below was in shade. It was almost as if some aerocraft were hovering high above the crag shining a light straight down. But if that were the case, it was so high we could neither see nor hear it.

The meadow grew busy with fraas and suurs who came out of the Cloister buildings to look at it. Most were silent—like Deolaters gazing upon a heavenly omen. But among a group of theoricians not far away an argument was gaining momentum, featuring words such as *laser, color,* and *wavelength.* That jogged my memory: I knew where I'd seen that grainy sort of light before: the guidestar lasers on the M & M.

And that was the key to the riddle. A laser beam could shine across a vast distance without spreading out very much. The thing that was shining this light on the Millenarian math didn't have to be nearby. It could be thousands of miles away. It could be—could *only* be—the alien spaceship.

Exclamations, and even a little bit of applause, rose up from the meadow. Looking more closely at the Millenarian math I saw that a column of smoke was rising from behind its walls. I swallowed hard and got very upset for just a moment, thinking that the laser was setting fire to the place! It was a death ray! Then my better sense got the upper hand. To burn things down, one would want an infrared laser, whose light would make things hot. By definition, this laser wasn't infrared, because we could see it. The smoke wasn't from burning buildings. The Thousanders were creating it. They were throwing grass or something onto fires, filling the space above their math with smoke and steam.

It was impossible to see a laser beam from the side if it was traversing empty space or clean air, but if you put smoke or dust in its way, the particles would scatter some of the light in all directions and make the ray stand out as a glittering line in space.

It worked. That ray might be thousands of miles long. We'd never be able to see most of it—the part that traversed the vacuum above the atmosphere. But the smoke made by the Thousanders enabled us to see the last few hundred feet, and to get a very good idea of which direction the light was coming from.

And of course I had an unfair advantage, since I knew the plane of the alien ship's orbit—which of the fixed stars it would pass in front of. I held my bolt up with one hand, making a screen to block out most of the light from the crag. My eyes adjusted to the dark, to the point where I could see the stars again.

And then I saw it arcing across the sky, just where I knew it'd be: a point of red light surrounded by a grainy nimbus caused by its passage through the atmosphere. I pointed. Others around me saw this and found it for themselves. The meadow became as silent as the Mynster during an Anathem.

The shooting star winked out and vanished into the black. The red glow was gone. A round of applause started up in the meadow, but it was tentative. Nervous. It died away before it really got going.

"I feel like a fool," Arsibalt said. He turned and looked at me. "When I think of all the things I've worried about and been afraid of in my life—and now it's plain that I've been scared of the wrong things."

They rang Voco at three o'clock in the morning.

No one minded the odd hour. No one was sleeping anyway. People showed up slow and late because most of them were carrying books and other things they thought they might need, supposing their names were called.

Statho Evoked seventeen.

"Lio."

"Tulia."

"Erasmas."

"Arsibalt."

"Tavener." And some other Tenners.

I stepped over the threshold into the chancel—a step I'd taken thousands of times to wind the clock. But when I wound the clock I always knew that a few minutes later Fraa Mentaxenes would open the door again. This time, I turned my back on three hundred faces I'd never see again—unless *they* got Evoked and sent to—well—wherever I was being sent.

I found myself with several I knew well, and some who were strangers to me: Hundreders.

The intonation of the names stopped. There had been so many that I'd lost count, and supposed we were finished. I looked at Statho, expecting him to move on to the next phase of the aut. He was staring at the list in his hand. His expression was difficult to read: his face and body had gone stiff. He blinked slowly and shifted the list toward the nearest candle as if having trouble reading it. He seemed to be scanning the same line over and over. Finally he forced himself to raise his gaze, and looked directly across the chancel at the Millenarians' screen.

"Voco," he said, but it came out husky and he had to clear his throat. "Voco Fraa Jad of the Millenarians."

Everything got quiet; or maybe it was blood raging in my ears.

There was a long wait. Then the door in the Thousanders' screen creaked open to reveal the silhouette of an old fraa. He stood there for a moment waiting for the dust to clear—that door didn't get opened very often. Then he stepped out into the chancel. Someone closed the door behind him.

Statho said a few more words to formally Evoke us. We said the words to answer the call. The avout behind the screens took up their anthem of mourning and farewell. All of them sang their hearts out. The Thousanders shook the Mynster with a mighty croaking bass line, so deep you felt more than heard it. That, even more than the singing of my Decenarian family, made the hairs prickle on my scalp, made my nose run and my eyes sting. The Thousanders were going to miss Fraa Jad and they were making sure he knew it in his bones.

I looked straight up, just as Paphlagon and Orolo had. The light of the candles only penetrated a short distance up the well. But I wasn't really doing this in an attempt to see something. I was doing it to prevent a deluge from running out of my nostrils and my eyes.

The others were moving around me. I lowered my chin to see what was happening. A junior hierarch was leading us out.

"There's a hypothesis, you know, that we just get taken to a gas chamber now," Arsibalt muttered.

"Shut up," I said. Not wanting to hear any more in this vein from him, I lingered, and let him go well ahead of me. Which took a while since he had made half of his bolt into a sack and was lugging a small library.

The hierarchs, all formally robed in purple, led us down the center aisle of the empty north nave and from there to the narthex just inside the Day Gate. We congregated below the Great Orrery. The Day Gate had been opened, but the plaza beyond was empty. No aerocraft was waiting for us there. No buses. Not even a pair of roller skates.

Junior hierarchs were circulating through the group handing things out. I got a shopping bag from a local department store. Inside were a pair of dungarees, a shirt, drawers, socks, and, on the bottom, a pair of walking shoes. A minute later I was handed a knapsack. Inside was a water bottle, a poly bag containing toiletries, and a money card.

There was also a wristwatch. It took me a while to understand why. Once we got more than a couple of miles from Saunt Edhar, we'd have no way of knowing the time.

Suur Trestanas addressed us. "Your destination is the Concent of Saunt Tredegarh," she announced.

"Is it a Convox?" someone asked.

"It is now," she answered. This killed all discussion for a minute as everyone absorbed that news.

"How are we to get there?" Tulia asked.

"Any way you can," said Trestanas.

"*What!?*" That or some variation of it came from all of the Evoked at once. Part of the romance of Voco—a small consolation for being ripped away from everyone you knew—was that you got whisked away in some kind of vehicle, as Fraa Paphlagon had been. Instead of which we'd been issued walking shoes.

"You are not to wear the bolt and the chord under the open sky, night or day," Trestanas went on. "Spheres are to be kept fist-sized or smaller and not used to make light. You are not to walk out of this gate all together—we'll have you emerge in groups of two or three. Later, if you want, you can meet up somewhere, away from the Concent. Preferably underneath something."

"What is the resolution of their surveillance?" Lio asked.

"We have no idea."

"Saunt Tredegarh's is two thousand miles away," Barb mentioned. In case this was of interest. Which it was.

"There are local organizations, connected with arks, that are trying to round up vehicles and drivers to get you there."

"Warden of Heaven people?" Arsibalt asked—he beat me to it.

"Some of them," Trestanas said.

"No, thanks!" someone called out. "One of those people tried to convert me during Apert. Her arguments were pathetic."

"Ho, ho, ho, ho, ho!" went someone very close to me.

I turned and looked. It was Fraa Jad, standing behind me with his shopping bag and his knapsack. He wasn't laughing that loudly, so no one else had noticed him. He smelled like smoke. He had not bothered to look into the shopping bag yet. He saw my head turn, and looked me in the eye—very amused. "The Powers That Be must be pissing their pants," he said, "or whatever they wear nowadays."

Everyone else was too stunned by all that had happened to say much. Here I had an advantage: I had gotten used to being stunned. Like Lio was used to being punched in the head.

I climbed up onto a stone bench that had been placed where visitors could sit on it and watch the orrery. "South of the concent, not far from the Century Gate, west of the river, there's a great roof on stilts that straddles a canal. Next to it is a machine-hall. You can't miss it. It's the biggest structure in the neighborhood by far. We can meet there under cover. Go there in small groups, like Suur Trestanas said. We'll convene there later and come up with a plan."

"What time shall we meet?" asked one of the Hundreders.

I considered it.

"Let's meet when we—I mean, when they—ring Provener."

Part 6

PEREGRIN

Peregrin: (1) In ancient usage, the epoch beginning with the destruction of the Temple of Orithena in -2621 and ending several decades later with the flourishing of the Golden Age of Ethras. (2) A theor who survived Orithena and wandered about the ancient world, sometimes alone and sometimes in the company of other such. (3) A Dialog supposedly dating to this epoch. Many were later written down and incorporated into the literature of the mathic world. (4) In modern usage, an avout who, under certain exceptional circumstances, leaves the confines of the math and travels through the Sæcular world while trying to observe the spirit, if not the letter, of the Discipline.

—THE DICTIONARY, *4th edition, A.R. 3000*

We took turns going into the men's and women's toilet chambers to change. The shoes immediately drove me crazy. I kicked them off and parked them under a bench, then found a clear place on the narthex floor where I could spread out my bolt and fold it up. That involved stooping and squatting—tricky, in dungarees. I couldn't believe people wore this stuff their whole lives!

Once I had my bolt reduced to a book-sized package, I wrapped my chord around it, put them into the department-store bag along with my balled-up sphere, and stuffed that into the bottom of the knapsack. Across the narthex, Lio was trying to perform some of his Vale-lore moves in his new clothes. He moved as if he'd just come down with a neurological disorder. Tulia's clothes didn't fit at all and she was negotiating a swap with one of the Centenarian suurs.

"Is this a Convox?"

"It is now."

There had only been eight Convoxes. The first had coincided with the Reconstitution. After that, one had been held at each Millennium to compile the edition of the Dictionary that would be used for the next thousand years, and to take care of other business of concern to the Thousanders. There had been one for the Big Nugget and one at the end of each Sack.

Barb became jumpy, then unruly, and then wild. None of the hierarchs knew what to make of him.

"He doesn't like change," Tulia reminded me. The unspoken message: he's your friend—he's your problem.

Barb didn't like being crowded either, so Lio and I crowded him. We crowded him into a corner where Arsibalt was encamped with his stack of books.

"Voco breaks the Discipline because the one Evoked goes forth alone, and from that point onward is immersed in the Sæcular world," Arsibalt intoned. "That's why they can't return. Convox is different. So many of us are taken at once that we can travel together and preserve the Discipline within our Peregrin group."

"Peregrin begins and ends at a math," Barb said, suddenly calm.

"Yes, Fraa Tavener."

"When we get to Saunt Tredegarh's—"

"We'll celebrate the aut of Inbrase," Arsibalt prompted him, "and—"

"And then we'll be together with other avout in the Convox," Barb guessed.

"And then—"

"And then when we're done doing whatever it is they want us to do, we make Peregrin back to Saunt Edhar," Barb went on.

"Yes, Fraa Tavener," said Arsibalt. I could sense him fending off the temptation to add *if we haven't been incinerated by an alien death ray or gassed by the Warden of Heaven.*

Barb calmed down. It wouldn't last. Once we left the Day Gate, we'd be contending with minor violations of the Discipline all the time. Barb would be certain to notice these and point them out. Why, oh why, had he been Evoked? He was just a brand-new fid! I was going to be babysitting him through the entire Convox.

As the small hours of the morning passed, though, and the lapis sphere that represented Arbre in the orrery ticked slowly around, I settled down a little bit and remembered that half of what I now knew about theorics was thanks to Barb. What would it say about me if I ditched him?

It was getting light outside. Half of the Evoked had already departed. The hierarchs were pairing Tenners with Hundreders because many of the latter would need help from the former in speaking Fluccish and coping with the Sæculum in general. Lio was summoned and went out with a couple of Hundreders. Arsibalt and Tulia were told to get ready.

I couldn't go out barefoot. My shoes were under a bench by the orrery. Fraa Jad had parked himself on that bench. Right above my shoes. His head was bent. His hands were folded in his lap. He must be doing some kind of profound Thousander meditation. If I disturbed him just so that I could fetch my shoes, he would turn me into a newt or something.

No one else wanted to disturb him either. Tulia, then Arsibalt, left with Hundreders in tow. There were only three Evoked left: Barb, Jad, and I. Jad was still in his bolt and chord.

Barb headed for Fraa Jad. I broke into a sprint, and caught up with him just as he arrived.

"Fraa Jad must change clothes," Barb announced, stretching his first-year Orth until it cracked.

Fraa Jad looked up. Until now I had thought that his hands were folded together in his lap. Now I saw that he was holding a disposable razor, still encased in its colorful package. I had one just like it in my bag. It was a common brand. Fraa Jad was reading the label. The big characters were Kinagrams, which he would never have seen before, but the fine print was in the same alphabet that we used.

"What principle explains the powers imputed by this document to the Dynaglide lubri-strip?" he asked. "Is it permanent, or ablative?"

"Ablative," I said.

"It is a violation of the Discipline for you to be reading that!" Barb complained.

"Shut up," Fraa Jad said.

"I don't mean in any way to be disrespectful," I tried, after a somewhat awkward and lengthy pause, "but—"

"Is it time to leave?" Fraa Jad asked, and checked the orrery as if it were a wristwatch.

"Yes."

Fraa Jad stood up and, in the same motion, stripped his bolt off over his head. Some of the hierarchs gasped and turned their backs.

Nothing happened for a little while. I rummaged in his shopping bag and found a pair of drawers, which I handed to him.

"Do I need to explain this?" I asked, pointing out the fly.

Fraa Jad took the garment from me and discovered how the fly worked. "Topology is destiny," he said, and put the drawers on. One leg at a time. It was hard to estimate his age. His skin was loose and mottled, but he balanced perfectly on one leg, then the other, as he put on the drawers.

The rest of getting Fraa Jad decent went by without notable incidents. I retrieved my shoes and tried once more to remember how to tie them. Barb seemed amazingly content to follow the command to shut up. I wondered why I had never tried this simple tactic with him before.

Stumbling and shuffling in our shoes, hitching our trousers up from time to time, we walked out the Day Gate. The plaza was empty. We crossed the causeway between the twin fountains and entered into the burgers' town. An old market had stood there until I'd been about six years old, when the authorities had renamed it the Olde Market, destroyed it, and built a new market devoted to selling T-shirts and other objects with pictures of the old market. Meanwhile, the people who had operated the little stalls in the old market had gone elsewhere and set up a thing on the edge of town that was now called the New Market even though it was actually the old market. Some casinos had gone up around the Olde Market, hoping to cater to people who wanted to visit it or who had business of one kind or another linked to the concent. But no one wanted to visit an Olde Market that was surrounded by casinos, and frankly the concent wasn't that much of an attraction, so the casinos were looking dirty and forlorn. Sometimes at night we could hear music playing from dance halls in their basements but they were awfully quiet at the moment.

"We can obtain breakfast in there," Barb said.

"Casino restaurants are expensive," I demurred.

"They have a breakfast buffet that you can go to for free. My father and I would eat there sometimes."

This made me sad but I could not dispute the logic, so I followed Barb and Jad followed me. The casino was a labyrinth of corridors that all looked the same. They saved money by keeping the lights dim and not washing the carpets; the mildew made us sneeze. We ended up in a windowless room below ground. Fleshy men, smelling like soap, sat alone or in pairs at tables. There was nothing to read. A speely display was mounted to the wall, showing feeds of news, weather, and sports. It was the first moving picture praxis that Fraa Jad had ever seen, and it took him some getting used to. Barb and I let him stare at it while we got food from the buffet. We put our trays down on a table and then I returned to Fraa Jad who was watching highlights of a ball game. A man at a nearby table was trying to draw him into conversation about one of the teams. Fraa Jad's T-shirt happened to be emblazoned with the logo of the same team and this had caused the man to jump to a whole set of wrong conclusions. I got between Fraa Jad's face and the speely and managed to break his concentration, then led him over to the buffet. Thousanders didn't eat much meat because there wasn't room to raise livestock on their crag. He seemed eager to make up for lost time. I tried to steer him toward cereal products but he knew what he wanted.

While we were eating, a news feed came up on the speely showing a Mathic stone tower, seen from a distance, at night, lit from above by a grainy red glow. The scene was very much like what the Thousanders' math had looked like last night. But the building on the feed was not one that I had ever seen.

"That is the Millenarians' spire in the Concent of Saunt Rambalf," Fraa Jad announced. "I have seen drawings of it."

Saunt Rambalf's was on another continent. We knew little of it because it had no orders in common with ours. I'd run across the name recently, but I could not remember exactly where—

"One of the three Inviolates," Barb said.

"Is that what you call us?" Jad asked.

Barb was right. The Flying Wedge monument inside our Year

Gate bore a plaque telling the story of the Third Sack and mentioning the three Thousander maths, in all the world, that had not been violated: Saunt Edhar, Saunt Rambalf, and—

"Saunt Tredegarh is the third," Barb continued.

As if the speely were responding to his voice, we now saw an image of a math that seemed to have been carved into the face of a stone bluff. It too was illuminated from above by red light.

"That's odd," I said. "Why would the aliens shine the light on the Three Inviolates? That is ancient history."

"They are telling us something," said Fraa Jad.

"What are they telling us? That they're really interested in the history of the Third Sack?"

"No," said Fraa Jad, "they are probably telling us that they have figured out that Edhar, Rambalf, and Tredegarh are where the Sæcular Power stored all of the nuclear waste."

I was glad we were speaking Orth.

We walked to a fueling station on the main road out of town and I bought a cartabla. They had them in different sizes and styles. The one I bought was about the size of a book. Its corners and edges were decorated with thick knobby pads meant to look like the tires of off-road vehicles. That's because this cartabla was meant for people who liked that kind of thing. It contained topographic maps. Ordinary cartablas had different decorations and they only showed roads and shopping centers.

When we got outside I turned it on. After a few seconds it flashed up an error message and then defaulted to a map of the whole continent. It didn't indicate our position as it ought to have done.

"Hey," I said to the attendant, back inside, "this thing's busted."

"No it's not."

"Yes it is. It can't fix our position."

"Oh, none of them can today. Believe me. Your cartabla works fine. Hey, it's showing you the map, isn't it?"

"Yeah, but . . ."

"He's right," said another customer, a driver who had just pulled into the station in a long-range drummon. "The satellites are on the blink. Mine can't get a fix. No one's can." He chuckled. "You just picked the wrong morning to buy a new cartabla!"

"So, this started last night?"

"Yeah, 'bout three in the morning. Don't worry. The Powers That Be depend on those things! Military. Can't get by without 'em. They'll get it all fixed in no time."

"I wonder if it has anything to do with the red lights shining on the—on the clocks last night," I said, just to see what they might say. "I saw it on the speely."

"That's one of their festivals—it's a ritual or something they do," said the attendant. "That's what I heard."

This was news to the other customer, and so I asked the attendant where he had heard it. He tapped a jeejah hanging on a lanyard around his neck. "Morning cast from my ark."

The natural question would now have been: *Warden of Heaven?* But showing more than the weakest curiosity might have pegged me as an escapee from a concent. So I just nodded and walked out of the fueling station. Then I started to lead Barb and Jad in the direction of the machine hall.

"The aliens are jamming the nav satellites," I announced.

"Or maybe they just shot them down!" said Barb.

"Let's buy a sextant, then," suggested Fraa Jad.

"Those have not been made in four thousand years," I told him.

"Let's build one then."

"I have no idea of all the parts and whatnot that go into a sextant."

He found this amusing. "Neither do I. I was assuming we would design it from first principles."

"Yeah!" snorted Barb. "It's just geometry, Raz!"

"In the present age, this continent is covered by a dense network of hard-surfaced roads replete with signs and other navigational aids," I announced.

"Oh," said Fraa Jad.

"Between that and this"—I waved the cartabla—"we can find

our way to Saunt Tredegarh without having to design a sextant from first principles."

Fraa Jad seemed a little put out by this. A minute later, though, we happened to pass an office supply store. I ran in and bought a protractor, then handed it to Fraa Jad to serve as the first component in his homemade sextant. He was deeply impressed. I realized that this was the first thing he'd seen extramuros that made sense to him. "Is that a Temple of Adrakhones?" he asked, gazing at the store.

"No," I said, and turned my back on it and walked away. "It is praxic. They need primitive trigonometry to build things like wheelchair ramps and doorstops."

"Nonetheless," he said, falling behind me, and looking back longingly, "they must have some perception—"

"Fraa Jad," I said, "they have no awareness of the Hylaean Theoric World."

"Oh. Really?"

"Really. Anyone out here who begins to see into the HTW suppresses it, goes crazy, or ends up at Saunt Edhar." I turned around and looked at him. "Where did you think Barb and I came from?"

Once we had gotten clear as to that, Barb and Jad were happy to follow me and discuss sextants as I led them on a wide arc around the west side of Saunt Edhar to the machine hall.

"You come and go at interesting times; I'll give you that," was how Cord greeted me.

We had interrupted her and her co-workers in the middle of some sort of convocation. Everyone was staring at us. One older man in particular. "Who's that guy and why does he hate me?" I asked, staring back at him.

"That would be the boss," Cord said. I noticed that her face was wet.

"Oh. Hmm. Sure. It didn't occur to me that you'd have one of those."

"Most people out here do, Raz," she said. "When a boss gives you that look, it's considered bad form to stare back the way you are doing."

"Oh, is it some kind of social dominance gesture?"

"Yeah. Also, busting into a private meeting in someone's place of employment is out of bounds."

"Well, as long as I have your boss's attention, maybe I should let him know that—"

"You called a big meeting here at midday?"

"Yeah."

"Or, as he would think of it, you—a total stranger—invited a whole lot of other total strangers to gather on his property—an active industrial site with lots of dangerous equipment—without asking him first."

"Well, this is really important, Cord. And it won't last long. Is that why you and your co-workers were having a meeting?"

"That was the first agenda item."

"Do you think he is going to physically assault me? Because I know a little vlor. Not as much as Lio but—"

"That would be an unusual way to handle it. Out here it would be a legal dispute. But you guys have your own separate law, so he can't touch you. And it sounds like the Powers That Be are leaning on him to let this thing happen. He'll negotiate with them for compensation. He's also negotiating with the insurance company to make sure that none of this voids his policy."

"Wow. Things are complicated out here."

Cord looked in the direction of the Præsidium and sniffled. "And they're not . . . in there?"

I thought about that for a while. "I guess my disappearance on Tenth Night probably looks as weird to you as your boss's insurance policy looks to me."

"Correct."

"Well, it wasn't personal. And it hurt me a lot. Maybe as much as this mess hurts you."

"That is unlikely," Cord said, "since ten seconds before you walked in here I got fired."

"That is wildly irrational behavior!" I protested. "Even by extramuros standards."

"Yes and no. Yes, it's crazy for me to get fired because of a decision you made without my knowledge. But no, in a way it's not, because I'm weird here. I'm a girl. I use the machines to make jewelry. I make parts for the Ita and get paid in jars of honey."

"Well, I'm really sorry—"

"Just stop," she suggested.

"If there's anything I can do—if you'd like to join the math—"

"The math you just got thrown out of?"

"I'm just saying, if there's anything I can do to make it up to you—"

"Give me an adventure."

In the moment that followed, Cord realized that this sounded weird, and lost her nerve. She held up her hands. "I'm not talking about some massive adventure. Just something that would make getting fired seem small. Something that I might remember when I'm old."

Now for the first time I reviewed everything that had happened in the last twelve hours. It made me a little dizzy.

"Raz?" she said, after a while.

"I can't predict the future," I said, "but based on what little I know so far, I'm afraid it has to be a massive adventure or nothing."

"Great!"

"Probably the kind of adventure that ends in a mass burial."

That quieted her down a little bit. But after a while, she said: "Do you need transportation? Tools? Stuff?"

"Our opponent is an alien starship packed with atomic bombs," I said. "We have a protractor."

"Okay, I'll go home and see if I can scrounge up a ruler and a piece of string."

"That'd be great."

"See you here at noon. If they'll let me back in, that is."

"I'll see to it that they do. Hey, Cord—"

"Yeah?"

"This is probably the wrong time to ask . . . but could you do me one favor?"

I went into the shade of the great roof over the canal and sat on a stack of wooden pallets, then took out the cartabla and figured out how to use its interface. This took longer than I'd expected because it wasn't made for literate people. I couldn't make any headway at all with its search functions, because of all its cack-handed efforts to assist me.

"Where the heck is Bly's Butte?" I asked Arsibalt when he showed up. It was half an hour before midday. About half of the Evoked had arrived. A small fleet of fetches and mobes had begun to form up: stolen, borrowed, or donated, I had no idea.

"I anticipated this," Arsibalt said.

"Bly's relics are all at Saunt Edhar," I reminded him.

"*Were,*" he corrected me.

"Excellent! What did you steal?"

"A rendering of the butte as it appeared thirteen hundred years ago."

"And some of his cosmographical notes?" I pleaded

No such luck: Arsibalt's face was all curiosity. "Why would you want Saunt Bly's cosmographical notes?"

"Because he ought to have noted the longitude and latitude of the place from which he was making the observations."

Then I remembered we had no way to determine our longitude and latitude anyway. But perhaps that information was entombed in the cartabla's user interface.

"Well, perhaps it's all for the best," Arsibalt sighed.

"*What!?*"

"We are supposed to go *directly* to Saunt Tredegarh's. Bly's Butte is not between here and there."

"I don't think it's that far out of the way."

"Didn't you just tell me you don't know where it is?"

"I have a rough idea."

"You can't even be certain that Orolo *went* to Bly's Butte. How are you going to persuade seventeen avout to make an illicit detour to search for a man they Anathematized a few months ago?"

"Arsibalt, I don't understand you. Why did you bother stealing Bly's relics if you had no intention of going to find Orolo?"

"At the time I stole them," he pointed out, "I didn't know it was a Convox."

It took me a moment to follow the logic. "You didn't know we'd be coming back."

"Correct."

"You reckoned, after we got finished doing whatever it is they wanted us to do—"

"We could find Orolo, and live as Ferals."

That was all interesting. Sort of poignant too. It did nothing, however, to solve the problem at hand.

"Arsibalt, have you noticed any pattern in the lives of the Saunts?"

"Quite a few. Which pattern would you like to draw to my attention?"

"A lot of them get Thrown Back before everyone figures out that they are Saunts."

"Supposing you're right," Arsibalt said, "Orolo's canonization is not going to happen for a long time; he's not a Saunt yet."

"Beg pardon," said a man who had lately been hovering nearby with his hands in his pockets, "are you the leader?"

He was looking at me. I naturally glanced around to see what fresh trouble Barb and Jad had gotten into. Barb was standing not far away, watching some birds that had built their nests up in the steel beams that supported the roof. He'd been doing this for a solid hour. Jad was squatting in a dusty patch, drawing diagrams using a broken tap as a stylus. Shortly after we'd arrived, Fraa Jad had wandered into the machine hall and figured out how to turn on a lathe. Cord's ex-boss almost *had* attacked me. Since then, both Jad and Barb had been reasonably well-behaved. So why was this extra asking me if I was the leader? He didn't seem angry or scared. More . . . lost.

I guessed that by *pretending* to be the leader I could make a few things go my way, at least for a little while, until they figured out I was faking it.

"Yes," I said, "I am called Fraa Erasmas."

"Oh, good to meet you. Ferman Beller," he said, and extended his hand a little uncertainly—he wasn't sure if we used that greeting. I shook his hand firmly and he relaxed. He was a stocky man in his fifth decade. "Nice cartabla you got there."

This seemed like an incredibly strange thing for him to say until I remembered that extras were allowed to have more than three possessions and that these often served as starting-points for small talk.

"Thanks," I tried. "Too bad it doesn't work."

He chuckled. "Don't worry. We'll get you there!" I guessed he was one of the locals who had volunteered to drive us. "Say, look, there's a guy over there wants to talk to you. Didn't know if we should, you know, let him approach."

I looked over and saw a man with a black stovepipe on his head, standing in the sun, glaring at me.

"Please send Sammann over," I said.

"You can't be serious!" Arsibalt hissed when Ferman was out of range.

"I sent for him."

"How would you go about sending for an Ita?"

"I asked Cord to do it for me."

"Is she here?" he asked, in a new tone of voice.

"I'm expecting her *and her boyfriend* to show up at any minute," I said, and jumped down off the stack of pallets. "Here, figure out where Bly's Butte is." I handed him the cartabla.

The bells of Provener flipped switches in my brain, as if I were one of those poor dogs that Saunts of old would wire up for psychological experiments. First I felt guilty: late again! Then my legs and arms ached for the labor of winding the clock. Next would be hunger for the midday meal. Finally, I felt wounded that they'd managed to wind the clock without us.

"We're going to hold much of the discussion in Orth because

many of us don't really speak Fluccish," I announced, from my pallet-stack podium, to the whole group: seventeen avout, one Ita, and a roster of extramuros people that grew and shrank according to their attention span and jeejah usage but averaged about a dozen. "Suur Tulia will translate some of what we say, but a lot of our conversation is going to be about stuff that is of interest only to avout. So you might want to have your own conversation about logistics—such as lunch." I saw Arsibalt nodding.

Then I switched to Orth. I was a little slow to get going because I was waiting for someone to point out that I was not actually the leader. But I had called this meeting, and I was standing on the stack of pallets.

And I was a Tenner. Our leader would have to be a Tenner who would be able to speak Fluccish and deal with the extramuros world. Not that I was an expert on that. But a Hundreder would be even more inept. Fraa Jad and the Hundreders couldn't very well choose which Tenner was going to be the leader, because they'd never met any of us until a few hours ago. For years, however, all of them had watched me and my team wind the clock, which gave me, Lio, and Arsibalt the advantage that our faces were familiar. Jesry, the natural leader, was gone. I had won Arsibalt's loyalty by speaking of lunch. Lio was too goofy and weird. So through no rational process whatsoever I was the leader. And I had no idea what I was going to say.

"We have to divide up among several vehicles," I said, stalling for time. "For now we'll stick with the same mixed groups of Tenners and Hundreders that were assigned in the Narthex this morning. We'll do that because it's simple," I added, because I could see Fraa Wyburt—a Tenner, older than me—getting ready to lodge an objection. "Swap things around later if you want. But each Tenner is responsible for making sure his Hundreders don't end up stranded in a vehicle with non-Orth speakers. I think we can all happily accept that responsibility," I said, looking Fraa Wyburt in the eye. He looked ready to plane me but decided to back down for reasons I could only guess at. "How will those groups be distributed among vehicles? My sib, Cord, the young woman in the vest with the tools, has offered to take some of us in her fetch. That's a Fluccish word. It is that industrial-looking vehicle that seems like a box on wheels. She wants me and her liaison-partner Rosk—the big man with the long hair—in there with her. Fraa Jad and Fraa Barb are with me. I have invited Sammann of the Ita to join us. I know some of you will object"—they were already objecting—"but that's why I'm putting him in the fetch with me."

"It's disrespectful to put an Ita in with a Thousander!" said Suur Rethlett—another Tenner.

"Fraa Jad," I said, "I apologize that we are discussing you as if you were not present. It goes without saying that you may choose whichever vehicle you want."

"We are supposed to maintain the Discipline during Peregrin!" Barb helpfully reminded us.

"Hey, you guys are scaring the extras," I joked. Because looking over the heads of my fraas and suurs I could see the extramuros people looking unnerved by our arguing. Tulia translated my last remark. The extras laughed. None of the avout did. But they did settle down a little.

"Fraa Erasmas, if I may?" said Arsibalt. I nodded. Arsibalt faced Barb but spoke loudly enough for all to hear: "We have been given two mutually contradictory instructions. One, the ancient standing order to preserve the Discipline during Peregrin. Two, a fresh order to get to Saunt Tredegarh by any means necessary. They have not provided us with a sealed train-coach or any other such vehicle that might serve as a mobile cloister. It is to be small private vehicles or nothing. And we don't know how to drive. I put it to you that the new order takes precedence over the old and that we must travel in the company of extras. And to travel with an Ita is certainly no worse than that. I say it is better, in that the Ita understand the Discipline as well as we do."

"Sammann's in Cord's fetch with me," I concluded, before Barb could let fly any of the objections that had been filling his quiver during Arsibalt's statement. "Fraa Jad's wherever he wants to be."

"I'll travel in the way you have suggested, and make a change if it is not satisfactory," said Fraa Jad. This silenced the remainder of the seventeen for a moment, simply because it was the first time most of them had heard his voice.

"That might happen immediately," I told him, "because the first destination of Cord's fetch will be Bly's Butte where I will try to find Orolo."

Now the extras really did have something to worry about, for the avout became quite loud and angry and my short tenure as self-appointed leader looked to be at an end. But before they pulled me down and Anathematized me I nodded to Sammann, who strode forward. I reached down and grabbed his hand and pulled him up to stand alongside me. The novel sight of a fraa touching an Ita broke the others' concentration for a moment. Then Sammann began to speak, which was so arresting that after the first few words he had a silent, almost rapt audience. A couple of Centenarian suurs plugged their ears and closed their eyes in silent protest; three others turned their backs on him.

"Fraa Spelikon told me to go to the Telescope of Saunts Mithra and Mylax and retrieve a photomnemonic tablet that Fraa Orolo had placed there hours before the starhenge was closed by the Warden Regulant," Sammann announced in correct but strangely accented Orth. "I obeyed. He did not issue any command as to information security relating to this tablet. So, before I gave it to him, I made a copy." And with that Sammann withdrew a photomnemonic tablet from a bag slung over his shoulder. "It contains a single image that Fraa Orolo created, but never got to see. I summon the image now," he said, manipulating its controls. "Fraa Erasmas, here, saw it a few minutes ago. The rest of you may view it if you wish." He handed it down to the nearest avout. Others clustered around, though some still refused even to acknowledge that Sammann was present.

"We need to be discreet and not show this to the extras," I said, "because I don't think they have any idea what we are up against." *We* meaning everyone on Arbre.

But no one heard me because by then they were all looking at the image on the tablet.

What the tablet showed did not force anyone to agree with me, but it was a huge distraction from the argument we'd been having. Those who were inclined to see things my way derived new confidence from it. The rest of them lost their nerve.

It took an hour to figure out who was going in which vehicle. I couldn't believe it could be so complicated. People kept changing their minds. Alliances formed, frayed, and dissolved. Inter-alliance coalitions snapped in and out of existence like virtual particles. Cord's big boxy fetch, which had three rows of seats, was to be occupied by her, Rosk, me, Barb, Jad, and Sammann. Ferman Beller had a large mobe that was made to travel on uneven surfaces. He would take Lio, Arsibalt, and three of the Hundreders who had decided to throw in with us. We thought we had pretty efficiently filled the two largest vehicles, but at the last minute another extra who had been making a lot of calls on his jeejah announced that he and his fetch were joining our caravan. The man's name was Ganelial Crade and he was pretty clearly some kind of Deolater from a counter-Bazian ark—whether Warden of Heaven or not, we didn't know yet. His vehicle was an open-back fetch whose bed was almost completely occupied by a motorized tricycle with fat, knobby tires. Only three people could fit into its cab. No one wanted to ride with Ganelial Crade. I was embarrassed on his behalf, though not so embarrassed that I was willing to climb into his vehicle. At the last minute, some younger associate of his stepped up, tossed a duffel bag into the back, and climbed into the cab with him. So that completed the Bly's Butte contingent.

The direct-to-Tredegarh contingent comprised four mobes, each with one owner/driver and one Tenner: Tulia, Wyburt, Rethlett, and Ostabon. Other seats in these vehicles were taken up by Hundreders who wanted no part of an Orolo expedition or by other extras who had volunteered to come on the journey.

With the exception of Cord and Rosk, all of the extras appeared to be part of religious groups, which made all of the avout more or less uncomfortable. I reckoned that if there had been a military base in this area the Sæcular Power might have ordered some soldiers to dress up as civilians and drive us around, but since there wasn't, they'd hit on the idea of relying on organizations that people were willing to volunteer for on short notice, which in this time and place meant arks. When I explained it to people in those terms, it seemed to settle them down a little bit. The Tenners sort of understood it. The Hundreders found it quite difficult to fathom and kept wanting to know more about the deologies espoused by their would-be drivers, which in no way shortened the process of getting them into vehicles.

Ganelial Crade was probably in his fourth decade, but you could mistake him for a younger man because he was slender and whiskerless. He announced that he knew the location of Bly's Butte and that he would lead us there and we should follow him. Then he got into his fetch and started the engine. Ferman Beller ambled over and grinned at him until he opened his window, then started talking to him. Pretty soon I could tell that they were disagreeing about something—mostly by watching Crade's passenger, who was glaring at Beller.

I got that mud-on-the-head sense of embarrassment again. Ganelial Crade had spoken with such confidence that I'd assumed he'd already gone over this plan with Ferman Beller and that the two of them had agreed on it. Now it was obvious that no such thing had ever happened. I'd been prepared to follow Crade wherever he led us.

I could now see that this business of being the leader was going to be a pain in the neck because people would always be trying to get me to do the wrong things or get rid of me altogether.

"Some leader!" I said, referring to myself.

"Huh?" asked Lio.

"Don't let me do stupid things any more," I ordered Lio, who looked baffled. I started walking towards Crade's fetch. Lio and Arsibalt followed at a distance. Crade and Beller were openly arguing now. I really wanted no part of this but I had been cornered into doing something.

The problem, I realized, was that Crade claimed to have knowledge we didn't have as to the location of Bly's Butte. That was my fault. I'd made the error of admitting that I didn't know exactly where it was. Inside the concent it was fine to admit ignorance, because that was the first step on the road to truth. Out here, it just gave people like Crade an opening to seize power.

"Excuse me!" I called out. Beller and Crade stopped arguing and looked at me. "One of my brothers has brought with him ancient documents from the concent that tell us where to go. By combining this knowledge with the skills of our Ita and the topographic maps on the cartabla, we can find our own way to the place we are going."

"I know exactly where your friend went," Crade began.

"We don't," I said, "but as I mentioned we can figure it out long before we get there."

"Just follow me and—"

"That is a brittle plan. If we lose you in traffic we will be in a bad way."

"If you lose me in traffic you can call me on my jeejah."

This hurt because Crade was being more rational than I was, but I couldn't back down at this point. "Mr. Crade, you may go on ahead if you like, and have the satisfaction of beating us there, but if you look in your rearview and notice that we are no longer visible, it is because we have decided to keep our own counsel as to how we should get there."

Crade and his passenger now hated me forever but at least this was over.

This plan, however, necessitated a shake-up that put me and Sammann in Ferman Beller's vehicle with Arsibalt. The three of us would navigate. Lio and a Hundreder moved to Cord's fetch to balance the load; they would follow. Ganelial Crade sprayed us with loose rocks as he gunned his fetch out into the open.

"That man behaves so much like the villain in a work of literature, it's almost funny," Arsibalt observed.

"Yes," said one of the Hundreders, "it's as if he'd never heard of foreshadowing."

"He probably *hasn't*," I said. "But please remember that our driver is the only extra in this vehicle and so let's show him the courtesy of speaking Fluccish at least part of the time."

"Go ahead," said the Hundreder, "and I'll see if I can parse it."

Fraa Carmolathu, as this Hundreder was called, was a little bit of a dork, but he had volunteered to go fetch Orolo, so he couldn't be all bad. He was five or ten years older than Orolo, and I speculated that he was a friend of Paphlagon.

"How many roads lead northeast, parallel to the mountains?" I asked Beller. I was hoping he'd say *only one.*

"Several," he said. "Which one do you want to take, boss?"

"By definition a butte is free-standing—not part of a range," Arsibalt said in Orth, "so—"

"It rises from the plateau south of the mountains," I announced in Fluccish. "We don't need to take a mountain road."

Beller put the vehicle into gear and pulled out. I waved goodbye to Tulia. She was watching us go, looking a little shocked. Our departure *had* been abrupt, but I was afraid that if we waited one more minute there would be another crisis. Tulia had elected to go directly to Tredegarh so that she could try to find Ala. Perhaps I ought to have done the same. But this was not an easy choice, and I thought I was choosing rightly. If all went well, we'd get to Tredegarh only a couple of days later than Tulia's contingent. She'd do a fine job of leading them there.

Before leaving town we stopped, or rather slowed down, at a place where we could get food without spending a lot of time. I remembered this kind of restaurant from my childhood but it was new to the Hundreders. I couldn't help seeing it as they did: the ambiguous conversation with the unseen serving-wench, the bags of hot-grease-scented food hurtling in through the window, condiments in packets, attempting to eat while lurching down a highway, volumes of messy litter that seemed to fill all the empty space in the mobe, a smell that outstayed its welcome.

Bazian Orthodox: The state religion of the Bazian Empire, which survived the Fall of Baz, erected, during the succeeding age, a mathic system parallel to and independent of that inaugurated by Cartas, and endured as one of Arbre's largest faiths.

Counter-Bazian: Religion rooted in the same scriptures, and honoring the same prophets, as Bazian Orthodoxy, but explicitly rejecting the authority, and certain teachings, of the Bazian Orthodox faith.

—THE DICTIONARY, *4th edition, A.R. 3000*

By the time we'd finished eating, we'd passed out of view of the Præsidium. We had left most of the slines' quarter behind us and were moving across a sort of tidal zone that was part of the city when the city was big and part of the country when it wasn't. Where a tidal zone would have driftwood, dead fish, and uprooted seaweed, this had stands of scrawny trees, animals killed by vehicles, and tousled jumpweed. Where the tidal zone would be littered with empty bottles and wrecked boats, this had empty bottles and abandoned fetches. The only thing of consequence was a complex where fuel trees that had been barged down from the mountains were chewed up and processed. There we were caught for a few minutes in a traffic jam of tanker-drummons. But few of these were going our way, and soon we had got clear of them and passed into the district of vegetable gardens and orchards that stretched beyond.

In my vehicle, besides me and Ferman Beller, were Arsibalt, Sammann, and two Hundreder Fraas, Carmolathu and Harbret. The other vehicle contained Cord, Rosk, Lio, Barb, Jad, and another Edharian from the Hundreder math: Fraa Criscan. I noted a statistical oddity, which was that there was only one female, and that was my sib, who was pretty unconventional as females went. Intramuros, we didn't often see the numbers get so skewed. Extramuros, of course, it depended on what religions and social mores prevailed at a given time. Naturally, I wondered how this had come about, and spent a little while reviewing my memories of the hour-long scramble to get people into vehicles. Of course, the biggest factor in determining who'd go in which group was how one thought about Orolo and the mission to go and find him. Perhaps there was something about this foray that smelled good to men and bad to women.

We numbered twelve, not counting Ganelial Crade. This was a common size for an athletic team or a small military unit. It had been speculated for a long time that this was a natural size for a hunting party of the Stone Age, and that men were predisposed to feel comfortable in a group of about that size. Anyway, whether it was a statistical anomaly or primitive behavior programmed into our sequences, this was what we'd ended up with. I spent a few minutes wondering whether Tulia and some of the other suurs in the straight-to-Tredegarh contingent hated me for letting it come out this way, then forgot about it, since we needed to think about navigation.

From the drawing that Arsibalt had supplied—which showed the profile of a range of mountains in the distance—and from certain clues in the story of Saunt Bly as recorded in the Chronicles, and from things that Sammann looked up on a kind of super-jeejah, we were able to identify three different isolated mountains on the cartabla, any one of which might have been Bly's Butte. They formed a triangle about twenty miles on a side, a couple of hundred miles from where we were now. It didn't seem that far away but when we showed it to Ferman he told us we shouldn't expect to reach it until tomorrow; the roads in that area, he explained, were "new gravel," and it would be slow going. We could get there today, but it would be dark and we wouldn't be able to do anything. Better to find a place to stay nearby and get an early start tomorrow.

I didn't understand "new gravel" until several hours later when we turned off the main highway and on to a road that had once been paved. It almost would have been faster to drive directly over the earth than to pick our way over this crazed puzzle of jagged slabs.

Arsibalt was uncomfortable being around Sammann, which I could tell because he was extremely polite when addressing him. Complaining of motion sickness, he moved up to the seat next to Ferman and talked to him in Fluccish. I sat behind him and tried to catch up on sleep. From time to time my eyelids would part as we caught air over a gap in the road and I'd get a dreamy glimpse of some religious fetish swinging from the control panel. I was no expert on arks, but I was pretty sure that Ferman was Bazian Ortho-dox. At some level this was just as crazy as believing in whatever Ganelial Crade believed, but it was a far more traditional and pre-dictable form of crazy.

Still, if a group of religious fanatics had wanted to abduct a few carloads of avout, they couldn't have done a slicker job of it. That's why I snapped awake when I heard Ferman Beller mention God.

Until now he'd avoided it, which I could not understand. If you sincerely believed in God, how could you form one thought, speak one sentence, without mentioning Him? Instead of which Deolaters like Beller would go on for hours without bringing God into the conversation at all. Maybe his God was remote from our doings. Or—more likely—maybe the presence of God was so obvious to him that he felt no more need to speak of it than did I to point out, all the time, that I was breathing air.

Frustration was in Beller's voice. Not angry or bitter. This was the gentle, genial frustration of an uncle who can't get something through a nephew's head. We seemed so smart. Why didn't we be-lieve in God?

"We're observing the Sconic Discipline," Arsibalt told him—happy, and a bit relieved, to've been given an opportunity to clear this up. He was too optimistic, I thought, too confident he could get Beller to see it our way. "It's not the same thing as not be-lieving in God. Though"—he hastily added—"I can see why it looks that way to one who's never been exposed to Sconic thought."

"I thought your Discipline came from Saunt Cartas," said Beller.

"Indeed. One can trace a direct line from the Cartasian princi-ples of the Old Mathic Age to many of our practices. But much has been added, and a few things have been taken away."

"So, I guess Scone was another Saunt who added something?"

"No, a scone is a little cake."

Beller chuckled in the forced, awkward way that extras did when someone told a joke that was not funny.

"I'm serious," Arsibalt said. "Sconism is named after the little tea-cakes. It is a system of thought that was discovered about halfway between the Rebirth and the Terrible Events. The high-water mark of Praxic Age civilization, if you will. A couple of hundred years earlier, the gates of the Old Maths had been flung open, the avout had gone forth and mingled with the Sæculars—mostly Sæculars of wealth and status. Lords and ladies. The globe, by this point, had been explored and charted. The laws of dynamics had been worked out and were just beginning to come into praxic use."

"The Mechanic Age," Beller tried, dredging up a word he'd been forced to memorize in some suvin a long time ago.

"Yes. Clever people could make a living, in those days, just by hanging around in salons, discussing metatheorics, writing books, tutoring the children of nobles and industrialists. It was the most harmonious relationship between, er—"

"Us and you?" Beller suggested.

"Yes, that had existed since the Golden Age of Ethras. Anyway, there was one great lady, named Baritoe, whose husband was a philandering idiot, but never mind, she took advantage of his absence to run a salon in her house. All the best metatheoricians knew to gather there at a particular time of day, when the scones were coming out of her ovens. People came and went over the years, so Lady Baritoe was the only constant. She wrote books, but, as she herself is careful to say, the ideas in them can't be attributed to any one person. Someone dubbed it Sconic thought and the name stuck."

"And it all got incorporated into your Discipline, what, a couple of hundred years later?"

"Yes, not in a very formal way though. More as a set of habits. Thinking-habits that many of the new avout already shared when they came in the gates."

"Such as not believing in God?" Beller asked.

And here—though we were driving on fair, level ground—I felt as I would've if we'd been on a mountain track with a thousand-foot cliff to one side, which Beller could have spilled us into with a twitch of the controls. Arsibalt was relaxed, though, which I marveled at, because he could be so high-strung about matters that were so much less dangerous.

"Studying this is sort of a pie-eating contest," Arsibalt began.

This was a Fluccish expression that Lio, Jesry, Arsibalt, and I used to mean a long thankless trudge through a pile of books. It completely wrong-footed Beller, who thought we were talking of scones, and so here Arsibalt had to spend a minute or two disentangling these two baked-goods references.

"I'll try to sketch it out," Arsibalt continued, once they'd gotten back on track. "Sconic thought was a third way between two unacceptable alternatives. By then it was well understood that we do all of our thinking up here in our brains." He tapped his head. "And that the brain gets its inputs from eyes, ears, and other sense organs. The naïve attitude is that your brain works directly with the real world. I look at this button on your control panel, I reach out and feel it with my hand—"

"Don't touch that!" Beller warned.

"I see *you* seeing it and having thoughts about it, and I conclude that it's really there, just as my eyes and fingers present it to me, and that when I think about it I'm thinking about the real thing."

"That all seems pretty obvious," Beller said.

Then there was an awkward silence, which Beller finally broke by saying—in good humor—"I guess that's why you called it naïve."

"At the opposite extreme, there were those who argued that everything we think we know about the world outside of our skulls is an illusion."

"Seems kind of smart-alecky more than anything else," Beller said after considering it for a bit.

"The Sconics didn't much care for it either. As I said, they developed a third attitude. 'When we think about the world—or about almost *anything*—' they said, 'what we are really thinking about is a bunch of data—givens—that have reached our brains from our eyes and ears and so forth.' To go back to my example, I am given a visual image of that button and I am given a memory of what it felt like when I touched it, but *that's all* I have to work with, as far as that button is concerned—it is *impossible, unthinkable,* for my brain to come to grips with the actual, physical button in and of itself because my brain simply does not have access to it. All that my brain can ever work with are the look and the feel—givens piped into our nerves."

"Well, I guess I see the point. It doesn't have that smart-aleckiness of the other one you mentioned. But it seems like a distinction without a difference," Beller said.

"It's not," Arsibalt said. "And here is where the pie-eating contest would begin, if you wanted to understand *why* it's not. Because, starting from this idea, the Sconics went on to develop a whole metatheorical system. It was so influential that no one has been able to do metatheorics since then without coming to grips with it. All subsequent metatheorics is a refutation, an amendment, or an extension of Sconic thought. And one of the most important conclusions you arrive at, if you make it to the end of the pie-eating contest, is that—"

"There is no God?"

"No, something different, and harder to sum up, which is that certain topics are simply out of bounds. The existence of God is one of those."

"What do you mean, out of bounds?"

"If you follow through the logical arguments of the Sconic system, you are led to the conclusion that our minds can't think in a productive or useful way about God, if by God you mean the Bazian Orthodox God which is clearly not spatiotemporal—not existing in space and time, that is."

"But God exists everywhere and in all times," Beller said.

"But what does it really mean to say that? Your God is more than this road, and that mountain, and all the other physical objects in the universe put together, isn't He?"

"Sure. Of course. Otherwise we'd just be nature-worshippers or something."

"So it's crucial to your definition of God that He is more than just a big pile of stuff."

"Of course."

"Well, that 'more' is by definition outside of space of time. And the Sconics demonstrated that we simply cannot think in a useful way about anything that, in principle, can't be experienced through our senses. And I can already see from the look on your face that you don't agree."

"I don't!" Beller affirmed.

"But that's beside the point. The point is that, after the Sconics, the kinds of people who did theorics and metatheorics stopped talking about God and certain other topics such as free will and what existed before the universe. And that is what I mean by the Sconic Discipline. By the time of the Reconstitution it had become ingrained. It was incorporated into our Discipline without much discussion, or even conscious awareness."

"Well, but with all the free time you've got—sitting there in your concents—couldn't *someone* be troubled in four thousand years to be aware of it? To discuss it?"

"We have less free time than you imagine," Arsibalt said gently, "but nevertheless, many people have devoted much thought to the matter, and founded Orders devoted to denying God, or believing in Him, and currents have surged back and forth in and among the maths. But none of it seems to have moved us away from the basic position of the Sconics."

"Do you believe in God?" Beller asked flat-out.

I leaned forward, fascinated.

"I *have* been reading a lot, lately, about things that are non-spatiotemporal—yet believed to exist." By this, I knew he meant mathematical objects in the Hylaean Theoric World.

"Doesn't that go against the Sconic Discipline?" Beller asked.

"Yes," Arsibalt said, "but that is perfectly all right, as long as one isn't going about it in a naïve way—as if Lady Baritoe had never written a word. A common complaint made about the Sconics is that they didn't know much about pure theorics. Many theoricians, looking at Baritoe's works, say 'wait just a minute, there's something missing here—we *can* relate directly to non-spatiotemporal objects when we prove theorems and so on.' The stuff I've been reading lately is all about that."

"So you can see God by doing theorics?"

"Not God," Arsibalt said, "not a God that any ark would recognize."

After that he managed to change the subject. He—like I—had wondered what the Powers That Be might have told Ferman and the others when they had put out the call for volunteers.

The answer seemed to be: not much. The Sæcular Power needed some sort of puzzle solved—the sort of thing that avout were good at. Some fraas and suurs would have to be moved from Point A to Point B so that they could work on this conundrum. People like Ferman Beller were naturally curious about us. They had all learned about the Reconstitution in their suvins, and they understood that we had an assigned role to play, however sporadically, in making their civilization work. They were fascinated to see the mechanism being invoked, at least once in their lives, and were proud to be a part of it even if they hadn't a clue as to why it was being engaged.

In the hottest part of the afternoon we pulled off into the shade of a line of trees that had once served as wind-break for a farm compound, now collapsed. We hadn't seen Crade in hours, but Cord's fetch was right behind us. Some of us walked around and some dozed. The mountains darkened the northwestern sky, though if you didn't know what they were you might mistake them for a storm front. On their opposite slope they caught most of the moisture blowing in from the ocean and funneled it into the river that ran through our concent. Consequently this side was arid. Only bunchgrass and low fragrant shrubs would grow here of their own accord. From age to age the Sæcular Power would irrigate it and people would live here growing grain and legumes, but we were now on the wane of such a cycle, as was obvious from the condition of the roads, the farmsteads, and what were shown on the cartabla as towns. The old irrigation ditches were fouled by whatever would grow in them, which was mostly things with thorns, spines, and detachable burrs. Lio and I went for a brisk walk along one of these, but we didn't say much as we were keeping an eye out for snakes.

Sammann kept looking as if he had something to say. We decided on a shake-up that put me and him in Cord's fetch, while Lio and Barb went to Ferman's mobe. Barb wanted to stay with Jad but we all knew that Jad must be getting a little weary of his company and so we insisted. Cord was tired of driving, so Rosk took the controls.

"Ferman Beller is communicating with a Bazian installation on one of those mountains," Sammann told me.

This was an odd phrasing, since Baz had been sacked fifty-two hundred years ago. "As in Bazian Orthodox?" I asked.

Sammann rolled his eyes. "Yes."

"A religious institution?"

"Or something."

"How do you know this?"

"Never mind. I just thought you might want to know that Ganelial Crade isn't the only one with an agenda."

I considered asking Sammann what *his* agenda was but decided to let it drop. He was probably wondering how a bunch of Bazian priests would treat an Ita.

My agenda was looking at the photomnenomic tablet, which I knew that everyone in this vehicle—except for Cord, who'd been driving—must have been studying. I'd only had a brief look at it before. Cord and I sat together in the back. The sun was shining in so we threw a blanket over our heads and huddled in the dark like a couple of kids playing campout.

This thing that Orolo had wanted so badly to take pictures of: would it be something that we would recognize as a ship? Until Sammann had showed me this tablet a few hours ago, all I had known was that it used bursts of plasma to change its velocity and that it could shine red lasers on things. For all I'd known, it could have been a hollowed-out asteroid. It could have been an alien life form, adapted to live in the vacuum of space, that shot bombs out of a sphincter. It could have been constructed out of things that we would not even recognize as matter; it could have been only half in this universe and half in some other. So I had made an effort to open my mind. I had been prepared to be confronted by some sort of image that I would not be able to understand at first. And it had, indeed, been a riddle. But not the kind of riddle I'd been expecting. I hadn't had time to study it, to puzzle over it, at the time. Now I had a good long look.

The image was streaked in the direction of the ship's motion. Fraa Orolo had probably set up the telescope to track it across the sky, but he'd had to make his best guess as to its direction and speed, and he hadn't gotten it exactly right, hence the motion blur. I guessed that this was only the last in a series of such images that Orolo had been making during the weeks leading up to Apert, each slightly better than the last as he learned how to track the target and how to calibrate the exposure. Sammann had already applied some kind of syntactic process to the image to reduce the blur and bring out many details that would have been lost otherwise.

It was an icosahedron. Twenty faces, each of them an equilateral triangle. That much I'd seen when Sammann had first shown it to me. And therein lay the puzzle, because such a shape could be either natural or artificial. Geometers loved icosahedrons, but so did nature; viruses, spores, and pollens had all been known to take this shape. So perhaps it *was* a space-adapted life form, or a giant crystal that had grown in a gas cloud.

"This thing can't be pressurized," I pointed out.

"Because the surfaces are all flat?" Cord said—more as statement than question. She dealt with compressed gases in her work, and knew in her bones that any vessel containing pressure must be rounded: a cylinder, a sphere, or a torus.

"Keep looking," Sammann advised us.

"The corners," Cord said, "the—what-do-you-call-'em—"

"Vertices," I said. Those twenty triangular facets came together at twelve vertices; each vertex joined five triangles. These seemed to bulge outward a little. At first I'd mistaken this for blur. But on a closer look I convinced myself that each vertex was a little sphere. And this drew my eye to the edges. The twelve vertices were joined by a network of thirty straight edges. And those too had a rounded, bulging look to them—

"There they are!" said Cord.

I knew exactly what she meant. "The shock absorbers," I said. For it was obvious, now: each of the thirty edges was a long slender shock absorber, just like the ones on the suspension of Cord's fetch, except bigger. The frame of this ship was just a network of thirty shock absorbers that came together at a dozen spherical vertices. The entire thing was one big distributed shock absorption system.

"There must be ball-and-socket joints in the corners, to make that work," Cord said.

"Yeah—otherwise the frame couldn't flex," I said. "But there's a big part of this I'm not getting."

"What are the flats made of? The triangles?" Cord said.

"Yeah. No point making a triangle out of things that can give, unless the stuff in the middle can give too—change its shape a little, when the shocks flex." So we spent a while puzzling over the twenty flat, triangular surfaces that accounted for the ship's surface area. These, I thought, looked a little funny. They looked rugged. Not smooth metal, but cobbled together.

"I could almost swear it's stucco."

"I was going to say concrete," Cord said.

"Think gravel," suggested Sammann.

"Okay," Cord said, "gravel has some give to it where concrete doesn't. But how's it held together?"

"There are a lot of little rocks floating around up there," I said. "In a way, gravel's the most plentiful solid thing you can obtain in space."

"Yeah, but—"

"But that doesn't answer your question," I admitted. "Who knows? Maybe they have woven some kind of mesh to hold them in place."

"Erosion control," Cord said, nodding.

"What?"

"You see it on the banks of rivers, where they're trying to stop erosion. They'll throw a bunch of rocks into a cube of wire mesh, then stack the cubes and wire 'em together."

"It's a good analogy," I said. "You need erosion control in space too."

"How do you figure?"

"Micrometeoroids and cosmic rays are always coming in from all directions. If you can surround your ship with a shell of cheap material—aka, gravel—you've cut down quite a bit on the problem."

"Hey, wait a sec," she said, "this one looks different." She was pointing to one face that had a circle inscribed in it. We hadn't noticed it at first, because it was around to one side, foreshortened, harder to make out. The circle was clearly made of different stuff: I had the feeling it was hard, smooth, and stiff.

"Not only that," I pointed out, "but—"

She'd caught it too: "No shocks around this one." The three edges outlining this face were sharp and simple.

"I've got it!" I said. "That one is the pusher plate."

"The what?"

I explained about the atomic bombs and the pusher plate. She accepted this much more readily than any of us had. The ship that Lio had shown us in the book had been a stack: pusher plate, shocks, crew quarters. This one was an envelope: the outer shell was one large distributed shock absorber, as well as a shield. And, I was beginning to realize, a shroud. A veil to hide whatever was suspended in the middle.

Once we'd identified the pusher plate—the stern of the ship—our eyes were naturally drawn to the face on the opposite, or forward end: its prow. This was hidden from view. But one of the adjoining shock absorbers was visible. And something was written on it. Printed there neatly was a line of glyphs that had to be an inscription in some language. Some of the glyphs, like circles and simple combinations of strokes, could easily be mistaken for characters in our Bazian alphabet. But others belonged to no alphabet that I had ever seen.

And yet they were so close to our letters that this alphabet seemed almost like a sib of ours. Some of them were Bazian letters turned upside-down or reflected in a mirror.

I flung the blanket off.

"Hey!" Cord complained, and closed her eyes.

Fraa Jad turned around and looked me in the face. He seemed ever so slightly amused.

"These people"—I did not call them aliens—"are related to us."

"We have started referring to them as the Cousins," announced Fraa Criscan, the Hundreder sitting next to Fraa Jad.

"What could possibly explain that!?" I demanded—as if they could possibly know such a thing.

"These others have been speculating about it," Fraa Jad said. "Wasting their time—as it is just a hypothesis."

"How big is this thing—has anyone tried to estimate its dimensions?" I asked.

"I know that from the settings of the telescope and the tablet," Sammann said "It is about three miles in diameter."

"Let me spare you having to work it out in your head," said Fraa Criscan, watching my face, mildly amused. "If you want to generate pseudogravity by spinning part of the ship—"

"Like those old doughnut-shaped space stations in spec-fic speelies?" I asked.

Criscan looked blank. "I've never seen a speely, but yes, I think we are talking about the same thing."

"Sorry."

"It's okay. If you are playing that game, and you want to generate the same level of gravity we have here on Arbre—and if there is such a thing hidden inside of this icosahedron—"

"Which is kind of what I was imagining," I allowed.

"Say it's two miles across. The radius is one mile. It would have to spin about once every eighty seconds to provide Arbre gravity."

"Seems reasonable. Doable," I said.

"What are you talking about?" Cord asked.

"Could you live on a merry-go-round that spun once every minute and a half?"

She shrugged. "Sure."

"Are you talking about where the Cousins came from?" shouted Rosk over his shoulder. He couldn't understand Orth but he could pick out some words and he could read our tones of voice.

"We're debating whether it is productive to have any such discussion at all," I said, but that was a little too complicated, shouted from the back of the fetch over road noise.

"In books and speelies, sometimes you see a fictional universe where an ancient race seeded a bunch of different star systems with colonies that lost touch with each other afterwards," Rosk volunteered.

The other avout in the vehicle looked as if they were biting their tongues.

"The problem is, Rosk, we have a fossil record—"

"That goes back billions of years, yeah, that is a problem with that idea," Rosk admitted. From which I guessed that others had already torn this idea limb from limb before his eyes, but that Rosk liked it too much to let go of it—he'd never been taught Diax's Rake.

Cord had put the blanket back over her head but she said, "Another idea that we were talking about earlier was, you know, the whole concept of parallel universes. Then Fraa Jad pointed out that this ship is quite clearly in *this* universe."

"What a killjoy," I remarked—in Fluccish, obviously.

"Yeah," she said. "It is a real drag hanging around with you people. So logical. Speaking of which—did you notice the geometry proof?"

"What?"

"They couldn't stop talking about it, earlier."

I ducked back under the blanket with her. She knew how to pan and zoom the image. She magnified one of the faces, then dragged it around until the screen was filled with something that looked like this, though a lot streakier and blurrier:

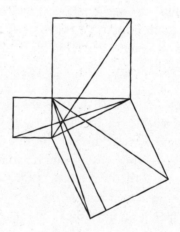

"That's certainly a weird thing to put on your ship," I said. I zoomed back out for a moment because I wanted to get a sense of where this diagram was located. It was centered on one of the icosahedron's faces, adjoining, and just aft of, the one that we had identified as the bow. If the ship's envelope was made of gravel, held in some kind of matrix, then this diagram had been built into this face as a sort of mosaic, by picking out darker pieces of gravel and setting them carefully into place. They'd put a lot of work into it.

"It's their emblem," I said. Only speculating. But no one spoke out against the idea. I zoomed back in and spent a while examining the network of lines. It was obviously a proof—almost certainly of the Adrakhonic Theorem. The sort of problem that fids worked all the time as an exercise. Just as if I were sitting in a chalk hall, trying to get the answer quicker than Jesry, I began to break it down into triangles and to look for right angles and other features that I could use to anchor a proof. Any fid from the Halls of Orithena probably would have gotten it by now, but my plane geometry was a little rusty—

Wait a minute! some part of my mind was saying.

I poked my head out from under the blanket, careful this time not to blind Cord.

"This is just plain creepy," I said.

"That's the same word Lio used!" Rosk shouted back.

"Why do you guys all think it's creepy?" Cord wanted to know.

"Please supply a definition of the oft-used Fluccish word *creepy*," said Fraa Jad.

I tried to explain it to the Thousander, but primitive emotional states were not what Orth was good at.

"An intuition of the numenous," Fraa Jad hazarded, "combined with a sense of dread."

"*Dread* is a strong word, but you are close."

Now I had to answer Cord's question. I made a few false starts. Then I saw Sammann watching me and I got an idea. "Sammann here is an expert on information. Communication, to him, means transmitting a series of characters."

"Like the letters on this shock absorber?" Cord asked.

"Exactly," I said, "but since the Cousins use different letters, and have a different language, a message from them would look to us like something written in a secret code. We'd have to decipher it and translate it into our language. Instead of which the Cousins have decided here to—to—"

"To bypass language," Sammann said, impatient with my floundering.

"Exactly! And instead they have gone directly to this picture."

"You think they put it there for us to see?" Cord asked.

"Why else would you go to the trouble to put something on the *outside* of your ship? They wanted to mark themselves with something they knew we'd understand. And *that* is what's creepy—the fact that they just *knew* in advance that we'd understand this."

"I don't understand it," Cord protested.

"*Yet*. But you know what it is. And we could get you to understand it a lot faster than we could decipher an alien language. It looks to me as though Fraa Jad has already worked it out." My eye had fallen on a leaf in his lap that bore a copy of the diagram, with some marks and notations that he had added as he had worked through the logic of the proof.

Logic. Proof. The Cousins had these—had them in common with us.

With us who lived in concents, that is.

Avout with nukes!

Roaming from star system to star system in a bomb-powered concent, making contact with their planet-bound brethren—

"Snap out of it, Raz!" I said to myself.

"Yes," said Fraa Jad, who'd been watching my face, "please do."

"They came," I said, "the Cousins did, and the Sæcular Power picked them up on radar. Tracked them. Worried about them. Took pictures of them. Saw that." I pointed to the proof on Fraa Jad's lap. "Recognized it as an avout thing. Got worried. Figured out that the ship had been detected—somehow—by at least one fraa: Orolo."

"I told him about it," Sammann said.

"What?"

Sammann looked uncomfortable. But I had gotten it all so badly wrong that he couldn't contain himself—he had to straighten me out. "A communication reached us from the Sæcular Power," he said.

"Us meaning the Ita?"

"A third-order reticule."

"Huh?"

"Never mind. We were told to go in secret—bypassing the hierarchs—to the concent's foremost cosmographer, and tell him of this thing."

"And then what?"

"There were no further instructions," Sammann said.

"So you chose Orolo."

Sammann shrugged. "I went to his vineyard one night while he was alone, cursing at his grapes, and told him this—told him I had stumbled across it while reviewing logs of routine mail-protocol traffic."

I didn't understand a word of his Ita gibberish but I got the gist of it. "So, part of your orders from the Sæcular Power were to make it seem that this was just you, acting on your own—"

"So that they could later deny that they had anything to do with it," Sammann said, "when it came time to crack down."

"I doubt that they were so premeditated," Fraa Jad put in, using a mild tone of voice, as Sammann and I had become heated—conspiratorial. "Let us get out the Rake," Jad went on. "The Sæcular Power had radar, but not pictures. To get pictures they needed telescopes and people who knew how to use them. They did not want to involve the hierarchs. So they devised the strategy that Sammann has just explained to us. It was only a means of getting some pictures of the thing as quickly and quietly as possible. But when they *did* get the pictures, they saw this." He rested the palm of his hand on the proof in his lap.

"And then they realized that they'd made a big mistake," I said, in a much calmer tone than before. "They had divulged the existence and nature of the Cousins to the last people in the world they'd want to know about them."

"Hence the closure of the starhenge and what happened to Orolo," Sammann said, "and hence me in this fetch, as I have no idea what they'll want to do to *me*."

I'd assumed until now that Sammann had obtained permission

to go on this journey. This was my first hint that it was more complicated than that. I found it strange to hear an Ita voicing fear of getting in trouble, since usually it was *we* who worried about *their* sneaky tricks—such as the one that had ensnared Orolo. But then my point of view snapped around and I saw it his way. Precisely because people believed the things they did about the Ita, no one was likely to believe Sammann's story or stand up for him if all of these doings broke out into the open.

"So you made this copy of the tablet and kept it so that you would have—"

"*Something,*" he said, "that I could leverage."

"And you showed yourself in Clesthyra's Eye. Announcing, in a deniable way, that you knew something—that you had information."

"Advertising," Sammann said, and the shape of his face changed, whiskers shifting on whiskers—his way of hinting at a smile.

"Well, it worked," I said, "and here you are, on the road to nowhere, being driven around by a bunch of Deolaters."

Cord got fed up with hearing Orth and moved up to the front of the fetch to sit with Rosk. I felt sorry—but some things were nearly impossible to talk about in Fluccish.

I was dying to ask Fraa Jad about the nuclear waste, but was reluctant to broach this topic with Sammann listening. So I drew my own copy of the proof on the Cousins' ship and began working it. Before long I got bogged down. Cord and Rosk started playing some music on the fetch's sound system, softly at first, more loudly when no one objected. This had to be the first time Fraa Jad had ever heard popular music. I cringed so hard I thought I'd get internal injuries. But the Thousander accepted it as calmly as he had the Dynaglide lubri-strip. I gave up trying to work the proof, and just looked out the window and listened to the music. In spite of all of my prejudices against extramuros culture, I kept being surprised by moments of beauty in these songs. Most of them were forgettable but one in ten sheltered some turn or inflection that proved that the person who had made it had achieved some kind of upsight—had, for a moment, got it. I wondered if this was a representative sampling, or if Cord was just unusually good at finding songs with beauty in them and loading only those onto her jeejah.

The music, the heat of the afternoon, the jouncing of the fetch, my lack of sleep, and shock at leaving the concent—with all of these affecting me at once, it was no wonder I couldn't work a proof. But as the day grew old and the sun came in more and more horizontally, as the dying towns and ruined irrigation systems came less and less frequently and the landscape was purified into high desert, spattered with stony ruins, I started thinking that something else was working on me.

I was used to Orolo being dead. Not literally dead and buried, of course, but dead to me. That was what Anathem did: killed an avout without damaging the body. Now, with only a few hours to get used to the idea, I was about to see Orolo again. At any moment, for all I knew, we might spy him hiking up one of these lonely crags to get ready for a night's observations. Or perhaps his emaciated corpse was waiting for us under a cairn thrown up by slines descended from those who'd eaten Saunt Bly's liver. Either way, it was impossible for me to think of anything else when I might be confronted by such a thing at any moment.

Cord's face was shining on me. She reached for a control and turned down the music, then repeated something. I had gone into a sort of trance, which I shattered by moving.

"Ferman's on the jeejah," she explained. "He wants to stop. Pee and parley."

Both sounded good to me. We pulled off at a wide place in the road along a curving grade, a third of the way into a descent that would, over the next half-hour, take us into a flat-bottomed valley that connected to the horizon. This was no valley of the wet and verdant type, but a failure in the land where withered creeks went to die and flash floods spent their rage on a supine waste. Spires and palisades of brown basalt hurled shadows much longer than they were tall. Two solitary mountains rose up perhaps twenty or thirty miles away. We gathered around the cartabla and convinced ourselves that those were two of the three candidates we'd chosen earlier. As for the third—well, it appeared that we had just driven around it and were now scouring its lower slopes.

Ferman wanted to talk to me in my capacity as leader. I shook off the last wisps of the near-coma I had sunk into, and drew myself up straight.

"I know you guys don't believe in God," he began, "but considering the way you live, well, I thought you might feel more at home staying with—"

"Bazian monks?" I hazarded.

"Yes, exactly." He was a little taken aback that I knew this. It was only a lucky guess. When Sammann had mentioned earlier that Ferman was talking to a "Bazian installation," I had imagined a cathedral or at any rate something opulent. But that was before I'd seen the landscape.

"A monastery," I said, "is on one of those mountains?"

"The closer of the two. You can see it about halfway up, on the northern flank."

With some hints from Ferman I was able to see a break in the mountain's slope, a sort of natural terrace sheltered under a crescent of dark green: trees, I assumed.

"I've been there for retreats," Ferman remarked. "Used to send my kids there every summer."

The concept of a retreat didn't make sense to me until I realized that it was how I lived my entire life.

Ferman misinterpreted my silence. He turned to face me and held up his hands, palms out. "Now, if you're not comfortable, let me tell you we have enough water and food and bedrolls and so on that we can camp anywhere we like. But I was thinking—"

"It's reasonable," I said, "if they'll accept women."

"The monks have their own cloister, separate from the camp. But girls stay at the camp all the time—they have women on the staff."

It had been a long day. The sun was going down. I was tired. I shrugged. "If nothing else," I said, "it might make for a good story or two, for us to tell when we get to Saunt Tredegarh."

Lio and Arsibalt had been hovering. They pounced on me as

soon as Ferman Beller started to walk away. They both had the somewhat tense and frayed look of people who'd just spent several hours cooped up with Barb. "Fraa Erasmas," Arsibalt began, "let's be realistic. Look at this landscape! There's no way anyone could live here on his own. How would one obtain food, water, medical care?"

"Trees are growing on one place on that mountain," I said. "That probably means that there is fresh water. People like Ferman send their kids here for summer camp—how bad can it be?"

"It's an oasis!" Lio said, having fun whipping out this exotic word.

"Yeah. And if the nearer butte has an *oasis* large enough for a monastery and a summer camp, why couldn't the farther one have a place where Ferals like Bly, Estemard, and Orolo could live in the shade and drink spring water?"

"That doesn't solve the problem of getting food," Arsibalt pointed out.

"Well, it's an improvement on the picture that I've been carrying around in my head," I said. I didn't have to explain this to the others because they'd had it in their heads too: desperate men living on the top of a mountain, eating lichens.

"There must be a way," I continued, "the Bazian monks do it."

"They are a larger community, and they are supported by alms," Arsibalt said.

"Orolo told me that Estemard had been sending him letters from Bly's Butte for years. And Saunt Bly managed to live there for a while—"

"Only because slines worshipped him." Lio pointed out.

"Well, maybe we'll find a bunch of slines bowing down to Orolo then. I don't know how it works. Maybe there's a tourist industry."

"Are you joking?" Arsibalt asked.

"Look at this wide spot in the road where we are stopped," I said.

"What of it?"

"Why do you suppose it's here?"

"I haven't the faintest idea, I'm not a praxic," Arsibalt said.

"So that vehicles can pass each other more easily?" Lio guessed.

I held out my arm, drawing their attention to the view. "It's here because of that."

"What? Because it's beautiful?"

"Yeah." And then I turned away from Arsibalt and looked at Lio, who started to walk away. I fell in alongside him. Arsibalt stayed behind to examine the view, as if he could discover some flaw in my logic by staring at it long enough.

"Did you get a chance to look at the icosahedron?" Lio asked me.

"Yeah. And I saw the proof—the geometry."

"You think these people are like us. That they will be sympathetic to our point of view as followers of Our Mother Hylaea," he said, trying these phrases on me for size.

I was already defensive—sensing a flank maneuver. "Well, I think that they are clearly trying to get at *something* by making the Adrakhonic Theorem into their emblem . . ."

"The ship is heavily armed," he said.

"Obviously!"

He was already shaking his head. "I'm not talking about the propulsion charges. They'd be almost useless as weapons. I'm talking about other things on that ship—things that become obvious when you look for them."

"I didn't see anything that looked remotely like a weapon."

"You can hide a lot of equipment on a mile-long shock absorber," he pointed out, "and who knows what's concealed under all that gravel."

"Can you give me an example?"

"The faces have regularly spaced features on them. I think that they are antennas."

"So? Obviously they're going to have antennas."

"They are phased arrays," he said. "Military stuff. Just what you'd want to aim an X-ray laser, or a high-velocity impactor. I'll need to consult books to know more. Also, I don't like the planets lined up on the nose."

"What do you mean?"

"There's a row of four disks painted on a forward shock. I think that they are depictions of planets. Like on a military aerocraft of the Praxic Age."

It took me a few moments to sort out the reference. "Wait a minute, you think that they are *kills?*"

Lio shrugged.

"Well, now, hold on a second!" I said. "Couldn't it be that it's something more benign? Maybe those are the home planets of the Cousins."

"I just think that everyone is too eager to look for happy, comforting interpretations—"

"And your role as a Warden Fendant-in-the-making is to be way more vigilant than that," I said, "and you're doing a great job."

"Thanks."

We walked along silently for a little while, strolling up and down the length of this wide place, occasionally passing others who were taking the opportunity to get a little bit of exercise. We happened upon Fraa Jad, who was walking alone. I decided that now was the moment.

"Fraa Lio," I said, "Fraa Jad has informed me that the Millenarian math at Saunt Edhar is one of three places where the Sæcular Power put all of its nuclear waste around the time of the Reconstitution. The other two are Rambalf and Tredegarh. Both of them were illuminated last night by a laser from the Cousins' ship."

Lio wasn't as surprised by this as I'd hoped. "Among Fendant types there is a suspicion that the Three Inviolates were allowed to remain unsacked for a reason. One hypothesis is that they are dumps for Everything Killers and other dangerous leftovers of the Praxic Age."

"Please. You speak of my home. Don't call it a dump," Fraa Jad said. But he was amused—not offended. He was being—if I could say this of a Thousander—playful.

"Have you seen the stuff?" Lio asked.

"Oh yes. It is in cylinders, in a cavern in the rock. We see it every day."

"Why?"

"Various reasons. For example, my avocation is thatcher."

"I don't recognize the word," I said.

"It is an ancient profession: one who makes roofs out of grass."

"What possible application could that have in a nuclear waste d—repository?"

"Condensation forms on the ceiling of the cavern and drips onto the tops of the cylinders. Over thousands of years it could corrode them—or, just as bad, form stalagmites whose weight would crush and rupture the containers. We have always maintained thatched roofs atop the cylinders to prevent this from happening."

This was all so weird that I couldn't think of anything to do other than to continue making polite chatter. "Oh, I see. Where do you get the grass? You don't have much room to grow grass up there, do you?"

"We don't need much. A properly made thatching lasts for a long time. I have yet to replace all of those that were put in place by my fid, Suur Avradale, a century ago."

Lio and I both walked on for a few paces before this hit us; then we exchanged a look, and wordlessly agreed not to say anything.

"He was just having us on," I said, the next time Lio and I could speak privately, which was at the retreat center, as we were dropping our bags in the cell we were to share. "He was getting back at us for calling his math a dump."

Lio said nothing.

"Lio! He's not that old!"

Lio put his bag down, stood up straighter than I could, and rotated his shoulders down and back, which was a way of recovering his equilibrium. As if he could defeat opponents just through superior posture. "Let's not worry about how old he is."

"You think he *is* that old."

"I said, let's not worry about it."

"I don't think we have to *worry* about it. But it would be *interesting* to know."

"Interesting?" Lio did the shoulder thing again. "Look. We're both talking bulshytt, would you agree?"

"Yeah, I agree," I said immediately.

"Enough of this. We have to talk straight—and then we have to shut up, if we don't want to get burned at the stake."

"Okay. You see this from a Fendant point of view. I take your point."

"Good. So we both know what we're *really* talking about now."

"That you can't live that long without repairing the sequences in the nuclei of your cells," I said.

"*Especially* if you work around radiation."

"I hadn't thought of that." I pondered it for a moment, replaying the earlier conversation with Jad. "How could he have possibly made such a slip? He must know how dangerous it is even to hint that he is—er—the sort of person who can do things like repairing his own cells."

"Are you kidding? It wasn't a slip. It was deliberate, Raz."

"He was letting us know—"

"He was entrusting us with his life," Lio said. "Haven't you noticed how he was sizing everyone up today? He *chose* us, my fraa."

"Wow! If that's really true, I'm honored."

"Well, enjoy being honored while you can," Lio said, "because that kind of honor doesn't come without obligations."

"What kind of obligations are you thinking of?"

"How should I know? I'm just saying that he was Evoked for a reason. He's expected to *do* something. He's starting to develop a strategy. And we're part of that strategy now. Soldiers. Pawns."

This shut me up for a little while; I could hardly think straight. Then I remembered something that somehow made it easier.

"We were already pawns anyway," I said.

"Yeah. And given the choice, I'd rather be a pawn of someone I can see," Lio said. And then he smiled the old Lio smile for the first time since last night. He had been more serious than I'd ever seen him. But the sight of those kills—if that was what they were—lined up on that ship had given him a lot to be serious about.

We avout liked to tell ourselves that we lived in a humble and austere manner, by contrast with Bazian prelates who strutted around in silk robes, enveloped in clouds of incense. But at least our buildings were made out of stone and didn't need a lot of upkeep. This place was all wooden: higher up the slope, a little ark and a ring of barracks that formed a sort of cloister, centered on a spring. Down closer to the road, two rows of cells with bunk beds and a large building with a dining hall and a few meeting rooms. The buildings were well taken care of, but it was obvious that they were in continual decay and that, if the people were to leave, the place would be a pile of kindling in a few decades.

We did not get to see how the monks lived. The cells where we stayed were clean but covered with graffiti scratched into the walls and bunks by the kids who came here by the coach-load during the summer. It was just dumb luck that no kids were there when we arrived; one group had departed a couple of days earlier, and another was expected soon. Of the half-dozen young adults who staffed the place, four had gone back to town during the break. The remaining two, and the Bazian priest who was in charge of the retreat center, had prepared a simple meal for us. After we'd deposited our bags in our cells and spent a few minutes cleaning up in the communal bathrooms, we convened in the dining hall and sat down at rows of folding tables much like the ones we used at Apert. The place smelled of art supplies.

The monks, we were told, numbered forty-three, which seemed like a small figure to us avout for whom a chapter was a hundred strong. Four of them came down to dine with us. It wasn't clear whether they had special status, like hierarchs, or were simply the only ones of the forty-three who had any curiosity about us. All of them were greybeards, and all wanted to meet Fraa Jad. Bazian Orthodox clerical Orth was about seventy percent the same as what we spoke.

After the exchange that Lio and I just had, you might think we'd have wanted to sit next to Fraa Jad, but in fact we had the opposite reaction and ended up sitting as far away from him as we could—as if we were secret agents in a speely, making a big point of preserving our cover, playing it cool. At the last minute, Arsibalt hustled in with several of the Hundreders; they'd been running a calca in one of the cabins. He had a wild look about him, desperate to talk. He had not been able to examine the photomnenomic tablet until late in the day. Now he'd seen the geometry proof blazoned on the Cousins' ship, and he was about to explode. I felt sorry for him when he came into the dining hall and found himself forced to choose between sitting with me and Lio, or with Fraa Jad and the Bazian monks. Ferman Beller, noting his indecision, stood up and beckoned him over. Arsibalt couldn't decline the invitation without giving offense, so he went and sat with Ferman.

We always opened our meals by invoking the memory of Saunt Cartas. The gist of it was that our minds might be nourished by all manner of ideas originating from thinkers dating all the way back to Cnoüs, but for the physical nourishment of our bodies we relied upon one another, joined in the Discipline that we owed to Cartas. Deolaters, on the other hand, all had different pre-meal rituals. Bazian Orthodoxy was a post-agrarian religion in which literal sacrifice had been replaced by symbolic; they opened their meals with a re-enactment in effigy of that, then praised their God for a while, then asked Him for goods and services. The priest who ran the retreat center launched into it out of habit, but got unnerved in the middle when he noticed that none of the avout were bowing their heads, just gazing at him curiously. I didn't think he was all that troubled by our not believing what he believed—he must have been used to that. He was more embarrassed that he'd committed a faux pas. So, when he was finished, he implored us to say whatever sort of blessing or invocation might be traditional in the math. As mentioned we were strangely lacking in sopranos and altos, but we were able to put together enough tenors, baritones, and basses to sing a very ancient and simple Invocation of Cartas. Fraa Jad handled the drone, and I could swear he made the silverware buzz on the tables.

The four monks seemed to enjoy this very much, and when we'd finished they stood up and did an equally ancient-sounding prayer. It must have dated back to the early centuries of their monastic age, just after the Fall of Baz, because their Old Orth was indistinguishable from ours, and it had obviously been composed in a time before the music of the maths and of the monasteries had diverged. If you didn't listen too carefully to the words, you could easily mistake this piece for one of ours.

The conversation during the meal had to be superficial compared to the events of the last twenty-four hours, given that we had to talk in Fluccish and couldn't mention the ship in earshot of our hosts. I became frustrated, then bored, then drowsy, and ate mostly in silence. Cord and Rosk talked to each other. They weren't religious, and I could tell they felt awkward here. One of the young women on the staff made lavish efforts to make them feel welcome, which mostly backfired. Sammann was absorbed in his jeejah, which he had somehow patched into the retreat center's communications system. Barb had found a list of the camp rules and was memorizing it. Our three Hundreders sat in a cluster and talked amongst themselves; they could not speak Fluccish and didn't have the Thousander glamor that had made Fraa Jad the center of attention with the Bazian monks. I noticed that Arsibalt was deep in conversation with Ferman, and that Cord and Rosk had shifted closer to them, so I wandered over to see what they were talking about. It seemed that Ferman had been thinking about the Sconics, and wanted to know more. Arsibalt, for lack of any other way to pass the time, had launched into a calca called "The Fly, the Bat, and the Worm," which was a traditional way of explaining the Sconic theory of time and space to fids. "Look at that fly crawling around on the table," Arsibalt said. "No, don't shoo it away. Just look at it. The size of its eyes."

Ferman Beller gave it a quick glance and then returned his eyes to his dinner. "Yeah, half of its body seems to be eyes."

"Thousands of separate eyes, actually. It doesn't seem as though it could possibly work." Arsibalt reached back behind himself and waved his hand around, nearly hitting me in the face. "Yet if I wave my hand back here, far away, it doesn't care—knows there is no threat. But if I bring my hand closer . . ."

Arsibalt brought his hand forward. The fly took off.

". . . somehow its microscopic brain takes signals from thousands of separate, primitive eyes and integrates them into a correct picture, not merely of space, but of spacetime. It knows where my hand is. Knows that if my hand keeps moving thus, it'll soon squash it—so it had better change its position."

"You think the Cousins have eyes like that?" Beller asked.

Arsibalt dodged sideways: "Maybe they're like bats instead. A bat would have detected my hand by listening for echoes."

Beller shrugged. "All right. Maybe the Cousins squeak like bats."

"On the other hand, when I shift my body to swat the fly, it creates a pattern of vibrations in the table that a creature—even a deaf and blind one, such as a worm—might feel . . ."

"Where is this going?" Beller asked.

"Let's do a thought experiment," Arsibalt said. "Consider a Protan fly. By that, I mean the pure, ideal form of a fly."

"Meaning what?"

"All eyes. No other sense organs."

"All right, I'm considering it," Beller said, trying to be good-humored.

"Now, a Protan bat."

"All ears?"

"Yes. Now a Protan worm."

"Meaning all touch?"

"Yes. No eyes, ears, or nose—just skin."

"Are we going to do all five senses?"

"It would start to become boring, so let's stop with three," Arsibalt said. "We place the fly, the bat, and the worm in a room with some object—let's say a candle. The fly sees its light. The bat squeals at it, and hears its echoes. The worm feels its warmth, and can crawl over it to feel its shape."

"It sounds like the old parable of the six blind men and the—"

"No!" said Arsibalt. "This is completely different. Almost the *opposite*. The six blind men all have the same sensory equipment—"

Beller nodded, seeing his mistake. "Yeah, but the fly, the bat, and the worm have different ones."

"And the six blind men disagree about what it is they are grop-ing—"

"But the fly, the bat, and the worm agree?" Beller asked, raising an eyebrow.

"You sound skeptical. Rightly so. But they are all sensing the same object, are they not?"

"Sure," Beller said, "but when you say that they agree with each other, I don't know what that means."

"It's a fascinating question, so let's explore it. Let's change the rules a little," said Arsibalt, "just to set the stakes a little higher, and make it so that they *have to* agree. The thing in the middle of the room isn't a candle. Now, it's a trap."

"A trap!?" Beller laughed.

Arsibalt got a proud look.

"What's the point of that?" Beller asked.

"Now there's a threat, you see. They have to figure out what it is or they'll be caught."

"Why not a hand coming down to swat them?"

"I thought of that," Arsibalt admitted, "but we have to make al-lowances for the poor worm, who senses things very slowly com-pared to the other two."

"Well," Beller said, "I expect they're all going to be caught in the trap sooner or later."

"They are *very* intelligent," Arsibalt put in.

"Still—"

"All right then, it is a huge cavern swarming with millions of flies, bats, and worms. Thousands of traps are scattered about the place. When a trap catches or kills a victim, the tragedy is witnessed by many others, who learn from it."

Beller considered it for a while as he served himself some more vegetables. After a while, he said, "Well, I expect that where you're going with it is that once enough time has gone by, and enough of these critters have been caught, the flies will learn what a trap looks like, the bats what it sounds like, the worms what it feels like."

"The traps are being planted by exterminators who are intent on killing everything. They keep disguising them, and coming up with new designs."

"All right," Beller said, "then the flies, bats, and worms have to get clever enough to detect traps that are disguised."

"A trap could look like anything," Arsibalt said, "so they must learn to look at any object in their environment and to puzzle out whether or not it could possibly function as a trap."

"Okay."

"Now, some of the traps are suspended from strings. The worms can't reach them or feel their vibrations."

"Too bad for the worms!" Beller said.

"The flies can't see anything at night."

"Poor flies."

"Some parts of the cavern are so noisy that the bats can't hear a thing."

"Well, it sounds as though the flies, the bats, and the worms had better learn to cooperate with one another," Beller said.

"How?" This was the sound of Arsibalt's trap closing on his leg.

"Uh, by communicating, I guess."

"Oh. And what exactly does the worm say to the bat?"

"What does all of this have to do with the Cousins?" Beller asked.

"It has everything to do with them!"

"You think that the Cousins are hybrid fly-bat-worm creatures?"

"No," Arsibalt said, "I think that *we* are."

"AAARGH!" Beller cried, to laughter from everyone.

Arsibalt threw up his hands as if to say *how could I make this any clearer?*

"Please explain!" Beller said. "I'm not used to this, my brain's getting tired."

"No, *you* explain. What does the worm say to the bat?"

"The worm can't even talk!"

"This is a side issue. The worms learn over time that they can squirm around into different shapes that the bats and flies can recognize."

"Fine. And—let me see—the flies could fly down and crawl around on the worms' backs and give them signals that way. Et cetera. So, I guess that each type of critter could invent signals that the other two could detect: worm-bat, bat-fly, and so on."

"Agreed. Now. What do they say to each other?"

"Well, hold on now, Arsibalt. You're skipping over a bunch of stuff! It's one thing to say a worm can squirm into a shape like C or S that could be recognized by a fly looking down. But that's an *alphabet*. Not a language."

Arsibalt shrugged. "But languages develop over time. Monkeys hooting at each other developed into some primitive speech: 'there's a snake under that rock' and so forth."

"Well, that's fine, if snakes and rocks is all you have to talk about."

"The world in this thought experiment," Arsibalt said, "is a vast, irregular cavern sprinkled with traps: some freshly laid and still dangerous, others that have already been sprung and may safely be ignored."

"You went out of your way to say that they were mechanical contraptions. Are you saying they're predictable?"

"You or I could inspect one and figure out how it worked."

"Well, in that case it comes down to saying 'this gear here engages with that gear, which rotates yonder shaft, which is connected to a spring,' and so on."

Arsibalt nodded. "Yes. That's the sort of thing the flies, bats, and worms would have to communicate to one another, in order to figure out what was a trap and what wasn't."

"All right. So, same way that monkeys in trees settled on words for 'rock' and 'snake,' they'd develop symbols—words—meaning 'shaft,' 'gear,' and so on."

"Would that be enough?" Arsibalt asked.

"Not for a complicated piece of clockwork. Let's see, you could have two gears that were close to each other, but they couldn't engage each other unless they were close enough for their teeth to mesh."

"Proximity. Distance. Measurement. How would the worm measure the distance between two shafts?"

"By stretching from one to the other."

"What if they were too far apart?"

"By crawling from one to the other, and keeping track of the distance it moved."

"The bat?"

"Timing the difference in echoes between the two shafts."

"The fly?"

"For the fly it's easy: compare the images coming into its eyes."

"Very well, let's say that the worm, the bat, and the fly have each observed the distance between the two shafts, just as you said. How do they compare notes?"

"The worm for example would tell what it knew by translating it into the squirming-alphabet you mentioned."

"And what does a fly say to another fly upon seeing all of this?"

"I don't know."

"It says 'the worm seems to be relating some kind of account of its wormy doings, but since I don't squirm on the ground and can't imagine what it would be like to be blind, I haven't the faintest idea what it's trying to tell me!'"

"Well, this is just what I was saying earlier," Beller complained, "they have to have a language—not just an alphabet."

Arsibalt asked, "What is the only sort of language that could possibly serve?"

Beller thought for a minute.

"What are they trying to convey to each other?" Arsibalt prompted him.

"Three-dimensional geometry," Beller said. "And, since parts of the clock are moving, you'd also need time."

"Everything that a worm could possibly say to a fly, or a fly to a bat, or a bat to a worm, would be gibberish," Arsibalt said, leading Beller forward.

"Kind of like saying 'blue' to a blind man."

"'Blue' to a blind man, *except for* descriptions of geometry and of time. That is the only language that these creatures could ever possibly share."

"This makes me think of that geometry proof on the Cousins' ship," Beller said. "Are you saying that we are like the worms, and the Cousins are like the bats? That geometry is the only way we can speak to each other?"

"Oh no," Arsibalt said. "That's not where I was going at all."

"Where are you going then?" Beller asked.

"You know how multicellular life evolved?"

"Er, single-celled organisms clumping together for mutual advantage?"

"Yes. And, in some cases, encapsulating one another."

"I've heard of the concept."

"That is what our brains are."

"*What!?*"

"Our brains are flies, bats, and worms that clumped together for mutual advantage. These parts of our brains are talking to each other all the time. Translating what they perceive, moment to moment, into the shared language of geometry. That's what a brain is. That's what it is to be conscious."

Beller spent a few seconds mastering the urge to run away screaming, then a few minutes pondering this. Arsibalt watched him closely the whole time.

"You don't mean *literally* that our brains evolved that way!" Beller protested

"Of course not."

"Oh. That's a relief."

"But I put it to you, Ferman, that our brains are functionally indistinguishable from ones that evolved thus."

"Because our brains have to be doing that kind of processing all the time, just—"

"Just in order for us to be conscious. To integrate our sensory perceptions into a coherent model of ourselves and our surroundings."

"Is this that Sconic stuff you were talking about earlier?"

Arsibalt nodded. "To a first approximation, yes. It is post-Sconic. Certain metatheoricians who had been strongly influenced by the Sconics came up with arguments like this one later, around the time of the First Harbinger." Which was a bit more detail than Ferman Beller really wanted to hear. But Arsibalt's eyes flicked in my direction, as if to confirm what I'd been suspecting: he had been reading up on this kind of thing as part of his research into the work that Evenedric had pursued later in his life. I lingered on the edge of that dialog until it started to wind down. Then I got up and headed straight for my bunk, planning to sleep good and hard. But Arsibalt, moving uncharacteristically fast, chased me out of the dining hall and ran me down.

"What's on your mind?" I asked him.

"Some of the Hundreders held a little calca just before dinner."

"I noticed."

"They couldn't get the numbers to add up."

"Which numbers?"

"That ship simply isn't big enough to travel between star systems in a reasonable amount of time. It can't possibly hold a sufficient number of atomic bombs to accelerate its own mass to relativistic velocity."

"Well," I said, "maybe it split off from a mother ship that we haven't seen yet, and that *is* that big."

"It doesn't look like it's that kind of vessel," Arsibalt said. "It is huge, with space to support tens of thousands of people indefinitely."

"Too big to be a shuttle—too small for interstellar cruising," I said.

"Precisely."

"Seems like you are making a lot of assumptions though."

"That is a fair criticism," he said with a shrug. But I could tell he had some other hypothesis.

"Okay. What do you think?" I asked him.

"I think it is from another cosmos," he said, "and *that* is why they Evoked Paphlagon."

We were at the door of my cabin.

"This cosmos we're living in has me flummoxed," I said. "I don't know whether I can start thinking about additional ones at this point in the day."

"Good night then, Fraa Erasmas."

"Good night, Fraa Arsibalt."

I woke to the sound of bells. I couldn't make sense of them. Then I remembered where I was and understood that they were not our bells, but those of the monks, rousing them for some punishingly early ritual.

My mind was about half sorted out. Many of the new ideas, events, people, and images that had come at me from every direction the day before had been squared away, like so many leaves rolled up and thrust into pigeonholes. Not that anything had really been settled. All of the questions that had been open when my head had hit the pillow were still pending. But in the intervening hours, my brain had been changing to fit the new shape of my world. I guess that's why we can't do anything else when we're sleeping: it's when we work hardest.

The peals faded slowly, until I couldn't tell whether I was hearing the bells themselves, or ringing in my ears. Enduring was a deep tone, solid, steady, but faint because distant. I knew somehow that I'd been hearing it for hours—that in those moments of semi-waking when I'd rolled over or pulled up the covers I'd marked this sound and wondered what it was before falling back to sleep. An obvious guess would be some nocturnal bird. But the tone was low, for an avian throat: like someone playing a ten-foot-long flute half-choked with rocks and water. And birds tended not to just sit in one place and make noise for half the night. Some kind of big amphibian, then, crazy for a mate, squatting on a rock by the spring and blowing wind through a quivering air-sac. But the sound was regular. Patterned. Perhaps the hum from a generator. An irrigation pump down in the valley. Trucks descending a grade using air brakes.

Curiosity and a full bladder were keeping me awake. Finally I got up, moving quietly so as not to disturb Lio, and tugged at my blanket. Out of habit, I was going to wrap it around myself. Then I hesitated, remembering that I was supposed to wear extramuros clothes. In the predawn gloom I couldn't even see the pile of trousers and underwear and whatnot I'd left on the floor last night. So I went back to plan A, peeled the blanket off the bed, wrapped it around myself, and went out.

The sound seemed to come from everywhere at once, but by the time I'd used the latrine and emerged into the cool morning air, I'd started to get an idea of where it came from: a stone retaining wall that the monks had built along a steep part of the mountain to prevent their road from crumbling into the valley. As I walked toward it my perceptions cleared suddenly and I shook my head in amazement at my own silliness in having imagined it was an amphibian or a truck. It was plainly a human voice. Singing. Or rather droning, for he had been stuck on the same note the whole time I'd been awake.

The note changed slightly. Okay, so it wasn't a drone. It was a chant. A very, very slow one.

Not wanting to stroll right up to Fraa Jad and disturb him, I maneuvered around on the soft wet grass of the retreat center's archery range until I was able to bring him in view at a distance of a couple of hundred feet. The retaining wall ran in straight segments joined by round, flat-topped towers about four feet in diameter. Fraa Jad had rescued his bolt from his luggage, plumped it up to winter thickness, and put it on, then climbed to the top of a pillar that had a fine view to the south across the desert. He was sitting there with his legs tucked under him and his arms outstretched. Off to the left, the sky was luminescent purplish, washed of stars. To the right, a few bright stars and a planet still shone, striving against the light of the coming day, succumbing one by one as the minutes went by.

I could have stood there watching and listening for hours. I got the idea—which might have been just my imagination—that Fraa Jad was singing a cosmographical chant: a requiem for the stars that were being swallowed up in the dawn. Certainly it was music of cosmographical slowness. Some of the notes went on for longer than I could hold my breath. He must have some trick of breathing and singing at the same time.

A single bell rang behind and above me at the monastery. A

priest's voice sang an invocation in Old Orth. A choir answered him. It was a call to the dawn aut, or something. I was crestfallen that their rituals were trampling on Fraa Jad's chant. But I had to admit that if Cord had been awake to see this, she'd have been hard put to see any difference between the two. Whatever Fraa Jad was chanting was rooted, I knew, in thousands of years' theorical research wedded to a musical tradition as old and as deep. But why put theorics into music at all? And why stay up all night sitting in a beautiful place chanting that music? There were easier ways to add two plus two.

I'd been singing bass since the eventful season, six years ago, when I'd fallen down the stairs from soprano. Where I lived, that meant lots of droning. When you spend three hours singing the same note, something happens to your brain. And that goes double when you have fallen into oscillatory lockstep with the others around you, and when you collectively have gotten your vocal chords tuned into the natural harmonics of the Mynster (to say nothing of the thousands of casks stacked against its walls). In all seriousness I believe that the physical vibration of your brain by sound waves creates changes in how the brain works. And if I were a craggy old Thousander—not a nineteen-year-old Tenner—I might just have the confidence to assert that when your brain is in that state it can think things it could never think otherwise. Which is a way of saying that I didn't think Fraa Jad had been up all night chanting just because he was a music lover. He was doing something.

I left Fraa Jad alone and went for a stroll while the sun came up. Clatters and hisses from the dining hall told me that the retreat center staff were up making breakfast, so I went to the cell and put on my extra costume, then went there to lend a hand. In some respects I might be helpless extramuros, but I knew how to cook. Fraa Jad and the rest of our group drifted in, one by one, and tried to help until they were ejected and commanded to eat.

In addition to the four who'd dined with us the night before, three more monks joined us for breakfast, including one very old one who wanted to talk to Fraa Jad, though he was quite hard of hearing. The rest of the avout left them alone. These monks seemed to consider it a high honor to talk to a Thousander and so why should we interfere? They weren't going to get another chance.

At the end of the meal they presented us with some books. I let Arsibalt accept them and make a nice speech. They liked what he said so much that it made me squirm a little, because it seemed he was encouraging them to see all sorts of natural connections between who we were and who they were. But no harm came of it. These people had been good to us, and they'd done it with open hearts, and no expectation of anything in return—I was pretty sure the Sæcular Power wasn't going to reimburse them! That's why Arsibalt's talk made me uneasy—he seemed to hold out the possibility that they *would* get something in return, namely, future contact between them and us. I stepped on his toe. He seemed to take my meaning. A few minutes later, we were on our way down the mountain, the monks' books having been added to Arsibalt's portable library.

○○○

Erasmas: A fraa at Saunt Baritoe's in the Fourteenth Century A.R. who, along with Suur Uthentine, founded the branch of metatheorics called Complex Protism.

—THE DICTIONARY, *4th edition, A.R. 3000*

Between the monastery and Bly's Butte, a very small river trickled through a very large canyon, spanned by only one bridge that was fit for use. Until we had crossed this, and come to a fork, we didn't need to think very hard about which direction we ought to go. The road to the left swung wide to avoid the mountain. The one to the right headed up the bank of a tributary toward a settlement marked on the cartabla as Samble. So we went that way, and, a little more than an hour after leaving the monastery, found ourselves approaching something that, from a distance, looked like a pot scourer dropped on the smooth southern flank of Bly's Butte. It was a carpet of scrubby trees. As we got closer we saw it had been cleaved and sorted by settlers' walls, rooves, and fences. Taller trees, obviously fawned over by generations who loved them for shade or beauty, stood in a rectangle around a plot of grass, at one end of which rose the acute wood-framed sky-altar of a counter-Bazian ark. Without any communication between the two vehicles, we found our way to that village green. When we climbed out, we heard singing from the ark. But we saw no people. The entire town—including Gane-lial Crade, whose fetch was parked in a patch of dirt behind the ark—was inside that building.

This didn't seem like a good place to look for Orolo or (assuming he was still alive) Estemard. But it did give us our first hint as to how a couple of Ferals might have been able to survive out here: by coming down into Samble to get things like food and medicine. How they might have paid for them was another question. But Fraa Carmolathu pointed out that Samble didn't make much economic sense to begin with. There weren't any other towns hereabouts, the land didn't support farming, there was little in the way of industry. He developed a theory that it was every bit as much a religious community as the monastery where we'd stayed last night. And if that were the case, perhaps Estemard and Orolo didn't have to pay for things with money, if instead they could provide useful services to the townsfolk.

"Or perhaps they are simply beggars," suggested Fraa Jad, "like certain Orders of old."

Most of the avout seemed more comfortable with the beggar hypothesis than with any suggestion that Estemard or Orolo might have been making himself useful to these kinds of people. It led to a lively discussion. All of our attempts to plane each other would have disturbed the service in the ark if it had been a quiet and contemplative kind of proceeding, but it was more raucous in that place than we could ever hope to be, with a lot of singing that sounded like shouting. A few of us separated ourselves from the discussion and spent a minute looking back and forth between the cartabla and the butte. Samble—which Fraa Carmolathu speculated might be an ancient weathered contraction of "Savant Bly"—stood at the beginning of a dirt road that spiraled around the butte to its top.

After a few minutes we identified the place where that road began: the dirt lot behind the ark. And at the moment there was no way to drive through it and get on that road. The lot was full of parked vehicles: a few shiny mobes such as might belong to whoever passed for Burgers in Samble, but mostly dust-covered fetches with big tires. There was an open lane up the center. The head of the road, though, was squarely blocked by Ganelial Crade's fetch.

According to the cartabla, it was only four miles to the top, and I was feeling restless, so I filled my water bottle from a pump in the middle of the green and started to walk up the road. Lio came with me. So did Fraa Criscan, who was the youngest of the Hundreders. It felt a little strange walking among the parked fetches of the faithful of Samble, but once we squeezed past Crade's and got onto the road, it curved around the flank of the butte, and the little town disappeared from view. A minute after that, we were no longer able to hear the shouting inside the ark, just the rush of a dry crackling wind coming at us from across the desert, carrying the sharp perfume of the tough resinous plants that grew down there. We gained altitude briskly and the temperature of the air dropped even as we warmed to the task. Once we had reached a point opposite to Samble, we were able to see all the way up to the top and make out a few buildings and the crippled skeletons of old aerial towers and polyhedral domes. We guessed they were military relics, which wasn't interesting, since, after a few thousand years of habitation, all landscapes were strewn with such things.

We spiraled up and around to a point where we could look down into Samble and wave to our friends below. The service in the ark showed no sign of winding down. We had assumed that the vehicles would catch up with us soon into our hike. In other words, we were only doing this to get some exercise—not as a way of getting to the top. But now it seemed we might get there before our vehicles did. For some reason this aroused our competitive instincts and made us hike faster. We found a shortcut that had been used by other hikers, and cut off one whole circuit of the mountain by scrambling straight up the slope for a couple of hundred feet.

"Did you know Fraa Paphlagon?" I asked Criscan when we

stopped at the top of the shortcut to drink water and marvel at our progress. The view was worth a few minutes.

"I was his fid," Criscan said. "You were Orolo's?"

I nodded. "Are you aware that Orolo was a fid of Paphlagon before Paphlagon came to you through the labyrinth?"

Fraa Criscan said nothing. For Paphlagon to have mentioned Orolo—or anything about his former life among the Tenners—to Criscan would have been a violation of the Discipline. But it was the sort of thing that could easily leak out when talking about one's work. I went on, "Paphlagon and another Tenner named Estemard worked together and raised Orolo. They left at the same time: Paphlagon via the labyrinth and Estemard via the Day Gate. Estemard came here."

Criscan asked, "What was Orolo's reputation? Before his Anathem, I mean."

"He was our best," I said—surprised by the question. "Why? What was Paphlagon's reputation?"

"Similar."

"But—?" Because I could tell that there was a "but" coming.

"His avocation was a bit strange. Instead of doing something with his hands like most people, he made a hobby of studying—"

"We know," I said. "The polycosm. And/or the Hylaean Theoric World."

"You looked at his writings," Criscan said.

"Twenty-year-old writings," I reminded him. "We have no idea what he's been up to recently."

Criscan said nothing for a few moments, then shrugged. "It seems highly relevant to the Convox, so I guess it's okay for me to talk to you about it."

"We won't tell on you," Lio promised him.

Criscan didn't catch the humor. "Have you ever noticed that when people are talking about the idea of the Hylaean Theoric World, they always end up drawing the same diagram?"

"Yeah—now that you mention it," I said.

"Two circles or boxes," Lio said. "An arrow from one to the other."

"One circle or box represents the Hylaean Theoric World," I said. "The arrow starts there and points to the other one, which represents this world."

"This cosmos," Criscan corrected me. "Or causal domain, if you will. And the arrow represents—?"

"A flow of information," Lio said. "Knowledge of triangles pouring into our brains."

"Cause-and-effect relationship," was my guess. I was recalling Orolo's talk of Causal Domain Shear.

"Those two amount to the same thing," Criscan reminded us. "That kind of diagram is an assertion that information about theorical forms can get to our cosmos from the HTW, and cause measurable effects here."

"Hold on, *measurable*? What kind of measurable are you talking about?" Lio asked. "You can't weigh a triangle. You can't pound in a nail with the Adrakhonic Theorem."

"But you can *think* about those things," Criscan said, "and thinking is a physical process that goes on in your nerve tissue."

"You can stick probes into the brain and measure it," I said.

"That's right," Criscan said, "and the whole premise of Protism is that those brain probes would show different results if there weren't this flow of information coming in from the Hylaean Theoric World."

"I guess that's so," Lio admitted, "but it sounds pretty sketchy when you put it that way."

"Never mind about that for now," Criscan said. We were on a steep part of the road, breathing hard and sweating as the sun shone down on us, and he didn't want to expend much energy on it. "Let's get back to that two-box diagram. Paphlagon was part of a tradition, going back to one Suur Uthentine at Saunt Baritoe's in the fourteenth century A.R., that asks 'why only two?' Supposedly it all started when Uthentine walked into a chalk hall and happened to see the conventional two-box diagram where it had been drawn up on a slate by one Fraa Erasmas."

Lio turned and looked at me.

"Yes," I said, "my namesake."

Criscan went on, "Uthentine said to Erasmas, 'I see you are teaching your fids about Directed Acyclic Graphs; when are you going to move on to ones that are a little more interesting?' To which Erasmas said, 'I beg your pardon, but that's no DAG, it is something else entirely.' This affronted Suur Uthentine, who was a theor who had devoted her whole career to the study of such things. 'I know a DAG when I see one,' she said. Erasmas was exasperated, but on reflection, he decided it might be worth following up on his suur's upsight. So Uthentine and Erasmas developed Complex Protism."

"As opposed to Simple?" I asked.

"Yes," Criscan said, "where Simple is the two-box kind. Complex can have any number of boxes and arrows, as long as the arrows never go round in a circle."

We had spiraled around to the shady side of the butte, and come to a stretch of road that had been covered with silt during seasonal rains—perfect for drawing diagrams. While we rested and sipped water, Criscan went on to give us a calca* about Complex Protism. The gist of it was that our cosmos, far from being the one and only causal domain reached by information from a unique and solitary Hylaean Theoric World, might be only one node in a web of cosmi through which information percolated, always moving in the same direction, as lamp oil moves through a wick. Other cosmi—perhaps not so different from ours—might reside up-Wick from ours, and feed information to us. And yet others might be down-Wick from us, and we might be supplying information to them. All of which was pretty far out—but at least it helped me understand why Paphlagon had been Evoked.

"Now I have a question for you Tenners," Criscan said, as we set out again. "What was Estemard like?"

"He walked out before we were Collected," I said, "so we didn't know him."

"Oh, that's all right," Criscan said, "we'll know soon enough."

We walked on silently for a few steps before Lio—casting a

---

* See Calca 3.

wary glance to the top of the butte, not so far away now—said, "I've been looking into Estemard a little. Maybe I should tell you what I know before we barge into his house."

"Good for you. What did you learn?" I asked.

"This might be one of those cases where someone walked out before he could be Thrown Back," Lio said.

"Really!? What was he doing?"

"His avocation was tiles," Lio said. "The really ornate tile work in the New Laundry was done by him."

"The geometric stuff," I said.

"Yes. But it seems he was using that as a sort of cover story to pursue an ancient geometry problem called the Teglon. It's a tiling problem, and it dates all the way back to the Temple of Orithena."

"Isn't that the problem that made a bunch of people crazy?" I asked.

"Metekoranes was standing on the Decagon in front of the Temple of Orithena, contemplating the Teglon, when the ash rolled over him," Criscan said.

I said, "It's the problem that Rabemekes was thinking about on the beach when the Bazian soldier ran him through with a spear."

Lio said, "Suur Charla of the Daughters of Hylaea thought she had the answer, scratched out on the dust of the road to Upper Colbon, when King Rooda's army marched through on their way to getting massacred. She never recovered her sanity. People's efforts to solve it have spun off entire sub-disciplines of theorics. And there are—have always been—some who paid more attention to it than was really good for them. The obsession gets passed down from one generation to the next."

"You're talking of the Lineage," Criscan said.

"Yes," Lio answered, with another nervous look up.

"Which lineage do you mean?" I asked.

"*The* Lineage, people call it," Criscan said, "or sometimes the Old Lineage."

"Well . . . give me some help. What concents is it based at?"

Criscan shook his head. "You're assuming it's like an Order. But this Lineage goes back farther than the Reconstitution—farther even than Saunt Cartas. Supposedly it was founded during the Peregrin period, by theors who had worked with Metekoranes."

"But who unlike him didn't end up under three hundred feet of pumice," Lio added.

"That's a whole different matter then," I said. "If that's really true, it's not of the mathic world at all."

"That's the problem," Lio said, "the Lineage was around for centuries before the whole idea of maths, fraas, and suurs. So you wouldn't expect it to operate according to any of the rules that we normally associate with our Orders."

"You are speaking of it in the present tense," I pointed out.

Criscan again looked uneasy, but he said nothing. Lio glanced up again, and slowed.

"Where is this going? Why are you guys so nervous?" I asked.

"Some came to suspect that Estemard was a *member*," Lio said.

"But Estemard was an Edharian," I said.

"That's part of the problem," Lio said.

"Problem?" I asked.

"Yes," said Criscan, "for me and you, anyway."

"Why—because you and I are Edharians?"

"Yes," Criscan said, with a flick of the eyes toward Lio.

"Well, Lio I trust with my life," I told him. "So you can say anything in front of him that you might say to me as a fellow Edharian."

"All right," Criscan said. "It doesn't surprise me that you've never heard about this, since you have only been in the Order of Saunt Edhar for a few months, and you're just a—er—"

"Just a Tenner?" I said. "Go ahead, I'm not offended." But I was, a little. Behind Criscan, Lio made a funny face that took the sting out of it.

"Otherwise you might have heard rumors about this kind of thing. Remarks."

"To what effect?"

"First of all, that Edharians in general are a little nutty—a little mystical."

"Of course I know some people like to say that," I said.

"All right," Criscan said. "Well, then you know that one of the reasons people look askance at us Edharians is that it seems as though our devotion to the Hylaean Theoric World might take precedence over our loyalty to the Discipline and the principles of the Reconstitution."

"Okay," I said, "I think that's unfair but I can see how some people might harbor such notions."

Lio added, "Or pretend to harbor them when it gave them a weapon to wave in Edharians' faces."

"Now," Criscan said, "imagine that there was—or was thought to be—a Lineage of what amounted to ultra-Edharians."

"Are you telling me that people think there's a connection between our Order and the Lineage?"

Criscan nodded. "Some have gone so far as to lodge the accusation that the Edharians are a sham—a false front whose real purpose is to act as a host body for an infestation of Teglon-worshippers."

Given the number of contributions Edharians had made to theorics over the millennia, I didn't have any trouble dismissing such a ludicrous claim, but one word caught my attention. "Worshippers," I repeated.

Criscan sighed. "The kinds of people who spread such rumors—" he began,

"Are the same ones who think that our belief in the HTW is tantamount to religion," I concluded. "And it suits their purposes to spread the idea that there is a secret cult at the heart of the Edharian order."

Criscan nodded.

"*Is* there?" Lio asked.

I'd have slugged him if I could have gotten away with it. Criscan didn't know about Lio's sense of humor and so he took it pretty badly.

"What did Estemard actually *do* when he was pursuing this avocation?" I asked Lio. "Was he reading books? Trying to solve the Teglon? Lighting candles and reciting spells?"

"Mostly reading books—very old ones," Lio said. "Very old ones that had been left behind by others who in their day had likewise been under suspicion of belonging to the Lineage."

"Seems interesting but harmless," I said.

"Also, people noticed that he was unduly interested in the Millenarians. During auts, he would take notes while the Thousanders sang."

"How can anyone really follow the meaning of those chants without taking notes?"

"And he went into the upper labyrinth a lot."

"Well," I admitted, "that's a bit odd . . . is it a part of the myth surrounding the Lineage that its members violate the Discipline—communicate across the boundaries of their maths?"

"Yes," Criscan said. "It fits in with the whole conspiracy-theory aspect. The slur on the Edharians in general is that they consider their work to be more profound, more important than anyone else's—that the pursuit of the truths in the Hylaean Theoric World takes precedence over the Discipline. So, if their pursuit of the truth requires that they communicate with avout in other maths—or with extras—they have no compunctions about doing so."

This was sounding more and more ridiculous by the moment, and I was beginning to think it was one of those nutty Hundreder fads. But I said nothing, because I was thinking about Orolo talking to Sammann in the vineyard and making illicit observations.

Lio snorted. "Extras? What kind of extras would care about a mystical, six-thousand-year-old theorics problem?"

"The kind we've been hanging around with the last two days," Criscan said.

We had come to a complete stop. I stepped forward up the road. "Well, if everything you're saying is true, we're not doing ourselves any favors by being out here."

Criscan took my meaning right away but Lio looked puzzled. I went on, "Saunt Tredegarh is filling up with avout from all over the world. The hierarchs must be keeping track of who has arrived, from which concent. And we—a group of mostly Edharians from, of all things, the Concent of Saunt Edhar—are going to be late . . ."

"Because we've been bending the rules—wandering among the Deolaters," Lio said, beginning to get it.

". . . looking for a couple of wayward fraas who exactly fit the stereotype that Criscan's been talking about."

Lio and I were at the summit a few minutes later. We had left Criscan huffing and puffing in our wake. All of the weird talk had made us nervous and we had practically run the rest of the way—not out of any practical need to hurry, simply to burn off energy.

The top of Bly's Butte looked as if it might have been a lovely place back in the days of Saunt Bly. It existed because there was a lens of hard rock that had resisted erosion and protected the softer stuff beneath it while everything for miles around had slowly washed down. There was enough room on top to construct a large house, say, the size of the one where Jesry's family lived. A lot of different structures had been crammed onto it over the millennia. The bottom strata were masonry: stones or bricks mortared directly onto the butte's hard summit. Later generations had poured synthetic stone directly atop those foundations to make small blockhouses, guard shacks, pillboxes, equipment enclosures, and foundations for aerials, dishes, and towers. These then had been modified: connections between them built, worn out, demolished or rusted away, replaced or buried under new work. The stone—synthetic and natural—was stained a deep ochre by the rust of all the metal structures that had been here at one time or another. For such a small area it was quite complicated—the sort of place children could have explored for hours. Lio and I were not so far out from being children that we couldn't be tempted. But we had plenty else on our minds. So we looked for signs of habitation. The most conspicuous of these was a reflecting telescope that stood on a high plinth that had once supported an aerial tower. We went there first. The telescope looked in some ways like an art project that Cord or one of her friends might have made in a welding shop from scraps of steel. But looking into it we could see a hand-ground mirror, well over twelve inches in diameter, that looked perfect, and it was easy to figure out that it had a polar axis drive cobbled together from motors, gearboxes, and bearings scavenged from who knows where. From there it was easy to follow a trail of evidence across the platform and down an external stairway to a lower platform on the southeast exposure of the complex. This had been kitted out with a grill for cooking meat, weatherproof poly chairs and table, and a big umbrella. Children's toys were stored with unchildlike neatness in a poly box, as if kids came up here sometimes, but not every day. A door led off this patio into a warren of small rooms—little more than equipment closets—that had been turned into a home. Whoever was living in this place, it wasn't Orolo. Judging from phototypes on the walls, it was an older man with a somewhat younger wife and at least two generations of offspring. Ikons were almost as numerous as snapshots and so this was obviously a Deolater family. We gathered these impressions over the course of a few seconds before we realized we were trespassing on someone's home. Then we felt stupid because this was such a typical avout mistake. We backed out so fast we almost knocked each other down.

The patio was a smooth slab of synthetic stone. Given that Estemard was such a zealous tiler, it seemed odd that he had not improved it. But now we noticed a stair that led up to a ledge where he had fashioned a kiln out of burnt bricks. Around it was strewn the detritus of many years' work: clay, molds, pots of glaze, and thousands of tiles and tile-shards in the same repertoire of simple geometric shapes as those that decorated the New Laundry at Edhar. Estemard hadn't got round to tiling his patio yet because he hadn't found the perfect configuration of tiles. He hadn't solved the Teglon.

"Clinically insane?" I asked Lio. "Or just well on his way?"

Criscan came up a different way. When he found us, he mentioned that he'd seen another, smaller habitation. We followed him as he backtracked around the southern limb of the complex.

We knew what it was instantly. All the earmarks of a pinprick math were plain to see. It was set off in a corner, reachable only by a long and somewhat challenging path, at the end of which stood a barrier—mostly symbolic, as it had been improvised recently from poly tarps and plywood—and a gate. Passing through the gate we found ourselves in a setting where we felt perfectly at home. It was another roofless slab. A broker of real estate might have called it a patio. We saw it as a miniature cloister. All vestiges of the Sæcular had been carefully scrubbed away; all that remained was the ancient, stained stone, and a few necessaries, all hand-made: a table and chair sheltered beneath a canvas stretched over a frame of timbers lashed together with many turns of string. A rusty paintbucket stood in the corner, lid held down with a stone. Lio opened it, wrinkled his nose, and announced that he had found Orolo's chamber pot. It was empty and dry. The ashes in the bottom of his brazier were cold. His water jug was empty and a wooden locker, which had once been used to store food, had been emptied of everything but seasonings, utensils, and matches.

A beat-up wooden door led to Orolo's cell, which for the most part was done up in similar style. The clock, however, was distinctly modern, with glowing digital readouts to a hundredth of a second. Bookshelves made of old stair treads and masonry blocks supported a few machine-printed books and hand-written leaves. One wall was covered by leaves: diagrams and notes Orolo had posted there using little dabs of tack. Another wall was covered by phototypes mostly showing various efforts that Orolo had made to capture images of the Cousins' ship using (we assumed) the home-made telescope above. The typical image was little more than a fat white streak against a background of smaller white streaks: the tracks of stars. In one corner of this mosaic, though, Orolo had posted several unrelated phototypes that he had torn from publications or printed using a syndev. At a glance, these seemed to depict nothing more than a big hole in the ground: an open-pit mine, perhaps.

The rest of the leaves formed an overlapping mosaic, with lines drawn from one to the next, diagramming a treelike system of connections. The uppermost leaf was labeled ORITHENA. Near its top was written the name of Adrakhones. From it, one arrow descended vertically to the name of Diax. This was a dead end. But a second arrow, angling down and off to the side, pointed to the name of Metekoranes, and from it, the tree ramified downward to include names from many places and centuries.

"Uh-oh," Lio said.

"I hate the looks of that," I admitted.

"It is Lineage stuff," put in Criscan.

The door opened, and there was violence. Not prolonged—it was finished in a second—and not severe. But it was definitely violence and it wrenched our minds so far out of the track we'd been following that there was no question of getting back to it any time soon.

Simply, a man burst in through the cell's door and Lio took him down. When it was finished, Lio was sitting on the man's chest and examining, with utmost fascination, a projectile weapon that he had just extracted from a holster on the man's hip. "Do you have any knives or anything like that?" Lio asked, and glanced at the door. More people were approaching. The foremost of these was Barb.

"Get off me!" the man shouted. It took a moment for it to sink in that he was speaking in Orth. "Give me that back!" We noticed that he was pretty old, although when he'd come in the door, he'd moved with the vigor of a younger man.

"Estemard carries a gun," Barb announced. "It is a local tradition. They don't consider it threatening."

"Well, I'm sure Estemard won't feel threatened by my carrying this one, then," Lio said. He rolled backward off Estemard and came up on his feet, gun in hand, pointed at the ceiling.

"You have no business in here." Estemard said, "And as for my gun, you'd better shoot me with it or hand it over."

Lio didn't even consider handing it over.

Now, through most of this I'd been so shocked, and then so confused, that I'd stood motionless. I had been afraid of doing anything for fear of doing the wrong thing. But the sight of my friends' faces outside nudged me to act, since I didn't wish to look tongue-tied or indecisive. "Since you have just asserted we have no business here," I pointed out, "an assertion we disagree with, by the way, it would not be in our interests to supply you with weapons."

By this time, other members of our Peregrin group had crowded onto the patio. Fraa Jad came in, shouldered Estemard out of his way, took in the cell at a glance, and began examining the leaves and phototypes Orolo had put on the wall. This, much more than being knocked down by Lio or planed by me, made Estemard realize he was outmatched. He got smaller somehow, and looked away. Unlike the rest of us, he'd only had a few minutes to get used to being in the presence of a Thousander.

"Lio, a lot of people carry sidearms out here." It was Cord. "I can see why you got the wrong idea, but take my word for it, he was not going to draw down on you." No one responded. "Come on, you bunch of sad sacks, it's picnic time!"

"Picnic?" I said.

"After we are finished with our service," Estemard said, "we have a cookout on the green, if the weather is good." Cord's intervention seemed to have cheered him up a little.

I glanced out the door and caught the eye of Arsibalt, out on the patio. He raised his eyebrows. *Yes. Estemard has become a Deolater.*

Back in the concent, we'd always pictured Ferals as long-haired wild men, but Estemard looked like a retired chemist out for a day hike.

Estemard held me in a careful gaze. "You must be Erasmas," he said. This seemed to settle something for him. He breathed deeply, shaking off the last vestiges of the shock he'd gone into when Lio had helped him to the floor. "Yes. All of you are invited to the picnic, if you promise not to assault people." Seeing the objection percolating through my brain toward my face, he smiled and added, "People who haven't assaulted you first, that is. And I doubt they will; they're more tolerant of avout than you are of them."

"Where's Orolo?"

Fraa Jad, still planted with his back to us, currently viewing the phototypes of the open-pit mine, startled us all by unlimbering his subsonic voice: "Orolo has gone north."

Estemard was astonished; then the smile crept back onto his face as he figured out how the Thousander had figured this out. "Fraa Jad has it right."

"We shall attend the *picnic*," Fraa Jad announced, pronouncing the Fluccish word with tweezers. "Lio, Erasmas, and I shall go down last, in the vehicle of Ganelial Crade."

This directive filtered out to the patio. People turned around and headed back toward the vehicles. Lio took the ammunition magazine out of the gun and handed them back separately to Estemard, who departed, reluctantly, with Criscan. As soon as they had passed out through the makeshift gate, Fraa Jad reached out and began plucking the leaves off the wall. Lio and I helped, and gave all that we'd harvested to Fraa Jad. He left most of the phototypes alone, but took the ones that depicted the big hole in the ground, and handed them to me.

The Thousander went out to Orolo's cloister and stuffed all of the leaves into the brazier. Then he reached into Orolo's food-locker and took out the matches. "I infer from the label that this is a fire-making praxis," he said.

We showed him how to use matches. He set fire to Orolo's leaves. We all stood around until they had turned to ash. Then Fraa Jad stirred the ashes with a stick.

"Time for *picnic*," he said.

As we spiraled down the butte, jostling and rocking in the open back of Ganelial Crade's fetch like so many bottles in a box, we were able to look down from time to time and see the picnic taking shape down on the village green of Samble. It appeared that these people took their picnics as seriously as they did their religious services.

Fraa Jad seemed to have other things on his mind, and said nothing until we were almost down to Samble. Then he pounded on the roof of the fetch's cab and, in Orth, asked Crade if he wouldn't mind waiting here for a few minutes. In really wild, barbarous-sounding Orth, Crade said that this would be fine.

It had never crossed my mind that someone like Crade would know our language. But it made sense. The counter-Bazians distrusted priests and other middlemen. They believed everyone should read the scriptures themselves. Almost all read translations into Fluccish. But it wasn't so farfetched to think that an especially fervent and isolated sect, such as the people of Samble, might learn Classical Orth so that they would no longer have to entrust their immortal souls to translators.

Fraa Jad let me know I should get out. I vaulted from the back of the fetch and then helped him down, more out of respect than any-thing, since he didn't seem to need much helping. We strolled about a hundred paces to a bend in the road where there was an especially nice view over the high desert to the mountains of the north, still patched with snow in places, and dappled by cloud-shadows. "We are just like Protas looking down over Ethras," he remarked.

I smiled but didn't laugh. The work of Protas was viewed as embarrassingly naïve by many. It was rarely mentioned except to be funny or ironic. But to deprecate it so was a trend that had come and gone a hundred times, and there was no telling what Fraa Jad, whose math had been sealed off for 690 years, might think of it. The more I stood and looked at him and followed his gaze northward to the clouds and the shadows that they cast on the flanks of the mountains, the more glad I became that I hadn't snickered.

"What do you think Orolo saw, when he looked out thus?" Fraa Jad asked.

"He was a great appreciator of beauty and loved to look at the mountains from the starhenge," I said.

"You think he saw beauty? That is a safe answer, since it is beautiful. But what was he thinking about? What connections did the beauty enable him to perceive?"

"I couldn't possibly answer that."

"Don't answer it. Ask it."

"More concretely, what do you want me to do?"

"Go north," he said. "Follow and find Orolo."

"Tredegarh is south and east."

"Tredegarh," he repeated, as if waking from a dream of it. "That is where I and the others shall go after the *picnic*."

"I have bent the rules quite a bit by coming here," I said. "We've lost a day—"

"A day. *A day!*" Fraa Jad, the Thousander, thought it was pretty funny that I should care about a day.

"Chasing Orolo around could take months," I said. "For being so late, I could be Thrown Back. Or at least given more chapters."

"Which chapter are you up to now?"

"Five."

"Nine" Fraa Jad said. For a moment I thought he was correcting me. Then I was afraid he was *sentencing* me. Finally I understood that he himself was all the way up to Chapter Nine.

He must have spent years on it.

Why? How had he gotten in that much trouble?

Had it made him crazy?

But if he was crazy or incorrigible, why had he, of all the Thousanders, been Evoked? After his Voco, why had his fraas and suurs sung the way they had—as though their hearts had been ripped out?

"I have a lot of questions," I said.

"The most efficient way for you to get answers is to go north."

I opened my mouth to repeat my earlier objection, but he held up a hand to stay me. "I shall make every effort to see to it you are not punished."

It was by no means clear to me that Fraa Jad would have any such power in a giant Convox, but I didn't have the strength of will to tell him as much to his face. Lacking that strength, I had but one way out of the conversation. "Fine. After the picnic I'll go north. Though I do not understand what that means."

"Then keep going north until you understand it," Fraa Jad said.

Part 7

FERAL

Reticule: (1) In Proto-, Old, and Middle Orth, a small bag or basket, netlike in its construction. (2) In early Praxic Orth, a gridlike network of lines or fine wires on an optical device. (3) In later Praxic and New Orth, two or more syntactic devices that are able to communicate with one another.

Reticulum: (1) When not capitalized, a reticule formed by the interconnection of two or more smaller reticules. (2) When capitalized, the largest reticulum, joining together the preponderance of all reticules in the world. Sometimes abbreviated to *Ret*.

—THE DICTIONARY, *4th edition, A.R. 3000*

There was no point trying to talk Cord out of going with me. We just climbed into her fetch and started as soon as the picnic was over. We had to backtrack thirty miles to find a north-going road that would not peter out before the mountains. At the first town on that road I used up my money card buying fuel, food, and warm clothes. Then I used up Fraa Jad's.

While we were loading the stuff into the fetch, Ganelial Crade pulled up. Sitting next to him was Sammann. Both were grinning, which was a novelty. They didn't have to announce that they were coming with us and we didn't have to discuss it. They got busy buying the same sorts of things we'd just bought. Crade had an ammunition can full of coins and Sammann had information in his jeejah that worked in lieu of money; I got the sense that each of them had obtained funds from his respective community. I wasn't happy to see Crade again. If it really was true that he was getting money for this journey from the people of Samble, it raised all sorts of questions as to what he was really up to.

Crade had reinstated the three-wheeler in the back of his fetch, so he didn't have much room left over; most of the bulky stuff went into Cord's fetch. We had no idea where we were going or what to plan for, but we all seemed to be carrying roughly the same picture in our heads, namely that Orolo had gone up into the mountains for some reason. It would be cold up there and we might have to camp, so we got things like winter bedrolls, tents, stoves, and fuel. Sammann had an idea that he might be able to track Orolo, and Crade was planning to make inquiries with some of his co-religionists along the way.

We all climbed back into our vehicles and headed north. It would be two hours' drive to the foothills, where Crade knew of places to camp. He led the way. This was a thing he felt a compulsion to do, and I was tired of fighting it. Cord was content to follow. Crade sitting upright at the controls, and Sammann hunched over the glowing screen of his super-jeejah, gave us the feeling that the two of them must be seeing to all of the details. I wouldn't have been comfortable following either of them alone, but together they'd never agree on anything, so I judged it was prudent.

I regretted parting from people like Arsibalt and Lio with whom I could talk about things. But once we turned north and started forging toward the mountains, the regret vanished and instead I felt relief. So much had been revealed to me over the course of the last twenty-four hours—not only about the Cousins' ship but even more so about the world I had lived in for ten and a half years—that it was too much for me to make sense of in one go. Just to name one example, the thatched roofs on the nuclear waste cylinders, alone, if I'd learned of it in the concent, would have taken me a little getting used to. I was much more at ease sitting next to my sib, staring out the windscreen, my sole responsibility being to chase a wild fraa across the waste. The night before, at the Bazian monastery, I had accommodated certain new, odd facts in my mind just by sleeping. A similar trick might work for me now: by doing something completely different for a few days, I might chance upon a better understanding than I could get by kneeling in a cell and concentrating on it, or having a wordy discussion in a chalk hall.

And even if all of that was completely wrong, I didn't care. I simply needed a break.

Cord spent a lot of time talking on the jeejah with Rosk. She'd kissed him goodbye on the Samble village green. He had to go back home and work. Now there were issues of some kind to be worked out. They didn't have just one long conversation on the jeejah. Instead they made and broke contact ten or so times. It got on my nerves and I wished we'd get to some wild reach where her link wouldn't work. But after a while I got used to it and started to wonder: if Rosk and Cord had to do so much communicating to rig for a few days' separation, what did that imply for me and Ala? I couldn't stop recalling the shocked look on Tulia's face as we had pulled out yesterday afternoon. Part of which, I was sure, came from her thinking I was being beastly to Ala.

"Is there currently a mechanism in place for sending letters?" I asked Cord during a breather between micro-conversations with Rosk.

"From here it'll take some doing, but the answer is yes," she said. Then she got a big smile. "You want to write to a girl, Raz?"

Since I'd never mentioned Ala to her and had asked my question in such a colorless way, I was shocked and then quite irritated that she had figured this out with no effort. She was still deriving joy from the look on my face when her jeejah twittered and gave me a few minutes to get my composure back.

"Tell me about her," Cord demanded, as soon as she disconnected.

"Ala. You met her. She's the one—"

"I remember Ala. I liked her!"

"Really? That was not obvious to me."

"That and so many other things," Cord said, in such an airy, innocent voice that it almost slipped by me. Then I had to spend a minute being silent and dignified.

"She and I have hated each other pretty much our whole lives," I said. "Especially recently. Then we started something. It was pretty sudden. Really wonderful though."

Cord gave me a grateful smile and almost swerved off the road.

"The next day she was Evoked. This was before we knew it was going to become a Convox, so in effect she was dead to me after that. This was, I guess, pretty upsetting to me. I sort of put it out of my mind by working. Then when I got Evoked yesterday—which seems like ten years ago now—it opened up the possibility that I might see her again. But then a few hours later I decided to make this little detour—which just turned into a bigger detour. As a matter of fact, I am technically a Feral now and so I might never see her again because of the way I just let Fraa Jad push me around. So you might say things are complicated. Hard to say just how long I'd have to spend on a jeejah with her, sorting this one out."

Cord took another call from Rosk then, and by the time she was finished, I was ready with more: "Mind you, I'm not just whining about my own situation here. Everything's confused. This is the biggest upheaval since the Third Sack. So many weird things are going on—it almost makes a mockery of the Discipline."

"But your way isn't just that set of rules," Cord said. "It's who you are—you follow that way for bigger reasons. And as long as you stay true to that, the confusion you're talking about will sort itself out eventually."

I would have been fine with that except for one problem: it sounded like the mentality that Edharians were accused of having by people who believed in all of that Lineage stuff that Criscan had been telling us about. So an instinct told me to say nothing.

Then Cord sprang the trap on me: "And likewise you could drive yourself crazy trying to sort through all of these ins and outs in your relationship with Ala, but if you send her a letter—which is a great idea—you shouldn't get into all of that. Just skip it."

"Skip it?"

"Yeah. Just tell her how you feel."

"I feel jerked around. That's how I feel. You want me to say that?"

"No, no, no. Tell her how you feel *about her*."

My gaze dropped to her jeejah, sitting on the seat between us, silent for once. "Are you sure you haven't been taking calls from Tulia on that thing? Because I have the feeling you guys have your own private reticule. Like—"

"Like the Ita?" This would have been insulting if I'd said it, but she thought it was hilarious. We both looked up the road at the back of Sammann's head silhouetted against his jeejah screen. "That's right," Cord said, "we're the girl Ita and if you don't do what we say, we're going to Throw the Book at you!"

Cord had a notebook that she used as a maintenance log for her fetch, so I used a blank page to begin a letter to Ala. This went about as badly as it was possible for a written document to go.

I tore it out and started again. I couldn't get used to the way the disposable poly pen shat pasty ink onto the slick machine-made paper. I tore it out and started yet again.

I had to suspend work on the fourth draft because Ganelial Crade had led us off the paved road and onto a dirt track better suited for his fetch than for Cord's. The lower, south-facing slopes of the mountains were covered with fuel tree plantations and criss-crossed with dirt roads such as this one, alive with rampaging log trucks, dusty and dangerous to us. We spent an unpleasant half-hour getting through that zone. Then we climbed to where the growing season was too short and the grades too steep for that industry, or indeed for any kind of economic activity save recreation.

He led us to a beautiful camping place at the edge of a tarn in the hills. People came here to hunt in the autumn, he said, but no one was here today. All of our equipment was new and we had to take it out of boxes and dispose of the wrappers and tags and in-struction manuals before we could do anything with it. We started a bonfire with these and sustained it with fallen dead timber. As the sun went down, this settled to a bed of coals on which we cooked cheeseburgs. Cord bedded down in her fetch and the three men got ready to share a tent. I stayed up late and finished my letter to Ala by firelight. Which was a good way to do it; the seventh draft was short and simple. I just kept asking myself: if fate had it that we'd never see each other again, what would I need to say to her?

The next day started out refreshingly devoid of great events, new people, and astonishing revelations. We got up slowly in the cold, lighted the stove, heated up some rations, and got on the road. Crade was happy. It was not in his nature to be that way but he was happy here and now, strutting all over the place telling us the best way to pack our bedrolls and attending to every detail of the camp stove as if it were a nuclear reactor. But he was much easier to be around in such circumstances, where he actually had some-thing to do with all of his energies. I decided that he was too intel-ligent for his circumstances and that he'd missed an opportunity to be an avout. If he'd been born among the slines he'd have ended up on a concent. Instead he'd landed among a sect that valued his brains too much to let him go. But his brains had no purpose there. Anyway, he was used to being the only smart person within a hundred miles and now that he'd been thrown together with other smart people he didn't know how to behave.

Sammann was badly out of his element—he could hardly pick up anything on his jeejah—but he managed well, as if prolonged suffering were a standard part of the Ita tool kit. He had a shoulder bag that was for him what Cord's vest was for her, and he kept pulling out useful tools and gadgets. Or so it seemed to me, as I was not used to owning things.

Cord was quiet unless I looked at her, whereupon she'd become grumpy. I was bored and impatient. When we finally got going again, I guessed it must be about midday. But according to the clock in Cord's fetch, midday was not for another three hours.

We went up into the mountains. This was new to me. *Any* travel would have been new to me. When I'd been a kid, before I'd been Collected, I'd left town a few times—tagging along on trips that my elders made to visit friends or kin in the near country. After I'd joined the Concent, of course, I hadn't traveled at all. And I hadn't missed it. I hadn't known what there was to miss. Up in those hills and mountains, seeing natural leads of open space through the forest, pale green meadows, old logging roads, abandoned fortresses, decrepit cabins, and collapsed palaces, I began to think of these as places I might go, if I had the time to stop and go for a walk. In that way the landscape was altogether different from the concent, all of whose paths had been trodden for thousands of years, and where going into the cellar of Shuf's Dowment seemed intrepid. It made me wonder where my mind might ramble, and where events might take me, now that circumstances had forced me to leave the concent and venture into such places.

Cord changed the music. The popular songs she'd been playing the previous days felt wrong here. Their beautiful parts did not stand comparison with what we could see out the windows, and their coarse parts jarred. She owned a recording of the music of the concent, which we sold in the market outside the Day Gate alongside our honey and our mead. She started playing random selections from it, beginning with a lament for the Third Sack. To Cord, this was just Selection Number 37. To me it was just about the most powerful piece of music we had. We sang it only once a year, at the end of a week spent fasting and reciting the names of the dead and the titles of the books burned. Somehow, the feeling was right: if the Cousins turned out to be hostile, they might Sack the world.

We came around a turn and were confronted by a wall of purple stone that went up until it disappeared in a cloud layer a mile above our heads. It must have stood there for a million years. Seeing it while I heard the lament, I felt what I can only describe as patriotism for my planet. Until this moment in history there had never been any call for such feelings because there'd never been anything beyond Arbre except for points of light in the sky. Now that had changed, and instead of thinking of myself as a member of the Provener team, or of the Decenarian math, or of the Edharian order, I felt like a citizen of the world and I was proud to be doing my little bit to protect it. I was comfortable being a Feral.

Casinos and speelies weren't the only new experiences you had when you went extramuros. Even if you traveled solo and stuck to the wild places—even if you never saw a strip mall or heard a word of Fluccish—you were getting information, not about the Sæcular world but about the world that had been there before it, the ground state that cultures and civilizations emerged from and collapsed back into. The wellsprings of the Sæcular—but also of the mathic world. The origin where, seven thousand years ago, those worlds had diverged.

⟨∘∘∘⟩

Sea of Seas: A relatively small but complex body of salt water, connected to Arbre's great oceans in three places by straits, and generally viewed as the cradle of classical civilization.

—THE DICTIONARY, *4th edition, A.R. 3000*

We crested the pass and descended into a small city, Norslof. This took me by surprise. I'd seen the cartabla. But in the fantasy map of the world that I carried in my head, the mountains went on much farther.

We had not found Orolo, but we had at least made one pass over the landscape. Along the way we had taken note of a few places where he might have gone. Most promising of these, to my mind, had been a small, tatterdemalion math constructed on a lookout tower originally put there to detect forest fires. It was a few miles off the road and a few thousand feet above it. We'd noticed it shortly after topping the pass. If it had been a full-sized concent they wouldn't have wanted anything to do with someone like Orolo, but such an out-of-the-way math might have welcomed an Orth-speaking wanderer who could bring them some new ideas.

We stopped to eat and use toilets at a big drummon-refueling station several miles outside of Norslof's commercial center. Here it was possible to rent rooms and it was permissible to sleep in one's vehicle. I had an idea that we might use it as a base from which to double back into the mountains and search for Orolo. I changed my mind when we walked into the mess hall, steamy and redolent of cured meats, and all of the long-range drummon operators turned to stare at us. It was obvious that they didn't get many customers such as us and that they preferred it that way. Part of it must have been that we were a group of four in a room full of singletons. But even if we'd come in one by one, we would have drawn stares. Sammann was dressed in normal-looking extramuros garb, but his long beard and hair were not the norm, and the bone structure of his face marked him ethnically. The men in this room would not be able to peg him as Ita—supposing they even knew what the Ita were— but they could tell he was not one of them. Cord did not dress or move like their women. Her repertoire of gestures and facial expressions was altogether disjoint from theirs. Ganelial, being an extra, ought to have blended—but somehow didn't. He belonged to a religious community that went to great lengths to preserve its apartness from the cultural baseline and he proclaimed as much in the way he carried himself and the looks he gave people. And I: I had no idea how I looked. Since leaving the concent I'd spent most of my time among extras who knew that I was an avout on Peregrin. Here I was trying to pass for something I wasn't, and it seemed best to assume I was doing a terrible job of it.

We might have drawn even more attention had it not been for the fact that there were speelies all over the place. They were mounted to the ceiling, angled down toward the tables. All of them ran the same feed in lockstep. At the moment we walked in the door, this showed a house burning down at night. It was surrounded by emergency workers. A close-up showed a woman leaning out of an upper-story window that was vomiting black smoke. She had a towel wrapped around her face. She dropped a baby. I kept watching to see what happened next, but instead the speely cycled back and showed the baby drop two more times in slow motion. Then that scene vanished and was replaced by images of a ball player making a clever play. But then it showed the same ball player breaking his leg later in the game. This too was repeated several times in slow motion so that you could see the leg bending at the site of the break. By the time we reached our table, the speelies were showing an extraordinarily beautiful man in expensive clothes being arrested by police. My companions glanced at the images from time to time, then looked away. It seemed that they had built up some kind of immunity. I couldn't keep my eyes off them, so I tried to sit in a position where there wasn't a speely directly in front of me. Still, every time the feed popped from one image to another, my eye jumped to it. I was like an ape in a tree, looking at whatever moved fastest in my environment.

We sat in the corner, ordered food, and talked quietly. The room, which had gone silent when we'd entered, slowly defrosted and was replenished by the normal low murmur of conversation. It occurred to me that we should not have chosen a corner table because this would make it impossible for us to get out quickly if there was some kind of trouble.

I missed Lio badly. He would have assessed the threats, if any, and thought about how to counter them. And he might have gotten it completely wrong, as he had with Estemard and his sidearm. But at least he would have taken care of these matters so that I could worry about other things.

Take Sammann as an example. When he'd joined us I'd been glad of his company, as he knew how to do so many things that I didn't. Which was all fine when it was just four of us camped by a tarn. But now that we were deep in the Sæcular world I recalled the ancient taboo against contact between avout and Ita, which we could not have been breaking any more flagrantly. Did these people know of that taboo? If so, did they understand why it had been instated? Were we, in other words, stirring memories and awakening fears of old? Would their police protect us from a mob—or join in with them?

Ganelial Crade started canvassing his local brethren on his jee-jah. This grew obnoxious, and when he noticed that we were all glaring at him, he got up and moved to an empty table. I asked Sammann if he could pull up any information on the lookout-tower math and he began to view maps and satellite photos on his jeejah that were much better than the stored charts on the cartabla. I'd rarely seen anything like these pictures, which must have been very like what the Cousins could see of Arbre from their ship. This answered a question that had been rattling around in my head since yesterday morning. "Hey," I said, "I think Orolo was looking at such pictures. He put a few up on the wall of his cell."

"It's too bad you didn't tell me that before," said Sammann curtly. Not for the first time I got the feeling that we avout were children and the Ita, far from being a subservient caste, were our minders. I was about to apologize. Then I got the feeling that once I started apologizing I'd never be able to stop. Somehow I managed to arrest my embarrassment before it reached the mud-on-the-head stage.

(on the speely: an old building being blown up; people celebrating)

"Okay, well, now that you mention it, Fraa Jad went out of his way to make sure I came away with them," I said, and pulled from my shirt pocket the folded-up phototypes of the big hole in the ground. I spread them out on the table. Three heads converged and bent over them. Even Ganelial Crade—who had taken to pacing back and forth as he yammered on his jeejah—slowed down for a look-see. But no light of recognition came into his face. "That looks like a mine. Probably in the tundra," he said, just to be saying something.

"The sun is shining almost straight down into it," I pointed out.

"So?"

"So it can't be at a high latitude."

Now it was Crade's turn to be embarrassed. He turned away and pretended to be extremely involved in his jeejah conversation.

(on the speely: phototypes of a kidnapped child, blurry footage of the kid being led out of a casino by a man in a big hat)

"I was wondering," I said to Sammann, "if you could, I don't know, use your jeejah to start scanning the globe and look for such features. I know it would be like finding a needle in a haystack. But if we were systematic about it, and if we worked in shifts for long enough—"

Sammann responded to my idea in much the same spirit as I had to Crade's suggestion that this thing was in the tundra. He held his jeejah up above the picture and took a phototype of the phototype. Then he spent a few seconds interacting with the machine. Then he showed me what had come up on its screen: a different picture of the same hole in the ground. Except now it was a live feed from the Reticulum.

"You found it," I said, because I wanted to go slowly and make sure I understood what was going on.

"A syntactic program available on the Reticulum found it," he corrected me. "It turns out to be a long way from here—on an island in the Sea of Seas."

"Can you tell me the name of the island?"

"Ecba."

"*Ecba!?*" I exclaimed.

"Is there a way to figure out what it is?" Cord asked.

Sammann zoomed in. But this was almost unnecessary. Now that I knew it was on Ecba, I was no longer inclined to see this hole as an open-pit mine. It was clearly an excavation—it was completely encircled by mounded-up earth that had been taken out of it. And a ramp spiraled around to its flat bottom. But it was too orderly, too prim for a mine. Its flat bottom was neatly gridded.

"It is an archaeological dig," I said. "A huge one."

"What's there on Ecba to dig up?" Cord asked.

"I can search for that," Sammann said, and got ready to do so.

"Wait! Zoom out. Again . . . and again," I asked him.

We could now see the dig as a pale scar several miles south-southeast of a huge, solitary mountain that ramped up out of a wrinkled sea. The upper slopes of the mountain were patched with snow but its summit had a scoop taken out of it: a caldera.

"That is Orithena," I said.

"The mountain?" Cord asked.

"No. The dig," I said. "Someone has been digging up the Temple of Orithena! It was buried by an eruption in Negative 2621."

"Who'd do that and why?" Cord asked.

Sammann zoomed back in. Now that I knew what to look for, I could see that the whole dig was surrounded by a wall. It was pierced in one place by a gate. Inside, several structures had been erected around a rectangular courtyard—a cloister. A tower sprouted from one of these.

"It's a math," I said. "Come to think of it, I once heard a story—probably from Arsibalt—that some order had gone to Ecba and started trying to dig their way down to the Temple of Orithena. I thought it was just a few eccentric fraas with shovels and wheelbarrows, though."

"I don't see any heavy equipment on the site," Crade pointed out. "A few people with shovels could dig a hole that deep if they kept at it long enough."

This left me a little irritated, since it ought to have been obvious to me; after all, our Mynster had been constructed in the same style. But Crade was right and there was nothing I could do but agree as vigorously as I could so that he wouldn't explain this any further.

"This is all very interesting," Sammann said, "but it's probably a dead end for us."

"I agree," I said. Ecba was on another continent; or, to be precise, it was in the Sea of Seas which lay among four continents on the opposite side of the world.

"Orolo is not in the mountains," Ganelial Crade announced, pocketing his jeejah. "He passed through here and kept right on going."

(on the speely: two very beautiful people getting married)

"How do you know this?" Sammann asked. I was glad of it. Crade was so sure of himself that I found it draining to confront him with even simple questions. Sammann seemed to derive wicked pleasure from doing so.

Crade rose to it. "He got a ride as far as here from some Samble folk who were going this way, and stayed the night before last in the back of my cousin's fetch, just a couple of miles from here."

"The back of his fetch? Doesn't your cousin have a spare bed?" Sammann asked.

"Yulassetar travels a lot," Crade answered, "the back of his fetch is nicer than his house."

"You say this happened the night before last?" I asked. "I had no idea we were so hot on his trail!"

"Getting colder every minute . . . Yulassetar helped him get outfitted yesterday morning, and then Orolo hitched a ride on a northbound drummon."

"Outfitted *how*?" Cord asked.

"With warm clothes," Crade said. "The *warmest* clothes. This is something Yul knows a lot about. It's what he does for a living. I'm sure that's why Orolo sought him out in Norslof."

"Why would Orolo want to keep going north?" I asked. "There's nothing there, am I right?"

Sammann pawed at my cartabla—which had a larger display than his jeejah—zoomed way out, and slewed it north and east. "Practically nothing but taiga, tundra, and ice between here and the North Pole. As far as economic activity is concerned, there are fuel tree plantations for the first couple of hundred miles. Beyond that, nothing but a few resource extraction camps."

The view on the cartabla seemed to contradict him, as it was densely netted with roads that came together at named places, many of which were ringed by concentric beltways. But all of these were depicted in the faint brown color used to denote ruins.

(on the speely: a fiery rocket launch from an equatorial swamp)

"Orolo's going to Ecba!" Cord proclaimed.

"What are you talking about?" Crade demanded.

"Ecba is not on this continent, you have to fly!" I said.

"He's going over the pole," she explained. "He's headed for the sledge port at Eighty-three North."

We were in the habit of referring to the Sæcular Power as if it were one thing down through the ages. This seemed simple-minded or even insulting to some extras—though they did essentially the same thing when they spoke of the Powers That Be. Of course we knew it was an over-simplification. But for us it was a useful convenience. Whatever empire, republic, despotate, papacy, anarchy, or depopulated wasteland lay beyond our walls at a given moment, we could slap this name on it and predicate certain things of it.

What you are reading does not attempt to set forth details as to how the Sæcular Power was constituted in my day. Such information can be had anywhere. It might even be interesting if you know nothing about the history of the world up to the Terrible Events; but if you have studied that, everything since will seem like repetition and all the particulars as to how the Sæcular Power of my day was organized will remind you of more or less ancient forerunners, but with less majesty and clarity since the ancients were all doing it for the first time and believed they were on to something.

But at this point I had to attend to one of those details. The Sæcular Power in my day was a federation. It broke down into political units that more or less agreed with Arbre's continents. One could travel freely within most of those units, but to cross from one to another one had to have documents. The documents were not that difficult to obtain—unless one was avout.

Since the Reconstitution, we had existed wholly apart from the legal system of the Sæcular Power. They had no records of us, no jurisdiction over us, no responsibility for us; they could not draft us into their armies, levy taxes on us, or even step through our gates except at Apert. Likewise they would not offer us assistance of any kind, except for protecting us from direct assault by mobs or armies if they felt like it. We didn't get pensions or medical care from the Sæcular Power—and we certainly didn't get identity documents.

It has become obvious during the writing of this that it might one day be read by people from other worlds. So I'll say that we considered ourselves to have ten continents but that the Cousins, or anyone else who came to us from beyond and looked at Arbre fresh, would have said we had only seven—and they would have been right. We counted ours as ten because the original tally had been made by explorers working outward from the Sea of Seas, who could only guess at what might lie more than a few days' march from its convoluted shores. It happened more than once that they bestowed distinct names on lands that were sundered by straits and gulfs, but that on further—and much later—exploration proved to be lobes of the same great land mass reaching toward the Sea of Seas from different quarters. But by that time the places had made their way into the classical myths and histories under the ancient names, which we could no more dislodge from the culture than we could withdraw one of the colossal foundation-stones that supported the Mynster.

Likewise, during the Rebirth, land had been found on the other side of the world from the Sea of Seas and had been proclaimed and mapped as a new continent. But centuries later it had been determined that the far northern reaches of that continent wrapped over the North Pole and thence extended south all the way to the Sea of Seas. It was not a new continent at all but a limb of the oldest and best-known continent, and no one had ever had a clue about it because even the aboriginal peoples who knew how to live in ice houses could not venture much above eighty degrees of latitude. To prove that the "old" and "new" continents were one, it was necessary to go all the way up to ninety degrees north latitude—the North Pole—and then descend to eighty or less on the other side. This had not been accomplished until the last century before the Terrible Events and it had not changed people's habit of referring to the place that Cord, Sammann, Ganelial Crade, and I were on now, and the land mass forming the northern boundary of the Sea of Seas, as two different continents. The ice cap separated the two even more absolutely than an ocean would have, and no normal person ever traveled between them that way. They flew in an aerocraft or did it in a ship.

But to do it by aerocraft or ship you'd have to pass through ports of entry and show documents. Orolo had none and no hope of getting any. So he was doing what was logical, which was to exploit the fact that the two continents were in fact one. Cord had been the first to put this whole picture together in her mind.

No. She'd been the *second*. The first had been Fraa Jad.

"The sledge trains! That's like something out of a children's storybook to me," Sammann said. "Do they still operate?"

"They were shut down for a while, but they are running again now," Crade confirmed. "The price of metals went up. People went back to stripping the Deep Ruins."

"We used to make parts for the sledge locomotives in the machine hall where I worked," Cord said. "We were the largest machine hall that was so far north, so they'd send the jobs to us. It's been a source of business for that shop for over a thousand years. We had to make them of special alloys that wouldn't shatter in the cold." And she went on in this vein for a minute or two; she could talk about alloys the way some girls talked about shoes. Crade and Sammann, who'd been so fascinated to hear about the sledge train idea at first, got less and less so the more Cord said of it.

In my mind I was replaying the memory of Fraa Jad in Orolo's cell yesterday. He couldn't have spent more than half a minute gazing at these phototypes before he'd figured it all out. Even if you were the kind of person who attributed nearly supernatural powers to the Thousanders, this seemed a little weird. He must have had some prior knowledge about this.

"This excavation," I said, tapping my finger on the phototype.

Everyone looked at me funny. I realized that I had just interrupted Cord's disquisition about alloys.

(on the speely: victims of a roadside massacre; their hysterical wives rending their clothes and rolling on the ground)

I continued, "I'll bet you my last energy bar that if you look it up, you'll find that it is 690 years old."

"You think they started digging this hole in 3000," said Ganelial Crade. "Why? You like round numbers?"

This was an extremely rare attempt by Crade to make a joke, and so etiquette required me to smirk at it for a moment before I answered. "I'm pretty sure Fraa Jad knew that this was going on. He recognized this as soon as he saw it. So, I'm thinking that this dig must have been launched during the most recent Millennial Convox. The Thousander math at Saunt Edhar would have sent delegates to that Convox and so they would have heard about it, and brought the knowledge back home with them—which is how Fraa Jad knew."

Sammann, as usual, was ready to play devil's advocate: "I'm not disagreeing, but even if you're right, it seems strange to me that Fraa Jad could take one look at this phototype and know that it was the Orithena dig. It could be any hole in the ground. There's nothing to peg it to Ecba."

Until now we had been attending mostly to the phototype that showed the entire dig on one sheet. The others were zoomed-in detail shots that hadn't made much sense before. Scanning them now, I was able to perceive the outlines of ancient building foundations, the stubs of columns, and flat areas of tiled floor. One of these was marked thus:

I pointed to it. "That's the analemma," I said. "The Temple of Orithena was a big camera obscura. It had a small hole in the roof that projected an image of the sun on the floor. As the seasons changed, the sun-spot hit the floor in a different place each day during their midday ritual—what we celebrate now as Provener. Over the course of the year it would trace this pattern on the floor."

"So, you think Fraa Jad noticed the analemma on this photo-type and said to himself 'Aha, this must be the Temple of Orithena?' That seems like pretty quick thinking to me," Cord said.

"Well, he's a pretty smart guy," I returned. This was not the most polite answer. Jesry would have planed me at this point. Cord was right to be skeptical about it. I wasn't willing to dig any deeper on this point, though. The speed with which Fraa Jad had recognized this hole in the ground suggested that he, and presumably the other Millenarians, knew a lot about it. I was worried that if we pulled any harder on this loose thread, it would lead us back to crazy talk about the Lineage.

"Oh, how interesting," Sammann said, gazing into his jeejah, "Erasmas wins his bet. This dig in the phototypes *was* started in A.R. 3000." He read another tidbit off the screen, then looked up and grinned at me. "It was started by Edharians!"

"Great!" I muttered, wishing I could take Sammann's jeejah and drop it down a toilet.

"It's a spinoff of Saunt Edhar. But a lot of other Edharian maths around the world contributed fraas and suurs to get it started."

"How many avout live there?" Cord asked. I could see her doing the calculation in her head: *if each avout moves twenty wheelbarrow loads of dirt per day, for 690 years, how big does the hole get?*

"I'll have to get back to you on that," Sammann said, grimacing. "Most of the information on this topic is crap."

"What do you mean by that?" Crade demanded. We all looked at him, because in an instant he had become markedly defensive.

Sammann raised his eyes from the screen of the jeejah and gazed interestedly at Crade. He let a few moments go by, then responded in a calm and matter-of-fact tone: "Anyone can post information on any topic. The vast majority of what's on the Reticulum is, therefore, crap. It has to be filtered. The filtering systems are ancient. My people have been improving them, and their interfaces, since the time of the Reconstitution. They are to us what the Mynster is to Fraa Erasmas and his kind. When I look at a given topic I don't just see information about that topic. I see meta-information that tells me what the filtering systems learned when they were conducting the search. If I look up *analemma,* the filtering system tells me that only a few sources have provided information about this and that they are mostly of high repute—they are avout. If I look up the name of a popular music star who just broke up with her boyfriend," Sammann continued, nodding at a tearful female on the speely, "the filtering system tells me that a vast amount of data has been posted on this topic quite recently, mostly of very low repute. When I look up the excavation of the Temple of Orithena on the Island of Ecba, the filtering system informs me that people of very high and very low repute have been posting on this topic, slowly but steadily, for seven centuries."

Sammann's explanation had failed if its purpose had been to settle Crade down. "What's an example of a person of high repute? Some fraa sitting in a concent?"

"Yes," Sammann said.

"And what would a low-repute source be?"

"A conspiracy theorist. Or anyone who makes a lot of long rambling posts that are only read by like-minded sorts."

"A Deolater?"

"That depends," Sammann said, "on what the Deolater is writing about."

"What if he's writing about Ecba? Orithena? The Teglon?" Crade asked, whacking his index finger into a phototype that depicted the ten-sided plaza in front of the ancient temple.

"The filters tell me that a lot has been posted in that vein," Sammann said, "as you appear to know very well. Sorting it out is difficult. When I see such a pattern emerging in the filter interface, my gut tells me that most of it is probably crap. It's a quick and superficial judgment. I could be wrong. I apologize if my choice of words offended you."

"You're forgiven," Crade snapped.

"Well!" I exclaimed, after a few moments' awkward silence had gone by. "This has been fascinating. It's good that we figured this out before we wasted a lot of time searching the mountains! Obviously, the whole premise of my search for Orolo has changed. None of you imagined he would be going to the other side of the world. So you'll all want to turn around and head back south at this point."

Everyone just looked at me. None of their faces was readable.

"Or so I imagine," I added.

"This changes nothing," Sammann said.

"I'm not about to ditch my sib in this dump," Cord said.

"You have to have two vehicles in case one breaks down in the cold," said Ganelial Crade. I couldn't argue with his logic. But I didn't for one moment think that this was his real reason for wanting to tag along. Not after he had let the word *Teglon* slip out.

"From here to Eighty-three North is two thousand miles on a great circle route," said Sammann, working his jeejah. "On the highway, it's twenty-five hundred and some."

"If you and Sammann learn to drive, Raz, so that we can switch off, we can make it in three or four days," Crade said.

"The road's bound to get worse as we go north," Cord said. "I would plan on it taking a week."

Crade was eager to dispute that with her but she added, "And we'll have to modify the vehicles."

So we encamped in the fueling station's back lot and set to work. Once the proprietors understood that we were just passing through en route to the far north, they became more comfortable with us and things got easier. They assumed we were just another crew of vagabonds going up to mine the ruins, and better equipped and financed than most.

The next day we used Cord's fetch to go out and buy new tires for Crade's. Then we used his to get tires for hers. The new tires were deeply grooved and had hobnails sticking out of them. Cord and Gnel (as Ganelial Crade now insisted we call him) worked together on some sort of tool-intensive project to replace the vehicles' coolants and lubricants with ones that would not freeze. Neither Sammann nor I knew much about working on vehicles, so we stood around and tried to be useful. Sammann used his jeejah to study the route north, reading logs posted by travelers who'd gone that way recently.

"Hey," I said to him at one point, "my mind keeps going back to an image I saw on that speely feed yesterday."

"The burning librarian?"

"No."

"The mudslide hitting the school?"

"No."

"The brain-damaged boy playing with the puppies?"

"No."

"Okay, I give up."

"A rocket taking off."

He looked at me. "And—what? Blowing up? Crashing into an orphanage?"

"No. That's the thing. It just took off."

"Did it have celebrities on board or—"

"Not that they showed. They'd show that, wouldn't they?"

"I wonder why they bothered to show it then. Rockets take off all the time."

"Well, I'm no judge of these things, but it looked like an especially big one."

For the first time Sammann seemed to take my meaning. "I'll see what I can find," he said.

An elderly but bustling lady—one of Gnel's co-religionists—came out with a cake that had been baked for us, then snared Gnel in a conversation that never seemed to end. While they were talking, a big, mud-splattered fetch with a wooden cabin on its back thundered into the fueling station, circled around us a couple of times, and claimed four parking spaces. The cake lady marched away, her face all pinched up. A big man with a beard shambled out of the cabin-fetch and came toward Gnel with his hands in his pockets, looking about curiously. When he got closer to Gnel he suddenly flashed a grin and extended his hand. Gnel extended his after a moment's hesitation and let the other heave it up and down for a while. They spoke for no more than a few seconds, then the newcomer began to pace around our little encampment taking a mental inventory of what we had and reconstructing in his mind what we'd been doing there. After a few minutes of that, he unfolded a sort of deployable counter from the side of his cabin-on-wheels and fired up a stove and began to make hot beverages for us.

"That's Yulassetar Crade. My cousin," Gnel told me as we watched him erect a little kitchen, blowing dust out of teacups and polishing pots with a rag from his pocket.

"What happened?" I asked.

"What are you talking about?" Gnel asked, nonplussed.

"It's obvious from the way that you and that lady react to him that there is some history. Some kind of trouble between you."

"Yul is a here—" Gnel began, and stopped himself before he had got to the end of the word. "An apostate."

I wanted to ask, *other than that, is he all right?* but I let it drop.

Yul made no effort to introduce himself, but when I approached him he turned to me with a smile and shook my hand before turning back to his chores. "Hold your arms out," he said, and when I complied he put a tray on them and then placed cups of hot stuff on the tray. "For your friends," he said.

I insisted that he come with me, though. So after giving Gnel a cup we went over to Sammann and I introduced the two of them. Then I talked Cord into sliding out from under her fetch. She stood up and dusted herself off and shook Yul's hand. They gave each other a funny look, which made me speculate that they might have crossed paths before. But neither one of them said anything about it. She accepted her cup and then they turned away from each other as if something embarrassing had happened.

Yulassetar Crade gave me a lift into town so that I could run a couple of errands. First, I mailed my letter to Ala, care of the Concent of Saunt Tredegarh. The woman at the post office gave me a lot of trouble because it wasn't properly addressed. Concents didn't have addresses for the same reason that I didn't have a passport. I knew I'd made a terrible mistake by not giving some sort of note to Arsibalt or Lio at the picnic in Samble. They could have smuggled it directly to Ala. Instead of which I had to mail this thing to the concent, where it would be intercepted by the hierarchs and—if they were sticking to the Discipline—kept out of Ala's knowledge until her next Apert, more than nine years from now. I could only imagine what she'd think of me at that time, reading this yellowed document written by a boy not yet twenty years of age.

The next stop on the itinerary was a place where we could get suitsacks: huge orange coveralls whose legs could be zipped together to make them into sleeping bags. These were made for people who hunted or scavenged in the far north. Each had a catalytic power unit built into it; as long as you kept some fuel in its bladder it would supply a modest trickle of power that was routed down the suits' arms and legs to warming-pads placed in the soles of the boots and the palms of the mittens. New ones could be pretty expensive, but Yul had helped Orolo get a cheap one the other day. He knew of places where you could get used ones that had been fixed up, and he knew tricks for making them more comfortable.

Once we'd taken care of that we set out in search of other gear and supplies we were going to need. Whenever I suggested going to an outdoorsy type of store, Yul winced and groaned, and then explained how better stuff could be had at one-tenth the price by using things you could buy at stores that sold housewares and groceries. He was always right, of course. He made his living as a wilderness guide, taking vacationers on trips to the mountains. Apparently he had no work at the moment, because he spent the whole day driving me around Norslof helping me improvise what we needed. When we were unable to get what we wanted at a store, he promised to supply us out of his own personal stock.

The driving consumed an unbelievable amount of time. The traffic was always bad, or so it seemed to me. But I wasn't used to the vehicular life of a city. When the traffic slowed to a stop, people in the mobes around us would look out the windows at Yul's ramshackle fetch. If they were grownups they would soon look the other way, but children loved to point and stare and laugh. And they were right to do so. Yul and I were an odd pair, compared to all of these people driving to school and to work.

At first Yul seemed to feel an obligation to be a good host—to provide entertainment during traffic jams. "Music?" he said distantly, as if music were something he had heard of once. Hearing no objection, he took to fiddling with the controls on his sound system as if they had broken off in his hands and were no longer attached to anything. Eventually he left it set on a random feed. Later, once he got to talking, I reached over and turned it off and he didn't notice.

Part of his job, I guessed, was to make people he'd just met (his clients) feel comfortable, which he did by telling stories. He was good at it. I tried to get him to talk about Orolo but he didn't have much to say. Orolo might be a lot of things to me but to Yul he was just another tenderfoot who needed advice on how to travel in the rough. This did, however, lead to the topic of getting around in the far north, which he knew a lot about.

Later I asked him if all of his travel had been in that direction and he scoffed and said that no, he'd spent years as a river guide in a region south of Samble that was gouged by deep sandstone canyons filled with spectacular rock formations. He told some good stories about such trips, but after a while became uncomfortable and stopped talking. Telling tales, it seemed, was a good way to loosen things up, a useful time-killer, but what he really wanted was a project into which he could pour his energies and his intelligence.

At some point during the day, he stopped referring to "you" as in "You're going to need extra fuel in case you have to melt snow to make drinking water" and began speaking of "we" as in "We should plan on at least four flat tires."

Yul's house was really just a dumping ground for stuff he couldn't fit into his fetch: camping equipment, vehicle parts, empty bottles, weapons, and books. The books were stacked in piles that came up to my hip. He didn't seem to own any shelves. A lot of them were fiction but he also had several geology-piles. Nailed to the wall were big blown-up phototypes of colorful sedimentary rock formations, sculpted by water and wind. In his cellar, where we went to mine more equipment, he had stacks of tabular rocks—slabs of sandstone—with fossils in them.

After we'd got everything he thought we'd need, and begun driving through another traffic jam back to the fueling station, I said to him, "You figured out that the world was old, didn't you?"

"Yeah," he said immediately. "I spent years on rafts going down those rivers. Years. The whole way, there's rocks strewn along the banks. Rocks the size of houses that fell off the canyon walls, higher up. Just looking down one of those canyons, you can see it happens all the time."

"You mean, rocks falling down."

"Yeah. It's like, if you're driving down this highway and you see skid marks on the pavement, like those right there, any idiot knows that skidding happens. If you see *lots* of skid marks, well, that means that skidding is *common*. If you see lots of fallen rocks in a canyon, then rock falls are common. So, I kept expecting to see one. Every day, I'd be drifting down the river on that raft with the clients, you know, and they'd be sleeping or talking about whatever they wanted to talk about, and I'd keep an eye on the canyon walls, waiting to see a rock fall."

"But you never did."

"Never. Not once."

"So you realized that the time scale had to be enormous."

"Yeah. I tried to figure it out once. I don't have the theorics. But I kept an eye on that river for five years and not a single rock fell down while I was running it. If Arbre is only five thousand years old—if all the rocks in that canyon have fallen down in that short a time—I should have seen some rocks fall."

"The people in your ark didn't like what you had to say about that," I guessed.

"There's a reason I got out of Samble."

That was the end of that conversation. It was the evening rush hour now and we drove in silence for a long time. I was fascinated by the little glimpses of other people's lives that I got through the windows of their mobes. Then I was struck by how different Yul's life seemed to be from theirs.

The way in which Yul had decided to join us on our journey north was strange to me. There had been no rational process: no marshaling of evidence, no weighing of options. But that was how Yul lived his whole life. He had not—I realized—been invited by Gnel to come out and pay us a visit at the fueling station. He had just shown up. He did a new thing with a new set of people every day of his life. And that made him just as different from the people in the traffic jam as I was.

So I looked with fascination at those people in their mobes, and tried to fathom what it would be like. Thousands of years ago, the work that people did had been broken down into jobs that were the same every day, in organizations where people were interchangeable parts. All of the story had been bled out of their lives. That was how it had to be; it was how you got a productive economy. But it would be easy to see a will at work behind this: not exactly an evil will, but a selfish will. The people who'd made the system thus were jealous, not of money and not of power but of story. If their employees came home at day's end with interesting stories to tell, it meant that something had gone wrong: a blackout, a strike, a spree killing. The Powers That Be would not suffer others to be in stories of their own unless they were fake stories that had been made up to motivate them. People who couldn't live without story had been driven into the concents or into jobs like Yul's. All others had to look somewhere outside of work for a feeling that they were part of a story, which I guessed was why Sæculars were so concerned with sports, and with religion. How else could you see yourself as part of an adventure? Something with a beginning, middle, and end in which you played a significant part? We avout had it ready-made because we were a part of this project of learning new things. Even if it didn't always move fast enough for people like Jesry, it did move. You could tell where you were and what you were doing in that story. Yul got all of this for free by living his stories from day to day, and the only drawback was that the world held his stories to be of small account. Perhaps that was why he felt such a compulsion to tell them, not just about his own exploits in the wilderness, but those of his mentors.

We at last reached the fueling station. Yul deployed his traveling kitchen and began to make supper. He made no formal announcement that he was coming with us, but this was obvious from the way he talked, and so after a while Gnel went into the station and struck a deal with the management for Cord to leave her fetch parked there for a couple of weeks. Cord began to move things from her fetch into Yul's. As he cooked, Yul observed this procedure closely, and soon began to complain, in a joking way, about the enormous volume of unnecessary clutter that Cord was, according to him, stuffing into his home-on-wheels. Cord soon began to volley the abuse back at him. Within about sixty seconds they were saying amazingly rude things to each other. I couldn't take part in their banter any more than I could get between two persons who were kissing or fighting, so I drifted over to Sammann.

"I found that rocket speely," he told me. "You were right about its being big. That's one of the largest rockets going nowadays."

"Anything else?"

"The payload," he said. "Its shape and size match those of a vehicle that is generally used to carry humans into space."

"How many humans?"

"Up to eight."

"Well, is there any information about who is on board, or why they're going up there?"

Sammann shook his head. "Not unless you count the absence of information as information."

"What do you mean by that?"

"According to the Powers That Be, the vehicle is unmanned. It's a test of a new system. Under syndev control."

I gave him a look. He grinned and held up his hands. "I know, I know! I've made inquiries on a few reticules known to me. In a few days maybe we'll have something."

"In a few days we'll be at the North Pole."

"In a few days," he said, "that might be a wise place to be."

The next morning, after a large breakfast prepared by Yul and Cord, we started the journey north. Cord's fetch stayed behind. Our caravan consisted of the Crade vehicles, that of Yulassetar containing most of the gear, that of Ganelial carrying his three-wheeler in the back.

The first leg was north and downhill to the coastal plain, a turn to the right when we neared salt water, and then a long sweeping leftward curve as we skirted a gulf of the northern ocean. At the head of that gulf lay what had been the greatest port in the world for a couple of centuries back in the First Millennium A.R. when the water had stayed ice-free all year round. Because of its location it had later become the "shallowest" of all ruins—the easiest to mine. Most of its great works—its viaducts, seawalls, and bridges—had been hammered apart by scavengers who had extracted the reinforcing bars buried in the synthetic stone and shipped the metal to places where it was needed. The rubble-mounds were forested with immense trees. The only remaining structure from that age was a suspension bridge over the great river that emptied into the head of the gulf; it was high enough above sea level that the resurgent pack ice had not crushed it. At this time of year there was no ice to be seen, but it was easy to make out the scars it had left along the rubble-banks. This port-ruin now functioned as a fishing village and drummon stop. A few hundred people lived here, at least in the summer. Once we left it behind and struck inland, heading almost due north, we saw only scattered settlements, which thinned and failed as we climbed into forested hills. We then descended into an unmistakably different landscape: taiga, a country too dry and cold for trees to grow much higher than a person's head. Almost all traffic had vanished from the highway. We drove for an hour without seeing any other vehicles. Finally we stopped in a rocky place near a river, pulled our vehicles round to where they couldn't be seen from the road, and slept in our suitsacks.

The next morning, the brand-new stove we had bought after leaving Samble stopped working. If Yul hadn't joined us, we'd have spent the rest of the trip eating cold energy bars. Yul, looking quietly triumphant, produced a thunderous breakfast on his battery of roaring industrial burners. Watching his cousin work, Gnel seemed proud, if exasperated. As if to say, *look at what fine people we can produce when they stop believing in our religion.*

Since there was almost no traffic on the road, I took driving lessons from Yul while Cord dismantled the stove. She diagnosed the problem as a clogged orifice, attributable to gunk that had precipitated from the fuel during the cold night.

"You're fuming," she pointed out a while later. I realized that I had withdrawn from the conversation. She and Yul had been talking, but I hadn't heard a word of their conversation. "What is the problem?"

"I just can't believe that in this day and age we are having a problem with chemical fuel," I said.

"Sorry. We should have bought the premium brand."

"No, it's not that. Nothing for you to be sorry about. I'm just pointing out that this stove is four-thousand-year-old praxis."

Cord was nonplussed. "Same goes for this fetch and everything in it," she said.

"Hey!" Yul cried, mock-wounded.

Cord scoffed, rolled her eyes, and turned her attention back to me. "Everything except for your sphere, that is. So?"

"I guess because I live in a place with almost zero praxis, it never occurs to me to think about such things," I said. "But at times like this, the absurdity hits me between the eyes. There's no reason to put up with junk like this. A stove with dangerous, unreliable chemical fuel. With orifices that clog. In four thousand years we could have made a better stove."

"Would I be able to take that stove apart and fix it?"

"You wouldn't have to, because it would never break."

"But I want to know if I could understand such a stove."

"You're the kind of person who could probably understand just about anything if you set your mind to it."

"Nice flattery, Raz, but you keep dodging the question."

"All right, I take your point. You're really asking if the average person could understand the workings of such a thing . . ."

"I don't know what an average person is. But look at Yul here. He built his stove himself. Didn't you, Yul?"

Yul was uneasy that Cord had suddenly made this conversation about him. But he deferred to her. He glanced away and nodded. "Yup. Got the burners from scavengers. Welded up the frame."

"And it worked," Cord said.

"I know," I said, and patted my belly.

"No, I mean the system worked!" Cord insisted.

"What system?"

She was exasperated. "The . . . the . . ."

"The non-system," Yul said. "The lack of a system."

"Yul knew that stoves like this were unreliable!" Cord said, nodding at the broken one. "He'd learned that from experience."

"Oh, bitter experience, my girl!" Yul proclaimed.

"He ran into some scavengers who'd found better burner heads in a ruin up north. Haggled with them. Figured out a way to hook them up. Probably has been tinkering with them ever since."

"Took me two years to make it run right," Yul admitted.

"And none of that would have been possible with some kind of technology that only an avout can understand," Cord concluded.

"Okay, okay," I said, and let it drop there. Letting the argument play out would have been a waste of breath. We, the theors, who had retreated (or, depending on how you liked your history, been herded) into the maths at the Reconstitution, had the power to change the physical world through praxis. Up to a point, ordinary people liked the changes we made. But the more clever the praxis became, the less people understood it and the more dependent they became on us—and they didn't like that at all.

Cord spent a while telling Yul what she knew about the Cousins, and about all that had happened during the journey from Saunt Edhar to Samble to Norslof. Yul took it pretty calmly, which irked me. I wanted to grab him by the shoulders and shake him and make him see, somehow, that this was an event of cosmic significance: the most important thing that had ever happened. But he listened to Cord's narration as if she were relating a story of how she had fixed a flat tire on her way to work. Perhaps it was a habit of wilderness guides to feign unnatural calm when people ran up to them with upsetting news.

Anyway, it gave me an opening to carry forward the stove argument in a way that wouldn't make Cord so irritated. When the conversation lapsed, I tried: "I see why you guys—or anyone—would feel more comfortable with a stove you could take apart and understand. And I'm fine with that—normally. But these are not normal times. If the Cousins turn out to be hostile, how can we oppose them? Because it looks like they came from a world that didn't have anything like the Reconstitution."

"A dictatorship of the theors," Yul said.

"It doesn't have to be a dictatorship! If you could see how theors behave in private, you'd know they could never be that organized."

But Cord was of one mind with Yul on this. "Once they get to the point where they're building ships like that one," she said, "it is a dictatorship in effect. You said yourself it would take the resources of a whole planet. How do you think they got their hands on those resources?"

In most cases Cord and I saw things the same way and the extra/avout split simply was not important to us, so when she talked this way it made me more upset than I cared to let on. I let it drop for a while. On these endless drives, it was nothing to let the conversation pause for an hour or two.

And there was something else going on, which was that everything had changed about Cord when Yul had showed up. These two simply knew what to do around each other. Whatever was going on between them, I wasn't part of it, and I felt jealous.

We passed through another ruin-city, almost as "shallow" as yesterday's and almost as thoroughly erased.

"The Cousins' praxis is nothing to jump up and down about,"

I said. "We haven't seen anything on that ship that couldn't have been built in our own Praxic Age. That makes me think that we could build a weapon that could disable their ship."

Cord smiled and the tension was gone. "You sound like Fraa Jad the other day!" she exclaimed, with obvious affection—for me.

"Oh really? What did the old man say?" I could hear the hurt draining out of my own speech.

She adopted a pretty good imitation of his grumbling voice. "'Their electrical systems could be disabled by a burst of whoz-amajigger fields.' Then Lio said, 'Begging your pardon, Fraa Jad, but we don't know how to make those.' 'Why, it's simple, just build a phrastic array of whatsit-field inducers.' 'Sorry, Fraa Jad, but no one knows those theorics any more and it takes thirty years' study to get up to speed!' and so on."

I laughed. But then—tallying the days in my head—I realized something: "They're probably reaching Tredegarh right now. Probably starting to talk about how to make those whatsit field inducers."

"I would hope so!"

"The Sæcular Power probably has tons of information about the Cousins that has been withheld from us until now. Maybe they've even been going up there and *talking* to the Cousins. I'll bet they are giving all of that information to the fraas and suurs at the Convox. I wish I was there. I'm tired of not understanding! Instead I'm helping Fraa Jad understand why a Throwback wants to visit a seven-century-old archaeological dig." I slapped the control panel helplessly.

"Hey!" Yul said in mock outrage and pretended to haul off and punch me in the shoulder.

"I guess that's part of being a pawn," I went on.

"Your vision of what the Convox is like sounds pretty romantic to me," Cord said. "Way too optimistic. Remember the first day at the machine-hall when we were trying to get seventeen people into six vehicles?"

"Vividly."

"This Convox thing is probably like that except a thousand times worse."

"Unless there's someone like me there," Yul said. "You should see the way I can get seventeen tourists into four rafts."

"Well, Yul's not at Tredegarh," Cord pointed out, "so you're not missing a thing. Just relax and enjoy the drive."

"Okay," I said, and laughed a little. "Your understanding of human nature is better than mine."

"What's her problem with me then?" Yul demanded.

As the drive went on, most of us bounced back and forth between the two vehicles. The exception was Gnel who always remained in his fetch, though sometimes he'd let Sammann drive it.

The next day, when Cord and I were alone together for a couple of hours, she told me that she and Yul had become boyfriend and girlfriend.

"Huh," I said, "I guess that explains why you two spend so much time out 'gathering firewood.'" I wasn't trying to be a smarty-pants, just trying to emulate the kind of banter that Cord and Yul exchanged so freely. But Cord became quite embarrassed and I realized that I had struck too close to home. I groped around for something else to say. "Well, now that you've told me, it seems like it was meant to be. I guess I just didn't see it because I had this idea that you were going out with Rosk."

Cord thought that was pretty silly. "Remember all those conversations I was having with him on my jeejah the other day?"

"Yes."

"Well, what we were really doing was breaking up."

"Well, Cord, I hate to be a pedantic avout, but I couldn't help overhearing your half of those conversations, and I don't think I heard a single word that was even remotely about breaking up."

She looked at me as if I were insane.

"All I'm saying," I said, holding up my hands, "is that I had no idea that that was what was going on."

"Neither did I," Cord said.

"Do you think . . ." I began, and stopped. I'd been about to say *Do you think that Rosk knows?* but I realized in the nick of time that it would be suicide. It seemed to me like a pretty irregular way to handle important relationships, but then I remembered how things had gone with me and Ala and decided I was in no position to criticize my sib on that score.

Cord and I had talked surprisingly little about our family—that is, the family I'd shared with her until I'd "gone to the clock." But what little I'd heard had left me amazed by how clever people were at finding ways to make each other crazy and miserable, whether it was those they were related to or a crowd of strangers they'd been thrown together with in a concent. Cord sometimes seemed eighty years old in her knowledge and experience and cynicism about such things. I couldn't help thinking she'd thrown up her hands at some point and decided to devote the rest of her life to mastering things, such as machines, that could be made sense of and fixed. No wonder she hated the idea of machines she couldn't understand. And no wonder she didn't waste a lot of time trying to understand things she couldn't—like why she was now Yul's girlfriend.

When the climate had been warmer, civilizations had sloshed back and forth across this glacier-planed landscape for a couple of thousand years like silt in a miner's pan, forming drifts of built-up stuff that stayed long after the people had departed. At any given moment during those millennia, a billion might have lived on this territory that now supported a few tens of thousands. How many bodies were buried up here, how many people's ashes scattered? Ten, twenty, fifty billion all told? Given that they all used electricity, how many miles of copper wire had been sewn through their buildings and under their pavements? How many man-years had been devoted to the one activity of pulling and stapling those wires into place? If one out of a thousand was an electrician, something like a billion man-years had been devoted to running wire from one point to another. After the weather had grown cold again and the civilizations had, over the course of a few centuries, shifted south—moving like glaciers—scavengers had begun coming up here to undo those billion man-years one tedious hour at a time, and retrieve those countless miles of wire yard by yard. Professional scavengers working on an industrial scale had gotten ninety percent of it quickly. I'd seen pictures of factories on tank treads that rolled across the north and engulfed whole city blocks at a time, treating the fabric of the ruins just as a mining robot would an ore-rich hill, grinding the buildings to rubble and sorting the shards according to density. The first ruins we had seen were the feces that those machines left along their paths.

Stripping ruins by hand was more expensive. When times were prosperous elsewhere, metals became precious enough that miners could make a life out of venturing to the deep ruins— far-flung cities of old, never reached by the factories-on-tank-treads—and extracting whatever was most valuable: copper wires, steel beams, plumbing, or what have you. The swag made its way toward the road we were driving in fitful stages, from one anarchic little tundra market-town to the next. Snowstorms and arctic pirate-bands might impede its progress but eventually it found the road and was piled on the backs of ramshackle drum-mons that seemed to consist of seventy-five percent rust by weight, held together only by rimes of ice and shaggy cloaks of dirty snow. These moved in caravans for protection, so it was hopeless to try to pass them, but they moved fast enough for our purposes and they afforded us the safety of the herd once they'd figured out we were pilgrims, not pirates. We stayed well back of them so that we'd have time to swerve whenever a rigid glyph of plumbing or a hairball of wire fell off onto the road. Our windscreen grew opaque with tire-flung mud-ice. We kept the side windows open so that we could reach out and wipe it off with rags on sticks. On the third day the rags froze; after that we kept the stove running with a pot of warm water on top of it, to thaw them out. Through our open windows we looked at ruins passing by. We learned to tell what age a place had been built by the character of its fortifi-cations: missile silos, three-mile-long runways, curtain walls, stone ramparts, acres of curled razor barbs, belts of sequence-engineered thorn trees, all more or less torn down and deranged by scavengers.

As the days went on, all of this stuff was dusted, then frosted, then choked, flattened, crushed, drowned, obliterated by ice. After that, the only things we saw that had been put there by humans were wrecks of former sledge ports: fluctuations of climate or of markets had left them defenseless long enough to die. The landscape a mile from the road was clean and white, that along the road was the most disgusting thing I'd seen the whole trip. The snow-piles along the sides of the road grew higher and blacker until our way became a carbon-black slit trench twenty feet deep, crammed with drummons moving about as fast as a healthy person could walk. After that there was no escape. We could have shut off our vehicles' engines and the drummon behind us would have shoved us all the way to the end of the road. They had snorkels to draw fresh air down into their cabs. We hadn't thought to so equip ourselves, and spent the last day breathing oily blue exhaust. When this became too sickening to endure we would swap drivers and climb up out of the trench (there were occasional ramps in the snow-walls) and simply walk alongside for a while (we had bought snowshoes, improvised from scavenged building materials, in one of the tundra markets) or ride on Gnel's three-wheeler.

It was on one of those trudges—the very last leg—that Yul finally asked me about the parking ramp dinosaur.

Ever since our day together in Norslof, it had been clear he'd wanted to get something off his chest. When he and Cord had suddenly become an item, he'd avoided being alone with me for a couple of days. But once it was clear that I was not going to go nonlinear, he'd begun a gentle search for opportunities to talk to me one-on-one. I'd assumed the topic was going to be him and Cord. But Yul was full of surprises.

"Some say it was a dinosaur, some say dragon," I told him. "One of the first things we were taught about the incident is that nothing can be known of it for certain—"

"Since all evidence was wiped out by the Incanters?"

"That's one story. The second thing we were taught, by the way, was that we should never discuss the incident with Sæculars."

He got a frustrated look.

"Sorry," I said, "that's just how it is. Most accounts agree that one group, let's call them Group A, started it, and Group B finished it. In popular folkore, A equals the so-called Rhetors and B equals the so-called Incanters. It happened three months before the opening of the Third Sack."

"But the dinosaur—or the dragon or whatever—really did appear in the parking ramp."

Yul and I were walking side-by-side on compacted snow, a stone's throw off to the right side of the drummon-jammed slit trench. Closer to it, conditions were dangerous because men, many of them intoxicated, were zipping back and forth on snow machines. The track that Yul and I were following appeared to have been laid down by such a machine a day or two earlier. We could tell where our fetches were in the trench because we'd learned to recognize the jury-rigged snorkels of the adjoining drummons. The traffic seemed to be accelerating slightly, so that we had to mush harder in order to keep pace. This was probably because we were only a couple of miles from the sledge port. We could see its antennas, its smoke, and its lights a couple of miles ahead. Even if the fetches outdistanced us, we'd be able to reach it on foot, so we weren't overly concerned about keeping up.

"It was only a couple of thousand feet away from Muncoster," I said. "There was a city there—as there is now. Overall level of affluence and praxic development, let's say nine on a scale of ten."

"Where are we today?" Yul asked.

"Let's say eight. But the society around Muncoster had peaked, though they didn't know it yet. Deolaters were gaining political influence."

"Which Ark?"

"I don't know. One of those that is aggressive about garnering power. They had an iconography—"

"A what?"

"Well," I said, "let's just say that they felt threatened by certain things that avout tend to believe."

"Such as that the world is old," Yul said.

"Yeah. There had been trouble at a couple of Annual Aperts, and bigger trouble at the Decennial of 2780. The Tenners' math got sacked a little on Tenth Night. But then things seemed to calm down. Apert was over. Things went back to normal. So, now, a parking ramp was then under construction within sight of the concent. It was part of a shopping center. The avout could see it going up, just by looking out the windows of their towers—Muncoster has a lot of towers. The ramp was finished a few months later. Sæculars went in there every day and parked their cars. No problem. Six years passed. The shopping center expanded. The workers had to make some structural changes to the parking ramp so that they could attach a new wing. One of them was up on the fourth level, using a pneumatic hammer to demolish part of the floor, when he noticed something embedded in the synthetic stone. It looked like a claw. Investigating, they removed more and more stone. It was a major safety issue since the building isn't structurally sound if there are such things as claws and bones in load-bearing members. They had to shore it up—the building was weakening, sagging, before their eyes. The more they uncovered, the worse it got. When all was said and done, they had uncovered a complete skeleton of a hundred-foot-long reptile embedded in synthetic stone that had only been poured four years earlier. The Deolaters didn't know what to make of it. There started to be serious unrest and violence around the walls of the concent. Then one night, chanting was heard from the Thousanders' tower. It went on all night. The next day, the parking ramp was back to normal. So the story goes."

"Do you believe it?" Yul asked.

"*Something* happened. There were—are—records."

"You mean, like, phototypes of the skeleton?"

"I'm referring more to things like the memories in the witnesses' minds. Piles of lumber used to shore up the structure. The paperwork at the lumberyard. A little bit of additional wear on the tires of the drummons that carried the lumber to the site."

"Like ripples spreading out," Yul said.

"Yeah. So if the skeleton suddenly vanishes, and there's no physical evidence it was ever there, what do you have left?"

"Only the records," Yul said, nodding vigorously, as if he understood it better than I. "The ripples, without the splash."

"The tires of the lumber drummon didn't suddenly get unworn. The paperwork at the lumberyard didn't vanish from the files. But now there is a conflict. The world isn't coherent any more—there are logical contradictions."

"Big piles of shoring lumber in front of a parking ramp that never needed to be shored up," Yul said.

"Yeah. And it's not that this is physically impossible. Obviously it is *possible* to have a pile of wood in front of a parking ramp, or some pieces of paper in a filing cabinet. But the problem—the issue it raises—is that the overall state of affairs just doesn't add up any more." I was remembering the pink dragon dialog with Orolo—realizing, all these months later, that his choice of a dragon to illustrate the point had been no accident. He'd been trying to remind us of the very incident Yul was talking about.

We heard a braying engine behind us and turned around to see Ganelial Crade headed our way on the three-wheeler. Yul and I exchanged a look that meant *let's not discuss this around him*. Yul bent down, scooped up a double handful of snow, and tried to pack it into a ball to throw at his cousin. It was too cold to pack though.

We reached the sledge port at Eighty-three North at two in the morning, which only meant that the sun was slightly lower in the sky than usual. The slit-road debouched into a plateau of pack ice a mile or two wide, and somewhat lower than the surrounding ice, so that it felt like being on the floor of a large meteorite crater. Here and there, housing modules rose on stilts that could be moved and adjusted when the ice flowed under them. The drummons tended to congregate around these. Each was the headquarters of a different scrap dealer, and the drivers would hustle from one to the next trying to get the best prices for their loads. Other structures served as hostels, eateries, or bordellos.

The place was dominated by the sledge train itself. The first time I saw this, with the low sun behind it, I mistook it for a factory. The locomotive looked like one of those city-eating scrap processors: a power plant and a village of housing modules built on a bridge that spanned the interval between two colossal tracks. In the train behind it were half a dozen sledges, each built on parallel runners that rode in the ruts of packed snow laid down by the locomotive's treads. The first of these was built to carry shipping containers. They were stacked four high, and an ungainly crane on wheels was laboring to begin a fifth layer. Behind it were a few sledges that simply consisted of great open boxes. Another crane, equipped with pincers easily big enough to snatch both of our vehicles at the same time, was clawing tangles of scrap metal from a pile on the snow and dropping them into these with heart-stopping crashes. The last sledge in the train was a flatbed: a mobile parking lot about half full of loaded drummons.

We spent a while blundering around, but from having talked to drummon operators at roadside stops we had a general notion of how the place worked and some good suggestions on how *not* to behave. From Sammann's research we already knew that another sledge train had departed two days earlier and that the one we were looking at would continue loading for another few days.

Getting about was a hazard because there were no established rights-of-way. Drummons and fetches just moved in straight lines toward whatever their jumped-up drivers wanted to reach. So we tended to use our vehicles even for short movements. We found the office-on-stilts that booked places on the flatbed, and arranged to have both of our vehicles loaded upon it. But we paid a little extra to get Gnel's fetch situated at the edge, rather than in the middle; that way, by deploying planks as ramps, we were able to get the three-wheeler on and off at will. It then became our means of moving around the sledge port, though it could only take two at a time and so at any given moment three of us would be marooned. So we rented one of the housing modules on the locomotive and marooned ourselves there. It was cheap. The toilet was a hole in the floor covered, when not used, by a trapdoor weighed down with slugs of scrap iron so that arctic gales wouldn't blow it open. A few trips up and down the sledge train in the three-wheeler sufficed to stock our little house with the rations and other goods we'd packed into the fetches, as well as a surprisingly comprehensive arsenal of projectile and edged weapons. Yulassetar and Ganelial Crade might disagree about religion, but in their relationship to arms they were the same mind in two different bodies. They even used the same types of cases to store their guns, and the same boxes for ammunition. Many at the sledge port carried weapons openly, and there was a place at the edge of "town" where people would go out and discharge weapons into the encircling ice-wall just to pass the time. On the whole, though, the place was more orderly and predictable than the territory we'd spent the last week driving though. As I was coming to understand, it had to be thus because it was a place of commerce.

Once we were settled in, Sammann and I took the three-wheeler and made the rounds of bars and brothels just to confirm that Orolo wasn't in any of them. Cord clambered around on the locomotive, admiring its workings, and Yul followed her. He claimed to be as interested in such things as Cord, but to me it was obvious that he expected she'd be raped if she went out alone.

We killed time for several days. I tried to read some theorics books I'd brought, but couldn't concentrate, and ended up sleeping for unreasonable amounts of time. Sammann had found a place near an office-module where he could get patchy connections to the Reticulum. He went there once a day, then came back to scan through the information he had acquired. Yul and Cord watched speelies on a tiny jeejah screen when they weren't "gathering firewood." Ganelial Crade read his scriptures in Old Bazian and began to signal interest in something that he had been polite enough to avoid and that I had been dreading: religion.

Sammann once saved me from a near brush with that by looking up suddenly from his jeejah, finding my face at the other end of the room, then dropping his gaze again to the screen. He'd recently come back from one of his data-foraging expeditions; there were still a few clots of ice dangling from his whiskers. I went over and squatted next to his chair.

"After we left Samble I began trying to obtain access to certain reticules," Sammann explained. "Normally these would have been closed to me, but I thought I might be able to get in if I explained what I was doing. It took a little while for my request to be considered. The people who control these were probably searching the Reticulum to obtain corroboration for my story."

"How would that work?" I asked.

Sammann was not happy that I'd inquired. Maybe he was tired of explaining such things to me; or maybe he still wished to preserve a little bit of respect for the Discipline that we had so flagrantly been violating. "Let's suppose there's a speelycaptor at the mess hall in that hellhole town where we bought snow tires."

"Norslof," I said.

"Whatever. This speelycaptor is there as a security measure. It sees us walking to the till to pay for our terrible food. That information goes on some reticule or other. Someone who studies the images can see that I was there on such-and-such a date with three other people. Then they can use other such techniques to figure out who those people are. One turns out to be Fraa Erasmas from Saunt Edhar. Thus the story I'm telling is corroborated."

"Okay, but how—"

"Never mind." Then, as if he'd grown weary of using that phrase, he caught himself short, closed his eyes for a moment, and tried again. "If you must know, they probably ran an asamocra on me."

"Asamocra?"

"Asynchronous, symmetrically anonymized, moderated open-cry repute auction. Don't even bother trying to parse that. The acronym is pre-Reconstitution. There hasn't been a true asamocra for 3600 years. Instead we do other things that serve the same purpose and we call them by the old name. In most cases, it takes a few days for a provably irreversible phase transition to occur in the reputon glass—never mind—and another day after that to make sure you aren't just being spoofed by ephemeral stochastic nucleation. The point being, I was not granted the access I wanted until recently." He smiled and a hunk of ice fell off his whiskers and landed on the control panel of his jeejah. "I was going to say 'until today' but this damned day never ends."

"Fine. I don't really understand anything you said but maybe we can save that for later."

"That would be good. The point is that I was trying to get information about that rocket launch you glimpsed on the speely."

"Ah. And have you succeeded?"

"I'd say yes. You might say no because you avout like your information tidily written down in a book and cross-checked by other avout. The information we trade in is noisy and ambiguous and suggestive. Often it's images or acoustical signatures instead of words."

"I accept your rebuke. What have you got?"

"Eight went up on that rocket."

"So the official statement was a lie as we suspected."

"Yes."

"Who were they?"

"I don't know. That's where things get noisy and ambiguous. This thing was very hush-hush. Military secrets and so forth. There is no passenger manifest that I can read to you. No stack of dossiers. All I have is ten seconds of really bad images from the collision-avoidance speelycaptor on the windscreen of some janitor's fetch, taken while he was parallel-parking in a tight spot a quarter of a mile away. Motion artifacts have been removed, of course."

Sammann caused the jeejah to begin playing back a snippet of—as advertised—terrible speely data. It showed a coach, with military markings, parked next to a large building. A door in the side of the building opened. Eight people in white coveralls came out and climbed into the coach. They were followed by others who looked like doctors and technicians. The interval between the building and the coach was about twenty feet, so we got to see them walk that far. Sammann made the thing run on infinite loop. The first couple of dozen times through, we focused all of our attention on the first four people in the white suits. Faces were impossible to make out, but it was surprising how much could be inferred from how people moved. Three of the white-suited people moved in an ever-shifting triangle around a fourth, who was bigger than all of them, with prepossessing hair. He carried himself erect and moved in a heedless line; the others scurried and weaved. His coverall was subtly different from the others': it had a pattern of stripes or markings crisscrossed over it, almost as if he'd been draped in a few yards of—

"Rope," I said, freezing the image and pointing to it. "I've seen something like that before—at Apert. There was an extra wearing something like that. He was a Warden of Heaven priest. That is their ceremonial garb."

By this point Cord had come over to watch the speely with us. She was standing behind Sammann's chair looking over his shoulder. "Those four who are bringing up the rear," she said, "they are avout."

Until now we'd only had eyes for the high priest and his three acolytes. The other half of the crew didn't do much: just walked in single file from the building to the coach. "What makes you say that?" I asked. "That is, other than the fact that they show zero interest in the guy with the rope. There is nothing to mark them as avout."

"Yes there is," Cord said. "The way they walk."

"What are you talking about!? We're all bipeds! We all walk the same way!" I protested. But Sammann had twisted around in his chair to grin up at Cord. He nodded enthusiastically.

"You two are nuts," I said.

"Cord is right," Sammann insisted.

"It couldn't have been more obvious at Apert," Cord said. "Extras swagger and slouch. They walk like they own the place." She got out from behind the chair and strode down the middle of the room in a rolling, easy gait. "Avout—and Ita—are more self-contained." She drew herself up and walked back to us with quick steps, not moving any air.

As crazy as this sounded, I had to admit that during Apert I'd been able to tell extras apart from fraas and suurs at a distance, partly based on how they moved. I turned my attention back to the screen. "Okay, I'll give you that one," I said. "The more I look at them, the more familiar that gait seems to me. Especially the tall one bringing up the rear. He is a dead ringer for—"

I couldn't get a word out for a few moments. Everyone looked at me to see if I was okay. I couldn't take my eyes off that speely. I watched it four more times, and each time I grew more certain of what—of *who*—I was seeing.

"Jesry," I said.

"Oh, my god!" Cord exclaimed.

"His blessings and mercy upon you," hissed Ganelial Crade, as was his custom when anyone used that word in an oath.

"That is absolutely your friend," Cord said.

"Fraa Jesry is in space with the Warden of Heaven!" I shouted, just to hear it.

"I'm sure they are having some fascinating discussions," said Sammann.

A couple of hours later, after we'd covered the windows and tried to sleep, the place began to hum and rumble, and there came a jerk that made half of our stuff fall to the floor. Gnel and I unzipped the legs of our suitsacks and ran out to the catwalk and looked down to see rimes of ice exploding into sparkling clouds as they were crushed by imperceptible shifting of the tread segments. We scurried to the end of the catwalk where a stair led down to near snow level, jumped off, got the three-wheeler started, and buzzed back to the flatbed. Explosive bangs resonated up and down the train as the locomotive budged forward and began to draw up slack. A couple of the flat-bed's boarding-ramps were dragging on the ice so that last-minute loading could proceed—it would be half an hour before the train was really moving. We blasted up one of these, veered around a drummon that was back-and-forthing into a tight slot, and found our way to Gnel's fetch. We ran the three-wheeler up the plank ramps and stowed the planks under the fetch. Then we spent a while drain-ing the coolants from all three vehicles' engines and storing it in poly jugs. By the time we were finished, the train was moving faster than we could walk in snowshoes, so we made our way forward along the system of catwalks that skirted the sledges and linked them together. Cord and Yul had pulled up the window-coverings to let the sun in, and were cooking a big celebratory breakfast. We were on our way to the North Pole. I was glad of that. But when I thought of Fraa Jesry in orbit I couldn't have felt more in the wrong place.

"Bastard!" I said. "That bastard!"

Everyone looked at me. We had pushed back from what, in these circumstances, counted as a huge breakfast.

Yulassetar Crade looked at Cord as if to say, *Your sib . . . your problem.*

"Who? What?" Cord asked.

"Jesry!"

"A few hours ago you were about to start weeping over Jesry. Now he's a bastard?"

"This is so typical," I said.

"He gets launched into space frequently?" Sammann asked.

"No. It's hard to explain, but . . . of all of us, *he* is the one they would pick."

"Who's *they?*" Cord asked. "Obviously this was not a Convox operation."

"True. But the Sæcular Power must have gone to the hierarchs at Tredegarh and said 'give us four of your best' and this is what they came up with." I shook my head.

"You must be proud . . . a little bit," Cord tried.

I put my hands over my face and sighed. "He gets to go meet aliens. I get to ride on a junk train." Then I uncovered my face and looked at Gnel. "What do you know about the Warden of Heaven?"

Gnel blinked. He froze for a moment. I had been avoiding religion for so long, and now I'd asked him a direct question about it! His cousin exhaled sharply and looked away, as if he were about to witness a traffic accident.

"They are heretics," he said mildly.

"Yes, but almost everyone is to you, aren't they?" I said. "Can you be any more specific?"

"You don't understand," Gnel said. "They aren't just any heretics. They are an offshoot of my faith." He looked at Yul. "Of *our* faith." Cord elbowed Yul just in case he'd missed this.

"Really?" I asked. "An offshoot of the Samblites?" This was news to the rest of us.

"Our faith was founded by Saunt Bly," Gnel claimed.

"Before or after you ate his—"

"That," said Gnel, "is an ancient lie invented to make us seem like a bunch of savages!"

"It's almost impossible to sauté a human liver without bruising it," Yul put in.

"Are you saying that Saunt Bly turned into a Deolater? Like Estemard?"

Gnel shook his head. "It's a shame you didn't have an opportunity to talk more with Estemard. He isn't a Deolater as you would define it—or as I would. Neither was Saunt Bly. And that's where we differ from the Warden of Heaven people."

"They think Bly *was* a Deolater?"

"Yes. Sort of a prophet, according to them, who found a proof of the existence of God and was Thrown Back because of it."

"That's funny because if anyone actually did prove the existence of God we'd just tell him 'nice proof, Fraa Bly' and start believing in God," I said.

Gnel gave me a cool stare, letting me know he didn't believe a word of it. "Be that as it may," he said levelly, "it's not the version put out by the Warden of Heaven."

My mind went back to Apert Eve and the discussion of iconographies with Grandsuur Tamura. "This is an instance of the Brumasian Iconography," I said.

"What?"

"The Warden of Heaven is putting out the story that there is a secret conspiracy in the mathic world."

"Yes," Gnel said.

"Something of great import—in this instance, the existence of God—has been discovered. Most of the avout are pure of heart and want to spread the news. But they are cruelly oppressed by this conspiracy which will stop at nothing to preserve the secret."

Gnel was getting ready to say something cautious but Yul spoke first: "You nailed it."

"That is disheartening," I said, "because of all the iconographies, the ones based on conspiracy theories are the hardest to root out."

"You don't say," Sammann said, looking me in the eye.

I got embarrassed and shut up for a bit. Cord broke the ice: "The Cousins' ship is still being kept secret. So we don't know what the Warden thinks about it. But we can guess. They'll see it as—"

"A miracle," Yul said.

"A visitation from another world, purer and better than ours," I guessed.

"Where the evil conspiracy doesn't exist," Cord said. "Come to reveal the truth."

"What about the laser light shining down on the Three Inviolates?" Sammann asked. "How would they interpret that?"

"Depends on whether they know that the Three Inviolates are nuclear waste dumps," I said.

"*What!?*" the Crades exclaimed.

"Even if they do know that," Cord said, "they'd probably give it a more spiritual interpretation."

Gnel was still a little off balance, but he put in, "The Warden of Heaven sees the Thousanders as the good guys."

"Of course," I said. "They know the truth but they can't get the word out because they're bottled up by conniving Tenners and Hundreders, is that it?"

"Yes," Gnel said. "So he would interpret the laser light as—"

"A blessing," Cord said.

"A benediction," I said.

"An invitation," Yul said.

"Boy, are they in for a surprise!" Sammann said delightedly.

"Probably. Maybe. We don't know. I just hope it isn't a nasty surprise for Jesry," I said.

"Jesry the bastard?" Cord said.

"Yeah," I said, and chuckled. "Jesry the bastard."

I was feeling good because it felt like we'd gotten through this without having to endure a sermon from Ganelial Crade; but my heart fell into my gut as Cord turned to him and asked, "Where did the Warden part company from your faith, Gnel?" The last part of this sentence was a little rushed and muffled because Yul had playfully reached around her shoulder to clap his hand over her mouth, and she was twisting his fingers backwards as she talked.

"We read the scriptures ourselves in the original Bazian," Gnel said, "so you might imagine that we are primitive fundamentalists. Maybe we are in that sense. But we aren't blind to what has happened in the mathic world—Old and New—in the last fifty centuries. The Word of God does not change. The Book does not suffer editing or translation. But what men know and understand outside of the Book changes all the time. That's what you avout do: try to understand God's creation without using the direct revelations given to us by God almost six thousand years ago. To us you're like people who've put out your own eyes and are now trying to explore a new continent. You're grievously handicapped—but for that reason you may have developed senses and faculties we lack."

After a few moments' silence, I said, "I'm just going to hold my tongue and not even get into all that is wrong in what you've just said. The gist of it seems to be that we aren't evil or misguided. You think that in the end we'll agree with the Book."

"Of course," said Gnel, "it has to be that way. But we don't think there's a secret conspiracy to hide the truth."

"He believes your confusion is genuine!" Yul translated. Gnel nodded.

"That's very considerate of you," I said.

"We preserved the notebooks of Saunt Bly," Gnel said. "I've read them myself. It's obvious he was no Deolater."

"Excuse me for saying so," Sammann said—this was always how he opened when he was going to insult someone—"isn't it a little nutty for a bunch of Deolaters to found a religion based on the writings of someone they know to have been an atheist?"

"We identify with his struggle," Gnel said, not the least bit insulted. "His struggle to find the truth."

"But don't you already *know* the truth?"

"We know those truths that are in the Book. Truths not therein we feel but we don't know."

"That sounds like something—" I began, then bit my tongue.

"That an avout would say? Like Estemard? Or Orolo?"

"Let's not bring him into this, please."

"Fine." Gnel shrugged. "Orolo kept to himself. Preserved the Discipline, as near as I could tell. I never talked to him."

Here I had to draw back. Count to ten. Take out the Rake. These people cared about eternal truths. Believed that some—but not all—such truths were written down in a book. That their book was right and the others wrong. This much they had in common with most of the other people who had ever lived. Fine—as long as they left me alone. Now they had this new wrinkle: they drew inspiration from a Saunt of the avout. It was not important that I be able to make sense of this.

"You feel the truth but you don't know it," Cord repeated. "Your service the other day, in Samble—we could hear your singing. It was very emotional."

Gnel nodded. "That's why Estemard attends—though he doesn't believe."

"He's not intellectually convinced of your arguments," Cord translated, "but he feels some of what you feel."

"That's exactly it!" Ganelial Crade was delighted. A strange thing to relate. But he was. As if he'd found a new convert.

"Well, even for one who doesn't believe, I can sort of understand the attraction," Cord said.

I gave her a look. Yul clapped his hands over his face. Cord became defensive. "I'm not saying I'm likely to join this ark. Just that it was remarkable, after driving through the middle of nowhere for hours, to come upon this building where people were gathered together and to feel the emotional bond that they shared. To know that they've been doing it for centuries."

"Our ark, our towns like Samble," Gnel said, "they are all dying. That's why those services are so emotionally intense."

This was the first thing he'd ever said that didn't bristle with confidence, so we were taken aback by it. Yul took his face out of his hands and blinked at his cousin.

"Dying because of the Warden of Heaven?" Sammann guessed.

"He preaches a simple, unsubtle creed. It spreads like a disease.

Those who adopt it turn around and spurn us as if we were the heretics. It is wiping us out," Gnel said, and aimed a none too friendly look at Yul.

This was all very interesting but I had other stuff to think about. *So Estemard has gone off the deep end. Has Orolo?*

I recalled the conversation I'd had with Orolo just before the starhenge had been closed—the one about beauty. The one that had saved my life. In retrospect it could be seen as the moment when Orolo's mind began to crack. As if he had started and I'd stopped being crazy at the same moment.

I shook it off. Orolo had been Thrown Back. He'd had only one place to seek refuge: Bly's Butte. Once there, he'd observed the Discipline. No singing in the ark for him. And he had gotten out of the place as soon as he'd been able to.

Well—

Wait a minute. *Not* as soon as he'd been able to. He had departed for the north only a couple of days before we had—the morning after the lasers had shone down upon the Three Inviolates. Why would that cause him to pack up his bolt, chord, and sphere, and hurry to Ecba, of all places?

Maybe in a few days I could just ask him.

○○○○○○○○○○○○○○○○○○○○○○○○○○○○○○○○○○○○○○○

Allswell: A naturally occurring chemical that, when present in sufficient concentrations in the brain, engenders the feeling that everything is fine. Isolated by theors in the First Century A.R. and made available as a pharmaceutical, it became ubiquitous when a common weed, subsequently known as blithe, was sequence-engineered to produce it as a byproduct of its metabolism. Blithe was subsequently made one of the Eleven.

—THE DICTIONARY, *4th edition, A.R. 3000*

The journey lasted about two days—or, up here, two waking-and-sleeping cycles. I was all of a sudden ready to get back to work. The journey from Samble to the sledge port had been a welcome respite from reading and thinking, but seeing Jesry had shocked me awake. I might be sleeping twelve hours at a time and watching speelies, but my friends were working as hard as ever and going off on dangerous missions. It was difficult for me to act on this, though. The continuous vibration and occasional jarring shifts of the sledge train were about as far as you could get from the cloister. Reading and writing were difficult; even watching speelies was hardly worth it. Going outside was out of the question. I could understand why so many people up here were substance abusers.

Before we'd departed, Sammann had done research on how to sneak across the border without documents. Economic migrants did this all the time and some of them had logged their experiences, which gave me a rough idea of what and what not to do. The most important thing *not* to do was to ride the sledge train the whole way. Apparently the sledge port on the other side was a much more fastidious operation than the one we'd passed through. Officials would board the train at an outpost a couple of degrees north of the port and make a sweep down the length of the train during the last few hours of the journey. You could try to hide from them but this was chancy. Instead, illegals tended to jump off the train just short of the outpost and make deals with local sledge-men who would spirit them past the border post.

These came in two categories. The older, more established smugglers had bigger, long-haul sledge trains that they would drive over the mountains to the icebound coast, a couple of hundred miles away. There was also a newer breed using small, nimble, short-range snow machines just to circumvent the sledge port itself. We were hoping to get me on one of those. But the little ones couldn't operate in foul weather. Of course, all of this smuggling could have been stopped if the Sæcular Power had been serious about doing so, but it seemed they were willing to look the other way as long as illegals showed them the courtesy of being a little bit sneaky.

Because of the Cousins' jamming the nav satellites we could

not know our latitude, but we could guess how far we'd come by dead reckoning. When we thought we were getting close, I put on all the warm stuff I had and topped off the fuel bladder in my suit-sack. The backpack I'd been issued at Voco was too small, too new, and too nice-looking, but Yul said he had an old one in his fetch that was bigger, with a metal frame. So we bundled our-selves up and made our way back over the catwalks to the flatbed in the rear. Our backs were to the wind but we staggered and flailed as the sledges bucked over ridges in the ice. We had to shovel three feet of snow off his vehicle. More snow began to fall while we were doing this, and at times it seemed to come down faster than we could get rid of it. But eventually we got into the back of Yul's fetch and found an old military backpack that wouldn't be too conspicuous in the company I'd soon be keeping. I transferred the contents of my little rucksack into it. We filled the remaining volume with energy bars, spare clothes, and other odds and ends, and strapped a pair of snowshoes to the sides just in case.

Back at the head of the train, Gnel supplied me with coins: enough to pay for passage if I haggled, not enough to stain me as rich. Sammann printed out a map of the region around the sledge port. Cord gave me a hug and a smack on the cheek. I went out on the catwalk, pulled the fake-fur fringe of my hood out to shield my face from wind blast, and looked out the left side of the train. Like a litter of cubs following their mother, three much smaller sledge trains were now shadowing us on that side. They'd materialized out of the storm in the last quarter of an hour. Each consisted of a tracked snow-crawler drawing a few sledges behind it. Some of those sledges were open boxes or flatbeds. These were for smug-gling goods, and indeed one was now being laden; it had pulled alongside the third sledge in our train, and men were throwing boxes and kicking gravid bags down into it. Others, though, were covered—tents had been pitched on their backs. I spied a couple of men in orange suitsacks vaulting down into one of those.

Sammann had given me one guideline and two rules. The guideline: get on a sledge with lots of other passengers. There's safety in numbers. Rule 1: don't let your feet touch the surface. You'll be abandoned and you'll die. Rule 2 I'll get to presently.

Gnel and I paced the catwalks for a quarter of an hour, hoping to see something smaller than these three trains. Tiny as they might have seemed next to the giant sledge train, they were quite a bit bigger than most vehicles you'd see on a road down south. They were probably bound west over the mountains. We did not see any of the smaller, more agile vehicles that made short-range smuggling runs in the vicinity of the sledge port. None of them was out today—probably because of the foul weather.

One sharp-eyed sledgeman spied me. He gunned his engine, coughing out a roil of black exhaust, and pulled alongside. He had only one sledge behind his crawler. He slid his window open and stuck his ruddy, hairy face out and quoted a price. I walked back a few steps so that I could look into his sledge. Empty. He quoted a lower price before I said a word.

It didn't feel right to jump into the first one that came along, so I shook my head, turned away, and headed back toward where a larger train was taking on passengers. This operation seemed more professional—if that word made any sense here—but I'd arrived late. The sledges were already crowded with what looked like organized bands of migrants whose stares suggested I wouldn't be welcome. And the price was high. A third, smaller train of mixed cargo and passenger sledges looked more promising: there were enough passengers aboard that I didn't fear being abandoned.

Seeing me and a couple of other singletons in negotiations with the driver of that train, the first sledgeman swooped in again. He pulled ahead so that I could look in through the flaps of the tent on his sledge and see that he'd taken on two passengers. The door of his crawler was hanging open, so I could see his control panel. A glowing screen was mounted above it, showing a jagged trace that scrolled horizontally as we moved: a sonic. Rule 2 was that I should never entrust myself to a sledge that lacked one. It used sound waves to probe the ice ahead for hidden crevasses. Most crevasses could be bridged by the tractor's long treads, but some might swallow it and everything in train behind it.

I asked the driver where he was headed: "Kolya," he answered. The longer, mixed passenger-cargo train was bound for another place called Imnash. The next icebreaker, we knew, was scheduled to leave from Kolya in thirty-one hours. So, having agreed on a price, I heaved my backpack down into the one-sledge train and became its third passenger. According to custom, I paid the driver half of the agreed-on fare up front and kept the other half in my pocket, payable on arrival. For another quarter of an hour he jockeyed for position along both flanks of the train, and managed to collect one more passenger on the right side. By that point, no one remained on the catwalks. All of the little sledge trains peeled away from the big one as if they'd received a common signal. I reckoned we must be drawing close to the outpost where the inspectors would board the train.

From fifty feet we could barely see the giant train; from a hundred it was invisible. A minute after that even the throbbing of its power plant had been muffled by the snow and drowned out by the higher-pitched note of our little train's motor.

This was hardly the sort of thing I'd had in mind when I'd walked out of the chancel at the big Voco two weeks earlier! Even when I'd made the decision to follow Orolo over the pole, I hadn't dreamed that the last leg of the journey was going to be like this. If someone had told me back at Samble that I was going to have to go on a ride like this one, I'd have come up with an excuse not to, and gone straight to Tredegarh. What wouldn't have been clear to me, though, back in Samble, was just how routine this all was. People did it all the time. All I needed to do was kill twenty-four hours, which was how long it would take for this contraption to reach the sea.

We four passengers sat on a pair of sideways-facing benches that could have accommodated eight. We all looked about the same in our suitsacks. Mine was new compared to theirs even though I'd been living in it for a week. Despite the trouble we'd gone to to outfit me with desperate-looking baggage, mine still gleamed in comparison with the first two passengers': poly shopping bags bound up with poly twine and reinforced with poly tape.

The last passenger had an old suitcase bound up in a neat gridwork of yellow rope.

The first two called themselves Laro and Dag, the last was Brajj, all of these being reasonably common extramuros names. I said my name was Vit. Further conversation was difficult over the engine noise and in any case these guys didn't seem very talkative. Laro and Dag huddled together under a blanket. I had the idea that they were brothers. Brajj, having entered last, sat closest to the flaps in the rear. Between his bulk (he was a little bigger than I) and his clumsy suitcase he claimed a lot of space. But it was space that we were glad to let him have because of the snow that swirled in from the sledge's coiling wake.

I'd left all my books with Cord. No one had a speely. There was nothing to see outside but swirling snow. I set my catalytic heater to the lowest power level that would keep my digits alive, folded my arms, propped my legs up on my pack, slumped down on the wooden bench, and tried not to think about how slowly time was passing.

It seemed like years since I'd been in the comfortable surroundings of the concent. But here on this sledge I'd gone into a daydream where I could practically see my fraas and suurs in front of me and hear their voices. From Arsibalt, Lio, and Jesry, I moved on to the decidedly more enjoyable image of Ala. I was fancying her at Tredegarh, a place of which I knew little except that it was older and much bigger than Saunt Edhar, and that the climate was better, the gardens and groves lusher and more fragrant. I had to interpolate a fantasy wherein I survived this trip, found Orolo, got back to Tredegarh, and was allowed in the gate as opposed to being Thrown Back or spending the next five years with nothing except the Book to keep me company. Having got those formalities out of the way, I conjured up a half-waking dream of a fine supper in a rich old Tredegarh refectory at which fraas and suurs from all over the world raised glasses of really good-tasting stuff to me and Ala for having made those pinhole camera observations. Then the daydream took a more private turn involving a long walk in a secluded garden . . . this made me drowsy. It was not turning out as I'd expected. Whatever part of my mind was in charge of daydreams was shaping this one to comfort me and lull me, not to arouse passions.

A shift in the sledge's attitude brought me just awake enough to know I'd been sleeping.

In going over the pole, we'd followed a stocky isthmus. Two tectonic plates had collided in the far north and pushed up a range of mountains that would have been tricky to pass over if they hadn't been buried under two miles of ice. During the last day or so the continent had broadened beneath us, but we had stayed to the right or (now that we were southbound) western side of it. Not all the way to the edge, for the western coast was a steep subduction-zone mountain range. There was very little level ground between it and the frozen sea, and most of that was covered in treacherous crevasse-riddled glaciers flowing down from the mountains. So instead the sledge train stayed some miles inland of the coastal range, tracking across a plateau with stable ice. That's where the sledge port stood. Roads ran south from there across ice, tundra, and taiga to connect up with the transportation network that ramified all the way to the Sea of Seas. But the first outpost going that way was hundreds of miles distant. Smugglers such as the man driving my sledge could not prosper carrying their passengers such a long way. Instead they veered to the right, or west, bypassing the sledge port and taking one of three passes that slashed through the coastal range to connect with ports on the shore of the ocean. These were reachable from the south via icebreakers.

Cord, Sammann, and the Crades would simply get into the fetches and drive south from the sledge port. If the weather had been better and the short-range smugglers had been operating today, I could have paid one of them to whisk me around the sledge port and drop me off on the road a few miles south where I could simply have climbed aboard Yul's fetch. Instead, my four companions would drive south without me for a couple of days into a more temperate zone, then swing west and cross the mountains to a harbor called Mahsht—the home port of the icebreaker fleet. In the meantime I would buy passage on an icebreaker or one of the convoy ships that followed in its wake. This would bring me down to Mahsht. Once we'd rendezvoused there, it would be only a few days' drive to the Sea of Seas. So what I was doing now was Plan B—Plan A being the short-range whisk-around—and frankly we hadn't discussed it in very much detail because we hadn't expected it to come out this way. I had a nagging feeling that I'd made the decision hastily and probably forgotten some important details, but during the first couple of hours on this little sledge train I'd had plenty of time to think it through and satisfy myself that it would turn out fine.

Anyway, when I sensed the sledge changing its attitude beneath me I took it as a sign that we were beginning the ascent to one of the three passes that connected the inland plateau to the coast. According to Sammann, one of these was considerably better than the other two, but was closed by avalanches from time to time. The sledge drivers never knew, from one day to the next, which one they would end up taking. They made up their minds on the spur of the moment based on what they heard from other smugglers on the wireless. Since our driver was in a separate vehicle, sealed up in a heated cab, there was no way for me to overhear his wireless traffic and get any sense of what was going on.

A few hours later, however, the sledge's velocity dwindled and it shambled to a halt. We passengers spent a minute or so learning how to move again. I checked my watch and was astonished to learn that we had been underway for sixteen hours. I must have slept eight or ten of them—no wonder I was stiff. Brajj hurled a tent-flap aside to flood our sledge with grey light, bright but directionless. The storm had broken, the air was free of snow, but clouds still screened the sky. We had paused on the flank of a mountain, but the surface beneath us was reasonably level—some sort of sledge track, I guessed, that traversed the slope through whatever pass our driver had decided to take.

Brajj showed no interest in getting out. I got to my feet and made as if I were going to climb over his outstretched legs, but he held up a hand to stay me. A moment later we heard a series of thuds from the sledge tractor followed by a peeling and cracking noise as its door was pushed open through a coating of ice. Feet descended steel stairs and crunched on snow. Brajj lowered his hand and drew in his legs: I was free to go. Only then did I remember Sammann's warning not to let my feet touch the surface, lest I be abandoned. Brajj, who seemed to have done this before, knew it wasn't prudent to venture out until the driver had exited the tractor.

We'd invested in snow goggles at Eighty-three. I pulled them down over my eyes and climbed off the sledge to find an unfamiliar man standing on the snow up next to the tractor, urinating on the uphill slope. I reasoned that there must be a bunk in the tractor and that two drivers must spell each other. Sure enough, the first driver now stuck his sleepy-looking face out the door, pulled on his goggles, and climbed out to join the other. They kept the door open, apparently so that they could listen to wireless traffic. This came through in rare bursts, weirdly modulated. I could understand enough to gather that it was sledge operators exchanging information about conditions in the passes, and who was where. But very little seemed to be getting through. When a transmission did erupt from the speaker, the two drivers stopped talking, turned toward the open door, and strained to follow it.

Laro and Dag climbed out and went to the other side—the downhill side—of the sledge. I heard exclamations from both of them. They began talking excitedly. The drivers looked annoyed since this made it difficult to follow the bursts of distorted speech on the wireless.

I went around to the other side. From here we had a fine view down a snow-covered slope, interrupted from place to place by spires of black stone, to a U-shaped valley. We were on its north side. To our right, it broadened and flattened as it debouched into the coastal strip. To our left it grew steeper as it ascended into white mountains. So we had made it over the summit of the coastal range and were descending toward one of the icebound ports.

But that wasn't what had drawn exclamations from Laro and

Dag. They were looking at a black snake, ten miles long, wreathed in steam, slithering up the valley toward the mountains: a convoy of heavy vehicles, jammed nose to tail. All the same color.

"Military," announced Brajj, climbing out of the sledge. He shook his head in amazement. "You'd think a war was starting."

"An exercise?" suggested Laro.

"Big one," said Brajj in a skeptical tone. "Wrong equipment." He spoke with such a combination of authority and derision that I guessed he must be retired military—or a deserter. He shook his head. "There's a mountain division on point," he said, and pointed to the head of the column, which, I now noticed, consisted of several score white vehicles running on treads. "After that it's all flatlanders." He chopped air, aiming for the first of the dark drummons, then swept his hand down-valley, encompassing the remainder of the column, trailing toward the frozen sea, which could be seen from here as a white, jumbled plateau crazed with blue fractures. A smear of yellow and brown marked the port we were trying to reach. A lane of black water had been gouged by an icebreaker but was already fading as the ice crowded in behind it.

I was not a praxic and not an Ita but I'd seen enough speelies as a kid, and heard enough from Sammann, to have a general idea of how the wireless worked. There was only so much bandwidth to go around. In most circumstances it was plentiful. This was true even in big cities. But military used lots of it, and sometimes jammed what it didn't use. The sledge operators up here in these mountains were accustomed to having a nearly infinite amount of bandwidth at their disposal, and had grown dependent on it—they were always swapping reports on the weather and on trail conditions. But at some point during today's journey our drivers must have noticed something new to them: transmissions got through rarely, and were of poor quality. Perhaps they had thought their equipment was malfunctioning until they had crested the pass and discovered this: hundreds, maybe thousands of military vehicles, commandeering every scrap of bandwidth.

Everything about this was so remarkable that we might have stood there for hours looking at it if Brajj hadn't turned to pay attention to our drivers. They were clambering over the tractor, knocking ice from various pieces of equipment, inspecting the treads, rattling the linkages between the tractor and our sledge, checking fluid levels in the engine. Brajj was a dour and calm man but he was extremely attentive, even skittish, to be standing on the snow at a time when both of the drivers had mounted the tractor. After a minute he simply became too uncomfortable and climbed back aboard. I was happy to follow his example. Only a few moments after I'd settled back into my place, we heard the door of the tractor thudding shut. We called out to Laro and Dag who were several paces behind the sledge, frozen in amazement at the sight of the convoy. We managed to get Dag's attention. He turned to look at us but still didn't seem to grasp what was happening until the engine of the tractor roared up, and a linkage clanked as it was put into gear. He smacked Laro on the shoulder, then took a couple of paces toward us, grabbing Laro by the collar as he went by and jerking him along in his wake. Brajj shifted closer to the back and thrust out an arm in case he had to pull them aboard. I got to my feet and moved closer to help. The tractor's engine roared louder and we heard the distinctive clanking of its treads beginning to move. Laro and Dag reached us at about the same time; Brajj and I each grabbed one of their hands and hauled them aboard. Their momentum carried them forward into the front of the sledge. The tread clanks had already built to a steady rhythm.

We weren't moving.

Brajj and I looked out at the snow. Then we looked at each other.

Both of us jumped out and ran around to the sides. The tractor was fifty feet away from us and picking up speed. The hitch that had linked it to our sledge was dragging on the snow behind it.

Brajj and I started running after it. The tracks supported our weight most of the time but every few steps we'd break through and sink to mid-thigh. In any event, I ran faster. I covered maybe a hundred feet before the side hatch swung open and the second driver emerged. He clambered out on to a sort of running board above the right tread, and let me see a long projectile weapon slung on his back.

"What are you doing!?" I shouted.

He reached into the cab, hauled out something bulky, and let it drop into the snow: a carton of energy bars. "We're going to have to take a different pass now," he called back. "It's farther. Steeper. We don't have enough fuel."

"So you're abandoning us!?"

He shook his head and dropped out another object: a can of suitsack fuel. "Going to see if we can beg some fuel from the military," he shouted—getting farther away—"down there. Then we'll come back up here and fetch you." Then he ducked back into the cab and closed the door behind himself.

The logic was clear enough: they had been surprised by the convoy. They couldn't get to safety without more fuel. If they took us with them on their begging expedition, it'd be obvious that they were smugglers and they would get in trouble. So they had to park us for a while. They knew we'd object. So they'd left us no choice.

Brajj had caught up with me. He had produced, from somewhere, a small weapon. But as he and I both understood, there was no point in taking potshots at the back side of the tractor. Only it, and the two men in it, could get us out of here.

When Brajj and I got back to the sledge dragging the fuel and the energy bars, we found Laro and Dag kneeling, face to face, holding each other's hands and mumbling so rapidly that I couldn't make out a single word. I had never seen any behavior quite like it and had to watch them for a few moments before I collected that they were praying. Then I felt embarrassed. I stepped back to get out of Brajj's way in case he wanted to join them, but the look on his face as he regarded the Deolaters was contemptuous. He caught my eye and jerked his head back toward the flaps. I joined him outside. Both of us were hooded, goggled, and swathed against the cold. Frost grew with visible speed on our face-masks as we talked.

Brajj had been checking his watch every few minutes since we had been abandoned. "It's been a quarter of an hour," he said. "If those guys haven't come back for us in two hours, we have to save ourselves."

"You really think they'd leave us here to die?"

Brajj chose not to answer that question but he did offer: "They might get into a situation where they have no choice. Maybe they can't get fuel. Maybe their tractor breaks down. Or the military commandeers it. Point being, we have to have our own plan."

"I have a pair of snowshoes—"

"I know. We have to make three more. Load up your water pouch."

The suitsacks had pouches on the front that could be stuffed with snow. Over time it would melt and become drinking water. That consumed energy, but it was sustainable as long as the body had food or the suitsack had fuel. We had both—for the time being. We packed ours as full of snow as we could. We replenished our fuel bladders from the cache that the drivers had left for us. Brajj interrupted the others' prayers and insisted they also take on water and fuel. Then he had us each eat a couple of energy bars. Only then did we get working.

The tent was held up by flexible metal poles. We collapsed it and drew them out. This had the side effect of getting Laro and Dag's attention. Our shelter was gone; they had no choice but to join in our plan. Brajj had a pocket tool with a little saw blade; he went to work cutting the tent poles into shorter segments. Once the others saw that there was work to be done, they joined in cheerfully. Dag, who was the sturdier of the two, took over the sawing of the tent poles. Brajj had Laro get to work scavenging every inch of rope and twine at our disposal. Then—perhaps leading by example—he undid the yellow rope that he had used to gird his suitcase. This turned out to be some thirty feet long. He undid the latches and dumped out the contents: hundreds of tiny vials, all packed in loose nodules of foam. I hadn't seen such things before but I guessed that these were pharmaceuticals. "Child support," Brajj explained, reading the look on my face.

The panels of the suitcase were a tough leathery material that we cut into slabs to make the platforms of the snowshoes. We bent the tent poles to make crude quadrangular frames and lashed the suitcase-panels to them using twine from Laro's and Dag's improvised baggage. This took a while because we had to do it with bare fingers, which went numb in a few seconds. The contents of Laro's and Dag's baggage were mostly old clothes, which they were willing to abandon, and keepsakes of their families, which they weren't. I pulled one of the benches off the sledge, flipped it upside down, and kicked its flimsy legs off. It would serve as a toboggan. We loaded it with the supplies and wrapped them up in what remained of the tent. My pack had already been stripped of its metal frame and of anything that would serve as rope. I added my energy bars and my stove to the supplies, threw away my extra clothes, and put my bolt, my chord, and my sphere (pilled down as small as it would go) into the cargo pockets on the body of my suitsack. I considered adding my chord to our stock of rope, but we seemed to have plenty—Laro had found a fifty-foot coil stored under one of the sledge's benches and we'd been able to make up another fifty by splicing together odds and ends from the tent's rigging and so on. That plus Brajj's thirty feet of yellow stuff gave us enough that we were able to rope ourselves together at intervals of thirty or forty feet, which Brajj explained would be useful if one of us lost his footing on a steep slope or fell into a crevasse.

These preparations consumed almost four hours, so we set out late according to Brajj's timetable. The convoy down below seemed as though it had not moved an inch. Brajj estimated that it was two thousand feet below us. He said that if "everything goes to hell" we should just "pull the ripcord" and let ourselves slide down the ice to the valley floor where we could throw ourselves on the mercy of the military. They might arrest us but they probably wouldn't let us die. It was a last resort, however, because if we tried it we stood a good chance of falling into a crevasse before we reached the bottom.

Brajj took the lead. He was armed with a length of tent-pole that he would use to probe the snow ahead of him for crevasses. At his hip he had his "sticker," a long, heavy-bladed knife. He claimed that if one of us fell into a crevasse he would throw himself down and jam this into the ice, anchoring himself so as to arrest our fall. He had me go last and saw to it that I was armed with an L-shaped piece of metal scavenged from the frame of my pack, which I was to use in the same manner. He even had me practice throwing myself down face-first and jamming the short leg of the thing into the ice. Dag, then Laro, were roped up between us. The toboggan trailed behind me.

The first part of the trek was balky and frustrating as the snow-shoes or the bindings that held them to the others' feet seemed to give out every few steps. The whole expedition seemed to have failed before it had started. But then I noticed we'd been going for a whole hour without pause. I sipped from the tube that ran down to my water-pouch and munched slowly on an energy bar. I looked around me and actually enjoyed the view.

Allswell! The thought hit me like a snowball in the nose. I'd been out of the concent for a little more than two weeks, eating extramuros food the whole time. Lio and Arsibalt and the others had probably made it to Tredegarh in less than a week—too brief a time for them to be affected. But I had been out long enough that the ubiquitous chemical must have taken up residence in my brain—subtly altering the way I thought about everything.

What would my fraas and suurs have said about the decisions I had been making recently? Nothing too polite. Just look at where those decisions had gotten me! And yet, even in the midst of this terrible situation, I'd been strolling around with nothing on my mind except for how pretty the view was!

I tried to force myself into a sterner frame of mind—tried to envision some bad outcomes so that I could lay plans. Brajj's "sticker" might serve as an anchor in a crisis—but he might just as well use it to cut himself free if one of us fell in. What should I do in that event?

But it was no use. Brajj had made himself the leader, and had made reasonable decisions to this point. There was no limit to the amount of time and energy I could put into spinning such alarming fantasies in my head. Better to attend to the here and now.

Or was that the Allswell talking?

For the first few hours we followed the tamped-down tracks left by the tractor, but then they veered downhill, following a cirque—a crescent-shaped vale cut by a tributary glacier—down toward the valley floor. This would take us straight to the military convoy, and so here we broke away from the trail and ventured across trackless snow for the first time. The first bit was slow going as we had to work our way up out of the cirque. By the time the slope began to level, I was ready to "pull the ripcord" in Brajj's phrase. If I threw myself on the mercy of some military drummon operator, what was the worst that could happen? I hadn't broken any laws. It was only my three companions who had to go to such ridiculous lengths to avoid the authorities' notice. But for better or worse I was roped up to them and couldn't cut myself free without endangering their lives and mine; I had to wait for *them* to pull the ripcord.

Then we crested a subsidiary ridge and came in view of the coastline. I was startled at how close it was. We had to shed some altitude but the horizontal distance didn't look that great. We could easily pick out individual buildings in the port and count the military transport ships moored at its piers. Military aerocraft were lined up at the edge of a dirty landing-strip wedged in between the coast and the foot of the mountains. We watched one take off and bank to the south.

One or two civilian ships were also in the harbor, and this gave us all the idea that if we could only get down there in one piece—which looked like less than a day's travel—we could buy passage on one of them and get out of here behind the next icebreaker. So we took a rest up there in preparation for what we all knew would be a long and arduous final push. I forced myself to eat two more energy bars. The things were starting to make me sick but perhaps that was just me worrying about the Allswell. I washed them down with water and refilled my snow pouches and my fuel bladder. Our supplies were holding up well. The sledge drivers had given us plenty—perhaps thinking that they might not be returning for a while. I was glad we had taken action—moved out instead of huddling in that tent not knowing if we'd live or die.

After an hour's rest we repacked the toboggan and got underway again. We descended into a round-bottomed cleft: another cirque that cut across our path and seemed to curve toward the port. Brajj decided to follow this one down. The risk was that it would become too steep for us to negotiate and that we'd have to backtrack. On a few occasions during the next couple of hours I became very worried about this, but then we would come around a bend, or crest a little rise, and get a view of the next mile or so and see that there was nothing we couldn't handle. On steeper bits the toboggan would try to run ahead of me, and then I would have my hands full for a while—the only remedy was to slew it round ahead of me and let it pull me downhill as I leaned back against its weight. At such times the others, who didn't have to contend with such a burden, would outdistance me. The rope joining me to Laro would draw taut and remind me of his impatience. I felt like reeling him in and smacking him. But Brajj kept our pace from running out of control. Even in stretches that looked smooth and safe he plodded along at the same rate, pausing every couple of steps to probe the snow ahead of him with his tent pole.

I had long since learned to distinguish Brajj's snowshoe prints from those of the others, and from time to time I would notice, to my indescribable annoyance, that they had diverged: Brajj had zigged for whatever reason, and Dag had zagged, and Laro followed in his kinsman's steps, obligating me to do the same, and hence pass over ground that Brajj had not probed.

We had probably shed three-quarters of the altitude needed to reach the port. It would be relatively easy going from here. Laro and Dag were laborers—they had plenty of energy left and yearned to push on past the plodding Brajj to a place where they could get a hot meal and peel off the accursed suitsacks.

It was on one of those steep bits where the toboggan had swung around in front of me and I was straining back against two ropes at once that I noticed myself being pulled out of balance. The tension on the rope that connected me to Laro was rapidly increasing. I planted my left snowshoe and pulled back, but the last hours' descent had turned my leg muscles into quivering flab. I collapsed to my knee, the rope at my waist pulling me forward. Just before I planted my face in the snow I collected a glimpse of Brajj standing up facing me, a hundred feet away, sticker in hand. Laro was sliding and tumbling down the slope, pulling me with him. Dag—who was roped between Brajj and Laro—was nowhere to be seen.

That remembered image was all I had to go on during the next little while, because I was face-down, being pulled along by Laro and by the toboggan. And—I realized—by Dag. He must have fallen into a crevasse! Why hadn't Brajj stopped his fall? The rope—the frayed yellow thirty-foot poly rope that had connected Brajj to Dag—must have snapped. Either that or Brajj had cut it with a swipe of his sticker. I was the only person who could stop this, and save Laro, Dag, and myself: I had to plunge that L-shaped piece of metal into the ice. I should have had it out and ready to use—should have been watching ahead for signs of trouble. But in order to free both hands to wrangle the toboggan I'd stuck it in one of the equipment loops on the outside of my suitsack. Was it still there? I kicked wildly with one leg and managed to roll over on my back. My head was plowing up a bow-wave of snow that buried my face. I snorted it out of my nose and stifled the urge to inhale. I groped around until I felt something hard, and pulled it out—or so I guessed. Through those mittens it was hard to tell what was going on. I got the pick pointed away from my body, flailed the legs again, and managed to roll over on my stomach. My head came up out of the snow and I heard Laro screaming something—he must have gone over the brink of the crevasse. I put all of my weight on top of that L-shaped hunk of metal and drove it down. It caught—sort of—and became a pivot; my body spun around it as the rope at my waist, now drawn by the combined weights of Laro and Dag, torqued me downhill. The pick tugged at my hands, but not all that hard. It didn't seem to be holding.

Or rather it held, but it held in a raft of snow that had broken loose and was now sliding down the hill beneath me.

This was just plain bad luck; if we'd been traversing packed snow, the pick would have had something firm in which to get purchase, but yesterday's storm had left the packed ice covered with powdery stuff that slid freely on top of it.

Another vicious jerk at my waist told me that the toboggan had just hurtled over the edge. I raised my face up out of this mini-avalanche and got the weird idea that I wasn't actually moving—because, of course, the snow around me was moving at the same speed as I. Then there was nothing under my toes. Nothing under my ankles. Nothing under my knees. My hips. The rope jerked me straight down with the weight of three men. I guess I did a sort of back-flip into the crevasse. But I only got to experience the terror of free fall for a fraction of a second before something terrible happened to my back and I stopped. The rope's force was pulling me down against something immobile and hard. Loose snow continued to pummel me for a while. I remembered a woolly story that Yul had told me about getting caught in an avalanche, the importance of swimming, of preserving air space in front of one's face. I couldn't swim, but I did get one arm up and crooked an elbow over my mouth and nose. The weight of snow on my body built steadily, the tension on the rope slackened. Most of the avalanche seemed to be parting around me—falling away to either side—as I remained stuck.

For some reason I heard Jesry's voice in my head saying, "Oh, so you're only being buried alive *a little bit*." What a jerk!

Then it stopped. I could hear my own heart beating, and nothing else.

I pushed outwards with my elbow. The snow moved a little and gave me a void in front of my face—air for a moment. More importantly it kept me from panicking, and let me open my eyes. There was dim blue-grey light. I could hear Arsibalt saying "Just enough to read by!" and Lio answering "If only you'd thought to bring a book."

For whatever reason, I was not falling any deeper into the crevasse. Yet. And I didn't think I'd fallen too far into it. Something had stopped my fall. I guessed that the toboggan had gotten lodged sideways between the crevasse walls and I'd fallen on it. Hard. I took a moment to wiggle my toes and my ankles, just to verify that I hadn't broken my spine. It would have been nice to explore with my hands but one was pinned at my side and the other—the one I'd crooked over my face—was hemmed in by snow. I was, however, able to move that one downwards over my body. I found the zipper pull for my front pocket and inched it open. Then I moved that hand up to my face and pulled my mitten off with my teeth. I reached my bare hand down into the open pocket and fished out my sphere.

Spheres don't have controls as such. They recognize gestures. You talk to them with your hands. My hand was a little stiff but I was able to make the unscrewing gesture that caused the sphere to get bigger. After a while this became a little scary because the sphere was stealing my air supply, claiming the void in front of my face and pressing on my chest. But I had the idea that the snow over me wasn't that deep. So I kept telling it to expand. And just when I thought my own sphere was going to squeeze the life out of me, I heard rushing noises—a small avalanche. I reversed the gesture. The sphere got small, the weight came off, and I found myself gazing up through clear air between walls of blue ice. The sky was visible. And so was Brajj, standing at the edge of the crevasse looking down at me. I'd fallen about twenty feet.

"You're avout," was the first thing he said to me.

"Yes."

"Got anything else in your bag of tricks? Because I have no rope. It all went down with those two Gheeths." He patted the length of yellow rope tied around his waist. Only a foot or so dangled below the knot. It had been severed at exactly the point where the blade of his sticker would have intercepted it in a moment of panic—or of calculation.

"I thought maybe you cut it," I said. I don't know why. I guess it was that weird avout compulsion to state facts.

"Maybe I did."

We looked at each other for a while. It occurred to me that Brajj was an exceptionally rational man—more so than some avout.

He was another like the Crades or Cord or Artisan Quin who was smart enough to be an avout but who for whatever reason had ended up extramuros. In his case it seemed that being alone out here with no bond to anyone else like him had made him utterly calculating and ruthless.

"Let's say you don't care whether I live or die," I said. "Let's say that every decision you've made has been based on self-interest. You kept us alive, brought us with you, and roped yourself to us because you knew that if you fell in we'd try to help you. But the minute one of us fell in you cut the rope to save yourself. You looked down into this crack out of simple curiosity. Nothing more. Then you saw my sphere. You know I'm avout. What's your decision?"

Brajj had found all of this faintly amusing. He rarely heard intelligent people state things clearly and he sort of enjoyed its novelty. He pondered my question for a minute or so, turning away at one point to look down the slope. Then he turned back to scrutinize me. "Move your legs," he said.

I did. "Arms." I did.

"Those Gheeths were more trouble than they were worth," he said.

"Is that an ethnic slur for what Laro and Dag are?"

"Ethnic slur? Yeah, it's an *ethnic slur*," he said in a mocking tone. "Gheeths are great for digging ditches and pulling weeds. Worse than useless up here. But *you* might keep me alive. How are you going to get out of there?"

For 3700 years, we had lived under a ban that prevented us from owning anything other than the bolt, the chord, and the sphere. Shelves of books had been written about the ingenious uses to which these objects had been put by avout who'd found themselves in trying circumstances. Many of the tricks had names: Saunt Ablavan's Ratchet. Ramgad's Contraption. The Lazy Fraa. I was no expert, but when we'd been younger, Jesry and I had leafed through some such books and practiced a few of those tricks, just for sport.

Chords and bolts were made of the same stuff: a fiber that could coil into a tight helix, becoming short and bulky and springy, or relax into a straight filament, becoming long, lean, and inelastic. In the winter we told the fibers in our bolts to coil up. They got much shorter but the bolt became thick and warm because of the pockets of air involved with those coils. In summer we straightened them and the bolts became long and sheer. Likewise the chord could be fat and yarn-like or long and thready.

I made my sphere about as big as my head, wrapped my bolt around it, and tied it together with my chord. Then I made the sphere get bigger and let the bolt expand with it. The sphere wedged itself between the walls. It could go up but it wouldn't go down, because the crevasse was wider at the top and narrower below. I pushed it up a short distance and it found a new equilibrium, a little higher. Then I expanded and pushed, expanded and pushed, a few inches at a time. The walls were surprisingly irregular, so all of this was more complicated than I'm making it sound. But once I got the hang of it, it went fast.

"Got it!" Brajj called. The sphere moved away from me, scraping against the ice walls. A panic came over me until I found my chord with a flailing arm. Then I let it slide through my hand until Brajj had pulled the sphere all the way out of the crevasse. Brajj and I were now linked by the chord. He jammed his sticker into the ice up there and wrapped my chord around its handle—or so he claimed.

I didn't want to lose our connection to the toboggan and to Laro and Dag, but I had to cut myself free of it to have any hope of bettering things. The end of my chord I joined to the loop of rope around my waist. Then I cut my way free from that loop. So I was free of the hundreds of pounds of stuff anchoring me to the bottom. The chord was now our only link to the toboggan and to Laro and Dag. I gave instructions to Brajj on how to make the sphere smaller. He threw it down to me. I wedged it between the crevasse walls again. This time—now that I had freedom to move—I was able to get astride it. For the first time since the accident I took my weight off whatever hard thing had stopped my fall and saved my life. Looking down at it, I verified that it was indeed the toboggan, wedged at an angle between the crevasse walls like a stick thrust between a monster's jaws. When I took my weight off it, it shifted, and a moment later it fell, tumbling another ten feet before getting wedged again. Braj had anchored his loop of the chord to his sticker, jammed in the ice, so we didn't lose it. I was able to extricate myself from the crevasse by expanding the sphere, which pushed me up as it inflated, while keeping the chord looped around one hand in case I fell off. Once I was out, we doubled the anchor by driving in my makeshift ice-axe, and secured the chord to that as well.

For a little while we were able to haul the rope up by causing the chord to get shorter (a simple implementation of Saunt Abla-van's Ratchet) but after a few minutes it ran out of stored energy. If I left it out in the sun for a while it would recharge, but we didn't have time. And it wasn't able to store a lot of energy anyway. So, after that, Brajj and I hauled using muscle power. Once we had got-ten the toboggan up on the surface, this became markedly easier. A few moments later, Laro's corpse could be seen deep down in the valley of blue light, emerging from the snow that had piled up in the bottom. The rope that trailed below him was no more than ten feet long, and ended in a botched knot. It had held well enough to drag down Laro, me, and the toboggan, but must have given way under the jerk when the toboggan and I came to rest. After that Dag must have free-fallen to the very bottom of the crevasse and been buried under falling snow. I hoped his death had been quicker than the long agonizing slide and tumble that had preceded it.

Brajj kept throwing me dirty looks as if to say *why are we doing this?* but I ignored him and kept pulling on the rope until we had brought Laro's body up to the brink of the crevasse.

As we were rolling him up onto the surface at last, he twitched, gasped, and called out the name of his deity.

Now I understood Brajj. He was smarter, more rational than I at the moment. He'd probably been wondering *what'll we do if he turns out to be alive?*

I just lay there on the snow for a few minutes, half dead. All the injuries I'd suffered in the fall were now making themselves obvious.

There was nothing to do but go on. Brajj was furious to have been burdened with an injured man, and kept stamping around in circles and gazing hungrily down the slope, wondering whether he should chance it alone. After a few minutes he decided to stay with us—for now.

Laro had a broken thigh, and his skull had taken a beating during the fall, creating some bloody lacerations. Between that and being buried in snow for a while, he was groggy.

One of Laro's snowshoes still dangled from his foot. I took it apart and used its pieces to splint his leg. Then I made my sphere big and flat on the snow.

The sphere is a porous membrane. Each pore is a little pump that can move air in or out. Like a self-inflating balloon. The spring constant—the stretchiness—of the membrane is controllable. If you turn the stretchiness way down (that is, make it stiff) and pump in lots of air, it becomes a hard little pill. What I did now was the opposite. I made it very stretchy and removed most of the air. I spread my bolt flat on the snow and dragged the flaccid sphere onto it. Then I got Brajj to help me roll Laro into the middle. He screamed and cried out to his mother and his deity as we were doing this. I took that as a good sign because he was seeming more alert. I rolled him in the sphere and then wrapped the bolt loosely around that, leaving his head exposed. The whole bundle I tied with my chord. Finally I inflated the sphere a little bit while telling the bolt not to stretch. The sphere expanded to form an air bed that coccooned Laro's whole body. The bundle was between two and three feet in diameter, and slid over the snow reasonably well, since I'd made the bolt sheer and smooth. I could never have pulled it up a slope, but going downhill ought to work.

I towed Laro and Brajj towed the toboggan. We tied ourselves together with the length of good rope that had formerly connected me to Laro, and set out in the same style as before, with Brajj going first and using his tent pole to probe for crevasses.

I tried not to think about the possibility that Dag might still be alive in the bottom of the crevasse.

Then I tried not to wonder how many other migrants' corpses

would be found strewn all over this territory if all the ice and snow ever melted.

Then I tried not to wonder if Orolo's might be among them.

For now I'd just have to settle for making sure *I* wasn't among them. I paid close attention to Brajj's footprints. If Brajj went into another crevasse, I might try to save him—which was why he'd kept me alive. But if I went in, Laro and I were both dead. So I stepped where he stepped.

After a few hours I lost track of what was happening. Everything I had was channeled into keeping my feet moving. There's not much point in trying to offer a description of the bleakness, the moral and physical misery. In those rare moments when I was lucid enough to think, I reminded myself that avout had been through far worse ordeals in the Third Sack and at other such times.

Since I was so groggy, I have no way of guessing when Brajj parted company with us. Laro's voice brought me to awareness. He was screaming and fighting with the sphere, trying to get out. I told Brajj we had to stop. Hearing no answer, I looked around and discovered that he was gone. The rope that had connected us had fallen victim to his sticker. And no wonder: we were on the floor of a valley that led straight to the port, a couple of miles away, and the ground was black and burnished smooth by all of the tires and treads that had passed over it. We were on the path of the military convoy. No worries about crevasses here. So Brajj had taken off. I never saw him again.

Laro was frantic to get out. Perhaps he'd been that way for a long time. I was worried he'd hurt himself flailing around. I inflated the sphere until he couldn't move at all, and then I knelt beside him and looked into his eyes and tried to talk some sense into him. This was monumentally difficult. I'd known some, such as Tulia, who could do it effortlessly—or at least she made it look that way. Yul simply would have bellowed into his face, used the force of his personality. But it was not a thing that came easily to me.

He wanted to know where Dag was. I told him Dag was dead, which did nothing to calm him down—but I couldn't lie to him and I was too exhausted to devise a better plan.

The sound of engines cut through the still, frigid air. It came from up-valley. A small convoy of military fetches was headed our way—detached from the huge procession to go back and run some errand at the port.

By the time they approached within hailing distance, Laro had got a grip on himself, if hopeless, uncontrollable sobbing could be so described. I relaxed the sphere, undid the chord, and dragged him free of the bundle, then got everything stowed back in my pockets.

Those guys in the military trucks were real pros. They came right over and picked us up. They took us into town. They didn't ask questions, at least none that I remember. Though I was not exactly in a mirthful frame of mind, I marked this down as being funny. With my simpleminded view of the Sæcular world, I'd assumed that the soldiers, simply because they looked sort of like cops with their uniforms and weapons, would act like cops, and arrest us. But it turned out that they couldn't have cared less about law enforcement, which made perfect sense once I thought about it for ten seconds. They took Laro to a charity clinic run by the local Kelx—a religion that was strong in these parts. Then they dropped me off at the edge of the water. I bought some decent food at a tavern and slept face-down on the table until I was ejected. Standing out there on the street I felt stretched thin, diluted, as if that pale arctic sunlight could shine right through me and give my heart a sunburn. But I could still walk and I had money—the sledge driver had never collected the second half of his fare. I bought passage to Mahsht on the next outbound transport, boarded it as soon as they'd let me, climbed into a bunk, and slept one more time in that horrible suitsack.

⦾⦾⦾⦾⦾⦾⦾⦾⦾⦾⦾⦾⦾⦾⦾⦾⦾⦾⦾⦾⦾⦾⦾⦾⦾⦾⦾

Kelx: (1) A religious faith created during the Sixteenth or Seventeenth Century A.R. The name is a contraction of the Orth *Ganakelux* meaning "Triangle Place," so called because of the symbolic importance of triangles in the faith's iconography. (2) An ark of the Kelx faith.

Kedev: A devotee of the Kelx or Triangle faith.

—THE DICTIONARY, *4th edition, A.R. 3000*

About halfway into the four-day cruise I had recovered to the point where I was capable of introspection. I spent a lot of time sitting very still in the ship's mess, eating. I had to sit still because I'd messed up my ribs and back in the fall, and it hurt to move—even to breathe. The food was good compared to energy bars. Perhaps I ate so much of it in hopes that it would bring up the level of Allswell in my blood and chase the dark thoughts from my head.

Getting me killed couldn't have been part of Fraa Jad's plan. Where then had it gone wrong? My foolish choices? The migrant traffic over the pole had been going on at least long enough for Jad to have heard about it—he'd known that a Feral like Orolo would take that route to Ecba. So it was an ancient and settled practice. We'd all underestimated its dangers precisely because it was so ancient. We'd assumed that nothing could go on for so long unless it was safe—the way avout would run things if we were in charge.

But we weren't in charge and it wasn't run that way.

Or maybe it was a safe and settled thing most of the time but the military convoy had thrown it into chaos.

Or maybe we'd just been unlucky.

"You look like you've been through a harrowing experience."

I snapped out of it, and looked up by rotating my eyeballs—not my head, as I had a terrible crick in the neck. A man was standing there looking at me. Probably in his third decade. I'd noticed him eyeing me the day before. Now he'd come over and said this to me as a way of striking up a conversation.

I'm sorry to say I broke out laughing. It took me a minute to get it under control.

Harrowing was a thing that we did—literally—to our tangles during the spring. We went through the beds on hands and knees identifying the weeds and rooting them out with hand-hoes, throwing the weeds on a pile to be burned, leaving nothing except churned-up soil, pulverizing the clods in our hands to leave a loose bed for expansion of the tangle plants' root systems. So when this stranger suggested I'd been through a harrowing experience, my mind went straight to that and I thought he was trying to say that I looked as if I'd been crawling through dirt. Which I did. Or perhaps that I looked like a heap of dead weeds. Which I also did. Finally I remembered that I was extramuros, where the old literal meaning of *harrowing* had been forgotten thousands of years ago, and it had become a cliché, uprooted from any concrete meaning.

None of this could be explained to the stranger, so all I could do was sit there and helplessly giggle—which made my ribs hurt—and hope he wouldn't take umbrage and slug me. But he was patient. He even looked a little pained to behold someone in such a pathetic state. Which was fortunate since he was a big man and could have slugged me hard.

This gave me an idea that stopped the giggle. "Hey," I said, "do you have any spare clothes? I'd buy them from you."

"You do need clean clothes," the stranger said. This brought me back to giggling. From time to time I'd get a whiff of myself. I knew it was bad. But I couldn't very well don my bolt.

"I have more clothes than I need and will gladly part with them," he said.

He had an odd way of talking. Quasi-literate Sæculars went to stores and bought prefabricated letters, machine-printed on heavy stock with nice pictures, and sent them to each other as emotional gestures. They were written in a stilted language that no one ever spoke aloud—except for this guy who was standing in front of me letting fly with words like *harrowing*.

He went on, "I don't ask for anything in return. But I do hope you'll join me for services—after you've changed."

So that was it. This guy wanted to convert me to his ark. He'd been watching me and had picked me out as a wretch—a soul ripe for saving.

I had nothing better to do, and it had become all too obvious that I needed to grow a little wiser in the ways of the Sæcular world. So I threw away my stinking clothes and my suitsack, bathed as best as I could while standing in front of a sink, and put on this guy's funny-smelling clothes. Then I went to a hot crowded cabin where his ark was holding its services. There were a dozen and a half devotees and one magister—a leathery man named Sark who apparently spent his life banging around on ships like this, ministering to sailors and fishermen.

This was a Kelx—a Triangle ark. Its adherents were called Kedevs. It was a completely different faith from that of Ganelial Crade. It had been invented about two thousand years ago by some ingenious prophet who must have been unusually self-effacing, since little was known about him and he wasn't worshipped as such. Like most faiths it was as fissured and fractured as the glaciers I'd been walking over lately. But all of its sects and schisms agreed that there was another world outside of and greater—in a sense, more real—than the one we lived in. That in this world there was a robber who had waylaid a family. He'd slain the father outright, raped and killed the mother, and taken their daughter with him as a hostage. Not long after, while trying to evade capture, he'd strangled the innocent girl. But he'd been caught anyway and locked up in a dungeon for a long time ("half of his life") while waiting for his case to come before a Magistrate. At the trial he had admitted his guilt. The Magistrate had asked if there was any reason why he should not be put to death. The Condemned Man had responded that there was such a reason, one that had come to him during his years in the dungeon. As he had meditated over his hideous crimes, the one thing he'd never been able to chase from his mind was the murder of the girl—the Innocent— because in her there had been the potential to do so many things that could now never be realized. In any soul, the Condemned Man argued, was the ability to create a whole world, as big and variegated as the one that he and the Magistrate lived in. But if this was true of the Innocent, it was true of the Condemned Man as well, and so he should not—no one should ever—be put to death.

The Magistrate upon hearing this had voiced skepticism that the Condemned Man really had it in him to generate a whole world. Taking up the challenge, the Condemned Man had begun to tell the tale of a world he had thought up in his mind and to relate the stories of its gods, heroes, and kings. This had taken up the whole day, so the Magistrate had adjourned the court. But he had warned the Condemned Man that his fate was still in the balance because the world he had invented seemed to be just as full of wars, crimes, and cruelty as the one that they lived in. The Condemned Man's stay of execution was only as good as the world he had invented. If the various troubles in that world could not be brought to a satisfactory conclusion in tomorrow's session, he would be executed at sundown.

The next day the Condemned Man had attempted to satisfy the Magistrate, and made a little headway, but in so doing introduced new troubles and gave birth to new characters no less morally ambiguous than the first lot. The Magistrate could not find sufficient grounds to execute him and so had continued the case to the next day, and the next, and the next.

The world that I lived in with Jesry and Lio and Arsibalt, Orolo and Jad, Ala and Tulia and Cord and all the others, was the very world that was being created from day to day in the mind of the Condemned Man in that courtroom. Sooner or later it would all end in a final judgment by the Magistrate. If that—if our—world seemed, on balance, like a decent place to him, he would let the Condemned Man live and our world would go on existing in his mind. If the world, as a whole, only reflected the Condemned Man's depravity, the Magistrate would have him executed and our world would cease to exist. We could help keep the Condemned Man alive and thus preserve the existence of ourselves and our world by striving at all times to make it a better place.

That's why Alwash—the big stranger—had given me his clothes. He was trying to prevent the end of the world.

Kelx was a contraction of the Orth words meaning "Triangle Place." Triangles figured in the faith's iconography. In the story just told there were three key characters: the Condemned Man, the Magistrate, and the Innocent. The Condemned Man represented a creative but flawed principle. The Magistrate represented judgment and goodness. The Innocent was inspiration that had the power to redeem the Condemned Man. Taken individually these each lacked something but taken as a triad they had created us and our world. Debates as to the nature of this triad had triggered a hundred wars, but in any case they all believed in one interpretation or other of the basic story. At this point in history the Kelx was very much under the heel of other faiths and had become especially bitter and apocalyptic. The premise of the whole faith was that sooner or later the Magistrate would make up his mind, and so the magisters—as their clergy were called—could get their flocks emotionally whipped up, as needed, by claiming that the judgment was near at hand.

Today's sermon was one of those. Kelxes didn't have long complicated services like the Bazians. The service consisted of a harangue from Magister Sark, followed by interviews with the Kedevs, concluded by another harangue. He wanted to know what each man in the cabin (we were all men) had done lately to make the world a better place. We might all be flawed—as how could we not since we originated in the mind of a rapist and murderer—and yet because of the pure inspiration that had impregnated the Condemned Man's soul from the Innocent at the moment of her death, we had the power to make the world better in a way that would please the all-seeing and -knowing Magistrate.

Crazy as this all was I found it sort of compelling in my weakened state, and tried the experiment of playing along with it for a while. This might sound very unlike an avout, but we were used to being presented with outlandish cosmographical hypotheses, and in our theorics we did this sort of thing all the time: that is, assume for the sake of argument that a hypothesis was true, and see where it led.

I'd known the tale of the Condemned Man for almost as long as I'd been alive, but sitting in this cabin I learned two things about the faith—or at least this sect—that I hadn't known before. One, that the events of our world, which happened in parallel (each person doing something different at the same time), were teased apart and narrated serially by the Condemned Man to the Magistrate.

There was no way to tell the stories of billions concurrently, so he broke them down into smaller, more manageable narratives and told them consecutively. So, for example, my trip down the glacier with Brajj and Laro and Dag had been related to the Magistrate as one self-contained tale, after which the Condemned Man had doubled back in time to tell the story of what, say, Ala had done that day. Or, if Ala hadn't done anything unusual—if she hadn't been presented, say, with any great choices—the Condemned Man might have said nothing of her and she might thus have avoided the Magistrate's scrutiny for the time being.

The full attention of the Magistrate was focused on only one such story at a time. When your story was being told, you were under the pitiless inspection of the Magistrate, who saw everything you did and knew everything you thought—so at such times it was important to make the correct choices! If you attended Kelx services often enough, you'd develop a sixth sense for when your story was being told to the Magistrate and you'd get better at making the right choices.

Second, the Inspiration that had passed from the Innocent to the Condemned Man at the moment of her death was viral. It passed from him into each of us. Each of us had the same power to create whole worlds. The hope was that one day there would be a Chosen One who would create a world that was perfect. If that ever happened, not only he and his world but all of the other worlds and their creators, back to the Condemned Man, would be saved recursively.

When Sark turned his hot gaze upon me and asked me what I had done of late to save the world, I, in a spirit of trying to play along, began to tell an edited version of the story of the descent of the glacier. I left out any mention of bolt, chord, and sphere. And I intended to leave out the story of Dag's death—or his being left for dead. But as I went on I found myself unable to tell the story without including that part of it. It just fell out of me, like an intestine that keeps uncoiling from the belly of a wounded animal. The whole thing had gone out of control. I'd intended to play along as a sort of intellectual parlor game but my emotions had taken over and dictated what I would say. Something about the whole setup of this ark, I realized (too late) was designed to play on such emotions. I wasn't the first stranger to walk into one of these meetings and spill his guts. They expected it. They counted on it. It was why the Kelx had lasted two thousand years.

When I'd finished, I looked over at Alwash, expecting to see a triumphant look on his face. Yeah, he'd gotten me but good. But he didn't look that way at all. Just serious, and a little sad. Like he'd known what would happen. He'd done it before. He'd had it done to him.

The silence that followed was long, but did not feel awkward. Then Magister Sark told me that it wasn't clear I had done anything wrong at all given the circumstances. I understood this to mean that when the Magistrate had heard the story of Brajj, "Vit," Laro, and Dag from the Condemned Man, he had not construed it to mean that the latter should be executed. At worst it was neutral testimony. I felt hugely relieved at this, and in the next moment hated myself for being emotionally manipulated by a witch doctor.

If I were still feeling bad about it, Sark concluded, I should try to put on a better showing the next time the Condemned Man saw fit to relate some part of my affairs in that celestial court.

Some of the others had even worse stories to tell to the magister. I could not believe some of what I heard. I wasn't the only first-timer in this congregation; it had been clear from the smirks on others' faces that they too had been dragooned into coming here. I suspected that some were embellishing their stories just to see if they could freak out the magister.

Apparently the rule for these services was that after all present had stated what they had to state, the magister would wind things up with a rip-roarer.

"It has been our way since of old to say that the day of the Magistrate's final judgment is coming. It is forever *coming*. But *today* I tell you that it is *here*. Signs and portents have made it plain! The Magistrate, or his bailiff, *has been sighted* in the heavens above! He has turned his red eye upon the avout in their concents and rendered his judgment upon them. Now he turns his eye upon the rest of us! The so-called Warden of Heaven has gone before him to make his entreaties, and the Magistrate has seen him for what he is, and cast him out in wrath! What shall he make of *you* who are gathered together in this cabin? On his final day before that court, of whom shall the Condemned Man speak? Shall he tell of you, Vit, and of your doings? To prove that he, and all his creations, are worthy of life, shall he tell of you, Traid, or you, Theras, or you, Everell? Shall it be your doings on the final day that tip the scales of judgment one way or the other?"

It was a tough question—was meant to be. Magister Sark had no intention of answering it. Instead he looked long and deep into each man's eyes.

Except for mine. I was staring at a bulkhead. Trying to figure out what he'd meant. The Magistrate had been seen in the heavens? The Warden of Heaven had been cast out in wrath? Was I supposed to read those statements literally?

If something bad had happened to the Warden of Heaven, what did it mean for Jesry?

I was desperate to know. I didn't dare ask.

When it was over, I was too drained to move. As the cabin emptied out I sat slumped against a steel bulkhead, letting the ship's engines jiggle my brain around.

One of the other Kedevs had been talking to Alwash. When the cabin was nearly empty they approached me. I sat up and tried to muster strength to fight back another religious harangue.

This new guy's name was Malter. "I was wondering," Malter said, "are you one of the avout?"

I did not move or speak. I was trying to remember what the Kelx thought of us.

"The reason I ask," Malter went on, "is that there were rumors going around town, before we shipped out, that an avout in disguise had come down the glacier in the last few days and got into trouble just like what you described."

I was startled. Not for long. It was easy to imagine Laro raving, to anyone who would listen, about his bizarre and tragic adventure with the avout who called himself Vit. Maybe I raised an eyebrow or something.

"I've always wanted to meet an avout," Malter said. "I think it would be an honor."

"Well," I said, "you just met one."

○○

Vout: An avout. Derogatory term used extramuros. Associated with Sæculars who subscribe to iconographies that paint the avout in an extremely negative way.

—THE DICTIONARY, *4th edition, A.R. 3000*

Mahsht was four times the size of the city around Saunt Edhar, and as such was the biggest city I'd yet been to in my peregrination—or my life, for that matter. To the great consternation of the regulars on this ship—the men who journeyed in transports like this one to and from the Arctic all the time—we were not given leave to enter the harbor and tie up at a pier as usual. Instead we had to stand off and keep station in the outer harbor. Word filtered down from the bridge that Mahsht had been thrown into disarray by the military convoys and that novel arrangements were being worked out from hour to hour.

I spent much of that day abovedecks, just looking at the place, and enjoying being in a part of the world where the weather wasn't trying to kill me. Even though Mahsht was farther north than Edhar, at fifty-seven degrees of latitude, its climate was moderate because of a river of warm water in the ocean. Having said that, it wasn't warm, just dependably chilly. You could be comfortable if you wore a jacket and stayed dry. Staying dry could be a bit of a project.

Mahsht was built around a fjord that forked into three arms. Each arm supported different kinds of facilities. One was military, and quite busy. One was commercial. It had been built around the end of the Praxic Age to handle cargo in steel boxes and hadn't changed much since then. Normally our ship would have put in at a passenger terminal in that district. The third was the oldest. It had been built up out of stone and brick a thousand years before the Reconstitution, during the age when ships moved under power of wind and were unloaded by hand. Apparently there was still a demand for such facilities because smaller vessels went in and out of its stone docks all the time.

The old town and the port facilities were built on filled tide flats, incised with networks of canals, narrow and irregular in Old Mahsht, gridded lanes in the commercial and military sectors. Much of the land that separated the arms of the fjord was too steep to build on. The spires and ridges of stone supported ancient castles, luxury casinos, and radar stations. The territory outside of town was steeper yet: a misty green-black wall with unrecognizable constructs scraped out of it, hanging at crazy angles a mile in the sky. Alwash explained to me that these were places where people paid to slide downhill on packed snow. It didn't appeal to me at the moment.

After a day, a tug came out and brought us to a wharf in Old Mahsht. According to the regulars, this had never happened before—they always went to the "new" commercial district. So, as much as I was absorbed in the workings of the tug and the shifting views of Old Mahsht's warehouses, arks, cathedrals, and town center, I had now to give some thought to how I was going to find Cord, Sammann, Gnel, and Yul—or how I could help them find me. Should I walk to the commercial port on the assumption they'd be waiting for me there? Or would they have already heard about the disruptions in traffic and be looking for me in Old Mahsht?

As soon as I came down the gangplank it was clear that Old Mahsht was the right place. Since the military part of town could not tolerate disarray and the commercial part found it unprofitable, all of the chaos had been pushed into the old town, which had become the kingdom of broken plans and improvisations. All of the city's proper lodgings had been claimed by contractors from the south who were involved in this project of moving the military north, so people were sleeping in mobes and fetches, or on the streets. Against them, all doors were locked and many were guarded, so they were channeled into such open places as could be found, such as the tops of the wharves, unbuilt stretches of tide flat, and lots where ancient warehouses had been demolished to make room for new projects that had never been realized. This is what the gangplank spewed me into. I shuffled down the ramp scanning the crowd for my friends. The longer I sought their faces, the lower I was pushed on the ramp and the less I could see. Then I was down in it and could see nothing. Having no plan, I let the currents of the multitude stir me around. When I sensed still pockets or eddies in the flow I sidled into them and stood and looked about. From what I've described so far you might think it was a scene of terrible poverty, but the more I observed the more it was plain to me that there was work to be had here, that people had come to find it, and that what I was seeing—what I had become *part of*—was a kind of prosperity. Young men queued to talk to important fellows who I assumed were buyers of labor. Many others had come to sell goods or services to those who'd found work, so people were cooking food in carts or on open fires, hawking mysterious effects from the pockets of their coats, or behaving in very strange ways that, as I slowly realized, meant that they were willing to sell their bodies. Old road-worn passenger coaches nudged through the crowds at slower than walking pace to discharge or take on passengers. The only wheeled transport that seemed to be of any practical use were pedal-powered cycles and motor scooters. Preachers of diverse arks commandeered pinch-points in the flow and shouted gospels and prophecies into crackling amps. There was a lot of uncollected garbage and open-air defecation, which made me glad it wasn't warmer.

The generous climate had long attracted immigrants, who came from all over the world, singly or in waves, and climbed up into fjords or mountain valleys to live as they pleased. Over time they developed their own modes of dress and even distinct racial characteristics. I bought food from a cart—it was easily the best food I'd had since my last supper at Saunt Edhar—and stood there eating it and watching the pageant. Long-haired mountain men, always alone. A huge family, moving in a tight formation, males in broad-brimmed hats, females in face-veils. A multi-racial group, all wearing red T-shirts, every head—men's and women's alike—shaved clean. A race, if that was the right word, of tall people with bony noses and prematurely white hair, hawking fresh shellfish packed in poly crates full of seaweed.

After I'd been off the ship for an hour, it had become evident that meeting up with Cord, Sammann, and the Crades could easily take more than one day. I started considering where I might sleep that night—for I had at last reached a latitude where the sun went down for a few hours at this time of year. I knew that there were no great concents this far north. But in a city as old as this one there had to be at least one small math—perhaps even one dating to the Old Mathic Age. Wondering if I should try to seek one out and talk my way in, I walked up a broad street that ran from the waterfront up to the Bazian cathedral, scanning the fronts of old buildings for Mathic architecture or anything that looked like a cloister.

Clamped to a black iron lamp post I noticed a speelycaptor, and this put me in mind of Sammann and his ability to obtain data from such devices. Perhaps I'd been going about this in the wrong way. It could be that Sammann was tracking me on speelycaptors but that my friends hadn't been able to catch up with me because I kept moving around. So I decided to remain still for a while in a conspicuous place and see if that helped. I had just bumped into Malter and Alwash, who had given me the address of a Kelx mission hostel where I might be able to sleep in a pinch, and as long as I had such a backup plan I thought it might be worth the gamble to sit and wait somewhere. I chose a spot in the open plaza before the cathedral, in direct view of a speelycaptor bracketed to the front of Old Mahsht's town hall.

That's where I got mugged.

Or at least I thought it was a mugging at first. My attention had been drawn to a street performer doing gymnastics about fifty feet away. "Hey, Vit!" someone said, behind me on the right. I turned my face straight into an onrushing fist.

While I was down, someone jerked my sweater up out of my trousers to bare my midsection. For some reason I thought of Lio, who'd been defeated at Apert when the slines had pulled his bolt over his head. So instead of protecting my face as I ought to have done I made a clumsy effort to push my sweater back down where it belonged. Someone's hands were busy down there, jerking something out of the waistband of my trousers.

It was my bolt, chord, and sphere. I'd made them up into a neat package and stuffed them into my trousers for safekeeping and covered them with the sweater.

Ground level makes for a lousy vantage point. Especially when you're on one side in a fetal position looking up out of the corner of one eye. But it seemed as though two men were playing tug-of-war with the package they'd stolen from me, trying to get it apart. The chord spiraled off and the bolt, which I'd pleated into a configuration called the Eight-fold Envelope, fell open. Out tumbled my pilled-up sphere. I caught it on the second bounce. A foot smashed down on my hand. "He's trying to use it!" someone cried. A man dropped on me, one knee to either side. At this point a reflex took over. Lio had taught me that once I'd been mounted I'd never get up again, and so when I sensed what was happening I twisted sideways, getting my back up and my belly down, and drew my knees up under me, so that by the time this guy's weight landed on me I was presenting my butt to him rather than my belly, and I had my legs under me where I could use them. My hand was still pinned to the ground by someone's foot, but my sphere was trapped between my hand and the pavement. I made it bigger. The expanding sphere forced the man's foot up, and when it became head-sized his foot rolled right off and my hand came free. I planted that hand under me and pushed as hard as I could with both arms and legs. The guy on top of me wrapped his arms around my trunk as I came up but I grabbed one of his pinkies in my fist and jerked it back. He screamed and let go. I surged forward without looking back. "He used a spell on me!" someone screamed. "The vout cast a spell on me!"

Part of me—not the wiser part—wanted to explain to that guy

what an idiot he was being, but most of me just wanted to put distance between myself and these mysterious attackers. How had they known I had been using the name Vit? I turned back to look at them. My passage through the crowd had left an open space in my wake. Several men were charging into it, coming for me. I'd never seen them before. There was something familiar in their faces, though: they belonged to the same ethnic group as Laro and Dag. Gheeths, as Brajj had called them.

They were having trouble keeping up with me but I could not outrun their voices: "Stop him! Stop the vout!" This didn't seem to have much effect. But then they got cleverer. "Murderer! Murderer! Stop him!" It turned out that this only made things easier for me since no one wanted to get in the way of a large, sprinting murderer. So then it became: "Thief! Thief! He stole an old lady's money!" That was when the crowd closed in and people started sticking legs out to trip me.

I jumped over a few of those, but it was obvious I had to get out of this crowded square, so I dodged into the first street I could reach that led away from it, then into an alley off that street. This was so narrow I could touch both sides, but at least I didn't have the feeling any more of being engulfed in a huge and hostile mob.

I heard the buzz of scooter engines. They were tracking me. Local scooter boys who knew the alley network were maneuvering to cut me off at the next intersection.

I tried a few doors but they were locked. Then I made the mistake of doing so in view of an armed guard who was standing in front of a money-changing house a few doors up. He unslung a weapon and muttered something into his collar. I backtracked, took the next side-alley that I could find, and ran down it for a hundred yards to a place where it bridged a narrow canal. A couple of scooter boys pulled up to block the bridge just as I reached it. Glancing down I saw some mucky canal-bottom exposed. The tide must be out. I jumped down without thinking, landed and rolled in the soft mud, felt pain but didn't break anything as far as I could tell. To one direction the canal curved back toward the town square. The other direction led to open sky: the waterfront. I began running that way, thinking that if I could get to the beach I might steal or beg a ride on a small boat. Even swimming would be safer than being in the middle of that crowd.

But I couldn't run very fast in the muck. And I was exhausted anyway. I'd forgotten to breathe. Bridges spanned the canal every couple of hundred feet, and I began to see people gathering on the bridges ahead of me, pointing at me excitedly.

I turned around to see a bigger crowd on the bridge behind. They had bottles and stones ready. Trying to run under those bridges would be suicide. The canal wall was vertical but the stonework was ancient and rough-cut; I tried to scale it. Scooter noise zeroed in on me and something hit me on the top of the head.

I woke up some time after landing in knee-deep water in the middle of the canal, and came up howling for air only to get hit by a dozen stones and bottles in as many seconds.

"Stop! Stop! The vout isn't going anywhere! Keep him penned in," said some kind of self-appointed leader: a stout Gheeth with shaggy hair. "Our witness is almost here!" he proclaimed.

So we all waited for the "witness." The crowd sorted itself. Most of them had been random people who had been drawn to the bridges or the canal-brink by simple curiosity or out of the belief that they were helping to collar a purse-snatcher. But those sorts drifted away or were pushed aside by new arrivals: Gheeths with jeejahs. So by the time that the witness arrived on the back of a pedal-powered cab, a minute or so later, a hundred percent of those staring down at me were Gheeths. And none of them believed that I was a purse-snatcher. What *did* they believe? I doubted most of them even cared.

The witness was Laro. His leg was in a military-issue cast. "That is him! I'll never forget his face. He used vout sorcery to save himself—but left our kinsman Dag for dead."

I looked at him like *you have got to be kidding* but the look on his face was so sincere it made me doubt my own version of the story.

"The cops are coming!" someone warned. Actually, we'd been hearing such warnings the whole time I'd been at bay here. I wished those cops would hurry. But I wasn't sure they'd treat me any better.

"Let's get this done!" someone shouted, and looked to the leader, who stepped to the brink. Sidling along next to him was a big guy holding a huge chunk of pavement above his head in both hands and staring at me intently.

The leader pointed down at me. "He's a vout. Laro testifies to it. These two found the evidence hidden under his clothes!"

Two young Gheeths—the pair who'd mugged me—were pushed to the front of the crowd so vigorously they almost fell in. They had my bolt, chord, and sphere. At the leader's prompting they raised these up for all to see. The crowd oohed and aahed at the exhibits as if they were nuclear bomb cores.

"The vout has broken the ancient law that keeps his kind apart. He has come among us as a spy. We all know what he did to poor Dag. We can only imagine what fate he had in store for Laro—had Laro not bravely fought his way free of the vout's snare. Are we going to stand for it?"

"No!" the crowd shouted.

"Are we going to get any justice from the cops?"

"No!"

"But are we going to see justice done?"

"Yes!"

The leader nodded at the big guy with the rock. He flung it down at me so ponderously that I was able to step out of its path with ease. But a score of smaller, faster projectiles came in its wake. Running back and forth just to make myself a moving target, I caught sight of a stone stairway in the canal about a hundred feet distant. If I could get to its top I'd at least be at street level again—not in this hopeless situation, down below the mob. I ran for it and took several more bottles and rocks in my back, but I had my arms folded behind my head to shield it.

I got to the top of those stairs all right, but they were waiting for me there. I'd scarcely ascended to street level before they'd tripped and shoved me down onto the street. One of them fell on me, or maybe it was a clumsy attempt to tackle me. I grabbed the lapel of his jacket and held him there, keeping him on top of me as a shield. People elbowed each other aside to get in and aim kicks at me, but most of them drew up short when they saw one of their own people in the way. Hands reached in to grab him and haul him to his feet. I ended up with his empty jacket clutched in my hand. I tried to get up but was pushed down. I went to a fetal position and clamped my arms over my head.

It was a few seconds later that I heard The Scream.

The Scream was definitely a human voice but it was unlike anything I'd ever heard. The only way I can convey just how disturbing it was, is to say that it fully expressed the way I was feeling. I even wondered, in my panicked and addled state, whether it might have escaped from my own throat. The Scream had the effect of making everyone stand still. They were no longer attacking me, no longer fighting to get within kicking distance. Instead, all stood around trying to figure out where The Scream had come from and what it portended.

I rolled over on my back. A space had opened up around me. Around me, that is, and a shaven-headed man in a red T-shirt.

He stepped toward me and drew something from his pocket that rapidly became large: a sphere. In a second he had expanded it to about five feet in diameter, leaving it somewhat flaccid. He doubled it over me. My head and feet stuck out to either end but the rest of me was shielded against further blows—at least as long as this man stood there holding the sphere in place. A gust of wind could dislodge it. But he took care of that by vaulting to its top and perching on it: a precarious pose even when you attempted it with both feet. He, however, was placing all of his weight on one foot, leaving the other drawn up beneath him. Sometimes, when we'd been younger, we'd tried to stand on our spheres as a kind of childish game. Some adults did it as an exercise to improve their balance and reflexes. This seemed an odd time and place for calisthenics, though.

It did have the useful side-effect of leaving the people around me even more nonplussed than they had been by The Scream. But after a few moments one young man spied my head—a tempting and obvious target—and stepped toward me, drawing back one leg to deliver a kick. I closed my eyes and braced myself. Above me I

heard a sharp, percussive sound. I opened my eyes to see my attacker falling backwards. A second later, moisture sprayed into my
face: a shower of blood. A few small pebbles or something rattled
to the pavement nearby. Blinking the blood out of my eyes, I perceived that they weren't pebbles but teeth.

Another scream emanated from the edge of the crowd. This
one was altogether different. It came from a person who was experiencing an amount of pain that was incredible, in the literal sense;
his scream sounded surprised, as in *I had no idea anything could be as
painful as whatever is happening to me now!* This got the attention of
everyone except for one Gheeth who was coming toward me and
my protector with an odd, fixed grin on his face, drawing a knife
from his pocket and flicking it open. This time I got a better view
of what happened. The man perched on the sphere above me faked
a snap-kick with his free leg and the other waved his knife at where
he supposed the kick was going; but before he even knew how
badly he'd missed, my protector had grabbed the hand holding the
knife and twisted it the wrong way—not simply by flicking his
wrist but by jumping off the sphere and doing a midair somersault
over the attacker's arm, whose joints and bones came undone in a
series of thuds and pops. The sphere rolled off me. The knife fell to
the ground and I tried to clap my hand down on top of it, but too
late—my protector kicked it away and it flew over the brink of the
canal and disappeared.

I was unshielded. But it hardly mattered because the crowd
had all moved in the direction of that horrible, astonished screaming. I pushed myself up on hands and knees and got to a kneeling
position.

The source of the screaming was an adult male Gheeth who
was being held in some sort of complicated wrestling grip by a
shaven-headed woman in a red T-shirt. A similar-looking man of
about eighteen was standing at her back, efficiently knocking down
anyone who approached. By the time I came in view of all this, the
mob had begun to hurl stones at these two. My protector abandoned me and slipped through the crowd to join the other two
redshirts and help bat away projectiles. They began to retreat.

Most of the mob went after them but some began to edge away; throwing stones at a lone avout might have been good sport for them but they wanted no part of whatever was going on now.

I turned, thinking I might just get out of here now, and found myself staring into the eyes of the Gheeth leader. He had a gun. It was aimed at me. "No," he said, "we haven't forgotten about you. Move!" He gestured with the gun in the direction that the crowd seemed to be moving. They were slowly pursuing the retreating redshirts down the edge of the canal toward a more open place a hundred feet away: a square where two streets met at canal's edge. "Turn around and march," he commanded.

I turned around and walked toward the square. Most of the mob had gone past us, so I was now in the outer fringes, the back lines, of a crowd of perhaps a hundred, all moving at a trot, then a run, after the three retreating redshirts, who by this point had dragged their hostage all the way into the square as they tried to get away from that overwhelmingly superior force of rock-throwing, knife-waving attackers.

My captor and I entered the square. The canal's edge was to my left, the square spread away from it to my right. War-cries now sounded from that direction. I'm using the term war-cry here to mean the unearthly scream that the first redshirt had uttered when he'd come out of nowhere to protect me. Now we heard ten of them at once. The first one, as I described, had simply paralyzed everyone. But in a short time we had learned to associate the sound with face-smashing, limb-twisting Vale-lore experts. A battle-line of redshirts had materialized on our right flank; they'd been poised in the square, waiting for the first three to draw us into position. All heads turned toward, all bodies swerved away from them. Each of the redshirts had sent one or two members of the mob down to the pavement with bloody lacerations before we could even take in the image. The line of redshirts pivoted to link up with the first three, who now released the man they'd been torturing. Beginning to understand that they were outflanked on the right and that the square in general was enemy territory, unable to move left because of the canal-edge, the mob turned back, hoping to withdraw the way they'd come. But another salvo of war-cries came from the rear as several redshirts vaulted up out of the canal. They'd been hiding down there, clinging to the rugged canal wall like rock-climbers, and we had unwittingly gone right past them. They sealed off the retreat. The only way out now for the mob was to squirt forward between the canal-edge and the redshirts into the square, or jump down into the canal. As soon as a few had escaped via these routes, everyone wanted to do it, and it flashed into a panic. The redshirts let them go. In a few moments almost all of my attackers had simply disappeared. The two lines of redshirts joined up and contracted to form a sparse ring about twenty feet in diameter. They faced outwards. Their heads never stopped moving. In the middle of the ring were three people: the gun-toting Gheeth leader, I, and a single redshirt who always moved so that he was between me and the muzzle of the gun.

A redshirted woman on the perimeter called out "Fusil" which was a ridiculously archaic Orth word meaning a long-barreled firearm. The redshirts to either side instantly turned their backs on her to look in other directions. Everyone else, though, did what came naturally: followed the woman's gaze to the top of a parked drummon on the edge of the square. A Gheeth had climbed up there with a long weapon and was training it in our direction. The woman who had called out "Fusil" skipped forward, raising her hands, and did a cartwheel that took her to the lid of a trash container. From there she sprang sideways, rolled, and came up near a drinking fountain on which she planted a foot to shove off and make a violent reversal of direction that took her toward a scraggly tree. She got a hand on that and swung round it, scampered to the top of a bench, disappeared into a little clot of pedestrians, reappeared a moment later sprinting directly toward the man with the gun but in a moment had changed course again to duck behind a kiosk. In this manner she made rapid progress toward the gunman atop the drummon. He was hard-pressed to aim his weapon at her with all these sudden changes in course. If I'd been in his shoes, I couldn't have fired, even to save my own life, because her gymnastics were so fascinating to watch.

A shot sounded. Not from the man on the drummon and not

from the leader in the ring behind me. It came from somewhere else: hard to pin down because it echoed from the fronts of buildings all around the square. My knees buckled.

Five feet away from me, something unpleasant happened to the Gheeth leader; a redshirt had used this distraction as an opportunity to take him down and disarm him.

The woman doing the gymnastics kept moving toward the gunman atop the drummon, who had frozen up and was looking all around trying to identify the source of the shot.

A second shot sounded. The gun spun loose from the would-be sniper's hands and clattered to the pavement. He grabbed his hand and howled. The redshirt woman stopped with the gymnastics, dropped into a normal sprinting gait, and went straight to the fallen weapon.

"Fusil!" called one of the other redshirts. He pointed across the canal. Again the two flanking him spun about to look in other directions. It took the rest of us a moment to see what he'd seen.

Across the canal was a food cart, prudently abandoned by its owner. A three-wheeler had drawn up behind it, using it and its array of signs and fluttering banners to provide visual cover. One man was operating the three-wheeler's controls: Ganelial Crade. Another was standing on its passenger platform: Yulassetar Crade. He was carrying a long weapon. He addressed himself to the sniper atop the drummon, bellowing across the canal. "The first shot was to make you freeze," he explained. "The second was to make you helpless. The third you're never going to know about. Show me your hands. *Show me your hands!*"

The Gheeth held up his hands—one of them bloody and misshapen.

"Run away!" Yul howled, and shouldered his rifle.

The Gheeth avalanched down over the front of the drummon, rolled around on the pavement for a few moments, then came up at a run.

"Raz, we gotta go!" Yul called. "The rest of you in the red shirts—whoever or whatever you are—you're welcome to come with. Maybe you want to be getting out of town as bad as we do."

There was a bridge over the canal at the square. Gnel zipped over it and came towards me. The circle of redshirts parted to let him in. He passed through the gap, eyeing them a little nervously, and pulled up alongside me. I wasn't moving too well. Yul bent down over me, grabbed my belt in his fist, just behind the small of my back, and heaved me aboard the three-wheeler like an unconscious rafter being pulled out of a river. It was extremely crowded now on this tiny vehicle. Gnel made a careful, sweeping turn into the square and headed up a street. He was wearing earphones plugged into a jeejah. Sammann must be feeding him instructions.

The redshirts followed us, jogging beside and behind the three-wheeler. Apparently they saw good sense in Yul's point that it was time to get out of town. Once it became clear which way we were going, they picked up the pace and threatened to outrun the three-wheeler, prompting Gnel to give it a little more throttle. Before long they were sprinting. We covered a mile in a few minutes, and came into a district of railway lines and warehouses that wasn't as crowded as the center of Old Mahsht. It was possible for full-sized vehicles to move about normally on the streets here. A pair of them came out of nowhere and nearly ran us down: Yul's and Gnel's fetches, driven by Cord and by Sammann respectively.

As we later established, the redshirts numbered twenty-five. We somehow got all of them onto the two fetches and the three-wheeler. I'd never seen people packed so tight. We had redshirts on the roof of Yul's fetch, elbows linked together to keep them from falling off.

Cord took all of this pretty calmly, considering that she couldn't have known, until just before they piled into the fetch, that she was going to be transporting a dozen and a half vlor experts in red T-shirts. As she drove us out of there, she kept looking over at me aghast. "It's okay," I told her. "They are avout—they must have been Evoked. I don't know what math they are from—obviously one that specializes in vlor—maybe an offshoot of Ringing Vale or some such—"

Behind me, an amused redshirt translated all of that into Orth and got a round of chuckles.

I got embarrassed. Horribly, mud-on-the-head embarrassed.

These people *were* from the Ringing Vale.

I tried to turn back to look at them but something impeded movement. Groping to explore, I discovered three hands, belonging to Valers behind or beside me, pressing wads of blood-soaked fabric against my face and scalp. Lacerations. I hadn't been aware of them. It wasn't the strangers crammed into her fetch that so disturbed Cord; it was my face.

During most of this I'd been having the wrong emotions. At the very beginning when the two Gheeths had mugged me, I'd been scared. Appropriately. That's why I'd run away. Then I had convinced myself that I could handle this somehow. I could evade the mob in streets or canals. I could talk some sense into Laro, plead my case. They didn't really mean to kill me; this couldn't be happening. The cops would get here any minute. Next had come a sort of dazed acceptance of my fate. Then the fraas and suurs of the Ringing Vale had arrived. Everything after that had been fascinating and sort of exhilarating, and I had surfed through it on some sort of chemical high: my body's reaction to injury and stress. A minute ago I'd greeted Cord with a big bloody hug as though nothing had happened.

A few minutes into the drive, though, I fell apart. All of my injuries began sending pain to my brain, like soldiers sounding off at roll call. Whatever convenient substances my glands had been squirting into my bloodstream were withdrawn, cold turkey. It was as if a trapdoor had opened beneath me. Just like that I became a shivering, weeping tangle of nerves, squirming and grunting in pain.

Twenty minutes' drive, under Sammann's direction, took us to a site on the left bank of a big river that flowed from the mountains down into the Old Mahsht fjord branch. It looked as though it might have been a broad sandbar in some earlier age, but had long ago been paved over and played host to a succession of industrial complexes, now in ruins. At one end of it was a recreational boat ramp and picnic ground with a couple of smelly latrines. We pulled in there and scared off some holiday-makers. I was carried out of Yul's fetch and laid out flat on a picnic table that they'd covered with camping pads to make it soft, and tarps to protect the camping pads from whatever was leaking out of me. Yul opened his medical kit, which like all of his other gear was not store-bought but improvised from found objects. Into a big, heavy-gauge poly bag he dumped white powder from a poly tube: salt and germicide. Then he filled it up with a couple of gallons of tap water and shook it for a minute, producing a sterilized normal saline solution. He tucked the bag under his arm and squeezed it hard against his ribs, shooting out a jet of fluid that he aimed into my wounds to flush them out. Picking a wound, he would yank off the gauze and sluice it until I screamed, then give it another thirty seconds. Gnel followed in his wake, working with something smelly. As he was using it on my split eyebrow I realized it was a tube of glue—the same stuff you'd use to stick the handle back onto a broken teacup. Wounds too big to glue were bridged with glass-fiber packing tape. At one point a Ringing Vale suur dug into me with a sewing needle and a length of fishing line from Gnel's tackle box. Once a wound had been hit with glue, tape, or fishing line, someone in a red T-shirt would slap petroleum jelly on it and cover it with something white. A Ringing Vale fraa, obviously a masseur, went over my whole body without so much as a by-your-leave, looking for broken bones and hemorrhages. If my spleen wasn't ruptured when he got to it, it was by the time he moved on to my liver. His verdict: mild concussion, three cracked ribs, spiral fracture of one arm bone, two small broken bones in one hand, and I could expect to pee blood for a while.

Enough time had gone by for me to be ashamed of how I'd fallen apart during the drive, so I put a lot of effort into not screaming any more than was strictly necessary. For some reason I was thinking of Lio. He'd worshipped all things Vale since before he'd even been Collected. He'd tracked down every book at Saunt Edhar that came from there, or that had been written by people who claimed to have visited the Vale or been beaten up by Valers. He'd have died of shame to know that I'd been less than totally immune to pain in the presence of these people.

Conversations I was dying to be a part of were taking place just out of earshot. Once they finished gluing my head together, I could look about and see Sammann talking to a senior fraa from the Vale, and a suur consoling Cord, who broke out crying whenever she turned her face in my direction. After a while, when it was decided I was going to live and so might be worth talking to, Fraa Osa—the First Among Equals of the Valers—came over to talk to me. With the exception of the seamstress, who was making long tedious work of a rambling slash on my calf, the wound-fixers raked up all their litter and drifted away. Yul went over and bear-hugged Cord and practically carried her over to the edge of the river where she had a good long soaking cry.

"Yesterday we were Evoked," said Fraa Osa. He was the first redshirt I had seen during the melee: the one who had covered me with his sphere and perched on it one-legged. He was probably in his fifth decade. "They said we should go to Tredegarh. We consulted a globe and determined that the most efficient route was via Mahsht."

The Ringing Vale was a hundred or so miles outside of Mahsht. From there a great circle route across the ocean would take one almost to Tredegarh, so this made sense as far as it went.

"Local people gave us transportation to Mahsht. We found it as you found it. Those of us who speak Fluccish sought transport on a ship. We were approached by your magister."

"My magister!?" I shouted. Then I saw the faintest trace of irony on Osa's face. He was half joking.

But only half. "Sark," he said. "He is well known to us. He comes to our Aperts, and speaks to us of his ideas." Osa shrugged and made a gentle bobbling motion with his hands, which I thought was his way of telling me that they tried to weigh Sark's preaching fairly. "In any case, he recognized us in the street. He told us that a lone avout was being pursued by a mob. We saw it as an emergence."

For a moment I thought he was slipping into broken Fluccish, trying to pronounce *emergency*. Then I remembered some of the Vale-lore that Lio had drummed into me over the years.

During the time of the Reconstitution, literally in the Year 0, when the sites of the first new maths were being surveyed so that the cornerstones of their Clocks and Mynsters could be laid down, a team of freshly sworn-in avout had journeyed to a remote place in the desert to begin such a project, only to find themselves under siege by mistrustful locals. For the place they'd been sent was covered with jumpweed plantations and they had stumbled upon a shack where the weed was being boiled down to make a concentrated, illegal drug. The avout were unarmed. They had been pulled together from all over the world and so had little in common with one another; most of them didn't even speak Orth. But it so happened that several of them were students of an ancient school of martial arts, which back in those days had no connection with the mathic world, even if it had been developed in monastic settings. Anyway, they had never used their skills outside of a gym, but they now found themselves thrust into a position where they had to take action. Some of their number were killed. Some of the martial artists performed well, others froze up and did no better than those who'd had no training at all. That sort of situation became known as an emergence. A few of the survivors went on to found the Ringing Vale math. According to Lio, they spent almost as much time thinking about the concept of emergence as they did in physical training—the idea being that all the training in the world was of no use, maybe even worse than useless, if you did not know when to use it, and knowing when to use it was a lot harder than it sounded, because sometimes, if you waited too long to go into action, it was too late, and other times, if you did it too early, you only made matters worse.

"The most salient feature of the enemy was its thoughtless aggression," Fraa Osa said. He reached into air and closed his hand as though grasping the wrist of an attacker who'd tried to punch him. It was an eloquent gesture, which was convenient for me, since Fraa Osa did not seem inclined to say more than that about the strategy they had used.

"You reckoned, as long as they are in such a mood, let's really give them something to be aggressive about," I said, trying to draw him out a little more. Fraa Osa smiled and nodded. "So you grabbed that one person and started, uh . . ."

Here for once I broke off instead of telling the truth, which was that they had been torturing that Gheeth. I didn't want to seem critical towards these people who had just risked their lives saving mine. Fraa Osa just kept smiling and nodding. "It is a nerve pressure technique," he said. "It seems to hurt a lot, but does no damage."

This raised all sorts of interesting questions: was there really a difference between hurting, and *seeming* to hurt? Was it permissible to torture someone if it didn't cause clinical injuries? But again there were all sorts of reasons not to pursue such questions now. "Well, anyway, it worked," I said. "The mob turned against you—you staged a false retreat and drew them into a trap—then you made them panic." More smiling and nodding. Fraa Osa simply was in no mood to wax eloquent about any of this. "And how long did you have in which to devise this plan?" I asked him.

"Not long enough."

"I beg your pardon?"

"There is no time in an emergence to think up plans. Much less to communicate them. Instead I told the others that we would emulate Lord Frode's cavalry at Second Rushy Flats, when they drew out Prince Terazyn's squadron. Except that the canal edge would substitute for the Tall Canes and that little square would take the place of Bloody Breaks. As you can see it does not take very much time to say these words."

I nodded as if I had some idea what he was talking about—which I didn't. I couldn't even guess which war he was alluding to, in what millennium.

"What's with the red T-shirts?" I asked, though I already had my suspicions. Fraa Osa grinned ruefully. "They were issued to us at Voco," he said. "Donated by a local ark. I look forward to reaching Tredegarh so that I can go back to the bolt and chord."

"Speaking of which—"

He shook his head. "Your bolt, chord, and sphere are lost. Perhaps we could have gotten them back—but we departed in some haste."

"Of course!" I said. "Not a big deal." And it wasn't, in one sense. Fraas and suurs lost theirs from time to time. New ones were issued. But losing mine in this way made me feel pretty bad. They'd been with me for more than ten years and they had a lot of memories associated with them. They'd been my last physical link to the Mathic world. Now that they were gone, I could be any old Sæcular. Which might be safer—no one could yank them out from concealment and wave them around and try to lynch me. But it made me feel lonely.

Sammann went over and had a few words with Yul who jumped up, fetched the rifle, grabbed it by the barrel, and after a few running steps gave it a mighty heave. Spinning end-over-end it flew about halfway across the river, then stabbed into the current and disappeared. About a minute later, two mobes full of Mahsht constables showed up and piled out of their wailing and flashing vehicles. Except for Fraa Osa and the suur who was sewing me together, all of the Ringing Vale avout sat on the ground, feet tucked under them, and looked serene. The constables mostly gaped at them. How many thousands of speelies had been produced about the fictional exploits of the Valers? The cops couldn't begin to think of them as suspects. They saw them more as tourist attractions. Zoo animals. Movie stars. What's more, the Valers knew as much, and knew how to exploit it. They showed us the meaning of posture, and pretended to meditate. The cops ate it up. The boss cop had a long and (at first) tense conversation with Yul and Fraa Osa. The suur with the needle kept running that string through my flesh and I gritted my teeth so hard I could hear them creaking. Finally she tied it off and walked away without a word—without even a look. I had an upsight: I might have warm feelings for these people because they had helped me and because I had seen way too many speelies about them before I'd been Collected. The Valers, however, had not been Evoked because they were nice guys.

Cord came over and stood with her hands in her pockets taking inventory of my bandages.

"See what a small percentage of my body they actually cover," I pointed out.

She was having none of it.

"Our plan didn't work out so well," I offered.

She looked off to the side and sniffled—the last emotional aftershock of a long day. "Not your fault. How could we have known?"

"I'm sorry to have put you through this. I don't understand how things could have gone so wrong."

She looked at me acutely and saw nothing, I guess, except for a stupid look on my face. "You don't have any idea what's going on, do you?"

"I guess not. Just that the military has been moving toward the pole." A memory popped into my head. "And a magister on the ship made some weird comment about the Warden of Heaven being cast out in wrath."

Even as I was saying this, an old rattletrap coach was pulling in off the road. At its controls was Magister Sark. It was one of those freakish coincidences that made some people believe in spirits and psychic phenomena. I explained it away by supposing that my unconscious mind had seen the coach out of the corner of my eye a few moments before I'd consciously recognized him.

"You still with me?" Cord asked.

"Yeah. Hey—what about Jesry? Is he okay?"

"We think so. We'll get you caught up."

We looked over at Yul, who had somehow managed to get the police captain laughing. Something had been decided between them. The official part of the conversation was over.

The captain came over and made a few appreciative remarks about how banged up I was and what a tough guy I must be, then asked if I wanted to pursue it—to press charges. Absolutely lying through my teeth, I said no. By doing so, I apparently closed a deal. The particulars were never explained to me, but the gist of it was that all of us were free to go. The leaders of that mob would get off free except for injuries and insults already suffered. And these constables would dodge a mountain of paperwork: paperwork that would have been ten times as bad as what they were used to simply because many of those concerned were avout and hence of tricky legal status.

Magister Sark had not been idle during all of these other goings-on. The coach belonged to his Kelx in Mahsht; it was painted all over with Triangle iconography. It was large enough to transport all of the Valers. Some other member of his Kelx had volunteered to drive them south to a bigger city, less chaotic than Mahsht at the moment, whence they could arrange transport to Tredegarh. This driver, he explained, was on his way, but because of the difficult conditions in town, we might have to wait for a little while.

The magister glanced at me as he was explaining these things, and for some reason I felt a thrill of resentment. I did not like being indebted to him, and did not relish the prospect of having to sit gratefully through another sales pitch for his faith while we waited for the driver to show up. But it seemed he was more interested in checking my status than starting a conversation, and as soon as he stopped looking my way I felt ashamed of the way I'd reacted. Was there really that much of a difference between the Kelx notion of having one's story related to the Magistrate, and the Valers' concept of emergence? They seemed to produce very similar behavior; I owed my life to the fact that Sark and Osa had been of one mind, earlier today in Mahsht.

I was on my feet by now; I limped over to him, held out my hand, and thanked him. He shook my hand firmly and said nothing.

"The Condemned Man had a good yarn to spin for the Magistrate today," I said. I guess I was trying to humor him.

His face darkened. "But he could not tell it without speaking too of the ones who behaved evilly. Yes, it is the case that—thanks to the spirit of the Innocent—some good was achieved. But I can scarcely believe that the Magistrate's ultimate judgment of this world was much shifted, either way, by what he heard from the Condemned Man today."

Not for the first time I was astonished by Magister Sark's ability to be intelligent and wise while spouting prehistoric nonsense. "For your own part, anyway," I pointed out, "it seems you chose in a way that reflects well on you and your world."

"The Innocent moved me," he insisted. "Give all credit to her."

"I give you my personal thanks," I said, "and ask you to relay it to the Innocent the next time you hear from her."

He shook his head in exasperation, then finally chuckled; though such a grim fellow was he that his chuckle was something between a gag and a cough. "You don't understand at all."

"Fair enough," I said. "I am in no shape for Dialog right now, but perhaps some other time I can try to explain to you how I see all of these matters."

His reaction was noncommittal, but he understood that the conversation was over. He wandered away. I collected some blank paper from Yul's fetch and began to scribble out notes to my friends at the Convox. Magister Sark got into a long conversation with Yul and Cord, interrupted from time to time by Ganelial Crade, who of course belonged to a completely different faith, and who paced back and forth at a distance, fuming, then darted in from time to time to dispute some fine point of deology.

A mobe swung through, dropped off the driver who would take the Valers south, and picked up Magister Sark. The Valers began to find seats aboard the coach. Fraa Osa was the last to board. I handed him a stack of notes. "For my friends at Tredegarh," I explained, "if you would not mind bearing them."

He bowed.

"You've already done me plenty of favors, so it is okay to say no," I went on.

"You did us a favor," he countered, "by creating an emergence nested within the larger emergence, and giving us an opportunity to train."

I said nothing. I was wondering what he meant by "the larger emergence," and reckoned he must be talking about the Cousins. He was sifting through the letters I'd given him. "You have many friends at the Convox!" he remarked, and looked up at me quizzically. This was probably an indirect way of asking *what the heck are you doing!?* but I ignored it. "The long one, there, is for a girl named Ala. The others are for some other fraas and suurs of mine—"

"Aah!" exclaimed Fraa Osa, holding one up. "You know the famous Jesry!"

I didn't even want to think about what was implied by Jesry's being famous, so I glided past it and directed his attention to the last letter in the stack. "Lio," I said, "Fraa Lio is a student of Vale-lore."

"Ah!" he exclaimed. As if Lio were unique; as if the world, for thousands of years, at any given moment, had not contained millions of vlor students.

"Mostly self-taught. But it is important to him. If this letter were handed to him by even the most junior member of the Ringing Vale math, it would be the greatest honor of his life. Uh, don't tell him I said that."

Fraa Osa bowed again. "I shall comply with all of your instructions." He put his foot on the coach's running board. "Here I say farewell—unless—?" And he looked between me and the coach.

I fell for it hard. I imagined the long ride on the coach full of authentic Ringing Vale avout, maybe a night or two in a room at a casino down south, a journey—safe and well-organized—to Tredegarh, reunion with my friends there. If these people could somehow get their hands on a plane, it could even happen in a day. I imagined all of that long and hard enough to savor it, to look forward to it.

But I knew it was all a daydream. That I had to pull back. That the longer I kept on this way the harder it was going to be.

"I want to climb on board that thing and go to Tredegarh with you like that water wants to find the ocean," I said, gesturing to the river. "But to quit in the middle"—*just because I'm beat up and homesick and scared*—"seems wrong. Fraa Jad—he's the Millenarian who sent me—would never understand."

This was the first thing that had happened all day that startled Fraa Osa. "A Thousander," he repeated.

"Yes."

"Then you had best finish the task."

"That's kind of what I'm thinking."

He bowed one more time—more deeply than before. Then he turned his back on me and climbed into the coach. I went to the latrine and peed blood and boarded Yul's fetch. Sammann was in there too. We pulled on to the main road and turned south. I slept.

They said I only slept for half an hour but it felt much longer. When I woke up I crawled into the back of the fetch, where it was darker, and Sammann showed me a speely on his jeejah.

Sammann was the only member of the crew who didn't make remarks or ask questions about my injuries and emotional state. This might make it sound like he was insensitive. Frankly, though, I could have done with a lot less sensitivity by that point in the day.

"There is not a lot of explanatory content connected to this data because of the way in which it was obtained," he warned as he was queueing it up.

The image quality was, as usual, terrible. It took me a minute even to be sure that it had been shot in color. Everything was either solid black (space, and shadows) or blinding white (anything with sun shining on it). As I slowly came to realize, it had been made by aiming a hand-held speelycaptor out a dirty window. "Outgassing," Sammann said, which meant little to me. He went on to explain that the materials used to build the space capsule had, in the vacuum of space, let go of vaporous byproducts that had congealed on the spacecraft windows. "You'd think they would have solved that problem," I said. "They built it in a rush," he answered.

A perfect circle, centered in a perfect equilateral triangle, dominated the view. "It's the back end of the alien ship," Sammann explained. "The pusher plate on the rear. They always kept it oriented toward the capsule—think about it."

After a few moments I tried: "They—the Cousins—couldn't be

sure that our space capsule wasn't carrying a nuclear warhead. So they kept the nuke-proof part of their ship aimed towards it."

"That's part of it," Sammann said, and gave me a wicked grin—egging me on.

"They could spit one of their own nukes out the back of that thing and blow up the space capsule any time they felt like it."

"You got it. Also: we can't get a good look at their ship from this angle. No way to gather military intelligence."

"Where's the hole that the nukes come out of?" I asked.

"Don't bother looking. You can't see it. It's tiny compared to the scale of the plate. It's closed by a shutter when it's not in use. You won't be able to see it until it opens."

"It's going to open!?"

"Maybe it's better if we just watch the speely." Sammann reached in and turned up the volume a bit. The sound track was a roar of ambient noise: whooshes, hums, buzzes, and drones at many different pitches. There was the occasional human word or phrase, shouted over the roar, but people spoke rarely, and when they did it tended to be in terse military jargon.

"Bogey," someone said, "two o'clock."

The image veered and zoomed, the big triangle expanding until its edge had become a straight division separating white from black. In the black part a grey blob was discernible: just a mess of pixels a few shades brighter than black. But it got brighter and bigger. "Incoming," someone confirmed.

The murk of noise took on new overtones. People were conversing. I thought I heard the cadences of an Orth sentence.

"Prepare for egress!" someone commanded, in a voice that meant business. For the first time, the speelycaptor turned away from the window and refocused to show the interior of the space capsule. This view was shockingly crisp, clear, and colorful after the endless dreary shot of the pusher plate. Several people were floating around in a confined space. Some were strapped into chairs before consoles. Some were gripping handles, the better to keep their faces pressed against windows. One of these was definitely Jesry. In the middle of the capsule was the big man with the hairdo.

He didn't look good. Weightlessness had made his hair go funny. His face was swollen and greenish; I could tell he was nauseated. He looked tired and uncaring—maybe from anti-nausea drugs? His impressive clothes were gone, revealing all sorts of things about his physique that no one except for his doctor really needed to know. A couple of people were striving to fit him into an outlandish garment consisting of a network of tubes in a matrix of stretchy fabric. It seemed that this project had been going on for a while, but just now they threw it into high gear and one of the others pushed himself away from a window and flew over to help jerk the thing on. The Warden of Heaven (I didn't know for a fact that this was he, but it seemed unmistakable) woke up enough to become indignant. He glared at the camera and lifted a finger. One of his aides drifted into position to block the view, and said, "Please give His Serenity some—"

"Some serenity?" cracked Jesry, off-camera.

Testy words were exchanged. The authoritative voice commanded them to shut up. The argument was replaced by technical conversation pertaining to the suit that they were building around the Warden of Heaven's body. One of the console-watchers called out updates on the approach of the bogey.

Jesry said, "You're about to become the first person ever to converse with aliens. What is your plan?"

The Warden of Heaven made some brief and indistinct response. He was farther from the microphone, he wasn't feeling well, and he'd seen enough of Jesry by this point to know that the conversation wasn't going to end well.

The speelycaptor swung round to point at the Warden again. They'd finished putting the tube-garment around his body and were building a space suit over that, one limb at a time.

Off-camera, Jesry answered: "How do you know that the Geometers are even going to recognize that concept?"

Another muffled, noncommittal response from the Warden (who, to be fair, couldn't talk well because they were mounting a headset on him).

"Geometers?" I asked.

"That's what people at the Convox have been calling the aliens, apparently," Sammann said.

"I would try to go in there with a mental checklist of basic observations I wanted to achieve," Jesry went on. "For example, do they take any precautions against infection? It would be quite significant if they were afraid of our germs—or if they weren't."

The Warden of Heaven deflected Jesry's suggestion with a humorous remark that his aides thought was funny.

"You ever look at bugs under a lens?" Jesry tried. "That'd be good preparation for this. They look so different from anything we normally experience that it's easy to be kind of stunned and bewildered by their appearance at first. But if you can get past that emotional reaction, you can see how they work. How do they transmit their weight to the ground? Count the orifices. Look for symmetries. Observe periodicities. By which I mean, how often do they breathe? From that, we can make inferences about their metabolism."

One of the aides cut Jesry short by telling him it was time to pray. The suit was all on now except for the helmet. The Warden's head—unrecognizable under the earphones, the mike, the heads-up goggles—poked up out of a huge, rigid carapace. He held hands with his aides as best he could through the bulky gloves. They closed their eyes and said something in unison. A loud metallic pop/crunch interrupted them. "Contact," someone called, "we have been grappled by a remote manipulator."

The speelycaptor swung past a crew member checking his watch and aimed back out the dirty window to focus on the bogey. This was a skeletal craft, altogether mechanical, no pressurized compartments where a Cousin might ride along: just a frame with half a dozen robot arms of various sizes, and thruster nozzles, spotlights, and dish antennas pointed every which way. One of its arms had reached out and grabbed an antenna bracket on the outside of the capsule.

Things happened fast now. The helmet had already been clamped down over the Warden of Heaven's head, and crew members had shooed away the aides and were manipulating the suit's controls. Through the bubble the Warden's eyes could be seen moving back and forth uncertainly, responding to inscrutable hisses and creaks from the suit as its systems came alive. His lips moved and he nodded and gave thumbs-up signs as communications were tested.

They pushed him through a pressure hatch at one end of the capsule, closed it behind him, and turned a wheel to dog it shut. He was in the airlock.

"Why's he going alone?" I asked.

"Supposedly that's how the Cousins—excuse me, the Geometers—wanted it," Sammann said. "Send one, they said."

"So we sent *him*?" I asked incredulously.

Sammann shrugged. "But that's part of the Geometers' strategy, isn't it? If we were allowed to send a whole delegation, we could hedge our bets. But if the whole planet is allowed to send only one representative, whom do we pick? That tells them a lot."

"Yeah, but why—?"

Sammann cut me off with an even more exaggerated shrug. "You seriously expect me to be able to explain why the Sæcular Power makes the decisions it makes?"

"Okay. Sorry. Never mind."

Hisses and clanks and terse utterances from the crew signaled the opening of the airlock's outer door. A small arm unfolded itself from the Geometers' robot probe and reached toward the ship, out of view of this window. When it drew back, a few moments later, it brought the Warden of Heaven with it. The arm's steely hand had gripped a metal bracket that projected from the suit's round shoulder—a lifting point. The Geometers understood our engineering, and knew a bracket for a bracket.

The bogey disengaged from the capsule and fired a puff of gas to get itself drifting away, then, after a few seconds, ignited larger thrusters that accelerated it toward the icosahedron. The Warden of Heaven waved back to us. "Everything is okay," he announced over the wireless. Then his voice was replaced by a harsh buzzing tone. A crew member turned it down. "They're jamming us," he announced. "His Serenity is on his own."

"No," said an aide, "God is with him."

The speelycaptor zoomed in on the Warden, being drawn backwards toward the icosahedron. He was getting harder to see, even at maximum zoom, but it looked like he was gesticulating, tapping his helmet and throwing up his hands in confusion. "Okay, we get it!" Jesry said. "You can't hear."

"I'm worried about his pulse. Way too high for a man his age," said a crew member.

"You've still got telemetry?" Jesry asked.

"Just barely. They jammed vox first. Now they are attacking the other channels . . . nope. Lost it. Bye-bye."

"The Geometers are some kind of military hardasses," Sammann said, perhaps unnecessarily.

The video went on with little further commentary until the robot probe and the Warden had shrunk to a tiny cluster of grey pixels. Then it cut out and went to black. Sammann paused it. "In the original, what follows is four hours of basically nothing," he said. "They just sit there and wait. Your friend Jesry baits the Warden's toadies into a philosophical debate and crushes them. After that, no one wants to talk. There is only one event of note, which is that after about one hour the jamming stops."

"Really? So they can talk to the Warden again?"

"I didn't say that. The jamming signals are turned off, but they can't get any data from the Warden's spacesuit. Most likely what it means is that the suit had been shut down."

"Because something happened to the Warden of Heaven or . . ."

"Most people think he got out of the suit. Since it was no longer necessary, it was turned off to conserve power."

"That implies . . ."

"That the Hedron—as people are calling it—has an atmosphere we can breathe, yes," Sammann said. "Or that the Warden was dead on arrival."

"The Warden of Heaven's dead?"

Sammann started the speely playing again. The time code in the corner had jumped forward a few hours.

"New signal from the Hedron," announced a tired crew member. "Repetitive pulses. Microwaves. High power. I'd say they are illuminating us with radar."

"Like they don't already know where we are!" someone scoffed.

"Cut the chatter!" ordered the voice I'd come to think of as the captain's. "Do you think they are acquiring us?"

"As in acquiring a target for a weapons launch," Sammann translated.

"It's definitely that kind of a narrow-beam signal," said the other, "but steady—not homing in."

"Activity on the base plate!" Jesry called. "Dead center."

The image once again wheeled to the huge circle-in-triangle. Then it zoomed. A dark mote was visible in the center. As the zoom went on, this grew and resolved itself as a circular pore.

"Give us some distance!" the captain ordered.

"Brace for emergency acceleration . . . three, two, one, now," said another voice, and then everything went out of whack for a minute. People and stuff flew around. Loud clunks and hisses sounded. Everything that was loose ended up plastered against the bulkhead closest to the icosahedron as the capsule accelerated away from it. The woman holding the speelycaptor did her share of gasping and cursing. But soon enough she got it pointed back out the window. "Something is coming out of that port!" Jesry announced, and once again we were treated to a long, veering zoom-in. But this time the hole wasn't crisp-edged and black. It was pinkish, its boundaries ill-defined. The pink part was moving; it separated itself from the base of the icosahedron. It had been cast off. It was adrift in space. The hole irised shut behind it.

"That doesn't look like a nuke," someone said.

"Understatement of the year," Sammann muttered.

"Move in on it."

"Brace for acceleration . . . three two, one, now." There was another messy scene as the capsule reversed its direction and began heading back toward the icosahedron. Yet again we had to wait as the indefatigable woman with the speelycaptor made her way back to that tiny, filthy window and re-acquired the shot.

She gasped.

So did I.

"What is it?" asked one of the voices. They couldn't see what she—what I—could see because they weren't peering at it through magnifying optics.

"It's him," said the woman holding the speelycaptor. "It's the Warden of Heaven!" She refrained from mentioning one important detail, which was that he was stark naked. "They threw the Warden of Heaven out the airlock!"

Sammann stopped it. "That has become the hip catch phrase of the moment," he told me. "Technically, though, it's not an airlock. It's the port where they spit out the little nukes."

The Warden at this point was still small and poorly resolved, but he had been getting bigger, and I had been steeling myself for what he would look like close-up. "I can keep playing it if you want," Sammann offered, none too enthusiastically, "or—"

"I've seen enough gore for one day, thanks," I said. "Don't you explode or something?"

"There was a little bit of that. By the time they got him back into the capsule—well, it was a mess."

"So the Geometers just—executed him?"

"This is not known. He might have died of natural causes. They found a burst aneurysm on autopsy."

"I imagine they found a *lot* of burst stuff!"

"Eew!" Cord said from up front.

"Exactly—so it's hard to say whether it blew before or after he was thrown out."

"Have the Geometers sent out any communications since this happened?"

"We'd have no way of knowing that. This speely was leaked. Other than that, the Powers That Be have managed to control information pretty effectively."

"Is *everyone* looking at this speely? Does the whole world know about it?"

"The Powers That Be have shut down most of the Reticulum in order to control propagation of this speely," Sammann said. "So only a few people have seen it. Most people, if they've heard any-thing, have only heard rumors."

"That's almost worse than facts," I said, and told him about Magister Sark. "When did this happen?" I asked.

"While we were going over the pole," he said. "The capsule landed a day later. Everyone except the Warden was safe and sound. Meanwhile the military had begun moving toward the poles, as you found out."

"Which makes no sense to me," I mentioned.

"I'm told that the Hedron is in an orbit that confines its ground track to a belt around the Equator . . ."

"Yes, and so if you go to the far north or south you can get out from under it—"

"And maybe out of reach of its weapons?"

"Depends on what kind of weapons they are. But the part that doesn't make sense to me is that the Geometers could change their orbit any time they wanted to. The first few months they were here, they were in a polar orbit, remember?"

"Yes, of course I remember," Sammann said.

"Then they changed and . . ."

"And what?" Sammann asked after a while, since I'd gone si-lent.

". . . and I saw—Ala and I saw—light from the nukes that they fired to make that change in their orbit. 'Plane change maneuvers are expensive.' For them to change *back* to a polar orbit *now*—where they could shoot down on our military forces at the poles—they'd have to fire that many nukes again." I looked at Sammann. "They're out of fuel."

"You mean . . . out of nukes?"

"Yeah. Nuclear bombs are the fuel that makes the ship go. They can only store so many of them. When they run low, they have to . . ."

"To go get more," Sammann said.

"Which means zeroing in on a technically advanced civiliza-tion and raiding them. Pillaging their stockpile of nuclear material. Which, in our case, means—"

"Edhar, Rambalf, and Tredegarh," Sammann said.

"That was the message they were sending on the night that the lasers shone down," I said, "the night I was Evoked."

"The night Fraa Orolo walked down off Bly's Butte," Cord put in, "and headed for Ecba."

Part 8

ORITHENA

The drive south went fast. We did it in four days and three nights. We were almost out of money, so we camped. Yul cooked our breakfasts and suppers. We saved our money for fuel and for lunch, passing through the mass-produced restaurants and fueling stations like ghosts.

During the first day or so, the landscape was dominated by endless tracts of fuel trees, relieved by small cities surrounding the plants where they were shredded and cooked to produce liquid fuel. Then we had two days of the most densely populated territory I had ever seen. The landscape was indistinguishable from that of the continent where we had started: the same signs and stores everywhere. The cities were so close that their fauxburbs touched one another and we never saw any open countryside, just pulsed along the highway-network from one traffic jam to the next. I saw several concents. They were always in the distance, for they tended to be built on hilltops or in ancient city centers that great highways swerved to avoid. One of these, by coincidence, happened to be Saunt Rambalf. It was built on an elevated mass of igneous rock several miles wide.

I thought about harrowing. When Alwash had used that word on me back on the ship, I'd thought it was funny. But after what had happened in Mahsht, I really did feel harrowed. Not in the sense of a weed that had been pulled out and burned, but in the sense of what was left after the harrowing had been finished: a plant, young, weak, survival still uncertain. But standing alone and alive, with nothing around it that might interfere with its growth or that could protect it from whatever blasts came its way tomorrow.

Late on the third day the landscape began to open up and to smell of something other, more ancient, than tires and fuel. We camped under trees and packed away our warm clothes. Breakfast the fourth day was made from things Cord and Yul had purchased from farmers. We drove into a landscape that had been settled and cultivated since the days of the Bazian Empire. Its population had, of course, waxed and waned countless times since then. Lately it had waned. The faux-burbs and then the cities had withered, leaving what I thought of as the intransigent strongholds of civilization: wealthy people's villas, maths, monasteries, arks, expensive restaurants, suvins, resorts, retreat centers, hospitals, governmental installations. Little stood between these save open country and surprisingly primitive agriculture. Tufts of scrawny, garishly colored businesses sprouted at road-junctions, just to keep the riffraff like us moving, but most of the buildings were stone or mud with slate or tile roofs. The landscape became more sere and open as we moved along. The roads shed lanes, then insensibly narrowed, grew rougher and more tortuous, until without having noticed any sudden transitions we found ourselves driving on endless one-lane tracks and stopping to avoid flocks of livestock so tough and emaciated they looked like jerky on the hoof.

Late on the fourth day we came over a little rise and beheld in the distance a naked mountain. Mountains for me had always borne dark green pelts, shaggy with mist. But this one looked as though acid had been poured on it and burned off everything alive. It had the same structure of ridges and cols as the mountains I was used to but it was as bald as the head of a Ringing Vale avout. The pink-orange light of the setting sun made it glow like flesh in candlelight. I was so taken by its appearance that I stared at it for quite a while before I realized that there was nothing behind it. A few more such mountains rose beyond it in the distance, but they rose from a flat and featureless geometric plane, dark grey: an ocean.

That night we camped on a beach beside the Sea of Seas. The next morning we drove the vehicles down a ramp onto the ferry that took us to the Island of Ecba.

Semantic Faculties: Factions within the mathic world, in the years following the Reconstitution, generally claiming descent from Halikaarn. So named because they believed that symbols could bear actual semantic content. The idea is traceable to Protas and to Hylaea before him. Compare **Syntactic Faculties.**

—THE DICTIONARY, 4th edition, A.R. 3000

The light through the tent-cloth roused, the surf on the beach lulled, and like a log rolling up and down in the breakers I'd rocked any number of times between sleeping and waking as I nursed a vague and uneventful dream about the Geometers. Some part of my mind had become obsessed with the remote manipulator arms on the probe that they had sent out to fetch the Warden of Heaven, and had been consuming vast dark energies dwelling on them, sharpening and embellishing my memories, building them up into a hybrid of seen and imagined, theorics and art, that encoded all sorts of weird ideas and fears and hopes. I fended off wakefulness as long as I could, since that would lose me the dream, and I lay there half-conscious, waiting for something to happen, willing the dream to move ahead, to reveal something; but I only grew more restless, for nothing occurred but what sprang from my own thinking: endlessly deeper study of the joints, bones, bearings, and actuators of those arms, which in my imagination had become as complex as my own arms and hands, and styled with the same organic curves as the parts of our clock that Cord used to make for Sammann. The only new thing that developed in that dreaming was that, at the very end, I turned my attention from the arms to the imaging devices that I guessed must be present on the bodies of those probes. But those lenses—supposing they were there—were guarded by clusters of spotlights, and when I tried to stare into them and meet the Geometers' gaze, all I could see was explosions of glare held apart by utter blackness.

Frustration succeeded in waking me up where daylight, the smell of cooking food, and the others' conversation had failed. I could not move matters forward save by waking up and doing something.

Ecba was beautiful, in a hot and harsh way. It had taken us a day simply to erect defenses against sun and heat. We'd found an east-facing cove north of a precipitous rocky headland that afforded us shade for much of the day, and Yul had showed us ways to anchor stakes deep in the sand, which enabled us to put up tarps that blocked the late afternoon sun. The only time we really got blasted with it was first thing in the morning, before the heat got too bad. A smaller island half a mile offshore broke and diffracted incoming surf, so waves here were small but unpredictable. The cove was too shallow and rock-bound to be of use to any but the smallest boats, so it had never, as far as we could tell, been settled or used for anything. We kept expecting someone to rush up, gaudy with insignias, and eject us, but it didn't happen. The place did not seem to be private property. It was not a park. It was simply there. Ecba's only real settlement (other than the math at Orithena) enveloped the ferry terminal, five miles away in a straight line, fifteen by the road that traversed the island's shore. A desalination plant, powered by the sun, made and sold water there. Yul had filled a couple of musty-smelling military surplus water bladders when we had arrived. Between that and the food we'd bought from farmers on the mainland, we wouldn't really have to make another supply run for a week.

The day after we'd made the camp and pitched the tarps had been, by unspoken, unanimous agreement, a time to rest. Beat-up books had appeared from bottoms of bags. Someone was always snoring, someone always swimming. I borrowed a pair of long-nosed pliers from Cord and yanked my stitches out, then sat in the surf up to my neck until the wounds went numb. There is more I could, but won't, say about healing. Watching my body marshal its forces of regeneration was fascinating at the time, and probably accounted for the weird dreams I had been having about the metallic limbs and crystal organs of the alien probe. There was the temptation to ponder and philosophize about the relationship between mind and body. But the Lorite in me said it would be a waste of time. More efficient to find a library and read what better thinkers had written on it.

Late yesterday, Yul had shattered the calm of the place by starting the engine of Cord's fetch, and some of us had gone for a dawdling, two-hour circumnavigation of the island. The location of the volcano was, of course, no secret; there was hardly a place from which it couldn't be seen. It was steep, which, as Fraa Haligastreme had taught me, meant that it was dangerous. Some volcanoes produced runny lava that spread out quickly; these were lens-shaped and safe, provided you could walk faster than the lava. Others made thick lava that moved slowly and built steep slopes; these were dangerous because pent-up pressure had no outlet except for explosions.

This island was the last stop on a ferry route that ran generally south-southeast from the mainland, so we'd steamed into it from the north. The terminal and town were built around the island's only surviving harbor, a bite chomped out of the northwest limb of the approximately round island. Our camp was in the northeast, in one of a series of closely spaced coves separated by fingers of hardened magma that had reached down from the caldera many centuries before Ecba had been settled. So all of our views, during those first few days, had been of the north face of the volcano, which looked regular and graceful—even if Haligastreme's voice was in my ear telling me it was dangerously steep. Yesterday's drive had taken us clockwise around the island, passing down its eastern shore, and after a few miles we had suddenly come in view of its south slope, which had exploded and collapsed in −2621, burying the Temple of Orithena, and filling in and obliterating a harbor on the island's southeastern coast into which the early physiologers—followers of Cnoüs from all round the Sea of Seas—had once voyaged in their galleys and sailing-ships. Anyone could see at a glance that it was the result of an explosion. The ash and rubble sloped straight from summit to sea. So slow had Ecba been to recover that the road, even now, faltered as it came up on to the rubble-fan, and became an informal dirt track for several miles. There were no signs, no buildings or improvements. At one point, though, as we had slowly rounded the island's southeastern curve, and had come to a place where we could look straight up into the yawning rupture in the volcano's cone, we had seen a separate track, teed into the coastal road, that ran straight uphill for some distance, then veered off into the first of a series of switch-backs. These ascended a bare slope whose skyline was reinforced by a dark wall. We hadn't needed Sammann's satellite imagery to know that this was the math that had been a-building there since 3000.

Halfway between us and it, at the beginning of the switchbacks, a few low buildings struggled to keep their roofs above the drifting ash. We had gone up there and found several avout running a sort of checkpoint and souvenir stand. They had all worn bolts and chords openly. We had told them no lies, but behaved as if we were tourists. They had been pleased to sell us things (soap made with volcanic ash) but had let us know we could not drive any farther up the road.

Later, as we had paused in town to pick up supplies, I had again seen bolted and chorded avout walking around openly. They had not seemed like hierarchs. This had been, then, a violation of the Discipline—as was letting avout run a souvenir stand. But too it let us know that relations between avout and extras were much friend-lier here than, say, in Mahsht. I had badly wanted to approach those avout and ask them if they knew of Orolo, but had checked myself, reasoning that they would still be here tomorrow, and it was better to sleep on it. And sleep on it I had, but this had booted me nothing but that endless, frustrating dream about remote manipulator arms.

Having slept so poorly, I didn't say much at breakfast until I came out with: "Suppose there *are* no biological Geometers—creatures with bodies like ours, sitting at the controls of those machines. What if they died long ago and left behind ships and probes that run an automated program?"

This turned out to be an absolute conversation-killer except in the case of Sammann, who seemed delighted by the idea. "So much the better for us," he said, which puzzled me for a moment until I perceived that by *us* he meant the Ita.

I considered it. "Makes you more useful to the Sæcular Power, you mean."

His face froze for a while and I knew I'd offended him. "Perhaps being useful to them isn't the *only* thing we care about," he suggested. "Perhaps the Ita can have other aspirations."

"Sorry."

"Think what a fascinating problem it would be, to interact with such a system!" he exclaimed. I had gotten off easy. He was so thrilled by this idea that he wasn't going to dwell on my slur. "At its lowest level, it would be a fully deterministic syndev. But it would express itself only in certain actions: movements of the ship, transmissions of data, and so on. Observables."

"We'd use *givens,* but go on."

"To grasp the workings of the syntactic program by analyzing those givens would be a sort of code-breaking effort. We Ita would have to have our own Convox."

"You could solve the Aboutness Problem once and for all," I suggested, half serious.

He lowered his gaze from enraptured study of the sky and stared at me. "You've studied the AP?"

I shrugged. "Probably not as much as you have. We learn about it when we study the early history of the Split."

"Between the followers of Saunt Proc and the disciples of Saunt Halikaarn."

"Yeah. Though it's a little unfair to call one group followers and the other disciples, if you see what I mean. Anyway, that's what we call the Split."

"Procians were more friendly to the syntactic point of view . . . or maybe I should have said Faanians . . ."

Sammann seemed a little shaky here, so I reminded him: "We're speaking, remember, of Aboutness. You and I can think *about* things. Symbols in our brains have meanings. The question is, can a syntactic device think about things, or merely process digits that have no Aboutness—no meaning—"

"No semantic content," Sammann said.

"Yes. Now, at the Concent of Saunt Muncoster, just after the Reconstitution, Faan was the FAE of the Syntactic Faculty—followers of Proc. She took the view that Aboutness didn't exist—was an illusion that any sufficiently advanced syndev creates for itself. By this time Evenedric was already dead but he like Halikaarn before him had taken the view that our minds could do things that syndevs couldn't—that Aboutness was real—"

"That our thoughts really did have semantic content over and above the ones and zeroes."

"Yes. It's related to the notion that our minds are capable of perceiving ideal forms in the Hylaean Theoric World."

"Would you people mind!?" Yul bellowed. "We're trying to have a campout here!"

"This is what we do to relax," Sammann shot back.

"Yeah," I said, "if we were *working,* we'd talk about things that were *tedious* and *complicated.*"

"It's worse than listening to preachers!" Yul complained, but Gnel refused to rise to the bait.

"Let me explain it in words you can understand, cousin," Gnel said. "If the aliens are just a big computer program, Sammann here can shut them down just by flipping one bit. The program won't even know it's being sabotaged."

"Only if it does not have Aboutness," I cautioned him. "If it's capable of understanding that its symbols are *about* something, then it'll know that Sammann is up to no good."

"It would have to have crazy security measures built in," Yul said, "what with all those nukes and so on."

"If it lacks Aboutness, it is incredibly vulnerable, so yes," Sammann said. "But systems with true Aboutness, or so the myth goes, should be much more difficult to deceive."

"Nah," Yul said, and looked at his cousin again. "You just have to deceive 'em in a different way."

"Apparently the Warden of Heaven was not very convincing," Gnel pointed out, "so maybe preaching isn't as easy as you think."

Cord cleared her throat and frowned at her bowl. "Uh, not that this isn't fascinating, but what is the plan for today?"

This produced a long silence. Cord followed up with, "I like it here, but it's beginning to feel creepy. Does anyone else think it's creepy?"

"You're talking to a bunch of guys," Yul said. "No one here is going to validate your feelings." She tossed sand at him.

"I've been doing some research," Sammann said, "which was creepy in itself, because I didn't understand why I should have such good Reticulum access in such a godforsaken place . . ."

"But you understand it now?" Gnel asked.

"Yes, I think so."

"What did you learn?"

"The whole island is a single parcel, owned by a single entity. Has been since the Old Mathic Age. Back in those days it was a petty principality. Got kicked back and forth between different empires from age to age. When kings and princes went out of style it would pass into the hands of a private owner or a trust. When they came back into fashion, it'd get a prince or a baron or something again. But nine hundred years ago it was purchased by a private foundation— that's a thing like a Dowment. And they must have had ties to the mathic world—"

"Because the Orithena dig—the new concent we saw yesterday— was sponsored by them?"

"Sponsored, or something," Sammann said.

"A single Apert—ten days—isn't long enough to organize such a big project," I pointed out. "This Dowment must have been a long time making its plans."

"It's not so hard," Cord said. "The Unarians have Apert once a year. It's easy to talk to them. Some graduate and become Tenners. Some of those become Hundreders, and so on. If these guys started working on it in 2800, by the time of the Millennial Convox of 3000 they could have had supporters everywhere except in Thousander maths."

I was uneasy with Cord's scenario because it sounded sneaky, but I couldn't dispute the facts she'd stated. I guess what troubled me about it was that we, the avout, liked to believe that we were the only long-term thinkers, the only ones capable of hatching plans over centuries, and her scenario envisioned a Dowment in the Sæcular world turning the tables on us.

Perhaps Sammann was harboring similar feelings. "It could just as well have worked the other direction," he said.

"What—" I exclaimed, "are you saying that a bunch of avout created a Dowment in the Sæcular world to buy them an island? That's outrageous."

But we all knew Sammann had won that exchange, because he was relaxed, satisfied. I was angry and off balance. Largely because this all fit so neatly into what I had been told, in recent weeks, about the Lineage.

Still, everyone seemed to be looking at me for a response. "If it's like you say, Sammann, then they—whoever *they* are—know we're here anyway. I think we should take the direct approach. Drive down there. I'll just walk up to the gate, knock, and state my business."

That got all of us on our feet, getting ready for the day, except for Gnel who just followed Sammann around. "There must be more information about what sort of entity bought the island. I mean, come on! How many things last nine hundred years in this world?"

"Lots of things," Sammann said. "As an example, that ark you belong to has lasted quite a bit longer . . ." He turned and searched Gnel's face. "That's your point, isn't it? You think this is some kind of religious institution?"

Gnel was a little taken aback, and seemed to back down. "I'm just saying, businesses don't last that long."

"But it's quite a stretch to go from that to saying that Ecba is run by a secret ark."

"When I see avout walking openly in the streets of the town," Gnel said, "it tells me we need to 'stretch' beyond normal explanations."

"We saw avout in the streets of Mahsht. Maybe the ones here just got Evoked or something," said Yul, getting into the act.

I don't think that this seemed plausible to any of us—Yul included—but it brought us to an impasse. "Many avout," I said, "especially Procian/Faanian ones, think that belief in the Hylaean Theoric World is basically a religion anyway. And I have reason to believe that the avout down there at Orithena are the ultimate fringe of HTW believers. So whether it's a religious community or not sort of depends on how you define your terms." I faltered as I said that last bit, just imagining how Orolo would plane me if he heard me talking Sphenic gibberish. Even Sammann turned to fix me with an incredulous look. But he didn't say anything, because I think he understood that I was just trying to get us moving. "Look," I said to Gnel, "Sammann's investigation just got started, and we've seen before that it can sometimes take a few days for him to get access to certain things. Whether or not they open the gates for me at Orithena, you'll have plenty of time to ask around and learn more in days to come."

"Yes," Gnel said, "but whether they open those gates for you depends on what you say. And that depends on what you know. So maybe it's better to wait for a couple of days."

"I know more than I'm saying," I said, "and I want to go there today."

○○

Metekoranes: A theor of ancient times, exceptionally gifted at plane geometry but usually silent in Dialogs, who was buried under volcanic ash in the eruption that destroyed Orithena. According to those traditions that believe in the existence of the Old Lineage, the founder (though probably unwittingly) of same.

—THE DICTIONARY, *4th edition, A.R. 3000*

Two hours later I was standing alone at the gates of Orithena.

The wall was twenty feet high, made of blocks of fine-grained, grey-brown stone that were all the same size and shape. As I stood there, sweating in the sun, waiting for an answer to my knock, I had more than enough time to examine these and to conclude that they had been cast in molds, using some process that fused loose volcanic ash into a sort of concrete. Each was about the size of a small wheelbarrow, say the largest that a couple of avout could move around using simple tools. Anyway the courses were extremely regular, since all of the blocks were clones. Some were slightly browner, some slightly greyer, but on the whole the wall looked as if it had been snapped together out of a child's building toy kit. The gates themselves were steel plates, which would last a good long while in this climate. After knocking, I stepped well back to get clear of the stored heat radiating from those panels, which were large enough to admit two of the largest drummons abreast. I turned and looked back at the souvenir stand, a few hundred feet down the hill. Cord, leaning back against the shady side of Yul's fetch, waved at me. Sammann took a picture on his jeejah.

The gate was framed between a pair of cylindrical bastions perforated with small gridded windows. The one on the left sported a tiny door, also of steel. After some time had passed, I ambled over and knocked on it. Framed in its upper half was a hatch, just about the size of my hand. Ten minutes or so later, I heard movement on the other side. A door opened, then slammed shut within the bastion. A latch scrabbled. The little hatch creaked open. The room on the other side of it was dark and, I guessed, delightfully cool. But my eyes were adjusted to the blasting sun of an Ecba noon, and I could see nothing.

"Know that you address a world that is not your own and into which you may not pass save that you make a solemn vow not to leave it again," said a woman's voice, speaking in locally accented Fluccish. This was what she was supposed to do. Gatekeepers in places like this had been saying this, or some variant of it, since Cartas.

"Greetings, my suur," I said, "let us speak in Orth if you please. I am Fraa Erasmas of the Edharian chapter of the Decenarian math of the Concent of Saunt Edhar."

A pause, then the hatch closed and was latched. I waited for a while. Then the hatch opened again and I heard a deeper, older woman's voice.

"I am Dymma," she said.

"Greetings, Suur Dymma. Fraa Erasmas at your service."

"That I am your suur, or you my fraa, is very much undecided in my mind, as you come so attired."

"I have traveled far," I returned. "My bolt, chord, and sphere were stolen from me as I made peregrin across the Sæculum."

"No Convox is summoned hither. We do not look for peregrins."

"It seems inhospitable," I said, "that Orithena, whence the first Peregrins departed, should not open her gates for one who has returned."

"Our duty is to the Discipline, not to any custom of hospitality. There are hotels in town; hospitality is their business." The little hatch made a noise as if she were getting ready to close it.

"What part of the Discipline permits avout to sell soap extramuros?" I asked. "Where does the Discipline state that bolted fraas may stroll about yonder town?"

"Your discourse belies your claim to be avout," said Dymma, "as a fraa would know that there are variations in the Discipline from one math to the next."

"Many avout would not know it since they never leave their own maths," I demurred.

"Precisely," Dymma said, and I could imagine her smirking in the dark at how deftly she had turned the point to her advantage—for I was on the outside, where no avout should be.

"I grant that your customs may differ from those of the rest of the mathic world," I began.

She interrupted me. "Not so much so that we would admit one who had not sworn the Vow."

"Did Orolo swear the Vow, then?"

A few seconds of silence. Then she closed the hatch.

I waited. After a while I turned back, waved to my friends, and pantomimed a big shrug. It was strangely difficult to reconnect with them, even in such a simple gesture, after having stared over the threshold of the math. I'd bid goodbye to them a few minutes ago as if I'd be back in time for lunch. But for all I knew I might end up spending the rest of my life there.

The hatch again. "State your business, you who style yourself Fraa Erasmas," said a man in Orth.

"Fraa Jad, Millenarian, would know Orolo's mind on certain matters, and sends me in quest of him."

"Orolo who was Thrown Back?"

"The same."

"One on whom the Anathem has been rung down may never more go into a math," the man pointed out. "And for that matter, one who has been Evoked, and despatched to Convox at Tredegarh, may not suddenly present himself at a different math on the other side of the world."

I had already suspected the answer before we reached Ecba. Certain clues had bolstered my hypothesis. But, strangely, what clinched it for me was the architecture of the place. No concessions to the Mathic style here. "The riddle that you pose is a trying one," I admitted, "however, on reflection, its answer is clear."

"Oh? What is its answer then?"

"This is not a math," I said.

"What is it if not a math?"

"The cloister of a lineage that was born a thousand years before Cartas and her Discipline."

"You are well come to Orithena, Fraa Erasmas."

Heavy bolts moved and the door swung open.

I stepped forward into Orithena, and into the Lineage.

At Saunt Edhar, Orolo had grown a little doughy, though he kept in decent shape by working in his vineyard and climbing the steps to the starhenge. At Bly's Butte, according to Estemard's phototypes, he had lost some of that weight and gone shaggy-headed and grown the obligatory Feral beard. But when I picked him up at the gates of Orithena and spun him around five times, his body felt solid, neither fat nor emaciated, and when I finally let him go, tears were making wet tracks down his tanned and clean-shaven cheeks. That was all I saw before my vision was blurred with tears, and then I had to break away and walk to and fro in the shade of the great wall to get my composure back. The Discipline had taught me nothing of how to cope with such an event: throwing my arms around a dead man. Perhaps it meant that I too was now dead to the mathic world, and had moved on to a sort of afterlife. Cord, Yul, Gnel and Sammann had served as my pallbearers.

It took a powerful effort of will to remember that they were still out there, wondering what was going on.

There was a little fountain in the cloister. Orolo fetched me a ladle of water. We sat together in the shade of the clock-tower as I drank. It tasted of sulfur.

Where to begin? "There's so much I would have said to you, Pa, if I could have, when you were Thrown Back. So much I wanted to say to you in the weeks following. But . . ."

"It all flows back."

"Beg pardon?"

"Those things flow back in time and as they do they change—your mind changes them—so that they no longer need talking about quite so much. Fine. Let's talk of what is fresh and interesting."

"All right. You're looking well."

"You aren't. Scars honorably earned, I hope?"

"Not really. Learned a lot though." But I did not really feel like telling him the story. We made idle chitchat for a few minutes until we both realized how ridiculous it was, then got up and began to prowl around. A younger fraa—if that was the correct term for one who lived in a math-that-was-not-a-math—brought me a bolt and chord, which I traded for my Sæcular clothes. Then Orolo led me away from the cloister along a broad path, beaten down by countless sandaled feet and barrow-wheels, to the edge of a pit big enough to swallow the Mynster of Saunt Edhar several times over. If we had built our monument by piling stone on stone, building up from the ground, they had built theirs by digging down, a shovel-load at a time. The walls of the hole were too steep, the soil too loose to be stable; they had shored it up using slabs of fused ash. A ramp spiraled down to the bottom. I started down it, but Orolo held me back. "You'll notice there are no people down there. It gets hotter as you descend. We dig at night. If you insist on going for a hike, we'll ascend." And he gestured up the mountainside.

I already knew from Sammann's pictures and from yesterday's

scouting trip that Orithena had two wall-systems, an inner and an outer. They coincided along the road, where the main gate stood. The huge twenty-foot wall enclosed the cloister where the avout lived, and the hole in the ground where they delved. The outer wall was much lower—perhaps six feet high—so, more symbolic than anything else. It reached thousands of feet up the mountainside, embracing a strip of ground that ran all the way to the volcano's caldera. It was clear from the pictures that mine-works had been created up at the top, possibly to extract energy from the volcano's heat. So there I reckoned it would be hot, foul-smelling, and dangerous. But the territory in between—what Orolo and I walked through—had been transformed into an oasis by the labor of the Lineage. Somehow they had found water and used it to raise vines, grain, and all manner of trees that yielded fruits and oils while casting dappled shade on the path up the mountain. The temperature dropped a little, the breeze freshened, with every step. The effort of climbing kept me warm, but when we reached a suitable altitude to stop, enjoy the view, and nibble at the fruits we'd pilfered along the way, my sweat dried instantly in the cool dry wind off the sea and I had to wrap myself up.

We passed beyond the upper limit of Orithena's orchards and wandered through a belt of twisted, gnarled trees to a sloping meadow dusted with what had looked, from a distance, like frost. But it was actually a carpet of tiny white wildflowers that somehow found a way to grow here. Colorful insects flew around but there weren't enough of them to be obnoxious. They were kept in check, I guessed, by the birds, who sang from perches in scrub-trees and bursts of spiky vegetation. We sat on the exposed root of a tree that must have been planted the spring after the volcano had gone off. Orolo explained that these trees, which were no taller than I, were in fact the oldest living things on Arbre.

Most of our conversation that afternoon consisted of such tour-guide stuff. In a way it was a great relief to chatter about birds and trees, and how many cubic feet of earth had been removed from the dig and how many of the Temple buildings had been excavated, rather than talking of such weighty affairs as the Geometers, the Convox, and the Lineage. Later we hiked down and supped at the Refectory with the hundred or so fraas and suurs who lived here. Their FAE, Fraa Landasher, the third of the three who'd interrogated me at the gate, formally bade me welcome and made a toast in my name. I drank more than my share of their wine, which was infinitely better than what Orolo made in his frostbitten vineyard at Saunt Edhar, and slept it off in a private cell.

I awoke sour, hung over, out of sorts, thinking it was late and that I'd overslept—but no, it was early, and the night shift of diggers were coming up out of the pit with their picks, trowels, brushes, and notebooks, singing hilarious marching-songs. They'd constructed a bathhouse where hot water was sluiced down from volcanic springs and routed through vertical shafts where you could get blasted clean in about ten seconds. I stood in one of those until I could no longer breathe, then stepped out and let my newmatter bolt pull the water off my skin. This helped a little. But what was really throwing me for a loop was the re-entry shock of being back in the mathic world, with its view of time so different from what I'd grown used to extramuros. Making it worse was that no one had explained the place's rules to me yet. In most ways it was like a Cartasian math. But they'd not made me swear a vow, and I got the sense that I could walk out the door whenever I chose. They just *pretended* it was a math when they were dealing with anyone who might not understand. Being avout was their cover story. And yet it was no lie, for they were as dedicated to their work as any who lived in Saunt Edhar. Perhaps more so, in that they wouldn't suffer that work to be impeded by rules, would not submit to the dictates of any Inquisition.

Fraa Landasher intercepted me coming out of the sluice-bath and introduced me to Suur Spry, a girl of about my age. Or rather reintroduced me, since she was the first person I'd spoken with yesterday at the gate. She reminded me disconcertingly of Ala. It was now or never, explained Landasher, for me to descend and see the ruins, for if we waited any longer it would be too hot. Suur Spry was to be my guide; she'd packed a basket of food that we could nibble on as we went. It was clear from the looks on their faces that they expected I'd be thrilled. And what would be more reasonable? Yet I had to feign gratitude because what I really wanted was to awaken Orolo and talk to him of pressing Sæcular matters.

Not having known what might happen at the gate, I'd made the plan yesterday with Cord, Yul, Gnel, and Sammann that if I was allowed to go inside, they should wait for an hour and then, if nothing happened, come back three days later, at which time I'd try to get word out to them as to what ought to be done next. I felt that my three days were flying by, and so in truth I did not want to go on a long tourist hike with some girl I'd only just met. It was in a peevish mood that I began to descend the ramp, carrying Suur Spry's picnic-basket on one arm.

It was in an altogether different mood, though, that I reached the bottom, kicked off my sandals, and felt under my bare feet the paving-stones on which Adrakhones had walked. The Temple steps where Diax had brandished his Rake. The Analemma where generations of physiologer-priests had celebrated Provener. And the tile-strewn Decagon where Metekoranes had stood, lost in thought, as the whole place was buried under ash.

"Did you find him?" I asked Spry, a few minutes later, as we were munching on some fruit and drinking water from the basket.

"Who—Metekoranes?"

"Yes."

"Yes. He was the first one we—I mean they, my forerunners— looked for. They found, standing upright, a—" She balked, looking awed and disgusted.

"Skeleton?"

"A cast," she said, "a cast of his whole body. You can look at it if you want. Of course it's just speculation that it is the actual Metekoranes. But it fits perfectly with the legend. He even had his head bowed, you know, as if he were looking at the tiles."

The plaza where we were enjoying our little picnic—the one where Metekoranes had been buried and cast in stone—was the Teglon made real. It was flat, decagonal, maybe two hundred feet across, paved in smooth slabs of marble. In ancient times the plaza had been plentifully supplied with tiles made of clay baked in molds.

There were seven molds, hence seven different shapes of tile. Their shapes were such that it was possible to fit them together in an infinite number of patterns. That's not possible with squares, or equilateral triangles; those fit together in repeating patterns, so there are no choices to make. But as long as you had more copies of the Teglon tiles, you could go on making choices forever. Hundreds of tiles were scattered around the place even now, and from place to place the modern-day Orithenans had been putting them together in little arrangements. I squatted down and looked at one, then looked questioningly at Spry. "Go ahead," she said, "it's a modern reproduction. We found the original molds!"

I picked up a tile for a closer look. This one happened to be four-sided: a rhombus. A groove was molded into its surface, curving from one of its sides to another. I carried it over to the nearest vertex of the Decagon and set it down; its obtuse angle fit perfectly into the corner.

"Ah," Suur Spry teased me, "going straight to the most difficult problem of all, huh?"

She was talking, of course, of the Teglon. She turned away and walked to the opposite vertex and set a tile down there. Meanwhile I scavenged a few other tiles, getting samples of all seven shapes. I chose one at random and set it next to the first. This one also had a groove curving from one side to another—all of the tiles were so made—and I rotated it until its groove mated with, and became a continuation of, the one on the first tile. Into the angle between them I was able to place a third. That created opportunities to slide in a fourth, a fifth, and so on. I was playing the Teglon. The objective of the game was to build the pattern outward from one vertex and pave the entire Decagon in such a way that the groove formed a continuous, unbroken curve from the first vertex to the last—the one directly opposite, where Suur Spry had put down a tile. Along the way, the curve had to pass across every tile in the entire Decagon. For the first little while, it was easy—it came naturally. But beyond a certain point, the two objectives—that of tiling the whole surface, and that of keeping the curve going—began to conflict. I had to leave a stretch of groove hanging unconnected for a while, then work my way back to it, steering the groove around to make the connection. That was satisfying. But a few minutes later I found myself with three such segments of marooned groove in different parts of the pattern, and despaired of ever finding an arrangement that would connect them all. On one level, this was all about the shape of the outer boundary, and how it developed. Tiles trapped in the middle were of no further interest to the game—or so you might think. But on the other hand, the way in which an interior tile had been laid down ended up determining the location of every other tile in the whole Decagon.

The ancient Orithenans suspected, but didn't know how to prove, that the tiles of the Teglon were aperiodic: that no pattern would ever repeat. Again, solving the Teglon would have been easy—it would have been automatic—with square or triangular tiles, or any tile system that was periodic. With aperiodic tiles, it was impossible, or at least very unlikely, unless you had some God-like ability to see the whole pattern in your head at once. Metekoranes had believed that the final pattern existed in the Hylaean Theoric World, and that the Teglon could only be solved by one who had developed the power of seeing into it.

Suur Spry was clearing her throat. I looked up. I was squatting at the edge of a system of tiles fifty feet wide. It was getting hot.

"Sorry," I said.

"Some people use sticks to push them around. Saves wear and tear on the back."

"We should probably get out of here, huh?"

"Soon," she allowed.

First, though, I followed her about as she showed me the remnants of the ancient buildings. All the roofs were gone, of course. Some pillars still stood, and a few courses of stone that had once been walls, now half-buried in blocks that had tumbled down from above. But mostly we were looking at foundations, floors, stairs, and plazas. Active parts of the dig were gridded with string, a geometric touch Adrakhones would have appreciated. The rocks were annotated with neatly brushed letters and numbers put down by diggers of centuries past. Up above, I knew, was a sort of museum where they'd placed many of the artifacts they had found, including presumably the cast of Metekoranes. I imagined that museum should be dark. Nicely ventilated. And cool. "Okay, let's get out of this barbecue pit," I proposed, and heard no argument from Suur Spry.

We had stayed later than expected. Partly because it had been fascinating. But—and this probably didn't say much for my character—mainly because this was the one thing I could do on this journey that would seem almost as cool as Jesry's space adventure.

My body had healed to the point where it was willing to cut me a little bit of slack, and so during the early part of the climb I was babbling about the Teglon just like all of those geometers of yore who'd gone crazy over it. Soon enough, though, my injuries began talking to me, and excitement was snuffed out by pain. The remainder of the hike was a long silent trudge. Another sluice-bath was called for. I fell asleep. When I woke up it was late afternoon. Orolo was on kitchen duty. I helped him. But we didn't really get to talk about anything. So more than one of my three days had been gobbled up just like that. Before we retired that evening I warned Orolo we must speak of important things the next day. So after breakfast the next morning we hiked back up to the meadow.

OOOOOOOOOOOOOOOOOOOOOOOOOOOOOOOOOOOOOOO

Sconic: One of a group of Praxic Age theors who gathered at the house of Lady Baritoe. They addressed the ramifications of the apparent fact that we do not perceive the physical universe directly, but only through the intermediation of our sensory organs.

—THE DICTIONARY, *4th edition, A.R. 3000*

"After I landed at Bly's Butte," Orolo said, "I was like one of those poor cosmographers, just after the Reconstitution, who couldn't use his atom smasher any more."

"Yes, I saw that telescope," I told him, "the pictures you tried to take of the icosahedron . . ."

He was shaking his head. "I could not see a thing with that. So, my work concerning the aliens had to be based on what I *could* observe."

This didn't make sense to me. "All right," I said, "what was that?"

He looked at me, mildly startled, as if it ought to have been obvious. "Myself."

I was nonplussed. Which only showed that I was dealing with the same old Orolo. "How would self-observation help you understand the Geometers?" I asked. For I had already mentioned to him that this was the term people were now using to denote the aliens.

"Well . . . the Sconics are not a bad place to start. Remember fly-bat-worm?"

I laughed. "Just got a refresher on that a couple of weeks ago. Arsibalt was explaining it to an extra who wanted to know why we didn't believe in God."

"Ah, but that's not what fly-bat-worm says," said Orolo. "It says only that pure thought alone doesn't enable us to draw any conclusions one way or another about things that are non-spatiotemporal—such as God."

"True."

"The same observations that the Sconics made about themselves must also be true of aliens' brains. No matter how different they might be from us in other respects, they must integrate sensory givens into a coherent model of what is around them—a model that must be hung on a spatiotemporal frame. And that, in a nutshell, is how they come to share our ideas about geometry."

"But they share more than that," I pointed out, "they appear to share the idea of Truth and of Proof."

"It is a reasonable enough supposition," Orolo said with a cautious shrug.

"More than that!" I protested. "They emblazoned the Adrakhonic Theorem on their ship!"

This was news to him. "Oh, really? How cheeky!"

"Didn't you see it?"

"I remind you that I was Thrown Back before I saw the last picture that I took of the alien ship."

"Of course. But I assumed you had taken other pictures before then—had been taking them for a long time."

"Streaks and blobs!" Orolo scoffed. "I was only learning how to capture a decent image of the thing."

"So you never saw the geometric proof—or the letters—or the four planets."

"That's correct," Orolo said.

"Well, there's much more that you have to know, if you want to think about the Geometers! All kinds of new givens!"

"I can see how excited you are about those new givens, Erasmas, and I wish you all the best in your study of them, but I'm afraid that for me it would all prove a distraction from the main line of the inquiry."

"The main line—I don't know what you mean."

"Evenedrician datonomy," Orolo said, as if this ought to have been quite obvious.

"Datonomy," I translated, "that would be study, or identification, of what is given?"

"Yes—givens in the sense of the basic thoughts and impressions that our minds have to work with. Saunt Evenedric pursued it late in his life, after he got locked out of *his* atom smasher. His immediate forerunner, of course, was Saunt Halikaarn. Halikaarn thought that Sconic thought was badly in need of an overhaul to bring it in line with all that had been discovered, since the time of Baritoe, about theorics and its marvelous applicability to the physical world."

"Well—how'd he make out?"

Orolo grimaced. "Many of the records were vaporized, but we think he was too busy demolishing Proc and kicking away all the ankle-biters Proc sent after him. The work fell to Evenedric."

"Has it been an important thing to the Lineage?"

Orolo gave me a queer look. "Not really. Oh, it's important in principle. But notoriously unsatisfying to work on. Except when great alien ships appear in orbit around one's planet."

"So, then . . . are you finding it satisfying *now*?"

"Let's be quite direct and say what we mean," Orolo said. "You fear that I'm navel-gazing. That on Bly's Butte I pursued this line of inquiry, not because it was really worthwhile, but simply because I didn't have hard givens about the Geometers. And that now that we have evidence that they are, or were, physically and mentally similar to us, this line of inquiry should be dropped."

"Yes," I said, "that's what I think."

"I happen to disagree," Orolo said. "But things have changed between us. We are no longer Pa and Fid but Fraa and Fraa, and fraas disagree, cordially, all the time."

"Thank you but it has certainly felt like a Pa/Fid conversation to this point."

"Largely because I have a bit of a head start on you."

I let this polite nothing pass without comment. "Listen, if I can tear you away from Evenedrician datonomy, we have to talk about Sæcular stuff for a minute."

"By all means," Orolo said.

"Several of us were Evoked to a Convox at Tredegarh," I said, for, unbelievably, Orolo had not yet expressed *any* curiosity as to why or how I'd turned up at Orithena. "One of the others was Fraa Jad, a Thousander. He accompanied me and Arsibalt and Lio to Bly's Butte—"

"And saw the leaves on the wall of my cell there."

"He—Jad—figured out quickly—*weirdly* quickly—that you had gone to Ecba and, I guess, that you had ideas about the Geometers that he wanted to know more of."

"It was neither quick nor weird," Orolo said. "All of these matters are connected. It would have been obvious to Fraa Jad as soon as he walked in."

"How? Do you guys communicate? Violate the Discipline?"

"What do you mean, 'you guys'? You are carrying around some melodramatic idea of the Lineage, aren't you?" Orolo said.

"Well, just look at this place!" I protested. "What is going on?"

"If I got interested in meteorology," Orolo said, "I'd spend a lot of time observing the weather. I would come to have much in common with other weather-watchers whom I'd never met. We would think similar thoughts as a natural result of observing the same phenomena. Nine-tenths of what you think of as mysterious Lineage machinations is explained by this."

"Except that instead of watching the weather you're thinking about Evendrician datonomy?"

"Close enough."

"But there was nothing about Evenedric or datonomy on the wall of your cell for Fraa Jad to see. Just material pertaining to Orithena, and a chart of the Lineage."

"What you identified as a chart of the Lineage was really a sort of family tree of those who have tried to make sense of the Hylaean Theoric World. And it turns out that if you trace the branches of that tree and, so to speak, prune off all the branches populated by fanatics, Enthusiasts, Deolaters, and dead-enders, you end up with something that doesn't look so much like a tree any more. It looks like a dowel. It starts with Cnoüs and runs through Metekoranes and Protas and some others, and about halfway along you encounter Evenedric."

"So Fraa Jad, looking at your tree-pruned-down-to-a-dowel, would guess immediately that you must be working on Evenedrician datonomy."

"And would assume I was doing so in hopes of gaining upsight as to how the Geometers' minds must be organized."

"What about Ecba? How'd he guess you went to Ecba?"

"This math was founded by people who lived in the same cells where Fraa Jad has spent his whole life. He would know or surmise that if I could get to this place they would let me in the gates and provide me with food and shelter—quite obviously a better existence than what I could manage at Bly's Butte."

"Okay." I was feeling relieved of a burden I'd been carrying since that day above Samble. "So there's not a conspiracy. The Lineage doesn't communicate through coded messages."

"We communicate all the time," Orolo said, "in the way I mentioned."

"Meteorologists watching the same cloud."

"That's good enough for this stage of our conversation," Orolo said. "But you haven't yet unburdened yourself of whatever terribly important-seeming message or mission you brought in the gates with you. What errand has Fraa Jad sent you on?"

"He said 'go north until you understand.' And I guess that part of the mission is accomplished now."

"Oh really? I'm pleased that you understand. I'm afraid I am still full of questions about these matters."

"You know what I mean!" I snapped. "He also implied I was to come back to Tredegarh later. That he'd see to it I didn't get in trouble. I guess he wanted me to fetch you. To bring you back to the Convox."

"In case I'd developed any ideas, concerning the Geometers, that might be useful," Orolo hazarded.

"Well, that's the point of a Convox," I reminded him, "to be useful."

Orolo shrugged. "I'm afraid I don't have enough givens to work with, concerning the Geometers."

"I'm sure that all the givens that there are to be had, are available at Tredegarh."

"They are probably collecting exactly the wrong sort of information," he said.

"So go there and tell them what to collect! Fraa Jad could use your help."

"For me and Fraa Jad and some others of like mind to try to change the behavior of this Sæcular/Mathic monstrosity called a Convox sounds like politics, which I am infamously bad at."

"Then let me try to help!" I said. "Tell me what you've been doing. I'll go back to the Convox and look for ways to use it."

The most charitable way to interpret the look Orolo now gave me was affectionate but concerned. He waited for my brain to catch up with my mouth.

"Okay," I said, "with a little help from some of the others, maybe." I was thinking of the conversation I'd had with Tulia before Eliger.

"I can't advise you on what to do at the Convox," he finally said, "however, I am happy to explain what I've been up to."

"Okay—I'll settle for that."

"It won't help you—in fact, it'll probably hurt you—at the Convox. Because it will sound crazy."

"Fine. I'm used to people thinking that we are crazy because of the whole HTW thing!"

Orolo raised an eyebrow. "You know, on balance I think that what I'm about to discuss with you is *less* crazy than that. But the HTW"—he nodded in the direction of the Orithena dig—"is a cozy and familiar form of craziness." He paused for a few moments, returning his gaze to me.

"Who are you talking to?" Orolo asked.

I was wrong-footed by this bizarre question, and took a moment to be certain I'd heard the question right. "I'm talking to Orolo," I said.

"What is this Orolo? If a Geometer landed here and engaged you in conversation, how would you characterize Orolo to it?"

"As the man—the very complicated, bipedal, slightly hot, animated entity—standing right over there."

"But depending on how a Geometer sees things, it might respond, 'I see nothing there but vacuum with a sparse dusting of probability waves.'"

"Well, 'vacuum with a sparse dusting of probability waves' is an accurate description of just about everything in the universe," I pointed out, "so if the Geometer was not able to recognize objects any more effectively than that, it could scarcely be considered a conscious being. After all, if it's having a conversation with me, it must recognize *me* as—"

"Not so fast," Orolo said, "let's say you are talking to the Geometer by typing into a jeejah, or something. It knows you only as a stream of digits. Now you have to use those digits to supply a description of Orolo—or of yourself—that it would recognize."

"Okay, I'd agree with the Geometer on some way to describe space. Then I'd say, 'Consider the volume of space five feet in front of my position, about six feet high, two wide, and two deep. The probability waves that we call matter are somewhat denser inside of that box than they are outside of it.' And so on."

"Denser, because there's a lot of meat in that box," Orolo said, slapping his abdomen, "but outside of it, only air."

"Yes. I should think any conscious entity should be able to recognize the meat/air boundary. What's on the inside of the boundary is Orolo."

"Funny that you have such firm opinions on what conscious beings ought to be able to do," Orolo warned me. "Let me see . . . what about this?" He held up a fold of his bolt.

"Just as I can describe the meat/air boundary, I can describe how bolt-stuff differs from both meat and air, and explain that Orolo is wrapped in bolt-stuff."

"There you go making assumptions!" Orolo chided me.

"Such as?"

"Let's say that the Geometer you're talking to has been inculcated in his civilization's equivalent of the Sconics. He'll say, 'Wait a minute, you can't really know, you're not allowed to make statements about, things in themselves—only about *your perceptions*.'"

"True."

"So you need to rephrase your statement in terms of the givens that are actually available to you."

"All right," I said, "instead of saying, 'Orolo is wrapped in bolt-stuff,' I'll say, 'When I gaze at Orolo from where I'm standing, I see mostly bolt, with bits of Orolo—his head and his hands—peeking out.' But I don't see why it matters."

"It matters because the Geometer can't stand where you are standing. It has to stand somewhere else, and see me from a different angle."

"Yes, but the bolt wraps all the way around your body!"

"How do you know I'm not naked in back?"

"Because I've seen a lot of bolts and I know how they work."

"But if you were a Geometer, seeing one for the first time—"

"I'd still be able to surmise that you were not naked in back, because if you were, the bolt would hang differently."

"What if I got rid of the bolt and stood here naked?"

"What if you did?"

"How would you describe me to the Geometer, then? What would meet your eye, and the Geometer's?"

"I would say to the Geometer 'From where I stand, all I see is Orolo-skin. From where you stand, O Geometer, the same is likely true.'"

"And why is it likely?"

"Because without skin your blood and guts would fall out. Since I can't see a puddle of blood and guts behind you, I can infer that your skin must be in place."

"Just as you infer that my bolt must continue all the way round me in back, from the way in which its visible part hangs."

"Yes, I guess it's the same general principle."

"Well, it seems that this process you call consciousness is somewhat more complex than you perhaps gave it credit for at first," Orolo said. "One must be able to take in givens from sparse dustings of probability waves in a vacuum—"

"I.e., see stuff."

"Yes, and perform the trick of integrating those givens into seemingly persistent objects that can be held in consciousness. But that's not all. You perceive only one side of me, but you are all the time drawing inferences about my other side—that my bolt continues round in back, that I have skin—inferences that reflect an innate understanding of theorical laws. You can't seem to make these inferences without performing little thought experiments in your head: 'if the bolt didn't continue round in back it would hang differently,' 'if Orolo had no skin his guts would fall out.' In each of those cases you are using your understanding of the laws of dynamics to explore a little counterfactual universe inside of your head, a universe where the bolt or the skin isn't there, and you are then running that universe in fast-forward, like a speely, to see what would happen.

"And that is not the only such activity that is going on in your mind when you describe me to the Geometers," Orolo went on, after a pause to swallow some water, "because you are forever making allowances for the fact that you and the Geometer are in different places, seeing me from different points of view, taking in different givens. From where you're standing you might be able to see the freckle on the left side of my nose, but you have the wit to understand that the Geometer can't see that freckle because of where it is standing. This is another way in which your consciousness is forever building counterfactual universes: 'if I were standing where the Geometer is, my view of the freckle would be blocked.' Your ability to have empathy with the Geometer—to imagine what it would be like to be someone else—isn't a mere courtesy. It is an innate process of consciousness."

"Wait a second," I said, "you're saying I can't predict the Geometers' inability to see the freckle without erecting a replica of the whole universe in my imagination?"

"Not *exactly* a replica," Orolo said. "*Almost* a replica, in which everything is the same, except for where you are standing."

"It seems to me that there are much simpler ways of getting that result. Perhaps I have a memory of what you look like when viewed from that side. I call up that image in my memory and say to myself, 'Hmm, no freckle.'"

"It is a perfectly reasonable thought," Orolo said, "but I must warn you that it does not really buy you much, if what you seek is a simple and easy-to-understand model of how the mind works."

"Why not? I'm only talking about memory."

Orolo chortled, then composed himself, and made an effort to be tactful. "Thus far we have spoken only of the present. We've talked only of space—not of time. Now you would like to bring memories into the discussion. You are proposing to pull up memories of how you perceived Orolo's nose from a different angle at a different time: 'I sat on his right last night at supper and couldn't see the freckle.'"

"It seems simple enough," I said.

"You might ask yourself what in your brain enables you to do such things."

"*What* things?"

"Take in some givens one evening at supper. Take in another set of givens now—or one second ago—two seconds ago—but always now! And say that all of them were—are—the same chap, Orolo."

"I don't see what the big deal is," I said. "It's just pattern recognition. Syntactic devices can do it."

"Can they? Give me an example."

"Well . . . I guess a simple example would be . . ." I looked around, and happened to notice the contrail of an aerocraft high overhead. "Radar tracking aerocraft in a crowded sky."

"Tell me how it works."

"The antenna spins around. It sends out pulses. Echoes come back to it. From the time lag of the echo, it can calculate the bogey's distance. And it knows in what direction the bogey lies—that's dead easy, it's just the same direction as the antenna is pointing when the echo hits it."

"It can only look in one direction at a time," Orolo said.

"Yeah, it's got extreme tunnel vision, and compensates for that by spinning around."

"A little bit like us," Orolo said.

We had begun descending the mountain, and were walking side by side. Orolo went on, "I can't see in all directions at once, but I glance to the side every so often to make sure you're still there."

"Yeah, I guess so," I said. "You have in your head a model of your surroundings that includes me off to your right side. You can maintain it for a while by holding down the fast-forward button. But every so often you have to update it with new givens, or it'll get out of whack with what is really going on."

"How does the radar system manage it?"

"Well, the antenna rotates once and takes in echoes from everything that's in the sky. It plots their positions. Then it rotates again and collects a new set of echoes. The new set is similar to the first one. But all of the bogeys are now in slightly different positions, because all of the aerocraft are moving, each at its own speed, each in its own direction."

"And I can see how a human observer, watching the bogeys plotted on a screen, would be able to assemble a mental model of where the aerocraft were and how they were moving," Orolo said, "in the same way as we stitch together frames of a speely to form a continuous story in our minds. But how does the syntactic device inside the radar system do it? It has nothing more than a list of numbers, updated from time to time."

"If there were only one bogey, it would be easy," I said.

"Agreed."

"Or just a few, widely separated, moving slowly, so that their paths didn't cross."

"Also agreed. But what of the hard case of many fast bogeys, close together, paths crossing?"

"A human observer could manage it easily—just like watching a speely," I said. "A syndev would have to do some of what a human brain does."

"And what is that, exactly?"

"We have a sense for what is plausible. Let's say there are two aerocraft, full of passengers, going just under the speed of sound, and that during the interval between two radar sweeps, their paths cross at right angles. The machine can't tell the bogeys apart. So there are a few possible interpretations of the givens. One is that both planes executed sharp right-angle turns at the same moment and veered off in new directions. Another is that they bounced off each other like rubber balls. The third interpretation is that the planes are at different altitudes, so they didn't collide, and both simply kept flying in a straight line. *That* interpretation is the simplest, and the only one consistent with the laws of dynamics. So the syndev must be programmed to evaluate the different interpretations of the givens and choose the one that is most plausible."

"So we have taught this device a little of what we know of the action principles that govern the movement of our cosmos through Hemn space, and commanded it to filter out possibilities that diverge from a plausible world-track," Orolo said.

"In a very crude way, I suppose. It doesn't really know how to apply action principles in Hemn space and all that."

"Do *we*?"

"Some of us do."

"Theors, yes. But a sline playing catch knows what the ball will do—more importantly, what it *can't* do—without knowing the first thing about theorics."

"Of course. Even animals can do that. Orolo, where is Evenedrician datonomy getting us? I see some connection to our pink dragon dialog back home, a few months ago, but—"

Orolo got a funny look on his face. He'd forgotten. "Oh yes. About you and your worrying."

"Yes."

"That's something animals can't do," he pointed out. "They react to immediate, concrete threats, but they don't worry about abstract threats years in the future. It takes the mind of an Erasmas to do that."

I laughed. "I haven't been doing it so much lately."

"Good!" He reached out and gave me an affectionate thud on the shoulder.

"Maybe it's the Allswell."

"No, it's that you have *real* things to worry about now. But please remind me how it went—the dialog about the pink nerve-gas-farting dragon?"

"We developed a theory that our minds were capable of envisioning possible futures as tracks through configuration space, and then rejecting ones that didn't follow a realistic action principle. Jesry complained it was a heavyweight solution to a lightweight problem. I agreed. Arsibalt objected."

"This was after Fraa Paphlagon had been Evoked, wasn't it?"

"Yes."

"Arsibalt had been reading Paphlagon."

"Yes."

"So tell me, Fraa Erasmas, are you still with Jesry, or with Arsibalt?"

"I still think it seems fanciful to think we are all the time erecting and tearing down counterfactual universes in our minds."

"I've become so used to it that it seems fanciful to think *otherwise*," Orolo said. "But perhaps we can go on another hike tomorrow and discuss it further." We were reaching the outskirts of the math.

"I'd like that," I said.

As we drew near enough to smell supper cooking, I recollected that I needed to get a message out to my friends the next day. But it was not the right moment to bring this up and so I resolved to mention it the next morning.

I had it in my mind that this would force Orolo to make a decision, but as soon as I explained it to him, he made a point that was embarrassingly obvious, once he'd made it: the three-day deadline was perfectly arbitrary, and hence the only sound approach was to brush it aside without any further mention. He called in Fraa Landasher, who proposed that my friends be invited into the math and allowed to lodge here for as long as it might take to sort things out. This was shocking until I reminded myself that things were done differently here and that Landasher was beholden to no one except, possibly, the dowment that owned Ecba. Then I felt sure that my four friends would have no interest in biding in such a place as this. But a couple of hours later, when I walked out of the gate and down to the souvenir shop to explain matters to them, they accepted unanimously and without discussion. That in itself made me a little nervous, so I accompanied them back to the cove and helped them strike camp, using the afternoon to provide them with a running lecture on mathic etiquette. I was especially worred that Ganelial Crade would preach to them. But soon, beginning with Yul and spreading quickly to the others, they began to make fun of me for being so worried about this, and I realized that I had offended them. So I said nothing more until we got back to Orithena. Cord, Yul, Gnel, and Sammann were let in through the gate and given rooms in a sort of guest lodge, set apart from the cloister, where they were allowed to keep jeejahs and other Sæcular goods. Dressed in their extramuros garb—but without the jeejahs—they joined us at dinner and were formally toasted and welcomed by Fraa Landasher.

The next morning I rousted them early and led them down to the dig for a tour. Gnel looked as if he were having some sort of Deolatrous epiphany, though in all fairness I'd probably had a similar look on my face when Suur Spry had taken me down there.

I asked Sammann if he'd learned anything more about who was running Ecba and he said "yes" and "it's boring." Some burger, just

after the Third Sack, had become an Enthusiast for all things Orithenan. He was very rich and so he'd bought the island and, to run it,
set up the foundation, complete with tedious bylaws that ran to a
thousand pages—it was meant to last forever and so the bylaws had
to cover every eventuality they could think of. Executive power lay
in the hands of a mixed Sæcular/Mathic board of governors, Sammann explained, warming to the task even as my attention was beginning to wander . . .

So getting my friends squared away at Orithena distracted me
for a couple of days. After that I resumed my walks up the mountain with Orolo.

Dialog: A discourse, usually in formal style, between Theors. "To be in Dialog" is to participate in such a discussion
extemporaneously. The term may also apply to a written
record of a historical Dialog; such documents are the cornerstone of the mathic literary tradition and are studied,
re-enacted, and memorized by fids. In the classic format, a
Dialog involves two principals and some number of onlookers who participate sporadically. Another common format
is the Triangular, featuring a savant, an ordinary person
who seeks knowledge, and an imbecile. There are countless
other classifications, including the suvinian, the Periklynian, and the peregrin.

—THE DICTIONARY, *4th edition, A.R. 3000*

"I know that our last conversation was not completely satisfactory
to you, Erasmas. I apologize for that. These ideas are unfinished. I
am tormented, or tantalized, by the sense that I'm almost in view of
something that is at the limit of my comprehension. I dream of being in the sea, treading water, trying to see a beacon on shore. But
the view is blocked by the crests of the waves. Sometimes, when
conditions are perfect, I can pop up high enough to glimpse it. But
then, before I can form any firm impression of what it is I'm seeing,

I sink back down of my own weight, and get slapped in the face by another wave."

"I feel that way all the time, when I am trying to understand something new," I said. "Then, one day, all of a sudden—"

"You just get it," Orolo said.

"Yeah. The idea is just there, fully formed."

"Many have noted this, of course. I believe it is related, in a deep way, to the sort of mental process I was speaking of the other day. The brain takes advantage of quantum effects; I'm sure of it."

"I know just enough about it to know that what you just said has been controversial for a long, long time."

This affected him not at all; but after I looked in his eye long enough, he finally gave a shrug. *So be it.* "Did Sammann ever talk to you of Saunt Grod's Machines?"

"No. What is it?"

"A syntactic device that made use of quantum theorics. Before the Second Sack, his forerunners and ours worked together on such things. Saunt Grod's Machines were extremely good at solving problems that involved sifting through many possible solutions at the same time. For example, the Lazy Peregrin."

"That's the one where a wandering fraa needs to visit several maths, scattered randomly around a map?"

"Yes, and the problem is to find the shortest route that will take him to all of the destinations."

"I kind of see what you mean," I said. "One *could* draw up an exhaustive list of every possible route—"

"But it takes forever to do it that way," Orolo said. "In a Saunt Grod's Machine, you could erect a sort of generalized model of the scenario, and configure the machine so that it would, in effect, examine all possible routes at the same time."

"So, this kind of machine, instead of existing in one fixed, knowable state at any given time, would be in a superposition of many quantum states."

"Yes, it's just like an elementary particle that might have spin up or spin down. It is in both states at the same time—"

"Until someone observes it," I said, "and the wavefunction collapses to one state or the other. So, I guess with a Saint Grod's Machine, one eventually makes some observation—"

"And the machine's wavefunction collapses to one particular state—which is the answer. The 'output,' I believe the Ita call it," Orolo said, smiling a little as he pronounced the unfamiliar bit of jargon.

"I agree that thinking often feels that way," I said. "You have a jumble of vague notions in your mind. Suddenly, bang! It all collapses into one clear answer that you know is right. But every time something happens suddenly, you can't simply chalk it up to quantum effects."

"I know," Orolo said. "Do you see where I'm going, though, when I speak of counterfactual cosmi?"

"I didn't really get it until you brought quantum theorics into the picture," I said. "But it's been obvious for a while that you have been developing a theory about how consciousness works. You have mentioned some different phenomena that any introspective person would recognize—I won't bother to go back and list them all—and you have tried to unify them . . ."

"My grand unification theory of consciousness," Orolo joked.

"Yes, you are saying that they are all rooted in a special ability that the brain has to erect models of counterfactual cosmi in the brain, and to play them forward in time, evaluate their plausibility, and so on. Which is utterly insane if you take the brain to be a normal syndev."

"Agreed," Orolo said. "It would require an immense amount of processing power just to erect the models—to say nothing of running them forward. Nature would have found some more efficient way to get the job done."

"But when you play the quantum card," I said, "it changes the game entirely. Now, all you need is to have one generalized model of the cosmos—like the generalized map that a Saint Grod's Machine uses to solve the Lazy Peregrin problem—permanently loaded up in your brain. That model can then exist in a vast number of possible states, and you can ask all sorts of questions of it."

"I'm glad that you now understand this in the same way that I do," Orolo said. "I do have one quibble, however."

"Oh boy," I said, "here goes."

"Traditions die hard, among the avout," Orolo said. "And for a very long time, it has been traditional to teach quantum theorics to fids in a particular way that is based on how it was construed by the theors who discovered it, way back in the time of the Harbingers. And that, Erasmas, is how you were taught as well. Even if I had never met you before today, I would know this from the language that you use to talk about these things: 'it exists in a superposition of states—observing it collapses the wavefunction' and so on."

"Yes. I know where you are going with this," I said. "There are whole orders of theors—have been for thousands of years—that use completely different models and terminology."

"Yes," Orolo said, "and can you guess which model, which terminology, I am partial to?"

"The more polycosmic the better, I assume."

"Of course! So, whenever I hear you talking of quantum phenomena using the old terminology—"

"The fid version?"

"Yes, I must mentally translate what you're saying into polycosmic terms. For example, the simple case of a particle that is either spin up or spin down—"

"You would say that, at the moment when the spin is observed—the moment when its spin has an effect on the rest of the cosmos—the cosmos bifurcates into two complete, separate, causally independent cosmi that then go their separate ways."

"You've almost got it. But it's better to say that those two cosmi exist *before* the measurement is made, and that they interfere with each other—there is a little bit of crosstalk between them—until the observation is made. And *then* they go their separate ways."

"And here," I said, "we could talk about how crazy this sounds to many people—"

Orolo shrugged. "Yet it is a model that a great many theors come to believe in sooner or later, because the alternatives turn out to be even crazier in the end."

"All right. So, I think I know what comes next. You want me to restate your theory of what the brain does in terms of the polycosmic interpretation of quantum theorics."

"If you would so indulge me," Orolo said, with a suggestion of a bow.

"Okay. Here goes," I said. "The premise, here, is that the brain is loaded up with a pretty accurate model of the cosmos that it lives in."

"At least, the local part of it," Orolo said. "It needn't have a good model of other galaxies, for example."

"Right. And to state it in the terminology of the old interpretation that fids are taught, the state of that model is a superposition of many possible present and future states of the cosmos—or at least of the model."

He held up a finger. "Not of *the* cosmos, but—?"

"But of hypothetical alternate cosmi differing slightly from *the* cosmos."

"Very good. Now, this generalized cosmos-model that each person carries around in his or her brain—do you have any idea how it would work? What it would look like?"

"Not in the slightest!" I said. "I don't know the first thing about the nerve cells and so on. How they could be rigged together to create such a model. How the model could be reconfigured, from moment to moment, to represent hypothetical scenarios."

"Fair enough," Orolo said, holding up his hands to placate me. "Let's leave nerve cells out of the discussion, then. The important thing about the model, though, is what?"

"That it can exist in many states at once, and that its wavefunction collapses from time to time to give a useful result."

"Yes. Now, in the polycosmic interpretation of how quantum theorics works, what does all of this look like?"

"There is no longer superposition. No wavefunction collapse. Just a lot of different copies of me—of my brain—each really existing in a different parallel cosmos. The cosmos model residing in each of those parallel brains is really, definitely in one state or another. And they interfere with one another."

He let me stew on that for a few moments. And then it came to me. Just like those ideas we had spoken of earlier—suddenly there in my head. "You don't even need the model any more, do you?"

Orolo just nodded, smiled, egged me on with little beckoning gestures.

I went on—seeing it as I was saying it. "It is so much simpler this way! My brain doesn't have to support this hugely detailed, accurate, configurable, quantum-superposition-supporting model of the cosmos any more! All it needs to do is to perceive—to reflect—the cosmos that it's really *in,* as it really *is.*"

"The variations—the myriad possible alternative scenarios—have been moved out of your brain," Orolo said, rapping on his skull with his knuckles, "and out into the polycosm, which is where they all exist anyway!" He opened his hand and extended it to the sky, as if releasing a bird. "All you have to do is perceive them."

"But each variant of me doesn't exist in perfect isolation from the others," I said, "or else it wouldn't work."

Orolo nodded. "Quantum interference—the crosstalk among similar quantum states—knits the different versions of your brain together."

"You're saying that my consciousness extends across multiple cosmi," I said. "That's a pretty wild statement."

"I'm saying *all* things do," Orolo said. "That comes with the polycosmic interpretation. The only thing exceptional about the brain is that it has found a way to *use* this."

Neither of us said a word as we picked our way down the path for the next quarter of an hour, and the sky receded to a deep violet. I had the illusion that, as it got darker, it moved away from us, expanding like a bubble, rushing away from Arbre at a million light-years an hour, and as it whooshed past stars, we began to see them.

One of the stars was moving. So discreetly, at first, that I had to stop, find my balance, and observe it closely to be sure. It was no illusion. The ancient animal part of my brain, so attuned to subtle, suspicious movement, had picked out this one star among the millions. It was in the western sky, not far above the horizon, hence diluted, at first, in twilight. But it rose slowly and steadily into the black. As it did, it changed its color and its size. Early on, it was a pinprick of white light, just like any other star, but as it rose toward the zenith it reddened. Then it broadened to a dot of orange, then flared yellow and threw out a comet-tail. Until that point my eyes had been playing any number of tricks on me and I'd misconceived its distance, its altitude, and its velocity. But the comet-tail shocked me into the right view: the thing was not high above us in space but descending into the atmosphere, dumping its energy into shredded, glowing air. Its rise had slowed as it neared the zenith, and it was clear it would lose all forward speed before it passed over our heads. The meteor's bearing had never changed: it was headed right at us, and the brighter and fatter it grew, the more it seemed to hang motionless in the sky, like a thrown ball that is coming straight at your head. For a minute it was a little sun, fixed in the sky and stabbing rays of incandescent air in all directions. Then it shrank and faded back through orange to a dull red, and became difficult to make out.

I realized I had tilted my head as far back as it would go, and was gazing vertically upwards.

At the risk of losing my fix on it, I dropped my chin and had a look around.

Orolo was a hundred feet downhill of me and running as fast as he could.

I gave up trying to track the thing in the sky and took off after him. By the time I caught up, we were almost at the edge of the pit.

"They deciphered my analemma!" he exclaimed between gasps.

We stopped at a rope that had been stretched at waist level from stake to stake around the edge of the pit, to prevent sleepy or drunk avout from falling into it. I looked up and cried out in shock as I saw something absolutely enormous, just above us, like a low cloud. But it was perfectly circular. I understood that it was a gigantic parachute. Its shroud lines converged on a glowing red load that hung far below it.

The lines went all quavery and the chute blurred, then began to drift sideways on a barely perceptible breeze. It had been cut loose. The hot red thing fell like a stone but then thrust out legs of blue fire and, a few seconds later, began to hiss, shockingly loud. It was aiming for the floor of the pit. Orolo and I followed the rope around to the top of the ramp. A crowd of fraas and suurs was building there, more fascinated than afraid. Orolo began pushing through them, headed for the ramp, shouting above the hiss of the rocket: "Fraa Landasher, open the gate! Yul, go out with your cousin and get your vehicles. Find the parachute and bring it back! Sammann, do you have your jeejah? Cord! Get all of your things and meet me at the bottom!" And he launched himself down the ramp, rushing alone into the dark to meet the Geometers.

I ran after him. My usual role in life. I'd lost sight of the probe—the ship—whatever it was—during all of this, but now it was suddenly there, dead level with me and only a few hundred feet away, dropping at a measured pace toward the Temple of Orithena. I was so stunned by its immediacy, its heat and noise, that I recoiled, lost my balance, and stumbled to my knees. In that posture I watched it descend the last hundred feet or so. Its attitude, its velocity were perfectly steady, but only by dint of a thousand minute twitches and wiggles of its rocket nozzles: something very sophisticated was controlling the thing, making a myriad decisions every second. It was headed for the Decagon. In the final half-second, a hell-storm of shattering tiles was kicked up by the plumes of hypersonic gas shooting from those engines. Crouching, insect-like legs took up the last of its velocity and the engines went dark. But they continued to hiss for a couple of seconds as some kind of gas was run through the engines, purging the lines, shrouding the probe in a cool bluish cloud.

Then Orithena was silent.

I picked myself up and began hurrying down the ramp as best I could while keeping my head turned sideways, the better to stare at the Geometers' probe. Its bottom was broad and saucer-shaped and still glowing a dull red-brown from the heat of re-entry. Above that it had a simple shape, like an inverted bucket, with a slightly domed top. Five tall narrow hatches had opened in its sides, revealing slots from which the bug-legs had unfolded. Atop its dome was some clutter I could not quite make out: presumably the mechanism for deploying and cutting free the parachute, maybe some antennas and sensors. I saw all sides of it as I chased Orolo down the spiral ramp, and never saw anything that looked like a window.

I caught up with him at the edge of the Decagon. He was sniffing the air. "Doesn't seem to be venting anything noxious," he said. "From the color of the exhaust, I'm guessing hydrogen/oxygen. Clean as a whistle."

Landasher came down alone. It seemed he had ordered the others to remain above. He had his mouth open to say something. He looked half-deranged, a man in over his head. Orolo cut him off: "Is the gate open?" Landasher didn't know. But above, we could now hear vehicles roaring around. I recognized them by their sounds: they were the ones we had brought over the pole. A light appeared at the top of the ramp.

"*Someone* opened them," Orolo said. "But they must be closed and bolted again, as soon as the vehicles and parachute are inside. You should prepare for an invasion."

"You think the Geometers are launching an—"

"No. I mean an invasion of the Panjandrums. This event will have been picked up on sensors. There is no telling how quickly the Sæcular Power may respond. Possibly within an hour."

"We cannot possibly keep the Sæcular Power out, if they wish to come in," Landasher said.

"As much time as possible. That is all I ask for," Orolo said.

The three-wheeler was coming down the ramp. As it drew closer I saw Cord at the controls, Sammann standing on the back, gripping Cord's shoulders to maintain his balance.

"What do you propose to do with that time?" Landasher demanded. Until now, he had always struck me as a wise and reasonable leader, but this evening he was under a lot of stress.

"Learn," Orolo said. "Learn of the Geometers, before the Sæcular Power takes this moment away from us."

The three-wheeler reached the bottom. Sammann hopped off, unslinging his jeejah from his shoulder. He aimed its sensors at the probe. Cord gunned the engine briefly and swung the machine around so that its headlight, too, was aimed at the probe. Then she hopped off and began to pull gear from the cargo shelf on the rear axle.

"What of—how do you know it is safe? What about infection!? Orolo? *Orolo!*" Landasher cried, for Cord's headlight gambit had offered a much better look at the thing, and Orolo was drifting toward it, fascinated.

"If *they* were afraid of being infected by *us,* they would not have come here," Orolo said. "If *we* are at risk of being infected by *them,* then we are at their mercy."

"Do you really fancy that bolting the gate is going to stop people who have helicopters?" Landasher asked.

"I have an idea about that," Orolo said. "Fraa Erasmas will see to it."

By the time I had got back up to the top of the ramp, Yul and Gnel had retrieved the parachute. They and a small crew of adventurous avout had wadded and stuffed much of it into the open back of Gnel's fetch, restraining it with a haphazard web of cargo straps and shroud lines. Still, an acre of parachute and a mile of shroud lines trailed in the dust behind the fetch as they drew up to the edge of the pit.

Now at this point we ought to have put on white body suits, gloves, respirators, and sealed the alien chute in sterile poly and sent it to a lab to be examined and analyzed down to the molecular level. But I had other orders. So I grabbed the edge of the chute—my first physical contact with an artifact from another star system—and felt it. To me, no expert on textiles, it felt like the same stuff we used to make parachutes on Arbre. Same story with the shroud lines. I did not think that they were what we called newmatter.

Quite a crowd had gathered around the fetch. They were respecting Landasher's order not to go into the pit. But he hadn't said anything about the parachute. I climbed up onto the top of the fetch and announced: "Each of you is responsible for one shroud line.

We'll pull the chute out and spread it on the ground. Form a ring around its edge. Choose your line. Then radiate. Spread the lines outwards, untangling them as you go. In ten minutes I would like to see the whole population of Orithena standing in a huge circle around this parachute, each holding the end of a line."

A pretty simple plan. It got quite a bit messier as they put it into practice. But they were smart people, and the less fussing and meddling I did, the better they showed themselves at dreaming up solutions to problems. Meanwhile I had Yul estimate the length of a single shroud line by counting fathoms with his arms.

Gnel drove his fetch out from under the spreading chute and down the ramp to the bottom of the pit. He had equipped it with a battery of high-powered lights that I had always found ridiculous. Tonight, he had finally found something to aim them at. I took a moment to glance down, and saw that Orolo and Cord had approached to within twenty feet of the probe.

Getting the Orithenans spread out around the chute took a little while. A supersonic jet screamed overhead and startled us.

Yul's measurement confirmed my general impression, which was that the shroud lines were something like half as long as the pit was wide. Once I explained the general plan to the Orithenans, they began to move toward the edge of the pit, parting to either side and circumventing the rim while keeping the shroud lines taut. The chute glided across the ground in fits and starts. We had to get a few people underneath it to coax and waft it over snags. But presently the leading edge of the fabric curled over the rim of the pit, and then the movement took on a life of its own as gravity helped it forward. I hoped the Orithenans on the ends of the lines would have the good sense to let go the ropes if they felt themselves being pulled toward the edge. But the chute wasn't nearly heavy enough to cause any such problems. Once all of the fabric had gone over the edge, and the Orithenans had spaced themselves evenly around it, the thing became quite manageable. The chute seemed to cover about half of the pit's area. The Orithenans by now had figured out the general idea, which was that we wanted to suspend the parachute above the Teglon plaza as a canopy. They began to move about en masse, adjusting its position and its altitude with no further direction from me. When it seemed right, I jogged around the perimeter urging them to move away from the hole and trace their shroud lines out as far as they could go, and to lash the ends around any solid anchors they could find. For about a third of them, this ended up being the top of the concent's outer wall. Other lines ended up finding purchase on trees, Cloister pillars, trestles, rocks, or sticks hammered into the ground.

Hearing an engine, I looked over to the top of the ramp and saw that Yul was gingerly driving his house-on-wheels down into the pit—the better, I guessed, to cook breakfast for the Geometers. I sprinted over and dived into the cabin with him. This sparked a general rebellion among the Orithenans who, ignoring Landasher's earlier order, followed us down on foot.

Yul and I drove down the ramp in silence. The look on his face was as if he were just on the verge of hysterical laughter. When we reached the bottom, he parked amid the ruins of the Temple, just near the Analemma. He shut off the engine. He turned to look at me and finally broke the silence. "I don't know how this is going to come out," he said, "but I sure am glad I came with you." And, before I could tell him how glad I was of his company, he was out the door, striding over to join Cord.

Radiant heat from the underside of the vehicle was making it difficult to approach. Yul went back to his fetch and got some reflective emergency blankets. Cord, Orolo, and I used these as bolts. Most of the vehicle was above us, so we put out a call for ladders.

It had been difficult to guess the thing's size before, but now I was able to borrow a measuring rod from the archaeological dig and measure it at about twenty feet in diameter. I hadn't brought anything to write with, but Sammann was using his jeejah in speelycaptor mode, taking everything down, so I called out the numbers.

A helicopter approached. We could hear it through the canopy. It circled the compound a few times, its downwash creating huge, eye-catching disturbances in the canopy. Then it withdrew to a higher altitude and hovered. It could not land here because of the parachute. All the land within the walls was built on or cultivated with trees and trellises. They'd have to land outside and knock on the door, or scale the wall.

So we had stalled them for a few minutes. But everyone felt desperately short of time now. Suddenly a dozen ladders were available—all different sizes, all hand-crafted of wood. The Orithenans began lashing them together to make a scaffold right next to the probe, on the side that seemed to have a sort of hatch. Cord clambered up and found a place to stand on a ladder that had been placed horizontally. I felt proud watching her. So much about this might have been overwhelming. At some level perhaps she *was* overwhelmed. But this probe was, after all, a machine. She could tell how it worked. And as long as she held her focus on that, none of the other stuff mattered.

"Talk to us!" Sammann called to her, staring at the screen of his jeejah as he lined up his shot.

"There is clearly a removable hatch," she said. "It is trapezoidal with rounded corners. Two feet wide at the base. One and a half at the top. Four high. Curved like the fuselage." She was doing a funny kind of dance, because the scaffold was still being improvised beneath her—she was poised between two ladder-rungs and the ladder kept shifting. She was casting an array of lapping shadows on what she wanted to see, so she fished a headlamp out of her vest, turned it on, and played its beam over the streaked and burned surface of the probe.

"Can we just go ahead and call it a door?" Sammann asked.

"Okay. There is Geometer-writing stenciled around the door. Letters about an inch high."

"Stenciled?" Sammann asked.

"Yeah." Cord stretched the band of the lamp over her head and adjusted its angle, freeing her hands.

"*Literally* stenciled?"

"Yeah. In the sense that they took a piece of paper with letter-shaped cutouts and held it up to the metal and slapped paint on it." I heard a series of metallic raps. Cord was touching a magnet to various places around the door. "None of this is ferrous." Then a screeching noise. "I can't scratch it with my steel knife blade. Maybe a high-temp stainless alloy."

"Fascinating," Orolo called. "Can you get it open?"

"I think that the stenciled messages are opening instructions," she said. "It is the same message—the same stencil—repeated in four places around the door. In each case, there is a line painted from it—"

"An arrow?" someone called. Others, who were standing where they could see it better, were more certain. "Those are arrows!"

"They don't look like our arrows," Cord said, "but maybe the Geometers do them differently. Each of them is aimed at a panel about the size of my hand. These panels appear to be held in place with fasteners—flush-head machine bolts—four per panel—I don't have the right tool to put into them but I can fake it with a daisy-head driver." She frisked herself.

"How do we know they are fasteners at all?" someone called. "We know nothing of these aliens and their praxis!"

"It's just obvious!" Cord called back. "I can see little burrs where some alien mechanic over-torqued them. The heads are knurled so aliens can turn 'em with their alien fingers when they are loose. The only question is: clockwise, or counterclockwise?"

She jammed a driver into place, whacked it once with the heel of her hand to seat it, and grunted as she applied torque. "Counterclockwise," she announced. For some reason this caused a cheer to run through the crowd of avout. "The Geometers are right-handed!" someone called, and everyone laughed.

Cord pocketed the bolts as she got them out. The little panel fell off and clattered through the scaffolding to the stone plaza, where someone snatched it up and peered at it like a page from a holy book. "Behind the panel is a cavity containing a T-handle," she announced. "But I'm going to remove the other three panels before I mess with it."

"Why?" someone asked—typical argumentative avout, I thought.

Going to work on another panel, Cord answered patiently: "It's like when you bolt the wheel onto your mobe, you take turns tightening the nuts to equalize the stress."

"What if there is a pressure differential?" Orolo asked.

"Another good reason to take it slow," Cord muttered. "We don't want anyone to get smashed by a flying door. As a matter of fact—" She looked out at the crowd of avout below.

Yul took her meaning. He cupped his hands around his mouth and bellowed: "MOVE BACK! Everyone get clear of the hatch. A hundred feet away. MOVE!" The voice was shockingly loud and authoritative. People moved, and opened up a corridor all the way to Gnel's fetch.

More aerocraft, of two or three different types, approached while Cord was undoing the panels. We could hear them landing on the other side of the wall. Someone called down news that soldiers were getting out, down on the road by the souvenir shop.

A thought occurred to me. "Sammann," I asked, "are you sending this out over the Reticulum?"

"Smile," Sammann answered, "right now a billion people are laughing at you."

I tried not to think about the soldiers and the billion people.

A hiss came from the probe. Cord jumped back and almost toppled from the scaffold. The hiss died away asymptotically over a few seconds. Cord laughed nervously. "One of the things that happens when you operate a T-handle," she said, "is that a pressure-equalizing valve opens up."

"Did air go in, or out?" Orolo asked.

"In." Cord operated the other three T-handles. "Uh-oh," she said, "here it comes!" And the door simply fell out and hit the ladder she was standing on. Yul got his arms up in time to steer it down to the ground. We all watched that. Then all looked to Cord, who was standing there, hands on hips, pelvis cocked to one side, aiming the beam of her headlamp into the probe.

"What's in there?" someone finally asked.

"A dead girl," she said, "with a box on her lap."

"Human or—"

"Close," Cord said, "but not from Arbre."

Cord crouched as if to enter the capsule, but then started as the scaffolding torqued, rocked, and rebounded. It was Yul. He had vaulted up to join her. He wasn't about to let his girl climb into an alien spaceship until he'd checked it for monsters. The scaffold had been about right for one, and had now reached maximum capacity; no one else was going up there as long as most of the space was claimed by an agitated Yulassetar Crade. Cord was mildly offended; she refused to move, so Yul had to drop to his knees and stick his head into the doorway down around the level of her thighs. It felt haphazard, hasty, and absolutely the wrong way to treat such priceless theorical evidence. If circumstances had been different, avout would have swarmed the ladders and restrained Yul, nothing would have been touched until all had been measured, phototyped, examined, analyzed. But the hovering and circling aerocraft, as well as other sound effects from above, had put everyone in a different frame of mind. "Yul!" Sammann shouted, and as soon as Yul turned around the Ita lobbed his jeejah up to the scaffold. Yul reached instinctively, snatched it out of the air, and thrust it into the capsule. It could see in the dark better than a human and so he ended up using its screen as a night vision device. That's how he noticed the dark stains in the clothing of the dead Geometer.

"She's wounded," he announced, "she's bleeding!" There were cries of alarm from some of the avout who assumed Yul must be talking of Cord, but soon it was clear that he was speaking of the Geometer in the capsule.

"Are you claiming he, she, is *alive*!?" Sammann asked.

"I don't know!" Yul said, turning his head to look down at us.

As long as he was out of the way, Cord thrust a leg into the doorway and leaned her head and upper body through. We heard a muffled exclamation. Yul relayed it: "Cord says she's still warm!"

All kinds of theorical questions were coming up in my mind—and probably the minds of all the others: how can you tell it's female? How do you know they even have sexes? What makes you think they have blood like we do, and that that's what is coming out of her? But, again, the stress and chaos relegated all such questions to a kind of intellectual quarantine.

Orolo pointed out, "If there is any possibility that she might be alive, we must do whatever we can to help her!"

That was all Yul needed to hear. He tossed the jeejah back to Sammann with one hand while giving Cord a knife with the other. "She's strapped in pretty good," he warned us. All we could see of Cord now was one leg, which twisted and pawed as she braced it against the scaffold. A minute passed. We stood, waiting, unable to help Cord, helpless to do anything about the banging, booming, and metallic screeching noises resounding from the gates and walls of the concent high above. Finally Cord gave a great heave and tumbled half out of the door. Yul reached in for the second heave. Like a rafting guide hauling a drowned customer from a river, he brought the Geometer out with the full power of both arms and legs, and ended up lying on his back with the alien sprawled full-length on top of him. Red liquid spilled down around his ribs and dripped through the rungs onto the ground. Twenty hands reached up to accept the weight of the Geometer as Yul rolled her sideways off his body. Three hands, one of them Orolo's, converged on her head, cradling it, taking great care it did not loll. I glimpsed the face. From fifty feet, anyone would have taken her for a native of this planet. Close up, there was no doubt that she was, as Cord had put it, "not from Arbre." There was no one thing about her face that would prove this. But the color and texture of her skin and hair, the bone structure, the sculpture of the outer ear, the shape of the teeth, were all just different enough.

It was out of the question to lay her down on the rocket-blasted ground, still hot and strewn with jagged tile-shards, so we looked around for the nearest flat surface that might serve. This turned out to be the empty bed of Gnel's fetch, about a hundred feet away. We carried the Geometer on our shoulders, quick-stepping as fast as we could without dropping her. Suur Maltha, the concent's physician, met us halfway and was probing the patient's neck with her finger-tips before we had even set her down. Gnel, thinking fast, got a camp pad rolled out just in time. We laid the Geometer down on it, head on the tailgate. She was in a loose, pale blue coverall, the back sodden with what was obviously blood. Suur Maltha ripped the garment open and explored the body with a stethoscope. "Even allowing for the fact that I can't be sure where the heart is, I hear no pulse. Just some very faint noises that I would identify as bowel sounds. Roll her over."

We got the Geometer on her stomach. Suur Maltha cut the fabric away. It was not just soaked with blood but perforated with many holes. Maltha used a cloth to swipe a mess of gore away from the back, revealing a constellation of large round puncture wounds, extending from the buttocks up halfway to the shoulder, mostly on the left side. Everyone inhaled and became silent. Suur Maltha regarded it for a few moments, mastering her own sense of shock, and then looked as if she might be about to deliver some clinical observation.

But Gnel beat her to it. "Shotgun blast," he diagnosed. "Heavy gauge—antipersonnel. Medium range." And then, though it wasn't really necessary, he delivered the verdict: "Some SOB shot this poor lady in the back. May God have mercy on her soul."

One of Maltha's assistants had had the presence of mind to shove a thermometer into an orifice that she had noticed down where the legs joined. "Body temp similar to ours," she announced. "She has been dead for maybe *minutes*."

The sky fell on us. Or so it seemed, for a few moments. Someone above had cut the shroud lines of the parachute and it had collapsed on our heads. Startling as all hell, but harmless. Everyone spread out and got busy pawing, dragging, stuffing, and wadding. There was no coherent plan. But eventually a lot of avout came together in the middle of the plaza, corralling a huge wad of chute-stuff which they pushed and rolled up the steps of the Temple to get it out of the way. When it was obvious that there was an oversupply of these chute-wranglers, I turned back towards the probe, meaning to go and give the people there an update. My inclination was to run. But soldiers in head-to-toe suits were coming down the ramp in force and I thought that running might only excite someone's chase instinct.

Orolo and Sammann were examining an artifact that had been in the capsule—the box that Cord had seen on the occupant's lap. It was made of some fibrous stuff, and it contained four transparent tubes filled with red liquid. Blood samples, we figured. Each was labeled with a different, single word in Geometer-writing, and a different circular ikon: a picture of a planet—not Arbre—as seen from space.

Soldiers yanked it out of our hands. They were all around us now. Each sported a bandolier loaded with what looked like oversized bracelets. Whenever they encountered an avout they'd yank one off and ratchet it around the avout's throat, whereupon it would come alive and flash a few times a second. Each collar had a different string of digits printed on its front, so once they'd captured a picture of you, they would know your face and your number. It didn't require a whole lot of imagination to guess that the collars had tracking and surveillance capabilities. But as sinister and dehumanizing as all of this was, nothing came of it, at least for now—it seemed that they only wanted to know who was where.

Fraa Landasher acquitted himself well, demanding—firmly but calmly—to know who was in charge, by what authority this was being done ("What law covers alien probes, by the way?") and so on. But the soldiers were all dressed in suits made for chemical and biological warfare, which didn't make engaging them in dialog any easier, and Landasher didn't know enough about the legal procedures of this time and place. He could have mounted a fine legal defense 6400 years ago but not today.

A contingent of four soldiers, distinguished by special insignias that had been hastily poly-taped onto their suits, approached the probe and started to unpack equipment. Two of them climbed up on the scaffold, shooed away the fraa who was inside of it, and began collecting samples and making phototypes of their own.

The soldiers had naturally come to the probe first. They communicated well with one another because their suits had wireless intercoms, but they couldn't hear or talk to us very fluently. When they did talk to us, it was to boss us around, and when they listened, it was with something worse than skepticism—as if their officers had issued a warning that the avout would try to cast spells on them. The ones who entered the probe might have noted some red fluid, but it wasn't as obvious as you might think—the capsule had very little uncluttered floor space, the lighting was poor, and the acceleration couches were upholstered in dark material that didn't show the stain. The face shields on the soldiers' helmets kept fogging up. Their gloved hands could not feel the sticky wetness, their air-filtration devices removed all odors. Standing near the probe, getting used to the collar snugged around my neck, I realized that a long time might actually go by before any of the soldiers became aware of the fact that a Geometer had come down in this capsule and was lying dead in the back of a fetch a hundred feet away. The billion people watching Sammann's feed over the Reticulum all knew this. The soldiers, isolated in their own secure, private reticule, had no idea. Sammann, Orolo, Cord, and I kept exchanging amazed and amused looks as we collectively realized this.

Yul distracted everyone for a while. He shoved away the soldiers who came to collar him, then, when they aimed weapons at him, negotiated a deal that he would collar himself. But once he'd put it on and the soldiers had walked away, he pulled the collar right off over his head. He had a thick neck and a small skull. The collar scraped his scalp and lacerated his ears, but he got it off. Then, having satisfied himself that he could do it, he pulled it back on again.

An officer finally noticed the small crowd of uncollared avout gathered around Gnel's fetch, and sent a squad over to take care of them. It seemed that we were free to move about as long as we didn't try to run away or interfere with the soldiers, so I followed them at a distance that I hoped they would consider polite.

Collared avout were being herded toward the Temple steps. Nearby, a line of soldiers was moving across the Teglon plaza, bent forward at the waist, picking up stray tiles and other debris that might go ballistic when they began landing things there. Big vertical-landing aerocraft were keeping station in the sky above, waiting for the landing zone to be prepared. I reckoned that the general plan was to load us on aerocraft and take us away to some kind of detention facility. The longer I could delay being on one of those flights, the better.

The squad leader did not show the least bit of curiosity as to what these half-dozen avout were doing in the back of the fetch, but only ordered them to move away from the vehicle and line up for collaring. The avout complied, looking nonplussed. A soldier circled around behind the fetch to check for stragglers. He saw the dead body, started, unslung his weapon—which drew the attention of his squad-mates—then relaxed and put the weapon back over his shoulder. He approached the fetch slowly. Something in his posture told me he was communicating with his mates on the wireless. I got in close enough to hear the squad leader saying to Suur Maltha—obviously the physician, since she was all stained with blood—"You have one casualty?"

"Yes."

"Do you require—"

"She's dead," Suur Maltha said, "we don't need a medic." She was speaking bluntly, a little sarcastically, astounded as I had been to realize that the soldiers *didn't know*. If they had only asked us, we would have told them; we wouldn't have been able to shut up. But they hadn't asked. They didn't care for our knowledge, our opinions. And so all of us—all the avout—were reacting in the same way to that: *to hell with them!*

The soldiers began to pop collars off their bandoliers and fit them around the necks of Maltha and her assistants. But halfway through they all stopped. Several of them raised gloves to helmets. I turned around and saw that all of the soldiers on the plaza and around the probe were behaving the same way. I reckoned the jig was up now. Some general, sitting in an office a thousand miles away where he had access to the civilian feeds, was screaming into a microphone that there was a dead alien in the back of the fetch. I supposed that in a moment all heads would turn in our direction, all soldiers would converge here.

But that was not what they did. Instead they all looked up into the sky.

Something was coming.

The hovering aerocraft had received the message too: the pitch of their engines changed, their lights shifted as they spun to new headings, banked, and sidled away, gaining altitude.

The soldiers by the fetch had turned inward on one another, though they kept glancing skywards.

"Hey!" I said. "Hey! *Look at me!*" I finally got the leader to swing his face shield in my direction. "Talk to us!" I shouted. "We can't hear! We don't know what's going on!"

". . . mumble mumble mumble EVACUATE!" he said.

Ganelial Crade didn't need to hear that twice. He swung himself up into the cab of the fetch and started the engine. Suur Maltha and one of her assistants climbed into the back with the "casualty." I decided to circle back to the probe first, just to make sure my friends there had gotten the same message—and to chivvy Orolo along if he decided to be difficult. All around the plaza, soldiers were waving their arms, herding avout toward the base of the ramp. Gnel's fetch was headed that way at slower than walking pace, pausing here and there to pick up slower-moving avout. Yul's vehicle had begun to do likewise, and I was comforted to see Cord in the front seat. But the ramp was already jammed with pedestrians, so the vehicles would not be able to go any faster than the slowest could walk.

Or run, as the case might be. "MOVE! MOVE!" someone was shouting. An officer had ripped his helmet off—alien infections be damned—and begun shouting into a loud-hailer. "If you can run, do so! If you can't, get on the truck!"

I ended up a straggler along with Sammann and Orolo. We jogged toward the ramp. I threw Sammann a questioning look. He shrugged. "They jammed the Ret as soon as they got here," he said, "and I can't penetrate their transmissions."

So I looked at Orolo, who was keeping an eye on the western sky as he jogged along. "You think something else is coming?" I asked.

"Since the probe was launched, about one orbital period has expired," he pointed out. "So, if the Geometers wanted to drop something on us at the next opportunity, then now would be the time to expect it."

"*Drop* something," I repeated.

"You saw what was done to that poor woman!" Orolo exclaimed. "There is insurrection—perhaps civil war—in the icosahedron. A faction that wishes to share information with us, and another that will kill to prevent it."

"Kill *us,* even?"

Orolo shrugged. We had reached the base of the ramp and got stuck in a traffic jam. Scanning the ramp circling round above us, I could see avout and soldiers, all mixed together, running. But some inscrutable law of traffic-jam dynamics dictated that those of us at the bottom were at a perfect standstill. All we could do was wait for it to clear. We were the last avout in the queue; behind us were two squads of soldiers bent under heavy packs, waiting stolidly, as was the timeless lot of soldiers. Behind them, Orithena was depopulated, empty except for the alien probe.

Orolo squared off in front of me and favored me with a bright grin. "Regarding our earlier conversation," he began, as if inviting me to dialog in the Refectory kitchen.

"Yes? You have something to add?"

"As to the actual substance, no," he confessed. "But things are about to become quite chaotic indeed, and it's possible we may get separated."

"I intend to stay by your side—"

"They may not give us a choice," he pointed out, running his finger around his collar. "My number is odd, yours is even—perhaps they'll sort us into different tents, or something."

The people in front of us finally began to move. Sammann, sensing we were trying to have some kind of private conversation, went ahead. We shouldered and jostled our way onto the lower stretches of the ramp. In a few moments we were walking, then jogging.

Orolo, still casting frequent glances at the western sky, went on: "If you find yourself at Tredegarh, let us say, talking to people of your experiences here, and you tell them about what we spoke of this afternoon, the kind of reaction you will get will depend quite strongly on who they are, what math they came from—"

"As in, Procian versus Halikaarnian?" I asked. "I'm used to that, Orolo."

"This is a little different," Orolo said. "Most people, Procians and Halikaarnians alike, will deem it nothing more than idle, metatheorical speculation. Harmless, except insofar as it is a waste of time. On the other hand, if you talk to someone like Fraa Jad . . ."

He paused. I thought it was only to catch his breath, for we really were running now. Above us, aerocraft were settling in for landings outside the front gates, and the noise of their engines forced Orolo to raise his voice. But when I glanced sideways at him, I thought I saw uncertainty on his face. Not something I'd learned to associate with Pa Orolo. "I think," he finally said, "I think that they all know this."

"Know what?"

"That what I told you earlier is true."

"Oh."

"That they've known it for at least a thousand years."

"Ah."

"And that . . . that they do experiments."

"*What!?*"

Orolo shrugged, and got a wry smile. "An analogy: when the theors lost their atom smashers, they turned to the sky and made cosmography their laboratory, the only place remaining to test their theories—to turn their philosophy into theorics. Likewise, when a lot of these people were put together on a crag with nothing to do except ponder the kinds of things you and I were talking of earlier, well . . . some of them, I believe, devised experiments to prove whether they were speaking truth or nonsense. And out of that arose, over time, through trial and error, a form of praxis." I looked at him and he winked at me.

"So, you think Fraa Jad sent me here to find out whether you knew?"

"I suspect so, yes," Orolo said. "Under normal circumstances they might simply have reached down and hauled me up into the Centenarian or Millenarian math, but . . ." He was scanning the western sky again. "Ah, here it comes now!" he exclaimed, delightedly, as if we had been waiting for a train, and he'd just spied it coming into the station.

A white streak sliced heaven in half, moving west to east, and ending, with no loss of speed, in the caldera of the volcano a few thousand feet above us.

In the moment before the sound reached us, Orolo remarked, "Clever. They don't trust their aim enough to score a perfect hit on the probe. But they know enough geology to—"

After that I could not hear anything for half an hour. Hearing was worse than useless; I was sorry I'd been born with ears.

Fraa Haligastreme had taught me some geological terms which I will use here. I can imagine Cord shaking her head in dismay, giving me a hard time for using dry technical language instead of writing about the emotional truth. But the emotional truth was a black chaos of shock and fear, and the only way to recount what happened in a sensible way is to give technical details that we only pieced together later.

So, the Geometers had thrown a rock at us. Actually, a long rod of some dense metal, but in principle nothing fancier than a rock. It penetrated a quarter of a mile into the solid cap of hardened lava on top of the volcano before it vaporized of its own kinetic energy, creating a huge burst of pressure that we knew as an earthquake. The pressure vented up along the wound that the rod had left through the rock, widening the hole as it roared out, founding systems of cracks that were immediately blown open by the underlying lava. This lava was wet, saturated with steam; the steam exploded into gas as the overburden was relieved, just as bubbles appear in a bottle of soda when the lid is removed. The lava, inflated by the steam, blew itself up into ash, most of which went straight up, which is why everything for a thousand miles downwind ended up buried in grey dust. But some of it came down the side of the mountain in the form of a cloud, rolling down the slope like an avalanche, and easy for us to see, since it was glowing orange. And once we had gotten over the shock of what we had seen and staggered back up to our feet after the leg-breaking jolt of the explosion and sprinted to the top of the ramp in a desperate mob, what we clearly saw was that this thing, this glowing cloud, was coming for us, and that it would simultaneously crush us like a sledgehammer and roast us like a flamethrower if we didn't get out of its path. The only way of doing that was to get on the aerocraft, which had landed on the open slope between the walls of the concent and the souvenir shop. There were exactly enough of these to carry the soldiers who had arrived in them, plus their gear. So they had chivalrously dropped their gear on the ground. They were abandoning everything they had brought with them, the better to carry passengers—avout—away from danger. They were even flinging armloads of gear—fire extinguishers, medical kits—out onto the ground to make room for more humans.

What it came down to then was a simple calculation of the type any theor could appreciate. The pilots of the craft knew how much weight they could lift off the ground and they knew how much a person weighed, on average. Dividing the latter into the former told them how many people might be allowed on each craft. To enforce that limit, the pilots had their sidearms out, and armed soldiers posted to either side of the doors. The soldiers, by and large, knew where to go: they simply returned to the same craft they'd arrived in. The Orithenans swarmed, streamed, surged in the open spaces among the aerocraft, tripping on or vaulting over abandoned gear. Pilots pointed at them one by one, hustled them aboard, and kept count. From time to time they figured out a way to throw out more equipment and accept another passenger. This had already been going on for some time before Orolo, Sammann, and I came running out the gates. Most of the places were already taken. Full craft were lifting off, some with desperate people hanging from their landing gear. The few who hadn't yet been chosen were running from one aerocraft to another, and I was heartened to see that many were finding spaces. I saw Gnel's and Yul's vehicles parked with lights on and engines running, but didn't see them—they must have made it! I'd lost track of Orolo, though. A running soldier grabbed my arm and hurled me toward an aerocraft that was revving up its engines. I staggered toward the door through a cloud of flying dirt. Hands grabbed me and hauled me inside as the craft's skids were leaving the ground. The soldier climbed on to the skid behind me. I spun around in the doorway to take in the scene below. I could not see Sammann and I could not see Orolo—good! Had they found places?

Only two craft remained on the ground. One of them lifted off, shedding two Orithenans who pawed desperately at the frame of its door but couldn't get a grip. At least ten other people had been left behind. Some sat despondently or lay crumpled on the ground where they had fallen. Some ran for the sea. One took off running toward the one remaining aerocraft, but he was too far away. Some part of me was thinking *why couldn't they only have taken a few more?* but the answer was obvious in the way my aerocraft was performing: engines screaming full tilt, yet gaining altitude no faster than a man could climb a ladder, and shedding a hail of small objects as people found odds and ends that could be hurled out the open door. A flashlight bounced off the back of my head and tumbled to the floor; I clawed it up and tossed it out.

It almost struck a bolted figure hurrying over the ground, harshly lit from behind by the lights of Gnel's fetch, bent under a heavy burden—light blue. The dead body of the Geometer, forgotten and abandoned in the back of Gnel's fetch. The man bent under it was headed straight for the only aerocraft still on the ground. Arms were reaching out from the door. The runner put on a last, mighty effort, planted both feet in the dust below the aerocraft, and gave a mighty leg-thrust to hurl the Geometer's body upward. Hands grasped it and hauled it aboard. The soldier in the doorway showed his teeth as he screamed something into his microphone. The aerocraft rose, leaving behind the man who had delivered the dead Geometer. I forced myself to look at him, and saw what I had expected and dreaded: it was Orolo, alone before the gates of Orithena.

We had enough altitude now that I could look over the walls and buildings of the concent and up the slope to see what was coming. It looked very much as Fraa Haligastreme had described it to us from ancient texts: heavy as stone, fluid as water, hot as a forge, and—now that it had fallen several thousand feet down a mountain—fast as a bullet train.

"No!" I screamed. "We have to go back!" Not that anyone could hear me. But a soldier behind me read my face, saw my eyes swing toward the cockpit. He calmly raised his sidearm and planted its muzzle in the center of my forehead.

My next thought was *do I have the guts to jump out so that Orolo could have my place?* but I knew that they would not set down again to pick him up. There was no time.

Orolo was looking about curiously. He seemed almost bored. He sidestepped to a position where he could get a clear view uphill through the open gates and see what was headed for him. That, I think, gave him a sense of how many more seconds he had. He picked up a trenching tool that had been discarded, and used its handle to slash an arc into the loose soil. He turned, again and again, joining one arc to another, until he had completed the graceful, neverending curve of the analemma. Then he tossed the tool aside and stood on the center, facing his fate.

The buildings of the concent imploded before the glowing cloud even reached them, for the avalanche was pushing an invisible pressure wave before it. Destruction washed across the full width of the concent in a few seconds, and slammed into the walls from the back side. The walls bulged, cracked, shed a few blocks, but held, until the glowing cloud hit them with its full force. Then they went down like a sand castle struck by a wave.

"No!" I screamed one more time, as Orolo withered under the pressure wave. He flopped to the ground like a hank of rope. For a moment, smoke shrouded him: radiant heat shining out as a harbinger of the glowing cloud. Our aerocraft rocked and skidded sideways on hard air. The cloud erupted from the gates, vaulted over the rubble of the wall, and fell on Orolo. For a fraction of a second he was a blossom of yellow flame in the stream of light, and then he was one with it. All that remained of what he'd been was a wisp of steam coiling above the torrent of fire.

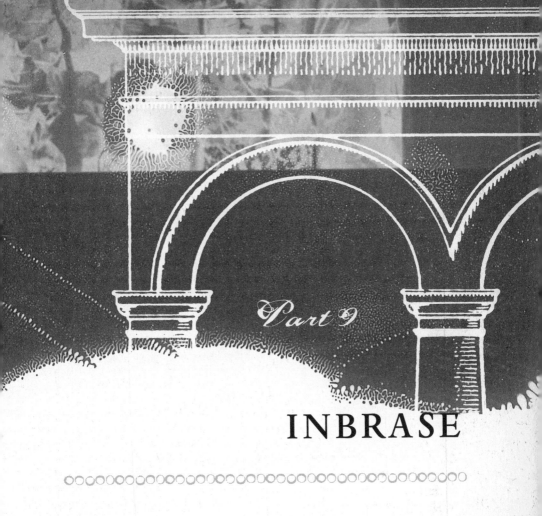

Part 9

INBRASE

Convox: A large convocation of avout from maths and concents all over the world. Normally celebrated only at Millennial Apert or following a sack, but also convened in highly exceptional circumstances at the request of the Sæcular Power.

—THE DICTIONARY, *4th edition, A.R. 3000*

Atide of milky light spilled in over the forests and the greens and congealed into sticky haze. It was a day without a dawn. The aerocraft's window had grown a million-edged network of tiny fractures that pulverized the light into a dust of rare colors. I was seeing it through the visor of a balloon suit. On the seat next to me was an orange suitcase that breathed and burbled like a torso, killing whatever came out of me. The avout and the Panjandrums who'd been summoned to Convox from all over Arbre were too important to risk infecting them with alien germs, and so I was living in a bubble until further notice.

This did not make sense. Why bring me to Tredegarh if there was any risk whatsoever? No dialog between rational people could have ended in the conclusion that I should be brought here—but only in a balloon suit. But as Orolo had said, the Convox was political, and made decisions by compromise. And it happened all the time that the compromise between two perfectly rational alternatives was something that made no sense at all.

So my first glimpse of the Precipice was through several layers of fogged, scratched, and cracked poly, and miles of haze: smoke, steam, or dust, I couldn't tell. The poets who wrote of it always seemed to behold the Precipice at dawn or sunset of a glorious day, and liked to wonder what the Thousanders were doing up in their turrets. They must not have known, or perhaps were too discreet to mention, that the lobe of granite beneath was riddled with tunnels for storage of nuclear waste, and that its Inviolateness was due not to the strength of its walls or the bravery of its defenders but to a deal between the mathic world and the Sæcular Power. I wondered what a poem would read like, written by one who saw the Precipice as I did now, knowing what I knew. A snort of laughter fogged my visor. But when it melted away, and gave me back again that stark, hazy, color-sapped prospect, I decided it could actually be a cool poem. The Precipice looked a thousand years older than anything on Ecba, and all of the stuff that so obscured my view gave me the same emotional distance as a cosmographer looking at a dust cloud through a telescope.

Tredegarh had been built somewhat farther away from the great cities of the late Praxic Age than Muncoster and Baritoe. That and the rugged look of the Precipice had given it the reputation of being isolated. The cities that surrounded Muncoster and Baritoe had, of course, fallen and been remade a dozen times since then, while similar ebbs and flows had lapped around Tredegarh; still, people in the mathic world insisted on thinking of it as a woodsy retreat. But we landed at a busy aerodrome no more than half an hour's walk from its Day Gate, and as we drove there I could see that what I'd identified as forests were really arboretums, and the pastures were really lawns for the pleasure of Sæculars who lived in great old houses tucked in at the verge of the woods.

The Day Gate was so lofty I didn't notice we'd passed through it. An inlaid road of red stone, wide enough to drive two mobes abreast, veered to the right and plunged under a huge Mathic pile that I mistook for the Mynster. But this was merely their Physicians' Commons, and the red road was a sign for illiterate patients and their visitors. I was being squired around on a motorized cart, since the suitcase grafted onto me was awkward to carry. My driver veered onto the red road and swung wide to dodge an old patient who was being aired out in a wheeled chair festooned with drip bags and readouts. We plunged through a portal arch, then turned off the red road into a service corridor. We hummed down long rows of chilly rooms with metal counters and sinister plumbing fixtures, then up a ramp and into a courtyard. This was about the size of the Cloister back home, but it felt smaller because the build-ings around it were higher. Planted in the corner of this space was a housing module, brand-new, with pipes and ducts snaking out of its windows and leading away to whirring machines, or through windows to a lab. I was directed to go inside and take off my suit. When the door closed behind me I heard it being locked from the outside, then the farting of a poly tape dispenser sealing the cracks all around. I kicked my way free of the suit and powered down the suitcase, then stuffed them under the bed. The module had a bedroom, a bath, and a kitchen/dining nook. The windows had been reinforced on the outside with metal mesh—so that if I turned out to be claustrophobic and prone to panic attacks I couldn't claw my way out—and sealed with thick, translucent poly sheeting.

Pretty bleak. Yet this was the first time I'd been alone for several weeks, and in that sense it could not have been more luxurious. I almost didn't know what to do with myself. I felt dizzy, and knew that I was about to fall apart. Then I didn't feel quite so private after all, since I guessed that I must be under surveillance. I couldn't stop thinking about the image of my sobbing face that I had inadvertently captured in Clesthyra's Eye after Orolo's Anathem—the *first* time he had died. Some instinct told me to burrow. I went into the bathroom, turned off the light, turned on the shower, and ducked under the water. Once the temperature had stabilized I collapsed back against the wall, sank down until I was all folded up over the drain, and utterly lost control of myself. A lot went down that drain.

I had been through adventures that might have made for good stories if Orolo hadn't been vaporized before my eyes. Our aerocraft, along with several others, had flown to the next island upwind and landed on a beach, scattering a crowd of locals who'd gathered there to drink wine and watch the eruption of Ecba. Other aerocraft had run out of fuel and ditched in the sea. Since they had jettisoned their life rafts to make room for passengers, many of these would have drowned had it not been for the avout, who could easily make their spheres into life buoys. A second wave of airborne commandoes had plucked them out of the water and brought them to the same beach where the rest of us had set down. This had been commandeered by the Sæcular Power and cordoned off. Tents had been dropped on us and we had erected our own camp: "New

Orithena," complete with a canvas cloister in the middle and a digital alarm clock on a stick, where Provener was celebrated. We had said the aut of requiem for Orolo and the others who had not survived. Meanwhile the military had pitched larger tents around us, marched us through naked, hosed us down with unspecified chemical solutions, given us plastic bags in which to void urine and excrement. We had spent a few days living off military rations, wearing paper coveralls that we were supposed to burn when they got dirty, being called in at random times to be interviewed, phototyped, and biometrically scanned.

Around noon on the second day, a big fixed-wing aerocraft had landed on a nearby road that had been made into a temporary aerodrome. A little while later, a caravan of vehicles had come up the beach, carrying civilians, some of whom had been dressed in bolts and chords. My name had been called. I'd walked to the camp gate, where I had encountered—across a safe, non-infectious expanse of empty sand—a contingent from Tredegarh. There had been a couple of dozen, all told. Until they had begun speaking to me in perfect Orth, I had not even recognized some of them as avout, because the style of their bolts and chords was so different from what we wore at Edhar. They originated from many different concents. I'd recognized only one of them: a Valer who'd helped save me in Mahsht. I'd caught her eye and made a hint of a bow, and she'd responded in kind.

The FAE of this group had said something about Orolo that was actually quite respectful and well put. He had then informed me that I would help them prepare the "givens" for shipment to the Convox, and return to Tredegarh with them the next day. By "givens," of course, he'd meant the box of vials and the body of the dead Geometer, both of which had been confiscated by the military and kept on ice in a special tent.

Meanwhile, Sammann had been having a similar conversation with one of his brethren; a small detachment of Ita, segregated in their own vehicle.

Thereafter it had mostly been work, which had probably been a good thing, since it had meant less brooding time for me. Since Orolo had traded the rest of his life for the theorical knowledge contained in the body of the Geometer, preparing it for shipment to Tredegarh had given me an opportunity to show it the same respect as I would have shown the body of Orolo, had we been able to give him a normal burial. Two lives had been sacrificed—one of Arbre, one of some other world—to bring us this knowledge.

In what free time I did have, I talked to Cord. At first, I only spoke of my feelings. Later, Cord began to share her views about what had happened, and it became obvious that she was interpreting the whole thing from a Kelx point of view. It seemed that Magister Sark had got himself a convert. His words, back in Mahsht, might have made only a faint impression on her, but something about what we had lived through at Orithena had made it all seem true in her mind. And this didn't seem like the right time for me to try to convince her otherwise. It was, I realized, like the broken stove all over again. What was the point of my having a truer explanation of these things if it could only be understood by avout who devoted their whole lives to theorics? Cord, independent soul that she was, wouldn't want to live her life under the sway of such ideas any more than she'd want to cook breakfast with a machine that she couldn't understand and fix.

Wrung out, purified, shaky but stronger, I wandered around my new home.

Half the kitchen was occupied by bottled water, palletized and stacked. The cupboards had been stocked with an odd mixture of extramuros groceries and fresh produce from the tangles and arboretums of Tredegarh. Some books had been left on the table: a few very ancient spec-fic novels (the originals, machine-stamped on cheap paper, were all dust; these had been copied out by hand on proper leaves) and a dog's breakfast of philosophy, metatheorics, quantum mechanics, and neurology. Some was famous stuff written by people like Protas, some had been produced by avout toiling in maths I'd never heard of. I concluded that some fid had been deputized to provide me with reading material and had run through a library blindfolded, pawing books off shelves at random.

On my bed lay a new bolt, chord, and sphere, wrapped and knotted into the traditional package. As I undid the knots and folds, kicked off the last of my Ecba garb, and got dressed, everything that had happened since I'd been walked out the Day Gate of Edhar began to seem dreamlike—as far back in the past as the time before I was Collected.

In the kitchen I culled all of the food from the Sæcular world, hiding it in the cupboards, and left the produce out where I could see and smell it. They'd provided me with everything I needed to make bread, so I set about it without thinking. The smell of it permeated the module and drove back the scents of fresh poly, carpet adhesive, and glueboard.

I tried to read one of the metatheorics books while the dough was rising. Just as I was beginning to doze off (the book was impenetrable and my body's clock was out of synch with the sun) someone tried to scare me to death by pounding on the walls of my trailer. I knew it was Arsibalt by the weight of the impacts. By his footfalls as he prowled around. By the methodical way he pounded on every bit of wall that presented itself—as if I could have missed it the first time.

I opened a window and shouted through steel mesh and cloudy poly-sheet. "It is not made of stone, like the buildings you are accustomed to, and so a little pounding goes a long way."

A vaguely Arsibalt-shaped ghost centered itself in the aperture. "Fraa Erasmas! How good it is to hear your voice, and squint at your indistinct form!"

"Likewise. Am I still even considered a fraa then?"

"They are far too busy to fit your Anathem into their schedules—don't flatter yourself."

A long silence.

"I am so terribly sorry," he said.

"Me too." Arsibalt seemed upset, so I nattered on for a while. "You should have seen me an hour ago! I was a mess," I said. "Am still."

"You were . . . there?"

"A couple of hundred feet away, I'd estimate."

Then he began weeping in earnest. I couldn't very well go and put my arms around him. I tried to think of something to say. It was harder, I saw, for him. Not that watching Orolo die had been *easy* for me. But if it had to happen, it was better to have been there and watched it. And better, as well, to have spent a couple of days afterwards with my friends on the beach.

After the contingent from Tredegarh had showed up and told me how it was going to be, I'd sat around a campfire with Cord, Yul, Gnel, and Sammann. It had not been necessary to point out that we five might never be together again.

"They wouldn't bring me back to Tredegarh just to Anathematize me," I speculated, "so I guess I'll go back to being what I was." I looked around at all of their faces, warm in firelight. "But I'll never be the same."

"No kidding," Yul said, "all those head injuries."

Ganelial Crade said, "I'm staying with these people."

This was so unexpected that we'd all been slow to work out what he meant: he was joining the Orithenans. "I've talked to Landasher about it," he went on, amused by how we were reacting. "He says they'll try me out for a while, and if I'm not too obnoxious, maybe I can stay."

Yul got up and went around the circle to hug his cousin from behind and pound him on the back. We all toasted him with our poly cups of dyed sugar water.

Heads turned next to Sammann, who threw up his hands and admitted, "All of this has been very good for my reputation and access." We all hurled mock abuse at him for a while. He soaked it up with a satisfied smile. "I'll be flying back to the Convox with Fraa Erasmas—probably in a different section of the plane, though." This moved me, and so I got up, walked over, and embraced him while I was still allowed to.

Finally attention turned to Cord and Yul, who were sitting on a cooler and leaning against each other. "Now that we are Arbre-leading experts on Geometer technology," Yul began, "we might go out and seek employment as such."

"Seriously," Cord said, "there are a lot of people here who want to ask us questions. Since the probe got destroyed, our memories of what we saw are important. We might even end up at Tredegarh."

"Yul's rig too," I remarked. I had a dim memory of its wreckage hurtling past Fraa Orolo. For once, Yul had nothing to say. He just gazed out over the sea and shook his head.

Cord reminded us, "My fetch should be safe at Norslof. Once things have settled down a little, we'll go back and collect it. Then we were thinking of going up into the mountains for a while—a delayed honeymoon."

A silence ensued. She let it stretch out just long enough before saying, "Oh, did I mention we're engaged?"

The previous evening, Yul had approached me with a conspiratorial look and drawn a shiny thing from his pocket: a metal ring that he had cut free from the rigging of the Geometers' parachute. He'd heated it in a campfire blown white-hot with an improvised bellows, and hammered it into a size that he hoped would fit Cord's finger.

"I was going to ask Cord to—well—you know. Not right away! But later, you know, when things are settled."

I'd realized that Yul was, in a way, asking my permission, so I'd moved to embrace him and said, "I know you'll take care of her." His hug had nearly broken my spine and I'd thought for a moment I'd have to summon one of the Valers to come and pry him off me.

After he'd calmed down a little, he'd let me look at the ring. "Not your normal jewel," he admitted, "but—being that it's from another world and all—it's the rarest, isn't it?"

"Yes," I assured him, "it's the rarest." Then both of us had involuntarily looked over at my sib.

He must have asked her earlier in the day, and she must have said yes. For a while, there was wild hugging, hollering, and running around. A mob of Orithenans gathered around us, drawn by a rumor that the wedding was going to happen *now*. They were followed by curious soldiers, followed in turn by Convox people who wanted to know what all the fuss was about. There was a kind of crazy momentum pushing us toward holding the ceremony that day, on the beach. But after a few minutes, everyone settled down, and it turned into a party. Orithenan suurs uprooted armloads of weedy flowers from the ditch along the road and braided them into garlands. The soldiers got into the spirit of things, producing booze from nowhere, and cheering Cord and Yul with gutsy noises. A helicopter mechanic gave Cord his favorite daisy-head screwdriver.

An hour later I was on the plane to Tredegarh.

Arsibalt was settling down a little. He drew a deep, shaky breath. "He accepted his fate quite calmly, it seemed."

"Yes."

"Do you know the meaning of the symbol he drew on the ground? The analemma?"

Something occurred to me. "Hey!" I said. "How do you know all of this stuff? Have they been letting you watch speelies?"

He was glad to have an excuse to declaim about something. It settled him right down. "I forget you know nothing of the Convox. Whenever they wish to say something to everyone—for example, when Jesry came back from space—they summon us to a so-called Plenary in the nave of the Unarians, the only place big enough to hold the entire Convox. Rules are relaxed; they show us speelies. Anyway, there was an all-day Plenary—most enervating—after the Visitation of Orithena."

"Is that what they're calling it?"

I could see him nodding. It was hard to make out details through the poly, but I feared he might be trying to grow a beard again.

"Well," I said, "I spent a few days with him before . . . before the events you saw on the speely. Of course, I saw the original Analemma, the ancient one on the Temple floor."

"Now *that* must have been something!" Arsibalt gushed.

"It was. Especially now that we can never go back," I said. "But as for the analemma that Orolo drew on the beach, I'm afraid I didn't get any special insight to decode the meaning of . . ."

"Is something the matter?" Arsibalt asked, a few seconds later. For I had trailed off.

"I just remembered something," I said. "A remark Orolo made. The last thing he said to me, before the probe fired its thrusters. 'They must have deciphered my analemma!'"

"'They' meaning the Geometers, presumably."

"Yeah. Too much was happening for me to ask him what it meant . . ."

"And then it was too late," Arsibalt said.

Orolo's death was still new enough that we had to stop talking for a few moments whenever it came up in conversation. But both of us were thinking. "A phototype on the wall of his cell, at Bly's Butte," I said, "showed the Analemma. The ancient one."

"Yes," Arsibalt said. "I remember seeing it."

"Almost as if it were the equivalent of a religious symbol to him," I said, "like the Triangle is to certain Arks."

"But that doesn't explain his remark about the Geometers 'deciphering' it," Arsibalt pointed out.

We sat there puzzling over it for a few more moments, but could make no headway.

"So," I said, "at the Plenary after Jesry came back from space . . . did you see what happened to the Warden of Heaven?"

"Did you?" he asked. Then both of us were silent for a minute, daring each other to say something funny and inappropriate. But somehow it didn't seem like the right time, yet.

"How are the others?"

He sighed. "I don't see much of them. We have all been assigned to different Laboratoria. Periklyne is absolute bedlam, of course. And we have chosen different Lucubs."

I could only guess at the meanings of those words. "But maybe you can at least tell me how they are doing?"

"You need to know it is different for Jesry and Ala," he began.

"Why?"

"Because they were summoned in Voco. They died, as do all whose names are called out thus, and they had to begin new lives. Some of them quite liked it. All of them got used to it. Then, suddenly, weeks later, the thing changed into a Convox."

"They had to undie."

"Yes. You should expect some awkwardness."

"Awkwardness! Well, at least something about this place will be familiar then."

Arsibalt cleared his throat instead of laughing.

"They are going to let you out of this contraption in no time," Jesry told me. Somewhat confounding Arsibalt's prediction, he came to visit me before my bread was even finished cooling.

He had spoken with such absolute confidence that I knew he had to be blowing this out of his rectal orifice. "What is the basis of your prediction?" I asked.

"The lasers were the wrong color," he said.

I repeated this sentence out loud, but could make nothing of it.

"The laser that shone down onto the Inviolates," he explained, "on the night that this turned into a Convox."

"It was red," I said—pretty stupid, but I was trying to dislodge loose bits of information from Jesry's brain by throwing rocks at it.

"Some here at Tredegarh are knowledgable about lasers," Jesry said. "They knew right away that something was funny. There are only so many gases, or combinations of gases, that can be used to make a red laser. Each generates a different wavelength. A laser expert can look at a spot of light and know right away what gas mixture was used as the lasing medium. They didn't recognize the color of the Geometers' laser."

"I don't see what—"

"Fortunately a cosmographer at Rambalf had the presence of mind to expose a photomnemonic tablet to that light," Jesry went on. "So we know its exact wavelength. And it has been confirmed that it doesn't match up with any naturally occurring spectral lines."

"That makes no sense! Those wavelengths fall out of quantum-mechanical calculations that are basic to *everything*!"

"But think of newmatter," Jesry said.

"Okay," I said, and considered it. If you messed around with how the nucleus was put together, it changed the way electrons orbited around it. Laser light was the result of an electron jumping from an orbit with a higher, to another with lower, energy. The energy difference determined the wavelength—the color—of the light. "Lasers made with newmatter have colors not found in nature," I allowed.

Jesry was silent, waiting for me to go the next step.

"So," I continued, "the Geometers have newmatter—they used it to make a laser."

He shifted posture. Through the plastic I could see nothing *but* posture. Yet I knew he was disagreeing with me. And for once, I knew why.

"But they *don't*," I continued. "At least, not in any meaningful way. I've handled their parachute. The shroud lines. The hatch. It was just regular stuff—too heavy, too weak."

He nodded. "What you couldn't know—what none of us knew, until a few hours ago—is that it is *all* newmatter. Everything that came down in that probe—all the hardware, all the flesh—is what we would call newmatter, in the sense that the nuclei are put together in a way that is not natural—not in this cosmos, anyway."

"But most of it was destroyed!" I protested. "Or at least buried in hundreds of feet of ash."

"The Orithenans, and your friends, came away with some fragments. We have a T-handle panel. Some bolts that Cord put in her pocket. Scraps of chute and shroud lines. The box of blood samples. And we have the entire body of the woman who was shot in the back, thanks to Saunt Orolo."

This almost slipped by me. Jesry hadn't mentioned Orolo until now. Certain nuances in his posture and voice told me he was grieving—but only because I'd known him my whole life. He was going to grieve in a funny, hidden way, over a long period of time.

I cleared my throat. "Are a lot of people referring to him that way, now?"

"Actually, fewer as time goes by. Right after they showed us the speely, it just flew out of people's mouths. His actions were so obviously those of a saunt that no one even had to think about it. In the last day or so, some are pulling back—reconsidering it."

"What's to reconsider!?"

He shrugged and threw up his hands. "Don't worry about it. You know how it is. No one wants to be hasty—to be called an Enthusiast. The Procians are probably cooking up radical new interpretations of what Orolo did in their Lucubs. Forget it. He made the sacrifice. We honor that by getting as much knowledge as we can out of the dead chick. And I'm trying to tell you that every nucleus of every atom in her, the shotgun balls in her guts, the clothing she wore, is newmatter—so the same is probably true of everything in the isocahedron."

"So the electrons around those nuclei behave correspondingly unnaturally," I said, "such as lasing at the wrong color."

"Electron behavior is basically synonymous with chemistry," Jesry put in. "That's why newmatter was invented: because monkeying around with nucleosynthesis gave us new elements and new chemistry to play around with."

"And the functioning of living organisms is founded on chemistry," I said.

Jesry was smarter than I. He must have known it. But he didn't let it show very often. No matter how many times I failed to get what he was talking about, he had this steady faith in my ability to understand what he understood. It was an endearing quality—his only one. Now, he shifted posture again, leaning in as if he were actually interested in what I had to say—letting me know I was on the right track.

"We can't interact *chemically* with the Geometers—or with any of their viruses or bacteria—because the laser was the wrong color!"

"Some simple interactions are doubtless possible," Jesry said. "An electron is an electron. So our atoms can form simple chemical bonds with theirs. But there's not the sophisticated biochemistry that germs use to go about their business."

"So, they could make noises that we could hear. See light reflecting from our bodies. Punch us in the nose, even . . ."

"Or rod us." This was the first time I'd heard *rod* employed as a verb, but I collected that he was talking of the projectile that had blasted Ecba.

"But not infect us," I said.

"Nor vice versa. Oh, over time, germs will evolve that can interact with both types of matter—knit the ecosystems together. But that'll take a long time, and we can stay ahead of it. So. You'll be out of that box soon."

"Do they have water? Oxygen?"

"Their hydrogen is identical to ours. Their oxygen is similar enough to give them water. We don't know whether we could breathe it. Carbon seems to be a little different. The metals and so on show greater divergence."

"How much more do you know about the Geometers?"

"Less than you. What was Orolo doing at Orithena?"

"Pursuing a line of inquiry that I don't fully understand."

"Consistent with a polycosmic interpretation of what's going on?"

"Totally."

"Tell me about it."

"I'm afraid to talk about it."

"Why?"

"Because I'm afraid I'll make a bloody hash of it."

Jesry did not respond, and I fancied he was eyeing me suspiciously through the plastic.

The real reason I didn't want to talk about it, of course, was because I was afraid it would lead straight to the Incanters. And I guessed that we were under surveillance.

"Some other time," I said, "when I'm fresher. We can go for a walk. Like when we used to hold theorical dialogs in Orolo's vineyard."

Orolo's vineyard, because of its south-facing slope, was one of those parts of Edhar that wasn't visible from any of the Warden Regulant's windows, and as such, was where we used to go when we were up to some kind of mayhem. Jesry got the message, and nodded.

"How's Ala?" I asked.

"Fine. I don't know when you'll see her, because after our Voco, she and I started having a liaison."

My ears caught fire and serrated bristles popped out of my spine.

Or at least it felt that way. But later when I checked out a mirror, I didn't seem any different, just a little more stupid-looking. Some higher, more modern part of my brain—that is, some part of it that had evolved more recently than five million years ago—thought it might be good to keep the conversation going. "Well. Thanks for letting me know. What's going to happen now, then?"

"Well, knowing her, she's going to make a decision. And until she's made it, neither one of us is probably going to hear from her."

I didn't say anything.

"She's busy, anyway," Jesry went on. I had the feeling that he was finished with me, bored, and really wanted to leave. But even he knew he couldn't just drop this bomb and walk away. So he filled a little time talking about the structure of the Convox and how it was organized. I heard little.

That's why he had paid me a visit so promptly. So that he could break this news to me while we were separated by steel mesh. Clever boy!

Because (as I reflected, after he had taken his leave) he knew me, and knew I'd brood on it, and be reasonable. Why *shouldn't* they have started a liaison? After Ala had been Evoked, I had thought of myself as available.

Not that it had gotten me anywhere!

I ate a piece of bread. Three avout in bubble suits came into the trailer. Two of them stole even more of my blood. The other stayed behind after the blood-stealers had made their getaway. She wrenched the head from her bubble suit and tossed it on the floor. Stuffed the gloves into that. Stuck her fingers through her hair, and felt her own scalp. "Stuffy in there," she explained, when she caught me looking. "Suur Maroa. Centenarian. Fifth Sconic. I'm from a little math you've never heard of. Can I have some of that bread?"

"Aren't you afraid you'll be contaminated?"

She glanced at her helmet, then back to me.

I thought Suur Maroa was pretty attractive, but she was fifteen years older than I, and I didn't trust myself at the moment; maybe

I'd have been attracted to any female who didn't treat me as an alien plague vector. So I got her a piece of bread. "What a godawful place!" she remarked, looking around. "Is this how extras live?"

"Most of them."

"You should be out of it soon, though." She inhaled deeply through her nose, and I could tell by the look on her face that she was thinking about what she smelled. Then she got an annoyed look, and shook her head. "Too many industrial byproducts in here," she muttered.

"What are you about?" I asked. "What do Fifth Sconics do? I'm sorry, I ought to know."

"Thank you," she said, accepting a piece of bread from my hand, touching me incidentally. She took a bite and stared off into space as she chewed it.

Avout who followed the Sconic Discipline had begun to splinter and fight immediately after the Reconstitution and to squabble over which sect had dibs on the names Sconics, Reformed Sconics, New Sconics, and so on. Eventually they had gone over to a numbering system. They were up into the low twenties now, so Fives were pretty well-established.

"I don't think that the differences between the Fives, the Fours, and the Sixes are germane here," she finally decided. She turned to look at me. "I just want to know how they smelled."

"Really?"

"Yeah. For example, you handled the parachute, right?"

"Yes."

"If you handled a big old parachute from a military depot on Arbre, you'd be able to smell it. Maybe it would smell musty from being wadded up in a sack for a long time."

"If only I'd had the presence of mind to pay more attention to that!" I said.

"It's all right," Suur Maroa said. She was a theor, used to setbacks. "You were kind of busy. Nice job, by the way."

"Oh thanks."

"When the cool girl—"

"Cord."

"Yeah, activated the pressure equalization valves on the hatch, air moved—?"

"*In* to the capsule," I said.

"So you didn't get to smell their atmosphere until *after* it had been mixed with ours."

"Correct."

"Damn."

"Maybe we should have waited," I said.

She aimed a sharp look at me. "I don't recommend you go around saying things like that!"

I was taken aback. She checked herself and went on in a lower voice: "This place is the world capital of know-it-alls. Everyone is jealous. Wishes they'd been there instead of you and a bunch of Lineage weirdos. Thinks they could have done better."

"Okay, never mind," I said. "We had to do what we did because we knew the military was coming to screw it up even worse."

"That's more like it," she said. "Back to the olfactory now: do you remember smelling anything, at any time?"

"Yes! We talked about it!"

"Not when that Ita had his speelycaptor on you, you didn't."

"Before Sammann arrived. The probe had just landed. Orolo smelled the plume from the engines. He wanted to know if they were using toxic propellants—"

"Wise of him. Some of them are frightening," Maroa put in.

"But we couldn't smell anything. Decided it was all steam. Hydrogen/oxygen."

"That is still a negative result."

"But later, there was a definite odor inside the probe," I said. "I remember it now. Associated with the body. I assumed it was some kind of bodily fluid."

"Assumed, because you didn't recognize the odor?" Suur Maroa asked, after she had thought about this for as long as she wanted to.

"It was totally new to me."

"So the Geometers' organic molecules *are* capable of interacting chemically with our olfactory systems," she concluded. "It's an interesting result. Theors have been breathing down my neck wanting me to answer it—because some of those reactions are quantum-mechanical in nature."

"Our noses are quantum devices?"

"Yes!" Maroa said, with a bright look that was close to a smile. "Little-known fact." She stood up and fetched her helmet. "It's a useful result. We should be able to get a sample from the body and expose it to olfactory tissue in a lab." She gave me the bright look again. "Thank you!" And, in a completely absurd departure ritual, she pulled her gloves on, and lowered her helmet over her head, which I was sorry to see the last of.

"Wait!" I said. "How could any of this be? How could the Geometers be so like us, and yet made of different matter?"

"You'll have to ask a cosmographer," she said. "My specialty is cornering vermin and taking them apart."

"What does that make me?" I asked, but she was too preoccupied getting her helmet on to catch the joke. She passed out into a kind of airlock that they'd erected outside my front door. The door closed and locked, and the tape dispenser started making rude noises again.

It got dark. I fretted over the contradiction. The Geometers looked like us, but were made of matter so fundamentally different that Maroa had entertained the possibility that we wouldn't even be able to smell it. Some at the Convox were afraid of space germs; Maroa sure wasn't.

My being stuck in this box was a byproduct of arguments that people were having in chalk halls a few hundred yards away. I should have paid better attention to Jesry's chitchat about what a Convox was.

Lio showed up late and made a hooting noise at the window. It was a fake bird call that we had used, back at Edhar, when we were out after curfew.

"I can't see you at all," I said.

"Just as well. Bumps and bruises mostly."

"Been working out with the Valers?"

"That would be much safer. No, I've been working out with

people who are as clumsy as I am. The Ringing Vale avout watch and laugh."

"Well, I hope you're giving as good as you're getting."

"That would be satisfying on one level," he allowed, "but no way to shine in the eyes of my instructors."

I felt funny talking to a blank square of plastic, so I turned off the lights and sat in the dark with him. For a long time. Thinking, not talking, about Orolo.

"Why are they teaching you how to fight?" I asked. "I thought they had that market cornered."

"You jumped straight to a pretty interesting question, Raz," he croaked. His voice had gotten all husky. "I don't know the answer yet. Just starting to get some ideas."

"Well, my body clock is screwed up, I'm going to be awake all night, and the books they left me are unreadable. My girlfriend ran off with Jesry. So, I'm happy to sit here and listen to your ideas."

"What books did they leave you?"

"A hodgepodge."

"Unlikely. There must be a common thread. You need to get on top of it before your first messal."

"Jesry used that word. I was trying to parse it."

"Comes from the diminutive of a Proto-Orth word meaning a flat surface on which food was served."

"So, 'small table'—"

"Think 'small dinner.' Turns out to be an important tradition here. It's really different from Edhar, Raz. The way we used to eat—everyone together in the Refectory, carrying their own food around, sitting wherever they felt like it—they have a word for that too, not so complimentary. It is seen as backward, chaotic. Only fids and a few weird, ascetic orders do it. Here it's all about messals. The maximum head count is seven. That's considered to be the largest number you can fit around a table such that everyone can hear, and people aren't always splitting off into side conversations."

"So, there's a dining hall somewhere with a lot of seven-person tables in it?"

"No, that'd be too noisy. Each messal is held in a small private room—called a messallan."

"So, there's a ring of these messallans, or something, around the Refectory kitchen?"

Lio was chuckling at my naïveté. Not in a mean way. He'd been in the same state of ignorance a few weeks ago. "Raz, you don't get how rich this place is. There is no Refectory—no one central kitchen. It's all dowments and chapterhouses."

"They have active dowments? I thought those were abolished—"

"In the Third Sack reforms," he said. "They were. But you know how Shuf's Dowment has been fixed up by the ROF? Well, imagine a concent with a hundred places like that—each of them bigger and nicer than Shuf's ever was. And don't get me started on the chapterhouses."

"I feel like a hick already."

"Just you wait."

"So there is a separate kitchen—" I stopped, unable to handle such a wild thought.

"A separate kitchen for each messallan—cooking just fourteen servings at a time!"

"I thought you said seven."

"The servitors have to eat too."

"What's a servitor?"

"*We* are!" Lio laughed. "When they let you out, you'll be paired with a senior fraa or suur—your doyn. A couple of hours ahead of time, you go to the dowment or chapterhouse where your doyn is assigned for messal, and you and the other servitors prepare the dinner. When the bells ring eventide, the doyns show up and sit down around the table and the servitors bring out the food. When you're not moving plates around, you stand behind your doyn with your back to the wall."

"That is *shocking*," I said. "I'm half convinced you're pulling my leg."

"I couldn't believe it myself, at first," Lio said, laughing. "Made me feel like such a hayseed. But the system works. You get to listen in on conversations you'd never get to be a part of otherwise. As years go by you move up and become a doyn and get a servitor of your own."

"What if your doyn is an idiot? What if it's a bad messal with the same boring conversation every evening? You can't get up and move to another table like we do at Edhar!"

"I wouldn't trade it for our system," Lio said. "It's not such an issue now, because the people who get invited to a Convox tend to be pretty interesting."

"So, who is your doyn?"

"She's the Warden Fendant of a small math on the top of a sky-scraper in a big city that is in the middle of a sectarian holy war."

"Interesting. And where is your messallan?"

Lio said, "My doyn and I rotate to a different one every evening. This is unusual."

"Hmm. I wonder where they'll put me."

"That's why you need to get on top of those books," Lio said. "You might get in trouble with your doyn if you're not prepared."

"Not prepared to do what—fold their napkin?"

"You're expected to understand what's going on. Sometimes, servitors even get to take part in the conversation."

"Oh. What an honor!"

"It might be a *great* honor, depending on who your doyn is. Imagine if Orolo were your doyn."

"I take your point. But that's out of the question."

Lio brooded for a while before answering. "That's another thing," he said, in a quiet voice. "The aut of Anathem has not been celebrated at Tredegarh for close to a thousand years."

"How can that be? This place must have twenty times the population of Edhar!"

"All the different chapters and dowments make it possible for weirdos and misfits to find homes," Lio said. "You and I grew up in a tough town, brother."

"Well, don't go soft on me now."

"That is unlikely," Lio said, "when I spend every day sparring with Valers."

This reminded me that he was exhausted. "Hey! Before you go—one question," I said.

"Yeah?"

"Why are we here? Isn't this Convox a sitting duck?"

"Yes."

"You'd think they'd have dispersed it."

"Ala's been busy," he said, "drawing up contingency plans for just that. But the order hasn't been given yet. Maybe they're worried it would look like a provocation."

"So—we are . . ."

"Hostages!" Lio said cheerfully. "Good night, Raz."

"'Night, Lio."

In spite of Lio's advice, I couldn't get a grip on the books that had been left for me. My brain was too jangled. I tried to skim the novels. These were easier to follow, but I couldn't fathom why I had been *assigned* to read such things. I got about twenty leaves into the third one, and the hero jumped through a portal to a parallel universe. The other two novels had also revolved around parallel-universe scenarios, so I reasoned that I was supposed to be thinking about that topic, and that the other books must relate to that theme. But all of a sudden my body decided it was time to sleep, and I was barely able to stagger over to bed before I lost consciousness.

I woke to bells ringing strange changes, and Tulia calling my name. Not in a happy way. For a moment I fancied I was back at Edhar. But when I opened one eye—just a slit—all I saw was trailer.

"My god!" Tulia exclaimed, from terrifyingly close range. I came awake to find her standing at the foot of my bed. No bubble suit. The look on her face was as if she'd found me sprawled in a gutter outside a bordello. I did some groping, and satisfied myself that most of me was covered by my bolt.

"What is your problem?" I muttered.

"You have to move *now*! *Instantly!* They are holding up Inbrase for you!"

That sounded serious, so I rolled out of bed and chased her out of the trailer. The airlock had been torn down; we trampled the plastic. She led me across the courtyard, under an arch, and down some ancient Mathic catacomb whose far end was sealed off by an iron grille—the sort of barrier used to separate one math from another. It sported a gate, which was being held open by a nervous-seeming fid who clanged it shut behind us as we burst through into a long straight lane guarded by twin rows of enormous page trees. This lane cut through the middle of a forest of them.

My feet had grown soft from wearing shoes and I kept mincing over stones and root-knuckles, so Tulia outran me. On its far side, the page-tree wood was bordered by a stone wall, thirty-odd feet high, pierced by a massive arch, where she paused to catch her breath and wait for me.

As I drew near, she turned to face me and raised her arms. I gave her a big hug, lifting her off the ground, and for some reason both of us broke out laughing. I loved her for that. She was the only one I'd met who was responding to Orolo's death with something other than sadness. Not that she wasn't sad. But she was proud of him, I thought, thrilled by what he had done, glad that I had survived and come back to be with my friends once more.

Then we were running again: through the arch and into a rolling green, splashed with coppices of great old trees, that seemed to extend for miles. Stone buildings rose up every few hundred feet, and a network of footpaths joined them. These must be the dowments and chapterhouses Lio had spoken of. I was more impressed by the lawns than anything else; at Edhar, we couldn't afford to waste ground this way.

The bells were getting marginally closer. As we came around the corner of an especially huge building—some sort of cloister/library complex—the Precipice finally came in view. Tulia led me to a broad tree-lined lane that would take us straight to it. Then I was able to see the Mynster complex massed at the base of the cliff.

The Precipice had been formed when a dome of granite, three thousand feet high, had shed its western face. Avout had cleaned up the mess below and used the crumbly bits to make buildings and walls. Since no artificial clock-tower could compete with the Precipice, they had built their Mynster at the base of the cliff and then cut tunnels and galleries and ledges into the granite above, sculpting the Precipice into their Clock, or vice versa. A succession of dials had been built over the millennia, each higher and larger than the last, and all of them still told time: all of them told me I was late.

"Inbrase," I gasped, "that's—"

"Your official induction to the Convox," Tulia said. "Everyone has to go through it—the formal end of your Peregrination—we did it weeks ago."

"A lot of trouble for one straggler."

She laughed once, sharply, but couldn't maintain it owing to air debt. "Don't flatter yourself, Raz! We've been doing these once a week. There's a hundred other peregrins from eight different maths—all waiting on you!"

The bells stopped ringing—a bad sign! We picked up our pace and ran silently for a few hundred yards.

"I thought everyone got here a long time ago!" I said.

"Only from big concents. You would not believe how isolated some are. There's even a contingent of Matarrhites!"

"So I'm with the Deolaters, eh?"

I was getting the picture that the chapterhouses closest to the Mynster were the oldest: ring around ring of cloister, gallery, walk, and yard. Glimpses, through Mathic gates and shouting arches, of chapterhouses so tiny, mean, and time-pitted that they must date back to the Reconstitution. New towers striving to make up in loftiness and brilliance what their ancient neighbors owned by dint of age, fame, and dignity.

"Another thing," Tulia said, "I almost forgot. Right after Inbrase there is going to be a Plenary."

"Arsibalt mentioned those—Jesry did one?"

"Yes. I wish I had more time, but . . . just remember it's all theater."

"Sounds like a warning!"

"Any time you get that many in a room, there's no dialog worthy of the name—it's all stilted. Filtered."

"Political?"

"Of course. Just—just don't try to out-politic these guys."

"Because I'm a complete idiot when it comes to—"

"Exactly."

We ran on silently for a few more strides, and she thought better of it. "Remember our conversation, Raz? Before Eliger?"

"You were going to nail down the political end of things," I recalled, "so that I could memorize more digits of pi."

"Something like that," she said, tossing off a chuckle just to be a good sport.

"And how's that plan working out?"

"Just tell the truth. Don't try to be tricky. It's not in you."

Half of the visible universe was now grey granite. We ran up steps whose only purpose was to support steps that held up other tiers and hierarchies and systems of steps. But at some point things flattened out. An entrance was dead ahead of us, but the wrong one. Peregrins were supposed to enter from the direction of the Day Gate, so we had to run a quarter of the way around the Mynster and go in the grandest of all the entrances, which I'd have stared at for half an hour if Tulia hadn't grabbed my chord like a leash and hauled me through. We ran through a lobby sort of thing and into a nave that was so large I thought we'd gone outdoors again. An aisle ran up the center. Three-quarters of the way along, I could see the tail end of a procession of avout, shuffling toward the chancel. Tulia dropped back, gave me a slap on the bottom that could have been heard from the top of the Precipice, and hissed: "Follow the guys in the loincloths! Do what they do!" At least thirty heads turned to stare; the pews were sparsely occupied with Sæculars.

I dropped to a brisk walk—needed to get my breathing under control—and timed it so that I caught up with half a dozen "guys in loincloths" just as they got to the screen at the head of the aisle. Following them through, I found myself sharing a big semicircular chamber—the chancel—with an assortment of hierarchs, a choir, the guys in the loincloths, and several other contingents of avout.

Inbrase was another one of our mathic auts. A formal program, hinged at several instants when coded movements were performed, ancient phrases called out, or symbolic objects manipulated in certain ways, and ventilated by musical entertainments and speeches from purpled hierarchs. A Sæcular would have seen it as ludicrous foppery if not outright witchcraft. I tried to get back into the spirit of things and see it as an avout was supposed to. That, after all, was the point of Inbrase: to get peregrins back into the mathic frame of mind. To that end, it was more fabulous and impressive than daily auts such as Provener. Or perhaps that was just how they did everything at Tredegarh. Their hierarchs really knew how to put on a show—to grab the audience in the way that great actors did in a theater. Their raiments were really something, and their numbers were intimidating; the Primate was flanked not just by his two Wardens but by echelons of other hierarchs, and not junior ones either, but people who had sub-entourages of their own, and looked as if they might have been Primates themselves. I was looking, I realized, at some sort of high council of Primates who had all been Evoked from their concents, presumably so that they could run the Convox. Or the mathic side of it, at least. Somewhere on the other side of a screen there must be a cabinet of Panjandrums who were as important in the Sæcular world as these hierarchs were in the mathic.

I felt like a scabby mendicant, and considered it a brilliant stroke of good fortune that I was standing next to an order of avout who wore only handkerchiefs. As I looked at those, however, I began to see that these were actually bolts that had frayed away to almost nothing. The loose fibers that dangled from their fraying ends had clumped together into ropy dreadlocks that these men (they were all men) used to tie the remaining snatches of fabric around their midsections. It was our tradition at Edhar to allow one end of the bolt to fray. The most ancient members of our order, however, when they succumbed to old age, might be buried in bolts with fringes a few inches long. In this order, it seemed, bolts were passed down from older to younger avout. Some of them must be thousands of years old. One of these strange half-naked fraas had a pot belly, and the rest were gaunt. They belonged to a race that tended to live near the Equator. Their hair was wild, but not so wild as their eyes, which stared into the space above the chancel floor without seeming to register anything. I got the feeling they weren't used to being indoors.

The other six contingents wore full-sized bolts in complicated wraps. That was all they had in common with one another. Each of the groups was accessorized with a completely different system of turbans, hats, hoods, footgear, under-bolts, over-bolts, and even jewelry. Plainly, we at Edhar were at the austere end of the spectrum. Perhaps only the Valers and the guys in the loincloths were more ascetic than we.

After we'd worked through the opening rounds of pomp, the Primate stepped up to say a few words. It was possible to hear people sighing and settling in the dark naves behind the screens. I risked looking down at myself and saw dirty bare feet, a rough, dull-colored bolt in the crudest possible wrap (the Just Got Up Special), scars that were still red, and bruises faded yellow-green. I was the token Feral.

One of the other Inbrase groups—the most numerous and dressed-up—stepped forward and sang a number. They had enough strong voices to pull off six-part polyphony without showing the strain. What a fine gesture, I thought. Then the group next to them rattled off a monophonic chant, using modes and tonalities I'd never heard before. I saw the next group worrying cheat sheets out of their bolts. Finally then, understanding came over me, and I got the feeling one gets only in an especially sadistic nightmare: I was perfectly trapped. Each group had to sing something! I was a group—of one! And it wasn't going to work for me to sheepishly wave my hands and beg off. No one at the Convox would think that was cute; no one would think it was funny.

It wouldn't be *that* bad, I told myself. Expectations would be low. I was a reasonably competent singer. If someone had stuck a piece of music in front of me and said "go!" I could have winged it—sight-read the thing. The hard part was deciding *what* to sing. Obviously these other groups had sorted it out weeks ago—chosen pieces that said something about who they were, what they thought about at their concents, what musical traditions they had developed to glorify the ideas most precious to them. The musical heritage of the Concent of Saunt Edhar could stand in the same ranks as those of much larger concents. I felt no insecurity there. A sizable contingent from Edhar had already arrived, though, and celebrated Inbrase. Arsibalt and Tulia had no doubt taken the matter in hand and organized a performance, anchored by Fraa Jad's world-shaking drone, that the rest of the Convox was still talking about at their messals. What, then, was left for me? Harmony and polyphony were out of the question. I wasn't good enough to blow everyone away with sheer skill. Best to be simple—not to overreach, not to make a fool of myself. Very few soloists were good enough that people would actually want to listen to them for more than a minute or two. I just had to do my bit, to show respect for the occasion, then step back and shut up.

But I didn't want to just rattle off some random scrap of lesson, which would have been easy, and would have sufficed, because—and I well know how insane this is going to sound—I wanted to touch Ala. Jesry was right about one thing: I was not going to see her until she had made up her mind. But she had to be somewhere in this Mynster, and she had no choice but to listen to what would come out of my mouth. Singing an old lesson we'd learned at Edhar might have evoked nostalgic feelings in her breast but it would be safe and dull. Jesry had been to space. But I was capable of having adventures of my own, learning new things, taking on qualities that Ala knew nothing of—yet. Was there a way of expressing that in music?

There might be. The Orithenans had used a system of computational chanting that, it was plain to see, was rooted in traditions that their founders had brought over from Edhar. To that point, it was clearly recognizable to any Edharian. It was a way of carrying out computations on patterns of information by permuting a given string of notes into new melodies. The permutation was done on the fly by following certain rules, defined using the formalism of cellular automata. After the Second Sack reforms, newly computerless avout had invented this kind of music. In some concents it had withered away, in others mutated into something else, but at Edhar it had always been practiced seriously. We'd all learned it as a sort of children's musical game. But at Orithena they had been doing new things with it, using it to solve problems. Or rather to solve *a* problem, the nature of which I didn't understand yet. Anyway, it *sounded* good—the results, for some reason, just tended to be more musical than the Edharian version, which was serviceable for computing things, but, as music, could be hard to take. I'd spent enough time among the Orithenans to hear some of it and to gain some familiarity with the system. I'd had one tune in particular stuck in my head during the flight to Tredegarh and my time in quarantine. Maybe if I sang it aloud, it would go away.

Once I'd thought of this, it was the obvious and easy choice. And so, when my turn came, I stepped forward and sang that piece. I sang it freely and easily, because I was not troubled by any second thoughts as to whether it was the right thing to do.

At least, not until it was too late. Because, when I had gotten a few phrases into it, a rumble of astonishment passed like a wave through one wedge of the audience. It wasn't loud, but it was unmistakable. I couldn't help glancing toward it, and then I faltered, and almost lost the melody, when I saw that it had come from behind the screen of the Thousanders.

Sensing I might have blundered into some kind of trouble, I did what any guilty fid would do: shot a furtive glance at the hierarchs. They were looking back at me. Most were glassy-eyed, but some were putting their heads together, starting a discussion. One of these, I noticed, was my old friend Varax the Inquisitor.

I actually derived a kind of relief then, from knowing that I was helpless—whatever basket of bugs I had overturned, I couldn't change the result now. Most of the audience heard nothing remarkable in this piece, and listened politely, so I concentrated on bringing it to a clean finish. But seeing movement in the corner of my eye, I glanced over to see that the guys in the loincloths—who'd appeared to've been ignoring the aut so far—had broken ranks, and shifted position so that all of them could get a clear view of me.

When I finished, there ought to have been silence—the polite response to a well-sung number. But some of the Thousanders were still muttering to one another. I even fancied I heard a snatch of music being sung back to me. In the vast swathes of pews behind the other screens, small knots of fraas and suurs were still talking about it, and being shushed by their neighbors.

The men in the loincloths stepped up and did a computational chant of their own. It was weird-sounding in the extreme, being built on modes completely different from ours. It was hard to believe that vocal cords could be trained to make such sounds. But I had the feeling that *as a computation* it was quite similar to what I'd done. When they got to the end of the sequence, the potbellied one sang a sort of coda that, if I understood it correctly, stated that this was only the latest phrase of a computation that his order had been carrying out continuously for thirty-six hundred years.

The last group were the Matarrhites: one of the very few Mathic orders that believed in God. They were the residuum of a Centenarian order that had gone hundred in the centuries just after the Reconstitution. They wore their bolts over their heads, completely covering their faces, except for a screen across the eyes. They sang a kind of dirge—a lament, I realized, for having been torn from the bosom of their concent, and a warning, as if we needed any, that they weren't going to hang out with us any more than they absolutely had to. It was well carried off, but struck me as whiny and a bit rude.

These performances were the next-to-last part of the aut of Inbrase. Though I hadn't fully understood it at the time, we had already, earlier in the aut, been struck off the register of peregrins and formally enrolled in the Convox. We had renewed our vows, and funny-looking documents, hand-written on animal skin, had been despatched to our home concents letting them know we'd arrived. The songs we'd just sung represented our first, albeit symbolic, contributions to whatever it was the Convox was supposed to be doing. All that remained was to stand there while everyone else—the thousands behind the screens—stood up to sing a canticle stating that our contributions were duly accepted and that they were glad to have us. During the final verse, the hierarchs began parading out through the screen into the Unarians' nave. We, the Inbrase groups, followed them in the same order as before. I brought up the rear. We had (at least symbolically) entered through the Day Gate and the visitors' nave, as Sæculars, and now, having become avout once more, we exited into a math. The canticle began to lose cohesion as the last of the hierarchs filed out, and by the time I stepped over the threshold, leaving the chancel empty behind me, the melody had been devoured by the shufflings and mutterings of the Convox taking their leave.

○○○

Tredegarh: One of the Big Three concents, named after Lord Tredegarh, a mid-to-late Praxic Age theor responsible for fundamental advances in thermodynamics.

—THE DICTIONARY, *4th edition, A.R. 3000*

I was on my own, back in the mathic world, officially decontaminated, free to pursue my own interests—for two seconds. Then: "Fraa Erasmas!" someone called out, as if I were being placed under arrest.

I stopped. I was at the head of the Unarian nave, which was huge and insanely magnificent. A couple of hundred avout were already in here. Hundreds more, as well as a few Sæculars, were pouring in through the entrance at the back, quick-walking toward the front to stake out the best pews.

The space between the front row and the screen, which ought to have been left open to provide a clear view of goings-on in the chancel, was cruddy with all sorts of Sæcular equipment. A scaffolding of newmatter tubes had been erected, framing but not blocking the screen, and burly fids were already at work carrying platform-slabs into it and slamming them into place, clamping them together to create a stage, raised above the level of the floor so that people in back could see it. Riggers payed out ropes, allowing a speely projection screen to unfurl until it filled most of the space above the stage. A test pattern flashed across this and was replaced by a live feed from a speelycaptor out in the nave, providing a magnified picture of the stage. Harsh lights began to come on, as if to say "under no circumstances look in this direction!" These were mounted high on scaffold-towers positioned here and there around the space. A bolted and chorded suur walked past me talking into a wireless headset.

The man who'd called out my name was a young hierarch whose sole charge was to channel me to one Fraa Lodoghir: a man in his sixth or seventh decade, dressed in something that was as far evolved from my bolt as a domestic fowl was from a prehistoric reptile. "Fraa Raz, my good young man!" he exclaimed, before the hierarch could trouble with a formal introduction. "Can't say how much I enjoyed your singing. Where did you pick up that ditty? Somewhere on your world travels?"

"Thank you," I said. "I heard it at Orithena and couldn't get it out of my head."

"Fascinating! Tell me, what are the people like there?"

"Like us, for the most part. At first they struck me as quite different. But the more I see of the different kinds of avout here—"

"Yes, I take your meaning!" Lodoghir said. "Those savages in the breechclouts—what tree did *they* fall out of?"

I didn't think it would be very productive for me to say that Fraa Lodoghir seemed more foreign to me than the "savages in the breechclouts," so I nodded.

"Has anyone explained to you that you're about to be the guest of honor at a Plenary?" Fraa Lodoghir asked me.

"It was mentioned but not explained."

Fraa Lodoghir seemed a little nonplussed by my way of talking, but after a moment's pause he went on, "Well, briefly then, I'm to be your loctor—"

"Loctor?"

"InterLOCuTOR," Fraa Lodoghir said, showing impatience, which he tried to mask with a chuckle. "You are much more formal in your pronunciation at Edhar! Good for you, sticking to your guns like that! Tell me, do you still say *savant,* or have you adopted *saunt* like the rest of us?"

"Saunt," I said. Fraa Lodoghir was doing so much talking that I didn't feel the need to say much.

"Splendid, well then, the idea is that the Convox have been crunching the numbers, analyzing the samples, perusing the speelies of the Visitation of Orithena, but there is some interest, naturally, in hearing from an eyewitness—which is why you're here. Rather than putting you to the trouble of preparing a lecture, we shall use the format of an extemporaneous dialog. I have some questions"—he rattled a sheaf of leaves—"handed to me by various interested parties, as well as some topics of my own that I'd like to pursue, should time permit."

As this dialog, or rather monolog, went on, the Plenary took shape. The suur with the headset shooed us up a stairway that had been rolled into place, and Fraa Lodoghir followed me up onto the stage-platform. Microphones were clipped to our bolts. Two mugs and a pitcher of water were placed on a little stand at the back of the stage. Other than that, there was no furniture. For some reason I did not feel the slightest bit nervous, and I did not think about what I was going to say. Instead I was musing about this funny structure that my loctor and I were standing on: a snatch of geometric plane held in a three-dimensional space grid. Like a geometer's fantasy, a modernized rendition of the Plane where the theors of Ethras used to have their dialogs.

"Do you have any questions, Fraa Erasmas?" my loctor asked me.

"Yes," I said, "who are you?"

He looked a bit regretful that I'd asked, but then his face hardened into a visage that—as I could see from a glance at the huge moving picture above us—was going to look much more impressive on a speely feed. More impressive than *mine,* anyway. "The First Among Equals of the Centenarian Chapter of the Order of Saunt Proc at Muncoster."

"Your microphone is live—*now*," said a fraa, flicking a switch on the apparatus clipped to my bolt, and then he performed the same service for Fraa Lodoghir. Lodoghir poured himself a mug of water, then took a draught, gazing at me over the rim of the mug, coolly curious to see what I was making of the news that my loctor was probably the most eminent Procian in the whole world. I have no idea what he saw.

"The Plenary begins," he said, in a voice that had somehow gone an octave deeper, and that was amplified all over the nave.

The crowd began to quiet down, and he gave them a few more moments to suspend conversations and take seats. I could see nothing, because of the lights; Fraa Lodoghir might have been the only other person on Arbre.

"My loctor," Fraa Lodoghir said, and then paused a moment for silence. "My loctor is Erasmas, formerly of the Decenarian chapter of something called the 'Edharian Order' in a place that, unless I've been misinformed, styles itself as the Concent of *Savant* Edhar."

A titter ran through the nave at this ridiculously old-fashioned pronunciation.

"Er, I think you *have* been misinformed—" I began, but my microphone wasn't in the right position or something, so my voice did not get amplified.

Meanwhile, Lodoghir was talking right over me. "They say it's up in the mountains. Tell me, don't you get cold, with nothing but that simple bolt between you and the elements?"

"No, we have shoes and—"

"Ah, for those of you who can't hear my loctor, he is very proud to announce that the Edharians do have shoes."

Finally I got the microphone aimed at my mouth. "Yes," I said. "Shoes—and manners." This got an appreciative rumble out of the crowd. "I'm still a member of the chapter and order you mentioned, and I may be addressed as Fraa."

"Oh, I beg your pardon! I've been looking into it, and have uncovered a different story: that you went Feral a day after the start of your peregrination, and rattled around the world for a bit until you fetched up in this place called Orithena, where I gather they welcome just about anyone."

"They were more hospitable than some places I could mention," I said. I thought about what Fraa Lodoghir had just said, looking for some way to break it down and plane him, but every word of it was factually correct—as he knew perfectly well.

He was trying to bait me into quibbling over how he'd phrased it. Then he'd crush me by quoting chapter and verse. He probably had the supporting documents right there in his hand.

That day on Bly's Butte, Fraa Jad had told me that when he got to Tredegarh, he'd make it all okay—prevent me from getting in trouble.

Had he failed? No. If he'd failed, they would not have permitted me to celebrate Inbrase. So Jad must have succeeded at *some* level. Along the way, maybe he'd made enemies.

Who were now *my* enemies.

"That is all correct," I said. "Yet here I am."

Fraa Lodoghir was off balance for a moment when he saw that his first gambit had failed, but like a fencer, he had a riposte. "That is extraordinary, for one who claims to know so much of manners. Thousands of avout are in this magnificent nave. Every one of them came straight to Tredegarh when he or she was summoned. Only one person in this room chose to go Feral, and to switch his allegiance to a society, an organization, that is not a part of the mathic world: the cult of Orithena. What in the world—or should I say, *who* in the world—induced you to make such a self-destructive choice?"

Now something funny happened inside of my head. Fraa Lodoghir had hit me with a sneak attack. He was good at this kind of thing and he had counters prepared for anything I might do to defend myself. My first reaction, naturally, had been to get flustered. But without knowing it, he'd just committed a tactical mistake: by making so much of my unauthorized and "self-destructive" peregrination, he had flooded my mind with memories of Mahsht and the sneak attack I had endured there: something so terrible that nothing Fraa Lodoghir could say to me could possibly be worse. His best efforts seemed kind of funny by comparison. Thinking of this made me calm, and in that calmness I noticed that Fraa Lodoghir had, with his last question, tipped his hand. He wanted me to blame it all on Fraa Jad. Give up the Thousander, he was saying, and all will be forgiven.

Only an hour ago, Tulia had warned me not to attempt to play politics—just to tell the truth. But some combination of stubbornness and calculation told me not to give Lodoghir what he wanted.

I thought of how the scene in Mahsht had ended, with the

onslaught of the Valers. How they had observed what was going on, and construed it as an emergence. I didn't have their training, but I knew an emergence when I saw one.

"I did it on my own," I said. "I accept the consequences of my decision. I knew that one such consequence might be Anathem. In that expectation I found my way to Orithena. There, I thought I might live in a Mathic style, even though Thrown Back. That I was returned to Tredegarh and allowed to celebrate Inbrase is a surprise and is an honor."

The Convox was as silent as it was invisible. It was just me and Lodoghir, floating in space on our scrap of plane.

Fraa Lodoghir had given up on getting Jad, and moved on to secondary targets. "I really don't understand how you think! You say that your objective was to live in the Mathic style? You were doing that already, weren't you?" He turned to face the crowd in the nave. "Perhaps he just wanted to do it someplace a bit warmer!"

The jest earned laughter from some but I could also hear an indignant strain out there beyond the lights. "Fraa Lodoghir wastes the time of the Convox!" a man called out. "The topic of this Plenary is the Visitation!"

"My loctor has asked me to address him by what he claims is the correct title of Fraa," Lodoghir said in return, "and as he seems to take such matters so seriously, I am merely attempting to get the facts straight."

"Well, I'm glad I was able to assist you," I said. "What would you like to know about the Visitation?"

"Since we've all watched the speely that was recorded by your Ita collaborator, I should think that what would be most productive would be for you to relate those parts of your experience that did *not* make it into the speely. What went on during those rare moments when you were able to tear yourself away from your Ita friend?"

He was giving me so much to object to, that I was forced to make a choice: I had to let the Ita-baiting go for now. The best I could do was give the Ita a name. "Sammann arrived and began to record images a few minutes after the probe landed," I began. "For several minutes, I saw what he saw."

"Not so fast, you're starting in the middle of the story!" Fraa Lodoghir complained, in an indulgent, fatherly style.

"Very well," I said, "how far back do you think it would be useful for me to go?"

"As much as I'm fascinated by the auts and folkways of the Cult of Orithena," Fraa Lodoghir said, "we ought to confine ourselves to the Visitation proper. Pray begin at the first moment when it penetrated your awareness that something extraordinary was happening."

"It looked like a meteorite—which is unusual, but not extraordinary," I said. "It didn't burn out instantly, so I thought it must be a big one. At first it was difficult to make sense of its trajectory—until I figured out that it was headed toward us. I can't tell you at what point I drew the conclusion that it was not a naturally occurring object. We began to run down the mountain. While we were en route, the probe's parachute deployed."

"Now, when you say 'we,' what size of group are you speaking of?"

Rather than wait for Fraa Lodoghir to drag this out of me, I volunteered: "Two. Orolo and I."

"*Saunt* Orolo! Yes, we know about *him*," Fraa Lodoghir said. "He's all over the speely, but we haven't known until now how he arrived at the scene. He was the first to reach the bottom of the hole, was he not?"

"If by 'hole' you mean the excavated Temple of Orithena, yes," I said.

"But that's at the *foot* of the volcano!" he exclaimed, in a tone of voice that somehow managed to accuse me of being such a simpleton that I did not know this.

"I'm aware of it," I said.

"But now we learn that you and Orolo were running down from the *top* of the volcano while the probe was parachuting into the hole."

"Yes."

"What of the others? Were they so entranced by contemplation of the Hylaean Theoric World that they were *unaware* that an alien space probe was dropping into the middle of their camp?"

"They stayed up at the rim of the excavation while Orolo ran down to the bottom alone."

"*Alone?*"

"Well, I followed him."

"What on earth were you and Orolo doing on the top of the volcano after dark?" Fraa Lodoghir managed, somehow, to ask this in a tone that elicited some titters from the audience.

"We weren't on the top—as ought to be obvious, if you think for a moment about what a volcano is."

This got a whole different kind of laugh. Even Fraa Lodoghir looked faintly amused. "But you *were* quite high up on its slopes."

"A couple of thousand feet."

"Above the cloud layer?" he asked, as if this were extremely significant.

"There *were* no clouds!"

"I ask you again: why? What were you doing?"

Here I hesitated. I'd have liked nothing better than to help propagate Orolo's ideas, and I'd never have a better opportunity, what with the whole Convox listening to me. But I'd only gotten to see a fragment of his argument. I didn't fully get what I'd heard. I knew enough, though, to know that it might lead to talk of Incanters.

"Orolo and I went up the mountain to talk," I said. "We became quite involved in our dialog, and didn't notice it was getting dark."

"When you choose to employ the word *dialog* it causes me to think that the topic was something more weighty than the charms of your new Orithenan girlfriend," Fraa Lodoghir said dryly.

Damn, he was good! How could he know so precisely what it would take to fluster me?

Bells began ringing, high up on the Precipice. It sounded like the call to Provener. How did they wind their clock here?

A memory came to me of Lio, a few months ago, winding the clock with two black eyes after he had asked me to punch him in the face. I tried to summon whatever Lio had learned to summon that day. I forced myself to go on as if the blows had never landed.

"This much of your statement is correct, that it was a serious theorical discussion."

"And what was so much on Orolo's mind that he had to drag you up a volcano to get it off his chest?"

I was rolling my eyes and shaking my head in amazement.

"Did it have anything to do with the Geometers?" he tried.

"Yes."

"Then I don't understand your reticence on this topic. If it relates to the Geometers, it is of interest to the Convox, is it not?"

"I'm reluctant because I only got to hear a small part of his thoughts and I fear I won't do them justice."

"Stipulated! Everyone has heard and understood your disclaimer now, so you have no reason to go on hoarding information."

"Because he was Anathematized, Orolo lost the ability to gather data about the Geometers. He never even saw the only good picture of their ship that he managed to take. So his thinking about them, from that point onward, had to be based on the only givens he still had access to—"

"I thought you just said he had access to *no* givens."

"None emanating from the icosahedron."

"So just what other kind of givens *are* there?"

"The givens that you and I are taking in all the time, simply by virtue of being conscious, and that we can observe and think about on our own, without any need for scientific instruments."

Fraa Lodoghir blinked in fake amazement. "Do you mean to claim that the subject of your dialog was *consciousness*?"

"Yes."

"Specifically, *Orolo's* consciousness? Since that, presumably, is the only one he has access to."

"His, and mine," I corrected him, "since I was part of the dialog too, and it was clear that Orolo's observations of *his* consciousness tallied with my observations of *mine*."

"But I thought you told me, only a minute ago, that this very same dialog was *about the Geometers!*"

"Yes."

"But you now contradict yourself by admitting it was about the features shared between your consciousness, and that of Orolo!"

"*And that of the Geometers*," I said, "because they clearly possess consciousness."

"Ohh," Fraa Lodoghir exclaimed, and got a faraway look in his eyes, as if trying to wrap his mind around something impossibly absurd. "Are you trying to say that just because you and Orolo are conscious, and the Geometers are too (which I'll give you for the sake of argument), that you can learn something about how the Geometers' minds work, simply by gazing at your own navel long enough?"

"Something like that."

"Well, I'm certain that the Lorites are going to have a field day with this. But to me it seems you are saying too little and too much at the same time!" Fraa Lodoghir complained. "Too little, because we here on Arbre have been gazing at our navels for six thousand years and still don't understand *ourselves*. So what does it boot us to be as in the dark about the Geometers as we are about our own minds? And too much, because you really are going too far in assuming that the Geometers would think like us at all."

"As to that last point, one can make strong arguments that all conscious beings must have certain mental processes in common."

"Strong arguments that no disciple of Halikaarn will examine too closely, I'm sure," Fraa Lodoghir said dryly, earning a chortle from every Procian at the Convox.

"As to your first point," I continued, "namely, that we still don't understand *ourselves* after six thousand years of introspection, I believe that Orolo was of the view that we might be able to settle some of those ancient questions now that we have access to conscious beings from other star systems."

This settled the crowd down, and they became so markedly quiet that I knew they must all be concentrating intensely. We had got to the heart of the matter. The Sphenic and Protan systems had been dueling for millennia, and continued the struggle here in this nave under the names of Procians and Halikaarnians, Lodoghir and Erasmas. The only thing they agreed on was the words I'd just put in Orolo's mouth: that the Geometers might tip the scales to one side or the other. Not necessarily because they would know the answers themselves—they might be just as confused as we were—but because of the new givens we could now obtain. And *that* was the true goal of many at this Convox. Never mind whatever mission statement the Sæcular Power had handed us.

Even Fraa Lodoghir knew to observe a few moments' silence, to give this the respect it deserved. Then he said: "If they were smart swarms of simple-minded bugs, or systems of pulsating energy fields, or plants speaking a chemical language to one another—something enormously different from us—then perhaps Orolo's lucubrations in the extinct pseudo-philosophy of Evenedric might provide us with a few moments' diversion. But the Geometers look like us. Orolo couldn't have known that this was the case, so we may forgive him for his temporary delusion."

"But *why* do they look like us?" I asked. Realizing, as I said it, that I was making a tactical error by asking a question—even a rhetorical one.

"Let me help you," Fraa Lodoghir said, magnanimously offering the hopelessly confused fid a helping hand, his giant face, on the screen above, a picture of amused beneficence. "We know that for months and months, before anyone else knew that the Geometers were up there, Orolo was up to something. Using the cosmographical devices at your concent to track the icosahedron."

"We know exactly what he was up to," I began.

Fraa Lodoghir cut me off: "We know what you were *told*: a story that many of your own fraas and suurs refuse to believe! And we know that Orolo was Thrown Back. That his fellow-cultists in the shadowy group known as the Lineage spirited him halfway around the world to Ecba: by an *amazing coincidence,* the place where the Geometers *just happened* to make their first landfall—and to do it on the *very evening* when this Orolo happened to mount a long and exhausting nocturnal expedition to the rarefied heights of an active volcano!"

"It's not long, it's not exhausting, and we didn't go up at night—" I tried to say. But he had reduced me once again to quibbling, and all I'd done was let him draw breath and get a sip of water.

"Help us now, Fraa Erasmas," Fraa Lodoghir said, in a perfectly reasonable tone. "Help us solve the riddle that has so bedeviled us."

"Who is 'us' in this case?" I demanded.

"Those, here at the Convox, who sense that there is something more to Orolo than what we've been allowed to see on the speely."

I couldn't keep the tiredness out of my voice as I answered. "What riddle are you speaking of?"

"How did Orolo signal the Geometers? What trick was he using to send them his secret messages?"

Here, if I'd been having a drink, I'd have spat it out. Fraa Lodoghir's statement raised a commotion: waves of murmuring, shock, anger, and derisive laughter clashed, lapped, and rolled from one end of the nave to the other. I was too dumbfounded to speak, but merely stood there looking at him for a long while, waiting for him to show signs of embarrassment and withdraw the accusation. But the look on his face was as pleasant, as unself-conscious as it could be. And as his calm, his confidence waxed, mine waned. I wanted so desperately to plane him!

But Orolo's words came back to me: *they deciphered my analemma!* As if he *had* somehow sent them a signal.

Why *else* would they have chosen to land at Orithena—the very place, in the whole world, where Orolo had sought sanctuary? Why else would Orolo have made the long and hazardous journey to Orithena?

Back to the matter at hand: I dared not enter a serious Dialog with Lodoghir, here, before this audience, on this topic. He'd plane me so badly they'd have to scrub my remains off the floor with a sandblaster. And he'd take Orolo down with me.

My dialog with Fraa Lodoghir was being witnessed by Sæculars. Important Sæculars. Panjandrums, as Orolo would call them. Maybe his sleazy tricks were actually *working* on them.

What was it people used to say of the Rhetors? That they had the power to alter the past, and that they did so every chance they got.

I had no power to duel a Rhetor. All I could do was speak the truth and hope it might be heard by friends who *could* wield such power.

"That's a novel suggestion," I said. "I don't know how you do things in the Order of Saunt Proc, but as an Edharian, I would look for *evidence*."

"What of the famous Steelyard?" Lodoghir asked.

"The Steelyard favors the simpler hypothesis. Orolo *not* sending secret messages to an alien starship is simpler than what you are proposing."

"Oh no, Fraa Erasmas," said Lodoghir with an indulgent chuckle, "I'll not let you slip that one past me. Try to remember that intelligent people are listening to us! If Orolo sending messages explains what is otherwise mysterious, then it *is* the simpler hypothesis!"

"What mysteries do you think it explains?"

"Three, to be exact. Mystery the First: that the probe landed on the ruins of Orithena, an otherwise desolate and uninteresting site whose most conspicuous feature is an analemma, clearly visible from space."

"*Anything* is clearly visible from space if you have good enough optics," I pointed out. "Remember that the Geometers decorated their ship with a proof of the Adrakhonic Theorem. What is more reasonable than for them to land on the Temple of Adrakhones?"

"They must know we're here," Lodoghir pointed out. "If they wanted to talk to theors, why not simply land at Tredegarh?"

"Why blast each other with shotguns? You can't burden me with responsibility for explaining everything that the Geometers do," I said.

"Mystery the Second: Orolo's suicide."

"No mystery there. He made a choice to preserve a priceless specimen."

"He weighed his own life against that specimen," Lodoghir said, making a scale-balancing gesture with his two hands. "Mystery the Third: he drew an analemma on the ground in the final instants of his life, and stood on it to meet the fate he had chosen."

I had nothing to say. It was a mystery to me as well.

"Orolo accepted his responsibility," Lodoghir said.

"You have completely lost me."

"Somehow, Orolo sent a message to the Geometers during those months when he was one of the only persons on Arbre who knew they were up there. I speculate that the message took the form of an analemma. A sign, telling the Geometers to make their landfall on the analemma that is—or used to be—so clearly visible at Orithena. Once Thrown Back, he went there, and waited. And lo, the Geometers *did* make landfall there. But not in the manner that Orolo had, perhaps naïvely, anticipated. A faction among the Geometers sent down an illicit probe. The alien woman sacrificed her life. The dominant faction retaliated by rodding Ecba, with deadly results at Orithena. Orolo understood that he bore responsibility for what had happened. Throwing the dead woman into the aerocraft was his self-imposed penance, and drawing the analemma on the ground was his way of admitting responsibility for what he had done."

As Lodoghir had proceeded through this indictment, his tone had changed: like an Inquisitor at first, but softening as he went on, so that by the time he reached the last part, he seemed regretful. Moved. I was spellbound. Perhaps this Rhetor *did* have magical powers to reach in and meddle with my brain—to change the past. But much more so, I was almost certain that he was right.

"You still have no evidence—only a good story," I finally said. "Even if you do find evidence, and prove you're right, what does it really say about Orolo? How could he have anticipated a civil war among the Geometers? The Geometer who gave the order to drop a rod on Ecba—doesn't he, or she, and not Orolo, deserve responsibility for the deaths below? So even if some elements of your hypothesis are proved, there is still room for dialog as to Orolo's state of mind when the glowing cloud struck him down. I think he was accepting a kind of responsibility, yes. But by planting himself on that analemma and waiting to die, I think he was saying something other than what you're trying to put in his mouth. I think he was saying 'I stand by what I did in spite of all this.'"

"A bit cheeky, wouldn't you say? Don't you think he ought to have deferred to the Sæcular Power? Let them weigh the evidence—make a considered judgment as to how best we ought to treat with the Geometers?" Lodoghir's eyes glanced to the side, as if to remind me that the Panjandrums were out there in the dark, listening for my answer.

And now I made the only move, out of this whole Dialog, that I was later proud of: I did *not* say what I was thinking: *the Warden of Heaven already tried that, remember?* But I didn't have to. A low murmur had begun to run through the audience, building toward mirth. All I had to do was sit silently and wait for the whole Convox to perceive just how ludicrous my loctor's statement really was. And—I sensed—this had been a considered move on his part.

"That depends," I said, "on how it all comes out in the end."

Lodoghir raised his eyebrows and turned away from me to face the speelycaptor. "And that," he said, "is the whole point of this Convox. I suppose we ought to get to work." He made a gesture. The microphones died and the speely screen went dark. Everyone in the nave began talking at once.

I was alone on the platform, and it was dark; Fraa Lodoghir had scurried down the steps, probably so that I could not tear his tongue out with my bare hands. The crew were already dismantling the stage. I took off my microphone, had a good long drink of water, and trudged down the steps, feeling as if I'd just spent an hour as a punching bag for Lio.

A few people seemed to be waiting for me. One in particular caught my eye, because he was a Sæcular, dressed in important-person clothes. He had made up his mind that he was going to be the first person to talk to me, so rather than wait for me to reach the bottom of the steps he bounded up and met me halfway. "Emman Beldo," he said, and then rattled off the name of some government ministry or other. "Would you mind telling me what the hell *that* was all about?"

He was younger than he looked in those clothes, I realized: only a few years older than I.

"Why don't you ask Fraa Lodoghir?" I suggested.

Emman Beldo chose to interpret that as dry humor. "I came here expecting to hear about the Geometers—" he began.

"And instead we talked about consciousness and analemmas."

"Yeah. Look. Don't get me wrong. I put in five years as a Unarian . . ."

"You're a literate, smart Burger, you read stuff and use your brain for a living, but still you can't fathom what just happened—"

"When we need to be talking about the *threat*! And how to address it!"

I lost focus for a moment, gazing down to the base of the stairs where a cluster of fraas and suurs all wanted to talk to me. I was trying to size them up without making eye contact. Some, I feared, styled themselves members of the Lineage and wanted to exchange secret handshakes with me. Others probably wanted to spend the whole afternoon telling me why Evenedric was wrong. There would be hard-core Halikaarnians furious because I had not managed to plane Fraa Lodoghir, and people like Suur Maroa who had specific questions about what I'd seen at Orithena. I was thinking it might be easier to have a regular job like Emman Beldo . . .

Fraa Lodoghir saved me—sort of. He pushed forward to the base of the steps. He had just finished a heated discussion with a senior hierarch. "Well, now you've gone and done it, Fraa Erasmas!" he said.

"Gone and done what, Fraa Lodoghir?"

"Gotten us relegated to the outer darkness—the arse-end of the mathic world, as far as I'm concerned."

"Wouldn't that be the Concent of *Savant* Edhar?"

"No, there's one place left that's even worse," he proclaimed. "The Plurality of Worlds Messal at Avrachon's Dowment. That is where we will be taking our sustenance until I can get the hierarchs to see reason."

"Who's this 'we' you're talking about?"

"You need to pay attention, Fraa Erasmas!"

"Attention to *what*?"

"Your place in the Convox!"

"And what is my place?"

"Standing behind me while I eat. Folding my napkin when I get up to use the toilet."

"*What!?*"

"You are my servitor, Fraa Erasmas, and I am your doyn. I like a damp face-cloth before dinner, warm but not too warm. See to it—if you don't want to spend the rest of the Convox studying the Book." He turned and strode out.

Emman Beldo was looking at me interestedly.

I should have been crushed by this terrible news, but I was a little punch-drunk, and it tickled me to see Fraa Lodoghir so irritated.

"Well," I said to Emman Beldo, "now you have a choice. If you want to learn about the threat posed by the Geometers, you can go anywhere except where I'm going. If you want an answer to why we spoke of such out-of-the-way topics during this Plenary, you can join me and Fraa Lodoghir at the arse-end of the mathic world."

"Oh, I'll be there!" he said. "My doyn wouldn't miss it."

"And who is your doyn?"

"You and I will address her as 'Madame Secretary,'" he cautioned me, "but her name is Ignetha Foral."

Part 10

MESSAL

Lorite: A member of an Order founded by Saunt Lora, who believed that all of the ideas that the human mind was capable of coming up with, had already been come up with. Lorites are, therefore, historians of thought who assist other avout in their work by making them aware of others who have thought similar things in the past, and thereby preventing them from reinventing the wheel.

—THE DICTIONARY, *4th edition, A.R. 3000*

"The Geometers have us pinned down like a biological sample on a table," said Ignetha Foral, after we had served the soup. "They can poke and prod us at their leisure, and observe our reactions. When we first became aware that they were in orbit around Arbre, we assumed that something was going to happen soon. But it has been maddeningly slow. The Geometers can get all the water they need from comets, all the stuff they need from asteroids. The only thing they can't do—we suspect—is go on interstellar voyages. But it could be that they aren't in that much of a hurry." She paused to whet her whistle. A bracelet gleamed on her wrist. It looked valuable but not gaudy. Everything about her confirmed what Tulia had told us, months ago, at Edhar: that she came from a moneyed Burger clan with old ties to the mathic world. It wasn't clear, yet, why she was here, and carrying the impressive-sounding title of "Madame Secretary." According to the information Tulia had dug up, she had been deposed from her Sæcular job by the Warden of Heaven. But that was old news. The Warden of Heaven had been thrown out of the airlock a few weeks ago. Perhaps, while I'd been distracted on Ecba, the Sæcular Power had reorganized itself, and she'd been dusted off and given a new job.

Having taken a bit of refreshment, Madame Secretary made eye contact with the other six at the table. "Or at least that's what I say to my colleagues who want to know why I'm *wasting my time* at this messal." She said this in a good-humored way. Fraa Lodoghir laughed richly. Everyone else was able to manage at least a chuckle except for Fraa Jad, who was staring at Ignetha Foral as if she were the aforementioned biological specimen. Ignetha Foral was sharp enough to notice this. "Fraa Jad," she said, inclining her head slightly in his direction, in a suggestion of a bow, "naturally takes the long view of things, and is probably thinking to himself that my colleagues must have dangerously short attention spans. But my *métier,* for better or worse, is the political workings of what you call the Sæcular Power. And to many in that world, this messal looks like a waste of some very good minds. The kindest thing some will say of it, is that it is a convenient place to which difficult, irrelevant, or incomprehensible persons may be exiled, so that they don't get in the way of the important business of the Convox. How would you at this table recommend that I counter the arguments of those who say it ought to be done away with? Suur Asquin?"

Suur Asquin was our host: the current Heritor of Avrachon's Dowment, hence its owner in all but name. Ignetha Foral had called on her first because she looked as though she had something to say, but also, I suspected, because it was the correct etiquette. For now, I was giving Suur Asquin the benefit of the doubt, because she had helped us make dinner, working side by side with her servitor, Tris. This was the very first Plurality of Worlds Messal, and so it had taken us a while to find our way around the kitchen, get the oven hot, and so forth.

"I believe I'd have an unfair advantage, Madame Secretary, since I live here. I'd answer the question by showing your colleagues around Avrachon's Dowment, which as you've all seen is a kind of museum . . ."

I was standing behind Fraa Lodoghir with my hands behind my back holding the knotted end of a rope that disappeared into a hole in the wall and ran thirty feet to the kitchen. Someone tugged on the other end of it, silently calling for me. I leaned forward to make sure that my doyn didn't need his chin wiped, then walked around the table, sidestepping in front of other servitors. Meanwhile Suur Asquin was trying to develop an argument that merely looking at the old scientific instruments scattered around the Dowment would convince the most skeptical extra that pure metatheorics was worthy of Sæcular support. Seemed obvious to me that she was using Hypotrochian Transquaestiation to assert that pure metatheorics would be the sole occupation of this messal, which I didn't agree with at all—but I mustn't speak unless spoken to, and I reckoned that the others here could take care of themselves. Fraa Tavener—aka Barb—was standing behind Fraa Jad, looking at Suur Asquin as a bird looks at a bug, just itching to jump in and plane her. I gave him a wink as I went by, but he was oblivious. I passed through a door, padded for silence, and entered a stretch of corridor that served as an airlock, or rather sound-lock. At its end was another padded door. I pushed through—it was hinged to swing both ways—and entered the kitchen, a sudden and shocking plunge into heat, noise, and light.

And smoke, since Arsibalt had set fire to something. I edged toward the sand bucket, but, not seeing any open flames, thought better of it. Suur Asquin could be heard over a speaker; the Sæcular Power had sent in Ita to rig up a one-way sound system so that we in the kitchen—and others far away, I had to assume—could hear every word spoken in the messallan.

"What's the problem?" I asked.

"No problem. Oh, this? I incinerated a cutlet. It's all right. We have more."

"Then why'd you yank me?"

He made a guilty glance at a plank on the wall with seven rope-ends dangling from it, all but one chalked with a servitor's name. "Because I'm *desperately* bored!" he said. "This conversation is *stupid!*"

"It's just getting started," I pointed out. "These are just the opening formalities."

"It's no wonder people want to abolish this messal, if this is a fair sample of—"

"How is yanking my rope going to help?"

"Oh, it's an old tradition here," Arsibalt said, "I've been reading up on it. If the dialog gets boring, the servitors show their disdain by voting with their feet—withdrawing to the kitchen. The doyns are supposed to notice this."

"The odds of that actually working with this group are about as high as that this dinner won't make them sick."

"Well, we must begin somewhere."

I went over to the ropes, picked up a lump of chalk, and wrote *"Emman Beldo"* under the one that was still unlabeled.

"Is that his name?"

"Yeah. He talked to me after Plenary."

"Why didn't he help cook?"

"One of his jobs is driving Madame Secretary around. He only got here five minutes ago. Anyway, extras can't cook."

"Raz speaks the truth!" said Suur Tris, coming in from the garden with a bolt-load of firewood. "Even you guys seem a little challenged." She hauled open the hatch of the oven's firebox and gazed on the coal-bed with a critical eye.

"We shall prove our worth anon," said Arsibalt, picking up a huge knife, like a barbarian warlord called to single combat. "This stove, your produce, your cuts of meat—all strange to us." And then, as if to say *speaking of strange* . . . Arsibalt and I both glanced over at a heavy stew-pot, which had been pushed to the back of the stove in hopes that the vapors belching out of it would stink less if they came from farther away.

Suur Tris was nudging coals around and darting bits of wood into the firebox as if it were brain surgery. We'd made fun of her for this until our efforts to manage it ourselves had produced the kinds of outcomes normally associated with strategic nuclear warfare. Now, we watched contritely.

"Kind of weird for Madame Secretary to open by saying the messal's a drain trap for losers," I said.

"Oh, I disagree. She's good!" Tris exclaimed. "She's trying to motivate them." Tris was podgy and not especially good-looking, but she had the personality of a beautiful girl because she'd been raised in a math.

"I wonder how that's going to work on my doyn," I said, "he'd like nothing more than to see this canceled, so he can go dine with cool people."

A bell jingled. We turned to look. Seven bells were mounted to the wall above the seven rope-ends; each was connected, by a long ribbon routed through the wall and under the floor, to the underside of the table in the messallan, where it terminated in a velvet pull. A doyn could summon his servitor, silently and invisibly, by yanking on the pull.

The bell rang once, paused, then began to jangle nonstop, more and more violently, until it looked like it was about to jump off the wall. It was labeled "Fraa Lodoghir."

I returned to the messallan, walked around behind him, and bent forward. "Get rid of this Edharian gruel," he breathed. "It is perfectly unpalatable."

"You should see what the Matarrhites are cooking up!" I muttered. Fraa Lodoghir glanced across the table at an avout—one of those who'd celebrated Inbrase with me, earlier in the day—whose face was covered by his or her bolt. The fabric had been drawn sideways over his or her head, as if to form a hood, but the hood had then been pulled down to cover the face, with an opening below through which food—if that was the correct word for what the Matarrhites put into their mouths during meals—could be introduced. "I'll have what *it's* having," Lodoghir hissed. "But not this!"

I glanced significantly at Fraa Jad who was shoveling the stuff into his mouth, then confiscated Lodoghir's serving and whisked it out of there, happy to have an excuse to go back to the kitchen. "Perfectly unpalatable," I repeated, heaving it into the compost.

"Perhaps we should slip him some Allswell," Arsibalt suggested.

"Or something stronger," I returned. But before we could develop this promising theme, the back door swung open and in walked a girl swathed in a hectare of heavy, scratchy-looking black bolt, lashed to her body with ten miles of chord. Her punched-in sphere was overflowing with mixed greens. Out of doors, she kept her head covered, but once she had set the greens down she swept her bolt back to reveal her perfectly smooth dome, all dotted with perspiration, since it was a warm day and she was overdressed. Arsibalt and I did not feel as easy around Suur Karvall as we did around Tris, so all banter stopped. "That's a lovely selection of greens," Tris began, but Karvall flinched and held up a bony, translucent hand, gesturing for silence.

Fraa Lodoghir had begun speaking. I reckoned that was why he'd wanted his "gruel" cleared away.

"Plurality of Worlds," he began, and let it resonate for a long moment. "Sounds impressive. I haven't the faintest idea what it means to some here. The mere fact of the Geometers' existence proves that there is at least one other world, and so on one level it is quite trivial. But since it appears that I am the token Procian at this messal, I shall play my role, and say this: we have nothing in common with the Geometers. No shared experiences, no common culture. Until that changes, we can't communicate with them. Why not? Because language is nothing more than a stream of symbols that are perfectly meaningless until we associate them, in our minds, *with* meaning: a process of acculturation. Until we share experiences with the Geometers, and thereby begin to develop a shared culture—in effect, to merge our culture with theirs—we cannot communicate with them, and their efforts to communicate with us will continue to be just as incomprehensible as the gestures they've made so far: throwing the Warden of Heaven out the airlock, dropping a fresh murder victim into a cult site, and rodding a volcano."

As soon as he paused, reactions came through on the speakers, several people talking over each other:

"I don't agree that those are incomprehensible."

"But they must have been watching our speelies!"

"You're missing the point of the Plurality of Worlds."

But Suur Asquin spoke last, and most distinctly. "Many other messals are addressing the topics you mentioned, Fraa Lodoghir. In the spirit of Madame Secretary's opening question: why should we have a separate Plurality of Worlds Messal?"

"Well, you might simply ask the hierarchs who brought it into existence!" Fraa Lodoghir answered a little disdainfully. "But if you want my answer as a Procian, why, it is quite straightforward: the arrival of the Geometers is a perfect laboratory experiment, as it were, to demonstrate and to explore the philosophy of Saunt Proc: put simply, that language, communication, indeed thought itself, are the manipulation of symbols to which meanings are assigned by culture—and *only* by culture. I only hope that they haven't watched so *many* of our speelies that their minds have been contaminated, and the experiment ruined."

"And this relates to our theme how?" Suur Asquin prodded him.

"She knows perfectly well," Suur Tris assured us, "she's just making sure it all gets spelled out for Ignetha Foral."

"Plurality of Worlds means a plurality of world cultures— cultures hermetically sealed off from one another until now—hence, for the time being, unable to communicate."

"According to Procians!" someone put in. I didn't recognize the oddly accented voice, so I thought it might be the Matarrhite.

"The purpose of this messal, accordingly, is to develop and, I would hope, implement a strategy for the Sæcular Power, assisted by the avout, to break down the plurality—which is the same thing as developing a shared language. We shall put ourselves out of business by making the Plurality of Worlds into One World."

"He hates this messal," I translated, "so he's trying to talk Ignetha Foral into turning it into something else: which would just happen to be a power base for the Procians."

Suur Karvall really hated it when we talked over the doyns, but she was going to have to get used to it. We were all standing around distributing the greens among half a dozen salad plates. Only six, because Matarrhites, apparently, didn't eat salad.

While making dinner, some of us servitors had had a good argument as to why a Matarrhite had been invited. One theory was simply that, because the Sæcular Power was religious, they wanted some Deolaters in on the discussion. The Matarrhites were going to have Convox clout way out of proportion to their significance in the mathic world, or so this argument went, because the Panjandrums felt more comfortable with them. The other theory was more in line with the notion, just voiced by Ignetha Foral, that this messal was a dumping ground.

Clanking sounds over the speaker told us that those servitors who were still in the messallan were collecting the soup bowls. This led to a break in the dialog; but we could hear an elderly woman's voice, speaking up, in a more informal mood, as the servitors worked: "I believe I can put your fears to rest, Fraa Lodoghir."

"Why, that's good of you, Grandsuur Moyra, but I don't remember voicing any fears!" said Fraa Lodoghir, trying and failing to sound jovial.

Moyra was Karvall's doyn, so, out of respect for Karvall, we actually did shut up for a moment.

Moyra returned, "I believe you did express concern that the Geometers had contaminated their own culture by watching too many of our speelies."

"Of course you are right! That's what I get for contradicting a Lorite!" Fraa Lodoghir said.

The door opened and in came Barb with seven bowls stacked on his arms.

"I think you ought to change my designation," said Moyra delicately, after considering this for a moment, "and now call me a meta-Lorite, or, in honor of this occasion, a Plurality of Worlds Lorite."

This got a murmur out of everyone—in the messallan and in the kitchen. Suur Karvall had drifted over to the speaker and was standing there rapt. Arsibalt had been chopping something; he stopped and poised his knife above the block.

"We Lorites are always making nuisances of ourselves," Moyra said, "by pointing out that this or that idea was already come up with by someone else, long ago. But now I do believe we shall have to broaden our sphere to include the Plurality of Worlds, and say 'I'm terribly sorry, Fraa Lodoghir, but your idea was actually dreamed up by a bug-eyed monster on Planet Zarzax ten million years ago!'"

Laughter around the table.

"Splendid!" Arsibalt said. He turned and looked at me.

"She's a closet Halikaarnian," I said.

"Exactly!"

Fraa Lodoghir had seen the same thing and was trying to lodge an objection: "I'd say you can't know such a thing until you communicate with that bug-eyed monster or his descendants . . ." And then he went on to reiterate what he'd said before. I rushed the salad out in the hopes that it would shut him up. Suur Moyra didn't seem quite taken with his arguments, and Ignetha Foral was beginning to look a little frosted.

Meanwhile, Arsibalt's doyn, who happened to be seated next to Fraa Jad, was leaning to exchange whispers with the Thousander. When first I'd seen this man, he'd struck me as oddly familiar. Only when Arsibalt told me his name had I realized where I'd seen him before: standing alone in the chancel of Saunt Edhar, looking straight up at me. This was Fraa Paphlagon.

Fraa Jad nodded. Paphlagon cleared his throat as Lodoghir began to wind down, and finally barged in: "Perhaps while we're proving that everything Saunt Proc ever wrote was just perfect, we can get some theorics done too!"

This shut even Lodoghir up, so there was a short pause. Paphlagon continued, "There's another reason for having a messal about the Plurality of Worlds: a reason that some would say is almost as fascinating as Fraa Lodoghir's remarks about syntax. It is a pure theorical reason. It is that the Geometers are made of different matter from us. Matter that is not native to this cosmos. And what is more, we have results just in from Laboratorium, concerning the tests that were performed on the four vials of fluid—assumed to be blood—on the Ecba probe. These four samples are made of different matter *from each other,* which is to say that each of them is as different from the other three, as it is from the matter *we* are made of."

"Fraa Paphlagon, I was only made aware of this as I was en route. I'm still absorbing it," said Ignetha Foral. "Say more, please, of what you mean when you speak of the matter being different?"

"The nuclei of the atoms are incompatible," he said. Then, surveying the faces at the table, he shifted back in his chair, grinned, and held up his hands like parallel blades, as if to say "imagine a nucleus." "Nuclei are forged in the hearts of stars. When the stars die, they explode, and the nuclei are thrown out as ash from a dead fire. These nuclei are positively charged. So, when things get cool enough, they attract electrons, and become atoms. Further cooling enables the atoms' electrons to interact with one another to form complexes called molecules, which are what everything is made of. But, again, the making of the world *begins* in the hearts of stars, where those nuclei are forged according to certain rules that only apply in very hot crowded places. The chemistry of the stuff we are made of reflects, in a roundabout way, those rules. Until we learned to make newmatter, every nucleus in our cosmos was made according to the set of rules that naturally obtains. But the Geometers are aware of—they are *made of*—four other slightly different, but totally incompatible, sets of rules for making nuclei."

"So," said Suur Asquin, "they too learned to make newmatter or—"

"Or they came from different cosmi," Fraa Paphlagon said. "Which makes a Plurality of Worlds Messal seem awfully relevant to me."

"This is bizarre—fantastical!" said a reedy voice with a heavy and strange accent. No one's lips were moving that we could see, so, by process of elimination, we turned to the Matarrhite, who was chalked up on the bell-board as one Zh'vaern, with no "Fraa" or "Suur" to give a clue as to sex. Zh'vaern turned slightly in his seat—I was guessing male, from the voice—and made a gesture. His servitor, a column of black fabric, loomed forward, grew a pseudopod, and took his plate—to the visible relief of those seated to either side. "I can hardly believe we are talking about a possibility so inconceivable as that other universes exist—and that the Geometers originate there!"

In this, Zh'vaern seemed to speak for the entire table.

Except for Jad. "The words fail. There is one universe, by the definition of *universe*. It is not the cosmos we see through our eyes and our telescopes—*that* is but a single Narrative, a thread winding through a Hemn space shared by many other Narratives besides ours. Each Narrative looks like a cosmos alone, to any consciousness that partakes of it. The Geometers came from other Narratives—until they came here, and joined ours."

Having dropped this bomb, Fraa Jad excused himself, and went to the toilet.

"What on *earth* is he going on about?" Fraa Lodoghir demanded. "It sounded like literary criticism!" But he did not speak scornfully; he was fascinated.

"So perhaps this messal has *already* turned into what its detractors claim of it," said Ignetha Foral. And having issued that challenge, she turned toward the topic of the research she had performed, years ago, as a Unarian.

Paphlagon was in his seventh decade, impressive-looking rather than handsome, no doubt accustomed to being the most senior, the most eminent person in any given room. He was sitting there with a trim, wry smile, staring at the center of the table—resigning himself, with all good humor, to being Fraa Jad's interpreter. "Fraa Jad," he said, "speaks of Hemn space. It's probably just as well he broached the subject early. Hemn space, or configuration space, is how almost all theors think about the world. During the Praxic Age, it became obvious that it was a better place for us to go about our work, so we decamped, left three-dimensional Adrakhonic space behind, and moved there. When you talk of parallel universes, you make as little sense to Fraa Jad as he does to you."

"Perhaps you can say a few words, then, about Hemn space, if it is so important," suggested Ignetha Foral.

Paphlagon got that wry look again, and sighed. "Madame Secretary, I am trying to think of a way to sum it up that will not turn this messal into a year-long theorics suvin."

And he gamely launched into a primer on Hemn space. He learned to look to Suur Moyra whenever he got stuck for a way of explaining some abstruse concept. More often than not, she was able to drag him out of trouble. She'd already shown herself to be good company. And the vast stock of knowledge that she, as a Lorite, carried around in her head made her good at explaining things; she could always reach back to a useful analogy or clear line of argument that some fraa or suur had written down in the more or less distant past.

I got yanked in the middle of it and, going back to the kitchen, found Emman Beldo on the other end of the rope. Zh'vaern's servitor was standing at the stove, stirring the mystery pot, and so Emman and I wordlessly agreed to retreat to the other end of the kitchen, near the open door to the garden. "What the hell are we talking about here?" Emman wanted to know. "Is this some kind of 'travel through the fourth dimension' scenario?"

"Oh, it's good that you asked," I said, "because it is precisely *not* that—Hemn space is anything *but*. You're talking about the old thing where a bunch of separate three-dimensional universes are stacked on top of each other, like leaves in a book, and you can move between them—"

Emman was nodding. "By figuring out some way to move through the fourth spatial dimension. But this Hemn space thing is something else?"

"In Hemn space, any point—which means any string of N numbers, where N is how many dimensions the Hemn space has—contains *all* the information needed to specify everything that can possibly be known about the system at a given moment."

"*What* system?"

"Whatever system the Hemn space describes," I said.

"Oh, I see," he said, "you're allowed to set up a Hemn space—"

"Any time you feel like it," I said, "to describe the states of any system you are interested in studying. When you are a fid, and your teacher sets a problem for you, your first step is always to set up the Hemn space appropriate to that problem."

"So what is the Hemn space that Jad's referring to, then?" Emman asked. "What is the system that his Hemn space gives all of the possible states of?"

"The cosmos," I said.

"Oh!"

"Which, to him, is one possible track through an absurdly gigantic Hemn space. But that very same Hemn space can have points in it that do not lie on the track that is the history of *our* cosmos."

"But they're perfectly legitimate points?"

"A few of them are—a tiny few, actually—but in a space so huge, 'a few' can be enough to make many whole universes."

"What about the *other* points? I mean the ones that aren't legitimate?"

"They describe situations that are incoherent somehow."

"A block of ice in the middle of a star," Arsibalt suggested.

"Yes," I said, "there is a point somewhere in Hemn space that describes a whole cosmos similar to ours, except that, somewhere in that cosmos, there's a block of ice in the middle of a star. But that situation is impossible."

Arsibalt translated, "There's no past history that could make it happen, so it can't be accessed by a plausible worldtrack."

"But if you can suppress your curiosity about those for a moment," I said to Emman, "the point I was getting at was that you can string the legitimate points—ones not visited by our worldtrack, but that make sense—into other worldtracks that make as much sense as ours."

"But they're not real," Emman said, "or are they?"

I balked.

Arsibalt said, "That is a rather profound question of metatheorics. All of the points in Hemn space are equally real—just as all possible (x, y, z) values are equally real—since they are nothing more than lists of numbers. So what is it that imbues one set of those points—one worldtrack—with what we call realness?"

Suur Tris had been clearing her throat, more and more loudly, the last few minutes, and now graduated to throwing things at us. To this was added the jingling of several bells. It was time to bring out the main course; other servitors had been picking up the slack for me and Emman. So we got very busy for a while. Several minutes later, the fourteen were all back in their formal positions, doyns at the table waiting for Suur Asquin to pick up her fork, servitors standing behind them.

Suur Asquin said, "I believe we have all decided—albeit with some reservations—to move over into Hemn space with Fraa Jad. And according to what we hear of it from Fraa Paphlagon and Suur Moyra, there should be no lack of room for us there!" All the doyns laughed dutifully. Barb snorted. Arsibalt and I rolled our eyes. Barb was clearly dying to plane Suur Asquin by explaining, in excruciating, dinner-wrecking detail, just how colossal the configuration space of the universe really was, complete with estimates of how many zeroes it would take to write down the number of states it could describe, how far said string of digits would extend, et cetera, but Arsibalt raised a hand, threatening to rest it on his shoulder: *steady, now.* Suur Asquin began to eat, and the others followed her lead. There was a little interlude during which some of the doyns (not Lodoghir) made the requisite comments on how tasty the food was. Then Suur Asquin continued, "But looking back on our discussion, I find myself puzzled by a remark that Fraa Paphlagon made before the topic of Hemn space was mentioned, concerning the different kinds of matter. Fraa Paphlagon, I believe you were citing this as evidence that the Geometers all came from different cosmi—or, to use Fraa Jad's term, different Narratives."

"A somewhat more conventional term would be *worldtracks*," Suur Moyra put in. "Use of *Narrative* is somewhat—well—*loaded.*"

"You're speaking my language now!" said Lodoghir, clearly delighted. "Who besides Fraa Jad uses *Narrative,* and what do they really mean by it?"

"It is rare," Moyra said, "and it is associated, in some people's minds, with the Lineage."

Fraa Jad appeared to be ignoring all of this.

"Terminology aside," Suur Asquin went on—a little brusquely— "what I don't quite understand is how it all fits together—what is the link that you see between the fact of the different kinds of matter, and the worldtracks?"

Paphlagon said, "The cosmogonic processes that lead to the creation of the stuff we are made of—the creation of protons and other matter, their clumping together to make stars, and the resulting nucleosynthesis—all seem to depend on the values of certain physical constants. The most familiar example is the speed of light, but there are several others—about twenty in all. Theors used to spend a lot of time measuring their precise values, back when we were allowed to have the necessary equipment. If these numbers had different values, the cosmos as we know it would not have come into being; it would just be an infinite cloud of cold dark gas or one big black hole or something else quite simple and dull. If you think of these constants of nature as knobs on the control panel of a machine, well, the knobs all have to be set in just the right positions or—"

Again Paphlagon looked to Moyra, who seemed ready: "Suur Demula likened it to a safe with a combination lock, the combination being about twenty numbers long."

"If I follow Demula's analogy," said Zh'vaern, "each of those twenty numbers is the value of one of those constants of nature, such as the speed of light."

"That is right. If you dial twenty numbers at random you never get the safe open; it is nothing more to you than an inert cube of iron. Even if you dial nineteen numbers correctly and get the other one wrong—nothing. You must get all of them correct. Then the door opens and out spills all of the complexity and beauty of the cosmos."

"Another analogy," Moyra continued, after a sip of water, "was developed by Saunt Conderline, who likened all of the sets of values of those twenty constants that *don't* produce complexity to an ocean a thousand miles wide and deep. The sets that *do,* are like an oil sheen, no wider than a leaf, floating on the top of that ocean: an exquisitely thin layer of possibilities that yield solid, stable matter suitable for making universes with living things in them."

"I favor Conderline's analogy," said Paphlagon. "The various life-supporting cosmi are different places on that oil-sheen. What the inventors of newmatter did was to devise ways to move around, just a little, to neighboring points on that oil-sheen, where matter had slightly different properties. Most of the newmatter they created was different from, but not really better than, naturally occurring matter. After a lot of patient toil, they were able to slide around to nearby regions of the oil-sheen where matter was better, more useful, than what nature has provided us. And I believe that Fraa Erasmas, here, already has an opinion on what the Geometers are made of."

So unready was I to hear my name called that I didn't even move for several seconds. Fraa Paphlagon was looking at me. In an effort to jog me out of my stupor, he added: "Your friend Fraa Jesry was kind enough to share your observations concerning the parachute."

"Yes," I said, and discovered that my throat needed clearing. "It was nothing special. Not as good as newmatter."

"If the Geometers had learned the art of making newmatter," Paphlagon translated, "they'd have made a better parachute."

"Or come up with a way to land the probe that was not so ridiculously primitive!" Barb sang out, drawing glares from the doyns. His name hadn't been called.

"Fraa Tavener makes an excellent point," said Fraa Jad, defusing the situation. "Perhaps he shall have more of interest to say later—when called upon."

"The point being, I take it," said Ignetha Foral, "that the Geometers—the four groups of them, I should say—each use whatever kind of matter is natural in the cosmos where they originated."

"The four have been given provisional names," announced Zh'vaern. "Antarcts, Pangees, Diasps, and Quators."

This was the first and probably the last time Zh'vaern was going to get a laugh out of the table.

"They all sound vaguely geographical," said Suur Asquin, "but—?"

"Four planets are depicted on their ship," Zh'vaern continued. "This is clearly visible on Saunt Orolo's Phototype. A planet is depicted on each of the four vials of blood that came in the probe. People have given them informal names inspired by their geographical peculiarities."

"So—let me guess—Pangee has one large continent?" asked Suur Asquin.

"Diasp a lot of islands, obviously," put in Lodoghir.

"On Quator, most of the landmasses are at low latitude," Zh'vaern said, "and Antarct's most unusual feature is a big ice continent at the South Pole." Then, perhaps anticipating another correction from Barb, he added: "Or whichever pole is situated at the bottom of the picture."

Barb snorted.

If Fraa Zh'vaern seemed strangely well-informed for a member of a fanatically reclusive sect of Deolaters who'd only arrived at the

Convox a few hours ago, it was because he had attended the same briefing as I had: a meeting in a chalk hall where a succession of fraas and suurs had gotten the Inbrase groups up to speed on diverse topics. Or (taking the more cynical view) fed us what some hierarchs wanted us to know. I was only beginning to get a feel for how *real* information diffused through the Convox.

This touched off a few minutes of banter, which made me impatient until I saw that Moyra and Paphlagon were using it as an opportunity to catch up with the others in cleaning their plates. Some of the servitors went back to the kitchen to look after dessert. It wasn't until we began to clear away the dinner plates that the conversation paused, and Suur Asquin, after an exchange of glances with Ignetha Foral, hemmed into her napkin and said: "Well. What I have collected, from what we heard a few minutes ago, is that none of the four Geometer races has invented newmatter—"

"Or wishes us to know that they have," Lodoghir put in.

"Yes, quite . . . but in any case, each of the four has originated from a cosmos, or a Narrative, or a worldtrack where the constants of nature are ever so slightly different from what they are here."

No one objected.

Ignetha Foral said, "That to me seems like an almost incredibly strange and remarkable finding, and I don't understand why we haven't heard more of it!"

"The results of the tests were not definitive until today's Laboratorium," Zh'vaern said.

"This messal seems to have been thrown together immediately afterwards—actually *during* Inbrase, as a matter of fact," said Lodoghir.

"There were some who had inklings of these results a day or two ago, in Lucub," said Paphlagon.

"Then we ought to have been *made aware of it* a day or two ago," said Ignetha Foral.

"It is in the nature of Lucub work that it does not get talked about as readily as what is done in Laboratorium," Suur Asquin pointed out, deftly playing her role as social facilitator, smoother-out of awkward bits. Jad looked at her as if she were a speed bump stretching across the road in front of his mobe.

"But there is another reason, which Madame Secretary might look on a little more benignly," said Suur Moyra. "The predominant hypothesis, until this morning, was that the propulsion system used by the Geometers to travel between star systems had changed their matter somehow."

"Changed their matter?"

"Yes. Locally altered the laws and constants of nature."

"Is that plausible?"

"Such a propulsion device was envisioned two thousand years ago, right here at Tredegarh," Moyra said. "I brought it up last week. The idea gained currency for a few days. So, you see, it is all my fault."

"The idea would not have gained currency," Fraa Jad announced, "but for that many were unsettled, disturbed by talk of other Narratives. They longed for an explanation that would not force them to learn a new way of thinking, and forgot the Rake."

"Most eloquent, Fraa Jad," said my doyn. "A fine example of the hidden currents that so often drive what pretends to be rational theoric discourse."

Fraa Jad fixed Lodoghir with a look that was hard to read—but not what you'd call warm.

I got yanked. I'd learned to recognize Emman's touch on the rope. Sure enough, he was waiting for me when I entered the kitchen. "The first thing Madame Secretary will say to me in the mobe on her way home is that I have to find my way into the right Lucub."

"You yanked the wrong guy then," I said, "I just got out of quarantine this morning."

"That's why you're perfect: you're going to be in the market."

The picture, as I'd pieced it together, was that mornings (ante Provener) were spent in Laboratorium. I would go to a specific place and work on a given job with others who'd been similarly assigned. Post Provener, but before Messal, was a part of the day called Periklyne, when people mixed and mingled and exchanged information (such as Laboratorium results) that could be further sorted and propagated in the messals. After Messal was Lucub—burning the midnight oil. Everyone was saying there was going to be a lot of Lucub activity tonight because so much of the workday had been wiped out by the Inbrase and the Plenary. Lucub tended to be where the action was anyway. Everyone here wanted to get things done, but many felt that the structure of Laboratorium, Messal, and so on was only getting in their way. Lucub was a way for them to exercise a little initiative. You might be working with a bunch of lunkheads all morning, the hierarchs might have assigned you to a real snoozer of a messal, but during Lucub you could do what you wanted.

"I'd be happy if you wanted to accompany me to Lucub," I told Emman—and I meant it. "But you have to understand that I can't guarantee—"

I was drowned out by indignant shushing from Arsibalt and Karvall.

Barb turned to me and announced: "They want you to be quiet, because they want to hear what is being said in the—"

I shushed Barb. Arsibalt shushed me. Karvall shushed him.

The topic seemed to have turned to the crux of the whole evening's discussion: how the idea of worldtracks and configuration space were related to the existence of different kinds of matter on "Pangee," "Diasp," "Antarct," "Quator," and Arbre.

"It was a strong meme, around the time of the Reconstitution," Moyra was saying, "that the constants of nature are *contingent*—not *necessary*. That is, they could have been otherwise, had the early history of the universe been somehow different. As a matter of fact, research into such ideas is how we got newmatter in the first place."

"So, if I'm following you," Ignetha Foral said, "the correctness of that idea—that those numbers are contingent—was proved. Proved by our ability to make newmatter."

"That is the usual interpretation," said Moyra.

"When you speak of 'early history of the universe,'" put in Lodoghir, "how early—"

"We are speaking of an infinitesimal snatch of time just after the Big Bang," Moyra said, "when the first elementary particles congealed out of a sea of energy."

"And the claim is, it happened to congeal *in a particular way*," Lodoghir said, "but it could have congealed a little differently—leading to a cosmos with different constants and different matter."

"Exactly," said Moyra.

"How can we translate what's just been said into the language that Fraa Jad prefers, of Narratives in configuration space?" asked Ignetha Foral.

"I'll take a crack at it," said Paphlagon. "If we traced *our* worldtrack—the series of points through configuration space that is the past, present, and future of our cosmos—*backwards* in time, we would observe configurations that were hotter and brighter, more closely packed—like running a photomnemonic tablet of an explosion in reverse. It would lead us into regions of Hemn space scarcely recognizable as a cosmos at all: the moments just after the Big Bang. At some point, proceeding backwards, we'd get to a configuration in which the physical constants we've been speaking of—"

"Those twenty numbers," said Suur Asquin.

"Yes, were *not even defined*. A place so different that those constants would be meaningless—they would have no value, because they still had the freedom to take on *any* value. Now, up until this point in the story I'm telling you, there really is no difference between the old one-universe picture, and the worldtrack-through-Hemn space picture."

"Not even when newmatter is taken into account?" asked Lodoghir.

"Not even then, because all the newmatter makers did was to build a machine that could create energies that high, and then make their own little Big Bangs in the lab. But what *is* new to us now, as of this morning's Laboratorium findings, is that if you, in the same manner, traced the worldtracks of Antarct, of Pangee, Diasp, and Quator backwards, you would find yourself in a very similar part of Hemn space."

"The Narratives converge," said Fraa Jad.

"As you go *backwards,* you mean," Zh'vaern said.

"There is no backwards," said Fraa Jad.

This occasioned a few moments of silence.

"Fraa Jad doesn't believe in the existence of time," Moyra said; but she sounded as if she were realizing it and saying it at the same moment.

"Ah, well! Important detail, that," said Suur Tris, in the kitchen, and for once no one shushed her. For some minutes, we'd all been standing around a set of dessert plates, ready to serve, waiting for the right moment.

"I don't recommend we get sidetracked on the question of whether time exists," said Paphlagon, to the almost audible relief of everyone else. "The point is that in that model that views the five cosmi—Arbre, and those of the four Geometer races—as trajectories in Hemn space, those trajectories are extremely close together in the vicinity of the Big Bang. And we might even ask whether they were *the same* up to a certain point, when something happened that made them split off from one another. Perhaps that is a question for another messal. Perhaps only Deolaters would dare to attempt it." In the kitchen, we risked glancing at Zh'vaern's servitor. "In any case, the different worldtracks ended up with slightly different physical constants. And so you could say that even if we were to sit in a room with a Geometer who seemed similar to us, the fact is that they would carry in the very nuclei of their atoms a sort of fingerprint that proved they came from a different Narrative."

"As our genetic sequences carry a record of every mutation, every adaptation, every ancestor to the first thing that ever lived," said Suur Moyra, "so the stuff of which they were made would encode what Fraa Jad calls the Narrative of their cosmos, back to the point in Hemn space when we all diverged."

"Farther," Fraa Jad said. Which was followed by the customary silence that followed most Jad-statements; but it was shattered, this time, by a laugh from Lodoghir.

"Ah, I see it! Finally! Oh, what a fool I've been, Fraa Jad, not to notice the game you've been playing. But now at last I see where you have been leading us, ever so subtly: to the Hylaean Theoric World!"

"Hmm, I don't know which is more annoying," I said, "Lodoghir's tone, or the fact that he figured this out before I did."

I'd been shocked, a few hours ago, when Lodoghir had wandered up to me during Periklyne and begun chit-chatting about our encounter on the Plenary stage. How could he come anywhere near me without body armor and a team of stun-gun-brandishing Inquisitors? How could he not have foreseen that I'd devote the rest of my life to plotting violent revenge? Which had forced me to understand that it really wasn't personal, for him: all the rhetorical tricks, the distortions, salted with outright lies, the appeals to emotion, were every bit as much parts of his tool kit as equations and syllogisms were of mine, and he didn't imagine I'd really object, any more than Jesry would if I pointed out an error in his theorics.

I had stared dumbly at Lodoghir throughout, judging the distance separating my knuckles and his teeth. I had had the vague idea that he was bossing me around a little, concerning this evening's messal, but I hadn't heard any of it. After a while he had lost interest, since I hadn't said a word, and had wandered off.

"I don't know how I'm going to make it through this, between him, and the Inquisition!" I said.

"You're *already* in trouble with the Inquisition?" Arsibalt asked, sounding amazed and appreciative at the same time.

"No—but Varax let me know he's watching me," I said.

"How in the world did he do that?"

"Earlier, I had a really annoying encounter with Lodoghir."

"Yes. I saw it."

"No, I mean I had a *second* one. And a few seconds later, guess who walked up to me?"

"Well, given the context in which you are telling the story," Arsibalt said, "I would have to guess it was Varax."

"Yeah."

"What did Varax say?"

"He said, 'I understand you're up to Chapter Five! Hope it didn't ruin your whole autumn.' And I told him that it had taken me a few weeks but I didn't blame him for what had happened."

"That was all?"

"Yeah. Maybe some chitchat afterwards."

"And how do you interpret these words of Varax?"

"He was saying 'don't pop your doyn in the nose, young man—I'm watching you.'"

"You're an idiot."

"*What!?*"

"You got it all wrong! This was a gift!"

"A *gift!?*"

Arsibalt explained: "A doyn has the power to discipline his servitor by assigning chapters in the Book. But you, Raz, hardened criminal that you are, are already up to Five. Lodoghir would have to give you Six: a very heavy punishment—"

"Which I could appeal," I said, getting it, "appeal to the Inquisition."

"Arsibalt's right," said Tris, who'd been listening (and who seemed to be looking at me in a whole new way, now that she knew I was up to Five). "It sounds to me like this Varax was giving you a big fat hint that the Inquisition would throw out any sentence from Lodoghir."

"They would almost have to," said Arsibalt.

I picked up Lodoghir's dessert and headed for the messallan in a whole new mood. The others followed me. We came into a room of flushed faces and bitten lips: a tableau of strained and awkward body language. Lodoghir had been having his usual effect on people.

"Just when I'd thought we were getting somewhere," Ignetha Foral was saying, "I see that once again the messal has been sidetracked into some old and tedious dispute between Procians and Halikaarnians. *Metatheorics!* Sometimes I wonder whether you in the mathic world really understand the stakes that are now in play."

Clearly I had come in at the wrong moment. But it was too late now, and others were piling up behind me, so I barged on in and gave my doyn his dessert just as he was saying, "I accept your rebuke, Madame Secretary, and I assure you that—"

"I don't accept it," said Fraa Jad.

"Nor should you!" put in Zh'vaern.

"These matters are important whether or not you take the trouble to understand them," Fraa Jad went on.

"How am I to distinguish this from the partisan bickering that goes on in the capital?" Ignetha Foral asked. Others at the table had been horrified by Fraa Jad's tone, but she seemed to find it bracing.

Fraa Jad ignored the question—it was none of his concern—and turned his energies to his dessert. Fraa Zh'vaern—who was surprising us all with his interest in the topic—took it up. "By examining the quality of the arguments."

"When the arguments come out of pure theorics, I am unable to make such judgments!" she pointed out.

"I would not assume that the existence of the Hylaean Theoric World comes out of what is called pure theorics," Lodoghir said. "It is as much a leap of faith as believing in God."

"As much as I admire the ingenuity with which you find a way to skewer Fraa Jad and Fraa Zh'vaern with the same sentence," said Ignetha Foral, "I must remind you that most of the people I work with believe in God, and so, among them, your gambit is likely to backfire."

"The hour is late," Suur Asquin pointed out—though no one seemed tired. "I propose that we take up the topic of the Hylaean Theoric World in tomorrow evening's messal."

Fraa Jad nodded, but it was hard to tell whether he was accepting the challenge, or really enjoying the cake.

Everything Killer: a weapons system of unusual praxic sophistication, thought to have been used to devastating effect in the Terrible Events. The belief is widely held, but unproved, that the complicity of theors in the development of this praxis led to universal agreement that they should henceforth be segregated from non-theorical society, a policy that when effected became synonymous with the Reconstitution.

—THE DICTIONARY, *4th edition, A.R. 3000*

"Have you all been enjoying your books?" Suur Moyra inquired, then seized a pan and began scraping dead vegetables into the compost. Karvall gasped—Moyra had sneaked in and ambushed us. She dropped the pot she'd been scrubbing, spun away from the sink, and ran over to take the pan out of her old doyn's frail hands. Arsibalt and I turned almost as adroitly to watch. Karvall might be swathed in a ton of black bolt, but, as we'd been noticing, the lashings that held it in place around her body were most intricate, and rewarded close examination. Even Barb looked. Emman Beldo was driving Ignetha Foral back to her lodgings. Zh'vaern's servitor, Orhan, was a hard man or woman to read with his or her head totally covered, but the wrinkles in his or her bolt told me his or her head was tracking Karvall. Tris took advantage of this to steal the best scrub-brush.

"Were you responsible for the books?" I asked.

"I had Karvall place them in your trailer," Moyra said, and gave me a smile.

"So *that's* where those came from," Tris said, then explained, "I found a stack of books in my cell this morning." From the way other servitors were now looking at Moyra, I guessed they'd had similar experiences.

"Wait a minute, that is chronologically impossible!" Barb pointed out, and then, showing a flash of the old Barb wit, added, "Unless you violated the rules of causality!"

"Oh, I've been trying to get this messal started for a few days," Moyra said. "Just ask Suur Asquin, she'll tell you what a pest I've made of myself. You don't really think something like this could be thrown together by a bunch of hierarchs passing notes around during Inbrase, do you?"

"Grandsuur Moyra," Arsibalt began, "if it wasn't this morning's Laboratorium results that brought this messal into being, what was it?"

"Well, if you weren't too busy flirting with these lovely suurs and horsing around in the kitchen, you might have heard me earlier, speaking of being a meta-Lorite."

"Or a Plurality of Worlds Lorite," I said.

"Ah, so you *were* paying attention!"

"I thought it was just an icebreaker."

"Who was *their* Evenedric, Fraa Arsibalt?"

"I beg your pardon?" Arsibalt was fascinated by the question, but soon had his hands full as Suur Tris dumped a huge greasy platter into his arms.

"Fraa Tavener, who was the Saunt Hemn on the planet of Quator? Tris, who was the Lady Baritoe of Antarct? Fraa Orhan, do they worship a God on Pangee, and is it the same as the God of the Matarrhites?"

"It *must* be, Grandsuur Moyra!" Orhan exclaimed, and made a gesture with his hand (I had decided he had to be male) that I'd seen before. Some kind of Deolater superstition.

"Fraa Erasmas, who discovered Halikaarn's Diagonal on the world of Diasp?"

"Because obviously they *did* think such thoughts, you're saying . . ." Arsibalt said.

"They must have done, to build that ship!" said Barb.

"Your minds are so much fresher, more agile than some of those who sit in that messallan," Moyra said. "I thought you might have ideas."

Suur Tris turned around and asked, "Are you saying that there would be one-to-one-correspondences between our Saunts and theirs? Like the same mind shared across multiple worlds?"

"I'm asking *you*," Moyra said.

I had nothing to say, being stricken with the all-too-familiar feeling of unease that came over me, lately, when conversations began to wander down this path. The last words Orolo had spoken to me, a few minutes before he'd died, had been a warning that the Thousanders knew about this stuff, and had been developing a praxis around it: in effect, that the legends of the Incanters were based in fact. And perhaps I'd fallen back into my old habit of worrying too much; but it seemed to me, now, that every conversation I was part of came dangerously close to this topic.

Arsibalt, unburdened by such cares, felt ready to have a go. He heaved the washed platter into a drying rack, wiped his hands on his bolt, and squared off. "Well. Any such hypothesis would have to be grounded in some account of *why* different minds in different worldtracks would think similar things. One could always look to a religious explanation," he went on, with a glance at Orhan, "but other than that . . . well . . ."

"You needn't be reticent about your belief in the HTW—remember who you're talking to! I've seen it all!"

"Yes, Grandsuur Moyra," Arsibalt said, with a dip of the head.

"How might the knowledge propagate from a common Theoric World—I won't call it Hylaean, since presumably there was no person named Hylaea on Quator—to the minds of different Saunts in different worlds? And is it still going on at this moment—between us, and them?" Moyra had been edging toward the back door as she tossed these mind bombs into the kitchen, and now almost collided with Emman Beldo, fresh in from escorting his doyn home.

"Well, it sounds as though the messal will discuss that tomorrow," I pointed out.

"Why wait? Don't be complacent!" Moyra shot back as she was storming out into the night. Karvall threw down a towel and scurried after her, drawing her bolt up over her head. Emman politely got out of her way, then swiveled to watch Karvall until there was nothing left to see. When he turned back around, he got a sponge in the face from Suur Tris.

"You can't just have these tracks wandering around in Hemn space—" said Emman.

"The way we're wandering around in the dark," I proposed. For we were attempting to find a suitable Lucub.

"With no rhyme or reason. Can you?"

"You mean the worldtracks? The Narratives?"

"I guess so—what is up with *that*, by the way?"

It was a vague question but I could tell what was on his mind.

"You mean, Fraa Jad's use of the word *Narrative*?"

"Yeah. That's going to be a hard one to sell to—"

"The Panjandrums?"

"Is that what you call people like my doyn?"

"Some of us."

"Well, they're pretty hardheaded. Don't go in for anything highfalutin."

"Well, let me see if I can come up with an example," I said. "Remember what Arsibalt said? The block of ice buried in the star?"

"Yeah, sure," he said. "There is a point in Hemn space that represents a cosmos that includes even that."

"The configuration of the cosmos encoded in that point," I said, "includes—along with all the stars and planets, the birds and the bees, the books and the speelies and everything else—one star that happens to have a big chunk of ice in the middle of it. That point, remember, is just a long string of numbers—coordinates in the space. No more or less real than any other possible string of numbers."

"Its realness—or unrealness in this case—has to grow out of some other consideration," Emman tried.

"You got it. And in this case, it is that the situation being described is so damned ridiculous."

"How could it ever *happen*, to begin with?" Emman demanded, getting into the spirit.

"*Happen*. That's the key word," I said, wishing I could explain this as confidently as Orolo. "What does it mean for something to happen?" That sounded pretty lame. "It's not just this situation—this isolated point in configuration space—that springs into being for a moment and then vanishes. It's not like you have a normal star, and then suddenly for one tick of the cosmic clock a block of ice materializes in the middle of it, and then, next tick, poof! It's gone without a trace."

"But it *could* happen, couldn't it, if you had a Hemn Space teleporter?"

"Mm, that's a useful thought experiment," I said. "You're thinking of a gadget from one of Moyra's novels. A magic booth where you could dial in any point in Hemn space, realize it, and then jump to another."

"Yeah. Regardless of the laws of theorics or whatever. Then you *could* make the ice block materialize. But then it would melt."

"It would melt," I corrected him, "if you let natural law take over from that point. But you could preserve it by making your Hemn Space teleporter jump to another point encoding the same cosmos, an instant later, but with the block of ice still included."

"Okay, I get it—but normally it would melt."

"So, Emman, the question is: what means 'normally'? Another way of putting it: if you look at the series of points you'd have to string together with your Hemn Space teleporter in order to see, outside the windows of the booth, a cosmos with a block of ice persisting in the middle of a star, how different would that series of points have to be from one that was a proper worldtrack?"

"Meaning, a worldtrack where natural laws were respected?"

"Yeah."

"I don't know."

We laughed. "Well," I said, "I'm now starting to understand some of what Orolo was saying to me about Saunt Evenedric. Evenedric studied datonomy—an outgrowth of Sconic philosophy—which means, what is given to us, what we observe. In the end, that's all we have to work with."

"I'll bite," Emman said, "what do we observe?"

"Not just world *points* that are coherent," I said, "so, no ice blocks in stars—but coherent *series* of such points: a worldtrack that *could have happened*."

"What's the difference?"

"It's not just that you can't have a block of ice in a star, but that you can't *get* it there, you can't *keep* it there—there is no coherent history that can include it. See, it's not just about what is *possible*—since anything is possible in Hemn space—but what is *compossible*, meaning all the other things that would have to be true in that universe, to have a block of ice in a star."

"Well, I actually think you could do it," Emman said. The praxic gears were turning in his head. This was what he did for a living; he'd been pulled out of his job at a rocket agency to serve as technical advisor to Ignetha Foral. "You could design a rocket—a missile with a warhead made of thick heat-resistant material with a block of ice embedded in it. Make this thing plunge into the star at high velocity. The heat-resistant material would burn away. But just after it did, for a moment, you'd have a block of ice embedded in a star."

"Okay, that's all possible," I said, "but it's a way of answering the question 'what other things would have to be true about a cosmos that included a block of ice in a star?' If you were to go to that cosmos and freeze it in that moment of time—"

"Okay," he said, "let's say the teleporter has a user interface feature that makes it easy to freeze time by looping back to the same point over and over."

"Fine. And if you did that and looked at the region around the ice, you'd see the heavy nuclei of the melted heat shield swirling around in the star-stuff. You'd see the trail of rocket exhaust in space, leading all the way back to the scorch marks on the launch pad. That launch pad has to be on a planet capable of supporting life smart enough to build rockets. Around that launch pad you'd see people who had spent years of their lives designing and building that rocket. Memories of that work, and of the launch, would be encoded in their neurons. Speelies of the launch would be stored in their reticules. And all of those memories and recordings would mostly agree with one another. All of those memories and recordings boil down to positions of atoms in space—so—"

"So those memories and recordings, you're saying, *are themselves* parts of the configuration encoded by that point in Hemn space," Emman said, loudly and firmly, as he knew he was getting it. "And that is what you mean about compossibility."

"Yes."

"Ice in a star could be encoded by *many* Hemn space points," he said, "but only a few of them—"

"A vanishingly tiny few," I said.

"Include all the records—coherent, mutually consistent records—of how it got to be there."

"Yes. When you go all praxic on me and dream up the ice missile delivery system, what you're really doing is figuring out what Narrative would create the set of conditions—the traces left behind in the cosmos by the execution of that project—that is compossible with ice in a star."

We walked on for a bit and he said, "Or to give a less dignified example, you can't look at Suur Karvall's outfit—"

"Without having to reconstruct in your mind the sequence of operations needed to tie all those knots."

"Or to untie them—"

"She's a Hundreder," I warned him, "and the Convox won't last forever."

"Don't get too attached. Yeah, I know. But I could still get a date with her in 3700—"

"Or become a fraa," I suggested.

"I might have to, after this. Hey, do you know where you're going?"

"Yeah. I'm following you."

"Well, *I've* been following *you*."

"Okay, that would mean that we're lost." And we stumbled about until we encountered a pair of grandsuurs out for a stroll, and asked them for directions to the Edharian chapterhouse.

"So," Emman said, after we'd set out on the right track, "the bottom line is that in any one particular cosmos—excuse me, on any one particular worldtrack—things make sense. The laws of nature are followed."

"Yes," I said. "That's what a worldtrack *is*—a sequence of Hemn space points strung together just so, to make it look like the laws of nature are preserved."

"I'm going to put that in teleporter terms, since that's how I'll be explaining it to people," he said. "The whole point of the teleporter is that it could take you to *any* other point at any moment. You could jump randomly from one cosmos to another. But only *one* point in Hemn space encodes the state that the cosmos *you're in now* will have *at the next tick of the clock,* if the laws of nature are followed—right?"

"You're on the right track," I said, "but—"

"Where I'm going with this," he said, "is as follows: the people to whom I have to explain this have heard of the laws of nature. Maybe even studied them a bit. They're comfortable with that. Now suddenly I come in and start talking about Hemn space. A new concept to them. I give them a big explanation—I talk about the teleporter, the ice in the star, and the scorch marks on the launch pad. Finally one of these people raises his hand and says, 'Mr. Beldo, you have squandered hours of our valuable time giving us a calca on Hemn space—what, pray tell, is the bottom line?' And my answer is, 'If you please, sir, the bottom line is that the laws of nature are followed in our cosmos.' And he's going to say—"

"He's going to say, 'We already knew that, you idiot, you're fired!'"

"Exactly! Which is when I have to run off and become a fraa, preferably in Karvall's math."

"So you are asking me—"

"What do we gain *that is consequential* by adopting the Hemn space model? You already mentioned it makes it easier to do theorics—but Panjandrums don't do theorics."

"Well, for one thing, it is actually *not* the case that, at any given point, there is *only one* next point that is consistent with the laws of nature."

"Oh, are you going to talk about quantum mechanics?"

"Yeah. An elementary particle can decay—which is compatible with the laws of nature—or it can *not* decay—which is *also* compatible with the laws of nature. But decaying and not decaying take us to two different points in Hemn space—"

"The worldtrack forks."

"Yeah. Worldtracks fork all the time, whenever quantum state reduction seems to occur—which is *a lot.*"

"But still, whatever worldtrack we happen to be on *still always obeys the laws of nature,*" he said.

"I'm afraid so."

"So, back to my original problem—"

"What does Hemn space get us? Well, for one thing, it makes it a heck of a lot easier to think about quantum mechanics."

"But Panjandrums don't think about quantum mechanics!"

I had nothing to say; I just felt like a clueless avout.

"So, do you think I should mention the Hemn space thing *at all?*"

"Let's ask Jesry," I proposed. "He's cool-looking." For we had reached the Edharian cloister, and I spied him on a path, drawing diagrams in the gravel with a stick while a fraa and a suur stood by watching and laughing delightedly. In the moonlight these people looked as though they'd been sketched in ash on a fireplace floor. Still, they cut altogether different figures. Jesry looked like a young prophet from some ancient scripture next to the fraa and the suur, who came from more cosmopolitan orders that went in for fancy wraps. This morning at Inbrase I'd felt like a real hick when I'd looked at how the other avout dressed. But that was just me. Put the same outfit on Jesry and he became awe-inspiringly rugged, simple, austere, and, well, manly. I understood, as I looked at him, why Fraa Lodoghir had been so keen to plane me. There was something about the Edharian contingent that impressed people. Orolo had made us into stars. Lodoghir had seen the Plenary as an opportunity to take one of us down a peg.

"Jesry," I called.

"Hi, Raz. I am not one of those people who think you sucked at the Plenary."

"Thanks. Name one thing we get by working in configuration space that we don't get any other way."

"Time," he said.

"Oh yeah," I said. "Time."

"I thought time didn't exist!" Emman said sarcastically.

Jesry looked at Emman for a few moments, then looked at me. "What, has your friend been talking to Fraa Jad?"

"It is nice that Hemn space gives us an account of time," I said, "but Emman will say that the Panjandrums he has to talk to already believe in the existence of time—"

"Poor, benighted fools!" Jesry exclaimed, getting a low, painful laugh out of Emman, and quizzical looks from his avout companions.

"So of what relevance to them is the Hemn space picture?" I continued.

"None whatsoever," Jesry said, "until strangers come to town from four different cosmi at once. Hey, can I get you guys something to drink?"

It was yet another of Jesry's annoying qualities that he did some of his finest work while drunk. We servitors had sampled our share of wine and beer in the kitchen, and I was just beginning to get my head clear, so I decided to drink water. Presently we found ourselves in the largest chalk hall of the local Edharian chapter—or at least I *assumed* it had to be the largest. The slate walls were covered with calculations I recognized. "They've got you doing cosmography?" I asked.

Jesry followed my gaze and focused on a table of figures chalked up on a slate. One column was longitude, another latitude—and seeing fifty-one degrees and change chalked up in the latter, I realized I was looking at the coordinates of Saunt Edhar.

"This morning's Laboratorium," he explained. "We had to check a bunch of calculations that the Ita did last night. All of the world's telescopes—including the M & M, as you can see—are to be pointed at the Geometers' ship tonight."

"All night long or—"

"No. In about half an hour. Something is going to happen," Jesry proclaimed in his usual confident baritone. I noticed Emman cringing. "Something that will give us a different view," Jesry went on, "more interesting than the pusher plate on its arse which I spent so many hours staring at."

"How do we know this?" I asked, though I was a little distracted by Emman's conspicuous nervousness.

"I don't," Jesry said, "I'm just inferring it."

Emman jerked his head toward the exit and we followed him out into the cloister.

"I'll tell you guys," he said, once we'd gotten out of earshot of the rest of the Lucub, "since the secret is going to be out in half an hour anyway. This is an idea that was cooked up at a very influential messal after the Visitation of Orithena."

"Were you in on it?" I asked.

"No—but it's why I was brought here," Emman said. "We have an old reconaissance bird up there in synchronous orbit. It's got loads of fuel on board, so that it can move around when we tell it to. We don't think the Geometers know about it. We've kept the bird silent, so it hasn't occurred to them to jam its frequencies. Well, earlier today we narrow-beamed a burst of commands to the thing and it fired up its thrusters and placed itself into a new orbit that will intercept that of the Hedron in half an hour." He used his toe to render the Geometers' ship in the gravel path: a crude polygon for the envelope of the icosahedron, a heel-stomp on one edge for the pusher plate. "This thing is always pointed at Arbre," he complained, tapping his toe on the pusher plate, "so we can't see the rest of the ship"—he swept his foot in an arc around the forward half—"which is where they keep all of the cool stuff. Obviously a deliberate move—this half has been like the dark side of the moon to us, so we've had to rely entirely on Saunt Orolo's Phototype." He stepped around to the flank of the diagram and swept out a long arc aimed at the bow. "Our bird," he said, "is approaching from this direction. It is radioactive as hell."

"The bird is?"

"Yeah, it draws power from radiothermal devices. The Geometers are going to notice this thing headed their way and they'll have no choice but to execute a maneuver—"

"To get the pusher plate—which is their shield—between themselves and the bogey," Jesry said.

"They'll have to spin the whole ship around," I translated, "exposing the 'cool stuff' to view from ground-based telescopes."

"And those telescopes are going to be ready."

"Is it even *possible* to spin something that big around in any reasonable amount of time?" I asked. "I'm trying to imagine how big the thrusters would have to be—"

Emman shrugged. "You ask a good question. We'll learn a lot just from observing its maneuver. Tomorrow we'll have lots of pictures to look at."

"Unless they get angry and nuke us," Jesry put in, while I was trying to think of a more delicate way of saying it.

"There's been some discussion of that," Emman admitted.

"Well, I should hope so!" I said.

"The Panjandrums are all sleeping in caves and bunkers."

"That's comforting," Jesry said.

Emman missed the sarcasm. "And the mathic world has experience in coping with nuclear aftermaths."

Jesry and I both turned to look in the direction of the Precipice, wondering how deep we could get in those tunnels, how fast.

"But this is all considered low-probability," Emman said. "What happened on Ecba was a serious provocation, if not an outright act of war. We have to make a serious response—show the Geometers we won't just sit passively while they drop rods on us."

"Will this bird actually hit the icosahedron?" I asked.

"Not unless they're stupid enough to get in its way. But it'll come close enough that they'll have to respond, as a precaution."

"Well!" Jesry said, after we had spent a minute absorbing all of this. "So much for getting anything done during Lucub."

"Yeah," I said, "I guess I *will* have that wine after all."

We took a bottle out onto the lawn between the Edharian and Eleventh Sconic cloisters. We knew where to look in the sky, so we arranged ourselves and lay in the grass waiting for the End of the World.

I really missed Ala. For a while I hadn't been thinking about her much. But she was the one I wanted to be next to when the nukes rained down.

At the appointed moment there was a tiny, momentary flash of light in the middle of the constellation where we knew the Hedron was. As though a spark had jumped between their ship and our "bird."

"They nailed it with something," Emman said.

"Directed energy weapon," Jesry intoned, as if he actually knew what he was talking about.

"X-ray laser, to be specific," said a nearby voice.

We sat up to see a stocky figure in an antique bolt-and-chord getup, shambling toward us on weary legs.

"Hello, Thistlehead!" I called out.

"Feel like a stroll while we await massive retaliation?"

"Sure," I said.

"I'm going to bed," Jesry said. I guessed he was lying. "No Lucub tonight." *Definitely* lying.

"Then I'm doing the same," said Emman Beldo, who knew when he was being gotten rid of. "Lots of work tomorrow."

"If we still exist," Jesry said.

"I really have to get in touch with Ala," I told Lio, after we had wandered for half an hour without saying a word. "I looked for her at Periklyne this afternoon but—"

"She wasn't there," Lio said, "she was getting ready for this."

"You mean aiming the telescopes or—"

"More the military side of it."

"How'd she get mixed up in *that*?"

"She's good. Someone noticed. The military gets what it asks for."

"How would you know? Are you mixed up in the military side too?"

Lio was silent. We walked for a few minutes more. "A few days ago they put me in a new Laboratorium," he said. I could tell that he'd been laboring to get it off his chest for a while.

"Oh really? What have they got you doing?"

"They dug up some old documents. *Really* old. We've been scraping them off. Getting familiar with them. Looking up old words, fallen from use."

"What kinds of documents?"

"Technical drawings. Specs. Manuals. Back-of-envelope sketches, even."

"For what?"

"They won't just come out and say, and no one is allowed to see the whole picture," Lio said, "but talking to some of the others, comparing notes in Lucub, taking into account the dates on the documents—just before the Terrible Events—we're all pretty sure that what we are looking at are the original plans for the Everything Killers."

I gave a little snort of laughter, simply out of habit. The Everything Killers were only ever mentioned in the same way as we might talk of God or Hell. But everything about Lio's tone and manner told me that he was being altogether literal. There was a long silence while I tried to absorb this news.

In an attempt to prove that he must be mistaken, I pointed out, "But that goes against everything—*everything*—that the world is based on!" Meaning the post-Reconstitution world. "If they're willing to do *that,* then nothing is real anymore."

"There are many who agree with you, of course," Lio said, "and that's why—" He exhaled, the breath coming out raggedly. "That's why I wanted to invite you to be part of my Lucub."

"What's the purpose of this Lucub?"

"Some people are thinking of going over to the Antarcts."

"Going over—as in joining forces with? With the *Geometers*!?"

"The Antarcts," he insisted. "It's been established, now, that the dead woman in the probe was from Antarct."

"Based on the blood samples in the tubes?"

He nodded. "But the projectiles in her body are from the Pangee cosmos."

"So people are guessing that the Antarcts are on our side—"

He nodded again. "And having some sort of conflict, up there, with the Pangees."

"So the idea is to forge an alliance between the avout, and the Antarcts?"

"You got it," Lio said.

"Wow! How exactly would you go about that? How would you even communicate with them? I mean, so that the Sæcular Power wouldn't know of it."

"Easy. Already been worked out." Then, knowing I'd never be satisfied with that, he added, "It's the guidestar lasers on the big telescopes. We can aim them at the icosahedron. They'll see the light but it can't be intercepted by anyone who's not right on the beam line."

I thought of the conversation I'd had with Lio months ago, when we had wondered whether it was really true, or just an old folk tale, that the Ita had us under continual surveillance. Idiotically, I looked around just in case any hidden microphones might somehow have popped into view. "Do the Ita—"

"Some of them are in on it," Lio said.

"What kind of relationship exactly do these people want to forge with the Antarcts?"

"We spend most of our time arguing about that. Too much time. There are some nut jobs, of course, who think we can go up there and live on their ship and it'll be like ascending to Heaven. Most are more reasonable. We'll set up our own communications to the Geometers and . . . conduct our own negotiations."

"But that is totally at odds with the Reconstitution!"

"Does the Reconstitution say anything about aliens? About multiple cosmi?"

I shut up, knowing when I was planed.

"Anyway," he went on.

I completed his sentence. "The Reconstitution is a dead letter anyway if they are dusting off the Everything Killers."

"The term *post-mathic* is being thrown around," Lio said. "People are talking about the Second Rebirth."

"Who's in on it?"

"Quite a few servitors. Not so many doyns, if you follow me."

"What orders? What maths?"

"Well . . . the Ringing Vale avout consider the Everything Killers to be dishonorable, if that helps you."

"Where does this Lucub meet? It sounds huge."

"It's a bunch of Lucubs. A network of cells. We talk to one another."

"What do *you* do, Lio?"

"Stand in the back of the room and look tough. Listen."

"What are you listening for?"

"There are some crazies," he said. "Well, not crazy, but *too* rational, if you know what I mean. No awareness of tactics. Of discretion."

"And what are those people saying?"

"That it's time for the smart people to be in charge. Time to take the power back from people like the Warden of Heaven."

"That kind of talk could lead to a Fourth Sack!" I said.

"Some people are way ahead of you," Lio said. "They are saying, 'Fine. Bring it on. The Geometers will intervene on our side.'"

"That is just shockingly reckless," I said.

"That's why I'm listening to those people," Lio said, "and reporting back to my Lucub group, which seems reasonable by comparison."

"Why would the Geometers reach down to stop a Sack?"

"People who believe this tend to be hard-core HTW types, I'm sorry to say. They've seen the Adrakhonic proof on Orolo's phototype. They assume that the Geometers are our brothers. The fact that the Geometers made their first landfall at Orithena just confirms this."

"Lio, I have a question."

"Okay."

"I've had zero contact with Ala. Jesry thinks it's because she's trying to get her liaisons sorted. But that doesn't seem like her. Does she know anything about this group?"

"She started it," Lio said.

Sphenics: A school of theors well represented in ancient Ethras, where they were hired by well-to-do families as tutors for their children. In many classic Dialogs, seen in opposition to Thelenes, Protas, or others of their school. Their most prominent champion was Uraloabus, who in the Dialog of the same name was planed so badly by Thelenes that he committed suicide on the spot. They disputed the views of Protas and, broadly speaking, preferred to believe that theorics took place entirely between the ears, with no recourse to external realities such as the Protan forms. The forerunners of Saunt Proc, the Syntactic Faculties, and the Procians.

—THE DICTIONARY, *4th edition, A.R. 3000*

Paphlagon's plate was clean; Lodoghir hadn't even picked up his fork. Hunger at last succeeded where throat-clearing, glares, exasperated sighs, and the *en masse* departure of the servitors had failed: Lodoghir fell silent, picked up his glass, and doused his flaming vocal chords.

Paphlagon was eerily calm—almost jolly. "If one were to examine a transcript of that, one would see an extraordinary, and quite lengthy, catalog of every rhetorical trick in the Sphenic book. We've seen appeals to mob sentiment: 'no one believes in the HTW any more,' 'everyone thinks Protism is crazy.' We've seen appeals to authority: 'refuted in the Twenty-ninth Century by no less than Saunt So-and-so.' Efforts to play on our personal insecurity: 'how can any person of sound mind take this seriously?' And many other techniques that I have forgotten the names of, as it has been so long since I studied the Sphenics. So. I must begin by applauding the rhetorical mastery that has given the rest of us an opportunity to enjoy this excellent meal and rest our voices. But I would be remiss if I did not point out that Fraa Lodoghir has yet to offer up a single argument, worthy of the name, against the proposition that there is a Hylaean Theoric World, that it is populated by mathematical entities—cnoöns, as we call them—that are non-spatial and non-temporal in nature, and that our minds have some capability of accessing them."

"Nor could I—ever!" exclaimed Fraa Lodoghir, whose jaw had been working at an astounding pace during the last few moments to get a bite of food squared away. "You Protists are ever so careful to frame the discussion so that it can't be touched by rational debate. I can't prove you're wrong any more than I can prove the non-existence of God!"

Paphlagon had some infighting skills of his own; he simply ignored what Lodoghir had just said. "A couple of weeks ago, at a Plenary, you and some of the other Procians floated the suggestion that the diagram of the Adrakhonic Theorem on the Geometers' ship was a forgery, inserted into Saunt Orolo's Phototype by Orolo himself, or someone else at Edhar. Do you now retract that allegation?" And Paphlagon glanced over his shoulder at an astoundingly high-resolution phototype of the Geometers' ship, taken last night by the largest optical telescope on Arbre, on which the diagram was clearly visible. The walls of the messallan were papered with such. The table was scattered with more.

"There is nothing wrong with mentioning hypotheses in the course of a discussion," Lodoghir said. "Clearly that particular one happened to be incorrect."

"I think he just said 'yes, I withdraw the allegation,'" said Tris, in the kitchen. I had gone back there ostensibly to fulfill my duties, but really to plow through heaps of more phototypes. Everyone in the Convox had been looking at them all day, but we weren't even close to being tired of it.

"It is *such* good fortune that this gambit worked," Emman reflected, gazing fixedly at a grainy close-up of a strut.

"You mean, that we did not get rodded?" Barb asked—sincerely.

"No, that we got pictures," Emman said. "Got them by doing something clever, *here*."

"Oh—you mean it is good fortune *politically?*" Karvall asked, a little uncertain.

"Yes! Yes!" Emman exclaimed. "The Convox is expensive! It makes the Powers That Be happy when it yields discernible results."

"Why is it expensive?" Tris asked. "We grow our own food."

Emman finally looked up from his pictures. He was checking Tris's face, in order to see whether she could possibly be serious.

Over the speaker, Paphlagon was saying: "the Adrakhonic Theorem is true *here*. It's apparently true in the four cosmi the Geometers came from. If their ship had turned up in some other cosmos, the same as ours, but devoid of sentient beings, would it be true *there?*"

"Not until the Geometers arrived to *say* it was true," said Lodoghir.

Back in the kitchen, I intervened before Emman could blurt out anything he might have to apologize for. "It must be expensive for people like Emman and Ignetha Foral to keep tabs on it," I pointed out.

"Of course," Emman said, "but even if you ignore that: there is a huge amount of mathic *effort* going into it. Thousands of avout working night and day. Sæculars don't like wasted effort. That goes double for Sæculars who know a thing or two about management."

Management was a Fluccish word. Faces went blank around the kitchen. I stepped in to translate: "Just because the Panjandrums know how to run cheeseburg stands, they think they know how to run a Convox. Lots of people putting in time with no results makes them nervous."

"Oh, I see," Tris said, uncertainly.

"How funny!" Karvall said, and went back to work.

Emman rolled his eyes.

"I admit I am no theor," Ignetha Foral was saying on the speaker, "but the more I hear of this, the less I understand your position, Fraa Lodoghir. Three is a prime number. It is prime today, was prime yesterday. A billion years ago, before there were brains to think about it, it was prime. And if all the brains were destroyed tomorrow, it would still be prime. Clearly its primeness has nothing to do with our brains."

"It has everything to do with our brains," Lodoghir insisted, "because we supply the definition of what it is to be a prime number!"

"No theor who attends to these matters can long escape the conclusion that the cnoöns exist independently of what may or may not be going on in peoples' brains at any given moment," Paphlagon said. "It is a simple application of the Steelyard. What is the simplest way of explaining the fact that theors working independently in different eras, different sub-disciplines, different cosmi even, time and time again prove the same results—results that do not contradict each other, even though reached by different proof-chains—results, some of which can be turned into theories that perfectly describe the behavior of the physical universe? The simplest answer is that the cnoöns really exist, and are not of this causal domain."

Arsibalt's bell jingled. I decided to go in with him. We took down a huge rendering of the icosahedron that had been pinned to a tapestry behind Paphlagon. Karvall and Tris came out and helped take the tapestry down, exposing a wall of dark grey slate, and a basket of chalk. The dialog had turned to an exposition of Complex versus Simple Protism, and so Arsibalt was called upon to draw on that slate the same sorts of diagrams that Fraa Criscan had drawn in the dust of the road up Bly's Butte when he had explained this topic to me and Lio some weeks earlier: the Freight Train, the Firing Squad, the Wick, and so on. I drifted back and forth between there and the kitchen as the exposition went on. Ignetha Foral had long been familiar with this material, but it was new to several of the others. Zh'vaern, in particular, asked several questions. Emman, for once, understood less of what was going on than his doyn, and so as he and I worked on garnishes for the desserts, I watched his face, and jumped in with little explanations when his eyes went out of focus.

I returned to the messallan to clear plates just as Paphlagon was explaining the Wick: "A fully generalized Directed Acyclic Graph, with no distinction made any more between, on the one hand, so-called theoric worlds, and, on the other, inhabited ones such as Arbre, Quator, and the rest. For the first time, we have arrows leading *away* from the Arbran Causal Domain *towards* other inhabited worlds."

"Do you mean to suggest," Lodoghir asked, as though not quite believing his ears, "that Arbre might be the Hylaean Theoric World of some *other* world that has people living on it?"

"Of *any number* of such worlds," Paphlagon said, "which might *themselves* be the HTWs of still other worlds."

"But how could we possibly verify such a hypothesis?" Lodoghir demanded.

"We could not," Jad admitted, in his first utterance of the whole evening, "unless those worlds came to us."

Lodoghir broke into rich laughter. "Fraa Jad! I commend you! What would this messal be without your punch lines? I don't agree with a word of what you're saying, but it does make for an entertaining—because completely unpredictable—mealtime!"

I heard the first part of this in person, the back half over the speaker in the kitchen, to which I had repaired with an armload of plates. Emman was standing over the counter where we had spread out the phototypes, thumbing something into his jeejah. He ignored me, but he did glance up and fix his gaze on nothing in particular as Ignetha Foral began to speak: "The material is interesting, the explanation well carried off, but I am at a loss, now. Yesterday evening we were told one story about how Plurality of Worlds might be understood, and it had to do with Hemn space and worldtracks."

"Which I spent all day explaining to rooms full of bureaucrats," Emman complained, with a theatrical yawn. "And now this!"

"Now," Ignetha Foral was saying, "we are hearing an altogether different account of it, which seems to have nothing to do with the first. I cannot help but wonder whether tomorrow's Messal will bring another story, and the day after that, yet another."

This touched off a round of not very interesting conversation in the messallan. The servitors pounced and cleared. Arsibalt trudged to the kitchen and busied himself at the keg. "I'd best fortify myself," he explained, to no one in particular, "as I am condemned to spend the remainder of the evening drawing light bubbles."

"What's a light bubble?" Emman asked me quietly.

"A diagram that shows how information—cause-and-effect—moves across space and time."

"Time, which doesn't exist?" Emman said, repeating what had become a stock joke.

"Yeah. But it's okay. Space doesn't exist either," I said. Emman threw me a sharp look, and decided I must be pulling his leg.

"So how's your friend Lio doing?" Emman asked, apropos of yesterday evening. It was noteworthy that he remembered Lio's name, since there had been no formal introduction, and little conversation. In the Convox, people met one another in myriad ways, though, so they might have crossed paths anywhere. I would not have given this a second thought if not for the substance of what Lio and I had talked about. Yesterday I'd felt easy around Emman. Today it was different. People I cared about were being drawn into—in Ala's case, perhaps *leading*—a subversive movement. Lio was trying to draw me into it even as Emman wanted to follow me to Lucub. Could it be that the Sæcular Power had got wind of it, and that

Emman's real mission was to ferret it out, using me as a way in? Not a very nice way to think—but that was the way I was going to have to think from now on.

I'd lain awake in my cell all night from a combination of jet lag and fear of a Fourth Sack. Good thing that most of the day had been a huge Plenary at which the story of last night's satellite gambit had been told, and phototypes and speelies exhibited. The back pews of the Unarian nave were dark, and roomy enough that I and scores of Lucub-weary avout had been able to stretch out full-length and catch up on sleep. When it was over, someone had shaken me awake. I had stood up, rubbed my eyes, looked across the Nave, and caught sight of Ala—the first time I'd seen her since she had stepped through the screen at Voco. She had been a hundred feet away, standing in a circle of taller avout, mostly men, all older, but seemingly holding her own in some kind of serious conversation. Some of the men had been Sæculars in military uniforms. I had decided that now was not the best time for me to bounce up to her and say hello.

"Hey! Raz! *Raz!* How many fingers am I holding up?" Emman was demanding. Tris and Karvall thought that was funny. "How's Lio doing?" he repeated.

"Busy," I said, "busy like all of us. He's been working out quite a bit with the Ringing Vale avout."

Emman shook his head. "Nice that they're getting exercise," he said. "Love to know what joint locks and nerve pinches are going to do against the World Burner."

My gaze went to the stack of phototypes. Emman slid a few out of the way and came up with a detail shot of a detachable pod bracketed to one of the shock absorbers. It was a squat grey metal egg, unmarked and undecorated. A structural lattice had been built around it to provide mountings for antennae, thrusters, and spherical tanks. Clearly the thing was meant to detach and move around under its own power. Holding it to the shock absorber was a system of brackets that reached through the lattice to engage the grey egg directly. This detail had drawn notice from the Convox. Calculations had been done on the size of those brackets. They were strangely oversized. They only needed to be so large if the thing they were holding—the grey egg—were massive. Unbelievably massive. This was no ordinary pressure vessel. Perhaps it had extremely thick walls? But the calculations made no sense if you assumed any sort of ordinary metal. The only way to sort it—to account for the sheer number of protons and neutrons in that thing—was to assume it was made from a metal so far out at the end of the table of elements that its nuclei—in any cosmos—were unstable. Fissionable.

This object was not just a tank. It was a thermonuclear device several orders of magnitude larger than the largest ever made on Arbre. The propellant tanks carried enough reaction mass to move it to an orbit antipodal to that of the mother ship. If it were detonated, it would shine enough radiant energy onto Arbre to set fire to whatever half of the planet could see it.

"I don't think that the Valers are really expecting to swarm over the World Burner in space suits and subdue it with fisticuffs," I said. "Actually, what impressed me most about them was their knowledge of military history and tactics."

Emman held up his hands in surrender. "Don't get me wrong. I would like to have them on my side."

Again, I couldn't help but see a hidden meaning. But then a bell rang. Like animals in a lab, we had learned to tell the bells apart, so we didn't have to look to know who it was for. Arsibalt took a final gulp from his flagon and hustled out.

Moyra's voice was coming through on the speaker: "Uthentine and Erasmas were Thousanders, so their treatise was not copied out into the mathic world until the Second Millennial Convox." She was speaking of the two avout who had developed the notion of Complex Protism. "Even then, it received scant notice until the Twenty-seventh Century, when Fraa Clathrand, a Centenarian— later in his life, a Millenarian—at Saunt Edhar, casting an eye over these diagrams, remarked on the isomorphism between the causality-arrows in these networks, and the flow of time."

"Isomorphism meaning—?" asked Zh'vaern.

"Sameness of form. Time flows, or seems to flow, in one direction,"

Paphlagon said. "Events in the past can cause events in the present, but not vice versa, and time never loops round in a circle. Fraa Clathrand pointed out something noteworthy, which is that information about the cnoöns—the givens that flow along all of these arrows—behaves *as if* the cnoöns were in the past."

Again, Emman was staring off into space, drawing connections in his head. "Paphlagon is also a Hundreder from Edhar, right?"

"Yeah," I said. "That's probably how he got interested in this topic—probably found Clathrand's manuscripts lying around somewhere."

"Twenty-seventh Century," Emman repeated. "So, Clathrand's works would've been distributed to the mathic world at large at the Apert of 2700?"

I nodded.

"Just eight decades before the rise of . . ." But he cut himself short and flicked his eyes nervously in my direction.

"Before the Third Sack," I corrected him.

In the messallan, Lodoghir had been demanding an explanation. Moyra finally settled him down: "The entire premise of Protism is that the cnoöns can change us, in the quite literal and physical sense that they make our nerve tissue behave differently. But the reverse is not true. Nothing that goes on in our nerve tissue can make four into a prime number. All Clathrand was saying was that things in our past can likewise affect us in the present, but nothing we do in the present can affect the events of the past. And so here it seems we might have a perfectly commonplace explanation of something in these diagrams that might otherwise seem a bit mystical—namely, the purity and changelessness of cnoöns."

And here, just as Arsibalt had predicted, the conversation turned into a tutorial about light bubbles, which was an old scheme used by theors to keep track of how knowledge, and cause-and-effect relationships, propagated from place to place over time.

"Very well," said Zh'vaern eventually, "I'll give you Clathrand's Contention that any one of these DAGs—the Strider, the Wick, and so on—can be isomorphic to some arrangement of things in space-time, influencing one another through propagation of information at the speed of light. But what does Clathrand's Contention *get* us? Is he *really* asserting that the cnoöns are in the past? That we are just, somehow, *remembering* them?"

"*Perceiving*—not remembering," Paphlagon corrected him. "A cosmographer who sees a star blow up perceives everything about it in his present—though intellectually he knows it happened thousands of years ago and the givens are only now reaching the objective of his telescope."

"Fine—but my question stands."

It was unusual for Zh'vaern to become so involved in the dialog. Emman and I confirmed as much by giving each other quizzical looks. Perhaps the Matarrhite was actually getting ready to say something?

"After the Apert of 2700, various theors tried to do various things with Clathrand's Contention," Moyra said, "each pursuing a different approach, depending on their understanding of time and their general approach to metatheorics. For example—"

"It is too late in the evening for a recitation of examples," said Ignetha Foral.

Which chilled the whole room, and seemed to end the discussion, until Zh'vaern, in the ensuing silence, blurted out: "Does this have anything to do with the Third Sack?"

A much longer silence followed.

It was one thing for me and Emman, standing back in the kitchen, to mention this under our breath. Even then, I'd felt excruciatingly awkward. But for Zh'vaern to raise the topic *in a messal* attended (and under surveillance) by Sæculars, went far, far beyond disastrously rude. To imply that the avout were in any way to blame for the Third Sack—*that* was mere dinner-party-wrecking rudeness. But to plant such notions in the minds of extremely powerful Sæculars was a kind of recklessness verging on treason.

Fraa Jad finally broke the silence with a chortling noise, so deep that it hardly came through on the sound system. "Zh'vaern violates a taboo!" he observed.

"I see no reason why the topic should be off limits," Zh'vaern said, not in the least embarrassed.

"How fared the Matarrhites in the Third Sack?" Jad asked.

"According to the iconography of the time, we, as Deolaters, had nothing to do with Rhetors or Incanters and so were considered—"

"Innocent of what *we* were guilty of?" said Asquin, who seemed to have chosen this moment to stop being nice.

"Anyway," Zh'vaern said, "we evacuated to an island, deep in the southern polar regions, and lived off the available plants, birds, and insects. That is where we developed our cuisine, which I know many of you find distasteful. We remember the Third Sack with every bite of food we take."

On the speaker I heard shifting, throat-clearing, and the clink of utensils for the first time since Zh'vaern had rolled his big stink-bomb into the middle of the table. But then he ruined it all by the way he volleyed the question back at Jad: "And your people? Edhar was one of the Inviolates, was it not?" Everyone tensed up again. Clathrand had come from Edhar; Zh'vaern seemed to have been developing a theory that Clathrand's work had been the basis for the exploits of the Incanters; now he was drawing attention to the fact that Jad's math had *somehow* managed to fend off the Sack for seven decades.

"Fascinating!" Emman exclaimed. "How could this get any worse?"

"I'm glad I'm not in there," Tris said.

"Arsibalt must be dying," I said. A small noise in the back of the kitchen drew our notice: Orhan, Zh'vaern's servitor, had been standing there silently the whole time. It was easy to forget he was there when you couldn't see his face.

"You just got to the Convox, Fraa Zh'vaern," said Suur Asquin, "and so we'll forgive you for not having heard, yet, what has become an open secret in the last few weeks: that the Three Inviolates are nuclear waste repositories, and as such were probably protected by the Sæcular Power."

If this was news to Zh'vaern, he didn't seem to find it very remarkable.

"This is going nowhere," announced Ignetha Foral. "Time to

move on. The purpose of the Convox—and of this messal—is to get things done. Not to make friends or have polite conversations. The policy of what you call the Sæcular Power toward the mathic world is what it is, and shall not be altered by a *faux pas* over dessert. The World Burner, you must know, has quite focused people's minds—at least where *I* work."

"Where would you like the conversation to go tomorrow, Madame Secretary?" asked Suur Asquin. I didn't have to see her face to know that the rebuke had really burned her.

"I want to know who—*what*—the Geometers are, and where they came from," said Ignetha Foral. "How they got here. If we have to discuss polycosmic metatheorics all evening long in order to answer those questions, so be it! But let us not speak of anything more that is not relevant to the matter at hand."

○○○

Rebirth: The historical event dividing the Old Mathic Age from the Praxic Age, usually dated at around -500, during which the gates of the maths were thrown open and the avout dispersed into the Sæcular world. Characterized by a sudden flowering of culture, theorical advancement, and exploration.

—THE DICTIONARY, *4th edition, A.R. 3000*

I'd been flattering myself that Fraa Jad might want to talk to me; he had, after all, sent me off on a mission that had almost killed me three times. But unlike Moyra he was not the type to hang around in the kitchen post-messal, rapping with the servitors and washing dishes. By the time we were done cleaning up, he was gone to wherever it was that the Convox stowed Thousanders when not in use.

It was just another reason I wanted to track down Lio. On the drive from Edhar to Bly's Butte, Fraa Jad had confided in both of us—or so we believed—by dropping the hint that he was unnaturally old. If I were going to seek out Jad and take the dialog to the next stage—whatever that might be—Lio should be there with me.

The only problem was that I seemed to have sprouted an entourage: Emman, Arsibalt, and Barb. If I led those three into a meeting of the seditious conspiracy of which Lio was now part, Arsibalt would black out and have to be dragged back to his cell, Barb would blab it to the whole Convox, and Emman would report us to the Panjandrums.

While mopping the kitchen floor, I hit on the idea of leading them to Jesry's Lucub instead. With luck, I could shed some or all of them there.

As we were informed while trying to find Jesry—in Emman's case, by a jeejah message, and for the rest of us, by coded bell-ringing from a carillon in the Precipice—Lucub had been canceled. Everything, in fact, except Laboratorium and Messal had been suspended until further notice, and the only reason we still had Messal was that we had to eat in order to work. The rest of the time, we were supposed to analyze the Geometers' ship. The Sæculars had syntactic systems for building and displaying three-dimensional models of complicated objects, and so the goal, now, was to create such a model, correct down to the last strut, hatch, and weld, of the starship orbiting our planet—or at least of its outer shell, which was all of it we could see. Emman was proficient in the use of this modeling system, and so he was called away to toil in a Laboratorium with a lot of Ita. As I understood it, he wasn't actually doing any modeling work—just getting the system to run. Those of us with theorical training had been assigned to new Laboratoria whose purpose was to pore over the phototypes from last night and integrate them into the model.

Some such tasks were more demanding than others. The propulsion system, with jets of plasma interacting with the pusher plate, was difficult even for a Jesry to understand. He'd been assigned to penetrate the mysteries of the X-ray laser batteries. I was on a team analyzing the large-scale dynamics of the entire ship. We assumed that, inside of the icosahedron, some part of it rotated to create pseudo-gravity. So it was a huge gyroscope. When it maneuvered—as it had been forced to, last night—gyroscopic forces must be induced between the spun and despun sections, and those must be managed by bearings of some description. How great were those forces? And how *did* the thing maneuver, anyway? No jets—no rocket thrusters—had fired. No propulsion charges had detonated. And yet the Hedron had spun around with remarkable adroitness. The only reasonable explanation was that it contained a set of momentum wheels—rapidly spinning gyroscopes—that could be used to store and release angular momentum. Imagine a circular railway built around the inner surface of the icosahedron, making a complete circuit, and a freight train running around it in an eternal loop. If the train applied its brakes, it would dump some of its angular momentum into the icosahedron and force it to spin. By releasing the brakes and hitting the throttle, it could reverse the effect. As of last night, it was obvious that the Hedron contained half a dozen such systems—two, running opposite directions, on each of three axes. How big might they be, how much power could they exchange with the ship? What might that imply about what they were made of? More generally, by making precise measurements of how the Hedron had maneuvered, what could we infer about the size, mass, and spin rate of the inhabited section that was hidden inside?

Arsibalt was put on a team using spectroscopy and other givens to figure out which parts of the ship had been forged in which cosmi; or had it all been made in one cosmos? Barb was assigned to make sense of a triangulated network of struts that had been observed projecting from the despun part of the ship. And so on. So six hours now went by during which I was completely absorbed in the problem to which I, and a team of five other theors, had been assigned. I didn't have a moment to think about anything else until someone pointed out that the sun was rising, and we received a message that food was to be had on the great plaza that spread before the Mynster, at the foot of the Precipice.

Walking there, I tried to force gyroscope problems out of my head for a few minutes and consider the larger picture. Ignetha Foral had made no secret of her impatience yesterday evening. We'd emerged from the messal to find ourselves in a Convox that had abruptly been reorganized—along Sæcular lines. All of us were like praxics now, working on small bits of a problem whose entirety we might never get to see. Was this a permanent change? How would it affect the move-ment Lio had spoken of? Was it a deliberate strategy by which the Panjandrums intended to snuff that movement out? What Lio had told me had made me anxious, and I'd been afraid of what I might learn if I ever found my way to Ala's Lucub. So I was relieved that it had been put into suspended animation. The conspiracy could have made no progress last night. But another part of me was concerned about how it might respond to being driven further underground.

Breakfast was being served out of doors, at long tables that the military had set up on the plaza. Convenient for us—but weirdly and intrusively Sæcular in style, and another hint that the Mathic hierarchs had lost or ceded power to the Panjandrums.

Emerging from the line with a hunk of bread, butter, and honey, I saw a small woman just in the act of taking a seat at an otherwise vacant table. I walked over quickly and took the seat across from her. The table was between us, so there was no awkwardness as to whether we should hug, kiss, or shake hands. She knew I was there, but remained huddled over her plate for a long moment, staring at her food, and, I thought, gathering her strength, before she raised her eyes and gazed into mine.

"Is this seat taken?" asked an approaching fraa in a complicated bolt, giving me the sort of ingratiating look I'd learned to associate with those who wanted to suck up to Edharians.

"Bugger off!" I said. He did.

"I sent you a couple of letters," I said. "Don't know if you got them."

"Osa handed one to me," she said. "I didn't open it until after what happened with Orolo."

"Why not?" I asked, trying to make my voice gentle. "I know about Jesry—"

The big eyes closed in pain—no—in exasperation, and she shook her head. "Forget about that. It's just that too much else has been going on. I've not wanted to get distracted." She leaned back against her folding chair, heaved a sigh. "After the Visitation of Orithena, I thought maybe I had better open up. Zoom out, as the extras say. I read your letter. I think—" Her brow folded. "I don't know what I think. It's like I've had three different lifetimes. Before Voco. Between Voco and Orolo's death. And since then. And your letter—which was a respectable piece of work, don't get me wrong—was written to an Ala two lifetimes gone."

"I think that we could all tell similar stories," I pointed out.

She shrugged, nodded, started to eat.

"Well," I tried, "tell me about your current life, then."

She looked at me, a little too long for comfort. "Lio told me that you spoke."

"Yes."

She finally broke eye contact, let her gaze wander over the breakfast tables, slowly filling up with weary fraas and suurs, and out over the lawns and towers of Tredegarh. "They brought me here to organize people. So that's what I've been doing."

"But not in the way they wanted?"

She shook her head quickly. "It's more complicated than that, Erasmas." It killed me to hear her speak my name. "Turns out that once you get an organization started, it takes on a life—lives by a logic—of its own. I suppose if I'd ever *done* this before, I'd have *known* it would be that way—would have planned for it."

"Well—don't beat yourself up."

"I'm *not* beating myself up. That's you putting emotions on me. Like clothes on a doll."

The old feeling—a curious mix of irritation, love, and desire to feel more of it—came over me.

"See, they knew from the start that the Convox was vulnerable. An obvious target, if the pact opened hostilities."

"The pact?"

"We call it PAQD now for Pangee-Antarct-Quator-Diasp. Less anthropomorphic than Geometers."

But they are anthropomorphic, I was tempted to say. But I stifled it.

"I know," she said, eyeing me, "they *are* anthropomorphic. Never mind. We call them the PAQD."

"Well, I had been wondering," I said. "Seems risky to put all the smart people in one square mile."

"Yeah, but what they have drilled into me, over and over, is that it's *all* about risk. The question is, what are the benefits that might be had in exchange for a given risk?"

To me this sounded like the kind of organizational bulshytt that was always being spouted by pompous extras who hadn't bothered to define their terms. But it seemed weirdly important to Ala that I listen, understand, and agree. She even reached out and put her hand on mine for a few moments, which focused my attention. So I went through a little pantomime of processing what she'd said and agreeing to it. "The benefit, here, being that maybe the Convox could do something halfway useful before it got blown up?" I asked.

That seemed to pass muster, so she plowed ahead. "I was assigned to risk mitigation, which is bulshytt meaning that if the PAQD does anything scary, this Convox is going to scatter like a bunch of flies when they see the flyswatter. And instead of scattering randomly, we are going to do it in a systematic, planned way—the Antiswarm, the Ita have been calling it—and we are going to stay on the Reticulum so that we can continue the essential functions of the Convox even as we are scurrying all over the place."

"Did you start on this right away? Just after you got Evoked?"

"Yes."

"So you knew from the outset that there was going to be a Convox."

She shook her head. "I knew they—we—were laying plans for one. I didn't know for sure it would actually happen—or who would be called. When it started to materialize, these plans that I'd been making came into sharper focus, took on depth. And then it became obvious to me—was unavoidable."

"*What* became obvious?"

"What did Fraa Corlandin teach us of the Rebirth?"

I shrugged. "You studied harder than I. The end of the Old Mathic Age. The gates of the old maths flung open—torn off their hinges, in some cases. The avout dispersed into the Sæculum—okay, I think I see where this is going now . . ."

"What the Sæcular Power had asked me to lay plans for—without understanding—was in many ways indistinguishable from a second Rebirth," Ala said. "Because, Raz, not only Tredegarh would open its gates. If it comes to war with the PAQD, all of the concents will have to disperse. The avout will move among—mingle with—blend into the general population. Yet we'll still be talking to one another over the Reticulum. Which means—"

"Ita," I said.

She nodded, and smiled, warming to the task, to the picture she was building. "Each cell of wandering avout has to include some Ita. And it won't be possible to maintain avout/Ita segregation any more. The Antiswarm will have tasks to carry out—not the kinds of things avout have traditionally done. Work of immediate Sæcular relevance."

"A second Praxic Age," I said.

"Exactly!" She'd become enthusiastic. I felt the excitement too. But I drew back from it, recollecting that it could only come to pass if we got into out-and-out war. She sensed this too, and clamped her face down into the kind of expression I imagined she wore when sitting in council with high military leaders. "It started," she said, in a much lower voice—and by *it* I knew she meant the thing Lio had told me of—"it started in meetings with cell leaders. See, the cells—the groups we're going to break into, if we trigger the Antiswarm—each has a leader. I've been meeting with those leaders, giving them their evacuation plans, familiarizing them with who's in their cells."

"So that's—"

"Preordained. Yes. Everyone in the Convox has already been assigned to a cell."

"But I haven't—"

"You haven't been informed," Ala said. "No one has—except for the cell leaders."

"You didn't want to upset people—distract them—there was no point in letting them know," I guessed.

"Which is about to change," she said, and looked around as if expecting it to change *now*. And indeed I noticed that several more military drummons had pulled onto the grounds and parked at one end of this open-air Refectory. Soldiers were setting up a sound system. "That's why we're all eating together." She snorted. "That's why I'm eating *at all*. First meal worthy of the name I've had in three days. Now I get to relax for a little—let things play out."

"What's going to happen?"

"Everyone's going to receive a pack, and instructions."

"It can't be random that we're doing this out of doors under a clear sky," I observed.

"Now you're thinking like Lio," she said approvingly, through a bite of bread. She swallowed and went on, "This is a deterrence strategy. The PAQD will see what we're up to, and it is hoped, guess that we're making preparations to disperse. And if they know that we are ready to disperse at a moment's notice, they'll have less incentive to attack Tredegarh."

"Makes sense," I said. "I guess I'll have many more questions about that in a minute. But you were saying something about the meetings with the cell leaders—?"

"Yes. You know how it is with avout. Nothing gets taken at face value. Everything is peeled back. Dialoged. I was meeting with these people in small groups—half a dozen cell leaders at a time. Explaining their powers and responsibilities, role-playing different scenarios. And it seemed as though every group had one or two who wanted to take it further than the others. To put it in bigger historical perspective, draw comparisons to the Rebirth, and so on. The thing that Lio told you about was an outgrowth of that. Some of these people—I simply couldn't answer all of their questions in the time allotted. So I put their names on a list and told them, 'Later we'll have a follow-up meeting to discuss your concerns, but it'll have to be a Lucub because I have no time otherwise.' And the timing just happened—and you can consider this lucky or unlucky, as you like—to coincide with the Visitation of Orithena."

We were distracted now, as the sound system came alive. A hierarch asked for "the following persons" to come to the front—to approach the trucks, where soldiers were breaking open pallet-loads of military rucksacks, prepacked and bulging. The hierarch had obviously never spoken into a sound amplification device before, but soon enough she got the hang of it and began to call out the names of fraas and suurs. Slowly, uncertainly at first, those who'd been called began to get up from their seats and move up the lanes between tables. Conversation paused for a little while, then resumed in an altogether different tone, as people began to exclaim about it, and to speculate.

"Okay," I said, "so here you are in a Lucub, in a chalk hall somewhere with all of the pickiest, most obstreperous cell leaders—"

"Who are wonderful, by the way!" Ala put in.

"I can imagine," I said. "But they are all wanting to go deep on these topics—at the same moment you are getting news of that poor woman from Antarct who sacrificed her life—"

"And of what Orolo did for her," she reminded me. And here she had to stop talking for a few moments, because grief had overtaken her in an unwary moment. We watched, or pretended to watch, avout coming back to their seats, each with a rucksack slung over one shoulder and a sort of badge or flasher hanging around the neck.

"Anyway," she said, and paused to clear her throat, which had gone husky. "It was the strangest thing I'd ever seen. I'd expected we'd talk until dawn, and never arrive at a consensus. But it was the opposite of that. We *walked in* with a consensus. Everyone just *knew* that we had to make contact with whatever faction had sent that woman down. And that even if the Sæculars wouldn't allow such a thing, well, once we had turned into the Antiswarm—"

"What could they do to stop us?"

"Exactly."

"Lio said something about using the guidestar lasers on the big telescopes to send signals?"

"Yes. It's being talked about. Some might even be *doing* it for all I know."

"Whose idea was that?"

She balked.

"Don't get me wrong!" I assured her. "It's a brilliant idea."

"It was Orolo's idea."

"But you couldn't have talked to him—!"

"Orolo actually *did* it," Ala said, reluctantly, watching me closely to see how I'd react. "From Edhar. Last year. One of Sammann's colleagues went up to the M & M and found the evidence."

"Evidence?"

"Orolo had programmed the guidestar laser on the M & M to sweep out an analemma in the sky."

A week or a month ago, I'd have denied it could possibly be true. But not now. "So Lodoghir was right," I sighed. "What he accused Orolo of, at the Plenary, was dead on."

"Either that," Ala said, "or he changed the past."

I didn't laugh.

She continued, "You should know, too, that Lodoghir is one of this group I've been telling you about."

"Fraa Erasmas of Edhar," called the voice on the speaker.

"Well," I said, "I guess I'd better go find out which cell you put me in."

She shook her head. "It's not like that. You won't know that until it's time."

"How can we meet up with our cell if we don't know who to look for?"

"If it happens—if the order goes out—your badge will come alive, and tell you where to go. When you get there," Ala said, "the other people you will see, are the rest of your cell."

I shrugged. "Seems sensible enough." Because she had suddenly become somber, and I couldn't guess why. She lunged across the table and grabbed my hand. "Look at me," she said. "Look at me."

When I looked at her I saw tears in her eyes, and a look on her face unlike any I'd ever seen before. Perhaps it was the same way my face had looked when I had gazed down out of the open door of the aerocraft and recognized Orolo. She was telling me something with that face that she did not have power to put in words. "When you come back to this table, I'll be gone," she said. "If I don't see you again before it happens"—and I sensed this was a certainty in her mind—"you have to know I made a terrible decision."

"Well, we all do, Ala! I should tell you about some of *my* recent terrible decisions!"

But she was already shaking me off, willing me to understand her words.

"Isn't there any way to change your mind? Fix it? Make amends?" I asked.

"No! I mean, I made a terrible decision in the way that Orolo made a terrible decision before the gates of Orithena."

It took me a few moments to see it. "Terrible," I said at last, "but *right*."

Then the tears came so hard she had to close her eyes and turn her back on me. She let go my hand and began to totter away, shoulders hunched as if she'd just been stabbed in the back. She seemed the smallest person in the Convox. Every instinct told me to run after her, put an arm around her bony shoulders. But I knew she'd break a chair over my head.

I walked up to the truck and got my rucksack and my badge: a rectangular slab, like a small photomnemonic tablet that had been blanked.

Then I went back to work estimating the inertia tensor of the Geometers' ship.

I slept most of the afternoon and woke up feeling terrible. Just when my body had adjusted to local time, I had messed it up by keeping odd hours.

I went early to Avrachon's Dowment. This evening's recipe called for a lot of peeling and chopping, so I brought a knife and cutting board around to the front veranda and worked there, partly to enjoy the last of the sunlight, but also partly in hopes I might intercept Fraa Jad on his way to messal. Avrachon's Dowment was a big stone house, not quite so fortress-like as some Mathic structures I could name, with balconies, cupolas and bow windows that made me wish I could be a member of it, just so that I could do my daily work in such charming and picturesque surrounds. As if the architect's sole objective had been to ignite envy in the hearts of avout, so that they'd scheme and maneuver to get into the place. I was fortunate that such an exceptional chain of events had made it possible for me even to sit on its veranda for an hour peeling vegetables. My conversation with Ala had reminded me that I had better take advantage of the opportunity while I could. The Dowment was situated on a knoll, so I had a good view over open lawns that rambled among other dowments and chapterhouses. Groups of avout came and went, some talking excitedly, some silent, hunched over, exhausted. Fraas and suurs were strewn at random over the grounds, wrapped in their bolts, pillowed on their spheres, sleeping. To see so many, clothed in such varied styles, reminded me again of the diversity of the mathic world—a thing I'd never been aware of, until I'd come here—and cast Ala's talk of a Second Rebirth in a different light. The idea of tearing the gates off the hinges was thrilling in a way, simply because it represented such a big change. But would it mean the end of all that the avout had built, in 3700 years? Would people in the future look with awe at empty Mynsters and think that we must have been crazy to walk away from such places?

I wondered who else might be assigned to my cell, and what tasks we might be assigned by those in charge of the Antiswarm. A reasonable guess was that I'd simply be with my new Laboratorium group, and that we'd go on doing the same sorts of things. Living in rooms in a casino in some random city, toiling over diagrams of the ship, eating Sæcular food brought up by illiterate servants in uniforms. The group included two impressive theors, one from Baritoe and one from a concent on the Sea of Seas. The others were tedious company and I didn't especially relish the idea of being sent on the road with them.

Occasionally I would glimpse one of the Ringing Vale contingent and my heart would beat a little faster as I imagined what it would be like to be in a cell with them! Rank fantasy, of course—I would be worse than useless in such company—but fun to daydream about. No telling what such a cell would be ordered to do. But it would certainly be more interesting than guessing inertia tensors. Probably something incredibly dangerous. So perhaps it was for the best that they were out of my league.

Or—in a similar yet very different vein—what would Fraa Jad's cell look like, and what sorts of tasks would they be assigned? How privileged I'd been, in retrospect, to have traveled in a Thousander's company for a couple of days! As far as I'd been able to make out, he was the only Millenarian in the Convox.

I'd settle for being in a cell with at least one of the old clock-winding team from Edhar. Yet I doubted that this would be the case. Ala was quite obviously troubled by some aspect of the decisions she had made regarding cell assignments, and though I could not know just what was eating at her so, it did serve as a warning that I should not lull myself into imagining a happy time on the road with old friends. The respect—I was tempted to call it awe—with which we Edharians were viewed by many at the Convox made it unlikely that several of us would be concentrated in one cell. They would spread us out among as many cells as possible. We would be leaders, and lonely in the same way Ala was.

Fraa Jad approached from the direction of the Precipice. I wondered if they had given him a billet up on top, in the Thousanders' math. If so, he must be spending a lot of time negotiating stairs. He recognized me from a distance and strolled right up.

"I found Orolo," I said, though of course Jad already knew this. He nodded.

"It is unfortunate—what happened," he said. "Orolo would have passed through the Labyrinths in due time, and become my fraa on the Crag, and it would have been good to work by his side, drink his wine, share his thoughts."

"His wine was terrible," I said.

"Share his thoughts, then."

"He seemed to understand quite a lot," I said. And I wanted to ask *how*—had he deciphered coded messages in the Thousanders' chants? But I didn't want to make a fool of myself. "He thinks—he thought—that you have developed a praxis. I can't help but imagine that this accounts for your great age."

"The destructive effects of radiation on living systems are traceable to interactions between individual particles—photons, neutrons—and molecules in the affected organism," he pointed out.

"Quantum events," I said.

"Yes, and so a cell that has just undergone a mutation, and one that has not, lie on Narratives that are separated by only a single forking in Hemn space."

"Aging," I said, "is due to transcription errors in the sequences of dividing cells—which are also quantum-level events—"

"Yes. It is not difficult to see how a plausible and internally consistent mythology could arise, according to which nuclear waste handlers invented a praxis to mend radiation damage, and later extended it to mitigate the effects of aging and so on."

And so on seemed to cover an awful lot of possibilities, but I thought better of pursuing this. "You're aware," I said, "of how explosive that mythology is, if it gains currency in the Sæculum?"

He shrugged. The Sæculum was none of his concern. But the Convox was a different matter. "Some here want badly to see that mythology promoted to fact. It would give them comfort."

"Zh'vaern was asking some weird questions about it," I said, and nodded at a procession of Matarrhites wafting across the lawn some distance away.

It was a gambit. I hoped to bond with Fraa Jad by giving him an opening to agree with me that those people were weird and obnoxious. But he slid around it. "There is more to be learned from them than from any others at the Convox."

"Really?"

"It would be impossible to pay too much attention to the cloaked ones."

Two Matarrhites detached themselves from the procession and set a course for Avrachon's Dowment. I watched Zh'vaern and Orhan come towards us for a few moments, wondering what Jad saw in them, then turned back to the Thousander. But he had slipped inside.

Zh'vaern and Orhan approached silently and entered the Dowment after greeting me, rather stiffly, on the veranda.

Arsibalt and Barb were a hundred feet behind them.

"Results?" I demanded.

"A piece of the PAQD ship is missing!" Barb announced.

"That structure you've been studying—"

"It's where the missing piece used to be attached!"

"What do you think it was?"

"The inter-cosmic transport drive, obviously!" Barb scoffed. "They didn't want us to see it, because it's top secret! So they parked it farther out in the solar system."

"How about your group, Arsibalt?"

"That ship is patched together from subassemblies built in all four of the PAQD cosmi," Arsibalt announced. "It is like an archaeological dig. The oldest part is from Pangee. Very little of it remains. There are only a very few odds and ends from Diasp. Most of the ship is made of material from the Antarct and Quator cosmi—of the two, we are fairly certain that Quator was visited more recently."

"Good stuff!" I said.

"How about you—what results have been produced by your group, Raz?" Barb asked.

I was collecting my things, getting ready to go inside. Arsibalt shuffled over to help me. "It sloshed," I said.

"Sloshed?"

"When the Hedron made its spin move the other evening, the rotation wasn't steady. It jiggled a little. We conclude that the spun part contains a large mass of standing water, and when you hit it with a sudden rotation, the water sloshes." And I went off into a long riff about the higher harmonics of the sloshing, and what it all meant. Barb lost interest and went inside.

"What were you discussing with Fraa Jad?" Arsibalt asked.

I didn't feel comfortable divulging the part of the talk that had been about praxis, so I answered—truthfully—"The Matarrhites. We're supposed to keep an eye on them—learn from them."

"Do you suppose he wants us to spy on them?" Arsibalt asked, fascinated. This gave me the idea that Arsibalt *wanted*, for some reason, to spy on them, and was looking for Jad's blessing.

"He said it would be impossible to pay too much attention to the cloaked ones."

"Is that how he phrased it!?"

"Pretty near."

"He said 'cloaked ones,' rather than 'Matarrhites'?"

"Yes."

"They're not Matarrhites at all!" Arsibalt said in an excited whisper.

"I'll take that if you don't mind," I said. For in his eagerness to help, he had reached for my cutting board. I confiscated the knife.

"You think I'm *so* profoundly insane that I can't be trusted with sharp objects!" Arsibalt said, crestfallen.

"Arsibalt! If they aren't Matarrhites, what are they? Panjandrums in disguise?"

He looked as if he were about to spill a great secret, but then Suur Tris came around, and he clammed up.

"I'll take your hypothesis under advisement," I said, "and weigh it on the Steelyard against the alternative—which is that the Matarrhites are Matarrhites."

○○

Syntactic Faculties: Factions within the mathic world, in the years following the Reconstitution, generally claiming descent from Proc. So named because they believed that language, theorics, etc., were essentially games played with symbols devoid of semantic content. The idea is traceable to the ancient Sphenics, who were frequent opponents of Thelenes and Protas on the Periklyne.

—THE DICTIONARY, *4th edition, A.R. 3000*

Fraa Lodoghir said, "We are on the third messal already. The first seemed to be about worldtracks in Hemn space as a way of understanding the physical universe. Which was unobjectionable to me, until it turned out to be a stalking horse for the Hylaean Theoric World. The second was a trip to the circus—except that instead of gawking at contortionists, jugglers, and prestidigitators, we marveled at the intellectual backflips, sword-swallowing, and misdirection in which devotees of the HTW must engage if they are not to be Thrown Back as a religious cult. That's quite all right, it was good to get it out of our systems, and I commend the Edharian plurality here for having, as it were, laid their cards on the messal. Ha.

But what may we now say about the matter at hand—which is, in case anyone has forgotten, the PAQD, their capabilities and intentions?"

"Why do they look like us, for one thing?" asked Suur Asquin. "That is the question that my mind returns to over and over again."

"Thank you, Suur Asquin!" I exclaimed back in the kitchen. I was scattering bread crumbs over the top of a casserole. "I can't believe how little attention has been paid to that minor detail."

"People simply don't know what to make of it—have no idea where to begin," said Suur Tris. And as if to confirm this, a welter of voices was coming through on the speaker. I hauled the oven door open and thrust the casserole in, arranging it on the center of a hand-forged iron rack. Fraa Lodoghir was going on about parallel evolution: how, on Arbre, physically similar but totally unrelated species had evolved to fill similar niches on different continents.

"Your point is well taken, Fraa Lodoghir," said Zh'vaern, "but I believe that the similarities are *too* close to be explained by parallel evolution. Why do the Geometers have five fingers, one of which is an opposable thumb? Why not seven fingers and two thumbs?"

"Do you have some knowledge of the PAQD that has been withheld from the rest of us?" demanded Lodoghir. "What you say is true of the one specimen *we have seen*—the Antarct woman. The other three Geometer species might have *seven* fingers, for all we know."

"Of course, you are correct," Zh'vaern said. "But the Antarct-Arbre correspondence, taken alone, seems too great to be accounted for by parallel evolution."

The point was argued all the way through the soup course. We servitors made our rounds, staggering and sidling through a messallan congested with rucksacks. For we had all been told that one should never let one's rucksack out of sight—so that, even if the dispersal order were accompanied by a power blackout, or some sort of disaster that filled the air with dust and smoke, one would be able to find it by touch. Since we servitors couldn't very well carry them up and down the serving corridor, we'd bent the rules by leaving ours lined up along the corridor wall. The doyns kept theirs behind the chairs in the messallan, and flipped their badges back over their shoulders to eat.

Ignetha Foral put a stop to the thumb-and-finger discourse with a glance at Suur Asquin, who silenced the room with another of her magisterial throat-clearings. "In the absence of further givens, the parallel-evolution hypothesis cannot be rationally evaluated."

"I agree," said Lodoghir in a wistful tone.

"The alternative hypothesis seems to be some sort of leakage of information through the Wick, if I have been taking up Fraa Paphlagon's argument?"

Fraa Paphlagon looked a bit uneasy. "The word *leakage* makes it sound like a malfunction. It is nothing of the kind—just normal flow or, if you will, percolation along the world-DAG."

"This percolation you speak of: until now, I fancied it was all theors seeing timeless truths about isosceles triangles," Lodoghir said. "I oughtn't to be surprised by the ever-escalating grandiosity of these claims, but aren't you now asking us to believe something even more colossal? Correct me if I'm wrong: but did you just try to link percolation of information through the Wick to biological evolution?"

An awkard pause.

"You *do* believe in evolution, don't you?" Lodoghir continued.

"Yes, though it might have sounded strange to someone like Protas, who had frankly mystical pagan views about the HTW and so on," said Paphlagon, "but any modern version of Protism must be reconcilable with long-established theories, not only of cosmography, but of evolution. However, I disagree with the *polemical* part of your statement, Fraa Lodoghir. It is not a larger claim, but a smaller, more reasonable one."

"Oh, I'm sorry! I thought that when you claimed more, it was a larger claim?"

"I am only claiming what is reasonable. That—as you yourself pointed out during your Plenary with Fraa Erasmas—tends to be the *smallest*, in the sense of least complicated, claim. What I claim is that information moves through the Wick in a manner that is somehow analogous to how it moves from past to present. As it moves, *one* of the things that it does is to excite physically measurable changes in nerve tissue . . ."

"That," Suur Asquin said, just to clarify, "being the part where we see truths about cnoöns."

"Yes," said Paphlagon, "whence we get the HTW and the theorical Protism that Fraa Lodoghir loves so well. But nerve tissue is *just tissue,* it is *just matter* obeying natural law. It is not magical or spiritual, no matter what you might think of my opinions on this."

"I am *so* relieved to hear you say so!" said Lodoghir. "I'll have you in the Procian camp by the time Fraa Erasmas brings me my dessert!"

Paphlagon held his tongue for a moment, dodging laughter, then went on. "I can't believe all of what I just said without positing some non-mystical, theorically understandable mechanism by which the 'more Hylaean' worlds can cause physical changes in the 'less Hylaean' worlds that lie 'downstream' of them in the Wick. And I see no prima facie reason to assume that *all* those interactions have to do with isosceles triangles and that the only matter in the whole cosmos that is ever affected just happens to be nerve tissue in the brains of theors! Now *that* would be an ambitious claim, and a rather strange one!"

"We agree on *something!*" said Lodoghir.

"A much more economical claim, in the Gardan's Steelyard sense, is that the mechanism—whatever it is—acts on *any* matter whether or not that matter is part of a living organism—or a theor! It's just that there is an observational bias at work."

A couple of heads nodded.

"Observational bias?" Zh'vaern asked.

Suur Asquin turned to him and said, "Starlight falls on Arbre all the time—even at high noon—but we would never know of the stars' existence if we slept all night."

"Yes," Paphlagon said, "and just as the cosmographer can only see stars in a dark sky, we can only observe the Hylaean Flow when it manifests itself as perceptions of cnoöns in our conscious minds. Like starlight at noon, it is *always* present, *always* working, but *only* noticed and identified as something remarkable in the context of pure theorics."

"Er, since you Edharians are so adept at burying assertions in your speeches, let me clarify something," Lodoghir said. "Did you just stake a claim that the Hylaean Flow is responsible for parallel evolution of Arbrans and Geometers?"

"Yes," said Paphlagon. "How's that for a speech?"

"Much more concise, thank you," Lodoghir said. "But you still believe in evolution!"

"Yes."

"Well, in that case, you must be saying that the Hylaean Flow has an effect on survival—or at least on the ability of specific organisms to propagate their sequences," Lodoghir said. "Because that's how we, and the Antarctans, ended up with five fingers, two nostrils, and all the rest."

"Fraa Lodoghir, you are doing my work for me!"

"*Someone* has to do it. Fraa Paphlagon, what *possible* scenario could justify all of that?"

"I don't know."

"You don't know?"

"The Visitation of Orithena was only ten days ago. Givens are still pouring in. You, Fraa Lodoghir, are now on the forefront of research into the next generation of Protism."

"I can't tell you how uneasy that makes me feel—really, I'd rather eat what Fraa Zh'vaern is eating. What *is* that?"

"At last Fraa Lodoghir asks a good question," said Arsibalt. Emman had yanked us; a boilover demanded our attention. We both knew exactly what Lodoghir was talking about. It was sitting on the stove, and we had been nervously edging around it all evening long. *Stewed hair with cubes of packing material and shards of exoskeleton,* or something. The hair seemed to be a vegetable. But what was really troubling Lodoghir and the others at the messal was the explosive crunching of the exoskeletons, or whatever they might be, between Zh'vaern's molars. We could actually hear these noises over the speaker.

Arsibalt looked around, verifying that Emman and I were the

only ones in the kitchen. "As a member of an ascetic, cloistered, contemplative order myself," he said, "I probably ought not level such criticisms against the poor Matarrhites—"

"Oh, go ahead!" Emman said. He was gamely trying to repair the ruptured casserole.

"All right, since you insist!" said Arsibalt. Protecting his hand with a fold of his bolt, he lifted the lid from the stewpot to divulge a bubbling morass of expired weeds, laced with dangerous-looking carapaces. "I think it's taking things just a little too far to selectively breed, over a period of millennia, foodstuffs that are offensive to all non-Matarrhites."

"I'll bet it's one of those not-as-bad-as-it-looks, -sounds, -feels, and -smells type of things," I said, holding my breath and approaching the pot.

"How much?"

"I beg your pardon?"

"How much do you bet?"

"Are you suggesting we try it?"

"I'm suggesting *you* try it."

"Why only me?"

"Because *you* proposed the wager, and *you* are the theor."

"What does that make *you*?"

"A scholar."

"So you'll take notes of my symptoms? Design my stained glass window, after I'm dead?"

"Yes, we'll place it right there," Arsibalt said, pointing to a smoke-hole in the wall, about the size of my hand.

Emman had drifted closer. Karvall and Tris had come in from the messallan and were standing very close to each other, watching.

Being watched by females changed everything. "What is the wager?" I said. "I am back down to three possessions." And it was one of the oldest rules in the mathic world that we weren't allowed to wager the bolt, chord, and sphere.

"Winner doesn't have to clean up tonight," Arsibalt proposed.

"Done," I said. This was easy; all I had to do, to win the bet, was to claim it wasn't that bad, and not throw up—at least, not in front of

Arsibalt. And even if I lost, I got all kinds of childish satisfaction out of Tris's and Karvall's exquisitely horrified reactions as I fished something out of the pulp and put it in my mouth. It was a cube of (I guessed) some curd-like, fermented substance, tangled up in wilted fronds, flecked with a few crunchy shards. While I was pursuing the latter with my tongue, the fronds slipped halfway down my gullet and made me swallow convulsively. They dragged the cube down with them, like seaweed killing a swimmer. I had to do a bit of coughing and gagging to get the vegetable matter back up into my mouth where I could chew it decently. This added some drama to the proceedings and made it that much more entertaining to the others. I held up a hand, signaling that all was well, and took my time chewing what was left—didn't want my innards slashed up by the sharp bits. Finally it all went down in a greasy, fibrous, thorny tangle. I put the odds at 60–40 that it wouldn't be coming back up. "You know," I claimed, "it's not that much worse than just standing over the pot and *wondering*."

"What's it taste like?" Tris asked.

"Ever put your tongue across battery terminals?"

"No, I've never even seen a battery."

"Mmm."

"Now, as to the wager—" Arsibalt said uncertainly.

"Yes," I said, "good luck with cleanup. Put your back into it when you are taking care of those casseroles, will you?"

Before Arsibalt could argue the point, his bell rang. Tris and Karvall were laughing at the look on his face as he slunk out of the kitchen.

In the messallan, the doyns had been asking Zh'vaern—much more circumspectly—about his food, but now Fraa Paphlagon took the bit in his teeth again: "Like cosmographers who sleep at day and work at night because that is when the stars can be seen, we are going to have to toil in the laboratory of consciousness, which is the only setting we know of where the effects of the Hylaean Flow are observable." And then he muttered something to Arsibalt. Then he added: "Though instead of one single HTW we should now speak of the Wick instead; the Flow percolates through a complex network of cosmi 'more theoric than' or 'prior to' ours."

Arsibalt returned to the kitchen. "Paphlagon doesn't want me. He wants you."

"Why would he want me?" I asked.

"I can't be sure," Arsibalt said, "but I was chatting with him yesterday and mentioned some of the conversations you had with Orolo."

"Oh. Thanks a *lot*!"

"So pick the shrapnel out of your teeth and get in there!"

And that was how I came to spend the entire main course recounting my two Ecba dialogs with Orolo: the first about how, according to him, consciousness was all about the the rapid and fluent creation of counterfactual worlds inside the brain, and the second in which he argued that this was not merely possible, not merely plausible, but in fact *easy*, if one thought of consciousness as spanning an ensemble of slightly different versions of the brain, each keeping track of a slightly different cosmos. Paphlagon ended up saying it better: "If Hemn space is the landscape, and one cosmos is a single geometric point in it, then a given consciousness is a spot of light moving, like a searchlight beam, over that landscape—brightly illuminating a set of points—of cosmi—that are close together, with a penumbra that rapidly feathers away to darkness at the edges. In the bright center of the beam, crosstalk occurs among many variants of the brain. Fewer contributions come in from the half-lit periphery, and none from the shadows beyond."

I gratefully stepped back against the wall, trying to fade into some shadows myself.

"I am indebted to Fraa Erasmas for allowing us to sit and eat, when so often we must interrupt our comestion with actual talk," Lodoghir finally said. "Perhaps we ought to trade places and allow the servitors to sit and eat in silence while they are lectured by doyns!"

Barb cackled. He had lately been showing more and more relish for Lodoghir's wit, furnishing me with the disturbing insight that perhaps Lodoghir was just a Barb who had become old. But after a moment's reflection I rejected such a miserable idea.

Lodoghir continued, "I'd like you to know that I fully took up

Paphlagon's earlier point about using consciousness as the laboratory for observing the so-called Hylaean Flow. But is this the best we can do? It is nothing more than a regurgitation of Evenedrician datonomy in its most primitive form!"

"I spent two years at Baritoe writing a treatise on Evenedrician datonomy," mentioned Ignetha Foral, sounding more amused than angry.

I got out of the room, which seemed more politic than laughing out loud. Back in the kitchen, I poured myself a drink and braced my arms on a counter, taking a load off my feet.

"Are you all right?" Karvall asked. She and I were the only servitors in the room.

"Just tired—that took a lot out of me."

"Well, I thought you spoke really well—for what that's worth."

"Thanks," I said, "it's worth a lot, actually."

"Grandsuur Moyra says we are doing something now."

"I beg your pardon?"

"She believes that the messal is on the verge of coming up with new ideas instead of just talking about old ones."

"Well, that's really something, from such a distinguished Lorite!"

"It's all because of the PAQD, she says. If they hadn't come and brought new givens, it might never have happened."

"Well, my friend Jesry will be pleased to hear it," I said. "He's wanted it all his life."

"What have you wanted all your life?" Karvall asked.

"Me? I don't know. To be as smart as Jesry, I guess."

"Tonight, you were as smart as anyone," she said.

"Thanks!" I said. "If that's true, it's all because of Orolo."

"*And* because you were brave."

"Some would call it stupid."

If I hadn't had that conversation with Ala at breakfast, I'd probably be falling in love with Karvall about now. But I was pretty sure Karvall *wasn't* in love with me—just stating facts as she saw them. To stand here and receive compliments from an attractive young woman was quite pleasant, but it was of a whole lesser order of experience from the continuous finger-in-an-electrical-socket buzz that I experienced during even brief interactions with Ala.

I ought to have volleyed some compliments back, but I was *not* brave in that moment. The Lorites had a kind of grandeur that intimidated. Their elaborate style—shaving the head, performing hours of knotwork just to get dressed—was, I knew, a way of showing respect for those who had gone before, of reminding themselves, every day, just how much work one had to do to get up to speed and be competent to sift new ideas from old. But my knowing that symbolism didn't make Karvall any more approachable.

We were distracted by Zh'vaern's strangely inflected voice on the speaker: "Because of the way we Matarrhites keep to ourselves, not even Suur Moyra might have heard of him we honor as Saunt Atamant."

"I don't recognize the name," Moyra said.

"He was, to us, the most gifted and meticulous introspectionist who ever lived."

"Introspectionist? Is that some sort of a job title within your Order?" Lodoghir asked, not unkindly.

"It might as well be," Zh'vaern returned. "He devoted the last thirty years of his life to looking at a copper bowl."

"What was so special about this bowl?" asked Ignetha Foral.

"Nothing. But he wrote, or rather dictated, ten treatises explaining all that went on in his mind as he gazed on it. Much of it has the same flavor as Orolo's meditations on counterfactuals: how Atamant's mind filled in the unseen back surface of the bowl with suppositions as to what it must look like. From such thoughts he developed a metatheorics of counterfactuals and compossibility that, to make a long story short, is perfectly compatible with all that was said during our first messal about Hemn space and worldtracks. He made the assertion that *all* possible worlds *really existed* and were every bit as real as our own. This caused many to dismiss him as a lunatic."

"But that is precisely what the polycosmic interpretation is positing," said Suur Asquin.

"Indeed."

"What of our second evening's discussion? Has Saunt Atamant anything to say about that?"

"I have been thinking about that very hard. You see, nine of his treatises are mostly about space. Only one is about time, but it is considered harder to read than the other nine put together! But if there is applicability of his work to the Hylaean Flow, it is hidden somewhere in the Tenth Treatise. I re-read it last night; this was my Lucub."

"And what did Atamant's copper bowl tell him of time?" Lodoghir asked.

"I should tell you first that he was knowledgeable about theorics. He knew that the laws of theorics were time-reversible, and that the only way to determine the direction of time's arrow was to measure the amount of disorder in a system. The cosmos seems oblivious to time. It only matters to us. Consciousness is time-constituting. We build time up out of instantaneous impressions that flow in through our sensory organs at each moment. Then they recede into the past. What is this thing we call the past? It is a system of records encoded in our nerve tissue—records that tell a consistent story."

"We have heard of these records before," Ignetha Foral pointed out. "They are essential to the Hemn space picture."

"Yes, Madame Secretary, but now let me add something new. It is rather well encapsulated by the thought experiment of the flies, bats, and worms. We don't give our consciousness sufficient credit for its ability to take in noisy, ambiguous, contradictory givens from the senses, and sort it out: to say 'this pattern of givens equals the copper bowl that is in front of me now and that was in front of me a moment ago,' to confer *thisness* on what we perceive. I know you may feel uncomfortable with religious language, but it seems miraculous that our consciousness can do this."

"But absolutely necessary from an evolutionary standpoint," Lodoghir pointed out.

"To be sure! But none the less remarkable for that. The ability of our consciousness to *see*—not just as a speelycaptor sees (by taking in and recording givens) but identifying things—copper bowls, melodies, faces, beauty, ideas—and making these things available to cognition—that ability, Atamant said, is the ultimate basis of all rational thought. And if consciousness can identify copper-bowlness, why can't it identify isosceles-triangleness, or Adrakhonic-theoremness?"

"What you are describing is nothing more than pattern recognition, and then assigning names to patterns," Lodoghir said.

"So the Syntactics would say," replied Zh'vaern. "But I would say that you have it backwards. You Procians have a theory—a model—of what consciousness is, and you make all else subordinate to it. Your theory becomes the ground of all possible assertions, and the processes of consciousness are seen as mere phenomena to be explained in the terms of that theory. Atamant says that you have fallen into the error of circular reasoning. You cannot develop your grounding theory of consciousness without making use of the power consciousness has of seizing on and conferring thisness on givens, and so it is incoherent and circular for you to then employ that theory to explain the fundamental workings of consciousness."

"I understand Atamant's point," Lodoghir said, "but by making such a move, does he not exile himself from rational theoric discourse? This power of consciousness takes on a sort of mystical status—it can't be challenged or examined, it just *is*."

"On the contrary, nothing could be more rational than to begin with what is given, with what we observe, and ask ourselves how we come to observe it, and investigate it in a thorough and meticulous style."

"Let me ask it this way, then: what results was Atamant able to deliver by following this program?"

"Once he made the decision to proceed in this way, he made a few false starts, went up some blind alleys. But the nub of it is this: consciousness is enacted in the physical world, on physical equipment—"

"Equipment?" Ignetha Foral asked sharply.

"Nerve tissue, or perhaps some artificial device of similar powers. The point being that it has what the Ita would call hardware. Yet Atamant's premise is that consciousness itself, not the equipment, is the primary reality. The full cosmos consists of the physical stuff *and* consciousness. Take away consciousness and it's only dust; add consciousness and you get things, ideas, and time. The story is long and winding, but eventually he found a fruitful line of inquiry rooted in the polycosmic interpretation of quantum mechanics. He quite reasonably applied this premise to his favorite topic—"

"The copper bowl?" Lodoghir asked.

"The complex of consciousness-phenomena that amounted to his perception of a copper bowl," Zh'vaern corrected him, "and proceeded to explain it within that framework." And Zh'vaern—uncharacteristically talkative this evening—proceeded to give us a calca summarizing Atamant's findings on the copper bowl. As he'd warned us, this had much in common with the dialogs I'd been reporting on a few minutes earlier, and led to the same basic conclusion. As a matter of fact, it was *so* repetitive that I wondered, at first, why he bothered with it, unless it was just to show off what a smart fellow Atamant was, and score one for the Matarrhite team. As a servitor, I was free to come and go. Zh'vaern eventually worked his way around to the assertion, which we'd heard before, that crosstalk among different cosmi around the time that their worldtracks diverged was routinely exploited by consciousness-bearing systems.

Lodoghir said, "Please explain something to me. I was under the impression that the kind of crosstalk you are speaking of could only occur between two cosmi that were *exactly* the same except for a difference in the quantum state of *one* particle."

"We can testify to that much," said Moyra, "because the situation you've just described is just the sort of thing that is studied in laboratory experiments. It is relatively easy to build an apparatus that embodies that kind of scenario—'does the particle have spin up or spin down,' 'does the photon pass through the left slit or the right slit,' and so on."

"Well, that's a relief!" Lodoghir said. "I was afraid you were about to claim that this crosstalk was the same thing as the Hylaean Flow."

"I believe that it is," Zh'vaern said. "It has to be."

Lodoghir looked affronted. "But Suur Moyra has just finished explaining that the only form of inter-cosmic crosstalk for which we have experimental evidence is that in which the two cosmi are the same except for the state of *one* particle. The Hylaean Flow, according to its devotees, joins cosmi that are altogether different!"

"If you look at the world through a straw, you will only see a tiny bit of it," Paphlagon said. "The kinds of experiments that Moyra spoke of are all perfectly sound—better than that, they are magnificent, in their way—but they only tell us of single-particle systems. If we could devise better experiments, we could presumably observe new phenomena."

Fraa Jad threw his napkin on the table and said: "Consciousness amplifies the weak signals that, like cobwebs spun between trees, web Narratives together. Moreover, it amplifies them *selectively* and in that way creates feedback loops that steer the Narratives."

Silence except for the sound of Arsibalt chalking that one down on the wall. I slipped into the messallan.

"Would you be so kind as to unpack that statement?" Suur Asquin finally said. Glancing at Arsibalt's handiwork, she said, "To begin with, what do you mean by amplifying weak signals?"

Fraa Jad looked as if he hardly knew where to begin, and couldn't be bothered, but Moyra was game: "The 'signals' are the interactions between cosmi that account for quantum effects. If you don't agree with the polycosmic interpretation, you must find some other explanation for those effects. But if you *do* agree with it, then, to make it compatible with what we have long known about quantum mechanics, you must buy into the premise that cosmi interfere with each other when their worldtracks are close together. If you restrict yourself to one particular cosmos, this crosstalk may be interpreted as a signal—a rather weak one, since it only concerns a few particles. If those particles are in an asteroid out in the middle of nowhere, it hardly matters. But when those particles happen to be at certain critical locations in the brain, why, then, the 'signals' can end up altering the behavior of the organism that is animated by that brain. That organism, all by itself, is vastly larger than anything that could normally be influenced by quantum interference. When one considers *societies* of such organisms that endure across long spans of time and in some cases develop world-altering technologies, one sees the meaning of Fraa Jad's assertion that consciousness amplifies the weak signals that web cosmi together."

Zh'vaern had been nodding vigorously: "This tallies with some Atamant that I was reading yesterday evening. Consciousness, he wrote, is non-spatiotemporal in nature. But it becomes involved with the spatiotemporal world when conscious beings react to their own cognitions and make efforts to communicate with *other* conscious beings—something that they can only do by involving their spatiotemporal bodies. This is how we get from a solipsistic world—one that is perceived by, and real to, only one subject—to the *intersubjective* world—the one where I can be certain that *you* see the copper bowl and that the thisness you attach to it harmonizes with mine."

"Thank you, Suur Moyra and Fraa Zh'vaern," said Ignetha Foral. "Assuming that Fraa Jad will maintain his gnomic ways, would you or anyone else care to take a crack at the second part of what he said?"

"I should be delighted to," said Fraa Lodoghir, "since Fraa Jad is sounding more and more Procian every time he opens his mouth!" This earned Lodoghir a lot of attention, which he reveled in for a few moments before going on: "By *selective* amplification, I believe Fraa Jad is saying that not *all* inter-cosmic crosstalk gets amplified—only *some* of it. To cite Suur Moyra's example, crosstalk affecting elementary particles in a rock in deep space has no effect."

"No *extraordinary* effect," Paphlagon corrected him, "no *unpredictable* effect. But, mind you, it accounts for *everything* about that rock: how it absorbs and re-radiates light, how its nuclei decay, and so on."

"But it all sort of averages out statistically, and you can't really tell one rock from another," Lodoghir said.

"Yes."

"The point being that the only crosstalk *capable* of being amplified by consciousness is that affecting nerve tissue."

"Or any other consciousness-bearing system," Paphlagon said.

"So there is a highly exclusive selection process at work *to begin with* in that, of all the crosstalk going on in a given instant between our cosmos and all the other cosmi that are sufficiently close to it to render such crosstalk possible, the stupefyingly enormous preponderance of it is only affecting rocks and other stuff that is not complex enough to respond to that crosstalk in a way we'd consider interesting."

"Yes," Paphlagon said.

"Let us then confine our discussion to the infinitesimally small fraction of the crosstalk that happens to impinge on nerve tissue. As I've just finished saying, this *already* gives us selectivity." Lodoghir nodded at the slate. "But, whether or not Fraa Jad intended to, he has opened the door to another kind of selection procedure that may be at work here. Our brains receive these 'signals,' yes. But they are more than passive receivers. They are not merely crystal radios! They compute. They cogitate. The *outcomes* of those cogitations can by no means be easily predicted from their inputs. And those outcomes are the conscious thoughts that we have, the decisions we put into effect, our social interactions with other conscious beings, and the behavior of societies down through the ages."

"Thank you, Fraa Lodoghir," said Ignetha Foral, and turned to scan the slate again. "And would anyone care to tackle 'feedback loops'?"

"We get those for free," Paphlagon said.

"What do you mean?"

"It's already there in the model we've been talking about, we don't have to add anything more. We've already seen how small signals, amplified by the special structures of nerve tissue and societies of conscious beings, can lead to changes in a Narrative—in the configuration of a cosmos—that are much larger than the original signals in question. The worldtracks veer, change their courses in response to those faint signals, and you could distinguish a cosmos that was populated by conscious organisms from one that wasn't by observing the way their worldtracks behaved. But recall that the signals in question only pass between cosmi whose worldtracks are close together. There is your feedback! Crosstalk steers the worldtracks of consciousness-bearing cosmi; worldtracks that steer close together exchange more crosstalk."

"So the feedback pulls worldtracks close to one another as time goes on?" Ignetha Foral asked. "Is this the explanation we've been looking for of why the Geometers look like us?"

"Not only that," put in Suur Asquin, "but of cnoöns and the HTW and all the rest, if I'm not mistaken."

"I am going to be a typical Lorite," Moyra said, "and caution you that *feedback* is a layman's term that covers a wide range of phenomena. Entire branches of theorics have been, and are still being, developed to study the behavior of systems that exhibit what laymen know as feedback. The most common behaviors in feedback systems are degenerate. Such as the howl from a public address system, or total chaos. Very few such systems yield stable behavior—or any sort of behavior that you or I could look at and say, 'see, it is doing *this* now.'"

"Thisness!" Zh'vaern exclaimed.

"But conversely," Moyra went on, "systems that *are* stable, in a tumultuous universe, generally *must* have some kind of feedback in order to exist."

Ignetha Foral nodded. "So if the feedback posited by Fraa Jad really is steering our worldtrack and those of the PAQD races together, it's not just *any* feedback but some very special, highly tuned species of it."

"We call something an attractor," Paphlagon said, "when it persists or recurs in a complex system."

"So if it is true that the PAQD share the Adrakhonic Theorem and other such theorical concepts with us," said Fraa Lodoghir, "those might be nothing more than attractors in the feedback system we have been describing."

"Or nothing *less*," said Fraa Jad.

We all let that one resonate for a minute. Lodoghir and Jad were staring at each other across the table; we all thought something was about to happen.

A Procian and a Halikaarnian were about to agree with each other.

Then Zh'vaern wrecked it. As if he didn't get what was going on at all; or perhaps the HTW simply was not that interesting to him. He couldn't get off the topic of Atamant's bowl.

"Atamant," he announced, "changed his bowl."

"I beg your pardon?" demanded Ignetha Foral.

"Yes. For thirty years, it had a scratch on the bottom. This is attested by phototypes. Then, during the final year of his meditation—shortly before his death—he made the scratch disappear."

Everyone had become very quiet.

"Translate that into polycosmic language, please?" asked Suur Asquin.

"He found his way to a cosmos the same as the one he'd been living in—except that in this cosmos the bowl wasn't scratched."

"But there were records—phototypes—of its having been scratched."

"Yes," said Zh'vaern. "so he had gone to a cosmos that included some inconsistent records. And that is the cosmos that *we* are in now."

"And how did he achieve this feat?" asked Moyra, as if she already guessed the answer.

"Either by changing the records, or else by shifting to a cosmos with a different future."

"Either he was a Rhetor, or an Incanter!" blurted a young voice. Barb. Performing his role as sayer of things no one else would say.

"That's not what I meant," said Moyra. *"How did he achieve it?"*

"He declined to share his secret," said Zh'vaern. "I thought that some here might have something to say of it." And he looked all around the table—but mostly at Jad and Lodoghir.

"If they do, they'll say it tomorrow," announced Ignetha Foral. "Tonight's messal has ended." And she pushed her chair back, casting a baleful glare at Zh'vaern. Emman burst through the door and snatched up her rucksack. Madame Secretary adjusted the badge around her neck as if it were just another item of jewelry, and stalked out, pursued by her servitor, who was grunting under the weight of two rucksacks.

I had grand plans for how I would spend the free time I'd won in my wager with Arsibalt. There were so many ways I wanted to use that gift that I could not decide where to start. I went back to my cell to fetch some notes and sat down on my pallet. Then I opened my eyes to find it was morning.

The hours of night had not gone to waste, though, for I awoke with ideas and intentions that had not been in my head when I'd closed my eyes. Given the sorts of things we'd been talking about lately at messal, it was hard not to think that while I'd lain unconscious, my mind had been busy rambling all over the local parts of Hemn space, exploring alternate versions of the world.

I went and found Arsibalt, who had slept less than I. He was inclined to surliness until I shared with him some of what I had been thinking about—if *thinking* was the right word for processes that had taken place without my volition while I had been unconscious.

For breakfast I had some dense, grainy buns and dried fruit. Afterwards, I went to a little stand of trees out behind the First Sconic chapterhouse. Arsibalt was waiting for me there, brandishing a shovel he'd borrowed from a garden shack. He scooped out a shallow depression in the earth, no larger than a serving-bowl. I lined it with a scrap of poly sheeting that I had scavenged from one of the middens that Sæcular people left everywhere they went—and that had lately begun to pock the grounds of this concent.

"Here goes nothing," I said, hitching up my bolt.

"The best experiments," he said, "are the simplest."

Analyzing the givens only took a few minutes. The rest of the day was spent making various preparations. How Arsibalt and I got others involved in that work, and the minor adventures each of us had during the day, would make for an amusing collection of anecdotes, but I have made the decision not to spell them out here because they are so trivial compared to what happened that evening. Before it was over, though, we had enlisted Emman, Tris, Barb, Karvall, Lio, and Sammann, and had talked Suur Asquin into looking the other way while we made some temporary alterations to her Dowment.

The fourth Plurality of Worlds Messal began normally: after a libation, soup was served. Barb and Emman went back to the kitchen. Not long after, Orhan was yanked. Tris followed him out. About a minute later I felt a coded sequence of tugs on my rope, which informed me that things had gone according to plan in the kitchen: the stew that Orhan had been cooking had "inadvertently" been knocked over by clumsy Barb. Between that distraction, and the racket that Tris and Emman had begun making with some pots and pans, Orhan would be unlikely to notice that sound was no longer coming out of the speaker.

I nodded across the table to Arsibalt.

"Excuse me, Fraa Zh'vaern, but you forgot to bless your food," Arsibalt announced, in a clear voice.

Conversation stopped. The messal had been unusually subdued to this point, as though all the doyns were trying to devise some way of restarting the dialog while avoiding the awkward territory that Zh'vaern had attempted to drag us into last night. Even in the rowdiest messal, though, any unasked-for statement from a servitor would have been shocking; Arsibalt's was doubly so because of what he'd said. As long as everyone was speechless, he went on: "I have been studying the beliefs and practices of the Matarrhites. They never take food without saying a prayer, which ends with a gesture. You have neither spoken the prayer nor made the gesture."

"What of it? I forgot," Zh'vaern said.

"You *always* forget," Arsibalt returned.

Ignetha Foral was giving Paphlagon a look that meant *when are you going to throw the Book at your servitor?* and indeed Paphlagon now threw down his napkin and made as if to push his chair back. But Fraa Jad reached out and clamped a hand on Paphlagon's arm.

"You always forget," Arsibalt repeated, "and, if you like, I can list any number of other ways in which you and Orhan have imperfectly simulated the behavior of Matarrhites. Is it because you're not actually Matarrhites?"

Beneath the hood, Zh'vaern's head moved. He was casting a glance at the door. *Not* the one through which he and the other doyns had entered, but the one through which Orhan had left.

"Your minder can't hear us," I told him, "the microphone wire has been cut by an Ita friend of mine. The feed no longer goes out."

Still Zh'vaern remained frozen and silent. I nodded at Suur Karvall, who pulled aside a tapestry to reveal a shiny mesh, woven of metal wires, with which we'd covered the wall. I stepped around toward Zh'vaern, stuck a toe under the edge of the carpet, and flipped it up to reveal more of the same on the floor. Zh'vaern took it all in. "It is a fencing material used in animal husbandry," I explained, "obtainable in bulk extramuros. It is conductive—and it is connected to ground."

"What is the meaning of all this?" demanded Ignetha Foral.

"We're in a Saunt Bucker's Basket!" exclaimed Moyra. Her life, as an extremely senior, semi-retired Lorite, probably didn't include many unexpected events, and so even something as mundane as discovering that she was surrounded by chicken wire seemed like quite an adventure. More than that, though, I believe she was pleased that the servitors had taken her exhortations to heart, and gone out and *done* something that the doyns never would have dreamed of. "It's a grounded mesh that prevents wireless signals from passing into or out of the room. It means we're informationally shielded from the rest of Arbre."

"In my world," said Zh'vaern, "we call it a Faraday cage." He stood up and shrugged his bolt off over his head, then tossed it to the floor. I was behind him and so could not see his face—only the looks of awe and astonishment on the faces of the others: the first Arbrans, with the possible exception of the Warden of Heaven, to gaze upon the face of a living alien. Judging from the back of his head and torso, I guessed he was of the same race as the dead woman who'd come down in the probe. Beneath a sort of undershirt, a small device was attached to his skin with poly tape. He reached under the garment, peeled it off, and threw it on the table along with a snarl of wires.

"I am Jules Verne Durand of Laterre—the world you know as Antarct. Orhan is from the world of Urnud, which you have designated Pangee. You had best get him inside the Faraday cage before—"

"Done," said a voice from the door: Lio, who had just come in, cheerfully flushed. "We have him in a separate Bucker's Basket in the pantry. Sammann found this on him." And he held up another wireless body transmitter.

"Well-wrought," said Jules Verne Durand, "but it has purchased you a few minutes only; those who listen will grow suspicious at the loss of contact."

"We have alerted Suur Ala that it might become necessary to evacuate the concent," Lio said.

"Good," said Jules Verne Durand, "for I am sorry to say that the ones of Urnud are a danger to you."

"And to you of Laterre as well, it would seem!" said Arsibalt. Since the doyns were all too speechless to rejoin the conversation, Arsibalt—who'd had time to prepare—was doing his bit to keep things going.

"It is true," said the Laterran. "I will tell you quickly that those of Urnud and of Tro—which you call Diasp—are of similar mind, and hostile to those of Fthos—which you call—"

"Quator, by process of elimination," said Lodoghir.

I'd worked my way round to a place where I could see Jules Verne Durand, and so was feeling some of the astonishment that the others had experienced a few moments earlier. First at the differences—then similarities, then differences again—between Laterran and Arbran faces. The closest comparison I can make is to how one reacts when conversing with one who has a birth defect that has subtly altered the geometry of the face—but without the deformity or loss of function that this would imply. And of course no comparison can be drawn to the way we felt knowing that we were looking on one who had traveled from another cosmos.

"What of you and your fellow Laterrans?" Lodoghir asked.

"Split between the Fthosians and the others."

"You, I take it, are loyal to the Urnud/Tro axis?" Lodoghir asked. "Otherwise, you would not have been sent here."

"I was sent here because I speak better Orth than anyone else—I am a linguist. A junior one, actually. And so they put me to work on Orth in the early days, when Orth was believed to be a minor language. They are suspicious of my loyalty—with good reason! Orhan, as you divined, is my watcher—my minder." He looked at Arsibalt. "You penetrated my disguise. Not surprising, really. But I should like to know how?"

Arsibalt looked to me. I said, "I ate some of your food yesterday. It passed through my digestive system unchanged."

"Of course, for your enzymes could not react with it," said Jules Verne Durand. "I commend you."

Ignetha Foral had finally recovered enough to join the conversation. "On behalf of the Supreme Council I welcome you and apologize for any mistreatment you have undergone at the hands of these young—"

"Stop. This is what you call bulshytt. No time," said the Laterran. "My mission—assigned to me by the military intelligence command of the Urnud/Tro axis—is to find out whether the legends of the Incanters are grounded in fact. The Urnud/Tro axis—which they call, in their languages, the Pedestal—is extremely fearful of this prospect; they contemplate a pre-emptive strike. Hence my questions of previous evenings, which I am aware were quite rude."

"How did you get here?" asked Paphlagon.

"A commando raid on the concent of the Matarrhites. We have ways of dropping small capsules onto your planet that cannot be noticed by your sensors. A team of soldiers, as well as a few civilian experts such as myself, were sent down, and seized that concent. The true Matarrhites are held there, unharmed, but incommunicado."

"That is an extraordinarily aggressive measure!" said Ignetha Foral.

"So it rightly seems to you who are not accustomed to encounters between different versions of the world, in different cosmi. But the Pedestal have been doing it for hundreds of years, and have become bold. When our scholars became aware of the Matarrhites, someone pointed out that their style of dress would make it easy for us to disguise ourselves and infiltrate the Convox. The order to proceed was given quickly."

"How do you travel between cosmi?" Paphlagon asked.

"There is little time," said Jules Verne Durand, "and I am no theor." He turned to Suur Moyra. "You will know of a certain way of thinking about gravity, likely dating to the time of the Harbingers, called by us General Relativity. Its premise is that mass-energy bends spacetime . . ."

"Geometrodynamics!" said Suur Moyra.

"If the equations of geometrodynamics are solved in the special case of a universe that happens to be rotating, it can be shown that a spaceship, if it travels far and fast enough—"

"Will travel backwards in time," said Paphlagon. "Yes. The result is known to us. We always considered it little more than a curiosity, though."

"On Laterre, the result was discovered by a kind of Saunt named Gödel: a friend of the Saunt who had earlier discovered geometrodynamics. The two of them were, you might say, fraas in the same math. For us, too, it was little more than a curiosity. For one thing, it was not clear at first that our cosmos rotated—"

"And if it doesn't rotate, the result is useless," said Paphlagon.

"Working in the same institute were others who invented a ship propelled by atomic bombs—sufficiently energetic to put this theory to the test."

"I see," said Paphlagon, "so Laterre constructed such a ship and—"

"No! We never did!"

"Just as Arbre never did—even though we had the same ideas!" Lio put in.

"But *on Urnud* it was different," said Jules Verne Durand. "They had geometrodynamics. They had the rotating-universe solution.

They had cosmographic evidence that their cosmos did in fact rotate. And they had the idea for the atomic ship. But *they* actually *built* several of them. They were driven to such measures because of a terrible war between two blocs of nations. The combat infected space; the whole solar system became a theatre of war. The last and largest of these ships was called *Daban Urnud*, which means 'Second Urnud.' It was designed to send a colony to a neighboring star system, only a quarter of a light-year away. But there was a mutiny and a change of command. It fell under the control of ones who understood the theorics that I spoke of. They chose to steer a different course: one that was intended to take them into the past of Urnud, where they hoped that they could undo the decisions that had led to the outbreak of the war. But when they reached the end of that journey, they found themselves, not in the past of Urnud, but in an altogether different cosmos, orbiting an Urnud-like planet—"

"Tro," said Arsibalt.

"Yes. This is how the universe protects herself—prevents violations of causality. If you attempt to do anything that would give you the power of violating the laws of cause-and-effect—to go back in time and kill your grandfather—"

"You simply find yourself in a different and separate causal domain? How extraordinary!" said Lodoghir.

The Laterran nodded. "One is shunted into an altogether different Narrative," he said, with a glance at Fraa Jad, "and thus causality is preserved."

"And now it seems they've made a habit of it!" said Lodoghir.

Jules Verne Durand considered it. "You say 'now' as if it came about quickly and easily, but there is much history between the First Advent—the Urnudan discovery of Tro—and the Fourth— which is what we are all living through now. The First Advent alone spanned a century and a half, and left Tro in ruins."

"Heavens!" exclaimed Lodoghir. "Are the Urnudans really *that* nasty?"

"Not quite. But it was the first time. Neither the Urnudans nor the Troäns had the sophisticated understanding of the polycosm that you seem to have developed here on Arbre. Everything was surprising, and therefore a source of terror. The Urnudans became involved in Troän politics too hastily. Disastrous events—almost all of them the Troäns' own fault—played out. They eventually rebuilt the *Daban Urnud* so that both races could live on it, and embarked on a second inter-cosmic voyage. They came to Laterre fifty years after the death of Gödel."

"Excuse me," said Ignetha Foral, "but why did the ship have to be changed so much?"

"Partly because it was worn out—used up," said Jules Verne Durand. "But it is mostly a question of food. Each race must maintain its own food supply—for reasons made obvious by Fraa Erasmas's experiment." He paused and looked around the messal. "It is my destiny, now, to starve to death in the midst of plenty, unless by diplomacy you can persuade those on the *Daban Urnud* to send down some food that I can digest."

Tris—who had returned to the messal early in the conversation—said, "We'll do all we can to preserve the Laterran victuals that are still in the kitchen!" and hustled out of the room.

Ignetha Foral added, "We shall make this a priority in any future communications with the Pedestal."

"Thank you," said the Laterran, "for one of my ancestry, death by starvation would be the most ignominious possible fate."

"What happened in the Second Advent—on Laterre?" asked Suur Moyra.

"I will skip the details. It was not as bad as Tro. But in every cosmos they visit, there is upheaval. The Advent lasts anywhere from twenty to a couple of hundred years. With or without your cooperation, the *Daban Urnud* will be rebuilt completely. None of your political institutions, none of your religions, will survive in their current form. Wars will be fought. Some of your people will be aboard the new version of the ship when it finally moves on to some other Narrative."

"As you were, I take it, when it left Laterre?" asked Lodoghir.

"Oh, no. That was my great-grandfather," said the visitor. "My ancestors lived through the voyage to Fthos and the Third

Advent. I was born on Fthos. Similar things will probably happen here."

"Assuming," said Ignetha Foral, "that they don't use the World Burner on us."

I was just learning to read Laterran facial expressions, but I was certain that what I saw on Jules Verne Durand's face was horror at the very mention. "This hideous thing was invented on Urnud, in their great war—though I must confess we had similar plans on Laterre."

"As did we," said Moyra.

"There is a suspicion, you see, planted deep in the minds of the Urnudans, that with each Advent they are finding themselves in a world that is more ideal—closer to what you would call the Hylaean Theoric World—than the last. I don't have time to recite all the particulars, but I myself have often thought that Urnud and Tro seemed like less perfect versions of Laterre, and that Fthos seemed to us what we were to Tro. Now we are come to yet a new world, and there is terrible apprehension among the Pedestal that those of Arbre will possess powers and qualities beyond their grasp—even their comprehension. They have exaggerated sensitivity to anything that has this seeming—"

"Hence the elaborate commando raid, this ambitious ruse to learn about the Incanters," said Lodoghir.

"And Rhetors," Paphlagon reminded him.

Moyra laughed. "It is Third Sack politics all over again! Except infinitely more dangerous."

"And the problem you—we—face is that there is nothing you can do to convince them that such things as Rhetors and Incanters *don't* exist," said Jules Verne Durand.

"Quickly—Atamant and the copper bowl?" asked Lodoghir.

"Loosely based on a philosopher of Laterre, named Edmund Husserl, and the copper ashtray he kept on his desk," said the Laterran. If I was reading his face right, he was feeling a bit sheepish. "I fictionalized his story quite heavily. The part about making the scratch disappear was, of course, a ruse to draw you out—to get you to state plainly whether anyone on Arbre possessed the power to do such things."

"Do you think that the ruse worked?" asked Ignetha Foral.

"The way you reacted made those who control me even more suspicious. I was directed to bear down harder on it this evening."

"So they are still undecided."

"Oh, I am quite certain they are decided *now*."

The floor jumped under our feet, and the air was suddenly dusty. The silence that followed was ended by a succession of concussive thuds. These rolled in over a span of perhaps a quarter of a minute—twenty of them in all. Lio announced, "No cause for alarm. This is according to plan. What you're hearing are controlled demolition charges, taking down sections of the outer wall—creating enough apertures for us to get out of the concent quickly, so we don't bunch up at the Day Gate. The evacuation is under way. Look at your badges."

I pulled mine out from under a fold of my bolt. It had come alive with a color map of my vicinity, just like the nav screen on a cartabla. My evacuation route was highlighted in purple. Superimposed over that was a cartoon rendering of a rucksack with a red flashing question mark.

The doyns took the momentous step of pushing their chairs back. They were looking at their badges, making remarks. Lio vaulted up onto the table and stamped his foot, very loud. They all looked up at him. "Stop talking," he said.

"But—" said Lodoghir.

"Not a word. Act!" And Lio gave that command in a voice I'd never heard from him before—though I had once heard something like it in the streets of Mahsht. He'd been training his voice, as well as his body—learning Vale-lore tricks of how to use it as a weapon. I sidestepped past a stream of doyns who were headed the other way, shouldering their rucksacks. I entered the corridor, where mine was waiting. I hoisted it to one shoulder and looked at my badge again. The rucksack cartoon had disappeared. I strode out to the kitchen. Tris and Lio were helping Jules Verne Durand package what was left of his food into bags and baskets.

I walked out the back of Avrachon's Dowment and into the midst of a total evacuation of the ancient concent of Tredegarh.

Thousands of feet above, aerocraft were landing on the tops of the Thousanders' towers.

All of this business with the badges and the rucksacks had seemed insultingly simpleminded to me and many others I'd talked to—as if the Convox were a summer camp for five-year-olds. In the course of a fifteen-minute jog across Tredegarh, I came to appreciate it. There was no plan, no procedure, so simple that it could not get massively screwed up when thousands of persons tried to carry it out at the same time. Doing it in the dark squared the amount of chaos, doing it in a hurry cubed it. People who had mislaid their badges and their rucksacks were wandering around in more or less panic—but they gravitated to sound trucks announcing "Come to me if you have lost your badge or your rucksack!" Others twisted ankles, hyperventilated, even suffered from heart trouble—military medics pounced on these. Grandfraas and grandsuurs who failed to keep up found themselves being carried on fids' backs. Running through the dark, mesmerized by their badges, people banged into one another in grand slapstick style, fell down, got bloody noses, argued as to whose fault it had been. I slowed to help a few victims, but the aid teams were astoundingly efficient—and quite rude about letting me know I should head for an exit rather than getting in their way. Ala had really put her stamp on this thing. As I gained confidence that the evacuation was basically working, I moved faster, and struck out across the giant page tree plantation, heavy with leaves that would never be harvested, toward a rugged gap that had been blasted through the ancient wall. The opening was choked with rubble. Lights shone through from extramuros, making the dusty air above the aperture glow blue-white, and casting long, flailing silhouettes behind the avout who were streaming through it, clambering over the rubble-pile, helped over tricky parts by soldiers who played flashlights over patches of rough footing and barked suggestions at any avout who stumbled or looked tentative. My badge told me to go through it, so I did, trying not to think about how many centuries the stones I trod had stood until tonight, the avout who'd cut them to shape and laid them in place.

Beyond the wall was a glacis, a belt of open territory that locals used as a park. This evening it had become a depot for military drummons: simple flatbeds whose backs had been covered by canvas awnings. At first I saw only the few that stood closest to the base of the rubble-pile, since these lay in the halo of light. But my badge was insisting that I penetrate the darkness beyond. When I did, I became aware that these drummons were scattered across what seemed like square miles of darkness. I heard their engines idling all around, and I saw cold light thrown off by glow buds, by the spheres of wandering avout, and by control panels reflecting in drivers' eyes. The vehicles themselves were running dark.

Something overtook me, parted around me, and moved on. I felt rather than heard it. It was a squad of Valers, swathed in black bolts, running silently through the night.

I jogged on for some minutes, taking a winding route, since my badge kept trying to get me to walk through parked drummons. Another blown wall section, with its mountain of light, passed by on my right, and I saw yet another swinging into view around the curve of the wall. All of these gaps continued to spew avout, so I didn't get the sense that I was late. Here and there I'd spy a lone fraa or suur, face illuminated by badge-light, approaching the open back of a drummon, eyes jumping between badge and vehicle, the face registering growing certainty: *yes, this is the one.* Hands reaching out of the dark to help them aboard, voices calling out to them in greeting. Everyone was strangely cheerful—not knowing what I and a few others now knew about what we were getting into.

Finally the purple line took me out beyond the last of the parked drummons. Only one vehicle remained that was large enough to carry a cell of any appreciable size: a coach, gaudy with phototypes of ecstatic gamblers. It must have been commandeered from a casino. I could not believe that this was my destination, but every time I tried to dodge around it, the purple line irritably re-vectored itself and told me to turn back around. So I approached the side door and gazed up the entry stair. A military driver was sitting there, lit by his jeejah. "Erasmas of Edhar?" he called out—apparently reading signals from my badge.

"Yes."

"Welcome to Cell 317," he said, and with a jerk of the head told me to come aboard. "Six down, five to go," he muttered, as I lurched past him. "Put your pack on the seat next to you—quick on, quick off."

The aisle of the coach and the undersurfaces of the luggage shelves were lined with strips that cast dim illumination on the seats and the people in them. It was sparsely occupied. Soldiers, talking on or busy with jeejahs, had claimed the first couple of rows. Officers, I thought. Then, after a few empty rows, I saw a face I recognized: Sammann, lit by his super-jeejah as usual. He glanced up and recognized me, but I didn't see the old familiar grin on his face. Instead his eyes darted back for a moment.

Gazing into the gloom that stretched behind him, I saw several rows of seats occupied by rucksacks. Next to each was a shaven head, bowed in concentration.

I stopped so hard that my pack's momentum nearly knocked me over. My mind said, *boy, did you ever get on the wrong coach, idiot!* and my legs tried to get me out of there before the driver could close the door and pull out.

Then I recalled that the driver had greeted me by name and told me to come aboard.

I glanced at Sammann, who adopted a sort of long-suffering expression that only an Ita could really pull off, and shrugged.

So I swung my pack down into an empty row and took a seat. Just before I sat down, I scanned the faces of the Valers. They were Fraa Osa, the FAE; Suur Vay, the one who'd sewn me back together with fishing line; Suur Esma, the one who had danced across the plaza in Mahsht, charging the sniper; and Fraa Gratho, the one who had placed his body between me and the Gheeth leader's gun and later disarmed him.

I sat motionless for a while, wondering how to get ready for whatever was to come, wishing it would just start.

Next on the coach was Jesry. He saw what I had seen. In his face I thought I read some of the same emotions, but less so; he'd already been picked to go to space, he was probably expecting something like this. As he walked past me, he socked me on the shoulder. "Good to be with you," he said, "there is no one I would rather be vaporized with, my fraa."

"You're getting your wish," I said, recalling the talk we'd had at Apert.

"More of it than I wished for," he returned, and banged down into the seat across the aisle from me.

A few minutes later we were joined by Fraa Jad, who sat alone behind the officers. He nodded to me, and I nodded back; but once he had made himself comfortable, the Valers came up the aisle one by one to introduce themselves to him and to pay their respects.

A young female Ita came in, followed by a very old male one. They stood around Sammann for a few minutes, reciting numbers to one another. I fancied that we were going to have three Ita in our cell, but then the two visitors walked off the coach and we did not see them again.

When Fraa Arsibalt arrived, he stood at the head of the aisle, next to the driver, and considered fleeing for a good half-minute. Finally he drew an enormous breath, as if trying to suck every last bit of air out of the coach, and marched stolidly up the aisle, taking a seat behind Jesry. "I had damned well better get my own stained-glass window for this."

"Maybe you'll get an Order—or a concent," I proposed.

"Yes, maybe—if such things continue to exist by the time the Advent is finished."

"Come off it, we are the Hylaean Theoric World of these people!" I said. "How can they possibly destroy us?"

"By getting us to destroy ourselves."

"That's it," said Jesry. "You, Arsibalt, just appointed yourself the morale officer for Cell 317."

Jesry didn't understand some of the remarks that Arsibalt and I had exchanged, and so we set about explaining what had happened at messal. In the middle of this, Jules Verne Durand came aboard, hung all about with a motley kit of bags, bottles, and baskets. His presence in the cell must have been a last-minute improvisation; Ala couldn't have planned on *him*. He looked slightly aghast for a minute, then—if I read his face right—cheered up. "My namesake would be unspeakably proud!" he announced, and walked the full length of the aisle, introducing himself as Jules to each member of Cell 317 in turn. "I shall be pleased to starve to death in such company!"

"That alien must have some namesake!" Jesry muttered after Jules had passed us.

"My friend, I'll tell you all about him during the adventures that are to come!" said Jules, who had overheard; Laterran ears were pretty sharp, apparently.

"Ten down, one to go," called the driver to someone who was evidently standing at the base of the steps.

"All right," said a familiar voice, "let's go!" Lio bounded up onto the coach. The door hissed shut behind him and we began to move. Lio, like Jules before him, worked his way down the aisle, somehow maintaining his balance even as the coach banked and jounced over rough ground. Those unknown to him got handshakes. Edharian clock-winders got spine-cracking hugs. Valers got bows—though I noticed that even Fraa Osa bowed more formally, more deeply, to Lio than Lio to him. This was my first clue that Lio was our cell leader.

We were at the aerodrome in twenty minutes. The escort of military police vehicles really helped speed up the trip. No hassles about tickets or security; we drove through a guarded gate right onto the taxiway and pulled up next to a fixed-wing military aerocraft, capable of carrying just about anything, but rigged for passengers tonight. The officers at the head of the coach were its flight crew. We filed out, crossed ten paces of open pavement, and clambered up a rolling stair onto the craft. I wasn't happy. I wasn't sad. Most of all, I wasn't surprised. I saw Ala's logic perfectly: once she had accepted that she was making the "terrible decision," the only way forward was really to make it—to take it all the way. To put all of her favorite people together. The risk was greater for her—the risk, that is, that we'd all be lost, and she'd spend the rest of her life knowing she'd been responsible for it. But the risk, for each of us individually, was less, because we could help one another through it. And if we died, we'd die in good company.

"Is there a way to send a message to Suur Ala?" I asked Sammann, after we'd all claimed seats, and the engines had revved up enough to mask my voice. "I want to tell her that she was right."

"Consider it done," said Sammann. "Is there anything else—as long as I have a channel open?"

I considered it. There was much I could—should—have said. "Is it a private channel?" I asked.

"Don't be ridiculous," he pointed out.

"No," I said, "nothing further."

Sammann shrugged and turned to his jeejah. The craft lunged forward. I fell into a seat, groped in the dark for the cold buckles, and strapped myself in.

Part 11

ADVENT

◦◦

Teglon: An extremely challenging geometry problem worked on at Orithena and, later, all over Arbre, by subsequent generations of theors. The objective is to tile a regular decagon with a set of seven different shapes of tiles, while observing certain rules.

—THE DICTIONARY, *4th edition, A.R. 3000*

Red light woke me, or kept me from sleeping in the first place. It was not the clear, cold blood-red of warnings and emergencies, but pink/orange, warm, diffuse. It was coming in through the windows of the aerocraft, which were few and tiny. I unbuckled myself, staggered over to one—for I'd lain wrong, and my limbs were tingling and floppy—and squinted out at a spectacular dawn above the same ice-scape I'd recently traversed on a sledge.

For a confused minute I fancied we might, for some reason, be headed back to Ecba. But I had no success matching the mountain ranges and glaciers below against those I recollected. Out of habit I looked for Sammann, hoping he could conjure up a map. But he was huddled with Jules Verne Durand. Both were wearing headsets. Sammann just listened. Jules alternated between listening and speaking, but he did a lot more of the latter. Sometimes he'd sketch on Sammann's jeejah, and Sammann would transmit the image.

I found myself irked. The Laterran's presence in Cell 317 had seemed like a medal pinned on our chests. Through him we would know things, be capable of deeds, beyond all other cells. But I hadn't bargained on the wireless link to the Reticulum that would make him fair game for any Panjandrum who was feeling curious about something. They were pumping him dry before he was rendered useless by inanition. I couldn't hear a word because of the noise of the plane, but I could tell he'd been at it for a while, and that he was tired, groping for words, doubling back midsentence to repair conjugations. Orth was a murderously difficult language and I thought it a kind of miracle that Jules spoke it as well as he did, having practiced it for only a couple of years (which, we'd calculated, was about how long the Geometers had been in a position to receive signals from Arbre). Either Laterrans were smarter than we, or he was prodigiously gifted.

Arsibalt was up, pacing the aisles. He joined me at the window and we began shouting at each other. From our recollected geography we convinced ourselves that we were descending from the pole along a more easterly meridian than the one that passed through Ecba. This was confirmed as we left the ice and the tundra behind and entered into more temperate places: there was a lot of forest down there, but few cities.

No wonder people were slow to get up; we'd jumped forward through more than half a dozen time zones. I'd fooled myself into thinking I'd had a full night's sleep. In fact, I might not have slept at all.

Lio had been sitting alone in the front row, trying to make friends with a military-style jeejah. I noticed he had set it aside, so I went up and sat next to him. "Jammed," he announced.

I turned and looked back at Sammann and Jules. They were peeling the phones off their heads. Sammann caught my eye and threw up his hands disgustedly. Jules, on the other hand, seemed relieved to have been cut free of the Ret; he sank back heavily in his seat, closed his eyes, and began to rub his face, then to massage his scalp.

I turned back to Lio. "Such a move must have been anticipated," I said. But he had got into one of those Lio-trances where he did not respond to words. I grabbed the jeejah, whacked him on the shoulder with it, threw up my hands, tossed it aside. He watched me curiously, then grinned. "The Ita can still make the Reticulum run on land lines and other things," he said. "When we stop moving, we can get patched in once more."

"What are your orders?" I asked.

"Go to ground—which we're doing now. All the other cells are doing it too."

"Then what?"

"At the place where we're going, there'll be equipment prepositioned. We're supposed to train on it."

"What kind of equipment?"

"Don't know, but here's a hint: Jesry is in charge of training."

I looked over at Jesry, who had commandeered a row of seats and constructed a sort of amphitheatre of documents all around himself. He was scanning these with an intensity that I had learned, long ago, never to interrupt.

"We're going into space," I concluded.

"Well," Lio said, "that *is* where the problem is."

I decided to take advantage of the noise, and of the fact that our wireless link was down. "What news of the Everything Killers?" I asked.

He looked as though in the earliest stages of airsickness. "I think I can tell you how they worked."

"Okay."

He pantomimed a punch to my face, pulled it so his knuckles met my cheek and nudged my head. "Violence is mostly about energy delivery. Fists, clubs, swords, bullets, death rays—their purpose is to dump energy into a person's body."

"What about poison?"

"I said *mostly*. Don't go Kefedokhles. Anyway, what's the most concentrated source of energy they knew about around the time of the Terrible Events?"

"Nuclear fission."

He nodded. "And the stupidest way of using it was to split a whole lot of nuclei in the air above a city, just burn everything. It works, but it's dirty and it destroys a lot of stuff that doesn't need destroying. Better to nuke the people only."

"How do you manage that?"

"The amount of fissile material you need to kill a person is microscopic. That's the easy part. The problem is delivering it to the right people."

"So, is this a dirty bomb type of scenario?"

"Much more elegant. They designed a reactor the size of a pinhead. It's a little mechanism, with moving parts, and a few different kinds of nuclear material in it. When it's turned off, it's almost totally inert. You could eat these reactors by the spoonful and it would be no worse than eating one of Suur Efemula's bran muffins. When the reactor goes to the 'on' configuration it sprays neutrons in every direction and kills—well—*everything* that is alive within a radius of—depending on exposure time—up to half a mile."

"Hence the name," I said. "What's the delivery mechanism?"

"Whatever you can dream up," he said.

"What causes them to turn on?"

He shrugged. "Body heat. Respiration. The sound of human voices. A timer. Certain genetic sequences. A radio transmission. The *absence* of a radio transmission. Shall I go on?"

"No. But what kinds of delivery mechanisms and triggers is the Sæcular Power looking at *now*?"

He got a distant look. "Remember, launching mass into space is expensive. With the amount of energy it takes to launch a single human, you could get thousands of Everything Killers into orbit. They'd be too small to show up on most radar. If you could get even a few of them into the vicinity of the *Daban Urnud* . . ."

"Yeah, I can see the strategy clearly. Which leads to the profoundly sickening thought—"

"Are *we* going to be asked to deliver these things?" Lio said. "I think the answer is no. If anything, we are going to be a diversion."

"We'll distract them," I translated, "while some other technique is used to deliver the Everything Killers."

Lio nodded.

"That's inspiring," I said.

He shrugged. "I could be wrong," he pointed out.

I felt like going outside and getting some fresh air. In lieu of which I walked up and down the aisles for a bit. Jules Verne Durand was asleep. Next to him, Sammann was bent over his jeejah. But I thought it was jammed? Looking over his shoulder, I saw he was making some sort of calculation.

Looking over Jesry's, I saw that he was, indeed, reading the manual for a space suit. This demanded a double-take. But it was as simple as that. Suur Vay was in an adjoining row, poring over many of the same documents, swapping them with Jesry from time to time. The other Valers were asleep. Fraa Jad was awake and chanting, though my ears were hard put to disentangle his drone from that of the engines. I went back to staring out the window.

We angled across a range of old, worn-down mountains and struck out over an expanse of brown that ran to the eastern horizon: the grass of the steppe, browned by the summer sun. The craft was descending. A river flashed beneath us. Then the industrial skirt of a modestly sized city. We landed at a military airbase that seemed to stretch on forever, since land here was as plentiful as it was flat, and there was no incentive to make things compact.

A canvas-backed military drummon came out to collect us. We had no windows, and could not see out the front, but through the aperture in the back we watched the streets of an ancient, none too prosperous city ramifying in our dust. There were more animals on highways than we were used to, more people carrying things that in other places might have been entrusted to wheels. Of a sudden, things got dense and old, all yellow brick adorned with polychrome tiles. A heavy shadow passed over our heads, as if we were being strafed. But no, we had only passed through an arch in a thick wall. Three successive gates were closed and bolted behind us. The vehicle stopped on a tiled plaza. We clambered out to find ourselves in a courtyard, embraced by an ancient building four stories high: stone, brick, and wrought iron, softened by cascades of flowering vines on trunks as thick as my waist. A fountain in the center supplied water for these and for gnarled fruit trees growing in pots and casting pools of shade on what would otherwise have been an unpleasant place to stand.

"Welcome to the Caravansery of Elkhazg," said a voice in cultured Orth. We turned to see an old man in the shade of a tree: a man who did not seem to belong here, in the sense that he was of an ethnic group one would expect to find in another part of Arbre. "I am the Heritor. My name is Magnath Foral, and I shall be pleased to serve as your host."

After introductions, Magnath Foral gave us a quick explanation of the history of Elkhazg. I made no effort to follow most of this, since I only needed a few cues and hints to reconstruct what I had been taught of the place as a fid. It was one of the oldest Cartasian maths, founded by fraas and suurs who had personally witnessed the Fall of Baz, and known Ma Cartas. They had trekked across forests and mountains to build this thing more or less out in the middle of nowhere, on an oxbow lake a few miles from the main course of a river. A trade route from the east crossed the river not far away—close enough to give them access to commerce when they needed it, not so close as to be a distraction or a menace. Centuries later, a rough winter followed by a stormy spring caused some trouble involving ice dams that altered the course of the river and turned the oxbow lake back into an active channel. The trade route adapted, choosing Elkhazg as the best place to make a crossing—since one of the side-effects of the math had been the development of a relatively stable and prosperous Sæcular community around its walls.

A certain kind of mathic personality would then have abandoned the place for something more remote, perhaps up in the mountains. The wardens of Elkhazg, though, weren't that way, and had come to notice that the goods being carried on the backs of the beasts passing over the river included not just fabrics, furs, and spices but books and scrolls. In a compromise that would have made Ma Cartas kick her way out of her chalcedony sarcophagus and come after them with a broken bottle, they had spun off a thriving side business in the form of a caravansery adjacent to the math, and a ferry across the river. The one tariff that they charged was that the fraas and suurs of Elkhazg be allowed to make a copy of every book and scroll that passed through. Books were copied whose meanings they did not even know. But they interpreted their mandate somewhat broadly and began, as well, to make copies of the geometrical designs that they saw on fabrics, pottery, and other goods. For these fraas and suurs had a particular interest in plane geometry and in tiling problems. So, to make a long story somewhat shorter, Elkhazg had become synonymous in the minds of theors all over the world with tiling problems. Important tile shapes and theorems about their properties were named after fraas and suurs who had lived here, or specific walls and floors in this complex.

It was no longer a math. At the time of the Rebirth its library had been dispersed and copied all over the world, and the building had fallen into private hands. It had not been made over into a new math at the time of the Reconstitution. Instead—as Magnath Foral did not come out and say, but as was easy enough to figure out—it had been taken over by a long-lived complex of financial interests similar to—quite likely the same as—the one that ran Ecba.

Fraa Jad skipped the intro and wandered off into some other courtyard. Elkhazg had been big and rich and its courtyards went on and on. Now it must appear as a large, rambling black hole in the population density map of the city, since the only people who dwelled here were Magnath Foral and another man who was his liaison-partner; some visiting avout (though these had all been sent packing yesterday); and a staff of janitors-cum-curators who looked after the place. For one of the problems with this kind of art—i.e., tiles cemented to stone walls—was that you couldn't cart it off to a museum.

My brain ought to have been shutting down, since I'd had essentially no rest since the shovel experiment at Tredegarh the day before, and the time since then had been freakishly eventful. But the visual environment of Elkhazg was overwhelmingly rich—would have been so even had I not known that every pattern of tiles was not merely a mesmerizing, intricate work of art, but a profound theorical statement as well, shouting at me in a language I was too tired or stupid to understand. This acted like a shot of jumpweed extract, or something, that kept me awake for another hour at the cost of some sanity. When I closed my eyes to get some respite from the relentless grandeur, questions crept out of the darkness. That our host had the same family name as Madame Secretary was, of course, interesting. Was it a coincidence that Cell 317 had ended up here? Of course not. What did it mean? Impossible to say. Should I even be trying to puzzle it out now? No—no more than I should be trying to grasp the significance of the tiling patterns that spread over every surface around me, and seemed to be trying to crawl beneath my closed eyelids and invade my brain.

One of the courtyards was a Decagon—of course. Fraa Jad

found it. The Teglon had already been solved on it, perhaps by some master geometer of yore, perhaps by a syndev. None of us had ever seen a full solution in person before, so we spent a while gawking. Stationed around the edges were baskets of extra Teglon tiles in a different color, which Fraa Jad was nudging around with his toe. It occurred to me I'd never seen him sleep. Maybe Thousanders did something else. We left him to the Teglon. Magnath Foral took the rest of us to the Old Cloister, which had not been remodeled in five thousand years. That is to say it lacked electricity or even plumbing. Each of us got a cell. Mine had a bed, and a lot of tiles. I closed some preposterously ancient and rickety shutters so that I'd not have to see, and consequently think about, the tiles, then sank to my knees and located the bed by groping.

"It occurred to me," said Arsibalt, the next time both of us were awake, "I don't think we have anything like this."

"*We* meaning—?"

"The modern, post-Reconstitution mathic world."

"And *this* meaning—?"

He held up his hands and gazed about in an *are you blind?* sort of gesture.

We were standing next to a table in an alcove on the ground floor, open to the cloister on one side. The floor of the cloister itself was covered with thousands of identical, horn-shaped, nine-sided tiles that had been joined together with machine-tool precision into a nonrepeating double-spiral pattern that was giving me motion sickness just looking at it. I turned my back on this and looked at a loaf of bread that was resting on the table. This was so fresh that steam was gushing out of the end—Arsibalt, an infamous heel-filcher, had already got to it. The loaf had been made by braiding several ropes of dough together in a non-trivial pattern that, I feared, had deep knot-theoretical significance and was named after some Elkhazgian Saunt. "I just don't think we have anything this ancient, this—well, *fantastic*," Arsibalt continued through a crunchy mouthful of bread-heel.

"There's more than one way to be Inviolate, I guess," I said, tearing off a hunk of bread, and sitting down at the table—which, inevitably, was ancient and covered with precision-cut tiles of diverse exotic woods. "You can simply stop being a math."

"And thereby become exempt from Sacks."

"Exactly."

"But what kind of entity owns something for four thousand years?"

"That's what I kept asking myself on Ecba."

"Ah, so you have a head start on me, Fraa Erasmas."

"I guess you could think of it that way."

"What conclusion have you reached?"

I stalled for a while by chewing the bread—which was possibly the best I'd ever had. "That I don't care," I finally said. "I don't need to know the bylaws, the org chart, the financial statements, the tedious history of the Lineage."

Arsibalt was horrified. "But how can you not be fascinated by—"

"I *am* fascinated," I insisted. "That's the problem. I am suffering from fascination burnout. Of all the things that are fascinating, I have to choose just one or two."

"Here's a candidate," announced Sammann, who had crossed into the cloister from an adjoining court where, I inferred, Reticulum access was to be had. He sat down next to me and laid his jeejah on the table. The screen was covered with the calculations I'd noticed him doing on the plane. "Chronology," he said. "According to Jules, the amount of time that has passed since the *Daban Urnud* embarked on its first inter-cosmic journey is 885 and a half years."

"Whose years?" Jesry asked, skittering down the stairs from his cell, homing in on the smell of the bread. He closed with it like a wrestler and ripped off a hunk.

"That, of course, is the whole question," Sammann said with a grin.

Arsibalt noticed a pitcher of water on a sideboard and began pouring it out into earthenware tumblers incised with geometric patterns.

"If Urnud years are anything like ours, that is a long time," I said. "Thank you, Fraa Arsibalt."

"The Urnudans, and later the Troäns, wandered for a *long* time between Advents. Jules thinks it explains why they are a little tetchy."

"Can we get a conversion factor—" Jesry said, in a tone that said *I'll be damned if I let this conversation wander.*

"That's what I've been working on," said Sammann, nodding thanks to Arsibalt. He took a draught of water. Elkhazg was in a climate that sucked the moisture out of you. "Problem is, Jules is a linguist. Hasn't paid a lot of attention to this. Knows the timeline in Urnud years—which is their standard unit up there—but not the conversion factor to Arbre years. Anyway, I was able to back it out from some clues—"

"What clues?" Jesry demanded.

"While the rest of us were evacuating Tredegarh, a unit of Valers assaulted the quarters of the so-called Matarrhites, and captured a lot of documents and syndevs before the Urnud/Tro guys could destroy them. My brethren are still virtualizing the syndevs—never mind—but some of the documents have timestamps in Urnud units, which can be matched against recent events on our calendar."

"Wait a moment, please, how can we even read a document in Urnudan?" Arsibalt asked, sitting down and helping himself to the other heel.

"We can't. But a cryptanalyst can easily see that many of the documents have the same format, which includes a string of characters readily decipherable as a timestamp. And they have a special, phonetic alphabet for transliterating proper names; they haul it out and dust it off whenever they encounter a new planet. This too is elementary to decipher. So if we see a document that has the phonetic transcription of *Jesry* and of his loctor at the Plenary—"

"We can infer it must be a report of the Plenary I participated in after I came back from space," Jesry said, "and we know the Arbre date of that event. Very well. I agree that such givens would enable you to begin estimating a conversion factor relating Arbran to Urnudan years."

"Yes," said Sammann. "And there is still some error margin, but I believe that, in Arbran years, the Urnudans began their inter-cosmic journey 910 years ago, plus or minus 20."

"Somewhere between 890 and 930 years ago," I translated, but that was the limit of my arithmetical powers so early in the morning. Sammann was glaring fiercely into my eyes, willing me to wake up a little faster, to go the next step, but mere calculation was not my strong suit, especially when I had an audience.

"Between 2760 and 2800 A.R.?" said a new voice: Lio, coming across the cloister with Jules Verne Durand. These two did not look as if they'd only just gotten up; I guessed Lio had been pumping the Laterran for information.

"Yes!" Sammann said. "The time of the Third Sack."

One of Magnath Foral's staff came out with a huge bowl of peeled and cut-up fruit and began ladling it into bowls, which we passed around.

Jules tore off a piece of bread and began to eat it. This surprised me at first, since he could not derive any nutritional value from it; but I reasoned it would fill his stomach and make him feel less hungry.

"Wait a second," Jesry said, "are you trying to develop a theory that there's a cause-and-effect relationship at work? That the Urnudans began their journey *because of* events that took place *here on Arbre?*"

"I'm just saying it is a coincidence that needs looking at," Sammann said.

We ate and thought. I had a head start on the eating, so I briefed Jesry and Lio—as well as others who drifted in, such as three of the Valers—on the conversations we'd had in the Plurality of Worlds Messal about the Wick and the idea that Arbre might be the HTW of other worlds, such as Urnud. The newcomers then had to be brought up to speed on the first part of this morning's conversation, so the conversation forked and devolved into a general hubbub for a couple of minutes.

"So information *could* flow from Arbre to Urnud, in that scenario," Jesry concluded, loudly enough to shut everyone up and retake the floor. "But why would the Third Sack trigger such behavior on the part of an Urnudan star captain?"

"Fraa Jesry, remember the margin of error that Sammann was careful to specify," Arsibalt said. "The trigger could have been anything that happened in this cosmos in the four decades beginning around 2760. And I'll remind you that this would include—"

"Events *leading up to* the Third Sack," I blurted.

Silence. Discomfort. Averted gazes. Except for Jules Verne Durand, who was staring right at me and nodding. I recalled his willingness to broach excruciating topics at Messal, and decided to draw strength from that. "I'm done tiptoeing around this topic," I said. "It all fits together. Fraa Clathrand of Edhar was the tip of an iceberg. Others back then—who knows how many thousands?—worked on a praxis of some kind. Procians and Halikaarnians alike. It's hard to know the truth of what this praxis was capable of. The parking ramp dinosaur hints at what it could do *when they made mistakes*. We know what the Sæculars thought of it, how they reacted. The records were destroyed, the practitioners massacred—except in the Three Inviolates. There's no telling what people like Fraa Jad have been up to since then. I'll bet they've just been nursing it along—"

"Keeping the pilot light burning," Lio called.

"Yeah," I said. "But something about what they did, circa 2760, when the praxis reached its zenith, sent out a signal that propagated down the Wick, and was noticed, somehow, by the theors of Urnud."

"It *drew* them here, you're saying," said Lio, "like a dinner bell."

"Like the fragrance of this bread," I said.

"Perhaps it's not just the smell of the bread that has drawn others to this room, Fraa Erasmas," Arsibalt suggested. "Perhaps it is the sound of the conversation. Half-overheard words, not understandable at a distance, but enough to pique the interest of any sentient person in range of the voices."

"You're saying that's what it might have been like to the Urnudan theors on that ship," I said, "when they received—I don't know—emanations, hints, signals, percolating down the Wick from Arbre."

"Precisely," said Arsibalt.

We all turned to Jules. He had removed some Laterran food from a bag and—having sated his appetite with stuff he could not digest—was now eating a few bites of what his body could use. He noticed the attention, shrugged, and swallowed. "Do not hold your breath waiting for an explanation from the Pedestal. Those of 900 years ago were rational theors, to be sure. But during the long, dark years of their wandering, it became something better recognizable as a priesthood. And the closer these priests get to their god, the more they fear it."

"I wonder if we might calm them down just a little by getting them to see they're not actually that close," Jesry said.

"What do you mean?" Yul asked.

"Fraa Jad's an interesting guy and all," Jesry said, "but he doesn't seem like a god, or even a prophet, to me. Whatever it is that he's doing when he chants, or plays Teglon all night, I don't think it is godlike. I think he's just picking up signals coming to Arbre from farther up the Wick."

By now everyone had showed up and eaten except for Fraa Jad. We found him sitting in the middle of the Decagon, eating some food that had been brought out to him by the staff. The Decagon looked altogether different. When we had passed across it yesterday, it had been paved in hand-sized clay tiles, dark brown, and grooved: just like the ones I'd played with at Orithena, except proportionally smaller. The groove seemed to run unbroken from one vertex to the opposite—I had not taken the time to verify this, but I assumed it was a correct solution. For those who wanted to try their hands at it, baskets of white porcelain tiles, marked with black glazed lines instead of grooves, had been stacked all around the edges. This morning, though, the baskets were empty, and Fraa Jad was enjoying his breakfast on a seamless white courtyard decorated with a wandering black line. During the night he had tiled the whole thing. When we understood this, we burst into applause. Arsibalt and Jesry were shouting as if at a ball game. The Valers approached Fraa Jad and bowed very low.

Out of curiosity, I backtracked to the outskirts of the Decagon and stepped off its edge—for the surface was several inches higher than the adjoining pavement. I squatted down and lifted up one of Jad's white tiles to expose a small patch of brown tiling underneath. Jad's was, as I'd expected, a wholly different solution of the Teglon—the positions of the older brown tiles didn't match up with those of the new ones, proving that Fraa Jad had not merely copied the older solution.

"It is the fourth," said a gentle voice. I looked up to find Magnath Foral watching me. He nodded at the tile in my hand. Looking more closely at the edge of the Decagon, I perceived, now, that underneath the brown tiles was a layer of green ones, and below that, one of terra-cotta.

"Well," I said, "I guess you need to bake up a new set of tiles."

Foral nodded, and said, deadpan: "I don't think there is any great hurry."

I set the white tile back into its place, stood up, and took a step up to the Decagon. It was open to the sky. I craned my neck and looked straight up. "Think they noticed?" I asked. Magnath Foral got a bemused look and said nothing.

Cell 317 moved on to convene in a courtyard we'd not visited yesterday. This one was circular, and roofed by a living bower. They had somehow trained half a dozen enormous flowering vines to arch across the top of the space and grapple with one another to form a stable dome of interlocked branches, fifty feet above the ground. Dappled light shone through it to illuminate the cool space below, but seen from above it would look like a hemisphere of solid green, freckled with color. Pallets of mysterious but expensive-looking stuff had been stationed around the edge of the yard. We devoted the remainder of the morning to breaking these open, getting rid of packaging materials, and drawing up an inventory: mindless labor that everyone badly needed.

That we'd be going into space was obvious from the nature of this stuff. By weight, it was ninety-nine percent containers. We were opening beautiful twenty-pound lockers to find pieces of equipment that weighed as much as dried flowers. We shed our bolts and chords in favor of nearly weightless charcoal-grey cover-alls. "It's all for the best," Jesry said, eyeing me. "In zero gravity, the bolt doesn't hang, if you get my meaning. Things would get ugly fast."

"Speak for yourself," I said. "Anything else I need to know?"

"If you get sick—which you will—it'll last for three days. After that, you get better or you get used to it. I'm not sure which."

"Do you think we'll even *have* three days?"

"If they were only sending us up as a diversion—"

"Just to get killed, you mean?"

"Yeah—then they could just send Procians."

Our conversation had begun to draw in others, such as the Val-ers, who did not understand Jesry's sense of humor. He cleared his throat and called out, "What is happening, my fraa?" to Lio.

Lio sprang to the top of a tarp-covered pallet, and everyone went silent.

"We're not allowed to know yet what the mission is," he began, "or why we're doing it. We just have to get there."

"Get where?" Yul demanded.

"That *Daban Urnud*," Lio said.

Not that we hadn't been paying attention, but: we were *really* paying attention now. Everyone seemed brighter. Especially Jules. "Food, here I come."

"How are we going to get aboard a heavily armed—" Arsibalt began to ask.

"We haven't been told that yet," Lio said. "Which is just fine, because simply getting off the ground is difficult enough. We can't use the normal launch sites. I would presume that the Pedestal have threatened to rod them if they notice launch preparations. That means we can't use the usual rockets, because those are tailor-made to be launched only from those sites. And that, in turn, means we can't use the usual space vehicles—such as the one you rode on, Jesry—because those can only be launched by said rockets. But there is an alternative. During the last big war, a family of ballistic missiles was developed. They use storable propellants and they launch from the backs of vehicles that ramble around the countryside on treads."

"That can't work," Jesry protested. "A ballistic missile doesn't get its payload to orbit. It merely throws a warhead at the other side of the world."

"But suppose you take off that warhead and replace it with something like this," Lio said. He jumped down, got a grip on the tarp, collected himself, and snapped it away with a forceful movement of the hips and the arms. Revealed was a piece of equipment not a great deal larger than a major household appliance. "A gazebo on top of a welding rig" was how Yul might have described it, if only he had been here. The "gazebo" was a very small one—though, as Lio demonstrated, it was large enough to house one person in a fetal position. Its roof was a lens of pressed sheet metal with some sort of hard coating. It was supported by four legs: spindly-looking, triangulated struts, like miniature radio towers.

So the gazebo had a roof and pillars, but it lacked a floor. In lieu of that were only three lugs projecting inward from a structural ring. At the moment, these were spanned by a sheet of plywood, which supported Lio's back as he curled up on top of it. Once he rolled out, though, he took the plywood away to reveal nothing below except for structural members and plumbing. There were two big tanks—a torus encircling a sphere—and several smaller ones, all spherical, and none larger than what you'd see on the shelves of a sporting goods store. These were profoundly ensnared in plumbing and cable-harnesses. Sticking out the bottom, like an insect's stinger, was a rocket nozzle, dismayingly small. "The real one will have a nozzle skirt bolted onto it," Lio informed us, "as big again as this whole stage."

"*Stage!?*" Sammann exclaimed. "You mean, as in—"

"Yes!" said Lio. "That's what I'm trying to tell you. I'm sorry I wasn't clearer. This is the upper stage of a rocket. There's one for each of us." Then, so that we could get a better view of the nozzle, he grabbed a strut with one hand and hauled up. The entire stage rocked back, exposing the underside.

"You've got to be kidding!" I exclaimed, and put my hand next to his and shouldered him out of the way. He let it drop into my hand. The entire stage weighed considerably less than I did. Then everyone else had to try it.

"Where's the rest of it?" Jesry asked.

There was an awkward silence.

"This is the whole thing," proclaimed Jules Verne Durand, understanding it perfectly, even though he was seeing it for the first time. "The conception is monyafeek!"

"Well, since you appear to be an expert on monyafeeks," Jesry said, "maybe you could tell us how four legs and a roof are going to contain a pressurized atmosphere!"

"It's not called a monyafeek," Lio protested mildly. "It's a—oh, never mind."

"We will have only space suits, am I right?" Jules asked, looking to Lio.

Lio nodded. "Jules gets it. Since we need space suits *anyway*, complete with life support and sanitation and all the rest, it'd be redundant to send up a pressurized capsule comprising extra copies of the same systems."

I was expecting Jesry to lodge further protests but he underwent a sudden conversion, and held up both hands to silence murmurs. "I have been there," he reminded us, "and I can tell you there is no part of the shared space capsule experience I'm eager to relive. You don't know the meaning of nasty until you've been blindsided by a drifting blob of someone else's vomit. Don't even get me started on what passes for toilets. How hard it is to see out those tiny windows. I think this is a great idea: each of us sealed up in our own personal spaceship, keeping our farts to ourselves, enjoying the panoramic view out the facemask."

"How long is it possible to live in a space suit?" I asked.

"You're going to love this," Jesry proclaimed, taking the floor with a nod from Lio. Jesry strode over to where he, with help from Fraa Gratho, had, for the last hour or so, been assembling space suits. He approached one that seemed to be complete, and slapped a green metal canister socketed into the suit's backpack. "Liquid oxygen! A whole four hours' supply, right here."

"Provided you show discipline in its use," put in Suur Vay.

"*Liquid!?* As in cryogenic?" Sammann asked.

"Of course."

"How long will it stay cold?"

"In space? It's not such an issue. It'll stay cold as long as the fuel cell has fuel to run the chiller." Slapping a red canister, he went on, "Liquid hydrogen. Easy on, easy off." He twisted it off, showed us some kind of complicated latching/gasket hardware, then twisted it back on.

"So we're competing against a fuel cell for the available oxygen?" Arsibalt asked.

"Think of it as coöperation."

"What about waste products?" someone asked, but Jesry was ready. "Carbon dioxide is scrubbed here." He twisted off a white can and waved it around. "When it's used up, slap on a new one. Then—you'll like this—take the old one over to the tender." He paced over to a separate piece of equipment that looked as if it belonged to the same genus, but a different species, from the space suits. It had color-coded sockets all over it for tanks and canisters. He jacked the scrubber onto one of these. "It bakes the CO_2 out of the scrubber. When this bar has changed color"—he pointed to an indicator on the side of the can—"it's ready to use again."

"This device is also a reservoir of air and fuel?" asked Suur Vay, eyeing the sockets for oxygen and hydrogen canisters.

"If it's available, this is where you'll get it," Jesry said. "It's meant to be connected to a water bladder and an energy supply—usually solar panels, but in our case, a little nuke. It breaks the water down into hydrogen and oxygen, liquefies them, and fills any tank you slap onto it. And it uses heat to recycle the scrubbers, as I was saying. Likewise, when your waste bags fill up—we'll discuss those later—you attach them here—" pointing fastidiously to an array of yellow fittings.

"Do you mean to say we'll be defecating inside the suits?" Arsibalt asked.

"Thank you for volunteering to demonstrate this amazing feature of the praxis!" Jesry proclaimed. "Lio and Raz, would you be so kind as to give your fraa some privacy?"

Lio and I collected Arsibalt's bolt from where he had left it, and held it up, stretched between us, to make a screen as Arsibalt shed his coverall. Meanwhile, Jesry fetched a double extra large space suit and trundled it over. It was suspended from a rolling contraption that he called the Donning Rig. The suit consisted of a big rigid construct, the Head and Torso Unit or, inevitably, HTU, whose upper back hinged open like a refrigerator door. Each arm and each leg was built up out of several short, stiff, bulbous pods, stacked like beads on a string. This gave it a different appearance from the space suits I remembered seeing in speelies, and on the Warden of Heaven: this one was bigger, more rounded, reassuringly solid. Another big difference, at least cosmetically, was that this suit—like all of the others that Jesry had been working on—was matte black.

Arsibalt stepped toward the Donning Rig, raising his hands to grasp a strategically located chin-up bar, and pulling/climbing to a step poised at the threshold of the suit's back door. He was surprisingly game. Perhaps he was remembering spec-fic speelies he used to watch before he was Collected, or perhaps he just didn't like being naked. With some help from Jesry he introduced one pointed toe, then the other, into the leg-holes at the base of the HTU, and lowered himself into them. As his feet descended, the hard segments rotated in different ways. Each bulb, it seemed, was joined to its neighbors by an airtight bearing. All of them could rotate independently, so that elbows and knees could bend normally without the need for a complex joint mechanism. Arsibalt looked even more roly-poly than usual now. He flexed one leg, than the other, giving us a look at how the segments allowed movement by rotating against each other.

"I want to you take notice of the bags ringing your thighs and waist," Jesry said, indicating some rubberish-looking stuff hanging limp from the inner walls of the HTU. "In a few minutes, those are going to rock your world."

"It is so noted," Arsibalt said, thrusting one hand, then the other, into the arm-constructs, which seemed to end in blunt hemispherical domes—handless stumps. All we could see now was his back and his arse. Jesry did us all the favor of slamming the door on that.

Now that our fraa was decent, Lio and I let the bolt drop, then migrated round to Arsibalt's front side. We could barely hear his muffled voice. Jesry jacked a wire into a socket on the chest and turned on an amplifier. We heard Arsibalt on a speaker: "There's much for my hands to learn about down here—I wish I could see what I was doing."

"We'll go over it," Jesry promised. He spoke distractedly, since he was busy examining an array of readouts on the front of the suit—making sure his fraa wasn't going to asphyxiate in there. I noticed others staring at Arsibalt's front and looking amused, so I came around to that side of him and discovered that a small flat-panel speely screen was planted in the middle of his chest. It was showing a live feed of Arsibalt's face, taken by a speelycaptor inside the helmet. It was quite distorted because shot through a fisheye lens at close range, but gave us something to look at other than the opaque smoked-glass face mask. "Pray tell, what are all these nozzles in front of my mouth?" Arsibalt asked, eyes downcast and scanning.

"Left, water. Right, food and, as warranted, pharmaceuticals. The big one in the middle is the scupper."

"The what?"

"You throw up into it. Don't miss."

"Ah." Arsibalt's eyes rose to look out the face-mask at where his hands ought to have been. He raised one arm until its stump was up where he could see it. A hatch popped open. We all jumped back as something like a giant metal spider sprang out of it, flailing its limbs. On a second look, this proved to be a skeletal hand: bones, joints, and tendons mimicking those of a natural hand, but all made of machined, black-anodized metal, and skinless, unless you counted the black rubber pads on the tips of the fingers. It all grew out of a wrist joint that was fixed to the end of the stump. At first, it twitched and flopped spasmodically. One by one, the joints seemed to come under Arsibalt's control, and it began to move like a real hand. His other arm came up, the hatch popped open, and another hand emerged from it. This one, though, was less human-looking; it was studded with small tools.

"Explain what you are doing with your hands," I requested.

"The ends of the arms are roomy," Arsibalt said. "There is a sort of glove, into which I can insert my hand. It is mechanically connected to the skeletal hand that you can all see."

"Pure mechanism?" Sammann asked. "No servos?"

"Strictly mechanical," said Jesry. "See for yourself." And we gathered round for a closer look. The skelehand was animated by a number of metallic ribbons and pushrods that all disappeared into the arm-stump where, we gathered, they were connected directly to the internal glove that Arsibalt was wearing.

"Simple, in a way," was Fraa Osa's verdict, "yet very complex."

"Yes. Except for the airtight seals, the whole thing could have been made by a medieval artisan with a lot of time on his hands," Jesry said. "Fortunately, the mathic world has a large number of medieval artisans. And, believe it or not, it's easier to build something like this than it is to make a pressurized space suit glove that's actually good for anything."

"There are other controls as well, in the end of the stump," Arsibalt volunteered. "If I withdraw my hand from the glove—" The skelehand wiggled, then went limp. It snapped back into its storage compartment in the end of the stump, and the hatch closed over it. "Now," Arsibalt said, "I'm groping around on the inner surface of the stump, which is replete with all manner of buttons and switches."

"Be careful with those," Jesry suggested. "Most of the suit's functions are controlled by voice commands, but there are manual overrides that you don't want to mess with."

"How are we to tell all of these buttons and whatnot apart, since we can't see them?" Arsibalt asked, and on the speely screen we could see his eyes wandering around uselessly as he felt his way around the inside of the stump.

"Most of them are a keyboard for entering alphanumeric data with the fingertips. Sammann will be able to use it immediately. The rest of us will have to hunt and peck."

"So," I asked, "overall, what do you think? How does it feel?"

"Surprisingly comfortable."

"As you've noticed, the suit touches you in relatively few places," Jesry said. "That is for comfort, and so that your core temp can be regulated by a simple air-conditioning system—obviates the tube garment that the Warden of Heaven had to wear. But where it touches you, it really grabs you—say the words *sanitary elimination cycle commence.*"

"Sanitary elimination cycle commence," Arsibalt repeated, with trepidation rising as he climbed to the end of this ungainly phrase. The words SANITARY ELIMINATION CYCLE appeared on a status panel below the speely of his face. His eyes got wide. "Oh, my god!" he exclaimed.

Everyone laughed. "Care to explain what's going on?" Jesry said.

"Those air bags you pointed out to me earlier—they inflated. Around my waist and upper thighs."

"Your pelvic region is now completely isolated from the rest of the suit," Jesry said.

"I'll say!"

"You can do whatever needs doing."

"I believe we can skip that part of the demonstration, Fraa Jesry."

"Have it your way. Say 'sanitary elimination cycle conclude.'"

Arsibalt said it, and we got to have another laugh as we saw and heard his reaction. "I'm being sprayed with warm water. Fore and aft."

"Yes. Boys and girls get the same treatment, like it or not," Jesry said. Jesry now hauled down a thick hose that was part of the donning rig, and jacked it into a not very dignified part of the suit's anatomy. "We don't have the infinite vacuum of space to draw on, so we fake it." He hit a switch and a vacuum cleaner howled for several seconds. More comedy on the speely screen. Arsibalt informed us that he was now being vigorously air-dried. Then: "It's over. The bags deflated."

"We know," Sammann said, reading the status panel.

"You spend some air every time you do this—so use it sparingly," Jesry cautioned us. "But the point is—"

"As long as the tender is up and running we can live in these things for a long time," I said.

"Yeah."

"This suit is altogether different from that worn by the Warden of Heaven," Fraa Osa pointed out. "More sophisticated."

"Beautifully machined," I said, wishing Cord could be here to admire the huge ring bearing that encircled Arsibalt's waist, just below the threshold of the back door, making it possible for him to swivel his hips and shoulders independently.

"It is literally unbelievable," was Arsibalt's verdict. "As highly as I rate our fraas and suurs of the Convox, I can't believe they could have designed something of such complexity on such short notice."

"They didn't," Jesry said, "this suit was designed, down to the last detail, twenty-six centuries ago."

"For the Big Nugget?" Sammann asked.

"Exactly. And *that* Convox had several years to devote to it. The plans were archived at Saunt Rab's, and preserved during the Third Sack by fraas and suurs who carried the books around on their backs their whole lives. Last year, when the Geometers dropped into orbit around Arbre, there was a whole round of Vocos that we at Edhar never heard about, just to dump talent into restarting the program. Money was spent on an inconceivable scale to build these"—he slapped Arsibalt's shoulder—"and those." He waved at the monyafeek. "Note the attachment points." He swiveled Arsibalt around so that the rest of us could see his back, and pointed out a triangular array of sockets, in the same configuration as the structural lugs on the monyafeek. "One plugs into the other—they become an integrated unit. So we don't need furniture—no acceleration couches. Air bags in the suit will inflate to cushion our bodies during launch."

"Impressive," Sammann said. "The only thing we won't be able to do in these things is sneak around."

Everyone looked at him blankly. He grinned, and waved at Arsibalt's chest, all lit up with speely feeds, alphanumeric displays, and status lights. "Pretty much rules out a covert operation."

Gratho stepped forward, grabbed a barely noticeable ridge projecting from the HTU at collarbone level, and pulled down. A retractable black screen deployed, slid down, and latched in place just above the waist bearing. All of the lights and displays were now concealed. Arsibalt was matte black from head to toe, as if he'd been sculpted out of damp carbon.

"It is remarkable," Osa pointed out, "when one considers that these were not even available when you, Fraa Jesry, went up with the Warden of Heaven."

Jesry nodded. "There are now sixteen of them."

"But there are eleven of us!" Arsibalt exclaimed, over his speaker. We'd forgotten he was there. His skelehand groped at his waist, found the latch for the screen, and yanked it back up to expose the speely. His familiar look of bulging-eyed surprise was comically magnified.

"That's right," said Jesry.

"The significance of that should be obvious," Lio said, "but I will spell it out: we can't screw this up. It is a similar story with the missile launchers. These were a military secret. There's no reason why the Pedestal—who have obtained almost all of their knowledge of Arbre from the leakage of popular culture into space—would know of their existence. They were specifically made to be hard to see from above. But as soon as one of them is launched, its thermal signature will be picked up on the Geometers' surveillance, and they'll know all about them. So they must be launched all at once, or not at all. There are a couple of hundred. They are all going to be sent up within the same ten-minute launch window, which happens to be three days from now. Eleven of them will be tipped with 'monyafeeks' carrying the members of this cell. Quite a few others will carry the equipment and consumables we'll be needing."

"And the remainder?" Sammann asked.

Lio said nothing, though he did throw a glance at me. Both of us were thinking of the Everything Killers. "Decoys and chaff," he said finally.

"What is it we're expected to do once we get up there?" Arsibalt asked.

"Consolidate a number of other payloads into a thrust platform—I won't dignify it as a 'vehicle'—that will inject us into a new orbit," Lio said, "an orbit that will bring us to a rendezvous with the *Daban Urnud*."

"We could have guessed that much," Jesry said. "What Fraa Arsibalt is really asking, is—"

Fraa Osa stepped forward, giving Lio an *if I may?* look. We hadn't heard much out of the Vale leader, so everyone got where they could see him. "The greatest difficulty for ones such as you shall be, not completion of the given tasks, but instead the humiliation and uncertainty that arise from not being able to know the entire plan. These emotions can hamper you. You must simply decide, now, either to proceed with the awareness that the entire plan might never be revealed to you—and, were it revealed, might have obvious defects—or to turn away and allow some other person to occupy the space suit that has been allotted to you." And then he stepped back. There was a minute of silence as all of us made our decisions. If that was the right word for what was going on in our heads. I didn't feel any of the emotions connected with real decision-making. To step away from this group at the moment was simply unthinkable. There was no decision to be made. Fraa Osa, who had devoted his entire life to preparing for such situations, no doubt knew this perfectly well. He wasn't *really* asking us to make a decision. He was telling us, in a reasonably diplomatic way, to shut up and concentrate on the matter at hand.

And so that is what we did eighteen hours a day until the truck came to pick us up and take us to the airfield. Though a casual observer might have thought we were working only half the time, and playing video games otherwise. Three of the cells that adjoined the courtyard had been equipped with syndevs hooked to big wraparound speely screens. In the center of each was a chair with disembodied spacesuit arms rigged to it. We'd take turns sitting in that chair with our hands stuck into the arms, groping at the controls. Projected on the screens around us was a simulation of what we might see out of our face-masks when we were floating around in low orbit, complete with all manner of readouts and indicators that, we were promised, would be superimposed on the view by the suit's built-in syndevs. The controls beneath our fingertips could be patched through to the thrusters on the monyafeeks so that, once we reached orbit, we'd be able to scoot around and accomplish certain tasks. Beneath the left hand was a little sphere that spun freely in a cradle; beneath the right, a mushroom-shaped stick that could be moved in four directions as well as pushed down or pulled up. The former controlled the suit's rotation, which was pretty easy to manage. The latter controlled translation—moving across space, as opposed to spinning in place. That would be tricky. Things in orbit didn't behave like what we were used to. Just to name one example: if I were pursuing another object in the same orbit, my natural instinct would be to fire a thruster that would kick me forward. But that would move me into a *higher* orbit, so the thing I was chasing would soon drop *below* me. Everything we knew down here was going to be wrong up there. Even for those of us who'd learned orbital mechanics at Orolo's feet, the only way for us to really grasp it was by playing this game.

"It is deceptive," was Jules's observation. He and I were in one of those cells together. I'd become good, early, at playing the game, since I knew the underlying theorics, so helping others learn it had become my role. "The left hand *seems* to make a great effect." He spun the little sphere. I closed my eyes and swallowed as the image on the screens—consisting of Arbre, and some other stuff in "orbit" around us—snapped around wildly. "However, in truth the six elements have not been changed in the slightest." He was referring to the row of six numbers lined up across the bottom of the simulated display: the same six numbers I'd once taught Barb about in the Refectory kitchen.

"That's right," I said, "you can spin around all you want and it won't change your orbital elements—which is all that *really* matters." A six-way indicator in the lower right began to flicker, which told me that Jules was using his other hand—the dexter, as he called it—to play with the mushroom, which he called a joycetick. The six orbital elements began to fluctuate. One of them changed from green to yellow. "Aha," I said, "you just screwed up your inclination. You're out of plane now."

"Very significant in the long run," he said, "and yet deceptively I observe no great difference now."

"Exactly. Let me run it forward, though, to show you what

happens." I had an instructor's control panel, which I used to fast-forward the simulation, compressing the next half hour into about ten seconds. The other satellites drifted so far away from us that they were lost to sight. "Once you get so far away that you can't see your friends—or can't tell them apart from all of the decoys—"

"I am pairdoo," he said flatly. "Can you make it run backward?"

"Of course." I ran the simulation back to just after he had messed up his inclination.

"How can I fix it—like so, perhaps?" he muttered, and tried something with the joycetick. The inclination got a little worse, and the eccentricity jumped through yellow to red. "Maird," he said, "I am fouled up now on *two* of the six."

"Try the reverse of what you just did," I suggested. He fired the opposite thruster, and the eccentricity improved, but semimajor axis got worse. "Quite a fine puzzle," he said. "Why did I study linguistics instead of celestial mechanics? Linguistics got me into this excellent mess—only physics can get me out."

"What's it like up there?" I asked him. He was getting frustrated and I thought he might benefit from a break.

"Oh, you have seen the model, I am sure. It is quite accurate, in the externals which can be viewed by your telescopes. Of course, most of the Forty Thousand never see any of that. Only the internals of the Orbstack where they live their whole lives." He was speaking of the living heart of the *Daban Urnud:* sixteen hollow spheres, each a bit less than a mile in diameter, clustered about a central axis that rotated to produce pseudogravity.

"That's what I'm asking about," I said. "What's that community of ten thousand Laterrans like?"

"Split, now, between the Fulcrum and the Pedestal." The Fulcrum was the opposition movement, led by Fthosians.

"But in normal times—"

"Until we came here, and the positions of Pedestal and Fulcrum became so hard, it was like a nice provincial town with perhaps a university or research lab. Each orb is half full of water. The water is covered with houseboats. On the roofs of them, we grow our own food—ah, I remember food!"

"Each race has four of the orbs, I assume?"

"Officially, yes, but there is of course some mixing of the communities. When the ship is not under acceleration, we can open certain doors to join neighboring orbs, and one moves freely between them. In one of the orbs of Laterre, we have a school."

"So there are children?"

"Of course we have children and raise them very, very well—education is everything to us."

"I wish we did a better job of that on Arbre," I said. "Extramuros, that is."

Jules thought about it, and shrugged. "Understand, I do not describe a utopia! We do not educate the young ones purely out of respect for noble ideals. We need them to stay alive, and to allow the voyaging of the *Daban Urnud* to continue. And there is competition between the children of Urnud, Tro, Laterre, and Fthos for the positions of power within the Command."

"Does that even extend to fields such as linguistics?" I asked.

"Yes, of course. I am a strategic asset! To make its way to new cosmi and to carry out new Advents is the Rayzon Det of the Command. And almost nothing is more useful to them, in an Advent, than a linguist."

"Of course," I said. "So, your nice town of ten thousand is big enough for people to marry, or whatever you do—"

"We marry," he confirmed. "Or at least, sufficient of us do, and have children, to maintain ten thousand."

"How about you?" I asked. "Are you married?"

"I *was*," he said.

So they had divorces too. "Any kids?"

"No. Not yet. Never, now."

"We'll get you back home," I told him. "Maybe you'll meet someone new up there."

"Not like her," he said. Then he got a wry look and shrugged. "When Lise and I were together, I always would have said such things. Sweet nothings. 'Oh, there is no one like you, my love.'" He sniffled, and looked away. "Not insincerely, of course."

"Of course not."

"But the manner of her passing made so clear, so bright, the truth of it—that there truly was no one like her. And in a community of only ten thousand, cut off forever from its roots in the home cosmos—well—I know them all, Raz. All the women of my age. And I can tell you as a matter of fact that in the cosmos where you and I are standing, there is no one like my Lise." Tears were running freely down his face now.

"I am terribly sorry," I said. "I feel such a fool. I didn't understand your wife was *dead.*"

"She is dead," he confirmed. "I have, you know, seen the pictures of her body—her face—all over the Convox."

"My god," I exclaimed. I wasn't in the habit of using religious oaths, but could think of nothing else strong enough. "The woman in the probe at Orithena—"

"She was my Lise," said Jules Verne Durand. "My wife. I have already told Sammann." And then he broke down altogether.

Jules and I were sitting together in the darkened cell, nothing to see by except simulated sunlight, reflecting from a simulated Arbre and a simulated moon. Simulated persons in spacesuits drifted silently around us. He was hunched over sobbing.

I remembered our Messal conversations about how we could interact in simple physical ways with the Geometers even if biological interaction was not possible. I went over and wrapped my arms around the Laterran until he stopped crying.

"He told me," I said to Sammann later.

He knew immediately who and what I was speaking of. He broke eye contact and shook his head. "How's he doing?"

"Better . . . he said something good."

"What's that?"

"I touched Orolo. Orolo touched Lise—gave himself up for her. When I touched Jules, it was like—"

"Closing a cycle."

"Yeah. I told him how we had prepared her body. The respect we showed it. He seemed to like hearing that."

"He told me on the plane," Sammann said. "Asked me not to tell the others."

"You have anyone like that, Sammann?" For in all the time we'd spent together, we'd never broached such topics.

He chuckled and shook his head. "Like *that*? No. Not like *that*. A few girlfriends sometimes. Otherwise, just family. Ita are—well—more family oriented." He stopped awkwardly. The contrast with avout was too obvious.

"Well, in that vein," I finally said, "could you help me close another cycle?"

He shrugged. "Be happy to try. What do you need?"

"You got a message off to Ala the other day. Just before the plane took off. I was sort of—shy."

"Because of the lack of privacy," he said. "Yeah, I could see that."

"Can you send her another?"

"Sure. But it won't be any more private than the last."

I sort of chuckled. "Yeah. Well, considering everything, that'll be acceptable."

"Okay. What do you want me to tell Ala?"

"That if I get to have a fourth life, I want to spend it with her."

"Whew!" he exclaimed, and his eyes glistened as if I'd slapped him. "Let me type that in before you change your mind."

"All we do now is go forward," I said, "there'll be no changing of minds."

Rod: Military slang. To bombard a target, typically on the surface of a planet, by dropping a rod of some dense material on it from orbit. The rod has no moving parts or explosives; its destructiveness is a consequence of its extremely high velocity.

—THE DICTIONARY, *4th edition, A.R. 3000*

I spent the entire journey to orbit convinced that the rocket had failed and that this was what dying was. The designers hadn't had time or budget to put in fripperies like windows, or even speely feeds: just a fairing, a thin outer shell whose functions were to shield the monyafeek from wind-blast; to block out all light, ensuring we'd make the trip in absolute darkness and ignorance; and to vibrate. The latter two functions combined to maximize the terror. Think of what you'd feel going down white water in a barrel. Keeping that in mind, think of being nailed into a rickety crate and then thrown from an overpass onto an eight-lane freeway at peak traffic. Now think of putting on a padded suit and being used for stick-fighting practice in the Ringing Vale. Finally, imagine having giant speakers glued to your skull and pure noise pumped into them at double the threshold for permanent hearing loss. Now pile all of those sensations on top of each other and imagine them going on for ten minutes.

The only favorable thing I could say about it was that it was much better than how I'd spent the preceding hour: lying on my back in the dark, wedged and strapped in a fetal position, and *expecting* to die. Compared to that, *actually dying* was turning out to be a piece of cake. Most unpleasant—and, in retrospect, most embarrassing—had been the philosophical musings with which I'd whiled away the time: that Orolo's death, and Lise's, had prepared me to accept my own. That it was good I'd sent that message to Ala. That even if I died in this cosmos I might go on living in another.

A stowaway hit me in the spine with a pipe. No, wait a second, that was the engine exploding. No, actually it had been the explosive charges blowing off the fairing. A system of cracks split the darkness into quadrants, then expanded to crowd it out. The four petals of the fairing fell aft and I found myself looking down at Arbre. Some of the buffeting's overtones (aero turbulence) lessened, others (combustion chamber instability) got worse. The acceleration, so far, had not been a big deal compared to the buffeting, but about then it became quite intense for half a minute or so as the missile's engine concluded its burn. Made it hard to appreciate the view. Another spine-crack told me that the booster had fallen off. Good riddance. It was just me and the monyafeek now. A few moments' drift and weightlessness came to a decisive end as the steering thrusters got a grip and snapped the stage into the correct orientation with a crispness that was reassuring even if it did make some of my internal organs swap places. Then a sense of steadily building weight as the monyafeek's engine came on for its long burn. To all appearances—the sky was black—I was out of the atmosphere, and the roof of the gazebo was doing nothing more than blocking my view ahead. But as the monyafeek's engine pushed me ahead toward orbital velocity, blades of plasma grew out from the roof's edges and twitched around my shoulders and feet, just close enough to make it interesting. This was the upper atmosphere being smashed out of the way with such violence that electrons were being torn loose from atoms.

At the launch site, just after I'd swallowed the Big Pill (an internal temperature transponder) and donned the suit, the avout who'd been pressed into service as launch crew had mummified me in kitchen wrap, stuffed me into the gazebo, bracing their shoulders against the soles of my feet, and strapped me together with packing tape. They had taken measurements with yardsticks: freebies from the local megastore. More tape work had ensued, until they'd compressed me into an envelope that matched the diagrams on their hastily printed, extensively hand-annotated documents. Then they had converged on me with cans of expanding foam insulation and foamed me into position, being sure to get the stuff between my knees and my chest, my heels and my butt, my wrists and my face. Once the foam had become rigid, someone had reached in and peeled the plastic back from my face shield so that I could see, patted me on the helmet, and stuck a box cutter into my skelehand. The importance of the measurements became obvious during the early minutes of the second stage burn, as I saw those jets of white-hot atmosphere playing within inches of my feet. But they faded as we climbed out of the atmosphere altogether. The entire gazebo sprang off (literally—it was spring-loaded) and drifted away, leaving me as hood ornament. Then I was powerfully tempted to get free of the packing material. But I knew the velocity-versus-time curve of this trajectory by heart, and knew I was still far from reaching orbital velocity. Most of the velocity gain was going to happen in the final part of the burn, when the monyafeek had left in its wake three-quarters or more of its mass in the form of expended propellants. The same thrust, pushing against a greatly reduced burden, would then yield acceleration that Lio had cheerfully described as "near-fatal." "But it's okay," he'd said, "you'll black out before anything really bad happens to you."

I tried to look around. During the last three days, I'd fantasized that the view would be fantastic. Inspiring. I'd be able to see the other rockets going up: two hundred of them, all arcing up and east on roughly parallel courses. But the suit had more air bags inside of it than Jesry had let on, and all of them had been pumped up to maximal inflation (meaning: I was lying on a bed of rocks), locking my head and torso into the attitude deemed least likely to end in death, paralysis, or organ failure. My spleen could rest easy; my eyes could see nothing but a starfield, and a bit of Arbre's glowing blue atmosphere down in the lower right. Those grew blurry as my eyes began to water, and the eyeballs themselves were mashed out of shape by their own weight, like Arsibalt sitting on a water balloon . . .

I was falling. I was hung over. I was not dead. My suit was talking to me. Had been for a bit. "Issue the 'Restraint Depressurize' command to deflate the restraint system and to commence the next stage of the operation," suggested a voice in Orth, over and over: some suur with good enunciation who'd been drafted to read canned messages into a recording device. I wanted to meet her.

"Ruzzin duzzle," I said, thinking that this would impress her.

The suit drew breath, then said, "Issue the 'Restraint Depressurize' command to—"

"Rustin Deplo!" I insisted. She was beginning to get on my nerves. Maybe I didn't want to meet her after all.

"Issue the 'Restraint—'"

"Restirraynt. Dee. Press. Your. Eyes."

The bags deflated. "Welcome to Low Arbre Orbit!" said the voice, in an altogether different tone.

My head and torso were now free to move about the HTU, but

my arms and legs were still taped and foamed. I got busy with that box cutter. It was slow going at first, but soon hunks of foam and snarls of tape were flying out of the monyafeek, drifting away, keeping station in my general vicinity. Eventually, because of their low mass and high drag, they'd re-enter and burn up. Until then, they'd make a lot of visual clutter to confuse the Geometers.

Speaking of clutter, I was beginning to see brilliant specks of light around me. There were two kinds: millions of tiny sparkles (strips of chaff sent up on other missiles) and dozens of large, steady beacons. Some of the latter were near enough that my eyeballs—gradually resuming their former shape—could resolve them as disks, or moons. Depending on where they, I, and the sun were situated, some looked like full moons, some like new ones, others somewhere in between.

There was a half moon off to my right, steadily getting larger as my orbit and it converged. It was a metallized poly balloon five hundred feet across, sent up in the same missile-barrage as I. By measuring its apparent size against the reticle on my face mask, I was able to estimate its distance: about two miles. This must be the one I was supposed to make for.

Feeling around inside the arm-stumps, I got my left hand on the trackball and my right on the stick. They were dead until I uttered another voice command, and confirmed it by flicking a switch. This brought the monyafeek's thrusters under my control. Up to now, the built-in guidance system had been managing them. And, assuming that the nearby balloon was the one that I was supposed to be aiming for, it seemed to have done a respectable job. But it had no eyes, no brain by which it could home in on the balloon. And as long as the Geometers kept jamming our nav satellites, it could only get me so close. From here on, my eyes would have to be the sensors and my brain the guidance system. I gave the trackball the tiniest rotation, just to verify that the system was working, and the thrusters spat blue light and spun me around to a new attitude. I got my bearings, squared Arbre's horizon below me, figured out which way was southeast (the direction of my orbital travel), made a mental calculation, thought about it one more time for good measure, and gave the joycetick a shot in two directions. The monyafeek hit me with a one-two punch. Other than that, nothing terrible happened, and I liked what the balloon was now doing in my visual field, so I was tempted to repeat. But I thought better of it. That was how we'd frequently got into trouble in the video game: by doing too much of the right thing.

I had a long-distance wireless transceiver, for use only in emergencies. I left it switched off. When the balloon was close enough for the short-range system to work, I said "Reticule scan," and a few moments later the suit came back with "Network joined," drowned out by Sammann's voice: "How was that for a ride?"

"I want my money back," I said, and suppressed a feeling of wild joy that came over me on hearing his—*anyone's*—voice. Glancing down at a display below my face mask (actually, projected into my eyeballs so that it *looked* that way), I saw ikons for myself, Sammann, and Fraa Gratho. But as I was looking, Esma's face and then Jules's were tacked on. I looked around to see two other monyafeeks converging on us. They were flying in improbably close formation. Actually, one of them—Esma—was *towing* the other. "I grappled Jules. He was drifting," Esma said. Fortunately, I had grown accustomed to the Valers' habit of modest understatement. I'd only just managed to get here *alone*. In the same time, Esma had tracked someone else, maneuvered to snag him, and brought him home.

"Jules? What's up? You okay? Is this what passes for a joke on Laterre?" Sammann asked.

"I locked him out of the reticule," Esma said. "He was speaking incoherently of cheese."

"Twenty minutes to line of sight," said an automated voice—referring to the time when the *Daban Urnud* would be able to see us. The balloon now was huge in my vision, and I could see Sammann hovering to one side of it in his monyafeek, Gratho in his about fifty feet away. Both looked strangely colorful and fuzzy, like toddlers' toys. The monyafeeks, and the other, non-human payloads that had been sent up at the same time, were surrounded by unruly clouds of fibrous netting that had been crammed into sealed capsules for the ride up, but that had popped open once we'd hit orbit, and expanded to ten times their former volume. We looked like drifting red pompoms.

"You guys performed the star check?" I asked.

"Yes," said Gratho, "but I invite you to verify our results."

I used the trackball to nudge myself around until I could see the vaguely circular constellation that outlined the Hoplite's shield, and compared its position to those of Arbre and of the balloon. This was a simple way of assuring that when our orbit took us around to where telescopes on the *Daban Urnud* might be able to see us, the balloon would be between us and them.

By now, the Geometers must know that something big was afoot. We had timed it, though, in such a way that Arbre had blocked their view of the two-hundred-missile launch. That was soon to change. Our orbit was almost perfectly circular—its eccentricity, a measure of how unround it was, was only 0.001—and it skimmed just above the atmosphere, at an altitude of a hundred miles. It took us around Arbre once every hour and a half. The *Daban Urnud*'s orbit was more elliptical, and its altitude ranged between fourteen and twenty-five *thousand* miles. It took ten times as long—about fifteen hours—to make one revolution. Imagine two runners circling a pond, one staying so close to the shore that his feet got wet, the other maintaining a distance of half a mile. The one on the inside would lap the one on the outside ten times for every circuit made by the other. Whenever we were lapping the *Daban Urnud*, they could look down and see us against the backdrop of Arbre. Soon, though, we would scoot around behind the planet and be lost to their view for anywhere from forty-five minutes to an hour. We had launched during one of those intervals of privacy; now it was halfway over.

Why hadn't we simply launched to a higher orbit? Because our patched-together launch system wasn't capable of dumping that much energy into a payload.

In a few minutes, when the *Daban Urnud* got line of sight to the cloud of stuff that had just been flung into orbit by those two hundred missiles, they'd see a few dozen balloons salted through a nebula of radar-jamming chaff—strips of metallized poly—hundreds of miles across, and rapidly getting bigger as orbits diverged. The chaff would make long-wavelength surveillance (radar) useless. They'd have to look at us in shorter wavelengths (light) which would necessarily mean sorting through a very large number of phototypes, looking for anything that wasn't a balloon or a strip of chaff. If we did this right, then even if they *did* manage to collect all of those pictures and inspect them in a reasonable span of time, they'd still see nothing—because we and all of our stuff would be hiding behind one of the balloons.

But this implied that a lot would have to happen in the next twenty minutes. I became so preoccupied that I almost forgot Jesry's first piece of advice: don't miss the scupper. The first spasms in my throat seized my attention, though, and I was able to lunge forward and bite down on the rubber orifice just in time. My breakfast was vacuumed away and freeze-dried into a waste bag somewhere. I returned to the task at hand. Fortunately—and a bit surprisingly—the Big Pill didn't come up. It must still be down in my gut somewhere, sending temperature and other biomedical data to the suit's processors.

After that, anyway, I felt better, and didn't throw up again for almost ten seconds.

By getting there first, Sammann had appointed himself Glommer, which meant that his job was to keep station under the balloon and secure the incoming payloads into a single, haphazardly connected mass. Payload number one was Jules Verne Durand. Esma towed him in and hit the brakes. Her monyafeek stopped, but Jules kept going, like a trailer jackknifing on an icy road. She had to back-thrust once more as the Laterran's rig tried to jerk her forward. As Gratho hovered watchfully, wondering whether this was an emergence, Sammann maneuvered closer, then spun in place. A long slender probe snapped out from his monyafeek, stretched across twenty feet of space in an eye-blink, and buried itself in the mass of red fuzz surrounding Jules's rig. "Nailed it!" Jules was now stretched between him and Esma. "Feel free to detach."

"De-grappling," Esma reported. "I'll try to find additional payloads." Her jets flared and the probe connecting her to Jules's fuzz-ball slid free.

Thus did Sammann begin his work as Glommer. The rest of us were Getters, meaning we'd move around using the maneuvering thrusters, latch on to payloads that drifted near, and bring them to the Glommer. I spun my rig around to look for any incoming payloads. Humans—of whom there ought to have been eleven—were color-coded red. The tender and its little nuke plant were also red, since we'd soon die without them. In addition, there were fifty monyafeeks carrying cargo. Their fuzzballs were blue. Their contents were interchangeable—each contained some water, some food, some fuel, and some other stuff we'd need. That's because we didn't expect to recover all of them. When I looked around, I saw what seemed like an impossibly huge number of red and blue fuzzballs, all drifting in the general vicinity. My brain told me, flat-out, that rounding them all up was impossible. It was a disaster. But the very least I could do was head for the nearest red one and make sure that whoever it was had survived the launch and was conscious. I began to line up for a rendezvous, but I'd barely begun to move before I saw maneuvering jets flash. Jesry's ikon came up on my display. "I'm good," he announced impatiently, "go look for something that can't take care of itself."

Beyond him, a blue payload was coming in. It was in the correct plane but its orbit was a little too eccentric, so it was losing altitude—probably doomed to re-enter and burn up in a few minutes. I got myself spun around facing "forward," i.e., in the direction that I, and all of this other stuff, were moving in our orbits around Arbre, and then made myself "vertical," so that the soles of my feet were pointed at Arbre and its horizon was parallel to a certain line projected across my face mask. The payload was slowly "falling" through my visual field. I used the stick to thrust backwards, slowing myself down. The payload stopped "falling," which meant I was now in the same doomed orbit that it was. A little more maneuvering took me to within twenty feet of the thing.

I was distracted for a moment by more visual clutter: a red payload, tumbling across my visual field from left to right, sideswiped a blue one. My eye was drawn to it. The red and the blue had stuck together. I reckoned it was one of the other cell members doing what I was doing. But if so, they weren't using a grapnel—just holding on to the net with a skelehand, or something. The red and the blue payload had merged into a slowly rotating binary star. I saw no sign of thrusters being fired—no evidence that the person was even conscious. "I think we might have someone in trouble here—an inadvertent collision," I reported.

"I see what you see and am coming to investigate," said Arsibalt.

"I'm a little closer," I offered, turning my head around and seeing Arsibalt on his way in. "I could—"

"No," he said, "go ahead and take the payload you've got."

So, to grips. But before I went to the next step, I couldn't help looking over toward the balloon. My pursuit of this payload had taken me well away from it, but I was heartened to see a number of blues and reds converging there. Suur Vay and Fraa Osa had linked half a dozen payloads into a big lazily spinning molecule of fuzz-balls and were hauling it in, getting ready to link it to a growing complex in the shelter of the balloon.

Arsibalt reported: "I'm closing on Fraa Jad. He has become entangled with a blue payload and he seems to be unconscious."

"What kind of orbital elements are you seeing?" Lio asked.

"His e is dangerously high," Arsibalt said, referring to the eccentricity of Jad's orbit. "He'll be in the soup in a few minutes."

"Be careful *you* don't get entangled, then!" Lio warned him.

"Rear grapnel camera on," I said, and the view out my face-mask was obscured by a virtual display in jewel-like laser colors: a green grid with red crosshairs in the middle. This was a feed from a speelycaptor aimed out the back of my monyafeek. I checked my pitch angle and then rotated the trackball until it had incremented by a hundred and eighty degrees. The payload swung into view. It was now directly behind me. "Grapnel One fire," I said, and felt a little kick in the tail as a small cylinder of compressed gas ruptured. The grapnel system was a long skinny tube of fabric, all telescoped in on itself like a stocking. When the gas exploded into it, the tube shot out straight and became a long rigid balloon. At its end was a warhead, rounded smooth on its tip so that it would plunge through the cloud of netting surrounding a payload, but spring-loaded with spines that sprang out when the tube reached the end of its travel, or when it smacked into something.

Based on my imperfect view through the rear camera, I was pretty certain it had all worked. But there was only one way to be sure. "Rear grapnel camera off," I said, and thrust forward. For a couple of seconds I don't think my heart beat at all. Then a jerk backwards told me my grapnel had engaged the netting. I allowed myself a shout of joy, then checked the balloon again.

Arsibalt reported, "Jad is welded to the payload. I'll never get them apart."

Lio: "What do you mean, welded?"

Arsibalt: "When he drifted into it, the blue plastic netting contacted the hot nozzle skirt on his monyafeek and melted—stuck fast. I'm attempting to grapple the two payloads as a unit."

Lio: "Do you have sufficient propellant to make the necessary burn?"

Arsibalt: "I'll tell you in a minute."

Lio: "I'm on my way. *Don't expend all your propellant.* We don't even know if Jad is still alive."

"Seventeen minutes to line of sight."

Plenty of time. I got myself oriented as before, with the payload trailing behind me, and thrust forward, undoing the damage I'd inflicted on my orbit a few moments earlier. It took more fuel—a longer burn—because I was moving double the mass now. Some nervousness here, because a long burn meant a large mistake, if I was doing it wrong. I kept an eye on the eccentricity readout at the bottom of my display. This was already about .005, but I had to make it less than .001 to stay in any kind of reasonable synch with everyone else.

In my earphones I could hear others making a similar calculation. Arsibalt, I gathered, had succeeded in grappling Jad and the payload Jad was stuck to, and was trying to do what I was doing, calling out numbers to Lio, who was maneuvering into position to rescue Arsibalt if that became necessary. Meanwhile Jesry was monitoring the traffic, calculating how much propellant was going to be needed, calling out suggestions that, as the adventure went on, hardened into commands. The distraction was severe, so I reluctantly shut off my wireless link and focused on my own situation.

Only once I'd burned my e down under .001 did I lift my hands from the controls and look around for the balloon. After a few moments' wild anxiety when I didn't think it was anywhere near me, I found it "above" and to my right, a thousand feet away, and slowly getting closer. A cluster of blue netting was forming up "below" it as other Cell 317ers brought in payloads. As long as I was so close, I took a look around to see if there were any others handy.

"Fifteen minutes to line of sight."

I'd lost contact with Arsibalt and Lio, but several other ikons came up on my display as I drifted in range of the reticule. I turned the sound back on, not without intense trepidation, since I did not know what news I was about to hear.

Screaming filled my ears—overloaded the electronics. I tried to remember how to turn down the volume. The tone was not that of a horror show; more like a sporting event where someone wins a close game with an improbable score just as time expires. Lio's ikon popped up. "Calm down! Calm down!" he insisted, appalled by the lapse of discipline. Arsibalt's ikon came up. "Sammann, prepare to grab Fraa Jad, please. He's unresponsive." His voice was weighed down with a kind of unnatural calm, but I sensed that if I checked his bio readouts they would reflect near-fatal excitement.

The balloon was rapidly getting bigger. I was too high, though—too far from Arbre—so I juked northwest, killing a bit of my orbital velocity, dropping to a lower altitude. I say "juke northwest" as if it were that simple, but now that I was towing a payload on the end of a twenty-foot grapnel, such moves were much more complicated; first I had to swing around to get on the payload's other side, *then* apply thrust. This slowed my convergence on the balloon.

Sammann said, "Got him. He's alive. Bio readouts are screwy though."

Everyone had been paying attention to Fraa Jad being towed in by Arsibalt. But suddenly all I heard was shouting. "Look out look out!" "*Damn* it!" "*That* was close!" and "Bad news—it's a red!"

Twisting my head around, I saw what they had been reacting to: a red payload had passed within a few yards of the balloon, moving at a high relative speed—fast enough to have done damage if it had been just a little bit "higher." It had come upon them so rapidly that no one had reacted in time to head it off, grapple it, and rein it in. It passed between me and the balloon, and I got a good look at it. "It's the nuke," I announced. Then I said to my suit, "Grapnel disengage."

"Disengaged," it returned.

I fired a little burst to pull myself free of the blue payload. "I'm on it," I announced, "someone grab this payload." The nuke was moving so fast that I reverted to instincts cultivated playing the video game in Elkhazg. I fired a lateral burst that—while it didn't solve the problem—slowed the rate at which the gap between me and the nuke was widening. Ikons were falling off my display as I shot out of range, and the sound was coming through as sporadic, disjointed packets. I was pretty sure I heard Arsibalt saying "wrong plane," which tallied with what I was thinking: this nuke's orbit was in a plane that differed from ours by a small angle, just because of some small error that had crept in during the chaos of launch.

One voice, anyway, came through clearly: "Thirteen minutes to line of sight."

I tried another maneuver, screwed it up desperately, and, with feelings that were close to panic, watched the nuke zoom across my field of vision. A moment later, Arbre whipped beneath me, and I realized I was spinning around. My hand must have brushed the trackball and set it spinning. I devoted a few moments to getting my attitude stabilized, then spun about carefully so that I wouldn't lose my fix on the nuke. Once I had that in hand, I glanced back toward the balloon. It was shockingly distant.

When I looked back toward the nuke, I couldn't see it. I'd lost it in sun-glare off the Equatorial Sea. Back-thrusting to lose altitude, I was able to find the red fuzzball again as it rose above the horizon.

No one else was anywhere near. They'd heard me saying I had the nuke, and assumed I could handle it.

"Calm down," I said to myself. Doing this slowly and getting it right on the next try would get me back to my friends quicker than making three hasty, failed attempts. I got myself stabilized so that the nuke was low in my field of vision and dead ahead, and forced myself to spend thirty seconds doing *nothing* except tracking it, observing how its motion differed from mine.

Definitely an error in the slant of its orbital plane. I had to fire the thrusters to match that error. Which I did—but in the process I messed up my semimajor axis and a couple of other elements in a way that would have killed me ten minutes later. Another sixty seconds' fussing got those squared away.

Plane change maneuvers are expensive.

I'd been forcing myself not to look for the balloon any more. Partly because I was afraid of what I'd see—my shelter, my friends, impossibly far away. But also because it simply didn't matter. Without the nuke, whose power would split water into hydrogen and oxygen, we would all asphyxiate within a couple of hours. If I lost my nerve and retreated to the balloon without it, my empty-handed arrival would be a death sentence for the whole cell.

I came near, but got slewed sideways at the last minute. Did a little spin move. Stopped myself, where "stopped" meant that the nuke and I were stationary with respect to each other. "Three minutes to line of sight," said the voice. I gave the controls the tiniest nudge, saw to my satisfaction that the nuke and I were converging. Just let it happen. Tried not to breathe so fast.

Rather than grappling the nuke, I spent a few moments maneuvering close enough that I could simply reach out with my skele-hand and grab the netting. Then I turned, making my best guess as to where the balloon might be, and saw—nothing. Or rather, too much. Our decoy strategy had backfired. At this distance, I had no way to distinguish true from false. There were three balloons about the same distance from me—none closer than ten miles. Even if I were to guess right, I wouldn't be able to reach it in three minutes. And if I guessed wrong, I'd use up so much thruster propellant in getting to it that I'd be marooned there.

On the other hand. The orbit that I, and the nuke, were in was a stable one. I double-checked the numbers, since all our lives depended on my judgment of this. The orbit's shape and size were such that it would not enter the atmosphere and burn up, at least not for a day or two.

What if I simply stayed with it? My oxygen supply was down to about two hours, but I could stretch it by calming down a little. I knew for a fact that the problem, here, was in the inclination of the orbit—the angle that the nuke and I were now making with respect to the equator. Ours was a little steeper than my comrades'. Consequently, my trajectory would only coincide with Cell 317's in two places—two points of intersection, occurring once every forty-five minutes, on opposite sides of the planet. Sort of like the proverbial stopped clock that's right twice daily. The last time it had been right had been about fifteen minutes ago, when the nuke had almost hit my friends, and I had gone after it. Since then, we'd been getting farther apart. But starting in another few minutes, we'd begin getting closer together again. And in half an hour, we should enjoy another near collision.

"One minute to line of sight."

The key to it all: what were my friends thinking? What were they saying right now over that wireless ret? I'd heard Arsibalt's voice saying that the nuke was in the wrong plane. They'd probably watched me drifting away, with mounting anxiety, and debated whether to send out a rescue team.

But they hadn't. Lio had given no such order. Not only that, they had fought off the temptation to switch on the long-range wireless.

If it had been anyone else, I wouldn't have been able to read their minds, nor they mine. But my fraas had been raised, trained, by Orolo. They had figured out—probably sooner than I had—that in forty-five minutes the nuke would reappear on the other side of Arbre. Just as important, they were relying on me—entrusting me with their lives—to figure out the same thing and to act accordingly.

And what did "act accordingly" mean? It meant stay calm and don't mess with the orbit that I was in. If I took no action, they'd be able to anticipate my position. If I *did* something, though, they'd have no way of predicting my whereabouts.

I didn't have much in the way of emergency supplies: just a blanket of metallized poly—like the emergency blanket they'd issued to Orolo after his Anathem—taped to the chest of my suit. It was to be used to block the light of the sun, where necessary, from striking our matte black suits with full force and overheating them, which would force the chiller to work harder and use more oxygen. I peeled mine loose and unfolded it—not easy with skelehands—and used it to cover as much of the nuke as I could, then snuggled beneath it.

"Line of sight established."

Supposing they were looking, the telescopes on the *Daban Urnud* could now see me, albeit as just another hunk of crud thrown up in the two-hundred-missile launch. Chaff.

Let's put this in perspective: the *Daban Urnud* was something like fourteen thousand miles away. At their closest approach to Arbre, the whole planet looked as big to them as a pie held at arm's length. At their farthest, the size of a saucer. For them to see my spread-out blanket, at this distance, was like trying to spot a gum wrapper from a hundred miles away. Worse—or, for me, better—it was like looking at a whole field covered with litter, trying to pick out a single gum wrapper from all the rest.

On the other hand, Lio—who had brought *Praxic Age Exoatmospheric Weapons Systems* with him to the Convox—had cautioned us not to get cocky, and Jules had added weight to this by telling us how the Urnudans, past masters of space warfare, had coupled syndevs to excellent telescopes, enabling them to sift through vast numbers of images to find things that didn't look right. Decoys, for example, were easy to detect because they were usually nothing more than balloons, whose huge size and light weight made them feel the drag of the evanescent atmosphere much more than real payloads.

So decoy orbits behaved a little differently from non-decoy ones.

Moreover, once the Urnudans had created a census of all the stuff that the two-hundred-missile-launch had flung into orbit, they would be in a position to notice if anything went missing, or changed to a new orbit. This could only happen if it had thrusters and guidance on board.

So in that sense we had already screwed up the mission. We had to fall back on safety in numbers: the hope that my blanket's sudden disappearance from the junk-cloud would not be noticed soon enough for the Pedestal to do anything about it.

But I was getting ahead of myself. In order for this blanket to suddenly disappear, I was going to have to rendezvous with the others.

That would be easier with oxygen. I closed my eyes, tried to relax, tried to stop thinking about the Pedestal and their admirable telescopes and their syndevs. Here was that rare circumstance where worrying too much actually *could* kill me.

Once my pulse had dropped to a more reasonable range, I found the keyboards in my arm-stumps and typed messages to Cord and to Ala, in case I died and the suit was recovered later with its memory intact.

The suit's syndev included an orbital theorics calculator, which one almost never had time to use in the heat of the moment, but I fired it up and used it to verify some of my hunches as to what I'd need to do when I drew within range of the others. It was infuriatingly difficult to concentrate, though. My brain had become like an old sponge that has sopped up more water than it can hold.

In zero gravity, there was almost no contact between the suit and the person wearing it. Air, at just the right temperature, circulated all around my naked body—it was like taking a bath in air. Behind my back was a small chemical plant going full tilt, but I was only aware of it as a source of gentle white noise. Other than that, I heard nothing except the beating of my own heart. Normally, I could get a jolt of excitement simply by opening my eyes and looking out the face-mask: *I'm in space!* But now all I could see was the back side of a crinkly blanket, as if I were poultry in a roasting pan. So it was not difficult to feel drowsy. My body and my mind had never had so many reasons to want rest; between jet lag and training, we'd slept very little at Elkhazg, and not at all in the last twenty-four hours. The last half hour had been absurdly stressful—just the kind of experience after which any sane person would want to crawl under the covers of a warm bed and cry himself to sleep.

The only thing that kept me from passing out instantly was fear of my own sleepiness. After the training we'd been through, I now knew the symptoms of carbon dioxide poisoning better than the alphabet. Nausea, check. Dizziness, check. Vomiting, check. Headache, check. But who *wouldn't* have all of those symptoms after being kicked up a hundred-mile-high staircase by a monyafeek? What came next? Oh, yeah—almost forgot—drowsiness and confusion.

I checked the readouts in my screen. Checked them again. Closed my eyes, waited for my vision to clear, checked them a third time. They were fine. Oxygen tank level was yellow—which was to be expected, after all the heavy breathing—but the oxygen content of the air I was breathing was fine and the CO_2 level was zero—the scrubber was taking all of it out.

But if I were drowsy and confused, might I be reading the numbers wrong?

I drifted off, but started awake every few minutes. Enough time had passed that I'd begun to second-guess what had happened just after the launch. I'd been so focused on what I'd been doing that when I'd noticed Jad bumping into the blue payload and getting stuck to it, I'd decided not to go check it out. That had been a mistake. I should have gone for it. Instead, Arsibalt had gone after Jad—and to judge from the way Jesry had been screaming when Arsibalt had made it back, he had just barely escaped with his life, and Jad's.

This was a bad plan. Who had come up with the idea of doing it this way?

I understood the logic. Arbre had two hundred missiles. No more. Each just barely capable of getting a tiny payload to a dangerously low and short-lived orbit. There was only so much we could do, working from that. We'd all studied the plan at Elkhazg, come to grips with it, nodded our heads, accepted it.

But that was one thing. To be up here with payloads zooming

around chaotically, bumping into each other, getting melted together—hiding under space blankets—there were so many ways this could have gone wrong.

Could *still* go wrong. Could be going wrong *now*.

What if I'd been a little hastier when I had reached the nuke, and made a bid to drag it back? We'd all have died.

I was worrying again. Actually, it was worse than that—even *more* pointless. Rather than worrying about the future—which could be changed—I was worrying about things that might have gone wrong in the past, and couldn't be changed in any case.

Leave that to the Incanters and the Rhetors, respectively.

Where were all of the Thousanders now? Gathered in a stadium, chanting?

"Raz!"

I opened my eyes. Had one of those moments when I simply couldn't figure out where I was—could not convince myself that the launch hadn't been a dream.

"Raz!"

One ikon was visible on the display: Fraa Jesry.

"Here," I said.

"It's great to hear your voice!" he exclaimed, sounding enormously relieved.

"Well, I'm touched to hear you say so, Jesry—"

"Shut up. I'm incoming. Get the blanket out of the way so you can get a clue what's going on."

"Are you sure? Aren't we in line of sight?"

"No."

"I think that we are in line of sight, Jesry."

"We were, *last* time. Now we're not."

"Last time?"

"We missed you the first time around. Crossed your path, but the altitude difference was too great. Couldn't raise you on the wireless."

"This is our *second* try?" I checked the time. He was right. Ninety minutes—not forty-five—had passed. My oxygen indicator had gone red. I'd slept through the first rendezvous!

I swiped the blanket out of the way. Saw a balloon, a mile away and rapidly getting closer. Tucked up under it was an ungainly structure of inflated grapnel-tubes with dozens of red and blue fuzz-balls caught up in it. A few space-suited figures on monyafeeks kept station nearby, all turned to look my direction. The row of ikons flashed up as I rejoined the reticule. But no one spoke except Jesry. He had come out alone.

"If I fail, remain calm and wait," he said. "There are two layers of backup plans."

"But they sent the best first, eh?" I kicked away from the nuke, very gently, and fired a grapnel into its net-cloud.

"Thanks, but for doing what you did, you get bragging rights, Raz." Jesry had floated in range. He spun about, collected himself, and fired a grapnel of his own.

"Maybe we can brag when we're old," I said. "What should I do?"

"Orient positive radial," he said. This meant that instead of fac-ing in the direction of our orbital movement as before, we had to swing around ninety degrees so that our backs were to Arbre. I did it, and bumped lightly against Jesry as we came around side by side.

"Rotate down forty-five degrees and fire a fifteen-second burst," Jesry said.

Fifteen seconds was huge, and, if the calculations had been wrong, would send us far off course with no propellant to get back. But I did it. Didn't even *think* of not taking the suggestion. This was Jesry. He'd been watching me, coolly, as I'd gone out to fetch the nuke. Had done the theorics in his head, and triple-checked it with the syndev. I swiveled and fired. Lost my visual in so doing.

"You are headed for us as if we were reeling you in on a line," Sammann proclaimed. But his tone of voice was all I really needed to hear.

"Take no action," Lio warned us. "You're passing under us—we are coming to grapple you—" And a moment later, two sudden yanks, and a cheer from the others, told me we'd been captured. I took my fingers off the thruster controls just to prevent my trembling hands' inadvertently firing the thrusters, and let Lio and Osa tow us in.

"Raz, you're secure," Lio said. "Sammann, final star check please?"

"We are still shielded by the balloon," Sammann said.

"Good," Lio said. "I'm sure everyone wishes to congratulate Fraa Erasmas, but don't. Save oxygen. Do it later. Arsibalt, you know what's next—let us know if you need to borrow oxygen from someone else."

The others had pulled on white overgarments of tough fabric to stop micrometeoroids and to reflect the heat of the sun. These made them look more like proper spacemen. One was given to me, and I put it on. Then, like the others, I snap-linked myself to this huge tangle of nets and payloads and grapnels and tried to sleep while Arsibalt and Lio got the tender online. This meant maneuvering it and the nuke close together and then connecting them. Already connected to the tender was a flexible water bladder. Other cell members had been busy during my absence scavenging water from the reservoirs on the blue payloads and transferring it into this bag, which had plumped out until it was bathtub-sized.

Arsibalt snap-linked himself to the control panel of the nuke and spent a lot of time motionless, which probably meant he was reading the instructions on the virtual screen inside his face-mask and going through checklists. After a while he got to work deploying some long poles that ended up sticking out from one side of the nuke like spines. Petals blossomed from near their ends, blocking our view of whatever was on the tips of those poles. Arsibalt returned to the control panel and worked for a few moments, then informed us, "I have powered up the reactor. Avoid the ends of the poles. They are hot."

"Hot, as in radioactive?" Jesry asked.

"No. Hot as in ouch. They are where the system radiates its waste heat into space." Then, after a pause: "But they're also radioactive."

No one said anything, but I'm sure I wasn't the only one who checked his oxygen supply. The water was now being split into hydrogen and oxygen. In a few hours we'd be able to replace our depleted air and fuel supplies, and swap used for fresh scrubbers, at the tender. Until then, we had to take it easy, and share what we had with others who needed it more. Esma, for example, had been responsible for scavenging water from payloads, and had used up a lot of her oxygen.

Lio said, "Everyone except Sammann and Gratho drink, eat, and sleep. If you absolutely can't sleep, review coming tasks. Sammann and Gratho, connect us."

Sammann and Gratho clambered free of their monyafeeks and took to shinnying around the payload-tangle. They found some kind of magic box, broke it free from the mess, and got it lashed into a position where it enjoyed a clear line of sight down to Arbre. A few minutes later Sammann announced that we were on the Reticulum. But I already suspected that based on new lights and jeejah-displays that had begun to flourish in my peripheral vision.

"Hello, Fraa Erasmas, this is Cell 87," said a voice in my ears. "Can you hear me?"

"Yes, Tulia, I can hear you fine. Good morning, or whatever it is where you are."

"Evening," she said. "We're in the equipment shed of a farm about a thousand miles southwest of Tredegarh. What took you guys so long?"

"We were enjoying the view and having a party," I said. "How have you been spending the time? What is it that Cell 87 does in that equipment shed?"

"Whatever makes things easier for you."

"Tulia, I've hardly ever known you to be so helpful, so compliant . . ."

"Looks like you need to urinate. What's the holdup?"

"I'll get right on it."

"Any particular reason your pulse is so rapid?"

"Gosh, I don't know, let me think . . ."

"Spare me," she said. "Here's a picture of the mess you're in—check it out while you're peeing." And just like that, my screen was filled with a three-dimensional rendering of a big silver sphere with a mess of struts, fuzzballs, and color-coded payloads tucked up against one side of it. "Here's where you are." My name flashed in yellow. "Here's where you need to be." A payload began flashing on the other side of the mess. "We worked out the most efficient route." A line snaked through, linking my name to the destination.

"That doesn't look so efficient," I began.

She cut me off. "There's stuff you don't know. Each of the others in your cell has to follow a different route to a different payload. This one is optimized to minimize interference."

"I stand corrected."

A flashing red box appeared about halfway along my route. "What's the red thing?" I asked.

She conferred with someone in the equipment shed, then answered, "One of the payloads has a sharp corner you'll want to avoid. No worries, we'll talk you through it."

"Gosh, thanks."

Rustling papers, she announced, "I'm going to talk you through the process of unstrapping yourself from the S2-35B."

"Up here, we call it a monyafeek."

"Whatever. Move your right hand up to the buckle above your left collarbone . . ."

I'll describe what we did next as if we'd just done it. In the act, though, it was—as the old joke goes—a whole hour's work packed into just one twenty-four-hour day.

It would have been twenty-four *days,* though, if not for our support cells on the ground, keeping track of what we were doing and coming up with ways to make it easier. During rest breaks—ruthlessly enforced by our private physicians—I learned that Arsibalt's support cell was in a drained swimming pool in a Kelx parochial suvin, and Lio's was on an unmarked drummon parked at a maintenance depot. And as slowly became plain, each of these cells was in turn being supported by networks of other cells out there in the Antiswarm.

Work began with disentangling and sorting the goods we'd hauled in during that first, feverish twenty minutes. Suur Vay tended to Jules Verne Durand and to Fraa Jad. Both ended up being fine. The Laterran was weak from lack of nutrition, and had suffered more from the ride up to orbit. It simply took him longer to become himself again. It wasn't really clear what had happened to Fraa Jad. He was unresponsive for a while, though his vital signs were in acceptable ranges and his eyes were open. Eventually, he requested that Suur Vay leave off pestering him. Then he dropped off the reticule and did nothing for an hour. Finally he began to move, and to take part in the unpacking. I wondered who was in *his* support cell.

The fuzz-balls we stripped off, wadded up, and got out of the way. The payloads we strapped together with poly ties, just so they wouldn't drift out from the shelter of the balloon and give away our position. We rigged the payload-cluster to a monyafeek, and used its thrusters for station-keeping. The balloon's low mass and high drag made it inevitable that we'd drift out from under its shelter unless we tapped the thrusters every so often to slow ourselves down. If we did this for more than a couple of days, we'd re-enter the atmosphere along with the balloon, and there would be a sort of race to see whether incineration or crushing deceleration would kill us first. But we had no intention of hanging around that long.

Arsibalt, Osa, and I assembled the decoy while the rest of Cell 317 assembled the Cold Black Mirror.

The decoy was erected on a base consisting of seven monyafeeks lashed together in a hexagonal array. We scavenged propellants from the blue payloads just as Suur Esma had earlier done with water, and loaded it into the decoy's tanks.

That took care of propulsion. On top of this platform we attached what looked like a big unruly wad of fabric—it was an inflatable structure—that had come up as a separate payload. There was a zipper in its side. We opened it, and stuffed in everything we didn't need: nets, leftover packing material, parts of other monyafeeks. Also there were four manikins dressed in coveralls. We closed the zipper to prevent all of that junk from drifting out, and opened it from time to time as members of the other team came to us with stuff they wanted to get rid of. But we didn't inflate it yet, because space on this side of the balloon was tight, and getting tighter as the Cold Black Mirror took shape.

My description of the Cold Black Mirror might make it sound heavy, but like everything else up here, it weighed practically nothing because it was slapped together of inflatable struts, memory wire, membranes, and aerogels. It was square, fifty feet on a side. Its upper surface was perfectly flat (it was a membrane stretched like a drumhead between knife edges) and perfectly reflective. It was made of stuff that would reflect not only visible light, but microwaves—the frequencies that the Geometers used for radar. When we ventured out from behind the balloon, we would keep it between us and the *Daban Urnud,* but angled, like a shed roof, so that their radar beams, as they swept across our vicinity, would be bounced off in some other direction. We'd still make a big echo, but it would never come anywhere near the *Daban Urnud,* and never show up on their screens.

As long as we were careful about which way the mirror was pointing, we would not be visible against the backdrop of space, because the mirror would be reflecting some other part of space, and all space looked more or less the same: black. If they just happened to zoom in on us with a really good telescope they might happen to notice a star or two in the wrong place, but this was unlikely.

When we passed between the *Daban Urnud* and the luminous surface of Arbre it would be a different matter, but we were hoping that a fifty-by-fifty-foot snatch of absolute blackness might go unnoticed on a backdrop eight thousand miles across. It would be like a single bacterium on a dinner plate.

If the mirror were permitted to get warm, it would emit infrared light that the Geometers might notice, and so most of the ingenuity that had been spent on its design had been devoted to keeping it cold. It was laced with solid-state chillers that were powered by the nuke. The nuke, as Jesry had mentioned, produced a lot of waste heat. This would show up like a casino on infrared, if we were dumb enough to shine it at the *Daban Urnud,* but as long as we kept the radiators hidden beneath the Cold Black Mirror and pointed in the direction of Arbre, the Geometers would not have a line of sight that would make it possible for them to see it.

Propulsion was, to get us started, three scavenged monyafeeks, and (for later) a reel of string. Our spacesuits would serve as living quarters, beds, toilets, Refectories, drugstores, and entertainment centers.

But not as cloisters. Space travel had any number of interesting features, but quiet contemplation was not among them. During Apert, and later when we had been Evoked, the worst part of the culture shock had been the jeejahs. There was no estimating how many times I'd said to myself *Thank Cartas I'm not chained to one of those awful things!* But this was like living inside of a jeejah: a super-ultra-mega jeejah whose screen wrapped all the way around my field of vision, whose speakers were jacked into my ears, whose microphone transmitted every word, breath, and sigh to attentive listeners on the other end of the line. Part of it was even *inside* of me: that huge temperature transponder.

We were only allowed to work for two hours before a mandatory rest break kicked in. And, as I began to suspect, round about the second or third such break, it wasn't so much to give our bodies a rest as it was to rest our souls from the bewildering, overwhelming, irritating barrage of information being pumped into our ears and eyes.

Strangely, when I got a moment's peace, I only wanted to talk to someone. In a normal way. "Tulia? You there?"

"I am *shocked* you haven't fallen asleep!" she joked. "You're behind schedule—get cracking and relax!"

I laughed not.

"Sorry," she said, "what's up?"

"Nothing. Just thinking, is all."

"Uh-oh."

"Are we the right people, out of all Arbre, to be up here doing this?"

"Uh, that decision has been made, and the answer is yes."

"But how did it get made? Wait a minute, I know: Ala rammed it through some committee."

"Maybe it wasn't so much a ramming kind of thing," Tulia said, and I had to smile at the distaste in her voice. "But you're right that Ala had a lot to do with it."

"Fine. No ramming. But I'll bet it wasn't all sweet persuasion either. Not all rational Dialog. Not with those people."

"You'd be surprised how far rational Dialog goes with wartime military."

"But the military must have been saying 'look, this is obviously a job for our guys. Commandos. Not a bunch of avout, a renegade Ita, and a starving alien.'"

"There was—is—a backup team," Tulia allowed. "I think it's all military. Same training as you guys."

"Then how did the decision get made to give *us* the suits, the monyafeeks—"

"Partly a language issue. Jules Verne Durand is a priceless asset. He speaks Orth. Not Fluccish. So the team would have to be at least part Orth-speaking. To make it bilingual would pose all sorts of problems."

"Hmm, so we were probably the backup option until Jules fell into our laps."

"He didn't fall into your lap," Tulia reminded me. "You went out and—"

"Be that as it may, I still find it amazing that the Panjandrums would even *entertain* the idea, given that they have commandos and astronauts who know this kind of thing *cold*."

"But Raz, you are *educable,* you can learn 'this kind of thing,' if by that you mean how to maneuver an S2-35B and how to assemble a Cold Black Mirror. You've spent your whole life, ever since you were Collected, becoming educable."

"Well, maybe you have a point there," I said, remembering the hitherto inconceivable sight of Fraa Arsibalt powering up a nuclear reactor.

"But the clincher—and here I'm just imagining how Ala would have framed the argument—is that the whole mission, the journey you and the others are going on, isn't going to be just this. When you get where you're going, who knows what you'll be called upon to do? And then you'll have to draw on everything you know—every aptitude you've ever acquired since you became a fid."

"Since I became a fid . . . now *that* seems like a long time ago!"

"Yeah," she said, "I was thinking about it the other day. Finding my way through that labyrinth. Coming out into the sun. Grand-suur Tamura taking me by the hand, making me a bowl of soup. And I remember when you were Collected."

"You showed me around the place," I recalled, "as if you'd lived there for a hundred years. I thought you were a Thousander."

I heard a sniffle on the other end of the link, and closed my eyes for a minute. The suit was built to handle just about every excretory function except for crying.

How could I ever have been so stupid as to think I could be in a liaison with Tulia? Now, *that* would have been a mess.

"You ever talk to Ala? Are you in touch with her?" I asked.

"I probably could if I had to," she said, "but I haven't tried."

"You've been busy," I said.

"Yeah. When your cell got shot into space, it made her really important. Really busy."

"Well . . . I hope she's busy figuring out what we're going to do when we get there."

"I'm sure she is," Tulia said. "You can't imagine how seriously Ala takes her responsibility for what she's—for what happened."

"In fact, I have a reasonably good idea," I said, "and I know she's worried we're all going to get killed. But if she could see how well the cell is working together, she'd take heart."

We dropped behind Arbre yet again. I'd lost track of how many times we had swung in and out of the *Daban Urnud's* line of sight. The others were strapping themselves down to the thrust struc-tures under the Cold Black Mirror. I was up underneath the decoy, running through the final seventeen items on a checklist that was two hundred lines long.

"Pulling the inflation lanyard," I proclaimed, and did. "It's done." I couldn't hear the hiss of escaping gas in space, but I could feel it in the hand that was gripping the frame of the decoy.

"Check," Lio said.

"Monitoring inflation process," I said, numbly reading the next line of technobulshytt. The listless wad of painted fabric, which we'd been using as a garbage receptacle for the last day, stirred, and began to show some backbone as internal struts filled with gas and began to stiffen. For a while I was afraid it was failing—not enough gas, or something—but finally, over the course of a few seconds, it snapped open.

"Status?" Lio demanded. Down under the mirror, he could see nothing.

"The status is, it's so beautiful I wish I could climb into it and go for a ride."

"Check."

"Commencing visual inspection," I said. I spent a minute clambering over the thing, admiring its origami "attitude thrusters," its paper-light, memory-wire-and-polyfilm "antennas," its hand-painted "scorch marks," and other marvels of stagecraft that Laboratoria at the Convox must have toiled over for weeks. I found a "thruster" that had failed to unfold, and popped it loose with my skele-fingers. Whacked on a creased strut until it inflated itself properly. Flicked off a clinging stripe of kitchen wrap. "It's good," I announced.

"Check."

The remaining items on the list were mostly valve openings and pressure checks down among the engines. I was conscious that a plumbing failure here would kill me, but had to get on with it.

"Ten minutes to line of sight."

The final step was to set a timer for five minutes, and to start the countdown. Lio's final "Check" was still in my ears when I felt a mighty yank on my safety line: Osa hauling me in. A few seconds later I was down beneath the Mirror and the others were strapping me down as if I were a homicidal maniac at the end of a day-long chase. All communications had devolved to a series of checklist items and clipped announcements.

"Eight minutes to line of sight." My suit's airbags inflated. Light flared as the Mirror's engines came on, and I felt the thrust against my back. As usual our faces were aimed in the wrong direction, so we could not see that anything was happening. But this time around, we had a speely feed to watch, so we were able to see the balloon and the decoy dwindling into the distance. By the time that the five-minute timer expired, the decoy was so far away that we could see nothing of it except for a single blue-white pixel as its engines fired.

A few minutes into its burn, the Geometers could see it too. Because by then the *Daban Urnud*'s orbit had taken it back into line of sight.

Our engines had performed their mission of kicking us into a new trajectory that would get us up to the same altitude as the Geometers. We'd never use them again. So we were back in free fall. The in-suit airbags deflated.

I loosened a couple of straps and twisted around so that I could see the decoy. Its engines continued to burn for another minute or so, as if it were making a spirited attempt to climb up out of low orbit and get on an intercept course with the *Daban Urnud*.

Then it blew up.

It was *supposed* to. Rather than wait for the Pedestal to do something about it—something we couldn't predict, something that might have unwanted side-effects on us—the designers of the mission had deliberately programmed the engines to open the wrong valve at the wrong moment. So it flew apart. There wasn't much in the way of fire, and obviously we couldn't hear the boom. The thing just turned into a rapidly expanding mess of smithereens, and ceased to exist. Only a few minutes later, we began to see streaks of fire drawn across the atmosphere below us as chunks of it began to re-enter. The Pedestal, we hoped, would think that our pathetic gambit had failed because of a malfunctioning rocket engine—which was all too plausible—and would put all of their sensors to work snapping pictures of the debris, greedily vacuuming up all the intelligence they could get before it was engulfed and burned by the atmosphere. The Cold Black Mirror they would not see.

The next phase of the journey lasted for several days. It couldn't have been more different from those first twenty-four hours. We no longer had that high-bandwidth link to the ground. Between that, and the fact that we didn't have much to do, things got quiet.

The burn that had taken us out from the shelter of the balloon had put us in a predicament, vis-à-vis the *Daban Urnud*, a little like that of a bird that is on a collision course with an aerocraft. We would definitely reach the *Daban Urnud* now, but if we didn't want to end up as a spray of freeze-dried flesh on its rubbly surface, we would need to slow down before we smacked into it.

Any other space mission would have done it with a brief rocket engine burn at the last minute, followed by some nice work with maneuvering thrusters. But since we were trying to sneak up, that wouldn't work. We needed a way of generating thrust that didn't involve a sudden brilliant ejaculation of white-hot gases.

The Convox had found the answer in the form of an electrodynamic tether, which was nothing more than a string with a weight on the end, with electricity running through it in one direction. The string was about five miles long. It was slender, but strong—similar to our chords. In order to keep it taut, we had to dangle a weight from the end. The weight turned out to be our spent and now useless monyafeeks, concealed under a smaller and simpler version of the Cold Black Mirror. So our first task, once we'd broken out from the shelter of the balloon, was to lash the monyafeeks together into a compact mass, to deploy another mirror above them, and to attach them to the end of the tether. We waited until Arbre was between us and the *Daban Urnud* before commencing the most ticklish—verging on insane—part of the operation, which was to throw ourselves into a spin and then use the resulting centrifugal force to pay out the five miles of line. This was sickening and terrifying for a few minutes, until we and the counterweight got a little farther apart. This slowed the rate at which we and the counterweight spun around our common center of gravity, so that Arbre was no longer whipping past us quite so frequently. By the time the counterweight was at the end of the string, the rotation had slowed to the point where we barely noticed it. From now on, we would spin exactly once during each orbit, which simply meant that the counterweight was always five miles "below" us, the string was oriented vertically, and the Cold Black Mirror was always "above" us—where we wanted it. This slow rotation yielded pseudogravity at a level of about a hundredth of what we felt on the surface of Arbre, so we and all of our stuff slowly "fell" upward—away from the planet—unless something stopped us. The something was the frame of inflated tube-struts that helped keep the Cold Black Mirror stretched out flat. We drifted up against it and remained caught there like litter pressed against a fence by an imperceptible breeze.

Shortly after completing this maneuver, we passed onto the night side of Arbre. This afforded us an excellent view when the Pedestal rodded all of the big orbital launch facilities around Arbre's equator. The planet was mostly black, with skeins and clots of light sprawling across the temperate parts of the landmasses where people tended to live. The incoming rods drew brilliant streaks across this backdrop, as if chthonic gods, trapped beneath Arbre's crust, were slicing their way to freedom with cutting torches. When a rod hit the ground its light was snuffed out for a moment, then reborn as a hemispherical bloom of warmer, redder light: comparable to a nuclear explosion, but without the radioactivity. We orbited over the very launch pad from which Jesry had begun his first journey into space, and got a perfect view of an orange fist reaching up toward us. Jesry was fussing over the tender at the time, but he paused in his labors for a few minutes to watch as we flew over.

I heard a little mechanical pop, and looked over to see that Arsibalt had just jacked a hard wire into the front of my suit. This was how we'd be talking to each other from now on. Even the short-range wireless was considered too much of a risk. Instead we physically connected ourselves, suit to suit, with wires. Likewise, we no longer had the 24/7 high-bandwidth link to the ground. Instead, Sammann was bringing up some kind of link that squirted information—slowly and sporadically—along a narrow line-of-sight beam that the Geometers would not be able to detect. So if Cell 87 had anything to say to me after this, they'd say it in the form of text messages that would flash up on the virtual screen inside my face-mask—but not immediately. We'd been told to expect delays on the order of two hours. And if we didn't hard-wire ourselves into the reticule, we'd not be able to send or receive anything.

"It is a high wire act," Arsibalt remarked. Out of habit I looked at his face-mask, but saw nothing except for the distorted reflection of a mushroom cloud. So I looked down at the screen mounted to his chest and saw his face, staring down at Arbre, then glancing up to make eye contact of a sort.

I collected myself for a moment. This was the first real—that is, private—conversation I'd had in days. Since I'd choked down the Big Pill and climbed into the suit, every sound I'd made, every beat of my heart, every swallow of water I'd taken had been recorded and transmitted somewhere in real time. I'd gotten into the habit of assuming that every word I spoke was being monitored by Panjandrums, discussed in committees, and archived for eternity. Hardly a way to have an honest or an interesting conversation. But I'd very quickly adjusted to not having Cell 87's voice in my ears. And now Arsibalt and I had the opportunity to talk. No one else was hard-wired to us. We were alone together, as if strolling through the page trees at Edhar.

High wire was a play on words: a literal description of the tether that we had just unreeled. But of course Arsibalt meant something else too. "Yes," I said, "as we have torn open one payload after another I have been keeping an eye out for anything that would serve as a—" And I checked myself on the verge of lapsing into astro-jargon. I'd been about to say "atmospheric re-entry and deceleration system" but it sounded as wrong here as it would have back among the page trees.

Arsibalt finished the sentence for me: "A way down."

"Yeah. And now that we've unpacked everything, and thrown away most of it—stripped down to the absolute basics—it's clear that there is nothing here that can get us back to Arbre. Never was." I thought about it as I watched another mushroom cloud skidding along below us, rapidly diluting itself and paling like dawn in the cold upper atmosphere.

Arsibalt picked up the thread I'd dropped: "So you told yourself that they would send up a re-entry vehicle for us later—launching it from, say, there, or there." He pointed at the mushroom cloud we'd just passed over, then at another, new one, burgeoning a few thousand miles to the east of it. "Or wherever that's going." He was obviously referring to another rod that was just now streaking across the atmosphere below us. I don't know what it hit. Maybe a rocket factory.

Of course, Arsibalt was making the point that we were all dead now—beyond rescue, unless we could make it to the *Daban Urnud*. I was irked, just a little, that he'd put this picture together a bit quicker than I had. And I was also thinking, *Here we go again*, bracing myself to spend the next ten hours hard-linked to Arsibalt, trying to talk him down from a condition of near-hysteria, persuading him to gulp sedatives from the supply that, I presumed, was stored somewhere in the suit.

But he wasn't being that way at all. He was grasping the truth of our situation as clearly as anyone could—more so than I'd done. But he wasn't upset. More bemused.

"When we were Evoked," I reminded him, "you said there was a rumor we'd just get taken off to a gas chamber."

"Indeed," he said, "but I was envisioning something much simpler—quicker—*less expensive.*"

It was the kind of joke that would only be ruined by my laughing out loud. I somewhat wished that Jesry and Lio could be in on it. But indeed, before too much longer, our conversation flagged. Arsibalt disconnected from me and began making the rounds, as if table-hopping in the Refectory.

He was connected to Jesry when Jesry applied power to the tether. This was a simple matter of pumping electrical current down the wire to its far end. Of course, in order to make an electrical circuit, there had to be some way for those electrons to get back up to the nuke. Normally that would have been provided by a second wire, parallel to the first—as in a lamp cord. Here, though, that would have defeated our purposes. Fortunately we were in the ionosphere—the extreme upper atmosphere, permanently ionized by the radiation of the sun, so that it conducted electricity. We got the return path for free. Current only flowed in one direction along that wire. Consequently, it interacted with Arbre's magnetic field in such a way as to generate thrust. Not a lot of it—not like a rocket engine—but, unlike a rocket engine, we could run it continuously for days, and gradually spiral in to the desired orbit: still, all this time later, the orbit that Ala and I had watched the *Daban Urnud* settle into by following a trail of sparks across a page in the Præsidium.

As long as Arsibalt was hard-wired to Jesry, he acted as communicator to the rest of us, getting our attention with sweeping arms and pantomiming a suggestion that we all grab on to something. Then he counted down with his finger. At "five," one of his skele-hands became redundant and he used it to grasp a bracket on the control panel of the nuke. At "one" he grabbed the bracket with his other hand as Jesry flipped a switch. The result was not dramatic, but it was perfectly obvious: we saw the tether adopt a slight bow, just like a taut string being acted on by wind. As it did, the Cold Black Mirror yawed around slightly and settled into a new angle, no longer looking straight down at the surface of Arbre but now canted almost imperceptibly sideways. And that was the whole event. We were under thrust now, as surely as if Jesry had fired a rocket engine. It was, though, a thrust too subtle for our bodies to feel it, and it would have to act on us for days to have any effect.

Once that had been done, I had a few moments to think about what Arsibalt had been saying. Even taking into account Jules's and Jad's medical troubles and my nuke escapade, it had to be said that the launch and the assembly of the Cold Black Mirror, the firing of the decoy and the deployment of the tether had all gone better than we'd had any right to expect. No one had turned up dead, or mysteriously failed to turn up at all. There'd been no accidents—no one drifting helplessly away—we'd recovered as many of the payloads as we needed. Since that had seemed like the most obviously fatal part of the journey, it had put me in too sunny a mood. But ten seconds' reflection sufficed to make it obvious that this was a suicide mission.

○○

Causal Domain: A collection of things mutually linked in a web of cause-and-effect relationships.
—THE DICTIONARY, *4th edition, A.R. 3000*

Social conventions evolved. I'd thought some might take it the wrong way if two or three of us jacked together for a private conversation. But I didn't feel thus when I noticed Lio talking to Osa or Sammann to Jules Verne Durand, and soon it became clear that everyone in the cell was happy to afford others privacy. Sammann strung a network of wires through the frame that everyone could connect to when it was necessary to have an all-hands meeting, and we agreed that we'd do so every eight hours. The intervals between those meetings were free time. Each of us tried to devote one out of three to sleeping, but this wasn't going so well. I thought I was the only one having trouble with it until Arsibalt drifted over during a rest period and connected himself to me.

"You sleeping, Raz?"

"Not any more."

"*Were* you sleeping?"

"No. Not really. How about you?"

Up to this point it had been the same, word for word, as the conversations we used to have in the middle of the night back when we had been newly Collected fids, lying in unfamiliar cells, trying to sleep. Now, though, it took a new turn. "Hard to say," Arsibalt said. "I don't feel as if I am going through normal sleeping and waking cycles up here. Frankly, I can't tell the difference between dreaming and waking any more."

"Well, what are you dreaming about?"

"About all that could have gone wrong—"

"But didn't?"

"Exactly, Raz."

"I haven't heard the whole story yet of how you rescued Jad."

"I'm not even certain that I could *relate* it coherently," he sighed. "It exists in my mind as a jumble of moments when I thought or did things—and every one of those moments, Raz, could have gone another way. And *all* of the other outcomes would have been bad ones. I'm certain of that. I replay it in my head over and over. And in every case, I happened to do the right thing."

"Well, it's kind of like the anthropic principle at work, isn't it?" I pointed out. "If anything had been a little different, you'd be dead—and so you wouldn't have a brain to remember it with."

Arsibalt said nothing for a while, then sighed. "That is as unsatisfactory as anthropic arguments *usually* are. I'd prefer the alternate explanation."

"Which is?"

"That I'm not only brilliant, but cool under pressure."

I decided to let this go. "I've had dreams," I admitted, "dreams in which everything is the same, except that you and Jad aren't here because you croaked."

"Yes, and I have had dreams in which I let Jad go because I couldn't drag him back, and watched him burn up in the atmosphere below me. And other dreams in which you didn't make it, Raz. We recovered the nuke, but you had simply vanished."

"But then you wake up—" I began.

"I wake up and see you and Jad. But the boundary between waking and dreaming is so indistinct here that sometimes I can't make out whether I've gone from dreaming to waking, or the other way round."

"I think I see where this is going," I said. "I might be dead. You might be dead. Jad might be dead—"

"We've become like Fraa Orolo's wandering 10,000-year math," Arsibalt proclaimed. "A causal domain cut off from the rest of the cosmos."

"Whew!"

"But there is a side effect that Orolo never warned us of," he continued, "which is that we've gone adrift. We don't exist in one state or another. Anything's possible, any history might have happened, until the gates swing open and we go into Apert."

"Either that," I said, "or we're just sleepy and worried."

"That is just another possibility that might be real," Arsibalt said.

When we weren't (according to most of us) dozing or (according to Arsibalt) drifting between distinct, but equally real, worldtracks, we were studying the *Daban Urnud*. A few paragraphs' worth of description from Jules Verne Durand, disseminated over the Reticulum, had given the Antiswarm enough information to build a three-dimensional model of the alien ship that, according to the Laterran, was eerily faithful.

Blow a balloon out of steel, almost a mile wide, and fill it half full of water. Repeat three more times. Place these four orbs at the corners of a square, close to one another, but not quite touching.

Repeat with four more orbs. Stack the new set atop the old. But give it a forty-five-degree twist, so that the upper orbs nestle into the clefts between the ones below, like fruits stacked at a green-grocer's.

Pile on two more such orb-squares, repeating the twist each time. Now you have sixteen orbs in a stack a little more than two miles high and a little less than two miles across. Running up the center of the stack is an empty space, a chimney about half a mile in diameter. Pack that chimney with all of the good stuff: all of the complicated, expensive, exquisitely designed praxis that we have long associated with space travel. Much of it is nothing but struc-ture: steel trusswork to grip those orbs and hold them securely in their places while the entire thing is spinning around at one revolu-tion per minute to create pseudogravity, maneuvering to dodge in-coming bogeys, managing the resultant slosh, accelerating under atomic power, or all of the above.

Once you're satisfied it's never going to fall apart structurally, weave in all of the other stuff: a storage magazine capable of hold-ing tens of thousands of nuclear propulsion charges. Reactors to supply power when the ship is far from any sun. Inconceivably com-plex plumbing and wiring. Pressurized corridors along which Urnu-dans, Troäns, Laterrans, and Fthosians can move from one orb to another. Trunk lines of optical fibers to pipe captured sunlight from the exterior of the icosahedron to the orbs, to shine on their rooftop farms.

The orbs themselves are comparatively simple. Inside of them, the water's free to find its own level. When the whole construct is spinning, the water flees to the outside and settles into a curve on which "gravity" is always equal to what it was on the home planet. When the ship is under power, the water settles into the aft part of the sphere and levels out. People live on the surface of the water in houseboats linked by a web of stretchy lines and held apart by tough air-bladders; when the shape of the water changes, there's always a bit of jostling. Like any proper boat, though, these are rigged for that; the cabinets have latches so that they don't fly open, the furniture is attached to the floor so it doesn't slide around. People live as their ancestors did on the home planet, and may go for days, weeks, without thinking very much about the fact that they're sealed in a metal balloon being spanked through space by A-bombs—as their families back on Urnud, Tro, Laterre, or Fthos might never think about the fact that they live on wet balls of rock hurtling through a vacuum.

This construct—the Orbstack—is a nice piece of work, but vulnerable to cosmic rays, wandering rocks, sunlight, and alien weaponry. So, frame walls of gravel around it, and while you're at it, hang the walls on a network of giant shock pistons. The Orbstack is suspended in its middle, webbed to it. Anything that relates to the rest of the universe—radar, telescopes, weapons systems, scout vehicles—lives on the outside, attached to the thirty shock pistons, or the twelve vertices where the shocks join together. Three of the vertices—the ones down around the pusher plate—are naked mechanisms, but the other nine are all complex space vehicles in themselves. Some are pressurized spheres where members of the Command float around weightless. Others have wide tunnels bored through them so that small vehicles, and space-suited persons, can pass between the interior of the icosahedron and the remainder of whatever cosmos the ship happens to be in. And one is an optical observatory, better than any on Arbre because it enjoys the vacuum of space.

All of this had been modeled, in more or less detail, by the minds of the Antiswarm during the days that my cell-mates and I had been assembling space suits and playing video games in Elkhazg. The model lived in our suits now. We could fly through it using the same controls—the trackball and the stick—that we had earlier used to steer the monyafeeks. From a distance it seemed impressively complete, with a kind of organic complexity about it; as I flew in closer, though, to explore the core of the Orbstack, I found hovering, semitransparent notes that had been posted by diffident avout, writing in perfect Orth, informing me, with regret, that everything beyond this point was pure conjecture.

Fraa Jad finally got his wish: a sextant. We had been supplied with a device consisting of a wide-angle lens, like Clesthyra's Eye, that was smart enough to recognize certain constellations. So it could know our attitude with respect to the so-called fixed stars. That in combination with the positions of the sun, the moon, and Arbre, and an accurate internal clock and ephemeris, gave this thing enough information to calculate our orbital elements. Fraa Jad seized this tool as soon as its presence was made known, and devoted hours to mastering its functions.

Now that our adventure had turned into an obvious do-or-die proposition, Jules had given up on trying to conserve what remained of his food, and was eating freely. So his energy level sprang back and his mood improved. Whenever he was awake, several others were jacked into his suit, asking him questions about internal details of the ship that had not made it into the model: for example, what the doors looked like, how to operate the latching mechanisms, how to tell a Fthosian from a Troän. I learned that the Geometers had a particular dread of fire in the zero-gravity parts of the ship, and that one could not go more than a hundred feet without encountering a locker stocked with respirators, fireproof suits, and extinguishers.

That still left a lot of free time. Two days in, I made a private connection with Jesry and told him what I knew of the Everything Killers. Jesry listened attentively, as in a chalk hall, and didn't say much. By watching his face on the speely screen I could tell that he was thinking about it hard—talking himself into why it made sense. It had been obvious to him that there was something we weren't being told. Otherwise, the mission made no sense on the face of it. I had given him something to think about. Until he'd thought about it—until he'd had a thought that wasn't obvious—he'd have nothing to say.

Text messages trickled in from Cell 87 and appeared on my screen. The first few were routine. Then they started getting weird.

Tulia: Settle an argument down here . . . what is your head count up there?

I pecked a message back: *Pardon me, but are you asking me how many of us are alive?* Then I fired the message off. Only after brooding over the exchange for a few minutes did I realize that I hadn't answered her question. By that time, though, we'd lost contact with the ground.

I called a meeting. We all jacked in.

"My support cell doesn't know how many of us are alive," I announced.

"Nor does mine," Jesry said immediately. "They claim I sent them a message a few hours ago implying that two of us were dead."

"Did you?"

"No."

"My support cell sent me no messages at all for quite a long time," said Suur Esma, "because they were convinced I had perished in the launch."

"It makes me wonder if something has gone wrong with the Antiswarm," I said. "All of these cells should be talking to each other on the Reticulum, right? Comparing notes?"

We looked at Sammann. New body language was required. Since faces could not be seen directly, we had gotten in the habit of shifting our bodies toward the interlocutor to let them know we were paying attention. So, nine space suits aimed themselves at Sammann. Fraa Jad, though, didn't seem interested. He had already jacked out of the meeting and was clambering to a different part of the space frame. But he had scarcely uttered a word since we had reached space, and so we paid him no mind. I was even starting to wonder if he had suffered brain damage.

"Something *has* gone wrong," Sammann affirmed.

"Did the Geometers find a way to jam the Reticulum?" Osa asked.

"No, the Ret—its physical layer, anyway—is working fine. But there's a low-level bug in the dynamics of the reputon space."

"In Ita talk," I said, "when you call something 'low-level,' you mean it's really important, right?"

"Yes."

"Can you say any more about what this means for us?" Lio requested.

"Early in the Reticulum—thousands of years ago—it became almost useless because it was cluttered with faulty, obsolete, or downright misleading information," Sammann said.

"Crap, you once called it," I reminded him.

"Yes—a technical term. So crap filtering became important. Businesses were built around it. Some of those businesses came up with a clever plan to make more money: they poisoned the well. They began to put crap on the Reticulum deliberately, forcing people to use their products to filter that crap back out. They created syndevs whose sole purpose was to spew crap into the Reticulum. But it had to be good crap."

"What is good crap?" Arsibalt asked in a politely incredulous tone.

"Well, *bad* crap would be an unformatted document consisting of random letters. *Good* crap would be a beautifully typeset, well-written document that contained a hundred correct, verifiable sentences and one that was subtly false. It's a lot harder to generate good crap. At first they had to hire humans to churn it out. They mostly did it by taking legitimate documents and inserting errors—swapping one name for another, say. But it didn't really take off until the military got interested."

"As a tactic for planting misinformation in the enemy's reticules, you mean," Osa said. "This I know about. You are referring to the Artificial Inanity programs of the mid–First Millennium A.R."

"Exactly!" Sammann said. "Artificial Inanity systems of enormous sophistication and power were built for exactly the purpose Fraa Osa has mentioned. In no time at all, the praxis leaked to the commercial sector and spread to the Rampant Orphan Botnet Ecologies. Never mind. The point is that there was a sort of Dark Age on the Reticulum that lasted until my Ita forerunners were able to bring matters in hand."

"So, are Artificial Inanity systems still active in the Rampant Orphan Botnet Ecologies?" asked Arsibalt, utterly fascinated.

"The ROBE evolved into something totally different early in the Second Millennium," Sammann said dismissively.

"What did it evolve into?" Jesry asked.

"No one is sure," Sammann said. "We only get hints when it finds ways to physically instantiate itself, which, fortunately, does not happen that often. But we digress. The functionality of Artificial Inanity still exists. You might say that those Ita who brought the Ret out of the Dark Age could only defeat it by co-opting it. So, to make a long story short, for every legitimate document floating around on the Reticulum, there are hundreds or thousands of bogus versions—bogons, as we call them."

"The only way to preserve the integrity of the defenses is to subject them to unceasing assault," Osa said, and any idiot could guess he was quoting some old Vale aphorism.

"Yes," Sammann said, "and it works so well that, most of the time, the users of the Reticulum don't know it's there. Just as you are not aware of the millions of germs trying and failing to attack your body every moment of every day. However, the recent events, and the stresses posed by the Antiswarm, appear to have introduced the low-level bug that I spoke of."

"So the practical consequence for us," Lio said, "is that—?"

"Our cells on the ground may be having difficulty distinguishing between legitimate messages and bogons. And some of the messages that flash up on our screens may be bogons as well."

"And this is all because a few bits got flipped in a syndev somewhere," Jesry said.

"It's slightly more complicated than you make it sound," Sammann retorted.

"But what Jesry's driving at," I said, "is that this ambiguity is ultimately caused by some number of logic gates or memory cells, somewhere, being in a state that is wrong, or at least ambiguous."

"I guess you could put it that way," Sammann said, and I could tell he was shrugging even if I couldn't see it. "But it'll all get sorted soon, and then we'll stop receiving goofy messages."

"No we won't," said Fraa Gratho.

"Why do you say that?" asked Lio.

"Behold," said Fraa Gratho, and extended his arm. Following the gesture, we found Fraa Jad at work on the wireless box that was our only link to the ground. He was stabbing it with a screwdriver again and again. From time to time a piece of shrapnel would float away from it, and he would fastidiously pluck it out of space with a skelehand so that it would not wander out from beneath the Cold Dark Mirror and return a radar echo.

When he was good and finished, he drifted back to the meeting and jacked himself in. Lio remained calm, and waited for him to speak.

Jad said, "The leakage was forcing choices, the making of which in no way improved matters."

Okay. So we were, in effect, locked in a room with a madman sorceror. That clarified things a little. We were silent for a while. We knew there was no point in requesting clarification. Fraa Jad had put it as clearly as he knew how. I saw Jesry looking my way in his speely display. *This is how the Incanters do it; he's doing it now.*

Sammann finally broke the silence. "It is most odd," he said, sounding strangely moved, "but I have been working up my nerve to do the same thing."

"What? Destroy the transmitter?" Lio asked.

"Yes. As a matter of fact, I dreamed a few hours ago I *had* done it. I felt good about it. When I woke up, I was surprised to find it intact."

"Why would you wish to destroy it?" Arsibalt asked.

"I've been observing its habits. Once every orbit, it comes into line of sight with a facility on the ground and establishes a link. Then it empties its buffer—clears its queue." He went on to translate these Ita terms into Orth. The queue was like a stack of leaves with messages written on them, which were transmitted down to Arbre whenever possible. They were sent down in the same order as they stood in the queue, like customers waiting in line at a store.

"So these things in the queue are, for example, the text messages I've been writing back to my support cell on the ground?" I asked.

"How many have you written?" he asked me.

"Maybe five."

"Lio?"

"More like ten."

"Osa?" Sammann polled everyone. None had written more than a few messages. "The number of items in the queue at this time," he announced, "is over fourteen hundred."

"What are they?" Arsibalt asked. "Can you read them?"

"No. They are all encrypted, and no one saw fit to give me the key. Most are quite small. Probably text messages, biomedical data, and associated bogons. But some of them are thousands of times larger. Since I am the only one here with knowledge of such things, I'll tell you what would be obvious to an Ita, which is that the large items are most likely recorded sound and video files."

I could think of any number of explanations for this but Arsibalt jumped directly to the most dramatic and, I had to admit, probably correct one: "Surveillance!"

Sammann made no objection. "I have been watching the behavior of the queue during my idle moments, of which I have many. The big files behave in certain remarkable ways. For one thing, they get priority over the little ones. The system advances them to the foremost position in the queue as soon as they are created. For another, the creation of these files seems to coincide with beginnings and ends of conversations. As an example, I saw Erasmas having a private conversation with Jesry a while ago, between about 1015 and 1030 hours. The next time Jesry connected himself to the reticule, which was only about fifteen minutes ago, a large file sprang into existence in the queue, and was promptly moved to the top. Time of creation, 1017. Last modified, 1030."

"Is this occurring with *all* of our conversations?" Lio asked. And the tone of his voice told me—as if I ever could have doubted it—that all of this was as new to him as it was to me.

"No. Only some."

"I propose an experiment," Jesry said. "Sammann, does it still work?"

"Oh yes. Fraa Jad destroyed only the transmitter. The syndev still functions as if nothing had changed."

"Are you monitoring the queue now?"

"Of course."

Jesry disconnected, and motioned for me to do the same. We formed a private connection. Jesry launched into a very old, well-worn dialog that we'd had to memorize as fids: a verbal proof that the square root of two was an irrational number. I did my best to hold up my end of it. When we were finished, we reconnected to the reticule and waited a few seconds. "Nothing," Sammann said.

Again we disconnected and formed a two-person link.

"Do you remember back at Edhar," I began, "when we and the other Incanters would sit around after dinner making Everything Killers out of cornstalks and shoelaces?"

"Of course," Jesry said, "those were really good Everything Killers because they could assassinate filthy Panjandrums like no one's business."

"That'll come in handy when we betray Arbre to the Pedestal," I pointed out.

And so on in that vein for a couple of minutes. Then we reconnected to the reticule. "There's a new file," Sammann announced, "at the head of the queue."

"Okay," I announced, "so the Panjandrums seem to be really keen on knowing if we talk about certain things like the Everything Killers."

"Ha!" Sammann exclaimed. "A new file has just been opened, and it is growing larger the longer . . . I . . . keep . . . talking."

The topic of the Everything Killers had not yet been broached to the group at large, and so some people had a lot of questions, which Lio fielded. Meanwhile, Jesry and I continued the experiment we had begun, breaking and re-establishing contact with the reticule a couple of dozen times over the course of the following half-hour. Every time we broke away, we'd try a few more words, just to see which topics triggered the automatic recording system. This was a haphazard business, but we were able to discover several more trigger words, including *attack, neutron, mass murder, insane, dishonor, unconscionable, refuse,* and *mutiny.*

Every time we reconnected, we heard more ideas for possible trigger words, since the conversation was quite naturally evolving in such a way that all the words listed above, and many more, were frequently put to use. Things were becoming extremely emotional, and it was good in a way that Jesry and I were able to jack in and out of it and treat its contents as an object of theorical study. But after a while it reached a point where we reckoned we had better join and stay joined.

Arsibalt had just asked a rather probing question of the Valers: where did their ultimate allegiance lie?

Fraa Osa was answering: "To my fraas and suurs of the Ringing Vale I have a loyalty that can never be dissolved precisely because it is no rational thing but a bond like that of family. And I will not waste oxygen by discussing all of the nesting and overlapping loyalty groups to which I belong: this cell, the Mathic world, the Convox, the people of Arbre, and the community, extending even beyond the limits of this cosmos, that unites us with the likes of Jules Verne Durand."

"Say zhoost," answered the Laterran, which we'd figured out was his way of expressing approval.

"To untangle all acting loyalties and obligations is not possible in the thick of an Emergence, and so one falls back on simple responses that arise from one's training."

Jules had not yet been exposed to this concept and so Osa gave him a brief tutorial on Emergence-ology, using as an example the decision tree that a swordfighter must traverse in order to make the correct move during a duel. It was obvious that such a thing was far too complex to be evaluated in a rational way during a rapid exchange of cuts and thrusts, and so it must be the case that swordfighters who survived more than one or two such encounters must be doing Something Different. The avout of the Ringing Vale had made the study and cultivation of that Something Different their sole occupation. Jules Verne Durand took the point readily. "The analogy works as well with complex board games. We have some on Laterre, similar to yours here in that the tree of possible moves and counter-moves rapidly becomes far too vast for the brain to sort through all possibilities. Ordinators—what you'd call syntactic devices—can play the game in this style, but successful human players appear to use some fundamentally different approach that relies on seeing the whole board and detecting certain patterns and applying certain rules of thumb."

"The Teglon," put in Fraa Jad. And he did not need to elaborate on this. We'd all seen the feat he had accomplished at Elkhazg, and it was obvious to all of us that it could not have been done by trial and error. Nor by building outwards from a single starting place. He'd had to grasp the whole pattern at once.

"This is dangerous," Jesry said flatly. "It leads to saying that we may abandon the Rake and behave like a bunch of Enthusiasts, and everything will work out just fine because we have achieved holistic oneness with the polycosm."

"What you say is indeed a problem," said Jules, "but no one here would dare argue that it is possible to win a swordfight or solve the Teglon by behaving so self-indulgently."

"Jesry is making a straw man argument," Arsibalt said. "He's raising a possible future issue. If we agree to proceed along these lines, and reach a point, somewhere down the line, where a difficult decision needs to be made, what grounds will we have for evaluating possible decisions, if we've already thrown rational analysis to the wind?"

"The ability to decide correctly at such moments must be cultivated over many years of disciplined practice and contemplation," said Fraa Osa. "No one would argue that a novice could solve the Teglon simply by trusting his feelings. Fraa Jad developed the ability to do it over many decades."

"Centuries," I corrected him, since I saw no benefit, now, in being coy about this. I heard a couple of surprised exclamations over the reticule, but no one said anything for or against the proposition.

Not even Fraa Jad. He did say this: "Those who think through possible outcomes with discipline, forge connections, in so doing, to other cosmi in which those outcomes are more than mere possibilities. Such a consciousness is measurably, quantitatively different from one that has not undertaken the same work and so, yes, is able to make correct decisions in an Emergence where an untrained mind would be of little use."

"Fine," Jesry said, "but where does it *get* us? What are we going to *do*?"

"I think it has already gotten us somewhere," I said. "When you and I re-joined this dialog a few minutes ago, passions were inflamed and people were still trying to frame the decision in terms of allegiances and loyalties. Fraa Osa has shown that any such approach will fail because we all belong to multiple groups with conflicting loyalties. This made the conversation less emotional. We've also developed an argument that it's not possible to work out all the moves in advance. But as you yourself pointed out, going on naïve emotion is bound to fail."

"So we must develop the same kind of decision-making ability that Fraa Jad employs when he solves the Teglon," said Jesry, "but that requires time and knowledge. We don't have time and we don't have much knowledge."

"We have two more days," said Lio.

"And there is much knowledge that we can infer," said Arsibalt.

"Such as?" Jesry asked in a skeptical tone.

"That Everything Killers might be planted in this equipment. That our purpose might be to deliver them to the *Daban Urnud*," Arsibalt said.

"Most of this equipment isn't going to make it to the *Daban Urnud*," Lio pointed out. He added, perfectly deadpan, "Those of you who've reviewed the Terminal Rendezvous Maneuver Plan will know as much."

"Just us, and our suits," Jesry said. "That's all that will make it to the ship—if we're lucky. And they—the ones who planned this—can't predict the fate of our suits. What if we get captured by the Pedestal? They might ditch our suits in space, or dismantle them."

"Your point is becoming clear," said Fraa Osa, "but it is important that you make it."

"Fine. *We* are the weapons. The Everything Killers have been planted inside our bodies. We all know how it was done."

"The giant pills," said Jules.

"Exactly: the core temperature transponders that we swallowed before takeoff," Jesry said. "Anyone pass theirs yet?"

"Come to think of it, no," said Arsibalt. "It seems to have taken up residence in my gut."

"There you have it," said Jesry. "Until those things are surgically removed, we are all living, breathing nuclear weapons."

"All," said Suur Vay, "except for Fraa Jad, and Jules Verne Durand."

This left all of us nonplussed, so she explained, "I believe you will find their core temperature transponders rattling around loose, somewhere inside their space suits."

"I threw mine up," explained Jules.

"I declined to swallow mine," said Jad.

"And as the cell physician, you knew this, Suur Vay, because their core temp readings have been obviously wrong?" asked Lio.

"Yes. And the incorrect readings caused their suits to respond in inappropriate ways, which is why both of them required medical attention following the launch."

"Why didn't you swallow your pill, Fraa Jad?" asked Arsibalt. "Did you know what it was?"

"I judged it wiser not to," was all that Fraa Jad was willing to supply in the way of an answer.

"This idea—that we've all been turned into nuclear weapons—is an amazing theory," I said, "but I simply don't believe that Ala would ever do such a thing."

"I'm guessing she didn't know," Lio said. "This must have been added onto the plan without her knowledge."

Fraa Osa said, "If I were the strategist in charge, I would go to Ala and say 'please assemble the team you deem most capable of getting aboard the *Daban Urnud*.' And her answer would come back: 'I will do it by making friends with those among the Geometers who are opposed to the Pedestal; they'll take our people in and offer them assistance.'"

"That is monstrous," I said.

"*Monstrous:* probably another trigger word," Jesry mused. I wanted to slug him. But he was making an excellent point.

Two days later we stripped off our white coveralls, then drew down the retractable shields to conceal the lights and displays on our suit-fronts. We were all matte black now. Like mountaineers, we roped ourselves together with a braided line that doubled as safety rope and communications wire. Jad, Jesry, and I had spent much of the last shift working with the sextant and making calculations. These culminated with Fraa Jad hanging off the underside of the nuke with a knife in one hand, sighting down the length of the tether as if it were a gun barrel, watching the constellations wheel behind it. At the instant when a particular star came into alignment with the tether, he slashed through it with a knife. The tether and the counterweight at its end flew off into space—and so did we, picking up a final momentum adjustment that would, we hoped, synch our orbit with that of the *Daban Urnud*.

Half an hour later, we all braced our feet against the underside of the Mirror and, at a signal from Lio, pushed it away—or jumped off, depending on your frame of reference. The Mirror glided out of the way to give us our first direct look at the *Daban Urnud*. It was so close to us, now, that we could hardly see anything: just a single triangular facet of the icosahedron, filling most of our visual field.

Essentially all of the Geometers' surveillance and remote sensing systems had been designed to look at things that were thousands of miles away. As Jesry and the others had learned when they had brought the Warden of Heaven here, the *Daban Urnud* did have short-range radars for illuminating things that were nearby, but there was no reason to keep them switched on unless visitors were expected. And we had not emerged from behind the Cold Black Mirror until we had approached too close even for those radars to work very well. This was partly luck. If our trajectory had been a little less precise, we'd have been forced to ditch the Mirror farther out, and thereby exposed ourselves to the scrutiny of those systems.

But Fraa Jad had wielded his knife at just the right instant. If he did nothing else for the rest of the mission he would still have earned his place.

In order to see us, they'd have to literally see us. Someone would have to look out a window, or (more likely) at a speelycaptor feed, and just happen to notice eleven matte-black humanoids gliding in against the background of space.

Its surface was like a shingle beach: flat, assembled from countless pieces of asteroids that had been scavenged from four different cosmi. Light glinted among the stones: the wire mesh that held them together. It seemed as though we were going to collide with a shock piston, which cut straight across our path like a horizon. But we cleared it by a few yards and found ourselves gliding along "above" a new face of the icosahedron, currently in shadow. Each of us was armed with a spring-loaded gun, and so at a signal from Lio, eleven grappling hooks shot out toward the rubble shield, trailing lines behind them. I'd estimate that half of them snagged in the mesh holding the rocks together. One by one the grapnel-lines went taut and began to pull back on those who'd fired them. This caused the ropes that joined us to go tight in a complex and unpredictable train of events, and so there were a few moments of bashing into one another and gratuitous entanglement as the whole cell came to the end of this improvised web of tethers. Our momentum caused us to swing forward and down toward the rubble, a scary development that was somewhat mitigated by the four Valers, who'd been issued cold gas thrusters that they held out before them like pistols and fired in the direction we didn't want to go. This led to further collisions and entanglements that bordered on the ridiculous, but did have the net effect of slowing us down some. As we got closer, we tried to get legs and/or arms out in front of ourselves to serve as shock absorbers. I was able to plant my right foot on a boulder. The impact torqued me around. I spun and punched another 4.5-billion-year-old rock with the stumpy end of my suit-arm just in time to avoid planting my face on it. Then various ropes jerked on me from multiple vectors and dragged me along for a short ways. But soon everyone stopped bouncing and dragging and managed to grip the wire mesh with their fingers, giving Cell 317 a secure purchase on the *Daban Urnud*.

○○○

Requiem: The aut celebrated to mark the death of an avout.

—THE DICTIONARY, *4th edition, A.R. 3000*

The darkness was nearly perfect. Arbre was on the other side of the ship, and shed no light here. A new moon, though, was swinging up through the cluttered horizon of the nearest shock piston, strewing faint light by which we cut ourselves apart and sorted ourselves out. Our magnetic boot-soles stuck faintly to the icosahedron, a rubble of nickel and iron. Moving like a man with gum on the soles of his shoes, Sammann made the rounds and checked our connections to the rope/wire.

"This facet will remain in darkness for another twenty minutes," Jesry informed us, "after which we have to move to that one." I supposed he was pointing at one of the three shock pistons that made up our local horizon, but I couldn't see him. As the *Daban Urnud* revolved around Arbre, the terminator—the dividing line between the sunlit and shaded halves of the icosahedron—crept around it. On any given facet, sunrise or sunset would be explosively sudden. We'd better not get caught in the open when it happened, because the citadel-like complexes that loomed over the twelve vertices had clear views over the surrounding facets.

"According to my equipment," announced Fraa Gratho, "we did not get illuminated by any short-range radar."

"They simply don't have it turned on," said Lio. "But sooner or later, they'll probably notice the monyafeeks that Fraa Jad cut loose, or the Cold Black Mirror, and then they'll go to a higher state of alert. So, which way to the World Burner?"

"Follow me," said Fraa Osa, and started walking. If walking was the right word for such a clumsy style of locomotion. I'd like to say we moved as drunks, but it would be an insult to every sloshed fraa who had staggered back to his cell in the dark. Much of our twenty minutes of darkness was burned moving the first couple of hundred feet. After that, though, we learned, if not what to do, then at least what *not* to do, and reached the nearest horizon with a few minutes' darkness to spare.

The shock piston was like a pipeline half-buried in the rubble, but reinforced with fin-like trusses to prevent it from buckling like a straw when it was under load. At its ends, about a mile away in either direction, it swelled like the end of a bone and developed into a heavy steel knuckle. Five such knuckles, coming together from different directions, formed the base of each vertex. Each vertex was different, but in general they had been cobbled together from a mess of domes, cylinders, gridwork, and antennae. Extravagant bouquets of silver parabolic horns flourished from their "tops," waiting for their turn to gaze into our sun and steal some of our light.

The triangular rubble-field across which we'd been walking didn't butt up hard against the shock piston, because there had to be some give in the system; a shock absorber that had been in effect welded to a stiff triangular plate all along its length would not be able to function. Instead the facet stopped ten feet short of the truss-work that enshrouded the shock, and was sewn to it by a system of cables that zigzagged over pulleys. At a glance, it looked awfully complicated, and made me think of sailboats, not starships. But since the Urnudans had been building such things for a thousand years I guessed they had come up with a way to make it work.

Light shone up from the chasm below. As we neared it we slowed, bent forward, and gazed into the interior of the icosahedron, a volume of some twenty-three cubic miles, softly illuminated by sunlight slitting in through other such gaps and scattering from the icosahedron's inner walls and the sixteen orbs. It was all as we'd seen it rendered on the model, but of course to see it in person was altogether different. The view was dominated by the nearest of the orbs, swinging by as fast as the second hand on a clock, helpfully painted with a huge numeral in the Urnudan writing system. I'd learned enough of this to translate it as number 5. Orb 5 housed high-ranking Troäns.

All of my instincts told me to fear the jump across the gap, because if I "fell in" I would drop for some vast distance before getting splattered on a rotating orb. But of course there was no gravity here, no down, nothing to fall into.

Osa went first, launching himself across the gap and getting himself established on the struts that lent strength to the shock piston. Vay was last on the line. Once we'd all made it over, we hand-over-handed our way across the shock out of concern that the snapping of our magnetic boots against its steel would create an obvious acoustical signature. There was a dizzy moment when our settled conception of up and down was challenged by the next facet swinging into view, defining a new level and a new horizon. Then we got used to it and floated across another gap using the same procedure as before. This was perhaps an overly cautious way to travel ten feet through space. But if we all did it at once, and jumped too hard, we might drift away.

Sun was striking the struts we had just passed over as we planted our feet on the next facet of the icosahedron, where we could be assured of a few hours' darkness. This was more time than we needed. Or, to speak truthfully, it was more than we had, since we only had an hour's oxygen remaining, and the tender was gone.

Two miles away—directly across the facet—was a hydrogen bomb the size of a six-story office building. It was essentially egg-shaped. But like a beetle caught in spider's webbing, its form was blurred by a fantastic tangle of strut-work and plumbing connecting it to the vertex-citadel. Indeed, that whole vertex appeared to have no practical use other than to serve as a support base for the World Burner. Even if it hadn't been so enormous, it would have been a difficult thing to miss, because it was all lit up.

Lit up for the benefit of a hundred people in space suits clambering around on it.

"Do you think they're getting ready to launch it?" Arsibalt asked.

"I don't think they're giving it a new paint job," Jesry said.

"Very well," Lio said. I didn't know who he was speaking to, or what he was giving his assent to. A click on the line suggested that someone had just jacked out.

Our view of the World Burner complex was interrupted, now, by four black-space-suited figures who had broken away from the rest of us. In the dark, with the suits in stealth mode, we could not tell one another apart, but something in the way that these four moved convinced me that they were the Ringing Vale contingent. They walked abreast, with one—presumably Fraa Osa—slightly ahead of the others. They were spreading a little farther apart with each step.

"Lio? What is happening?" I asked.

"An Emergence," he reasoned.

When the four Valers were spaced about twenty feet apart, Fraa Osa deployed his skelehands and, like a steppe rider in a shootout, drew a pair of pistol-like objects—the cold gas thrusters—from holsters bracketed to the hips of his suit. The other three did likewise. Then, to all appearances, Fraa Osa fell on his face. He planted his feet next to each other and let his momentum carry his body forward, peeling his magnetic soles loose from the rubble. As soon as he lost that connection to the icosahedron, his feet swung up and his whole body pivoted in space until he was prone. And in the same moment he began to glide headfirst toward the World Burner. He was holding both arms down to his sides, pointing the cold gas guns toward his feet, using them to thrust himself across the rubble plane, like a low-flying superhero. Vay, Esma, and Gratho were all doing likewise. In their wake we could see a roiling in the light, like heat waves, as the plumes of clear gas dissolved into space. At first their movement was achingly gradual, but they rapidly picked up speed, sometimes porpoising up, then correcting it with a calm inflection of the wrist, spreading out as they vectored themselves toward different parts of the World Burner complex, sliding with a kind of wicked, silent beauty over the glossy purple-blue rubble plane. We were able to see them only in silhouette against the lights of the sprawling complex—and that only for the first few moments of their flight. Then they were as invisible to us as they were to the space-suited Geometers swarming over the bomb.

Lio announced, "We have perhaps only a few minutes to get inside and find something to breathe before every door in the *Daban Urnud* is locked against us."

"What about the Valers?" Arsibalt said.

"I think it would be wisest to assume that they and everyone working on the World Burner are as good as dead," Lio said, after a moment's thought.

"They are attacking *now?*" I asked.

"They are *boarding it* now," Lio said.

Or—technically speaking—reminded me. For we had discussed this eventuality. *"What if, when we come in sight of the World Burner, we see evidence that the Geometers are just about to launch it?"*

"Ah, well, of course that would change everything, we'd have to fork to a completely different branch of the plan, not a moment to spare!" I knew we'd gone over it. But I had filed it, in my head, under the category of "things very unlikely to happen, hence safely forgotten." Lio, however, had not forgotten. "If the Valers can manage to get aboard the World Burner covertly, they'll hide, and take no further action until just before their air supply runs out. That's to give the rest of us time to find a way in. But if the World Burner launches—or if someone sees them, and raises the alarm—well—"

"Bad things will happen," Jesry snapped.

"So we might or might not have a little time," I said.

"Which means, we should act as if we have none at all," Lio returned. "Jules?" For the Laterran had been silent for a long time. "You still with us?"

"Pardon me," Jules returned. "I am amazed, thinking of the havoc that our friends of the Ringing Vale are about to unleash. It is an inconceivable nightmare for the Pedestal, the worst embarrassment they will have suffered in one thousand years. My loyalties are torn several ways, you know."

"No matter how much conflict is in your soul," I said, "you can't possibly object to the destruction of the World Burner, can you?"

"No," said Jules softly, but distinctly. "In that my feelings are unalloyed. What a shame, if some of those working on it are slain!

But to work on such a horrible device—" He did not finish the sentence, but I knew that, inside his space suit, he was shrugging.

"So mainly you just don't want to introduce Everything Killers to the *Daban Urnud*," I said.

"That is certainly correct."

Lio broke in: "I never thought I'd hear myself saying this, but: take us to your leader,"

"I beg your pardon?"

"Point us to the Urnudans. Then your work is done. You can go home and get a decent meal."

"Which is more than we can say for ourselves," Arsibalt pointed out.

"Yes," Jules said, "the irony. No food for you. Not here!"

"So then," Lio said, "what is your decision?" All of us shared his impatience, if for no other reason than that we were running out of air. I'd like to report that I was still thinking coolly, applying the Rake to everything that was clattering through my mind. But in truth I was stunned and bewildered and—if this made sense—hurt by the sudden departure of Osa, Vay, Esma, and Gratho. I'd known, of course, that there were various contingency plans. Had never fooled myself that I could know all of them. But I'd been telling myself all along that the Valers would always be with us. When I'd first seen them on the coach at Tredegarh I'd been horrified by the idea that I was about to be sent off on the kind of mission where such persons might be needed. But over the days since, I had grown used to—and proud of—being on just such a mission. Now, here we were, at its most critical moment, and the Valers were suddenly gone, without explanation, without even a "goodbye and good luck!" The logic of the decision they'd made was unassailable—what could be more important than disabling the World Burner? But where did it leave the rest of us?

"Is it possible," I heard myself saying, "that we are a spent delivery mechanism? Like those boosters that threw us into space—to be dumped into the sea?"

"That's totally plausible," Jesry said without hesitation. "We did our lessons well and played some clever tricks to get the four Valers here. That job is done. Now, here we are. No food, no oxygen, no communications, and no way home."

"You overestimate the importance of the World Burner," Jad announced. "It is a bluff. Its existence forces our military to act in ways it would not otherwise. Its destruction would give Arbre back a measure of freedom. But what use the Sæcular Power would make of that freedom is yet to be known, and our actions may yet be of some importance. We go on."

"Jules?" Lio said. "How about it?"

"It is tempting to drop through this opening before us, no?" Jules said. For we had instinctively turned our backs on the World Burner, as if this would protect us from whatever was about to erupt there. Once more we were gazing down into the gap, watching Orbs 6 and 7 rotate past, glimpsing the Core in the cleft between them. "But then we are in the light, where we may be seen. And the Orbstack rotates with too much velocity for us ever to catch it. No. We must go in via the Core. But to enter the Core, we must first go in at a vertex." He toddled around until he was gazing at the vertex that, as we faced the shock piston, was to our left. "That is the observatory. You've studied the pictures." He toddled right. "*That* one is a military command post."

"Does the observatory have airlocks?" Arsibalt asked. For all of us were now looking leftward—no one felt up to invading a military command post, not after we'd lost our Valers.

"Oh yes, you are looking at one," said Jules, and began walking toward it. We fell in step.

"Er—I am?"

"The dome that houses the telescope is, itself, a great airlock," Jules explained.

"Makes sense," Jesry said. "To work on the telescope, they'd want to flood the dome with air. Then, when they were ready to make observations, they'd evacuate it and expose it to space." Which is where I normally would have become irritated with Jesry for lecturing the rest of us. But it went by me. I was fascinated, dumbfounded, by an idea I had not dared to think of for a week: taking my suit off. Being able to touch my face.

Arsibalt was on the same track: "The way I smell will probably seem funny when I reminisce about it years hence."

"Yes," Lio said, "if odors can travel between cosmi, everything down-Wick of us is about to die."

"Thanks for the preview," Jesry said.

"Let's not get ahead of ourselves," I suggested.

Sammann asked, "Is anyone going to be on duty in this observatory?"

"Perhaps not physically there," Jules said. "The telescopes are controlled remotely on our version of the Reticulum. But the big one will be in use, certainly—making a survey of your lovely cosmos, which is all new to us."

The vertex was looming mountainously as we carried on this conversation. Old instincts warned me that we had an exhausting climb ahead of us. But, of course, it was no climb at all, because we were weightless. Without having to discuss it we made for the "highest" and largest of the domes, which, as Jules had promised, was open. It was a spherical shell, split into two hemispheres, which had spread apart on tracks to expose a multi-segmented mirror with a diameter of some thirty feet. We all clambered through the gap between the hemispheres, which was wide enough to throw a three-bedroom house through, and hand-over-handed ourselves "down" to the level of the trusses and gimbals that supported the mirror—all following, I think, a sort of instinct to get indoors, under cover, away from the terrible exposure we had been living with for so long. Jules pointed out a hatch by which we could gain entry to the pressurized regions of the vertex once the dome had been closed and filled with air. There was even a nice big red panic button that we could slam to emergency-pressurize the dome. But he advised us not to use it, because this would trigger alarms all over the *Daban Urnud*. Instead he pulled himself up on the struts that held the telescope's objective suspended at the mirror's focal point. He peeled the reflective blanket off his chest and stuffed it in there, then clambered "down" to rejoin us. Meanwhile, the rest of us tried to stay calm and control our breathing. Arsibalt, who used more oxygen than anyone else, was down to ten minutes. Sammann had twenty-five; the two of them swapped oxygen tanks. I had eighteen. Lio suggested we all try to eat as much as possible; if we were separated from our suits, we'd have no food left except for a few energy bars that we could carry with us. So I sucked more gruel from the nozzle and made a prolonged and labored effort not to throw it right back up into the scupper.

"Hello!" called Jules, more as an exclamation than a greeting. It took us a moment to understand that he was responding to a face that had appeared in the porthole of the hatch: some cosmographer come to see why the big scope had gone dark. Based on Jules's lessons, I guessed, from the hue of her eyes and the shape of her nostrils, that she was Fthosian. And, though it would take some time to learn Fthosian facial expressions, I reckoned I had now seen two of them: befuddlement followed by shock as a matte black space suit of unfamiliar design loomed in her window. Jules grabbed handles flanking the hatch and pressed his face plate against the glass. Then we all had to turn down the volume in our phones as he began to holler in what I assumed was Fthosian. The woman inside got the idea and pressed her ear against the window. Sound would not travel through the vacuum of space, but, by shouting loud enough, Jules could excite vibrations in his face-mask that would be transmitted by direct contact into the glass of the porthole and thence into the cosmographer's ear.

He repeated himself. He somehow managed to sound more cheerful than desperate. His tone seemed to say it was all in good sport. The woman's lips moved as she shouted back.

The dome illuminated. I reckoned she'd hit the light switch, to get a better look at what was going on. But on second thought this light was pouring in through the gap between the hemispheres. The sun must have risen? We'd been warned of explosive sunrises. But this seemed explosive in more ways than one; the light flared, faded, and flared brighter. It burbled and boiled. A silent concussion passed through the frame of the icosahedron. Lio sprang up so smartly that he almost committed the fatal mistake of flying straight up out of the dome and off into space. But he caught himself short by gripping the comm wire that linked him to the rest of us, and swung around above the telescope mirror until he finally contrived to stop himself short on the edge of a dome-half. The light, which was slowly dying, reflected in his face mask. "The World Burner," he said, "I think they must have blown the propellant tanks." Then, with a sudden exclamation, he pushed off and glided back "down" to what I was thinking of as the floor of the dome. For the giant hemispheres had gone into movement, and the slit between them was narrowing decisively. The lights really *did* come on now.

The slit disappeared with a clunk, felt not heard. For better or worse, we were trapped here now. I kept eyeing the big red emergency button. I had eight minutes.

A readout on my display began to change: outside air pressure, which had been a red zero ever since I'd been launched into the vacuum of space, was climbing up toward the yellow zone. Jules had noticed the same thing; he went over to a grated vent near the hatch and reached for it. His arm was batted aside by inrushing air.

"Thank Cartas," Arsibalt said, "I don't care what cosmos this air came from. I just want to breathe it."

"While we are waiting, re-acquaint yourselves with the doffing procedure," Lio told us. "And show yourselves." He pulled up the screen that had been hiding his readouts. The rest of us did likewise. For the first time in a couple of hours we were able to see one another's faces on the speely screens and to check one another's readouts. I could not see everyone in the group, because we were distributed around a cluttered and complex space "beneath" the mirror supports. But I could see Jesry, who had two minutes. I had five. I swapped canisters with him; it was taking a long time to pressurize the dome.

A few minutes later the external pressure readout finally changed from yellow to green: good enough to breathe. Just as my oxygen supply indicator was going from red (extreme danger) to black (you are dead). With my last lungful of Arbre air I spoke the command that opened my suit to the surrounding atmosphere. My ears popped. My nose stung, and registered a funny smell: that of something, *anything*, other than my own body. Lio, who'd been keeping a sharp eye on my readouts (I had less oxygen than anyone else that I could see), stepped behind me and hauled the back of my suit open. I withdrew my arms, got a grip on the rim of the HTU, and pulled myself, stark naked, out of the accursed thing. I breathed alien air. My comrades watched me with no small interest. The only other Arbran to have breathed this stuff had been the Warden of Heaven, who apparently hadn't lasted more than a few minutes. My hands flew to my face. I kneaded it, scratched my nose, rubbed a week's sleep from my eyes, ran my fingers up into my hair. Could have thought of more edifying things to do, but it was a biological imperative.

Lio groped on his front, found a switch, flicked it. "Can you hear me?"

"Yeah, I can hear you." The others took to groping for their switches.

"Not that it makes a difference—since we all have to get out—but what is it like, my fraa?"

"My heart is pounding like crazy," I said, and paused, since to say that much had worn me out. "I thought I was just excited, but—maybe this air doesn't work for us." I was speaking in bursts between gasps for air; my body was telling me to breathe faster. "I can see why the Warden of Heaven blew an aneurysm."

"Raz?"

Breathe, breathe. "Yeah?" Breathe breathe breathe . . .

"Get me out of this thing!" Lio insisted.

Jesry grabbed Lio, spun him around, yanked his door open. Lio got out of his suit as if it were on fire. He floated over with a mad look on his face. All my habits from home told me to get out of Lio's way when he approached in that mood, but I simply didn't have the strength. His arms, which had subjected me to so much rough treatment over the years, came around me in a bear hug. He pressed his ear against my chest. His scalp was like thistles. I felt his rib cage begin heaving. Jesry and Arsibalt and Jules were swimming free of their suits. Jules went straight to the hatch, threw a lever, and shoved it open. Everything faded—not to darkness but to a washed-out yellow-gray, as if too much light were shining through it.

Fraa Jad and I were floating in a white corridor. I was naked. He was dressed in one of the grey coveralls we'd brought up in our kit. Evidence suggested he had been rummaging in a steel locker set into the wall. Two clumps of silvery fabric were floating near him. He teased one open. It turned out to have arms and legs. From time to time he glanced my way. When he noticed me looking at him, he tossed me a grey packet in a poly bag: another folded-up coverall. "Put this on," he said. "Then, over it, the silver garment."

"Are we going to put out a fire?"

"In a manner of speaking."

The effort of tearing open the poly wrapper set my heart pounding. Pulling on the coverall plunged me deep into oxygen debt. Once I had recovered enough to get a few words out, I asked, "Where are the others?"

"There is a Narrative, not terribly dissimilar to the one you and I are perceiving, in which they went to explore the ship. Their plan is to surrender peacefully whenever someone notices them."

"Is there any particular reason they left us behind?"

"Emergence from the suit after so long. Finding oneself in a confined space after having grown accustomed to the unobstructed vastness. Breathing an atmosphere from a different cosmos. Effects of long-term weightlessness. General stress and excitement. All of these induce a syndrome that lasts for a few minutes, a kind of going into shock, that can produce confusion or even loss of consciousness. Soon it passes, if one is healthy. I infer that it was too much for the Warden of Heaven."

"So," I tried, "after we doffed the suits, we were all confused or unconscious for a few minutes. Meaning—in your system of thought—we lost our grip on the Narrative. Stopped tracking it. Whatever faculty of consciousness enables it continuously to do the fly-bat-worm trick—it shut down for a while, there."

"Yes. And the others regained consciousness in a worldtrack in which you and I are dead."

"Dead."

"That is what I told you."

"So that's why they left us behind," I said. "They *didn't* leave us behind, because, in their worldtrack, we never even made it here."

"Yes. Put this on." He handed me a full-face respirator.

"What of the Fthosian astronomer? Won't she summon the authorities, or something?"

"She went with Jules. He is talking to her. He has a gift for that kind of thing."

"So Lio, Arsibalt, Jesry, and Sammann are just wandering around the ship *openly*, looking for someone to surrender to?"

"Such a worldtrack exists."

"It's pretty bizarre."

"Not at all. Such occurrences are common in the confusion of war."

"How about *this* worldtrack? What are the four of them doing in the Narrative that you and I are in?"

"I'm in *several*," Fraa Jad said, "a state of affairs that is not easy to sustain. Your questions hardly make it easier. So here is a simple answer. The others are all dead."

"I don't wish to abide in a worldtrack where my friends are all dead," I said. "Take me back to the other one."

"There is no taking, and there is no back," Jad said. "Only going, and forward."

"I don't want to be in a Narrative where my friends are dead," I insisted.

"Then you have two choices: put yourself out the airlock, or follow me." And Fraa Jad pulled the respirator over his face, terminating our conversation. He handed me a fire extinguisher, and took one for himself. Then he shoved off down the corridor.

Now my mind did something absurd, namely, attended to the nuts and bolts of the ship instead of things that were truly important. It was as though some Barb-like part of me had stepped to the fore, elbowed my soul out of the way, and directed all of my energies and faculties toward those things that Barb would find interesting, such as door-latching mechanisms. Subsystems responsible for irrelevancies such as grieving for my friends, fearing death, being confused about the worldtracks, and wanting to strangle Fraa Jad, were starved of resources.

There were many doors, all closed but not locked. This was, according to Jules, the usual state of affairs here. These outer reaches of the ship were divided into separate, independently pressurized compartments so that a meteor strike in one wouldn't beggar its neighbors. Consequently, one spent an inordinate amount of time opening and closing doors. These were domed round hatches about three feet in diameter, with heavy bank-vault-like latching mechanisms. One opened them by grabbing two symmetrical handles and pulling them opposite ways, which was handy in zero gravity where planting one's feet and using one's body weight were not supported by theorical law. The effort always left me panting for breath in Fraa Jad's wake. One of the questions I had meant to annoy him with had been, *Why me? Can't you do whatever it is you are doing alone, so that I can be in a Narrative where my friends are alive?* And maybe this was the answer. I'd been picked out for the same reason that the hierarchs at Edhar had made me part of the bell-ringing team: I was a lummox. I could open heavy doors. It seemed preferable to doing nothing, so I floated ahead of Fraa Jad and applied myself to it. Every time I hauled one open I expected to find myself staring down the muzzle of an Urnudan space marine's weapon, but there simply weren't that many people here in the observatory, and when we did finally encounter someone in a corridor, she gasped and got out of our way. The firefighter disguise was so simple, so obvious, I'd assumed it could never work. But it had worked perfectly on the first person we'd met, which probably meant it would work as well on the next hundred.

That corridor led to a spherical chamber that apparently served as the foyer for the whole vertex. We had to pass through it, anyway, to get out of this vertex and reach other parts of the

Daban Urnud. As we discovered by trial and error, one of its exits communicated with a very long tubular shaft. "The Tendon," I announced, when I discovered it. Fraa Jad nodded and launched himself down it.

The stupendous icosahedron and its imposing vertex-citadels had accounted for almost all of my impressions of the ship until now. Their size and their strangeness made it easy to forget that essentially all of the *Daban Urnud's* complexity and population lay elsewhere: in the spinning Orbstack. Until now, Fraa Jad and I had been like a couple of barbarians kicking down doors in an abandoned guardhouse on the frontier of an empire. Here, though, we had set out on the road that would take us to the capital. There were a dozen Tendons. Six radiated from each of the mighty bearings at the ends of the Orbstack. The Orbstack was like a monkey using its arms and legs to brace itself in the middle of a packing crate. Sometimes an arm had to push, sometimes it had to pull. It flexed to absorb shocks. It was alive: a bundle of bones that gave strength, muscles that reacted, vessels that transported materials, nerves that communicated, and skin that protected all of the rest. The Tendons had to perform all of the same functions, and so shared much of that complexity. All that Fraa Jad and I could see of this Tendon was the inner surface of a ten-foot-diameter shaft, but we knew from talking to Jules that the Tendon as a whole was more than a hundred feet wide, and crammed with structure and detail hidden from our view—but richly hinted at by a bewilderingly various series of hatches, valve-wheels, wiring panels, display screens, control panels, and signs that shimmered by us as we flew along. Since it was impossible for novices such as we to get aimed perfectly down the center, we strayed from side to side as we went along. Whenever we came in slapping range of a likely-looking handhold we'd give it a bit of abuse and earn some speed, then take a lot of deep breaths while coasting to the next. About halfway along, we encountered a group of four Geometers who, when they saw us coming, grabbed handholds and crouched against the wall to make way. As we flew by, they shouted what I assumed were questions, which we had little choice but to ignore.

The hatch at the end opened onto a domed chamber about a hundred feet across: by far the largest open volume we had yet seen. I knew it had to be the forward bearing chamber. This was confirmed by the fact that it had a navel in its floor, perhaps twenty feet across, and everything that we could see on the other side of it was rotating. We had reached the forward end of the Core. Surrounding but invisible to us was the immense bearing that connected the spinning Orbstack to the non-spinning complex of icosahedron and Tendons that guarded it.

It was a mess. Half a dozen Tendon-shafts were plumbed into this thing via huge portals shot into its domed "ceiling." Fraa Jad and I had just emerged from one of them. The adjacent one was the focus of a huge amount of activity and attention—it looked like one of those pits in great cities where stocks are traded. This, of course, was the Tendon that led to the World Burner complex, or what was left of it now that the Valers had got to it. People were flying in to, or issuing from, it at a rate of about two per second—it was like watching the entrance of a hornet's nest in high summer. Most of those going into it were carrying weapons or tools. Some of those coming out were injured. The ingoing and outcoming streams collided in the bearing chamber, and others tried to sort things out, to tell people where to go, what to do, without much result that I could discern, save that they ended up arguing with each other. I was just as happy I couldn't understand what they were saying. The chaos made it almost too easy for me and Fraa Jad to move around without attracting notice. In fact, my only problem was distinguishing the Thousander from *other* men in firefighting gear. But after a brief moment of anxiety when I feared I'd lost him, I spied a likely-looking firefighter gazing in my direction and pointing toward what I had begun to think of as the floor of the chamber: the flat surface with the big hole in the middle of it.

The hole was getting smaller.

As Jules had explained, wherever the *Daban Urnud*'s architects had needed to forge a connection between major parts of the Core, they had used a ball valve, which was just a sphere with a fat hole drilled through the middle, held captive in a spherical cavity bridging the two spaces in question. The sphere couldn't go anywhere, but it was free to rotate. Depending on how the hole in its middle was aligned, it could allow free passage or form an impregnable barrier. Such a valve was set into the "floor" of this chamber. It was so huge that, at first, I hadn't seen it for what it was. But now that it had gone into motion, its nature and its function were perfectly obvious. It moved ponderously, but by the time Fraa Jad managed to draw my attention to it, the thing was already about half closed, like an eyeball slowly drifting into sleep.

Fraa Jad planted his feet against a soldier's backside and shoved off, driving the soldier toward the ceiling and Jad down toward the ball valve. I was already near a sort of ladder or catwalk, which I pushed off against to propel myself after him. When we got to the ball valve, the aperture had narrowed to perhaps three feet at its widest—plenty of room to squeeze through. But we had used up all of our momentum just getting there, and our aim had been miserable. After some feverish banging around we drifted through the aperture and found ourselves hovering in the bore of the sphere, watching the eye at its other end get smaller. There were no handholds that we could use to move ourselves along. If we didn't reach the other end by the time it closed, we'd be imprisoned until the next time they opened the valve.

I was too out of breath to do much anyway. I aimed my fire extinguisher back the way we'd come and pulled the trigger. The recoil forced it back against me; I took the force with my arms and felt myself tumbling backwards. But I was moving. I slammed into the socket-wall at the end, scrabbled for a handhold on the rim of the hole, and pulled myself through. A second later Fraa Jad squirted through on a snowy plume of fire retardant. I grabbed his ankle, which slowed him down quite a bit. We found ourselves adrift and slowly tumbling at the forward extremity of the two-mile-long, hundred-foot-diameter shaft that ran the length of the Orbstack. We had made it to the Core. And if any of those we'd left behind in the bearing chamber had found our behavior suspicious, they had not been adroit enough to follow us through the ball valve. Smaller hatches—airlocks, made for one person at a time—were planted around it so that people could pass between Core and bearing chamber even when the ball valve was closed. I kept a nervous eye on those, half expecting a space cop to fly out and accost us, but then reasoned that it simply wasn't going to happen. Jules's words of a few minutes ago came back to me. What the Valers had done—what *we* had done—had been the worst military embarrassment these people had suffered in a thousand years. The bomb was still on fire, the disaster only getting started. The Valers might still be alive and fighting. So they weren't going to make a big deal about a couple of firefighters acting weird.

Our panicky flight through the valve had imbued us with momentum that carried us outward toward the wall of the Core, which was rotating about as fast as the second hand on a clock. This meant that when we drifted into the wall, it was moving past us at a brisk walking pace. This part of the Core wall was covered with a grid with convenient hand-sized holes between the bars, so we did what came naturally and grabbed it. The effect was gentle but inexorable acceleration that made our feet spin out to find purchase on the grid. We were now rotating along with everything else. Here our body weight was less than that of a newborn infant. But it was the most "gravity" we had known for a long time, and took a little getting used to.

We clung to it for a couple of minutes, gasping for air, trying not to black out. Then Fraa Jad, never one to discuss his plans and intentions with his traveling companions, pushed off and glided along the Core wall, headed for the first of the four great Nexi that were spaced evenly along its length. Travel was easier in micro- than in zero gravity, because we slowly "fell" to the Core wall where we could always push off and get another dose of momentum. Available was a sort of rapid transit system, consisting of a moving conveyor-belt-cum-ladder that glided up one side of the Core and down the other. Most of the people we could see—perhaps a hundred, heavily skewed toward soldiers and firefighters—were using it. The rungs were elastic, so that when you grabbed one it didn't simply jerk your arm from its socket. Tired as I was, I was tempted to have a go, but didn't want to make a spectacle of myself.

Fraa Jad showed no interest. We moved more slowly than those who were using it, which worked to our advantage: some of them shouted questions at us as they glided by, but none was inquisitive enough to jump off and pursue the conversation.

In a few minutes we came to the station in the Core where the forward-most Orbs—One, Five, Nine, and Thirteen—were connected. Each of these stood at the head of a stack of four. So, Orbs One through Four were for the Urnudans. Five through Eight were Troän, Nine through Twelve were Laterran, and the rest Fthosian. By convention, the lowest-number Orb in each stack—the ones that connected here, at the heads of the stacks—were for the highest-ranking members of their respective races. So this Nexus was the most convenient place for the Geometers' VIPs to meet. From where we were, it didn't look like much: just four cavernous holes in the wall, the termini of perpendicular shafts leading out to the Orbs. According to Jules, though, if we were to look at it from the outside, we would see that this part of the Core was wrapped in a doughnut of offices, meeting-chambers, and ring-corridors where the Command had its offices. Several hatches in the Core wall hinted at this. But conflict between Pedestal and Fulcrum had led to a division of the Command torus into parts of unequal size. Hatches had been locked, partitions welded into place, guards posted, cables severed.

None of which concerned us very much, since the space we were in served only as a service corridor or elevator shaft, rarely visited or thought about by the Command. Of much greater interest to us were the four huge orifices in the Core wall. As we drifted into the Nexus we were able to gaze into these and see tubular shafts, each about twenty feet in diameter, each leading "down" about a quarter of a mile. At the "bottom" of each was another huge ball valve, currently closed. Beyond each such valve was an inhabited Orb a mile wide.

It wasn't difficult to identify the shaft leading to Orb One. A large numeral was painted on the Core wall next to it. The numeral was Urnudan, but any sentient being from any cosmos could recognize it as the glyph that represented unity, 1, a single copy of something. I, however, did not have time to linger and contemplate its profound meaning, as Fraa Jad had already located a ladder bracketed to the wall of the shaft, and begun to descend it.

I followed him. Gravity slowly came on as we went. It's hard to describe how terrible this made me feel. The only thing that kept me from passing out was fear I'd let go of the rungs and fall down on top of Fraa Jad. During the worst spell, a voice drilled into my awareness and made my skull buzz. Fraa Jad had begun to sing some Thousander chant like the one that had kept me awake at the Bazian monastery on the night we had been Evoked. It gave my consciousness something to hold on to, like the steel ladder-rung that I was gripping with my hand: my only hard tangible link to the giant complex spinning around me. And in the same way that the rung kept me from falling, the sound of Jad's voice in my skull kept my mind from floating away to wherever it had gone when I'd passed out in the observatory and awoken on the wrong worldtrack.

I kept descending.

I was crouching atop a giant steel navel with my head between my knees, trying not to pass out.

Fraa Jad was punching numbers into a keypad mounted to the wall.

The sphere began to rotate beneath me.

"How did you know the code?" I asked.

"I selected a number at random," he said.

I'd heard only four beeps from the keypad. Only a four-digit number. Only ten thousand possible combinations. So if there were ten thousand Jads in ten thousand branches of the worldtrack . . . and if I were lucky enough to be with the right one . . .

Sunlight was shining through the bore of the valve. I flattened myself on it and gazed down on open water, vegetation, and buildings from an altitude of half a mile.

This time, the bore of the valve had ladder-rungs on it. We climbed down them even as the valve was snapping to its final position, and exited onto a ring-shaped catwalk hung from the ceiling of the orb, surrounding the aperture—the oculus at the top of a vast spherical dome, a little sky above a little world. A stairway led up to it. Men with weapons were running up the stairway, intent on saying hello to us. Fraa Jad, seeing this, pulled off his respirator. No point in maintaining the disguise now. I did likewise.

Two soldiers, peering down shotgun barrels, reached the catwalk. One of them moved aggressively toward Fraa Jad. I stepped forward, instinctively, holding up my hands. My attention was drawn to a small silver object in Fraa Jad's hand—like a jeejah, of all things! The other soldier pivoted toward me and swung the butt of his weapon around, catching me in the jaw. I toppled backward over the rail and felt my old friend, zero gravity, taking me back into its embrace as I went into free fall down the middle of the orb. Something went extremely wrong in my guts. A moment later I heard the boom of a shotgun. Had I been shot? Not likely, given my situation. My vision whited out again, and my viscera caught on fire and melted.

They had shot Fraa Jad. The Everything Killers had been turned on. I had become a nuclear weapon, a dark sun spraying fatal radiance onto the dwellings and cultivated terraces of the Urnudan community below.

We had accomplished our mission.

○○○○○○○○○○○○○○○○○○○○○○○○○○○○○○○○○○○○○○

Harbinger: One of a series of three calamities that engulfed most of Arbre during the last decades of the Praxic Age and later came to be seen as precursors or warnings of the Terrible Events. The precise nature of the Harbingers is difficult to sort out because of destruction of records (many of which were stored on syntactic devices that later ceased functioning) but it is generally agreed that the First Harbinger was a worldwide outbreak of violent revolutions, the Second was a world war, and the Third was a genocide.

—THE DICTIONARY, *4th edition, A.R. 3000*

"We have come," said the man in the robes. "We have answered your call." He was speaking Orth. Not as well as Jules Verne Durand, but well enough to make me think he had been studying it for almost as long. As long as we didn't snow him with arcane tenses and intricate sentence structures, he would be able to keep up.

I say "we," but I didn't expect to do much talking. "Why am I here?" I'd asked Fraa Jad, as we had approached the gate of the building that floated in the center of Orb One.

"To serve as amanuensis," he had replied.

"These people can build self-sufficient intercosmic starships, but they don't have recording devices?"

"An amanuensis is more than a recording device. An amanuensis is a consciousness-bearing system, and so what it observes in its cosmos has effects in others, in the manner we spoke of at Avrachon's Dowment."

"*You're* a consciousness-bearing system. And you seem to be much better at playing this polycosmic chess game than I am. So doesn't that make me exiguous?"

"Much pruning has taken place in recent weeks. I am now absent in many versions of the cosmos where you are present."

"You mean, you're dead and I'm alive."

"Absent and present express it better, but if you insist on using those terms, I won't quibble."

"Fraa Jad?"

"Yes, Fraa Erasmas?"

"What happens to us after we die?"

"You already know as much of it as I do."

About then the conversation had been interrupted as we had been ushered into the room featuring the man in the robes. Knowing nothing of Urnudan culture put me at a disadvantage in trying to puzzle out who this man was. The room offered no clues. It was a sphere with a flat floor, like a smallish planetarium. I guessed that it was situated near the geometric center of the Orb. The inner surface was matte, and glowed softly with piped-in sunlight. The circular floor had a chair in the middle, surrounded by a ring-shaped bench. A few receptacles, charged with steaming fluids, were arranged on the bench. Otherwise the room was featureless and undecorated. I felt at home here.

"We have answered your call."

What was Fraa Jad going to say to that? A few possible responses strayed into my head: *Well, what took you so long?* or *What the hell are you talking about?* But Fraa Jad answered in a shrewdly noncommittal way by saying, "Then I have come to bid you welcome."

The man turned sideways and extended an arm toward the circular bench. The robes unfurled and hung from his arm like a banner. They were mostly white, but elaborately decorated. I wanted to say that they were brocade or embroidery, but life among bolt-wearing ascetics had left me with a deeply impoverished vocabulary where the decorative arts were concerned, so I'll just say that they were fancy. "Please," the man said, "we have tea. A purely symbolic offering, since your bodies can do nothing with it, but . . ."

"We shall be pleased to drink your tea," Fraa Jad said.

So we repaired to the circular bench and took seats. I let Fraa Jad and our host sit relatively close, facing each other, and arranged myself somewhat farther away. Our host picked up his teacup and made what I guessed was some kind of polite ceremonial gesture with it, which Fraa Jad and I tried to copy. Then we all sipped. It was no worse and no better than what "Zh'vaern" used to eat at Messal. I didn't think I'd be taking any home with me.

The man drew some notes from a pocket in his robe and consulted them from time to time as he delivered the following. "I am called Gan Odru. In the history of the *Daban Urnud*, I am the forty-third person to bear the title of Gan; Odru is my given name. The closest translation of *Gan* into Orth is 'Admiral.' This only approximates its meaning. In our military system, one class of officers were responsible for the trees, another for the forest."

"Tactics and strategy respectively," Fraa Jad said.

"Exactly. 'Gan' was the highest-ranking strategic officer, responsible for direction of a whole fleet, and reporting to civilian authorities, when there were any. Command of specific vessels was delegated by the Gan to tactical officers with the rank of Prag, or what you would call a captain. I apologize for perhaps boring you with this, but it is a way to explain the manner in which the *Daban Urnud* has behaved toward Arbre."

"It is in no way boring," said Fraa Jad, and glanced over my way to verify that I was doing my job: which as far as I could tell was merely to remain conscious.

"The first Gan of the *Daban Urnud* was entrusted with the responsibility to establish a colony on another star system," Gan Odru continued. "As links to Urnud became more tenuous with distance, his responsibilities grew, and he became the supreme authority, answerable to no one. But he was a strange kind of Gan in that his fleet consisted of but one ship and so his staff consisted of but one Prag, and inasmuch as the Prag had no real tactical decisions to make—as the war had been left far behind—the relationship between Gan and Prag became unstable, and evolved. A simple way to express it is that the Gan became somewhat like your avout, and the Prag like your Sæcular Power. This state of affairs came about over the course of but a single generation, but proved extraordinarily stable, and has not changed since. The clothing that I wear is but little changed from the formal dress uniforms worn by the Gans of Urnud's ocean-going fleets thousands of years ago. Though, of course, they did not wear them aboard ship, since it is difficult to swim in robes."

Humor was the last thing I was looking for here and so astonishment got the better of mirth and I chuckled too little and too late.

"The second Gan was weakened by illness and served for only six years. The third was a young protégé of the first; he had a long career, and through the force of his personality and his uncommon intelligence, gained back some of the power that his office had ceded to that of the Prags. Late in his career, he became aware of your summons, and made the decision to alter the trajectory of the *Daban Urnud* so that it would—as he conceived it—fly into the past. For the signals that he and the others heard, they conceived as ancestral voices calling them home to make the Urnud that should have been but that, through its leaders' follies, it had failed to become.

"I suppose you have already some notion of the wanderings that followed, the Advents at Tro, Earth, and Fthos and their consequences. My purpose is not to rehearse all of that history but to give an account of our actions here."

"It will be useful," Fraa Jad said, "to know what occurred with the Warden of Heaven."

"For a long time," said Gan Odru, shifting into a lower gear, as he was now making it up as he went along instead of reading from notes, "the relationship between the Gans and the Prags has been poisoned. The Prags have said that the third Gan was simply wrong. That all the wanderings of the *Daban Urnud* have been without meaning—simply the endless consequence of an ancient mistake. Believing that, they saw their only purpose as self-preservation. Those who think this way want only to settle down somewhere and go on living. And, with each Advent, some do. We have left Urnudans behind on Tro, Troäns behind on Earth, and so on. They find ways to live even though those cosmi are not their own. So, of the cynical ones, the ones who believe it is all a meaningless error, a large fraction are bled off at each Advent. At the same time we are joined by ones from the new cosmos who believe in the quest. So the ship is rebuilt and departs for the next cosmos. At first the Gans have power and the Prags do their bidding. But the journey is long, the quest is forgotten as generations go by, the Prags gain, the Gans lose, power. The Pedestal and the Fulcrum have long been our names for these two tendencies. And so here you see me, virtually alone in this place of ceremony, doing what my predecessors did, but with little respect and no power.

"Thus came we to Arbre. Prag Eshwar, my counterpart, and her followers saw your planet as just another civilization to be raided for its resources, so that the ship could be rebuilt and the journey extended. Yet Eshwar is an intelligent woman who has read our histories and well knows that, in an Advent, the Pedestal and the Prag tend to lose power to the Fulcrum and the Gan. Already she was choosing tactics to forestall this.

"When the Warden of Heaven came to us, it was obvious that he was a fool, a charlatan. We already knew as much, of course, from our surveillance of Arbre's popular culture. And the Prag had already devised a plan, to draw comparisons between me and this

Warden of Heaven. To make his foolishness, his falseness, rub off on me.

"So the Warden of Heaven was brought here in his spacesuit. He kept wanting to take it off. We advised against it. When he came in to this room, he saw it as a kind of holy place, and insisted that the risk of removing his suit was acceptable. That his god would watch over him and keep him safe. So, off came the suit. He became short of breath. Our physicians tried to reassemble the suit around him but this did not help matters, for he had already suffered the bursting of a major blood vessel. The physicians next tried to put him in a cold hyperbaric chamber, a therapy in which they are well practiced. He was stripped naked and readied for the procedure, but it was too late—he died. A debate followed as to what should be done with the body. While some of us debated, overzealous researchers took samples of his blood and tissues, and commenced an autopsy. So the body had already been desecrated, if you will. Prag Eshwar made the decision that any effort to apologize would be taken as a sign of weakness and that any sharing of information would only benefit Arbre. And too, for internal political reasons, she was inclined to show contempt, or at least disregard, for the body—because she had made it into a symbol for *me*. Hence the style in which the Warden of Heaven was returned."

"But it backfired," I said, "didn't it?"

"Yes. Those of the Fulcrum were embarrassed and ashamed, and conceived a plan to make an exchange of blood for blood. As we had taken samples of blood from the Warden of Heaven's body, they would convey samples of our blood to the surface of Arbre. We had detected signals from the planet, which, as we later learned, had been sent by Fraa Orolo. These took the form of an analemma. Jules Verne Durand had become the foremost authority on Orth and on the avout. He was covertly sympathetic to the Fulcrum. He interpreted Orolo's signal as pointing to Ecba, and suggested that it would have profound symbolic value to deliver the samples there. He even volunteered to go down on the probe. But at about the same time he was ordered to go on the raid to the concent of the Matarrhites, and so was no longer available. Lise went in his stead—without his knowledge, of course. For she had learned much of the avout, and even a few words of Orth, from Jules. It went wrong and she was shot while boarding the probe, as you know."

We let a few moments pass untroubled by words.

"Since then things have moved fast. I would say that Prag Eshwar has done what Prags do, which is—"

"React tactically, with no thought of strategy," Jad said.

"Yes. It led us to this pass. Thirty-one have been slain by your fraas and suurs—from the Ringing Vale, I presume?"

Fraa Jad made no response, but Gan Odru looked my way, and I nodded. He continued, "Eighty-seven more are held hostage—your colleagues herded them into a chamber and welded the doors shut."

"A misinterpretation," Fraa Jad said. "Such people do not take hostages, so the eighty-seven were put in that room to keep them safely out of the way."

"Prag Eshwar interprets it, rightly or wrongly, as hostage-taking, and prepares a response with one hand. With her other hand she has reached out to me and asked me to discuss matters with you. She is shaken. I don't really know why. The large bomb that was destroyed has always been a weapon of last resort; no one would seriously consider using it."

"Pardon me, Gan Odru, but the Pedestal was getting ready to launch it," I blurted.

"As a *threat*, yes—to hang above your planet and exert pressure. But that is its only real use. I don't understand why its loss has shaken Prag Eshwar so deeply."

"It didn't," Fraa Jad said. "Prag Eshwar sensed terrible danger."

"How would you know this?" Gan Odru asked politely.

Fraa Jad ignored the question. "She might explain it by claiming that she had a nightmare, or that sudden inspiration struck her in the bath, or that she has a gut feeling that tells her she ought to steer a safer course."

"And is this something that you brought about!?" Gan Odru said, more as exclamation than as question. He was getting very little satisfaction from Fraa Jad, and so turned to look at me. I can't guess what he saw on my face. Some mix of bemusement and shock. For I had just seen a glimpse of an alternate Narrative in which we had visited appalling destruction upon one of the Orbs.

"That we might send a signal to Prag Eshwar—is that such a difficult thing to believe for you, Gan Odru, the Heritor of a tradition, a thousand years old, founded on the belief that my predecessors summoned you hither?"

"I suppose not. But it is so easy, after all this time, to harbor doubts. To think of it as a religion whose god has died."

"It is good to doubt it," Fraa Jad said. "After all, the Warden of Heaven's mistake was failure to doubt. But one must choose the target of one's doubt with care. Your third Gan detected a flow of information from another cosmos, and saw it as cryptic messages from his ancestors. Your Prags, ever since, have doubted both halves of the story. You disbelieve only one half: that the signal came from your ancestors. But you may still believe *that the signal exists* while discarding the third Gan's incorrect notions as to its source. Believe, then, that information—the Hylaean Flow—passes between cosmi."

"But if I may ask—have you learned the power to modulate that signal, to send messages thus?"

I was all ears. But Fraa Jad said nothing. Gan Odru waited for a few moments, then said, "I suppose we've already established that, haven't we? You apparently got inside Prag Eshwar's head somehow."

"What signal did the third Gan receive nine centuries ago?" I asked.

"A prophecy of terrible devastation. Robed priests massacred, churches torn down, books burning."

"What gave him the idea it was from the past?"

"The churches were enormous. The books, written in unfamiliar script. On some of their burning leaves were geometrical proofs unknown to us—but later verified by our theors. On Urnud we had legends of a lost, mythic Golden Age. He assumed that he was being given a window into it."

"But what he was really seeing was the Third Sack," I said.

"Yes, so it seems," said Gan Odru. "And my question is: did you send us the visions, or did it just happen?"

We have come . . . we have answered your call. Was he the last priest of a false religion? Was he no different from the Warden of Heaven?

"The answer is not known to me," said Fraa Jad. He turned to look at me. "You shall have to search for it yourself."

"What about *you?*" I asked him.

"I am finished here," Fraa Jad said.

Part 12

REQUIEM

Something was pressing hard against my back—accelerating me forward. That couldn't be good.

No, it was just gravity, or some reasonable facsimile, pulling me down against some flat firm thing. I was monstrously cold. I started to shiver.

"Pulse and respiration are looking more normal," said a voice in Orth. "Blood oxygenation coming up." Jules was translating this into some other language. "Core temp is getting into a range compatible with consciousness."

That would, perhaps, be *my* consciousness they were talking about. I opened my eyes. The glare faded. I was in a small but nice enough room. Jules Verne Durand was seated on the edge of my bed, looking clean and sleek. This more than anything else confirmed the vague impression that a lot of time had passed. I was hooked up to a bunch of stuff. A tube was cinched under my nose, blowing something cold, dry, and sweet into my nostrils. A physician—from Arbre!—was glancing back and forth between me and a jeejah. A woman in a white coat—a Laterran—was looking on, running a big piece of equipment that was circulating warm water to—well—you wouldn't believe me if I told you, and then you'd wish I'd kept such details to myself.

"You have questions, my friend," Jules said, "but perhaps you should wait until—"

"He's fine," said the Arbran. He was dressed in a bolt and chord. He had a tube strapped across his upper lip. He shifted his attention to me. "You're fine—as far as I can tell. How do you feel?"

"Unbelievably cold."

"That'll change. Do you know your name?"

"Fraa Erasmas of Edhar."

"Do you know where you are?"

"I would guess on one of the orbs on the *Daban Urnud*. But there are some things I don't understand."

"I am Fraa Sildanic of Rambalf," said the physician, "and I need to tend to your comrades. I need Jules to come with me as interpreter, and Dr. Guo here to supervise the core warming procedure. Speaking of which, we'll be needing that."

Dr. Guo now punctuated this statement in the most dramatic way you can possibly imagine by reaching up under my blankets from the foot of the bed and disconnecting me from the core warmer. For the first time in a long time, I uttered a religious oath.

"Sorry," said Fraa Sildanic.

"I'll live. So—"

"So we are going to have to leave your questions unanswered," Fraa Sildanic continued, "but one is waiting outside who will, I think, be happy to lay it all out for you."

They left. Through the opening door I glimpsed a pleasant view over open water, with green growing things all over the place, soon blocked by a small figure coming in at speed. A moment later, Ala was lying full-length on top of me, sobbing.

She sobbed and I shivered. The opening half-hour was all about raising my core temp and getting her calmed down. We made a great team that way; Ala was just what the doctor ordered as a way to raise my temperature, and using me as a mattress seemed to be good for what ailed her. During the bone-breaking shivering that hit its peak about fifteen minutes in, she clung to me as if I were an amusement park ride, and kept me from vibrating right off the bed. This kind of thing gave way, in due course, to other fascinating biological phenomena, which I can't set down here without turning this into a different kind of document.

"Okay," she finally said, "I'll report to Fraa Sildanic that you have excellent blood flow to all of your extremities." It was the first complete sentence that had come out of her mouth. We'd been together for an hour and a half.

I laughed. "I was thinking Heaven? But Heaven wouldn't have

these." I tugged gently at the hissing tube under her nose. She snorted, and batted my hand away. "Oxygen from Arbre?" I asked.

"Obviously."

"How did it—and *you*—get here?"

She sighed, seeing that I was determined to ask tedious questions. She pushed herself up, straddled me. I raised my knees and she leaned back against them. Snatched a pillow, propped herself up, got comfortable, fiddled with her oxygen tube. She looked at me, and once again the *I'm in Heaven* hypothesis floated to the top. But it couldn't be. You had to *deserve* Heaven.

"After you went up," she said, "the Pedestal rodded all of our space launch infrastructure."

"I'm aware of it."

"Oh yes. I forgot. You had a vantage point. So, we got the message that they were extremely cross with us over the two-hundred-missile launch. But they had fallen for the decoy—the inflatable thing you launched. They sent us detailed phototypes of the wreckage. Were they ever triumphant!"

"Maybe they were only *pretending* to fall for it."

"We considered that. But, remember—a few days later, you guys were able to just walk right in."

"Well, it was a *little* more difficult than you make it sound!" I was trying to laugh, but it was hard, with her weight on my tummy.

"I get that," she said immediately, "but what I'm trying to say is—"

"The Pedestal hadn't taken any extraordinary precautions," I agreed, "they were totally surprised."

"Yes. So, one moment, they are feeling triumphant. The next, out of nowhere, all of a sudden, their World Burner has been wrecked. A bunch of their people are dead. One of the twelve Vertices has been seized by Arbran commandos."

"Wow! The Valers did all that?"

"They sneaked onto the World Burner and planted three of the four shaped charges they had with them. Then they headed for a certain window—"

"Pardon me, a window?"

"That vertex is a sort of command post and maintenance depot for all things World Burner. There is a conference room with windows that look out over the bomb. Osa and company had a plan, apparently, to rendezvous there. Along the way, they were noticed, and came under assault by the maintenance workers who were out there in space suits. But the workers didn't have weapons per se."

"Neither did the Valers," I said.

She gave me a sort of pitying look. Maybe with a trace of affection. "Okay," I said, "Valers don't need weapons."

"The Geometers' space suits are soft. Ours are hard. Just imagine."

"Okay," I said, "I'd almost rather not. But I can see how it would come out."

"Suur Vay died. She took on five guys, one of whom happened to be carrying a plasma cutter. Uh, it's a very unpleasant story. She and the five all ended up dead. But, largely because of her intervention, the other three Valers made it to that window."

She paused for a moment, letting me absorb that. I had really hated Suur Vay when she had sewn me up after Mahsht, but when I remembered that picnic-table surgery now, it made me want to cry.

Once we'd given Suur Vay a decent moment of silence, Ala went on: "So, imagine this from the point of view of the big bosses inside the conference room. They see a large number of their people converted to floating corpses before their eyes. There's nothing they can do about it. Fraa Osa trudges right up to the window and slaps on a shaped charge, right up against the glass. They're not certain what it is. He makes a gesture. The World Burner explodes in three places: the primary detonator, the inertial guidance system, and the propellant tanks. There is a huge secondary detonation as the tanks rupture."

"That we noticed."

"Fraa Gratho is killed by a piece of flying debris."

"Damn it!" My eyes were stinging. "He stood between me and a bullet . . ."

"I know," she said softly.

After another silence, she went on, "So, the bosses now understand the nature of the object that's been slapped on their window. They get the message and open an airlock. Esma comes inside. Osa stays where he is—he's the gun to their heads. Esma stays in her suit. She herds all the Geometers she can find into the conference room, locks the door, welds it shut with Saunt Loy's Powder. Now, Osa joins her, bringing the shaped charge with him. They lock the doors into the vertex, sealing it off from the rest of the *Daban Urnud*, and weld those too. They detonate the fourth charge in such a way that most of the vertex vents its atmosphere to space. Now it can't be approached except by people in space suits. They hole up in one of the few rooms that still has an atmosphere. Their suits are out of air now, so they climb out of them, and suffer the usual symptoms."

"What is up with that, by the way?"

She shrugged. "Hemoglobin is a classy molecule. Finely tuned to do what it does—take oxygen from the lungs and get it to every cell in the body. If you give it oxygen that is only a little bit different from what it's used to, well, it still works—just not as well. It's like being at high altitude. You get short of breath, woozy, can't think straight."

"Hallucinations?"

"Maybe. Why? Did you hallucinate?"

"Never mind . . . but wait a second, Jules can get along just fine on Arbre air."

"You acclimatize. Your body responds by generating more red blood cells. After a week or two, you can handle it. So, as an example, some of the people who live on the *Daban Urnud* rarely leave their home orb. They have trouble going into common areas of the ship, where the air is a mixture. Others are used to it."

"Like the Fthosian cosmographer who let us in the airlock at the observatory."

"Exactly. When she saw you guys gasping for breath and starting to lose consciousness, she recognized what was going on. Sounded an alarm."

"She did?" I said.

She gave me that pitying-but-affectionate look again. "What, you were hoping you'd managed to sneak aboard?"

"I, er, thought we had done exactly that!"

She grabbed my hand and kissed it. "I think your ego can be satisfied by what you *did* accomplish, which people are going to be celebrating for a long time."

"Okay," I said, feeling it was time to change the subject away from my ego. "She sounded an alarm."

"Yes. Of course, there were lots of other alarms going off at the same time because of the Valers' mayhem," Ala said, "but some medics came to the observatory and found you unconscious, but alive. Fortunately for you, the physicians around here are used to dealing with such problems. They put you on oxygen, which seemed to help. But they had no way to be sure; they'd never treated Arbrans, they were worried you were going to suffer brain damage. Better safe than sorry. So they put you on ice in a hyperbaric chamber."

"On ice?"

"Yeah. Literally. Dropped your body temperature to limit brain damage while oxygenating your blood as best they could with Laterran air. You've been unconscious for a week."

"What about Osa and Esma, holed up in that vertex?"

She let a long moment pass before saying, "Well, Raz, they died. The Urnudans figured out where they were. Blew a hole in the wall. All the air escaped into space."

I lay there for a minute.

"Well," I finally said, "I guess they went out like real Valers."

"Yes."

I laughed in a not-funny way. "And—like a true non-Valer—I lived."

"And I'm glad you did." And here she started crying again. It wasn't sadness over the dead Valers. Nor joy that the rest of us had lived. It was shame and hurt that she had sent us into a situation where we easily *could* have died; that the responsibilities placed on her shoulders, and the logic of the situation, had left her no alternative to the Terrible Decision. For the rest of her life—of *our* life, I hoped—she'd be waking up sweaty in the middle of the night over this. But it was a hurt she'd have to keep to herself, since most people she might share it with would not extend her much sympathy. *"You sent your friends to do what!? While you sat on the ground, safe!?"* So it was going to be a private thing between us, I knew, forever. I squirmed free and held her for a bit.

Once it felt right to go back to the story, I said, "How long did Osa and Esma remain locked up in that room before—before it happened?"

"Two days."

"Two days!?"

"The Pedestal assumed that the place was booby-trapped, and/or that there might be other Valers lurking in it. But they had to do something, since the hostages were running out of air. It was either that, or watch their people die on the speely."

"So they were scared to death."

"Yes," Ala said, "I think so. Maybe shocked is a better word. Because they had thought for a while that they had us locked down in Tredegarh, which they had infiltrated. Then you and your friends unmasked Jules Verne Durand, so they lost their eyes and ears on the ground. At the same moment, the Convox—and all of the other big concents—dispersed into the Antiswarm."

"That was a great idea! Who dreamed that up?"

She blushed, and fought back a smile, but wasn't happy with my turning the attention to her, so went on: "They are really afraid of the Thousanders—the Incanters—and must have noticed that all of the Millenarian maths had been emptied out. Where did all of those Thousanders go? What are they cooking up? Then, the two-hundred-missile launch. Very upsetting. A lot of data to process. Zillions of bogeys to track. They think they see a ship—it blows up—they think they've dodged a bullet. But a few days after that, out of nowhere, comes this horrifying and devastating attack on their biggest strategic asset. For two days afterwards, it is all that they can think of—they are worried sick about the hostages trapped in that vertex. Not only that, but some other dudes in black suits manage to gain entry to the ship, and are only foiled because they can't breathe the air—"

"They mistook us for another squad of Valers?"

"What would you think, in their place? And the biggest concern of all in their minds, I believe, was that they couldn't know how many others were out there. For all they knew, there were a hundred more of you on the way, with more weapons. So, the result of it all was that—"

"They decided to negotiate."

"Yes. To initiate four-way talks among the Pedestal, the Fulcrum, and the Magisteria."

"Pardon me, what was that last one?"

"The Magisteria."

"Meaning—?"

"This happened after you left Arbre. One magisterium is the Sæcular Power. The other is the Mathic world—now the Antiswarm. The two of them together are—well—"

"Running the world?"

"You could say that." She shrugged. "Until we come up with a better system, anyway."

"And would you, Ala, be one of those people who is currently running the world?"

"I'm here, aren't I?" She didn't appreciate my humor.

"As part of the delegation?"

"A wall-crawler. An aide. And the only reason I made the cut was that the military likes me, they think I'm cool."

I was about to point out a much better explanation, which was that she had been responsible for sending Cell 317 on a successful mission, but she read it on my face and glanced away. She didn't want to hear it mentioned. "There are four dozen of us," she said hurriedly. "We brought doctors. Oxygen."

"Food?"

"Of course."

"How did you get here?"

"Geometers came down and picked us up. Once we reached the *Daban Urnud*, we came straight here, of course."

"Hmm," I reflected, "shouldn't have brought up the subject of food."

"Are you hungry?" she asked, as if it were astonishing that I would be.

"Obviously."

"Why didn't you say so—we brought five hampers of absolutely the best food for you guys!"

"Why five?"

"One for each of you. Not counting Jules, of course—he's been stuffing his face since he got here."

"Um. Just to prove I don't have brain damage, would you name the five, please?"

"You, Lio, Jesry, Arsibalt, and Sammann."

"And—what of Jad?"

She was so aghast that my social instincts got the better of my brain, and I backed down. "Sorry, Ala, I've been through a lot of weird stuff, my memory is a little blurry."

"No, *I'm* sorry," she said, "maybe it is a result of the trauma." She looked a little quivery, scrunched her face, mastered it.

"Why? What trauma?"

"Of seeing him float away. Knowing what happened to him."

"When did I see him float away?"

"Well, he never regained consciousness after the two-hundred-missile launch," Ala said softly. "You saw him collide with a payload. He got stuck to it. You made the decision to go after him—to try to help. But it was tricky. The grapnel missed. You were running out of time. Arsibalt was coming to help. But then you nearly got sideswiped by the nuke. Jad drifted away. Re-entered the atmosphere. And burned up over Arbre."

"Oh yeah," I said, "how could I have forgotten?" I said it sarcastically, of course. But I was carefully watching Ala's face as I did. The circumstances of my recent life were such that I was more exquisitely attuned to Ala's facial expressions than to anything else in the Five Known Cosmi. She believed—better, she *knew*—that what she'd just reminded me of was true.

There were, I was sure, records down on Arbre to prove it.

○○○

Rhetor: A legendary figure, associated in folklore with Procian orders, said to have the power of altering the past by manipulating memories and other physical records.

—THE DICTIONARY, *4th edition, A.R. 3000*

All I could think of was getting to the food. First, though, I had to stop being naked. Ala slipped out, as though it were perfectly all right to see me nude, but watching me dress would be indecent. The Arbran delegation had brought us bolts and chords and spheres. The four Geometer races were more or less fascinated by the avout, and might take it the wrong way if we attempted to hide what we were.

Once I got properly wrapped, the hospital staff helped me don a backpack carrying a tank of Arbre oxygen that was connected to the tube beneath my nose. Then I followed a series of pictographic signs to a terrace on the roof of the hospital, where I found Lio and Jesry elbow-deep in their hampers. Fraa Sildanic was there. With a resigned and hopeless air, he cautioned me not to eat too fast lest I get sick. I ignored him as heartily as my fraas were doing. After a few minutes, I actually managed to lift my gaze from my bowl, and look out at the artificial world around me.

The four orbs of a given stack were so close that they almost kissed, and were linked by portals, a little bit like cars on a passenger train. When the *Daban Urnud* was maneuvering or accelerating, the portals had to be closed and dogged shut, but they were open today.

Laterrans lived in Orbs Nine through Twelve. The hospital was in Ten, not far from the portal that joined it to Eleven. This rooftop terrace, like all other outdoor surfaces, was intensively cultivated. A bit of space had been cleared for tables and benches. The tops of these, though, were slabs of glass, and vegetables grew in trays underneath. Bowers arched over our heads, supporting vines laden with clusters of green fruit. As long as one maintained focus on what was near to hand, it looked like a garden on Arbre. But the long view was different. The hospital consisted of half a dozen houseboats lashed together. Each had three stories below the waterline and three above. Flexible gangways linked them to one another and to neighboring houseboats, which spread across the water to form a circular mat that seemed to cover every square foot of the water's surface. But because "gravity" here was a fiction created by spin, the surface—what our inner ears, or a plumb bob, would identify as level—was curved. So the circular mat of boats was dished into a trough. Our inner ears told us that we were at its lowest point. If we gazed across it to the other side, rather less than a mile away, our eyes gave us the alarming news that the water was above us. But if we were to make the journey blindfolded, it would feel like walking over level ground—we'd have no sense of climbing uphill.

Of the orb's inner surface, about half was under water. The remainder constituted the "sky." This was blue, and had a sun in it. The blue was painted on, but it was possible to forget this unless you looked at the portals to Orbs Eleven and Nine. These hung in the firmament like very strange astronomical bodies, and were linked by cable-chair systems to houseboats below. The sun was a bundle of optical fibers bringing processed and filtered light that had been harvested by parabolic horns on the exterior of the icosahedron. The fibers were fixed in place on the ceiling of the orb, but by routing the light to different fibers at different times of day, they created the illusion that the sun was moving across the sky. At night it got dark, but, as Jules had explained, fiber-pipes were hard-routed to indoor growing facilities in the cellars of many houseboats so that plants could grow around the clock. The system was so productive that these Geometers were capable of sustaining a population density like that of a moderately crowded city solely on what was produced in the city itself.

It was good, in a way, that the view from the hospital roof afforded so many remarkable things to look at and talk about, because otherwise the conversation would have been paralyzingly awkward. Lio's and Jesry's faces were stiff. Oh, they had cracked huge smiles when they'd seen me. And I could not have been happier to see them. We'd shared those feelings immediately and without words. But then their faces had closed up like fists, as much as forbidding me to say anything out loud.

We were eating too hard to talk much anyway. Fraa Sildanic and another Arbran medic kept coming and going. And, though I didn't wish to think ill of our Laterran hosts, I had no way of knowing whether this terrace might be wired with listening devices. Half of the Laterrans were pro-Pedestal. Even the pro-Fulcrum ones, though, might not take kindly to the role we had played in assaulting the *Daban Urnud*. Some might have had friends or relatives who had been slain by the Valers. To divulge in casual conversation that a Thousander had breached the hull and then vanished would be the worst thing that could happen right now. Once I had sated my hunger a little bit, I began to get physically anxious about it.

When Arsibalt showed up, and made for his hamper like a piece of earth-moving equipment, I waited until his mouth was crammed before raising my glass and saying, "To Fraa Jad. Even as we think of the four Valers who died, let's not forget the one who sacrificed his life in the first ten minutes of the mission, before he even made it out of Arbre's atmosphere."

"To the late Fraa Jad," Jesry echoed, so quickly and forcefully that I knew he must be thinking along similar lines.

"I'll never be able to erase the memory of his fiery plunge into the atmosphere," Lio added with a patently fake sincerity that almost made me blow the libation out of my nose. I was keeping an eye on Arsibalt, who had stopped chewing, and was staring at us, eyes a-bulge, trying to make out if this was some kind of extremely dark and elaborate humor. I caught his eye and glanced up: an old signal from Edhar, where we would, by a flick of the eyes at the Warden Regulant's windows, say *shut up and play along*. He nodded, letting me know he had taken my meaning, but the look on his face made his shock and confusion plain. I shrugged as a way of letting him know he was in good company.

Sammann showed up, dressed in the traditional Ita costume,

and, showing remarkable self-control, went around and shook our hands and gave each of us a squeeze or pat on the shoulder before tearing open his hamper, full of infinitely better- and spicier-smelling foods than anything we had. We let him eat. He went about this in the same quiet, contemplative style I had once grown used to, watching him take his lunches on the top of the Pinnacle at Edhar. His face showed no curiosity as to why there were five people and five hampers, instead of some other number. In fact, he was altogether reserved and impassive, which, combined with his formal Ita garb, stirred up all sorts of old habits and social conventions that had long since settled to the bottom of my consciousness.

"Earlier we were raising a toast to the memory of the late Fraa Jad and the others who died," I told him, when he paused in his eating and reached for his glass. He gave a curt nod, raised the glass, and said, "Very well. To our departed comrades." *Yes, I know too.*

"Am I the only one who suffers from funny neurological sequelae?" Arsibalt asked, still a bit rattled.

"You mean, brain damage?" Jesry asked in a helpful tone.

"That would depend on whether it is as permanent as what ails you," Arsibalt fired back.

"Some of my memories are a little sketchy," Lio offered.

Sammann cleared his throat and glared at him.

"But the longer I'm awake, the more coherent I seem to get," Lio added. Sammann returned his focus to the food.

Jules Verne Durand stopped by, took in the scene, and beamed. "Ah!" he exclaimed. "When I saw the five of you, out of your spacesuits, gasping for air, like beached fish, in the observatory, I feared I would never be able to look on a scene such as this one."

We all raised glasses his way, and beckoned for him to join us.

"What of the others—I mean, what was done with the four corpses?" Jesry asked. Five sets of Arbran eyes went to the Laterran's face. But if Jules noted any discrepancy in the figures, he didn't show it. "This became a topic of negotiation," Jules said. "The bodies of the four Valers have been frozen. As you can guess, there are those of the Pedestal who wish to dissect them as biological specimens." A cloud passed over his face, and he paused for a few moments. We all knew he was remembering his wife Lise, whose body had been subjected to the biological-specimen treatment at the Convox. After getting his poise back, he went on: "The diplomats of Arbre have said in the strongest terms that this would be unacceptable—that the remains are to be treated as sacred and handed over, undisturbed, to this delegation of which you are now a part. This will occur at the opening ceremonies, which are to take place in Orb Four in about two hours." *The Pedestal doesn't know yet about the Everything Killers lodged in your bodies, and I haven't spilled the beans—but it's really making me nervous.*

Had even more Everything Killers been brought up by the delegation? Were hundreds, thousands of them now salted around the *Daban Urnud?* Were there some in the delegation who had the power to trigger them? I "remembered"—if that was the right word for something that had not happened in this cosmos—the silver box in Fraa Jad's hand. The detonator. Who of the four dozen were carrying them? More to the point, who would press the trigger? To a certain kind of mind, this would make for an acceptable trade. At the cost of four dozen Arbran lives, the *Daban Urnud* would be sterilized, or at least crippled to the point where its survivors would have no choice but to surrender unconditionally. Much cheaper than fighting a war with them.

For more than one reason, I was no longer hungry.

Everyone else was thinking similar thoughts, and so conversation was not exactly sparkling. In fact, it was nonexistent. The silence became conspicuous. I wondered what a blind visitor would think of the place, for the sonic environment was distinctly odd. The air didn't move much in these orbs. Each was warmed and cooled on a different diurnal schedule so that the expanding and contracting air would slosh back and forth through the portals and stir faint breezes down below. But it never blew hard enough to raise waves, or even to blow a leaf from a table. Sound carried in that still air, and it ricocheted strangely from the ceiling of the orb. We heard someone rehearsing a tricky passage on a bowed instrument, children arguing, a group of women laughing, an air-powered tool cycling. The air felt dense, the place closed-in, deadening, stifling. Or perhaps that was just the food catching up with me.

"Orb Four is Urnudan," Lio finally said, waking us all up.

"Yes," Jules said heavily, "and all of you will be there." *Nothing personal, but I want you walking bombs out of my orb as soon as possible.*

"It is the highest-numbered of the Urnudan orbs," Arsibalt observed, "meaning—if I understand the convention—the farthest aft, the most residential, the, er . . ."

"Lowest in the hierarchy, yes," said Jules. "The oldest, the most important stuff, the highest in the Command, are in Orb One." *That's the one you'd want to nuke.*

"Will we be visiting Orb One?" Lio asked. *Are we going to have an opportunity to nuke it?*

"I would be astonished," said Jules, "the people there are very strange and hardly ever come out."

We all looked at each other.

"Yes," said Jules, "they are a little like your Thousanders."

"Fitting," said Arsibalt, "since their journey has lasted for a thousand years."

"It is doubly unfortunate that Fraa Jad perished during the launch, then," I said, "since Orb One sounds like a place he would make a beeline for—that is, in a Narrative where he had made it here with someone like me to open doors for him."

"What do you imagine he'd do once he reached it?" asked Jesry, keenly interested.

"Depends on what kind of reception we got when we came in the door," I pointed out. "If things went badly wrong, we would not survive, and our consciousnesses would no longer track that Narrative."

Sammann chopped this off by clearing his throat again.

"How long will it take for us to get from here to Orb Four?" Jesry asked. I think he was the only one capable of speech; Lio and Arsibalt were gobsmacked.

"We should leave as soon as convenient," Jules replied. "An advance party is already there." *Everything Killers are already in Orb Four, nothing can be done about it.*

We began wrapping up our food, repacking our hampers. "How many Orth interpreters are there?" Arsibalt asked. *Do we get to hang out with you?*

"With my level of skill, there is only I." *I'm about to become extremely busy, I won't be able to talk to you after this.*

"What kind of people make up the Arbran delegation?" Lio asked. *Who's got his finger on the Everything Killers' trigger?*

"Quite a funny mix, if you ask me. Leaders of Arks. Entertainers. Captains of commerce. Philanthropists such as Magnath Foral. Avout. Ita. Citizens—including a couple well known to you." This was directed at me.

"You're kidding," I said, momentarily forgetting about all of the grim subtext. "Cord and Yul?"

He nodded. "Because of their role during the Visitation of Orithena—watched by so many on the speely that you, Sammann, put on the Reticulum—it was seen as fitting that they come here, as representatives of the people." *The politicians are pimping them to the mass media.*

"Understood," said Lio. "But among all of those pop singers and witch doctors, there must be at least *some* actual representatives of the Sæcular Power?"

"Four of the military, who strike me as honorable." *Not the ones who will trigger the EKs* "Ten of the government—including our old friend Madame Secretary."

"Those Forals really get around," I couldn't help saying. Sammann raised an eyebrow at me. Jules went on to rattle off a list of the names and titles of the Sæcular Power contingent, going out of his way to identify some of them as mere aides. ". . . and finally our old friend Emman Beldo, to whom, I sense, there is more than meets the eye." *He's the one.*

Whatever praxis would be used to trigger the EKs, it would be advanced, possibly nothing more than a prototype. It would have to be disguised as something innocuous. They would need someone like Emman to operate it. And he would take his orders from, presumably, the highest-ranking Panjandrum in the delegation. Not Ignetha Foral. She was here on Lineage business, of that I had no doubt. Whatever her nominal title and brief might be in the Sæcular Power, she and her cousin—or whatever he was—Magnath had not come all this way to follow the whims of whatever Panjandrum happened to have most lately gained the upper hand in the infinite clown-fight that was Sæcular politics.

Did the Forals know about Fraa Jad? Were they working with him? Had they framed a plan together during our stay at Elkhazg?

There was so much to think about that my mind shut off, and all I did for the better part of the next half-hour was take in new sensations. I had turned into Artisan Flec's speelycaptor: all eyes, no brain. With my Eagle-Rez, my SteadiHand, and my DynaZoom, I dumbly watched and recorded our discharge from the hospital. Paperwork, it seemed, was one of those Protic attractors that remained common and unchanged across all cosmi. We were given over into the care of a squad of five nose-tube-wearing Troäns in the same getups as the goons who had assaulted me and Jad in my dream, hallucination, or alternate polycosmic incarnation. Lio ogled their weapons, which tended toward sticks, aerosol cans, and electrical devices—apparently, high-energy projectiles were frowned on in a pressurized environment. They gave us a good looking-over in return, paying special attention to Lio—they'd been doing research on who was who, and some of the Valer mystique had rubbed off on him.

Two of the soldiers and Jules went ahead of us, three followed. We crossed a gangplank into someone's garden and I looked through an open window, from arm's length away, at a Laterran man washing dishes. He ignored me. From there we crossed into a school playground. The kids stopped playing for a few moments and watched us go by. Some said hello; we smiled, bowed, and returned the greeting. This went over well. From there we crossed to a houseboat where a couple of women were transplanting vegetables. And so it went. The community did not waste space on streets. Their transportation system was a network of rights-of-way thrown over the roofs and terraces of the houseboats. Anyone could walk anywhere, and a social convention dictated that people simply ignore each other. Heavy goods were moved around on skinny, deep-draught gondolas maneuvering through narrow leads of open water—whose existence came as a surprise, because they tunneled under flexible bowers, and so, from the hospital terrace, had looked only like dark green veins and arteries ramifying through the town.

In a few minutes we came to a boat that served as the terminal of the cable-chair system. We rode up to the hole in the sky two by two, each Arbran accompanied by a Troän soldier, until all had collected in the portal that joined Ten to Eleven. The wind was blowing in our faces strongly enough to sting our eyes and whip our bolts around.

While waiting for the others to catch up, I stood in the portal and looked at the theatrical machinery behind the blue scrim of the fake sky, the bundles of glass fibers that piped in the light. The sun was bright, but cold; all the infrared had been filtered out of it. Warmth came instead from the sky itself, which radiated gentle heat like an extremely low-temperature broiler. We felt it strongly here, and were glad of the wind.

Then another chair ride down to Orb Eleven's houseboat-mat, a walk across, and a similar ride up to the next portal and into Orb Twelve: the highest-numbered, farthest-aft of the four Laterran orbs. Hence, there was no next portal; we had reached the caboose. But the sky supported a tubular catwalk-cum-ladder that took us "up" and around to a portal in the "highest" part of the sky—the zenith. Gravity here was noticeably weaker because we were closer to the Core. We tarried on the ring-shaped catwalk below the portal, which, down to the last rivet, was just like the one in Orb One where Fraa Jad had taken a shotgun blast. I looked around and saw details I clearly "remembered," and I perched my butt on the railing to check it against my "memory" of being knocked over it.

Jules had to identify himself at a speely terminal and state his business to someone in a language that I assumed was Urnudan. The leader of the soldiers chimed in with bursts of gruff talk. We five had to take turns standing in front of the machine and have our faces scanned. While we waited, we examined the ball valve, which felt, and therefore looked, as if it were in the ceiling, straight above our heads. It was old hat to me. In its design I recognized the massive, thunderous praxic style—call it Heavy Intercosmic Urnudan Space Bunker—that dominated the look of the ship as seen from the outside and the Core, but was mercifully absent from the orbs.

That great steel eye would not open for us today. Instead we would use a round hatch just wide enough to admit Arsibalt, or a Troän grunt in his cumbrous gear-web. This eventually swung open by remote command, and we queued up to climb through it.

"A threat," Jesry snorted, and nodded at the colossal ball valve. I knew his tone: disgusted that he'd been so long figuring it out. I must have looked baffled. "Come on," he said, "why would a praxic design it that way? Why use a ball valve instead of some other kind?"

"A ball valve works even when there is a large pressure difference between its two sides," I said, "so the Command could evacuate the Core—open it to space—and then open this valve and kill the whole orb. Is that what you're thinking?"

Jesry nodded.

"Fraa Jesry, your explanation is unreasonably cynical," said Arsibalt, who'd been listening.

"Oh, I'm sure there are other reasons for it," Jesry said, "but it is a threat all the same."

One by one we ascended a ladder through the small side hatch, up a short vertical tube, and through a second hatch—an airlock—and collected on another ring-catwalk on the bore of the vertical shaft that rose twelve hundred feet "above" us to the Core. I checked out the keypad: just where I remembered it.

Lio had passed through first, and was donning a sort of padded blindfold. Jules handed them to the rest of us as we emerged from the airlock. "Why?" I asked sharply.

"So you don't get sick from the effects of Coriolis," he said. "But, in case you do—" And he handed me a bag. "Come to think of it, take two—the way you were eating."

I took a last look up before putting on the blindfold. We were getting ready to ascend a dauntingly tall ladder. But I knew that "gravity" would get weaker the higher we went, so it wouldn't be that arduous. We would, however, be experiencing powerful, disorienting inertial effects as we moved closer to the axis. Hence the concern about motion sickness.

I groped for the lowest rung. "Slow," Jules said, "settle on each step and wait for it to feel correct before moving to the next."

Since the whole ladder was enclosed in a tubular cage, there was scant danger of falling. I took the rungs slowly as recommended, listening for movement from Lio, who was above me, before going to the next. But above a certain point the rungs became mostly symbolic. A flick of the wrist or finger floated us to the next one up. Still the Troän soldier at the top maintained the same steady pace—he'd learned the hard way that those who climbed too fast would soon be reaching for their bags.

I was thinking about that keypad. What if Fraa Jad had punched in one of the 9,999 *wrong* numbers? What if he had attempted it several times? Eventually a red light would have gone on in some security bunker. They'd have turned on a speelycaptor and seen a live feed of two firefighters screwing around with the keypad. They'd have sent someone to shoo them off. That person probably would not have been issued a shotgun—just the nonlethal weapons that our escorts were toting.

Jesry's words came back to me: *A threat.* He was right. Opening that ball valve had been a way of putting a gun to the head of the whole Orb. No wonder those soldiers had simply rushed up and blown us away! In a cosmos where Fraa Jad knew—or guessed—the number on the keypad, we were sure to get killed. Freeing me, apparently, to end up somewhere else.

But what would have happened in all of the vastly more numerous cosmi where he'd punched in the *wrong* random number? We would have been taken alive.

What would have happened next in those cosmi?

We'd have been detained for a while—then taken to parley with Gan Odru.

My ears told me I had emerged from the top of the shaft, my hand pawed in the air but didn't find a next rung. Instead the Troän intercepted it, hauled me out, hauled back the other way to kill the momentum he'd conferred on me, and guided me to something I could grab. I peeled up my blindfold and saw that I had emerged into the Core. The ball valve leading to the aft bearing chamber was just a stone's throw behind us. Its length in the other direction was inestimable, but I knew it to be two and a quarter miles. It was as I "remembered" it: glowing tubes strung down its inner surface emitted filtered sunlight, and the conveyor belt ran endlessly with well-lubed clicking and humming noises.

Three other well-shafts were plumbed into the Core at this nexus. The one directly "above" or opposite us led into Orb Four; it looked like a direct, straight-line continuation of the shaft we had just finished climbing. A ring-ladder ran around the Core wall, providing access to all of them. Those who were practiced at this kind of thing could simply jump across.

There was a wait. To begin with, those below me on the ladder had to catch up. Moreover, a traffic jam had already developed in the shaft to Orb Four. There were safety rules governing how many were allowed to use the ladder at once, being enforced by a soldier stationed at the top rung. Some other delegation was going down ahead of us—though from our point of view they appeared to be ascending the ladder feet-first—and we would have to wait until they had reached the bottom.

So, Lio and I began screwing around. We decided to see if we could make ourselves motionless in the center of the Core. The goal was to place oneself near the middle of the big tunnel while killing one's spin so that the whole ship would rotate around one's body. This had to be done through some combination of jumping off from the wall just so, and then swimming in the air to make adjustments. Desperately clumsy would be a fair description of our first five minutes' efforts. From there we moved on to dangerously incompetent, as, while flailing around, I kicked Lio in the face and gave him a bloody nose. The Troän soldiers watched with mounting amusement. They couldn't understand a word we were saying, but they knew exactly what we were trying to do. After I kicked Lio, they took pity on us—or perhaps they were just scared that we'd get seriously hurt and they'd be blamed. One of them beckoned me over. He grabbed my chord in one hand and my bolt, at the scruff of my neck, at the other, and gave me a gentle push combined with a little torque. When I swam to a halt in the middle of the tunnel, I saw I was closer than I had ever been to achieving the goal.

Hearing voices in Fluccish, I looked up the Core to see a contingent of perhaps two dozen coming to join us. Most were floating down the middle of the Core instead of using the conveyors, so even if they hadn't been speaking Fluccish I'd have known them for tourists. One of these suddenly bounded ahead of the group, drawing a rebuke from a soldier.

Cord hand-over-handed her way along the tunnel wall and launched herself at me from a hundred feet away. I feared the impending collision, but fortunately air resistance slowed her flight, so that when we banged bodies it was no more violent than walking into someone. We had a long zero-gravity hug. Another Arbran was not far behind her: a young Sæcular man. I didn't recognize him, but I had the oddest feeling that I was *expected* to. He was slowly tumbling on all three axes as he drifted toward me and my sib, flailing his arms and legs as if that would help. For that, he was very impressively dressed and coiffed. One of our soldier escorts reached out and gave him a push on the knee that stopped his tumbling and slowed his trajectory to something not quite so meteoric. He came to a near-stop with respect to me and Cord. Gazing at him past Cord's right ear, which was pressed so hard against my cheek that I was pretty sure her earrings were drawing blood, I saw him raise a speelycaptor and draw a bead on us. "In the chilly heart of the alien starship," he intoned, in a beautifully modulated baritone, "a heartwarming reunion between brother and sister. Cord, the Sæcular half of the heroic pair, shows profound relief as she—"

I was just beginning to have some profound—but not quite so heartwarming—emotions of my own when the man with the speelycaptor was somehow, almost magically, replaced by Yulassetar Crade. Associated with the miracle were a few sound effects: a meaty *thwomp,* and a sharp exhalation—a sort of bark—from the man with the speelycaptor. Yul had simply launched himself at the guy from some distance away, and body-checked him at full speed, stopping on a dime in midair as he transferred all of his energy into the target.

"Conservation of momentum," he announced, "it's not just a good idea—it's the law!" Far away, I heard a thud and a squawk as the man with the hairdo impacted on the end-cap. This was almost drowned out, though, by chuckling and what I took to be appreciative commentary from our soldier-escorts. If I'd been startled, at first, to learn that Yulassetar Crade had been made part of—of all things—a diplomatic legation, I saw the genius of it now.

Once Cord had settled down enough to release me, I drifted over and bumped bodies (more gently) and shared a hug with Yul too. Sammann had emerged from the Orb Twelve shaft by now, and greeted them both in high spirits. Of course, there was much more that I wanted to say to Cord and Yul, but the man with the speelycaptor had crawled back close enough to get us in his sights—though from a more respectful distance—and this made me clam up. "We'll talk," I said, and Yul nodded. Cord, for now, seemed content merely to look at me, her face a maze of questions. I couldn't help wondering what she saw. I was probably drawn and pasty. She, by contrast, had gone to some effort to dress up for the occasion: all the milled titanium jewelry was on display, she had gotten a new haircut and raided a women's clothing store. But she'd had the good sense not to get too girly, and she still seemed like Cord: barefoot, with a pair of fancy shoes buckled together in the belt of her frock.

Others filtered in: a couple of ridiculously beautiful persons I didn't recognize. Some old men. The Forals, drifting along arm in arm as if members of their family had been going on zero-gravity perambulations for centuries. Three avout, one of whom I recognized: Fraa Lodoghir.

I flew right at him. Spying me inbound, he excused himself from his two companions and waited for me at a handhold on the tunnel wall. We wasted no time on pleasantries. "You know what became of Fraa Jad?" I asked him.

His face spoke even more eloquently than his voice knew how to do—which was saying a lot. He knew. *He knew.* Not the false cover story. He knew what I knew—which probably meant he knew a lot *more* than I knew—and he was apprehensive that I was getting ready to blurt something out. But I shut my mouth at that point, and with a flick of the eyes let him know I meant to be discreet.

"Yes," said Lodoghir. "What can avout of lesser powers make of it? What does Fraa Jad's fate mean, what does it entail, for us? What lessons may we derive from it, what changes ought we to make in our own conduct?"

"Yes, Pa Lodoghir," I said dutifully, "it is for such answers that I have come to you." I could only pray he would catch the sarcasm, but he made no sign.

"In a way, a man such as Fraa Jad lives his whole life in preparation for such a moment, does he not? All the profound thoughts that pass through his consciousness, all the skills and powers that he develops, are shaped toward a culmination. We only see that culmination, though, in retrospect."

"Beautiful—but let's talk of the *prospect*. What lies ahead—and how does Fraa Jad's fate reshape it for us? Or do we go on as if it had never occurred?"

"The practical consequence for me is continuing and ever more effective coöperation between the tendencies known to the vulgar as Rhetors and Incanters," Lodoghir said. "Procians and Halikaarnians have worked together in the recent past, as you know, with results that have been profoundly startling to those few who are aware of them." He was staring directly into my eyes as he said this. I knew he was talking about the rerouting of worldtracks that, among other things, had placed Fraa Jad at the *Daban Urnud* at the same time as his death was recorded above Arbre.

"Such as our unveiling of the spy Zh'vaern," I said, just to throw any surveillors off the scent.

"Yes," he said, with a tiny, negative shake of the head. "And this serves as a sign that such coöperation must and should continue."

"What is the object of that coöperation, pray tell?"

"Inter-cosmic peace and unity," he returned, so piously that I wanted to laugh—but I'd never give him that satisfaction.

"On what terms?"

"Funny you should ask," he said. "While you were in suspended animation, some of us have been discussing that very topic." And he nodded a bit impatiently, toward the muzzle of the Orb Four shaft, where everyone else was gathering.

"Do you think that Fraa Jad's fate affected the outcome of those negotiations?"

"Oh yes," said Fraa Lodoghir, "it was more influential than I can say."

I was beginning to feel a little conspicuous and I could see I'd get nothing more out of Lodoghir, so I turned and accompanied him to the head of the Orb Four shaft.

"I see we have some big-time Procians," Jesry said, nodding at Lodoghir and his two companions.

"Yeah," I said, and did a double-take. I had just realized that Lodoghir's companions were both Thousanders.

"They should be in their element," Jesry continued.

"Politics and diplomacy? No doubt," I said.

"And they'll come in handy if we need to change the past."

"More than they've already changed it, you mean?" I returned—which I figured we could get away with, since it would sound like routine Procian-bashing. "But seriously, Fraa Lodoghir has paid close attention to the story of Fraa Jad and has all sorts of profound thoughts about what it means."

"I will *so* look forward to hearing them," Jesry deadpanned. "Does he have any practical suggestions as well?"

"Somehow we didn't get around to that," I said.

"Hmm. So does that mean it's our department?"

"That's what I'm afraid of."

The trip down to Orb Four took a while because of the safety regulations.

"I wouldn't have thought it possible," said Arsibalt's voice, somewhere on the other side of my blindfold, as we descended. "But this is *already* banal!"

"What? Your feet in my face?" For he kept wanting to descend too fast, and was always threatening to step on my hands.

"No. Our interactions with the Geometers."

I descended a few more rungs in silence, thinking about it. I knew better than to argue. Instead I compiled a mental list of all that I'd seen on the *Daban Urnud* that had struck me as, to use Arsibalt's word, banal: the red emergency button on the observatory hatch. The bowel-warming machine. Paperwork at the hospital. The Laterran man washing his dishes. Smudgy handprints on ladder-rungs. "Yeah," I said, "if it weren't for the fact that we can't eat the food, it would be no more exotic than visiting a foreign country on Arbre."

"*Less so!*" Arsibalt said. "A foreign country on Arbre might be pre-Praxic in some way, with a strange religion or ethnic customs, but—"

"But this place has been sterilized of all that, it's a technocracy."

"Exactly. And the more technocratic it becomes, the more closely it converges on what we are."

"It's true," I said.

"When do we get to the good part?" he demanded.

"What do you have in mind, Arsibalt? Like in a spec-fic speely, where something amazingly cool-to-look-at happens?"

"That would help," he allowed. We descended a few more rungs in silence. Then he added, in a more moderate tone: "It's just that—I want to say, 'All right, already! I get it! The Hylaean Flow brings about convergent development of consciousness-bearing systems across worldtracks!' But where is the payoff? There's got to be more to it than this big ship roaming from cosmos to cosmos collecting sample populations and embalming them in steel spheres."

"Maybe they share some of your feelings," I suggested. "They *have* been doing it for a thousand years—a lot more time to get sick of it than you've had. You only *woke up* a couple of hours ago!"

"Well, that is a good point," Arsibalt said, "but Raz, I am apprehensive that they're *not* sick of it. They've turned it into a sort of religious quest. They come here with unrealistic expectations."

"Ssh!" Jesry exclaimed. He was just below me. He continued, in a voice that could have been heard in all twelve Orbs, "Arsibalt, if you keep running your mouth this way, Fraa Lodoghir will have to erase everyone's memory!"

"Memory of what?" Lio said. "I don't remember anything."

"Then it is not because of any Rhetor sorcery," called out Fraa Lodoghir, "but because failed attempts at wit fade so quickly from the memory."

"*What* are you people talking about!?" demanded Yul, in Fluccish. "You're spooking the superstars."

"We're talking about what it all means," I said. "Why we're the same as them."

"Maybe they are weirder than you think," Yul suggested.

"Until they let us visit Orb One, we'll never know."

"So go to Orb One," Yul said.

"He's already been there," Jesry cracked.

We reached the bottom and climbed down an airlock-shaft just like the others and found ourselves looking straight down on the houseboat-mat of Orb Four. This had an elliptical pool of open water in the middle: a touch of luxury we hadn't seen in any of the Laterran orbs. Perhaps the Urnudans had agriculture even more productive than the others, and could afford to waste a bit of space on decoration. The pool was surrounded by a plaza, much of which was now covered with tables.

"It is a center for the holding of meetings," Jules explained.

My mind went straight back to Arsibalt's complaints about the banality. *The aliens have conference centers!*

They had welded stairs to their sky, and painted them blue. We clanked down them, getting heavier as we went. The architecture of the houseboats below was not markedly different from what we'd seen in the Laterran orbs. There were only so many ways to build a flat-roofed structure that could float. Many of the decorative flourishes that might distinguish one style of architecture from another were buried under cataracts of fruit-bearing vines and layered canopies of orchard-trees. Our path across the houseboat complex was a narrow, but straight and unmistakable, boulevard to the elliptical pool; here, we did not ramble from one terrace to the next. Still, we did encounter the occasional Urnudan pedestrian, and as I looked at their faces I tried to resist the temptation to perceive them as mere rough drafts of superior beings from higher up the Wick. As we drew near and passed them by, they averted their gaze, got out of our way, and stood patiently in what looked to me like submissive postures.

"How much of what we're seeing is native Urnudan culture," I wondered out loud to Lio, who had fallen in step next to me, "and how much is a consequence of living on a military spaceship for a thousand years?"

"Same difference, maybe," Lio pointed out, "since only the Urnudans built ships like this in the first place."

The boulevard debouched into the plaza surrounding the meeting pool. This—as we had clearly seen from above—was partitioned into four quadrants of equal size. In turn, it was enclosed by four glass-walled pavilions that curved around it like eyebrows.

"Check out the weatherstripping on the doors!" Yul remarked, nodding at a pavilion entrance. "Those things are aquariums." And indeed, through the glass walls we could see Fthosians, who were not equipped with nose tubes, speed-walking with documents or talking into their versions of jeejahs. "They check their breathing gear at the door," Cord observed, and pointed to a rack just inside that heavily weatherstripped door where dozens of tank-packs had been hung up.

Jesry nudged me. "Translators!" he said, and pointed to a windowed mezzanine above the main deck of the "aquarium." A few Fthosian men and women, fiddling with headsets, sat at consoles that overlooked the pool. And as if to confirm this, Urnudan stewards began to circulate through our delegation carrying trays of earbuds: red for Orth, blue for Fluccish. I stuffed a red one into my ear and heard in it the familiar tones of Jules Verne Durand. With a quick look around, I picked him out in the translators' booth atop the Laterran pavilion. "The Command welcomes the Arbran delegation and requests that you gather at the water's edge for opening ceremonies," he was saying. I got the impression, from his tone of voice, that he'd already said it a hundred times.

We had joined up with a part of the Arbran contingent that had arrived earlier to get things sorted before the stars, journalists, and space commandos showed up to make it complicated. Ala was one of those. The Panjandrums and their aides had also preceded us, and were waiting near the water's edge in an inflated poly bubble the size of a housing module, just off to our left as we emerged from the boulevard. Behind it was a clutter of equipment including compressed air tanks that must have been brought up on the ship from Arbre. So this was meant to be a makeshift pavilion, symbolically placing our Panjandrums on the same footing as the Geometer dignitaries. It was made of the same kind of milky poly sheeting that had covered the windows of my quarantine trailer at Tredegarh. I could make out vague shapes of dark-suited figures around a table—I thought of them as doyns—and others, servitors, hovering round the edges or darting in to handle documents.

I spent a while watching Ala run in and out of that tent, sometimes gazing off at the fake sky as she talked on a headset, other times peeling it off her head and holding her hand over the microphone as she talked to someone face to face. I was overcome by recollection of the time she and I had spent together that morning, and could not think of much else. I thought that I was like a man lame in one leg, who had learned to move about well enough that all awareness of his disability had passed out of his mind. And yet, when he tried to go on a journey, he kept finding himself back where he had started, since his weak leg made him go in circles. But if he found a partner who was weak in the other leg, and the two of them set out as companions . . .

Cord goosed me. I nearly toppled into the water and she had to pull me back by my bolt.

"She's beautiful," she said before I could get huffy.

"Yeah. Thanks. She most definitely is," I said. "She's the one for me."

"Have you told her?"

"Yeah. Actually *telling* her isn't the problem. You can ease up on me as far as *telling* her is concerned."

"Oh. Good."

"The problem is all of these other circumstances."

"They are some pretty interesting circumstances!"

"I'm sorry you got swept up in it like this. It's not what I wanted."

"But it was never about what you wanted," she said. "Look, cuz, even if I croak, it was a good trade."

"How can you say that, Cord, what about—"

She shook her head, reached out, and put her fingertips to my lips. "No. Stop. We are not discussing it."

I took her hand between mine and held it for a moment. "Okay," I said, "it's your life. I'll shut up."

"Don't just shut up. *Believe* it, cuz."

"HEY!" called a gruff voice. "What do you think you're doing, holding hands with my girl?"

"Hey Yul, what have you been up to since Ecba?"

"Time went by fast," he said, ambling closer and standing behind Cord, who leaned comfortably against him. "We got a lot of free aerocraft rides. Saw the world. Spent a lot of time answering questions. After three days, I laid down the law. Said I wouldn't answer any question I had answered already. They took it hard, at first. Forced them to get organized. But after that, it was better for everyone. They put us up in a hotel in the capital."

"An actual hotel," Cord wanted me to understand, "not a casino."

"Days would go by with nothing—we'd go see museums," Yul said. "Then all of a sudden they'd get excited and call us back in, and we'd spend a few hours trying to remember whether the buttons on the control panel were round or square."

"They even hypnotized us," Cord said.

"Then someone ratted us out to the media," Yul said bleakly, and cast a wary look round for the man with the speelycaptor. "Less said about that, the better."

"They moved us to a place just outside Tredegarh, then, for a couple of days," Cord said.

"Right before they blew the walls," Yul added. "Then we Antiswarmed to an old missile base in the desert. I liked that. No media. Lots of hiking." He sighed helplessly. "But now we're here. No hiking in this place."

"Did they give you anything before you boarded the ship?"

"Like a big pill?" Yul said. "Like this?" He held out his hand, the Everything Killer resting in the middle of his palm. I jerked my hand out and clasped his and shook it. He looked surprised. When we let go, I made sure that pill was in my hand.

"You want mine?" Cord said. "They said it was a tracking device—for our safety. But I didn't want to be tracked, and, well—"

"If you wanted safety you wouldn't have come," I said.

"Exactly." She handed me her pill, a little more discreetly than Yul had done.

"What are they really?" Yul asked. I was drawing up a lie when I happened to glance up, and saw him looking at me in a way that said he would brook no deception.

"Weapons," I mouthed. Yul nodded and looked away. Cord looked nauseated. I took my leave, tucking the pills into a fold of my bolt, for I had just noticed Emman Beldo emerging from the inflatable with an aide of, to judge from body language, lesser stature. I yanked out my earbud and tossed it aside. Emman saw me headed his way and told the other to get lost. I met him at the edge of the pool.

"Just a second," were his first words. Around his neck he had a little electronic device on a lanyard. He turned it on and it began to talk, emitting random syllables and word-fragments in Orth. It sounded like Emman and a couple of other people, recorded and run through a blender. "What is it?" I asked, and before I had reached the end of this short utterance my own voice had been thrown into the blender too. I answered my own question: "A means of defeating surveillance," I said, "so we can talk freely."

He made no sign that I was right or wrong, but only looked at me interestedly. "*You've* been through some changes," he pointed out, making an effort to speak distinctly above the murmur of Emman- and Erasmas-gibberish.

I peeled back my bolt fold and let him see what I'd collected from Yul and Cord. "Under what circumstances," I said, "are you planning to turn these on?"

"Under the circumstance that I am given the order to do so," he answered, with a glance back toward the tent.

"You know what I mean."

"It is clearly a measure of last resort," Emman said, "when diplomacy fails and it looks like we are about to be killed or taken hostage."

"I just wonder whether the Panjandrums are even competent to render such judgments," I said.

"I know paying attention to Sæcular politics isn't your game," he said, "but it has gotten a little better since our gracious hosts threw the Warden of Heaven out the airlock. And even more so since the Antiswarm started throwing its weight around."

"Well, I wouldn't know about that, would I?" I pointed out. "Since I've been otherwise engaged the last two weeks."

Emman snorted. "No kidding! Nice job, by the way."

"Thanks. Some day I'll tell you stories. But for now—just how, exactly, did the Antiswarm throw its weight around?"

"They didn't have to say much," Emman told me. "It was obvious."

"*What* was?"

He took a deep breath, sighed it out. "Look. Thirty-seven hundred years ago, the avout were herded into maths because of fear of their ability to change the world through praxis." He nodded helpfully at where I had tucked the Everything Killers. "Because of clever stunts like that, I guess. So praxis stopped, or at least slowed down to a rate of change that could be understood, managed, controlled. Fine—until these guys showed up." He raised his head and gazed around. "Turned out that all we'd been doing was losing the arms race to cosmi that hadn't imposed any such limits on their avout. And guess what? When Arbre decided to fight back a little, who delivered the counterpunch? Our military? The Sæcular Power? Nope. *You* guys in the bolts and chords. So the Antiswarm has garnered a lot of clout just by doing a lot and saying very little. Hence the concept of the two Magisteria, which is—"

"I've heard of it," I said.

He and I stood there for a few moments, gazing across the elliptical pond at the opposite shore, where processions of Urnudan and Troän dignitaries were emerging from their pavilions, making their way toward the water. The garble-box around Emman's neck, however, did not know how to shut up.

"So that is the Narrative everyone is working with now?" I asked him.

He looked at me alertly. "I guess you could think of it that way."

"Well," I said, "if this thing goes all pear-shaped and some Panjandrum gives you the order to activate the EKs, it'd be a shame if that Panjandrum and you turned out to have the Narrative all wrong, wouldn't it?"

"What do you mean?" he asked sharply.

"Thirty-seven hundred years ago they rounded us up, yeah. But they didn't take away our ability to mess with newmatter. In consequence of which, we had the First Sack. Fine. No more newmatter, except for a few exemptions that got grandfathered in: factories where the stuff still gets made, staffed by ex-avout who get Evoked when they are needed. Time passes. We're still allowed to do sequence manipulation. Things get a little spooky. There's a Second Sack. No more sequence work, no more syndevs in the concents, except for a few exemptions that get grandfathered in: the Ita, the clocks, the page trees, and the library grapes, and maybe some labs on the outside, staffed by skeleton crews of Evoked and concent-trained praxics like you. Fine. Things are under control *now*, right? Not much the avout can do if they have *nothing*, no syndevs, no tools at all except for rakes and shovels, and are being watched over by an Inquisition. Now we're *really* under the Sæcular Power's thumb—until two and half millennia later, when it turns out that sufficiently smart people locked up on crags with *nothing* to do but think can actually come up with forms of praxis that require *no* tools and are all the more terrifying for that. So we have a Third Sack—the worst of all, much more savage than the others. Seventy years later the mathic world gets reëstablished. But, you have to ask yourself the obvious question . . ."

"What got grandfathered in?" Emman said, completing the sentence for me. "What were the special exemptions?" And then there was silence except for the babble coming out of his jammer.

Each of us was waiting for the other to finish the sentence—to answer the question. I hoped he might know—and that he might be so forthcoming as to share the answer with me. But from the look on his face it was plain that this was not the case.

So I had to follow the logic myself. Fortunately, Magnath and Ignetha Foral chose this moment to come down to the water's edge—as it had become obvious that something was about to happen. I looked at them, and Emman Beldo looked with me.

"Those guys," he said.

"Those guys," I affirmed.

"The Lineage?"

"Not *exactly* the Lineage—since that goes all the way back to the time of Metekoranes—but a kind of Sæcular incarnation of it, a dowment that was established and funded around the time of the Third Sack. Tied into the mathic world in all sorts of ways. Owns Ecba and Elkhazg and probably other places besides."

"Maybe it looks that way to you," Emman said, "but I can promise you that most of what you call the Panjandrums have never heard of this dowment. It is nothing to them—exerts no influence. Magnath Foral—if they've heard his name at all—is just a dried-up, blue-blooded art collector."

"But that's how it *would* happen," I said. "They would set this thing up after the Third Sack. It would be famous and influential for about ten minutes. But after a few wars, revolutions, and Dark Ages, it would be forgotten. It would become what it is."

"And what is it?" Emman asked me.

"I'm still trying to figure that out," I said. "But I think that what I'm saying is that—"

"We Sæculars are in over our heads here?" Emman suggested. "I'm comfortable with you saying that."

"But are you comfortable with the practical consequence," I asked him, "which is—"

"That if I get the order," he said, with a flick of the eyes at the place where I'd secreted the Everything Killers, "maybe I should ignore it, because it was issued by a clueless Sæcular who has been working from the wrong Narrative?"

"Exactly," I said. And I noticed him rubbing his jeejah with his thumb. He had gotten a new jeejah since Tredegarh. Most unusual. From hanging around with Cord, I knew some of the terminology: Emman's jeejah had been milled from a solid billet of alloy, not molded in poly or stamped out of sheet material. Very expensive. Not mass-produced.

"Nice, huh?" He'd caught me looking.

"I've seen one before," I said.

"Where?" he asked sharply.

"Jad had one."

"How could you know that? It was issued to him immediately before the launch. He burned up before you could talk to him."

I just stared at him, hardly knowing where to begin.

"Is this one of those in-over-my-head things?" he asked.

"More or less. Tell me, how many more of those things?"

"Up here? At least one." And he turned his head toward the inflatable. The outer door of its airlock had been unzipped, and a series of men and women in impressive clothes were emerging, patting their heads self-consciously as they got used to the feel of their nose-tubes. "The third one—the bald man—has one just like it."

My right arm departed the conversation. Ala had made off with it. The rest of me caught up just in time to avoid dislocation of the shoulder joint. "You should wear your earbud," she told me, "then you'd know we're in the middle of an aut!" She slapped a bud into my hand and I wormed it into my ear. Music had begun to play from a band on the other side of the ellipse. I looked across and saw four long boxes—coffins—being borne down to the water's edge by a mixed contingent of Urnudan, Troän, Laterran, and Fthosian soldiers.

Ala led me round behind the inflatable, where Arsibalt, Jesry, and Lio were standing at three corners of another coffin. "For once, I'm not the latest!" Lio said wonderingly.

"Leadership has changed you," I said, and reported to my corner. We picked up the coffin, which I knew must contain the remains of Lise.

All of these coffins smacked me into a whole different frame of mind. We carried Lise out from behind the inflatable, centered her in the road that led to the water's edge, and set her down as we waited for the procession on the opposite side to finish. The music, of course, sounded strange to our ears, but no stranger than a lot of stuff you might hear on Arbre. Music, it seemed, was one of those places where the Hylaean Flow was especially strong—composers in different cosmi were hearing the same things in their heads. It was a funeral march. Very slow and grim. Hard to say whether this was a reflection of Urnudan culture, or a sort of reminder that the four in those coffins had slain a lot of Geometers and that we'd best keep that in mind before we got to celebrating them.

It almost worked. I actually started to feel guilty for having delivered the Valers to the *Daban Urnud*. Then I happened to glance down at the coffin beside my knee, and wondered who up here had shot Jules's wife in the back. Who had given the order to rod Ecba? Who was responsible for killing Orolo? Was he or she standing around this pool? Not the sorts of things I should have been thinking at a peace conference. But there wouldn't have been a need for one if we hadn't been killing each other.

The soldiers carried the coffins of Osa, Esma, Vay, and Gratho quite slowly, stopping for a few beats after each pace. My mind wandered, as it always did during long auts, and I found myself thinking about those four Valers, recalling my first impressions of them in Mahsht, when I'd been cornered, and hadn't understood, yet, what they were. The scenes played in my head like speelies: Osa, perched one-legged atop the sphere that sheltered me, fending off attackers with snap-kicks. Esma dancing across the plaza toward the sniper while Gratho made his body into a bullet-shield for me. Vay fixing me up afterwards—so efficiently, so ruthlessly that snot had run out of my nose and tears from my eyes.

Were doing so, for I was weeping now. Trying to imagine their last moments. Especially Suur Vay, out on the icosahedron, in single combat against several terrified men with cutting tools. Alone, in the dark, the blue face of Arbre thousands of miles away, knowing in the last moments she'd never breathe its air again, never hear the thousand brooks of the Ringing Vale.

"Raz?" It was Ala's voice. She had her hand—more gently, this time—on my elbow. I wiped my face dry with my bolt, got a moment's clear view before things got all misty again. The honor guard across the pool had set the Valers' coffins down and were standing there expectantly. "Time to go," Ala said. Lio, Jesry, and Arsibalt were all looking at me, all crying too. We all bent our knees, got a grip on the coffin, raised it off the deck.

"Sing something," Ala suggested. We looked at her helplessly until she said the name of a chant that we used for the aut of Requiem at Edhar. Arsibalt started it, giving us the pitch in his clear tenor, and we all joined in with our parts. We all had to do some improvising, but few noticed and none cared. As we came out in view of the Laterran pavilion, Jules Verne Durand went off the air. I glanced up through the windows of the translators' booth and saw other Laterrans rushing to his side to lay hands on him. We all sang louder.

"So much for the Orth translation," Jesry said, once we had reached the water and set Lise down. But he said it in a simple and plaintive way that did not make me want to hurt him.

"It's okay," Lio said, "that's the good thing about an aut. The words don't matter." And he rested his hand absent-mindedly on the lid of the coffin.

The soldiers on the opposite bank transferred the coffins of the Valers onto a sort of flatboat. They could simply have marched them around to us, but there seemed to be something in the act of crossing the water that was of ceremonial meaning here. "I get it," Arsibalt said, "it represents the cosmos. The gulf between us." There was more music. The raft was staffed by four women in robes, who began rowing it across. The music was much easier on the ears than the funeral march: different instruments with softer tones, and a solo by a Laterran woman who stood at the edge of the water and seemed to make the whole orb resonate with the power of her voice. It was a good going-home piece, I reckoned.

When the ladies were halfway finished rowing across, Jesry spoke up: "Not setting any speed records, are they?"

"Yeah," Lio said, "I was just thinking the same thing. Give *us* a boat! We could take 'em!"

It wasn't *that* funny, but our bodies thought it was, and we had to do a lot of work in the next couple of minutes trying to avoid laughing so obviously as to create a diplomatic incident. When the boat finally arrived, we took the coffins off, then loaded Lise's on board. To the accompaniment of more music, those slow-rowing ladies took her in a long arc to the Laterran shore, where she was brought off by half a dozen civilian pallbearers—friends of Jules and of Lise, I guessed—while Jules, supported by a couple of friends, looked on. Then in four separate trips we carried the Valers' coffins back to the staging area behind the inflatable. Meanwhile Lise was conveyed into the Laterran pavilion so that Jules could have a private moment with her. The oar-ladies rowed back to the Urnudan shore. Fraa Lodoghir and Gan Odru, from opposite sides of the pond, each said a few words reminding us about the others who had died in the little war that we had come here to conclude: on Arbre, the ones who had been killed in the rod attacks, and up here, the ones who had fallen to the Valers.

After a moment of silence, we broke for an intermission, and food and drinks were brought out on trays by stewards. Apparently, the need to eat after a funeral was as universal as the Adrakhonic Theorem. The boat ladies went to work refitting their barge with a table, draped with blue cloth, and arrayed with piles of documents.

"Raz."

I had been waiting for my crack at a food tray, but turned around to discover Emman a few paces away, just in the act of underhanding something to me. Reflexes took over and I pawed it out of the air. It was another one of those conversation-jamming machines.

"I stole it from a Procian," he explained.

"Won't the Procian be needing it?" I asked, my face—I hoped—the picture of mock concern.

"Nah. Redundant."

The conversation jammer turned into a conversation piece, as my friends gathered round to play with it and chuckle at the funny sounds it made. Yul got it to generate random, profane sentences by cursing into it. But after a few minutes, the voice of Jules Verne Durand—hoarse, but composed—was in our ears telling us that the next phase of the aut was about to begin. Once again we convened at the water's edge and heard speeches from the four leaders who would be putting pens to paper in a few minutes: first Gan Odru. Then Prag Eshwar: a stocky woman, more grand-auntish than I had envisioned, in a military uniform. Then the Arbran foreign minister, and finally one of the Thousanders who had been hanging around with Fraa Lodoghir. As each of the speakers finished, they stepped aboard the barge. When our Thousander had joined the first three, the oar-ladies rowed them out into the middle. They all took up pens and began to sign. All watched in silence for a few moments. But the signing was lengthy, and so, soon enough, people began muttering to one another. Conversations flourished all over, and people began to mill around.

It might sound like an odd thing to do, but I strayed around behind the inflatable and counted the coffins. One, two, three, four.

"Taking inventory?"

I turned around to find that Fraa Lodoghir had followed me.

I flicked on the conversation jammer, which emitted a stream of profanity in Yul's voice as I said, "It's the only way for me to be sure who is still dead."

"You can be sure now," he said. "It's over. The tally will not change."

"Can you bring people back as well as make them disappear?"

"Not without undoing that." He nodded at the barge where they were signing the peace.

"I see," I said.

"You were hoping to get Saunt Orolo back?" he asked gently.

"Yes."

Lodoghir said nothing. But I was able to work it out for myself. "But if Orolo's alive, it means Lise is buried at Ecba. We don't get the intelligence gleaned from her remains—none of this happens. Peace is only compatible with Lise and Orolo being dead—and staying that way."

"I'm sorry," Lodoghir said. "There are certain worldtracks—certain states of affairs—that are only compatible with certain persons' being . . . absent."

"That's the word Fraa Jad used," I said, "before he turned up absent."

Fraa Lodoghir looked as if steeling himself to hear some sophomoric outburst from me. I continued, "How *about* Fraa Jad? Any chance he'll be *present* again?"

"His tragic demise is extensively recorded," said Fraa Lodoghir, "but I'd not presume to say what an Incanter is and is not capable of." And his gaze fell away from my face and traveled across the milling crowd until it had come to rest, or so I thought, on Magnath Foral. For once, the Heritor of Elkhazg did not have Madame Secretary at his side—she was tending to official duties—and so I walked directly over to him.

"Did you—did *we*—summon them here?" I asked him. "Did we call the Urnudans forth? Or is it the case that some Urnudan, a thousand years ago, saw a geometric proof in a dream, and turned that into a religion—decided that he had been called to a higher world?"

Magnath Foral heard me out, then turned his face toward the water, drawing my attention to the peace that was being signed there. "Behold," he said. "There are two Arbrans on that vessel, of coequal dignity. Such a state of affairs has not existed since the golden age of Ethras. The walls of Tredegarh have been brought down. The avout have escaped from their prisons. Ita mingle and work by their sides. If all of these things had occurred as the result of a summoning such as you suppose, would it not be a great thing for the Lineage to have brought about? Oh, I should very much like to claim such credit. Long have my predecessors and I waited for such a culmination. What honors would decorate the Lineage were it all true! But it did not come to pass in any such clean and straightforward manner. I do not know the answer, Fraa Erasmas. Nor will any born of this cosmos until we have taken ship on a vessel such as this, and journeyed on to the next."

Part 13

RECONSTITUTION

Upsight: A sudden, usually unlooked-for moment of clear understanding.

—THE DICTIONARY, *4th edition, A.R. 3000*

The need for stakes was insatiable. Our volunteers were fashioning them from anything they could find: reinforcing bar cut from buildings that had been splashed across the landscape, twisted angle irons sawed from toppled gantries, splinters of blown-apart trees. Lashed into bundles, they piled up before the flaps of my tent and threatened to block me in.

"I need to deliver those to the survey team on the rim," I said, "would you like to walk with me?"

Artisan Quin had been sitting in a fetch for six days with Barb. My proposal sounded good to him. We pushed through mildewy canvas and came out into the white light of an overcast morning. Each of us shouldered as many stake-bundles as he thought he could carry, and we began to trudge uphill. Our early trails down from the rim had already been turned into gullies by erosion, so new arrivals were cutting terraces and properly switchbacked paths into the dirt. Hard work, and a good way to sort mere vacationers from those who would stick it out and make their livings at Orolo.

"The first draft of everything is going to be wood and earth," I told him, as we passed by a mixed team of avout and Sæculars pounding sharpened logs into the ground. "By the time I die, we should have a rough idea of how the place works. Later generations can begin planning how to do it all over again in stone."

Quin looked dismayed for a moment. Then his face relaxed as he understood that I was talking about dying of old age. "Where are you going to get the stone from?" he asked. "All I see is mud."

I stopped and turned back to face the crater. It had filled with water as soon as it had cooled down, and so, with the altitude we'd already gained, we could easily see its general shape: an ellipse, oriented northwest to southeast—the direction in which the rod had been traveling. We were above its southeastern end. Its most obvious feature was an island of rubble that rose from the brown water a few hundred yards offshore. But I directed his attention to a barely visible notch in the coastline, miles away. "The river that filled it spills in over yonder, near the other end," I said. "It's not easy to make out from here. But if you go up that river a couple of miles, you come to a place where the impact touched off a landslide that exposed a face of limestone. Enough for our descendants to build whatever they want."

Quin nodded, and we resumed climbing. He was silent for a while. Finally he asked, "Are you going to *have* descendants?"

I laughed. "It's already happening! People started getting pregnant during the Antiswarm. We started eating normal food and the men stopped being sterile. The first avout baby was born last week. I heard about it on the Reticulum. Oh, you'll find our access is a little spotty. For a while Sammann—he's our ex-Ita—was keeping it running all by himself. But more ex-Ita show up here every day. We have a couple of dozen now."

Quin wasn't interested in that part of it. He interrupted me: "So, Barb could one day be a father."

"Yes. He could." Then—better late than never—I worked out the implication: "You could be a grandfather."

Quin picked up the pace—suddenly eager to get Saunt Orolo's constructed *now*. Huffing along in his wake, I added: "Of course, that raises the ancient breeding issue. But we know enough now that we can prevent a forking of the race into two species. It puts some responsibility on us to make places like this welcoming for what we used to call extras."

"What are you going to call them—us—now?" Quin asked.

"I have no idea. What matters is that, under the Second Reconstitution, there are two coequal Magisteria. People can come up with words for them later."

We had reached a place where the crater's formerly knifelike edge had already softened to a round shoulder under the action of rain and wind. It was dotted with a few opportunistic weeds and etched with colored lines strung between stakes. "The boundaries will run wherever we put them. Here's one." I plucked at a red string.

Quin was aghast. "How can you just *do* that? Go out and stake a claim? The lawyers must be going crazy."

"We have a small army of Procians running their mouths for us. The lawyers don't stand a chance."

"So everything on this side of the string is your property?"

"Yes. The walls will run parallel to it, just inside."

"So you'll still have walls?"

"Yes. With gateways—but no gates," I said.

"Then why bother building the walls?"

"They have symbolic content," I said. "They say, 'you're passing into a different Magisterium now, and there are certain things you must leave behind.'" But I knew I was not being altogether forthright. Half a mile away I could make out half a dozen people in bolts, peering through instruments and pounding in stakes: Lio and the crowd of ex-Ringing Vale avout he ran with now. I knew exactly what they were discussing: when war breaks out between the Magisteria and we plug the holes in the wall with gates, we'll want interlocking fields of fire between this bastion and the next to repel any assault on the intervening stretch of wall . . .

I whistled between my fingers. They looked over at us. I pointed to the bundles of stakes that Quin and I had just dropped. A couple of the Valers began sprinting to fetch them. Quin and I turned to descend the way we'd come. But we were pulled up short by an answering whistle, which I recognized as Lio's. I looked his way. He gestured down the outer slope of the crater wall, trying to get me to see something. There wasn't much to reward looking: just a long slope of boiled earth, burned wood, shredded insulation, and pulverized stone. Farther away, a flat place where pilgrims like Quin had parked their vehicles. Finally, though, I saw what Lio wanted me to see: a vein of yellow starblossom rushing up the slope.

"What is it?" Quin asked.

"Barbarian invasion," I said. "Long story." I waved to Lio.

Quin and I turned around and began the descent into the crater. We had enough time to go on a detour to a certain terrace that my Edharian fraas and suurs and I had built soon after we had come to this place. Unlike most of the terraces, which were beginning to sprout plants that would eventually grow up into tangles, this one was covered with scrap-metal trellises that would one day support library vines. Some months ago, Fraa Haligastreme had paid us a visit from Edhar, and he'd brought with him root stock from Orolo's old vineyard. We'd planted it in the ground beneath these trellises, and since then visited it frequently to see whether the vines, in a fit of pique, were committing suicide. But they were sending out new growth all over the place. We were near the equator, but almost two miles high, so the sun was intense but the weather was cool. Who would've thought that rockets and grapevines liked the same sorts of places?

As we were walking back down to the lake's edge, Quin—who had been silent for a while—cleared his throat. "You mentioned that there were certain things you have to leave behind when you enter this new Magisterium," he reminded me. "Does that include religion?"

One measure of how much things had changed was that this didn't make me the least bit nervous. "I'm glad you brought that up," I said. "I noticed that Artisan Flec came with you."

"Flec's been going through rough times," Quin wanted me to know. "His wife divorced him. Business hasn't been so good. The whole Warden of Heaven thing sent him into a tailspin. He just needed to get out of town. Then, Barb spent the whole drive, er . . ."

"Planing him?"

"Yeah. Anyway, I just want to say, if his presence here is not appropriate . . ."

"The rule of thumb we've been using is that Deolaters are welcome as long as they're not certain they're right," I said. "As soon as you're sure you're right, there's no point in your being here."

"Flec's not sure of *anything* now," Quin assured me. Then, after a minute: "Can you even *have* an Ark, if you're not sure you're right? Isn't it just a social club, in that case?"

I slowed, and pointed to an outcropping of bedrock that protruded from the curving wall of the crater. Smoke was braiding up from a fire that had been kindled on its top, before the entrance of a tent. My fraa was up there burning his breakfast. "Flec should hike up to Arsibalt's Dowment," I suggested. "It is going to be a center for working on that sort of thing."

Quin made a wry grin. "I'm not sure if Flec wants to *work* on it."

"He just wants to be *told*?"

"Yes. Or at least, that's what he's used to—what he's comfortable with."

"I have a few Laterran friends now," I said, "and one of them, the other day, was telling me about a philosopher named Emerson who had some useful upsights about the difference between poets and mystics. I'm thinking that it's just as applicable in our cosmos as it is in his."

"I'll bite. What's the difference?"

"The mystic nails a symbol to one meaning that was true for a moment but soon becomes false. The poet, on the other hand, sees that truth *while it's true* but understands that symbols are always in flux and that their meanings are fleeting."

"Someone here must have said something like that once," Quin said.

"Oh, yes. It's a great time to be a Lorite. We have a whole contingent of them here, gearing up for the great project of absorbing the knowledge from the four new cosmi." I looked toward the tent-cloister where Karvall and Moyra and their fraas and suurs had encamped, but they'd not emerged from under canvas yet. Probably still tying their outfits on. "Anyway, my point is that guys like Flec have a weakness, almost a kind of addiction, for the mystical, as opposed to poetic, way of using their minds. And there's an optimistic side of me that says such a person could break that addiction, be retrained to think like a poet, and accept the fluxional nature of symbols and meaning."

"Okay, but what's the pessimistic side telling you?"

"That the poet's way is a feature of the brain, a specific organ or faculty, that you either have or you don't. And that those who have it are doomed to be at war forever with those who don't."

"Well," Quin said, "it sounds like you're going to be spending a lot of time up on that rock with Arsibalt."

"Well, someone has to keep the poor guy company."

"For guys like me and Flec, do you have anything? Besides hammering stakes into mud?"

"We *are* actually building some permanent structures," I said, "mostly on the island. The new Magisterium needs a headquarters. A capitol. You came just in time to watch the cornerstone being laid."

"When will that happen?"

I slowed again and checked the position of the bright place in the sky. The sun was almost ready to burn through. "Noon sharp."

"You have a clock?"

"Working on it."

"Why today? Is this a special day in your calendar?"

"It will be after today," I said. "Day Zero, Year Zero."

Chance or luck had endowed us with half of a causeway to the island: a launch gantry that had gone down like a tall tree in a gust of wind. It was twisted, fractured, and half melted, but still more than able to bear the weight of humans and wheelbarrows. Halfway from shore to island, it ramped beneath the surface. Beyond there we had extended it with pontoons of closed-cell foam, anchored by scavenged cables to the submerged part of the gantry. The last few hundred yards still had to be managed on small boats. Yul liked to swim it. "We would like to build a simple cable-car system," I told Quin, as we rowed across the gap, "but it is a serious praxic challenge to anchor a tower in the soil of the island, which is still loose. That might be something where father and son could work together." For Quin, Barb, and I were all crossing together. I don't think Barb had come along for the companionship so much as because the breeze had shifted and carried the scent of cooking food from island to shore. From his perch in the bow, Barb had already identified the barbecue pits and other such attractions he would be visiting first. "You have an oven!" he exclaimed, pointing to a smoking masonry dome that had just interrupted the skyline.

"That was the first permanent thing we built. Arsibalt started it and Tris finished it. Later we'll build a kitchen, then a Refectory around it."

"How about messallans?" Barb asked.

"Maybe a couple of those too," I allowed, "for those who just can't get along without servitors."

"So, this will become the Concent of Saunt Orolo?" Quin asked me.

I hesitated, and shipped the oars, not wanting to clobber Yul, who was wading out to come and tow us in. "It'll be the *something* of Saunt Orolo," I assured Quin. "But we are a little uneasy with the word *Concent*. We need a new word. Hey, Barb!" For Barb was about to jump off and wade to shore in quest of food. He didn't hear me, but Yul—who had his big wet hand clamped on our gunwale now—touched Barb's arm, and pointed to me. Barb turned around. "I will not drown," he assured me, as if calming a fretful child, "my clothes are made from non-absorbent fibers."

"You won't eat, either. That food is for later."

"How much later?"

"You're going to have to sit through two auts," I said. "One at noon. The second immediately after. Then, for the rest of the day, we eat."

"What time is it?"

"Let's go ask Jesry."

Jesry's clock was taking shape on the summit of the island. It was another of those projects that would not be finished in our natural lifetimes—but at least it was ticking! Jesry's ideas on how to build "the real one" were so advanced that I could not understand half of them. But we had insisted he have something working for today. He and Cord had been toiling for a couple of months, building and breaking prototypes. The pace of the work had quickened as Cord had gathered in more tools. When Barb, Quin, and I hiked to the top, Cord was absent, having been called away to other preparations. Jesry was up there alone with his machines, like a half-mad holy hermit, watching through goggles as a spot of blinding light crept across a slab of synthetic stone. It was cast by a parabolic mirror that we had all taken a hand in grinding. "Lucky the sun came out," he said, by way of greeting.

"It often does, this time of day," I said.

"You ready?"

"Yeah, Arsibalt is a few minutes behind us, and I saw Tulia and Karvall putting their heads together, so . . ."

"Not for that," he said. "I mean, are you ready for the other thing?"

"Oh, that?"

"Yeah, *that*."

"Sure," I said, "never been readier."

"You, my fraa, are a liar."

"How much time?" I asked, feeling a change of subject was in order.

He pulled his goggles back down over his eyes, judged the distance between the spot of light and a length of wire that lay helpless in its path. "A quarter of an hour," he decreed. "See you there."

"Okay, Jesry."

"Raz? Any Deolaters down there?"

"Probably. Why?"

"Then ask them to pray that this contraption doesn't fall apart in the next fifteen minutes."

"Will do."

We got to the site of the aut by following the trigger line down from the clock. The island had very little flat space, but we had created one just big enough for the cornerstone by scraping it out with hand tools and pounding it flat. Above it Yul had welded together a tripod from scrap steel. The stone—a fragment of the actual rod that the Geometers had thrown from space—was suspended from the tripod's apex. It had been shaped to a cube by avout stonemasons, of whom we already had several. OF SAVANT OROLO was carved into one face—we'd fill in the blank later, when we'd found a suitable word—and YEAR 0 OF THE SECOND RECONSTITUTION was on another. On a third face—which would be hidden when the structure was built—we'd all been scratching our names. I invited Barb and Quin to add theirs.

Barb got so involved in it that I don't think he heard a word or a note of the aut and the music that Arsibalt, Tulia, and Karvall had put together for us. But neither did I. I had other matters on my mind, and was too busy, anyway, marveling at all who'd showed up for the event: Ganelial Crade. Ferman Beller, with a couple of Bazian monks in tow. Three of Jesry's siblings. Estemard and his wife. A contingent of Orithenans. Fraa Paphlagon and Emman Beldo. Geometers of all four races, equipped with nose tubes.

As noon drew near, we launched into a version of the Hylaean Anathem that Arsibalt had chosen for what he called its "temporal elasticity," meaning that if the clock malfunctioned we'd be able to cover it up. But at some point—I have no idea whether it was even close to true solar noon—I saw Jesry spring up out of his clock-hovel, fling his goggles aside, and take off toward us at a run. I could tell by his gait that the news was good. The trigger line was getting noticeably tighter. I looked over at Yul, who was under the tripod, and drew my thumb across my throat. He grabbed Barb in a bear hug and jerked him back to safety. A moment later, a mechanism snapped and the stone dropped into its place with a thud that we all felt in our ankles. There was applause and cheering, which I didn't really get to take part in since Arsibalt—presiding at a lectern, and leading the Anathem—was staring into my eyes and jerking his head in the direction of a tent a short ways up the hill. "Okay," I mouthed, and obeyed.

Yul reached the tent a few moments after I did. He helped me change into a fancy Tredegarh-style bolt while I helped him put on a formal going-to-Ark suit. And both of us proved so incompetent at our respective tasks that these preparations outlasted the aut, and led to audible restlessness and rude comments from the crowd milling around just on the other side of the canvas. Emman Beldo had to tear himself away from bothering Suur Karvall, come into the tent, and intervene on Yul's behalf. Meanwhile my overwraps were pleated and fixed into place by, of all people, Fraa Lodoghir, who had showed up probably to make sure that Saunt Orolo's would include an influential Procian faculty.

Yul and I dithered and swapped after-yous at the threshold—which was obviated when the threshold ceased to exist. Lio and some of the Valers had lost patience, cut the tent's guy ropes, and swept it off over our heads, like unveiling a couple of statues.

And, as a matter of fact, statues is probably what we acted like when we caught sight of Ala and Cord, who had done a much better job of getting dressed. I'd expected that my bride would be garlanded with starblossom and other invasive species. But I understood, now, that Quin's fetch had been loaded with proper flowers, raised in faraway fields and hothouses.

The aut was a little complicated, since I had to give away Yul's bride, but it had all been worked out by better minds. Cord and Yul were joined in matrimony by Magister Sark, who pulled it off pretty well, considering he'd been up until three A.M. in Dialog with Arsibalt over bottles of wine. He used the occasion to uncork one of his amazing, exasperating sermons, filled with wisdom and upsight and human truths, fettered to a cosmographical scheme that had been blown out of the water four thousand years ago.

When Sark's part of the ceremony was complete, I, seconded by Jesry, and Ala, backed up by Tulia, came together in the presence of Fraa Paphlagon, and, to the accompaniment of a joyous song, and the distant rumble of Ma Cartas rolling over in her chalcedony sarcophagus, joined ourselves together in a Perelithian liaison.

It was traditional for the presiding fraa or suur to deliver some remarks, so we came to a place in the aut when all of the avout fell silent and turned their eyes to Fraa Paphlagon. This could have been awkward, since there was no avoiding the fact that the listeners would view his words, not entirely in their own light, but as a counterbalance to what Magister Sark had said. I thought it good that Paphlagon did not try to sneak around this.

"Since we pride ourselves on our Dialogs, let me welcome Magister Sark as a respected interlocutor. In his words I clearly see the traces left, thousands of years ago, when one of his forebears hit on an upsight and a way of expressing it that, for that moment, were true. As when the parts of a clock tick into alignment, and a pin falls into a slot, and something happens: a gate swings open, there's a little Apert, and through it, a glimpse into the next cosmos. Or—in light of recent developments—perhaps I should say *a* next cosmos." As he was saying this, Paphlagon looked around and made eye contact with Urnudans, Troäns, Laterrans, and Fthosians. "Those who were there when that gate opened, knew it for a real upsight, wrote it down, made it part of their religion—which is a way of saying that they did all that was in their power to pass it on to the ones they loved. We can, on some other occasion, have a lively debate as to whether they succeeded; I regret to say that in my case they did not."

I couldn't help looking over at Ganelial Crade to see how he was reacting. I saw no trace of the old fuming resentment that had used to come over him when he felt that we were disrespecting his beliefs. Something had changed for him at Orithena.

"We are gathered at a place named after Fraa Orolo, who was a fid of mine for a little while," Paphlagon continued. "When he was only a little older than some of you," and here he looked at me and Ala, then Jesry, Tulia, and the others who had come from Edhar or from the Convox, "he spoke to me once of why he had made Eliger with my Order. For he could have left the mathic world at Apert and found a life in the Sæculum, or, having decided to remain a fraa, he might just as well have joined the New Circle. Orolo said that the more he knew of the complexity of the mind, and the cosmos with which it was inextricably and mysteriously bound up, the more inclined he was to see it as a kind of miracle—not in quite the same sense that our Deolaters use the term, for he considered it altogether natural. He meant rather that the evolution of our minds from bits of inanimate matter was more beautiful and more extraordinary than any of the miracles cataloged down through the ages by the religions of our world. And so he had an instinctive skepticism of any system of thought, religious or theorical, that pretended to encompass that miracle, and in so doing sought to draw limits around it. That's why he'd chosen the path that he had. Now the coming of our friends from Urnud, Tro, Earth, and Fthos has demonstrated certain things about how the polycosm works that we had only speculated about before. We must all of us re-examine everything we know and believe in the light of these revelations. That is the work that begins here now. It is a great and gradual beginning that encompasses many smaller but no less beautiful beginnings—such as the union of Ala and Erasmas."

I almost missed my cue. But I felt Ala swinging around toward me. We came together, there on the rubble, and found each other. You might find it odd that a story like this one ends with a kiss, as if it were a popular speely, or a comedy acted out on a stage. But in that we started so many things in that moment, we brought to their ends many others that have been the subject matter of this account, and so here is where I draw a line across the leaf and call it the end.

GLOSSARY

A.R.: Year of the Reconstitution. Arbre's dating system defines Year 0 as the year in which the Reconstitution took place; any year prior to that is assigned a negative number, any year that is expressed as a positive number or, equivalently, followed by A.R., happened afterwards.

Adrakhonic Theorem: An ancient theorem from plane geometry, attributed to Adrakhones, the founder of the Temple of Orithena, stating that, in a right triangle, the square of the hypotenuse is equal to the sum of the squares of the other two sides. Equivalent to the Pythagorean Theorem on Earth.

Allswell: A naturally occurring chemical that, when present in sufficient concentrations in the brain, engenders the feeling that everything is basically fine. Its level may be artificially adjusted by, e.g., consuming blithe.

Analemma: A shape like a slender, elongated figure eight, observed by astronomers who track the way the sun's apparent movement across the sky varies from day to day over the course of a year.

Anathem: (1) In Proto-Orth, a poetic or musical invocation of Our Mother Hylaea, used in the aut of Provener, or (2) an aut by which an incorrigible fraa or suur is ejected from the mathic world.

Apert: The aut in which a math opens its gates for a period of ten days, during which time the avout are free to come and go extramuros, and Sæculars are free to come in, sightsee, and talk to the avout. Depending on the math, Apert is celebrated every one, ten, hundred, or thousand years.

Arbortect: One who genetically engineers new species of trees.

Arbre: The name of the planet on which *Anathem* is set.

Ark: Equivalent to a church, temple, synaogue, etc., on Earth.

Atlanian: See **Liaison, Atlanian.**

Aut: A rite observed in the mathic world. Some of the more important and commonly celebrated auts are Provener, Eliger, Regred, and Requiem. Rarely celebrated rites include Anathem, Voco, and Inbrase.

Avout: A person sworn to the Cartasian Discipline and therefore dwelling in the mathic, as opposed to Sæcular, world.

Baritoe, Saunt: (1) A noblewoman of the mid-Praxic Age, the hostess and the leader of the Sconics. (2) A concent of the same name, one of the Big Three.

Baz: Ancient city-state that later created an empire encompassing the known world.

Bazian Orthodox: The state religion of the Bazian Empire, which survived the Fall of Baz, erected, during the succeeding age, a mathic system parallel to and independent of that inaugurated by Cartas, and endured as one of Arbre's largest faiths.

Big Three: The Concents of Saunt Muncoster, Saunt Tredegarh, and Saunt Baritoe, all relatively old, wealthy, distinguished, and close together.

Blithe: A weed that was genetically altered to produce the brain chemical known as Allswell. Forbidden to the avout.

Bly, Saunt: A theor of the Concent of Saunt Edhar who was Thrown Back and lived out the remainder of his days as a Feral on a butte, later known as Bly's Butte. According to legend, he was worshipped as a god by the local slines, who eventually killed him and ate his liver.

Book, The: A tome filled with subtly incoherent material, which misbehaving avout are forced to study as a form of penance. Divided into chapters, the difficulty of which grows exponentially.

Bulshytt: Speech (typically but not necessarily commercial or political) that employs euphemism, convenient vagueness, numbing repetition, and other such rhetorical subterfuges to create the impression that something has been said.

Calca: An explanation, definition, or lesson that is instrumental in developing some larger theme, but that has been moved aside from the main body of the dialog and encapsulated in a footnote or appendix.

Cartabla: A portable location-finding and map-display gadget, like a GPS unit on Earth.

Cartas, Saunt: An educated Bazian noblewoman who, after the Fall of Baz, founded the first math and created the Discipline that was followed all throughout the Old Mathic Age and, with certain renovations, in the mathic world following the Reconstitution.

Cartasian Discipline: The set of rules prescribed by Saunt Cartas, who is credited with having brought the mathic world into being following the Fall of Baz. An avout is a person who has taken an oath to observe the Discipline.

Causal Domain: A collection of things mutually linked in a web of cause-and-effect relationships.

Centenarian: An avout sworn not to emerge from the math or to have contact with the outside world until the next Centennial Apert. Informally, "Hundreder."

Chapter: Local organizational unit of an Order of avout. Orders generally span the entire mathic world, and may have local Chapters in any number of different maths and concents. Commonly, as for example at Edhar, a math will comprise two or more distinct Chapters, belonging to different Orders.

Chronicle: Log of all events, great and small, taking place within a math or concent. Assiduously maintained and archived by hierarchs.

Chronochasm: In Mathic architecture, the space in the interior of a clock tower housing the workings of the clock and related equipment such as dials, bells, etc.

Cnoön: According to Protan metatheorics, the pure, eternal, changeless entities, such as geometric shapes, theorems, numbers, etc., that belong to another plane of existence (the Hylaean Theoric World) and that are somehow perceived or discovered (as opposed to fabricated) by working theors.

Cnoüs: Ancient historical figure famous for having a vision in which he claimed to see into another, higher world. The vision was interpreted in two different and incompatible ways by his daughters Hylaea and Deät.

Collect: Used as a verb, to accept a newcomer into a math from extramuros during Apert. Typically the newcomer is within a few years of his or her tenth birthday. Used as a noun to denote such a newcomer.

Concent: A relatively large community of avout in which two or more maths exist side by side. In general, Centenarian and Millenarian orders are only to be found in concents, as practical considerations make it difficult for them to exist as freestanding maths.

Convox: A large convocation of avout from maths and concents all over the world. Normally celebrated only at Millennial Apert or following a sack, but also convened in highly exceptional circumstances at the request of the Sæcular Power.

Cosmi: Plural of cosmos. A coinage necessary for discoursing of polycosmic theorics.

Cosmographer: In Earth terms, an astronomer/astrophysicist/cosmologist.

Counter-Bazian: Religion rooted in the same scriptures, and honoring the same prophets, as Bazian Orthodoxy, but explicitly rejecting the authority, and certain teachings, of the Bazian Orthodox faith.

DAG: See **Directed Acyclic Graph**.

Datonomy: An approach to philosophy rooted in the work of the Sconics and based on rigorous study of data, or, literally, givens, meaning what is given to our minds by our sensory apparatus.

Deät: One of the two daughers of Cnoüs, the other being Hylaea. She interpreted her father's vision as meaning that he had glimpsed a heavenly spiritual kingdom populated by angelic beings and ruled by a supreme creator.

Decenarian: An avout sworn not to emerge from the math or to have contact with the outside world until the next Decennial Apert. Informally, "Tenner."

Deolater: One who favors Deät's interpretation of her father Cnoüs's vision and therefore believes in a Heaven with a God in it. Compare **Physiologer**.

Dialog, Peregrin: A Dialog in which two participants of roughly equal knowledge and intelligence develop an idea by talking to each other, typically while out walking around.

Dialog, Periklynian: A competitive Dialog in which each participant seeks to destroy the other's position (see **Plane**).

Dialog, Suvinian: A Dialog in which a mentor instructs a fid, usually by asking the fid questions, as opposed to speaking discursively.

Dialog: A discourse, usually in formal style, between theors. "To be in Dialog" is to participate in such a discussion extemporaneously. The term may also apply to a written record of a historical Dialog; such documents are the cornerstone of the mathic literary tradition and are studied, re-enacted, and memorized by fids. In the classic format, a Dialog involves two principals and some number of onlookers who participate sporadically. Another common format is the Triangular, featuring a savant, an ordinary person who seeks knowledge, and an imbecile. There are countless other classifications, including the suvinian, the Periklynian, and the peregrin.

Diax's Rake: A pithy phrase, uttered by Diax on the steps of the Temple of Orithena when he was driving out the fortune-tellers with a gardener's rake. Its general import is that one should never believe a thing only because one wishes that it were true. After this event, most Physiologers accepted the Rake and, in Diax's terminology, thus became Theors. The remainder became known as Enthusiasts.

Diax: An early physiologer at the Temple of Orithena, credited with driving out the Enthusiasts, founding theorics, and placing it on a solid, rigorous intellectual footing.

Directed Acyclic Graph: An arrangement of nodes connected by one-way links (think boxes connected by arrows) so arranged that it is not possible to follow the links around in a circle.

Discipline: See **Cartasian Discipline**.

Dowment: In its most general usage, any wealth accumulated and held by a Lineage in the mathic world. Almost always used to refer to a building and its contents.

Doyn: At Concents that observe the mealtime tradition of the Messal, a senior avout who has the privilege of sitting at the table and being waited on by a servitor.

Drummon: A large wheeled vehicle used extramuros to transport heavy freight on roads.

Ecba: A volcanic island in the Sea of Seas, home of the Temple of Orithena until the catastrophic eruption of -2621.

Edhar: A Saunt belonging to the Evenedrician order who in 297 established a new order and later founded a concent, where he lived until he died; both the order and the concent ended up being named after him. The full name of the latter is "The Concent of Saunt Edhar" but in common usage this is often shortened to "Saunt Edhar" or simply "Edhar."

Eleven: The list of plants forbidden intramuros, typically because of their undesirable pharmacological properties. The Discipline states that any specimen noticed growing in the math is to be uprooted and burned without delay, and that the event is to be noted in the Chronicle.

Eliger: The aut by which a fid chooses, and is chosen by, a specific chapter in his or her math, and thereby ceases to be a fid. Typically celebrated within a few years of the age of twenty.

Enthusiast: Disparaging term for those early Physiologers at Orithena who were driven out by Diax because of their unwillingness or inability to think rigorously.

Erasmas: A fraa at Saunt Baritoe's in the Fourteenth Century A.R. who, along with Uthentine, founded the branch of metatheorics called Complex Protism. Also, his namesake, a fraa at Saunt Edhar's in the Thirty-seventh Century who narrates *Anathem*.

Ethras: A relatively prosperous and powerful city-state in the ancient world that, during its Golden Age (circa -2600 to -2300) was home to many theors, including Thelenes and Protas. The site of many important Dialogs studied, re-enacted, and memorized by fids.

Etrevanean: See **Liaison, Etrevanean**.

Evenedric: A protégé of Halikaarn, credited with carrying Halikaarn's work forward into the time of the Reconstitution and helping to found the Semantic Faculties.

Evenedricians: An early offshoot of the Halikaarnians.

Everything Killer: A weapons system of unusual praxic sophistication, thought to have been used to devastating effect in the Terrible Events. The belief is widely held, but unproved, that the complicity of theors in the development of this praxis led to universal agreement that they should henceforth be segregated from non-theorical society, a policy that when effected became synonymous with the Reconstitution.

Evoke: To call out an avout in the aut of Voco.

Extra: Slightly disparaging term used by avout to refer to Sæcular people.

Extramuros: The world outside the walls of the math; the Sæcular world.

Faanians: An early offshoot of the Procians.

Fendant: See **Warden Fendant**.

Feral: A literate and theorically minded person who dwells in the Sæculum, cut off from contact with the mathic world. Typically an ex-avout who has renounced his or her vows or been Thrown Back, though the term is also technically applicable to autodidacts who have never been avout.

Fetch: A wheeled vehicle used extramuros, typically by artisans, to transport small amounts of freight, tools, etc. Typically larger and less comfortable than a mobe.

Fid: A young avout; an avout who has not yet joined an Order. See **Eliger**.

Fluccish: The dominant global language of the Sæcular world. Derived from an ancient "barbarian" (i.e., non-Orth) language, its vocabulary overlaps with that of Orth when dealing with abstractions, technical, medical, or legal terms. When extramuros culture is largely illiterate or aliterate (which is most of the time), it is written in short-lived, ad hoc writing systems such as Kinagrams or Logotype, but it can also be transcribed using the same alphabet as is employed for Orth.

Fraa: A male avout.

Gardan's Steelyard: (1) A rule of thumb stating that when one is comparing two hypotheses, preference should be given to the one that is simpler. Also referred to as Saunt Gardan's Steelyard or simply the Steelyard.

Gheeth: An informal term, verging on an ethnic slur, for a particular ethnic group in the Sæcular world.

Graduation: A procedure by which an avout belonging to a Unarian, Decenarian, or Centenarian math may move up to (respectively) the adjoining Decenarian, Centenarian, or Millenarian math, traditionally by passing through a labyrinth that bridges the two maths in question.

Grandfraa: An informal term of respect by which an avout might address a very senior fraa, especially, but not necessarily, one who has celebrated the aut of Regred.

Grandsuur: An informal term of respect by which an avout might address a very senior suur, especially, but not necessarily, one who has celebrated the aut of Regred.

HTW: See **Hylaean Theoric World**.

Halikaarn: A Saunt from the last decades of the Praxic Age who clashed with his contemporary, Proc. Sometimes called Saunt Halikaarn the Great. Broadly speaking, Halikaarn is seen as the standard-bearer of the school of theorics promulgated thousands of years earlier by Protas and Thelenes and carried forward after his death by his disciple Evenedric and the Semantic Faculties.

Halikaarnian: Of, or relating to, Saunt Halikaarn or any of the Orders that claim descent from the Semantic Faculties. Frequently seen as natural opponents of Procians and Faanians.

Harbinger: One of a series of three calamities that engulfed most of Arbre during the last decades of the Praxic Age and later came to be seen as precursors or warnings of the Terrible Events. The precise nature of the Harbingers is difficult to sort out because of destruction of records (many of which were stored on syntactic devices that later ceased functioning) but it is generally agreed that the First Harbinger was a worldwide outbreak of violent revolutions, the Second was a world war, and the Third was a genocide.

Hemn space: What is called configuration, state, or phase space on Earth.

Hierarch: One of a specialized caste of avout whose responsibilities include the administration of maths and concents, interaction with the Sæcular world and with hierarchs in other maths, defense of the math from Sæcular molestation, policing, and maintenance of the Discipline.

Hundred, to go: To lose one's mind, to become mentally unsound, to stray iredeemably from the path of theorics.

Hundreder: Informal term for a Centenarian (see).

Hylaea: One of the two daughters of Cnoüs, the other being Deät. She interpreted her father's vision as meaning that he had glimpsed a higher and more perfect world (the Hylaean Theoric World or HTW) populated by pure geometric forms, crudely copied by geometers in this world.

Hylaean Theoric World: The name used by most adherents of Protism to denote the higher plane of existence populated by perfect geometric forms, theorems, and other pure ideas (cnoöns)

Hypotrochian Transquaestiation: Only one of a very large number of rhetorical tactics drilled into fids, particularly those under the tutelage of Procians. It means to change the subject in such a way as to assert, implicitly, that a controversial point has already been settled one way or the other.

Iconography: An oversimplified and, in most cases, wildly inaccurate schema used by Sæculars to make sense of what little they know of the mathic world, often taking the form of a conspiracy theory or an allusion to characters and situations from popular entertainments.

Icosahedron: A roughly spherical geometric figure with twenty faces, each of which is an equilateral triangle.

Inbrase: A rarely celebrated aut in which Peregrins are welcomed back into the mathic world following a journey through the Sæculum.

Incanter: A legendary figure, associated in folklore with Halikaarnian orders, said to be able to alter physical reality by the incantation of certain coded words or phrases.

Inquisition: Global body charged with maintaining uniform standards of the Discipline across all maths and concents, typically acting through the Wardens Regulant.

Inviolate: One of the three Millenarian maths that was never breached during the seven decades of the Third Sack. The Three Inviolates were at the Concents of Saunt Edhar, Saunt Rambalf, and Saunt Tredegarh.

Ita: A caste dwelling in the mathic world but segregated from the avout, responsible for all functions having to do with syntactic devices and the Reticulum.

Jeejah: Ubiquitous handheld electronic device used by Sæculars, combining functions of mobile telephone, camera, network browser, etc. Forbidden in the mathic world.

Jumpweed: A ubiquitous weed that when chewed acts as a stimulant. Psychoactive in larger doses. One of the Eleven.

Kedev: A devotee of the Kelx or Triangle faith.

Kefedokhles: A smug, pedantic interlocutor.

Kelx: (1) A religious faith created during the Sixteenth or Seventeenth Century A.R. The name is a contraction of the Orth *Ganakelux* meaning "Triangle place," so called because of the symbolic importance of triangles in the faith's iconography. (2) An ark of the Kelx faith.

Kinagrams: A simple set of ideograms used by Sæculars in place of a written language per se.

Laboratorium: At a Convox, a daily work session, typically in the morning, in which the attendees gather in groups to which they have been assigned by the hierarchs and pursue specific projects.

Lesper's Coordinates: Also called Saunt Lesper's Coordinates. Equivalent to Cartesian coordinates on Earth.

Liaison, Atlanian: An unusual type of liaison between a Tenner and a partner who dwells extramuros, therefore only capable of being consummated every ten years.

Liaison, Etrevanean: A liaison roughly equivalent to going steady in the Sæcular world.

Liaison, Perelithian: A liaison equivalent to marriage in the Sæcular world.

Liaison, Tivian: The most casual and ephemeral type of liaison.

Liaison: A relationship, typically sexual or at least romantic, in the mathic world.

Lineage, Old: According to some traditions, an unbroken chain of mentors and fids beginning with Metekoranes and extending all the way to the era in which *Anathem* is set, and as such, constituting a community of theors more ancient than, and separate from, the mathic tradition founded by Saunt Cartas.

Lineage: In general, a chronological sequence of avout who, prior to the Third Sack reforms, acquired and held property exceeding the bolt, chord, and sphere, each conferring the property upon a chosen heir at the moment of death. In this sense, frequently connected with Dowments. Also, sometimes used as a shorthand term for the Old Lineage; see **Lineage, Old**.

Loctor: Informal contraction of Interlocutor, meaning one's partner in a Dialog.

Logotype: A simple writing system used by Sæculars but, during the time in which *Anathem* is set, being rendered obsolete by Kinagrams.

Lorite: A member of an Order founded by Saunt Lora, who believed that all of the ideas that the human mind was capable of coming up with had already been come up with. Lorites are, therefore, historians of thought who assist other avout in their work by making them aware of others who have thought similar things in the past, and thereby preventing them from re-inventing the wheel.

Lucub: At a Convox, an informal work group that, on the members' own initiative, meets in the evening to "burn the midnight oil" on some topic of shared interest.

Ma: An informal term of respect by which a fid might address a more senior suur.

Magister: Title bestowed on the clergy of the Kelx faith.

Matarrhite: One of an Order founded at the Centenarian math of the Concent of Saunt Beedle's between the Second and Third Centennial Aperts. One of the few explicitly religious Orders of avout. Reclusive even by the standards of the mathic world. During the Third Sack they fled to an island in the southern polar regions, where they developed various distinctive cultural traits, including bolts that covered their entire bodies and an austere cuisine based on the limited range of edible things in their environment.

Math: A relatively small community of avout (typically fewer than a hundred, sometimes as small as one). In general, all members of a given math celebrate Apert on the same schedule, i.e., all of them are either Unarians, Decenarians, Centenarians, or Millenarians. Compare **Concent**.

Messal: At certain (typically larger and older) concents, the traditional way of taking the evening meal, in which no more than seven senior avout (doyns) are waited on by an equal number of junior avout (servitors).

Metatheorics: Equivalent to metaphysics on Earth. The part of human thought that addresses questions so fundamental that they must be settled before one can even begin to do productive work in theorics.

Metekoranes: A theor of ancient times who was buried under volcanic ash in the eruption that destroyed Orithena. According to some traditions, the founder (probably unwittingly) of the Old Lineage. See **Lineage, Old**.

Millenarian: An avout sworn not to emerge from the math or to have contact with the outside world until the next Millennial Apert. Informally, "Thousander."

Mobe: A wheeled passenger vehicle used extramuros.

Muncoster, Saunt: (1) A theor of the late Praxic Age, responsible for crucial advances in what is called, on Earth, general relativity. (2) One of the Big Three concents.

Mynster: At many concents, the large centrally located building that houses the clock and that serves as the venue for auts and other gatherings of the entire population.

Mystagogue: One who is fond of mysterious thinking and obfuscatory cant. In the Old Mathic Age, an all too powerful faction during the centuries leading to the Rebirth. Since then, a pejorative term.

Newmatter: A form of matter whose atomic nuclei were artificially synthesized and which therefore has physical properties not found in naturally occurring elements or their compounds.

One Hundred and Sixty-four: A list of plants allowed to be cultivated within maths by the version of the Discipline current at the time in which *Anathem* is set. Expanded from shorter lists found in earlier versions of the Discipline dating all the way back to Saunt Cartas. The plants on the list are deemed adequate to supply all nutritional requirements of the avout as well as filling other needs including medicinal, shade, erosion control, etc. Compare **Eleven**.

One-off: Informal term for a Unarian (see).

Orithena: A temple founded in ancient times by Adrakhones on the Isle of Ecba, later populated by physiologers who migrated there from all over the ancient world. Destroyed by a volcanic eruption in -2621, excavated, beginning in 3000, by avout who founded a new math around the perimeter of the dig.

Orth: The classical language used by all classes of people in the Bazian Empire and, during the Old Mathic Age, used intramuros in both Cartasian maths and Bazian Orthodox monasteries. The language of science and learned discourse in the Praxic Age. In a revived and modernized form, the language used at almost all times by the avout. May also denote the alphabet used to write it.

Pa: An informal term of respect by which a fid might address a more senior fraa.

Panjandrum: Fraa Orolo's pejorative term for a high-ranking official of the Sæcular Power.

Penance: Tedious or unpleasant chore assigned as punishment by the Warden Regulant to avout who have violated the Discipline.

Peregrin: (1) In ancient usage, the epoch beginning with the destruction of the Temple of Orithena in -2621 and ending several decades later with the flourishing of the Golden Age of Ethras. (2) A theor who survived Orithena and wandered about the ancient world, sometimes alone and sometimes in the company of other such. (3) A Dialog supposedly dating to this epoch. Many were later written down and incorporated into the literature of the mathic world. (4) In modern usage, an avout who, under certain exceptional circumstances, leaves the confines of the math and travels through the Sæcular world while trying to observe the spirit, if not the letter, of the Discipline.

Perelithian Liaison: See **Liaison, Perelithian**.

Periklyne: An open area in the ancient city-state of Ethras, home to the market, where Golden Age theors were wont to congregate and engage one another in Dialog.

Physiologer: In the span of time between Cnoüs and Diax, a thinker who followed the Hylaean Way, i.e., who favored Hylaea's interpretation of her father's vision. The forerunners of theors and the founders of the Temple of Orithena. Compare **Deolater**.

Plane: Used as a verb, utterly to destroy an opponent's position in the course of a Dialog.

Plenary: In a Convox, an event in which all attendees come together in the same room at the same time for some purpose.

Polycosm: Two or more universes (cosmi), especially when considered as a system that includes the possibility of interactions between cosmi.

Præsidium: In Mathic architecture, the tallest structure in a concent, typically the clock tower.

Praxic Age: Period of Arbre's history beginning in the century after the Rebirth (therefore, approximately -500) and ending with the Terrible Events and the Reconstitution (the year 0). So called because the inhabitants of the old mathic system, who had dispersed into the Sæcular world after the Rebirth, put their theorics to work exploring the globe and creating technology.

Praxic: An applied scientist, an engineer.

Praxis: Technology.

Primate: The highest-ranking hierarch in a math or concent.

Proc: A late Praxic Age metatheorician, the standard-bearer in his age of the theorical lineage traceable to the Sphenics, and the progenitor of all orders that trace their descent to the Syntactic (as opposed to Semantic) Faculties of the early post-Reconstitution maths. Contrast with **Halikaarn**.

Procian: Of, or relating to, Saunt Proc or any of the Orders that claim descent from the Syntactic Faculties. Frequently seen as natural opponents of Halikaarnians.

Protan: Of or relating to the ancient Ethran philosopher Protas.

Protas: A student of Thelenes during the Golden Age of Ethras, later the most important theor in Arbran history. Building on the foundation laid by Hylaea and later strengthened by the Orithenans, developed the notion that the objects and ideas that humans perceive and think about are imperfect manifestations of pure, ideal forms that exist in another plane of existence.

Protism, Complex: A relatively recent (Fourteenth Century A.R.) interpretation of traditional ("Simple") Protism, positing more than two (possibly infinitely many) causal domains linked in a Directed Acyclic Graph or DAG, known, in the most general case, as the Wick. Information about cnoöns is assumed to flow through the DAG from "more Hylaean" to "less Hylaean" cosmi.

Protism, Simple: A retroactive coinage used by Uthentine and Erasmas to contrast the traditional conception of Protism, which consisted of one Hylaean Theoric World having a causal relationship to the cosmos in which Arbre is embedded, to their new scheme, which they dubbed Complex Protism. See **Protism, Complex**.

Protism: The philosophy of Protas. More specifically, the notion that theors perceive pure ideas from another realm of existence known as the Hylaean Theoric World.

Provener: The most commonly observed aut of the mathic world, typically celebrated every day at noon, and linked to the winding of a clock.

Rake: See **Diax's Rake**.

Rambalf: A concent. One of the Three Inviolates.

Rebirth: The historical event dividing the Old Mathic Age from the Praxic Age, usually dated at around -500, during which the gates of the maths were thrown open and the avout dispersed into the Sæcular world. Characterized by a sudden flowering of culture, theorical advancement, and exploration.

Reconstitution: The state of affairs that came into being following the Terrible Events, whereby almost all learned and literate persons were concentrated together in maths and concents.

Regred: The aut by which a senior avout withdraws from active service and goes into retirement.

Regulant: See **Warden Regulant**.

Requiem: The aut celebrated to mark the death of an avout.

Ret: See **Reticulum**.

Reticule: A network; two or more syntactic devices that are able to communicate with one another.

Reticulum: The largest reticulum, joining together the preponderance of all reticules in the world.

Rhetor: A legendary figure, associated in folklore with Procian orders, said to have the power of altering the past by manipulating memories and other physical records.

Ringing Vale: A mountain valley that gave its name to a math founded there in 17 A.R., specializing in study and developments of martial arts and related topics. See **Vale-Lore**.

Rod: Military slang. To bombard a target, typically on the surface of a planet, by dropping a rod of some dense material on it from orbit. The rod has no moving parts or explosives; its destructiveness is a consequence of its extremely high velocity.

Sæcular: Of or pertaining to the non-mathic world.

Sæcular Power: Whatever entity currently wields power in the non-mathic world.

Sæculum: The Sæcular world.

Sack: A breach of the terms of the Reconstitution in which maths or concents are forcibly violated and despoiled by Sæcular interlopers. Normally used only to refer to Sacks-General, in which most or all of the maths and concents are sacked at the same time.

Samblites: A religious sect tracing its origin back to Saunt Bly, and centered on Bly's Butte, not far from the Concent of Saunt Edhar.

Sarthian: Steppe-dwelling horse archers of ancient times, held responsible for the Fall and Sack of Baz, which ended the Bazian Empire and inaugurated the Old Mathic Age.

Saunt: A title bestowed on great thinkers.

Sconic: One of a group of Praxic Age theors who gathered at the house of Lady Baritoe. They addressed the ramifications of the apparent fact that we do not perceive the physical universe directly, but only through the intermediation of our sensory organs.

Sea of Seas: A relatively small but complex body of salt water, connected to Arbre's great oceans in three places by straits, generally viewed as the cradle of classical civilization.

Semantic Faculties: Factions within the mathic world, in the years following the Reconstitution, generally claiming descent from Halikaarn. So named because they believed that symbols could bear actual semantic content. The idea is traceable to Protas and to Hylaea before him. Compare **Syntactic Faculties**.

Sequence: The genetic code of a living organism. In various usages, equivalent to *gene, genetic,* or *DNA* on Earth.

Servitor: At Concents that observe the mealtime tradition of the Messal, a junior avout who is assigned to wait on a doyn.

Sline: An extramuros person with no special education, skills, aspirations, or hope of acquiring same, generally construed as belonging to the lowest social class.

Sphenics: A school of theors well represented in ancient Ethras, where they were hired by well-to-do families as tutors for their children. In many classic Dialogs, seen in opposition to Thelenes, Protas, or others of their school. Their most prominent champion was Uraloabus, who in the Dialog of the same name was planed so badly by Thelenes that he committed suicide on the spot. They disputed the views of Protas and, broadly speaking, preferred to believe that theorics took place entirely between the ears, with no recourse to external realities such as the Protan forms. The forerunners of Saunt Proc, the Syntactic Faculties, and the Procians.

Starhenge: In Earth terms, an observatory, esp. one with multiple telescopes.

Steelyard: See **Gardan's Steelyard**.

Suur: A female avout.

Suvin: A school.

Syndev: Contraction of Syntactic Device. A computer.

Syntactic Device: In Earth terms, a computer.

Syntactic Faculties: Factions within the mathic world, in the years following the Reconstitution, generally claiming descent from Proc. So named because they believed that language, theorics, etc., were essentially games played with symbols devoid of semantic content. The idea is traceable to the ancient Sphenics, who were frequent opponents of Thelenes and Protas on the Periklyne.

Tangle: A cultivated plot, roughly hexagonal in plan, supporting a particular set of more or less genetically engineered food-bearing plant species that, taken together, supply all of the nutritional requirements for a single avout. A web of symbiotic relationships among the species bolsters the health and productivity of the plants while preventing exhaustion of the soil. In concents that employ the tangle system, each avout is responsible for maintenance of one tangle; the produce of all of the tangles is pooled to supply food for the concent. Since a math cannot observe the Discipline when it is dependent on Sæcular trade for foodstuffs, the tangle is a fundamental enabling technology for the Reconstitution.

Teglon: An extremely challenging geometry problem worked on at Orithena and later, all over Arbre, by subsequent generations of theors. The objective is to tile a regular decagon with a set of seven different shapes of tiles, while observing certain rules.

Tenner: Informal term for Decenarian (see).

Tenth Night: The traditional conclusion of an Apert, held on its tenth and final night. A feast served by the math to any and all extramuros visitors who wish to attend. Also used to transact certain necessary items of business with the Sæcular Power, such as formal transfer of new Collects from Sæcular to mathic jurisdiction.

Terrible Events: A poorly documented worldwide catastrophe thought to have begun in the year -5. Whatever it was, it terminated the Praxic Age and led immediately to the Reconstitution.

Thelenes: A great theor of the Golden Age of Ethras, protagonist of many Dialogs, mentor to Protas. Executed by the Ethran authorities for irreligious, or at least disrespectful, teachings.

Theor: Any practitioner of theorics, which see.

Theorician: Nearly equivalent to theor, but with slightly different connotations. "theorician" tends to be used of one who is devoted to highly specific, detailed, technical work, e.g., carrying out elaborate computations.

Theorics: Roughly equivalent to mathematics, logic, science, and philosophy on Earth. The term can fairly be applied to any intellectual work that is pursued in a rigorous and disciplined manner; it was coined by Diax to distinguish those who observed the Rake from those who engaged in wishful or magical thinking.

Thousander: Informal term for a Millenarian (see).

Throw Back: An informal term meaning to subject an avout to the aut of Anathem.

Throwback: An ex-avout who was Anathematized.

Tredegarh: One of the Big Three concents, named after Lord Tredegarh, a mid-to-late Praxic Age theor responsible for fundamental advances in thermodynamics.

Triangle Ark: Alternate term for the Kelx faith or one of its arks.

Unarian: An avout sworn not to emerge from the math or to have contact with the outside world until the next Annual Apert. Informally, "One-off."

Upsight: A sudden, usually unlooked-for moment of clear understanding.

Uraloabus: Prominent Sphenic theor of the Golden Age of Ethras who, if the account of Protas is to be credited, committed suicide after being planed by Thelenes.

Uthentine: A suur at Saunt Baritoe's in the Fourteenth Century A.R. who, along with Erasmas, founded the branch of metatheorics called Complex Protism.

Vale-lore: Martial arts. Associated with the Ringing Vale (see).

Valer: An avout of the Ringing Vale; one who has, therefore, devoted his or her entire life to the martial arts.

Vlor: An informal contraction of Vale-lore (see).

Voco: A rarely celebrated aut by which the Sæcular Power Evokes (calls forth from the math) an avout whose talents are needed in the Sæcular world. Except in very unusual cases, the one Evoked never returns to the mathic world.

Vout: An avout. Derogatory term used extramuros. Associated with Sæculars who subscribe to iconographies that paint the avout in an extremely negative way.

Warden Fendant: A hierarch charged with defending the math or concent from Sæcular interlopers, by all means up to and including physical violence, and typically overseeing a staff of more junior hierarchs trained to carry out such functions.

Warden of Heaven: During the years leading up to the time in which *Anathem* is set, a popular religious leader who obtained Sæcular power by claiming to embody the wisdom of the mathic world.

Warden Regulant: A hierarch charged with maintaining the Discipline intramuros, empowered to conduct investigations and to mete out penance. Technically subordinate to the Primate but ultimately answerable to the Inquisition, and empowered to depose the Primate in certain exceptional circumstances.

Wick: In Complex Protism, a fully generalized Directed Acyclic Graph in which a large (possibly infinite) number of cosmi are linked by a more or less complicated web of cause-and-effect relationships. Information flows from cosmi that are more "up-Wick" to those that are more "down-Wick" but not vice versa.

CALCA I: *Cutting the Cake*

A supplement to *Anathem* by Neal Stephenson

"LET'S SAY THAT EACH serving will be a square, the same width as the spatula. Go ahead and cut in one corner of the pan."

Dath cut the cake thus:

and then made more cuts thus, to produce the four servings I'd asked for:

"I can't believe you're doing this!" Arsibalt muttered.

"If it worked for Thelenes . . ." I muttered back. "Now shut up," and I turned my attention back to Dath who was awaiting further instructions. "How many servings do we have there?" I asked him.

"Four," he said, slightly unnerved by my ridiculously easy question.

"Now, what if you cut a similar figure but with sides twice as long? So instead of each side being two units—two spatula-widths—it would be—?"

"Four units?"

"Yes. We have four servings here already—if you doubled the size of the figure, how many people could we serve then?"

"Well, two times four would be eight."

"I agree that two times four is eight. Go ahead and try it," I said. Dath made more cuts thus:

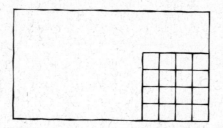

Halfway through, he saw his error and made a wry face, but I encouraged him to keep going until he was finished. "Sixteen," he said. "We actually have sixteen servings. Not eight."

"So, just to review: when we cut a square grid that is two units on a side, we get how many servings?"

"Four."

"And you just told me that a *four*-unit grid gives us *sixteen*. But what if we only wanted *eight* servings? How many units would our grid have to be?"

"Three?" Dath said, cautiously. Then his eyes dropped to the cake and he counted it out. "No, that gives nine servings."

"But we're getting warmer. And now an important thing has changed, which is that you know you don't know."

Dath's eyebrows went up. "That's important?"

"It's important *to us in here*," I said.

I couldn't remember what Thelenes had done next when he had done this with a slave-boy on the Plane six millennia ago, and had to ask Orolo.

I spun the cake around, presenting Dath with an unmarked corner. "Go ahead and cut one square big enough for four servings. You don't have to cut the individual servings out of it."

"Can I make lines on the frosting?" he asked.

"If it helps."

With some hints and nudges from Cord, Dath produced a square like this:

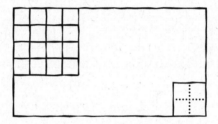

"Good," I said, "now add three more squares just like it."

Extending lines he'd already made and adding some new ones, Dath enlarged it to this:

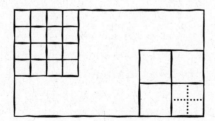

"Now, remind me, how many servings can we get out of that whole area?"

"Sixteen."

"All right. Now look only at the square in the lower right-hand corner."

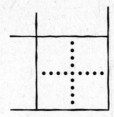

"Is there a way you can divide it exactly in half with only one cut?"

He got ready to slice along one of the dotted lines, but I shook my head. "Arsibalt here is very particular about his cake and he wants to be sure no one gets a larger slice than him."

"Thank you very *much,* wise Thelenes," Arsibalt put in.

I ignored him. "Can you make one cut that's guaranteed to satisfy him? The pieces don't have to be square. Other shapes are okay—like triangles."

With that hint, Dath made a cut like this:

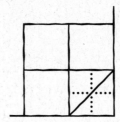

"Now, do the others the same," I said. He made it like this:

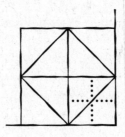

"When you made the first diagonal cut, you cut a square exactly in half, right?"

"Right."

"And is the same true of the other three diagonal cuts and the other three squares?"

"Of course."

"So, let's say I rotate the pan and you look at it this way":

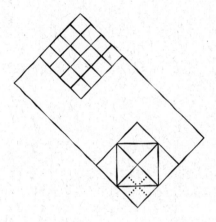

"What shape do you see in the middle there?"

"A square."

"And how many servings worth of cake are contained in that square?"

"I don't know."

"Well, it's made up of four triangles, right?"

"Yeah."

"Each of those triangles is half of a small square, right?"

"Right."

"And how many servings in a small square?"

"Four."

"So each triangle has enough cake for how many servings?"

"Two."

"And the square that's made up from four such triangles has enough cake for—"

"Eight servings," he said, and then realized: "which is the problem we were trying to solve before!"

"We've been trying to solve it the whole time," I corrected him, "it just takes a minute or two. So, can you cut us eight servings then, please?"

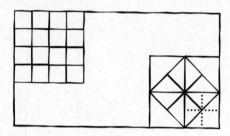

"That's it," I said.

"We can eat now?"

"Yes. Do you see what just happened?"

"Uh . . . I cut eight equal servings of cake?"

"You make it sound easy . . . but it was hard, in a way," I said. "Remember, a few minutes ago, you knew how to cut four servings. That was easy. You knew how to cut sixteen. That was easy too. Nine, no problem. But you didn't know how to cut *eight*. It seemed impossible. But by thinking it through, we were able to come up with an answer. And not just an approximate answer, but one that is perfectly correct."

CALCA 2: *Hemn (Configuration) Space*

A supplement to *Anathem* by Neal Stephenson

IT JUST SO HAPPENED that in our comings and goings we had kicked over an empty wine bottle, which was resting on the kitchen's floor like this:

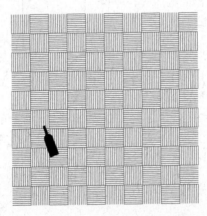

The floor had been built up out of strips of wood, set on edge in a gridlike pattern, which put me in mind of a coordinate plane.

"Get a slate and a piece of chalk," I said to Barb.

I felt a little guilty bossing him around like this, but I was cross at him for not helping me with the drain. He didn't seem to mind, and it didn't take him long to fulfill the request, since slates and chalks were all over the kitchen. We used them to write out recipes and lists of ingredients.

"Now indulge me for a second and write down the coordinates of that bottle on the floor."

"Coordinates?"

"Yes. Think of this pattern as a Lesper's coordinate grid. Let's say each square in the floor pattern is one unit. I'll put a potato down here, to mark out the origin."

"Well, in that case the bottle is at about (2, 3)," Barb said, and worked with the chalk for a moment. Then he tipped the slate my way:

x	y
2	3

"Now, this is already a configuration space—just about the simplest one you could possibly imagine," I told him. "And the bottle's location, (2, 3), is a point in that space."

"It's the same as regular two-dimensional space then," he complained. "Why didn't you say so?"

"Can you add another column?"

"Sure."

x	y	
2	3	

"Notice that the bottle isn't straight. It's rotated by something like a tenth of p—or in the units you used to use extramuros, about twenty degrees. That rotation is going to become a third coordinate in the configuration space—a third column on your slate."

Barb went to work with the chalk and produced this:

x	y	∠
2	3	20

"Okay, now it's starting to look like something different from plain old two-dimensional space," he said. "Now it's got three dimensions, and the third one isn't normal. It's like something I had to learn once in my suvin—"

"Polar coordinates?" I asked, impressed that he knew this. Quin must have spent a lot of money to send him to a good suvin.

"Yeah! An angle, instead of a distance."

"Okay, let's learn something about how this space behaves," I proposed. "I'll move the bottle, and whenever I say 'mark,' you punch in its current coordinates."

I dragged the bottle a short distance while giving it a bit of a twist. "Mark."

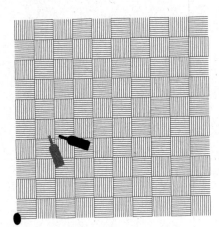

x	y	∠
2	3	20
3	3.5	70

"Mark. Mark. Mark . . ."

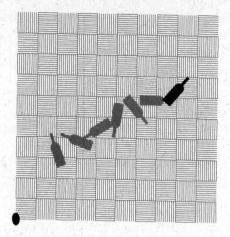

x	y	∠
2	3.	20
3	3.5	70
4	4.	120
5	4.5	170
6	5.	220
7	5.5	270
8	6.	320

I said, "So, this set of points in configuration space is like what we'd get if I accidentally kicked the bottle and sent it skidding and spinning across the floor. Would you agree?"

"Sure. That's kind of what I was thinking!"

"But I moved it in slow motion to make it easier for you to take down the data."

Barb didn't know what to make of this very weak attempt at humor. After an awkward pause, I plowed ahead: "Can you make a plot now? A three-dimensional plot of those numbers?"

"Sure," Barb said uncertainly, "but it's going to be weird."

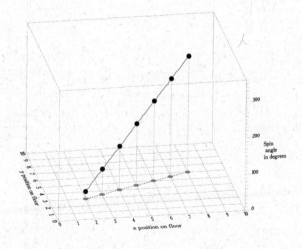

"The dotted line track on the bottom shows just the x and the y," Barb explained. "The track that it made across the floor."

"That's okay—it'd be confusing otherwise, if you're not used to configuration space," I said. "Because part of it—the xy track that you plotted with a dotted line—looks just like something that we all recognize from Adrakhonic space; it just shows where the bottle went on the floor. But the third dimension, showing the angle, is a completely different story. It doesn't show a literal distance in space. It shows an angular displacement—a rotation—of the bottle. Once you understand that, you can read it directly off the graph and say 'yeah, I see, it started out at twenty degrees and spun around to three hundred and some degrees while it was skidding across the floor.' But if you don't know the secret code, it doesn't make any sense."

"So what's it good for?"

"Well, imagine you had a more complicated state of affairs than one bottle on the floor. Suppose you had a bottle, and a potato. Then you'd need a ten-dimensional configuration space to represent the state of the bottle-potato system."

"Ten!?"

"Five for the bottle and five for the potato."

"How do you get five!? We're only using three dimensions for the bottle!"

"Yeah, but we are cheating by leaving out two of its rotational degrees of freedom," I said.

"Meaning—?"

I squatted down and put my hand on the bottle. The label happened to be pointed toward the floor. I rolled it over. "See, I'm rotating it around its long axis so that I can read the label," I pointed out. "That rotation is a completely separate, independent number from the kick-spinning rotation that you plotted on your slate. So we need an extra dimension for it." Grabbing the bottle, and keeping its heel pressed against the floor, I now tilted it up so that its neck was pointed up from the floor at an angle, like an artillery piece. "And what I'm doing here is yet another completely independent rotation."

"So we're up to five," Barb said, "for the bottle alone."

"Yeah. To be fully general, we'd want to add a sixth dimension, to keep track of vertical movement," I said, and raised the bottle up off the floor. "So that would make six dimensions in our configuration space just to represent the position and orientation of the bottle." I set the bottle down again. "But as long as we keep it on the floor we can get along with five."

"Okay," Barb said. He only said this when he totally got something.

"I'm glad you think so. Thinking in six dimensions is difficult."

"I just think of it as six columns on my slate, instead of three," he said. "But I don't understand why we need six completely new dimensions for the potato. Why don't we just re-use the six that we've already got for the bottle?"

"We sort of do," I said, "but we keep the numbers in separate columns. That way, each row of the chart specifies everything there is to know about the bottle/potato system at a given moment. Each row—that series of twelve numbers giving the x, the y, and the z position of the bottle, its kick-spin angle, its label-reading angle, and its tilt-up angle, and the same six numbers for the potato—is a point in the twelve-dimensional configuration space. And one of the ways it starts to get convenient for theors is when we link points together to make trajectories in configuration space."

"When you say 'trajectory' I think of something flying through the air," Barb said, "but I don't follow what you mean when you use that word in this twelve-dimensional space that isn't like a space at all."

"Well, let's make it ultrasimple and restrict the bottle and the potato to the x-axis," I said, "and ignore their rotations." I moved them around thus:

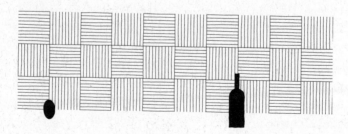

"Can you use your slate to record their x positions?" I asked.

"Sure," he said, and after a few moments, showed me this:

Bottle's x	Potato's x
7	1

"I'm going to smash them into each other," I said, "in slow motion, of course. Try to make a record of their positions, if you would." And, much as before, I began to move the potato and the bottle in small increments, calling out "Mark" when I wanted him to add a new line to his chart.

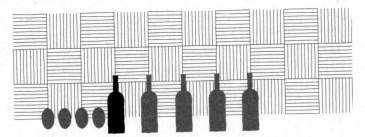

"The bottle's moving faster," he observed, as we worked.

"Yeah. Twice as fast." I ended up holding the potato on top of the bottle at 3.

Bottle's x	Potato's x
7	1.
6	1.5
5	2.
4	2.5
3	3.

"They just hit each other," I said, "and so now they are going to bounce apart. But they are going to move slower, because the potato got mashed in the collision and some energy was lost." With a little over-the-shoulder coaching from me, Barb added several post-smashup points to the table:

Bottle's x	Potato's x
7	1.
6	1.5
5	2.
4	2.5
3	3.
3.2	2.5
3.4	2.
3.6	1.5
3.8	1.

"There," I said, letting go of the projectiles, and clambering back up to my feet. "Now, all of this action happened along a straight line. So, this is a one-dimensional situation, if you keep thinking in Saunt Lesper's coordinates. Saunt Hemn, though, would do something here that might strike you as strange. Hemn would think of each row of the table as specifying a point in a *two-dimensional* configuration space."

"Treat each pair as a point," Barb translated, "so, the beginning point is (7, 1) and so on."

"That's right. Can you make a plot of that for me?"

"Sure. It's trivial."

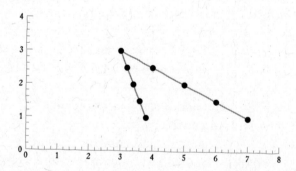

"That's weird!" Barb exclaimed. "It's like Saunt Hemn has turned the whole situation inside out."

"Well, give me the chalk for a minute and I'll annotate it in ways that will help you make sense of it," I said. A few minutes later, we had something that looked like this:

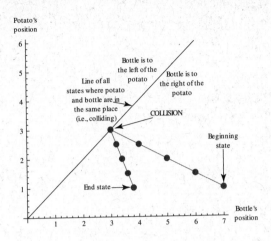

"The collision line," I said, "is nothing other than the set of all points where the bottle and the potato happen to be at the same place—where their coordinates are equal to each other. And any theor, looking at this plot, even without knowledge of the physical situation—the bottle, the potato, the floor—can see right away that there is something special about that line. The state of the system progresses in an orderly and predictable fashion until it touches that line. Then something exceptional happens. The trajectory makes a hairpin turn. The points become more closely spaced—this means that the objects are moving more slowly, which means that the system has lost energy somehow. I don't expect you to be bowled over by this, but maybe this can give you an inkling of why theors like to use configuration space as a way to think about physical systems."

"There's got to be more to it than that," Barb said. "We could have just plotted this in a simpler way."

"This *is* simpler," I insisted. "It is closer to the truth."

"Are you talking about the Hylaean Theoric World now?" Barb asked, half whispering and half gloating, as if this were just about the naughtiest thing that a fraa could do.

"I'm an Edharian," I answered. "No matter what some people around here might think . . . that's what I am. And naturally we seek to express what we are thinking in the simplest, most elegant way possible. In many—no, most—cases that are interesting to theors, Saunt Hemn's configuration space does that better than Saunt Lesper's space of x, y, and z coordinates, which you've been forced to work in until now."

Something occurred to Barb: "The bottle and the potato each had six numbers—six coordinates in Hemn space."

"Yes, in general it takes six numbers to represent the position of something."

"A satellite in orbit needs six numbers too!"

"Yes—the orbital elements. A satellite in orbit *always* needs a six-dimensional Hemn space, no matter which coordinate system you use. If you're using Saunt Lesper's Coordinates, it leads to the problem you were complaining of earlier—"

"The xs and ys and zs don't really tell you anything!"

"Yes. But if you transform it into a *different* six-dimensional space, using six different numbers, it becomes very clear, the same way that the bottle-potato scenario became clear when we chose an appropriate space in which to plot it. For a satellite, those six numbers are the eccentricity, the inclination, the argument of perihelion, and three others with complicated names that I'm not going to rattle off now. But just to name a couple of them: the eccentricity tells you, at a glance, whether or not the orbit is stable. The inclination tells you whether it's polar or equatorial. And so on."

CALCA 3: *Complex Versus Simple Protism*

A supplement to *Anathem* by Neal Stephenson

"HERE'S THAT TWO-BOX DIAGRAM we've all seen," Criscan began, and drew something like this in the dust:

"The arrow says that entities in the Hylaean Theoric World are capable of causing effects within the Arbran Causal Domain but not vice versa. And if you take the trouble to unpack what it is that people are asserting when they chalk one of these up on a slate, it boils down to a small set of premises that define what we call Protism. And I know that you two are well aware of these, but with your indulgence I'm going to run through them briefly just so that we can be sure we are starting from the same place."

"Please do," I said.

"Be my guest," Lio said.

"All right. The first assertion is: entities that are the subject matter of theorics exist independently of human perceptions, definitions, and constructions. Theors don't create them; theors merely discover them. And the second premise is that the human mind is capable of perceiving such entities; which is exactly what theors are doing, when they discover them."

"We're with you so far," I said.

"Very well," Criscan said, "now, if you want to proceed beyond merely rattling off those two premises, you need to supply an account of how it is that the human mind is capable of obtaining knowledge about theorical entities, which, according to the first premise, are non-spatiotemporal and do not stand in a normal causal relationship to the entities that make up the cosmos as we know it. And various arguments have been put forward over the millennia as metatheoricians have tried to supply that account. For example, Halikaarn took a lot of heat from the Procians because he thought that our brains contained an organ that was responsible for this."

"An organ? Like a gland, or something?" Lio asked.

"Some interpreted it that way, which helps explain why he took so much heat for it. But this was probably a translation error. Halikaarn was pre-Reconstitution, of course, so he was not writing in Orth but in one of the minor languages of his day. The person who translated his works into Fluccish did him a disservice by choosing the wrong word. Halikaarn wasn't thinking of something like a gland. He was thinking of a faculty, an inherent ability of the brain, not localized in any one specific lump of tissue."

"That's a little easier to take seriously," I said. "Fine." Because I had the sense that Criscan was getting ready to veer off into a long tedious defense of Halikaarn. "So how does this faculty figure into his account of what's happening in this diagram?"

"There is some other type of given, other than what we can detect with our eyes, ears, and so on, that somehow reaches the Arbran Causal Domain and that is perceived by Halikaarn's Organ," Criscan said.

"That almost raises more questions than it answers," Lio pointed out.

"It doesn't answer any questions at all," Criscan returned, "this is not really an attempt to answer questions but a way of setting one's pieces out on the board, agreeing on terminology, and so on. So. The theorical entities in the HTW—triangles, theorems, and other pure concepts—are called cnoöns."

"Cnoöns, check!" Lio said.

"Between us and the HTW is a relationship, the details of which are subject to further debate, which Halikaarn didn't name, but it's symbolized by this arrow, and so people have ended up calling it Halikaarn's Arrow."

"Halikaarn's Arrow, check!"

"A Halikaarn's Arrow is a one-way conduit for givens about the cnoöns. These givens enter the Arbran Causal Domain through a poorly understood process called the Hylaean Flow and there impinge on Halikaarn's Organ, which is how we become aware of them."

"Hylaean Flow, check!"

Criscan had decided that he didn't like Lio very much, but was making a visible effort to tolerate him. I stepped into the position of interlocutor, shouldering Lio aside. Lio reacted melodramatically, sprawling off to the shoulder of the road as if he had been struck by a speeding fetch. I ignored him. "So," I said to Criscan, "now that we have the terminology bolted down, where are we going with it?"

"Now we're going to skip ahead a millennium and a half," Criscan said, "and talk about the move that Erasmas and Uthentine made, when they decided to see what happened if they construed this diagram as just one, particularly simple example of a Directed Acyclic Graph or DAG. Here 'directed' just means 'arrows are unidirectional.' The modifier 'acyclic' means that the arrows can't go around in a circle, i.e., if we have an arrow from A to B, we can't also have an arrow from B to A."

"Why bother stipulating that, I wonder?"

"The property of being acyclic is required in order to preserve the fundamental doctrine of Protism: that the cnoöns are changeless. If it were possible for the arrows to go around in a circle, it would mean that events in our universe could alter things in the Hylaean Theoric World."

"Of course," I said, "pardon me, that's obvious now that you mention it."

"This diagram," said Criscan, drawing my attention back to his two-box sketch, "just seems wrong, to a metatheorician."

"What do you mean, just seems wrong? How can you get away with statements like that?"

"It is a legitimate move in metatheorics. You have to be continually asking yourself, 'why are things thus, and not some other way?' And if you apply that test to this diagram, you immediately run into a problem: there are exactly two worlds. Not one, not many, but two. One might draw such a diagram having only one world—the Arbran Causal Domain—and zero arrows. That would draw very few objections from metatheoricians (at least, those who are not Protists). One might, on the other hand, assert 'there are lots of worlds' and then set out to make a case for why that is plausible. But to say 'there are two worlds—and only two!' seems no more supportable than to say 'there are exactly 173 worlds, and all those people who claim that there are only 172 of them are lunatics.'"

"Okay, if you put it that way, I agree that there is a certain odor of crankiness about it. Like when Deolaters claim that there are thirty-seven books making up their scripture but that anyone who proposes a different number must die."

"Yes, and this accounts, at least in part, for the way Protism raises hackles in some quarters. So the Erasmas/Uthentine move is simply to say 'what's true of one DAG ought to be true of another' and to consider other DAGs having other numbers of worlds."

Criscan took up his stick again, and scratched out a diagram like this one:

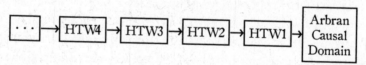

"They called this one the Freight Train," Criscan announced. "In the Freight Train topology, there is a (possibly infinite) plurality of Hylaean Theoric Worlds that stand in a hierarchical relationship, each 'more Protan' than the last and 'less Protan' than the next. This introduces the notion of Analog Protism. In Simple Protism, being Protan is a binary, digital property."

"A world is either Protan, or it isn't," I translated.

"Yes. Here, on the other hand, gradations of Protanness are possible."

"Not just possible," I pointed out, "they are required."

"Yes," Criscan said, a little distractedly, for he was already at work making another diagram.

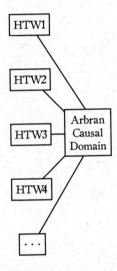

"This is the Firing Squad," he said. "In the Firing Squad topology, some number of Hylaean Theoric Worlds are connected by direct linkages to the Arbran Causal Domain. This introduces the notion of separate Protan domains that have nothing to do with one another. In Simple Protism, all possible theoric entities are lumped together in one box labeled 'Hylaean Theoric World,' which seems to imply that, within that box, they can stand in cause-and-effect relationships to one another. But perhaps this is not the case, and each mathematical entity should be isolated in a separate World as above."

He now spent a while drawing a much more complex diagram:

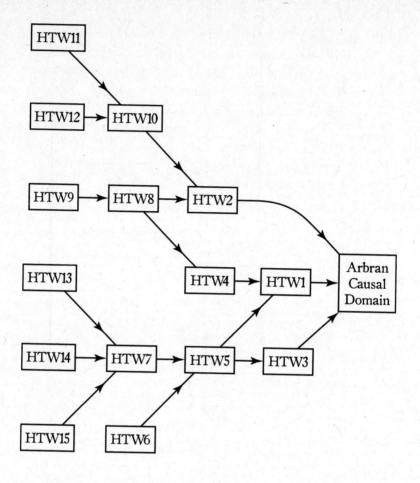

"The Reverse Delta," Criscan said. "It has the topology of a river delta, but the arrows run backwards, hence the name. The Reverse Delta is most easily summed up by saying that it combines the properties of the Freight Train and Firing Squad topologies."

"Got it," I said, after a moment's thought—for Criscan, I sensed, was testing me. "It's got Analog Protism—many gradations of Protanness—and it's got the idea, from the Firing Squad, that different cnoöns might have nothing to do with one another—might come from altogether different Theoric Worlds."

Criscan did not respond one way or the other, since he was busy with his stick again. "The Strider," he proclaimed.

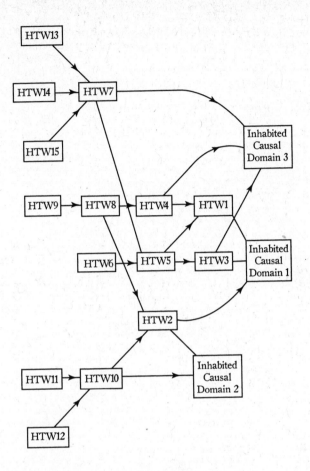

"Strider? In what way does it stride?" I asked.

"It's named after a kind of tree—a tropical species that connects to the ground through multiple root systems. As you can see, it is similar to a Reverse Delta topology. The only difference is that the Strider contains more than one inhabited cosmos. You'll note I changed the name."

"Yes. Up until now, it's always ended with arrows going to the Arbran Causal Domain. But here you are assuming a polycosmic scheme—multiple inhabited cosmi, causally disconnected from one another."

"That's right. Causally disconnected, but—and this is important—

non-causally *correlated* in that they share knowledge of the same cnoöns. The inhabitants of these other cosmi receive the Hylaean Flow from the same sources as ours. As a result they could, for example, have the Adrakhonic Theorem for the same reason we do.

"And this finally leads us to the Wick."

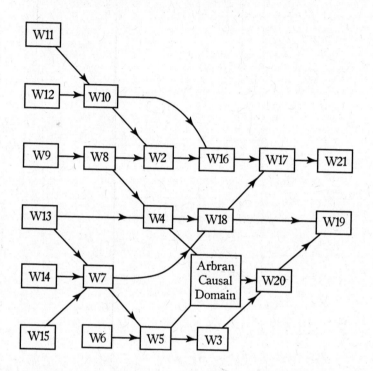

"The Wick is a fully generalized DAG," Criscan said. "The Hylaean Flow moves through it from left to right—from more Protan to less Protan worlds—but here we are taking Analog Protism to its logical extreme in that no distinction is drawn between types of worlds."

"I see ours there," I said, pointing to the one labeled "Arbran Causal Domain."

"Yes," Criscan said, "I did that just to distinguish it from the others. But it's no different in principle or in kind from any of the other cosmi in this diagram; here, all worlds are potentially habitable cosmi that would look similar to the one that we live in."

"Okay, so you have completely dispensed with the idea that there might be a special HTW full of pure ideas," I said.

Criscan shrugged. "Perhaps there's something like that *somewhere*, way off to the left, but you're basically right. This is a network of cosmi like ours. And there is one thing about it that is not shown on any of the other topologies I've drawn, which is—"

"I think I see it," I said, and tapped my toe on the "Arbran Causal Domain" box. "In the Wick, we are shown as a source of the Hylaean Flow for other worlds."

"Exactly," Criscan said. "The Wick introduces the notion that our world might, in effect, be the HTW of some other world."

"Or might be *seen* that way," Lio corrected him, "if there was no one in that world, yet, who had thought up the idea of Complex Protism."

"Yes," said Criscan, a little surprised to hear such a good point from someone he had written off as a tiresome clown.

"It makes you wonder about the Cousins," I said, thinking back to a wild notion that Arsibalt had raised last night: that the Cousins might have come, not just from another solar system, but from another cosmos.

"Yes," Criscan said, "it makes you wonder about the Cousins."

ACKNOWLEDGMENTS

ANATHEM COULD NOT HAVE been written had the following not come first:

- the Millennium Clock project being carried out by Danny Hillis and his collaborators at the Long Now Foundation, including Stewart Brand and Alexander Rose.
- a philosophical lineage that can be traced from Thales through Plato, Leibniz, Kant, Gödel, and Husserl.
- the Orion project of the late 1950s and early 1960s.

The author is, therefore, indebted to many more people than can comfortably be listed on a traditional acknowledgments page. The premise of the story, as well as the simple fact that it is a work of fiction, rule out the use of footnotes. This is unfortunate in a way, since many readers will presumably wish to know where the ideas being discussed by the characters actually originated, and how to learn more about them. Accordingly, detailed acknowledgments, complete with links to other resources, may be found at www.nealstephenson.com/anathemacknowledgments.